SELECT EDITIONS

Selected and Edited by Reader's Digest

SELECT EDITIONS

Selected and Edited by
Reader's Digest

Reader's Digest | New York • Montreal

FROM THE EDITORS

What would you do for family? And what would they do for you—or *to* you? Family can inspire a wide range of emotions, and in this volume our authors have (coincidentally!) tapped into that fact. From missing family heirlooms to found family members, from tragic loss to joyous new bonds, the terrific tales in this volume will, we suspect, have you both laughing and crying.

2 Sisters Detective Agency by James Patterson and Candice Fox kicks off the volume with a rollicking thriller featuring two stepsisters who didn't know about each other. Patterson is the world's number one author, and we're proud to include his latest in this volume.

Next comes Louisa Leaman's *The Lost and Found Necklace,* which follows a young woman's journey to uncover the truth about her family's history while also gaining some insight into herself.

Our third entry, *Girl in Ice* by Erica Ferencik, is an imaginative tale of adventure and suspense that takes place near the remote Arctic Circle. Trust us, you have not read a book like this before!

To finish up the volume we've got *The Family You Make* by Jill Shalvis, a sweet tale about finding love and family in new and sometimes unexpected places. It's an uplifting story at a time when, really, who couldn't use some feel-good fare?

We are so pleased to share this volume with you, our SE family. Enjoy!

Inside
SELECT EDITIONS

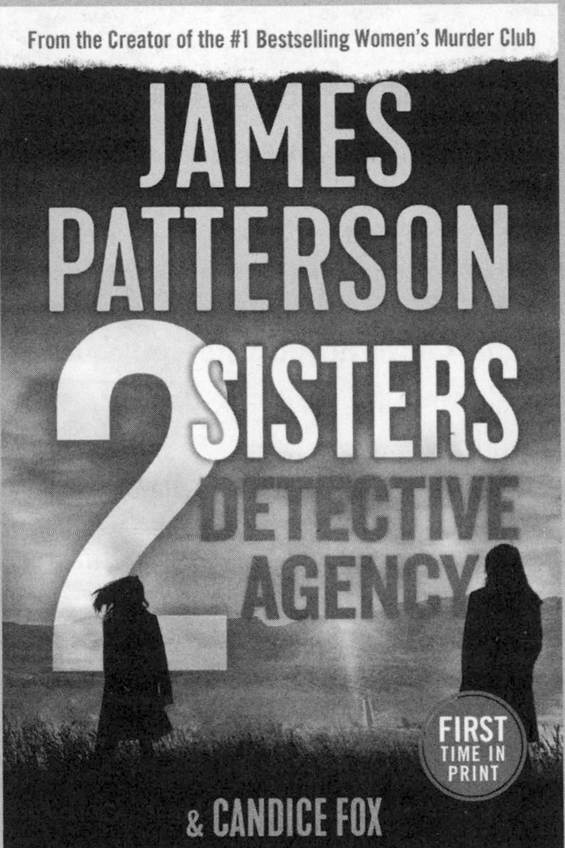
From the Creator of the #1 Bestselling Women's Murder Club
JAMES PATTERSON
2 SISTERS DETECTIVE AGENCY
FIRST TIME IN PRINT
& CANDICE FOX

Prologue

She was a killer.

Jacob Kanular knew it, as soon as the girl put the gun to his head. It was the way she angled the barrel of the revolver: straight down from forehead to neck so that when she pulled the trigger, the bullet would pass cleanly through his brain to his spinal column. She wasn't trying to scare him. Wasn't messing around by putting the gun against his temple. Whoever she was, she knew how to kill.

This was the only rational thought Jacob could manage. Everything else was just desperate internal screams. For himself. For his wife. For his baby.

There were five of them—three males, two females—and they were young and angry. There was at least one phone filming, illuminating snippets of what was happening next to him. They were binding his daughter, Beatrice, and wife, Neina, to chairs. A Taser zapped, threateningly, in Beaty's face. Jacob looked at the girl with the gun on him, and his thoughts focused on what he'd do to these people if he survived. But the duct tape across his mouth prevented him from speaking.

"I could kill you," the girl said, as though she could read his thoughts. She seemed to really be weighing it up, tapping on the trigger so he could feel the vibration through the metal, through his electrified skin. An eighth of an inch from death. "But I'm a nice girl. So I'll teach you a lesson instead."

The others heard what she said and came for him. They pushed Jacob's chair over, and he lay strapped to it in his boxer shorts, trying to fold himself in two to defend against the blows. The girl took a golf club from the bag in the hall and came back, raised it over her shoulder with professional ease, and smashed it into his ribs. He tried to focus on a cold emotionless thought to get him through. He saw a curl of blond hair poking out from beneath her hood. He squeezed his eyes shut and thought about that curl, as they kicked him half to death.

Beyond the huge glass windows, the ocean off Palos Verdes was calm and gray and flat, sparkling with moonlight. The girl with the curl grabbed a hank of his hair and lifted his head.

"You learned any manners yet?" she asked.

"Hey, Ash. Look," someone said.

Ash, Jacob thought.

"Oh, man." A boy's voice. "She's not breathing right."

"Chill. She's faking it."

Through the pounding in his head, Jacob strained to listen, and in the hot bedroom air he could pick out Beaty's wheezes and coughs and groans. She hadn't had an asthma attack since she was four years old. Six years since he'd heard that hellish noise. They didn't even keep an inhaler in the house anymore.

The girl leader stepped on Jacob. He felt the rubber grip of her boot. "If she dies, it's on you."

Then they were gone, the sound of their running footsteps echoing off the high ceilings.

In the darkness of the car, Neina spoke for the first time, sitting in the back seat with their daughter in her lap. Jacob could hardly hear his wife's voice over Beaty's struggling breaths. The garage door seemed to take a year to slide up and let them free. There was still tape hanging from his left wrist as he gripped the wheel and floored it for the nearest hospital.

"Who the hell were they?" Neina cried.

"I don't know," he said honestly.

Chapter 1

"Your Honor," I said. "My client is an artist."

The courtroom had been rippling gently with the sounds of conversations between the clients waiting in the stalls and their defenders, and of family members moving in and out of the wide double doors. At my words, the room fell silent. Judge Mackavin rested his chin on his palm, a single eyebrow raised.

"Get on with it, Rhonda," the judge said as I soaked in the dramatic silence I'd created. Everyone was looking at me—for once a spectacle based on my words rather than my appearance.

As big as I am—260 pounds, some of it well-earned muscle and some of it long-maintained fat—there's no point trying to fit in with the crowd. The pink hair was just the latest shade in a rotating kaleidoscope of colors I applied to my half-shaved, wavy quiff, and I always wore rock band shirts in the courtroom under my blazer.

"Mr. Reece Donovan comes from a long line of artists," I said, gesturing to my client, who slumped meekly in his chair. "His mother, Veronica, is a talented glassblower. His father sold portrait sketches on Main Street in Littleton as a youth. For the entirety of his sixteen years, this young man has been lectured by his parents on the importance of art as a commentary on the folly of humankind, and—"

"Counselor." Judge Mackavin leaned forward in his big leather chair. "You're not about to tell me that what young Mr. Donovan did was performance art, are you?"

There was a cough at the back of the crowded room. The only sound. Young Reece Donovan chewed his fingernails and looked like he wanted the ground to open up and swallow him.

"Hear me out," I said. "I'm just getting momentum."

"From the brief of evidence I have here," the judge said, lifting a page from those spread before him, "I'm to understand that Mr. Donovan was so upset by his mom's plan to marry her boyfriend that he filled the sprinkler system at the Colorado National Golf Club with red paint and rigged it to go off in the middle of their ceremony on the ninth green. Is that right?"

"That's correct, Your Honor," I said.

"I see." He nodded. "And his ingenious plan worked, it says here. He bathed the entire wedding party in paint, turning the ceremony into what visually resembled a bloodbath."

The judge held a picture of the dripping, mortified wedding party, snapped by the photographer moments after the sprinkler system launched. It looked like a scene from a horror film.

"It's a striking image, Judge," I said. "Some would say *bold*. Some would say *inspired*."

"He also managed to douse seventeen golfers standing at various stations on the course."

"Mr. Donovan didn't realize the whole sprinkler system was connected," I said. "He thought he'd isolated the ninth green."

The entire courtroom looked at my young client, who was wringing his long, slender fingers. In the front row of the audience, his mother and new stepfather looked exhausted. They'd forgiven him, but it had been hard work. I'd seen that expression on countless sets of parents over the course of my career.

"You know I support artistic expression in all its forms, Rhonda." Mackavin looked pointedly at my flamingo-pink hair and Metallica shirt. "But you're right out on the ledge here."

"The kid was angry," I said. "He wanted to make a statement. Yes, a lot of people got painted, but they were painted *red*, Your Honor. The color of passion. Of love! Of lifeblood, desire, longevity. An informed choice, I'm sure you'll agree. And Judge, where would modern expressionism be without Jackson Pollock's reckless determination to splash everything within ten feet of him with paint?"

The judge stifled a laugh, shook his head.

"Damages to the golf course, the sprinkler system, and the other golfers in attendance are into the tens of thousands of dollars," the judge said, regaining his frown.

"We're aware, Your Honor, and my client is remorseful."

The judge looked at me. A small smile played about his lips.

"I'm willing to reward your creativity, Rhonda, in trying to pass Mr. Donovan's actions off as anything more than pure idiocy," Mackavin said. "You've amused me, which is not easy. Four hundred hours of community service." The judge waved me away. "And tell the artist to keep it in the studio."

I turned and smiled at my client, but like the judge's, my humor was short-lived. Across the room, I spied my next client, a handsome young man in an expensive blue suit, being led out from the holding rooms. Unlike the slouching, fidgeting juvenile offenders lined up on the bench behind the rail, Thad Forrester was cuffed. The bailiff escorted him to the end of the row and uncuffed him, and I felt dread at the center of my stomach as I headed over to greet the most dangerous kid on my list.

THAD looked me over from head to foot as I approached, obviously skeptical, on the edge of disbelieving laughter. I get that look a lot, and not only from entitled frat boys up on rape charges. Thad would be just one in a crowd of people who'd underestimated me based on my appearance that morning.

"Mr. Forrester." I injected as little warmth into my words as possible. "I'm Rhonda Bird, your public defender."

"You can't be serious." He snorted. "Is this what passes for legal aid these days?"

"This is exactly what passes for legal aid these days," I said. "Passes with summa cum laude and a fifty-thousand-dollar research grant."

I hadn't actually taken the research grant, or the Ph.D. offer. I'd wanted to get out there, into the courtroom, among the young and vulnerable people who I felt so deserved my service. People like Reece Donovan. Not people like Thad Forrester.

He smirked. "You should have spent the grant money on a personal trainer. And what the hell are you wearing? You look like you just stepped out of some lame-ass rock concert."

"You shouldn't judge people by their appearance," I said. "The Metallica shirt doesn't make me any less of a lawyer, just like your Hugo Boss one doesn't make you any less of a rapist." Thad shook his head ruefully. I checked off his attendance on my clipboard. "I assume, because you're on my list, your expensive lawyer from New York hasn't arrived yet."

"That's right. So you need to get this thing canceled."

"It's an advisement hearing," I said. "The judge is just going to tell you what you're charged with."

Thad's charges were laid out vaguely on my list, but I'd heard the story from other lawyers in the courthouse halls. Thad's arrest related to an incident six months earlier, in which a local college sophomore had been found lying half-naked in the bushes outside a frat-house party in the early hours of the morning. The girl hadn't reported a sexual assault, probably because she couldn't remember it, but pictures of her involved in sexual activity while obviously unconscious had circulated on the phones of some young men on campus in the following weeks. The girl had made an attempt on her own life, which had brought the whole tragedy to the attention of the police. The police had acquired the photographs and identified a scar on the wrist of her assailant as identical to that on Thad Forrester.

"You don't need a pricey lawyer for this stage," I told Thad. "No rulings will be made on your case today."

"How about you let *me* decide what I need," the kid snapped, with the tone of someone used to giving commands. "I've had friends wrapped up in this kind of crap before. Every second I'm in the courtroom is being analyzed, and the last thing I want is to be associated with some freaky fat clown for my first hearing."

I smiled. "Mr. Forrester, from the brief of evidence attached to your file, these charges don't look like crap at all. That's your wrist in those pictures. Even this 'fat clown' can see that."

"It won't matter," he said with a smile. "We have a plan."

I backed up. I could see the rest of the case playing out as others had so many times before. There would be a large financial offer from the Forrester family to the girl's in exchange for a withdrawal of the charges. If her family didn't bite, Thad's expensive legal team would invade the girl's life like a disease, going after her sexual history, her family life, her friends. Every slipup she'd had since she was in grade school would be exposed and examined under hot lights.

I'd dealt with scum like Thad a hundred times across my career as a juvenile public defender. I had to defend them, but that didn't mean I had to stop them from digging their own graves. I matched Thad's smile with my own.

Because I also had a plan. I would have the advisement hearing postponed, as he'd demanded, and then I'd bring him to an interview room at the back of the courthouse under the guise of having him sign release papers. There, while he relaxed, already mentally detached from the fat clown with the pink hair, I'd get Thad chatting about the night he assaulted the girl at the frat party, challenge his manhood, poke and prod him until he snapped. Little boys with big mouths like Thad didn't want to listen—especially to women. They wanted to talk. They wanted to be listened to. Obeyed. And I knew the recording light on the camera in interview room 3 wasn't working.

"Wait here while I go get a coffee, little boy," I said as the next client and her defender shuffled their way up to the tables before the judge. I gave Thad one last look as I turned to walk out of the courtroom.

That's when I saw his attacker approaching.

I'd seen the brief of evidence against Thad Forrester, including the photographs of his victim he'd taken with his phone. Constance Jones's heart-shaped face was obviously a product of her father, a man I recognized now striding toward me up the courtroom's center aisle. At first I thought that he was coming for me. It's not uncommon for me to get berated for providing counsel to the young killers, thugs, and creeps of the Watkins region outside Denver. But one look in Mr. Jones's cold eyes told me exactly where he was going. Constance's father was heading for Thad. I noticed a bulge at his hip.

Most people think you can't get a gun into a courtroom unless you're a cop, a bailiff, or a US marshal. Anyone who's spent enough time in courthouses, however, knows there are a thousand ways to do it if you're determined. You could sneak the gun in through the air-conditioning vents on the rooftop or mix it with equipment used by the thousands of workers who service the building throughout the year—plumbers, electricians, cleaners, audio technicians, and repair crews. Hell, you could send it in on a coffee-and-sandwich cart while the vendor is out taking a leak. However Mr. Jones had done it, I realized I was the only thing standing between him and his vengeance.

I made my decision. I spun as Mr. Jones shoved past me and launched myself toward him, barreling into his back. He was a big man, but I was bigger. We slammed onto the courtroom carpet together. I heard gasps all around us. Mr. Jones reached for his gun. I grabbed his hand as he squeezed off a bullet, the shot smacking harmlessly into the ceiling.

I ripped the gun from his hand and threw it aside, then sucker punched him as he tried to roll underneath me. When he doubled over, I grabbed his arm and twisted it behind his back.

"Bailiff!" I cried, looking up. Everyone had frozen, including the bailiffs near the row of defendants. "Little help here?"

They rushed to my assistance. I handed off to them a sweating, swearing Mr. Jones, protesting, "He raped my daughter! That boy raped my daughter!" I stood watching as the courtroom guards dragged the furious father away.

My phone rang in my pocket. I walked out, ignoring the uncomfortable congratulations I caught on my way. I waited until I was outside the courtroom to pull the device from the pocket of my torn blazer.

"Hello?"

"Uh, is this Rhonda Bird?"

"It is. What do you want?" I said sharply.

"I'm calling about your father, Ms. Bird," the voice said, obviously cowed by my tone. "I'm sorry to have to tell you this over the phone, but he's dead."

He couldn't look at her. That's what scared him.

Jacob stood at the windows of his daughter's hospital room and gazed out at the parking lot, watching nurses arriving for the morning shift. He couldn't look at his daughter, Beatrice, lying stiff in the bed behind him.

All her life, he'd spent every possible minute watching her. Those early days when she would sleep on his chest, her tiny hand gripping his shirt. Watching her had always been his greatest joy, but now he feared what he saw would be the last memory of her burned into his brain. And it was all his fault.

The doctor and Neina were sitting on the edge of Beaty's bed. *They always sit when it's bad news,* Jacob thought.

"The severe asthma attack caused respiratory failure that starved Beatrice's brain of oxygen for a dangerous period," the doctor was saying. "Essentially, to protect itself, the organ shut down. We're not getting any brain activity showing up on our scans. But that doesn't mean—"

"She's brain-dead?" Neina's voice was quivering. "Is that what you're saying? How do you know that?"

"She's not brain-dead. We can't rule that out, but we're not ruling it in either. Not enough time has passed for us to . . . Look, Mr. and Mrs. Kanular, you need to maintain hope. The best thing you can do for your daughter is to be here with her, talking to her, letting her know you are a united front."

Jacob turned from the window and gathered his wife into his arms. He said words he didn't believe. "We're gonna get through this, Neina. All three of us. We're going to be fine. She'll come back to us."

When Jacob had found Neina, when he'd decided to marry her and have a child, he'd wanted only the best for her and the baby. The big house. The fancy cars. Vacations in the Bahamas. It had all been for them. For years he'd traveled the world with only what he could carry in a bag. He'd done bad things in those years. Caused a lot of pain. A thought pushed at him, that the things he had done during those years had caused this. That this was his punishment.

But no. Punishment was something you submitted to. He finally looked at Beaty in the bed. She was fighting her way back from the darkness. He knew it. He'd fight too.

When the doctor left, Jacob put the first step of his plan into action. "Neinie," he said. "We're not going to report the break-in to the police."

"What?" She stared up at him, her mouth falling open.

"We're going to tell them Beaty had a nightmare, that she woke and the asthma attack was upon her. It worsened as we drove to the hospital. We won't mention the home invasion."

"Are you insane? These monsters attacked us! They nearly killed our child, Jake!"

"Listen to me," he said. "These attackers were highly sophisticated. They knew what they were doing. They cut the power, bypassed security. This wasn't their first time. If we bring in the police now, we might be inviting more trouble."

"Jake, are you kidding me?"

"Neina, there were five of them. The cops aren't going to catch them all at once. If we leave even one of them out there, running loose, they'll come for us."

"Jake—"

"Just stay here with Beaty. I'll handle it."

He tightened his grip on her arms. Not painfully. Just enough to let her feel his certainty, his determination. She could trust him to make them safe. She'd always been able to do that.

Neina nodded, and Jacob held her to him again.

At the house, he stood in his kitchen, looking at the black streak the fire had left on the wall behind the stove. They'd tossed an aerosol can of something in there while they trashed the place. The sprinkler system had kicked in, dousing everything. His boots crunched over broken glass as he made his way to the stairs and down to the ground floor. He crossed the lavish game room, skirting around the pool table, and took the stairs by the bar down to the basement. The wide space was home to a few boxes, Beaty's bike, a treadmill, a desk. He went to a large wine rack on the east wall and flipped a hidden switch, and the rack slid sideways to reveal a narrow alcove.

The smell hit him first. Gun oil and the musty scent of used banknotes. In the alcove, stacks of unmarked bills bound in elastic bands reached knee height, consuming the floor space beneath the lowest of several wall shelves. On the shelf above the hoard of cash lay his passports and a battered old laptop that contained information to make the FBI's counterterrorism squad believe all their Christmases had come at once. Beside the laptop was a torn and dusty backpack. That tattered black backpack had accompanied him to Madrid, Belfast, Sydney, Honolulu.

Jacob reached for the second shelf, where, along with a few other weapons, the Barrett M82 sniper rifle he had used on his last job lay patiently waiting, as though it had known all this time that he wasn't done with his old life. He hadn't lined a man up in the crosshairs in twenty years, hadn't taken a job to kill political rivals, ex-lovers, despised public figures, or criminal adversaries. But the time had come to kill again.

Jacob picked up the gun and loaded it.

Chapter 2

Twenty-five years. That was how long it had been since I'd seen or spoken to my father. I walked away from the courtroom in a daze, through the bustling courthouse halls and to the parking lot. I forgot all about Thad Forrester and Constance Jones's father, and the murder attempt I'd just thwarted. In a space toward the back of the lot, my lovingly restored 1972 Buick Skylark with a leopard-print paint job bulged from the tiny space, its big square bumper hanging out over the adjacent sidewalk. I climbed into the car, making the suspension sing.

"Are you still there?" the voice asked.

"I'm here. This is . . ." I fumbled for words. "Wow. *Wow*. What happened?"

"Heart attack in his office. His health was not at premium levels."

An image of my father from two and a half decades earlier flashed. The fixed chandelier of blue-gray cigar smoke hanging from his office ceiling. The bottle of whiskey and crystal glass on the edge of the table, take-out wrappers crunched down in the trash can under pill containers and bottles of Pepto Bismol. The place had always looked like a tornado had swept through it, depositing betting slips for horse races everywhere.

"Sorry," I said. "I didn't catch your name. Or who you are."

"I'm Ira Abelman, your father's attorney." I heard papers being shuffled. "Ms. Bird, I'm going to have to ask you to come to Los Angeles to see about Earl's estate."

"Oh, believe me, you can wrap it up without me being there," I said, suddenly and undeniably grounded in the situation. "I'd be absolutely stunned if he's left me anything. But if he has, just donate it to a charity of your choice."

I made a move to hang up, strangely angry with the lawyer for delivering the message. His voice stopped me.

"Ms. Bird, you are absolutely *required* here in Los Angeles."

"What do you mean? Why am I required there?"

There was a silence. My stomach sank.

"Let me guess," I said. "He's riddled with debt, and I'll have to be there because it has all fallen to me. I'm his only living relative so I'll have to assume the liability. How much is it?"

"Ms. Bird, I've been instructed to explain everything only once you arrive here in person," Abelman said.

I felt suddenly, crushingly exhausted, the last time I had seen my father turning over in my mind. I'd been thirteen, sitting in a big car like the one I now owned, squashed against the door by his bulk. I'd been excited. My parents' divorce had been rough. My father had packed his bags and walked out one cold, snowy night and left my mother to explain to me that Earl had picked up a girlfriend in California on his latest business trip, and he was leaving us for her. When my father called and asked me to go out for coffee with him two weeks later, I'd been buzzed. In my mind, we were going to bond, to negotiate our new, exciting future together as

Daughter and Divorced Dad. He was going to tell me he was renting a cool new apartment in downtown Denver, and I could come hang out with him there whenever I wanted.

We hadn't gone for coffee. He'd driven me to the courthouse, where he'd had a notary witness me signing over some stocks he had held in my name. After he'd reclaimed the stocks, he'd dropped me back home. I never saw him again.

Something was pressing at me now, an instinct I couldn't deny. "Something's wrong," I said. "This feels like a trap."

There was a small sigh on the line. When the lawyer spoke again, his tone was sympathetic. It was the voice of a man who had dealt with my father for a long time.

"You'll understand when you get here," Abelman said.

"I'm coming," I told him.

It didn't take long for Jacob to figure out who his attackers were once he had locked back into hunter mode.

As a young man, he'd wandered from job to job, his senses ticking all the time. Every interaction was a puzzle, every face a mask of clues. Did the woman at the hotel counter recognize him from an Interpol alert? Was the man across the café an FBI agent surveilling him? It had been a long time since Jacob had employed such heightened awareness of his movements, but it was easy to resume the behavior. Being a killer and fugitive was like riding a bike. The muscles remembered.

He walked now through the bustling shopping mall toward the security office. He was sure he was on the right track as he followed the signs to a narrow hall between a juice bar and a sushi place.

In his retirement, Jacob lived a quiet life. He had a volunteer job at the local community college, teaching trade skills and joinery to young people. He'd learned carpentry while stalking a target for six months in Alaska on a rare long-term job. He didn't stop to chat with the other fathers when he dropped Beaty at school. He passed politely on dinner-party invitations, didn't return friendly calls or texts. He didn't have golfing buddies, fishing buddies, or buddies of any kind. He let Neina attend functions alone, and while she had complained in the early years, after a while she had stopped trying to push him. He went through life offending no one and befriending no one.

Which made it easy to remember the last time he'd offended someone. The girl who had attacked them in his house had accused him of needing to learn manners. There was only one thing remotely rude he'd done recently. A mistake caused by the pressures of time.

At the security office, a lone man in a black-and-white uniform lounged behind the counter, one hand hidden in a bag of Cheetos, the other tapping away on the PC on the desk.

"Excuse me," Jacob said. "I don't mean to bother you. I know you're probably busy."

"What's up, pal?"

"I was just in T.J.Maxx on the first floor, and there are a bunch of kids in there. I saw one of them slip a pair of sunglasses into his backpack. I tried to alert staff at the store, but they were all busy."

"Oh, man." The mall cop shot upward in his seat. "Thanks for telling me. I'm on it. I'm on it!"

Jacob stood back as the mall cop thrust open the barn door of the security office and bounded away. When the man had disappeared, Jacob reached over the counter and flipped the lock, walked to the desk, and settled into the chair. He knew the exact time and date he was looking for. He clicked through the security cameras on the PC until he found the northeast corner of the mall parking lot at 9:47 a.m. two Tuesdays earlier.

There he was on the screen, pulling his Tesla into an empty space, ignoring the little red convertible Mustang that had been waiting patiently for the spot to be vacated. He'd been in a hurry to get into the mall. Beaty had called him from school in tears—she'd forgotten to bring a roll of blue craft board needed for a group project that day. Jacob watched a petite girl with blond ringlet curls stand up in the passenger seat of the convertible.

The footage had no sound, but Jacob could see her yelling after him as he jogged toward the mall entrance. He remembered the moment distinctly, could hear her voice in his mind.

Hey, jackass! That was our spot!

He didn't typically do something like that—take people's parking spots or cut in line. People remembered that kind of thing, and he avoided being remembered.

In the video footage, Jacob watched the girl jabbering excitedly to the teenage boy in the driver's seat and pointing angrily at Jacob's car. He watched as she took out her phone and tapped something into the device as the driver pulled away.

He knew she was writing down his license plate number.

Jacob paused the footage, zoomed in, and noted the license plate of the red convertible.

"See you soon," he said.

Ashton Willisee let the back door of the Beverly Hills Playhouse close behind him. The parking lot was almost empty. He'd sat for ten minutes on the stage in theater room 6 after class had finished, staring at the empty seats, visualizing.

Ashton thought the creative visualization stuff was probably baloney, but he'd been taking classes for a year and only had one unsuccessful audition for a toilet paper commercial to show for it, so he figured he'd give it a whirl.

As he walked to his car at the far edge of the lot, a light distracted him. Two spots from his red Mustang convertible, a battered white Econoline van sat idling, the cabin light glowing brightly. Silhouetted against the light, a man in a ball cap stood, poring over a map.

"Hey, mate," the man said as Ashton moved toward his car. Heavy Australian accent. "Could I borrow you for a sec?"

"Yeah, sure." Ashton started walking over.

"Is that Gregory Way over there?" the man asked. "I'm looking for a place on the corner of Gregory and Arnaz."

"That's Robertson," Ashton said, taking out his phone. He pulled up Google Maps as he walked. "Gregory Way is—"

He was interrupted by a hiss sound, and the shocking sensation of a fine mist of liquid hitting his face. At first he thought the man had sneezed. Then Ashton saw a hand emerge whip fast from beneath the map, and the unlabeled aerosol can.

Then he saw nothing.

Ashton woke to the sensation of the van thumping over a pothole in the road. There was no telling how long he had been lying there, facedown on the rough carpet. His mind whizzed backward in terror. He remembered the van. The nondescript Econoline—anonymous serial killer van of the ages. He remembered the man, ball cap pulled low. He remembered the Australian accent. The hiss of whatever paralyzing chemical he'd been sprayed with.

Ashton curled into a ball, eyes wide in the dim light. His wrists were bound with something thin, like wire. There was tape on his mouth. He shifted, looked around him. A case lay beside him, hard and black, three-quarters the length of his body. An unzipped duffel bag, which he could see held pliers, drills, clamps. A folding chair and sheets of plastic.

Ashton told himself that he could talk his way out of this. The guy probably wasn't a serial killer. Why pick off a rich kid from Beverly Hills and cause a media sensation when you could grab homeless kids from Culver City without anyone batting an eye? So if he knew Ashton's family had money, that meant the guy was a businessman. This was a kidnapping.

The van stopped. Ashton swallowed down sobs as the man crunched through what sounded like gravel outside the van.

The doors opened, and Ashton was dragged and dropped onto the ground. He spotted dark mountains. A distant road, the red and yellow lights of passing motorists. Too far to hear his scream. He still couldn't see the guy's face.

The man caught Ashton's wrists, cut the tie. Ashton ripped the tape off his mouth and scrabbled away on the ground, almost crawling right over the edge of a gaping ravine.

He thought of running, but the van blocked both him and the man on an outcrop of rock with only a narrow escape route on either side. Ashton let a few sobs escape as the man went back to the van and returned with a huge black rifle.

"Oh, please. Please no." Ashton's voice was high, thin. "Listen! Listen! Listen! I know what this is."

"You do, huh?"

Ashton didn't recognize the voice. He cowered on the edge of the cliff.

"I-i-if you look in the contacts list on my phone," Ashton stammered, "you'll get my parents. They can have the money here in-in-in—"

"Do you recognize me yet?" the man asked.

Ashton's stomach sank. A person didn't kidnap someone who knew them. "This is a mistake!" he cried.

The man shifted the rifle in his grip. "There's no mistake, Ashton," he said.

"I don't know you!" Ashton pleaded. "I've never seen you before in my life! I— Don't hurt me. I'm just a kid!"

A *thunk* sound. A spray of dirt. Ashton realized with sickening clarity that the guy had shot the ground an inch away from the toe of his right sneaker. The rifle had a suppressor on it.

Ashton backed onto the last few inches on the edge of the cliff. There was nowhere to go. *Thunk, thunk*. He screamed and curled into a ball on the ground.

"Just a kid, Ashton?" the guy said. "Just a child? An innocent child? Tell me, what do children deserve, Ashton?"

Another spray of dirt. The guy had shot into the ground near his face. Ashton drew his arms up over his head and face, too terrified to move. It was the sound that drew him out of it. He expected another *thunk* from the suppressor, but instead there was a *blip*. A short, high-pitched wail. Ashton blinked through tears. Down on the distant road, blue and red lights.

The guy's silhouette was watching the distant lights too. Paused, calculating. Ashton gripped the ground for dear life, his teeth clenched, his clothes soaked through with sweat.

"Go," the guy told him.

Ashton didn't have to hear the word twice. He fast-crawled toward the van, squeezed past it, then bolted down a slope beside the cliff. He ran blindly, thinking only of getting away.

Another *thunk* behind him. Another into the boulders of granite on either side of him. He followed the narrow trail, stumbling over rocks, falling and getting up and pulling himself onward as the shots followed him into the night.

Chapter 3

There was a beautiful young Black woman sitting in the waiting room of Ira Abelman's office on Wilshire Boulevard in Central Los Angeles. I guessed her to be around twenty-five. She was the first Angeleno I'd seen up close. True to the city of beautiful people, she was tall and rake thin, and I'd bet she paid her hairdresser more than I paid my mechanic.

She gave me the Fat Person Look-Over and turned back to her phone, clicking a moody selfie of herself.

I sank into a chair two down from the beauty in Abelman's waiting room. I felt only a mild sense of annoyance as she took a *Diet Right* magazine from the coffee table before us and slapped it suggestively on the chair between us.

I'd set my expectations of my father's debt at a hundred grand. If I sold my condo in Watkins, that might give me enough to stave off debt collectors for a while. Then I'd probably have to make some unwelcome business decisions. Being a public defender paid my bills, but it wouldn't pay my father's. I'd never been in it for the money. I liked helping young people who were stuck in a criminal jam. I felt like those early offenses—usually fueled by plain stupidity, emotional overreaction, or the spirit of adventure—could make or break a kid and determine whether they became a lifelong criminal. When I helped a kid and got them a second chance, I felt like I was actually doing that corny thing all lawyers profess to want to do: making a difference in people's lives.

But shouldering my father's mistakes might mean giving that up for higher-paying legal work. I sat staring at my feet as the minutes ticked by, trying to remind myself that it wasn't good practice to hate someone who was dead.

Abelman, a small man in a suit with terrible hair plugs, emerged as the young woman was taking her sixth or seventh selfie and I was sucking on an overchewed fingernail.

"Ladies," he said gravely, gesturing to his inner office.

"Huh?" the girl said. She looked at me.

I shrugged. Abelman had disappeared back into his office.

"This is *my* appointment," she said, giving me another completely uninhibited dressing-down with her big Bambi eyes. "You can wait. I was here first."

"Ladies!" Abelman called. "I haven't got all day!"

The beauty huffed as she entered Abelman's office ahead of me. The trepidation that had followed me all the way from Colorado was thumping in my temples now, alarm bells ringing. I lowered myself cautiously into a chair in front of Abelman's desk, next to the one where the pissed-off beauty slumped.

"I've been trying to figure out a way to do this properly for the past three days," Abelman said. He raised his hands, held them wide, helpless. "There's no gentle way to go about it. So I've decided I'm just going to say it straight up."

I gripped the arms of my chair. When I looked over, I saw the young woman was gripping hers too.

"You two are sisters," Abelman announced.

I released my grip on the arms of my chair. An unfamiliar sensation rushed through me. It was a strange, giddy relief. I found myself looking over at the young woman with an astonishment so heavy I was able to completely ignore the twisted expression she had on her face as she looked back at me.

"Whoa" was all I could say.

"Wait." The girl pointed at my face. "You're my dad's . . ."

"This is Rhonda Bird," Abelman told her, gesturing to me. "Early's daughter with his first wife, Liz Savva." Abelman gestured to the girl. "This is Baby—uh . . ."

"Baby?" I scoffed.

The girl glared at me.

"Barbara Ann Bird." Abelman rolled his eyes. "Everyone calls her Baby. I've dealt with the family since she was born, fifteen years ago."

"You must mean twenty, twenty-five years," I said.

"No," Abelman said knowingly. "I don't."

"She's . . ." I felt my mouth gaping open. "You're *fifteen?*"

"Not only is she fifteen, Ms. Bird," Abelman said, "but she's also now your legal charge."

"What?" Baby and I said together.

Abelman picked up a manila file and extracted a single sheet of paper, holding it up as he read. "'I instruct my lawyer, Mr. Ira Abelman, to inform my daughter Rhonda Mavis Bird of the existence of my second child, Barbara Ann Bird, on the occasion of my death. Should Barbara be under the age of eighteen, it is my wish that Rhonda assume full custody and legal responsibility for Barbara from that point onward.'" He put the paper down. "Early told me it would be best to inform you of this decision in person, Ms. Bird, which is why I was reluctant to share this information over the phone. He was concerned that if I explained this to you from afar, there was a chance you would not come to Los Angeles to assume care of Baby."

"This is not happening," Baby said. "This is *not happening.*"

"I can't be someone's mom," I said. I got up and grabbed the folder from under Abelman's hands and started shuffling through it. "There should be a letter to me, telling me why—"

"There isn't one," Abelman said.

"This is a joke. Dad is . . . He's joking. Is he here?"

"I assure you, Ms. Bird, Early is deceased."

"Where's your real mom?" I asked Baby, who was staring out the window, mouth hanging open.

"She is also deceased," Abelman answered for the girl. "Ms. Bird, as of now, this young woman is officially in your care. You're her guardian. There's no way around it."

Baby got up and ran out of the room. I stared after her in disbelief, and felt a strange panicky sense of horror as I heard the outer door slam after her.

My child is running away, I thought. "She's not my child," I said aloud.

"Well, if I know one thing, it's that she's not *my* child," Abelman said. "This is why I don't do family law. I made an exception for Early. He said that you'd take care of it."

"The guy didn't even know me." I headed for the door. "He wouldn't have recognized me if he ran into me on the street."

"I'm sure he would have. You look just like him."

"Thanks."

"Here's Earl's wallet. Inside is Baby's credit card," Abelman said, pushing a fat leather wallet toward me. "I wouldn't give that to her if I were you."

I took the wallet and turned again to leave.

"Before you go!" Abelman shouted. He tossed me a key. "You better go secure your father's office. It's in Koreatown. Baby knows the address."

"Secure it?"

"Yeah." He looked at me meaningfully. "I'd suggest you do that as soon as possible."

I HEARD the girl before I saw her. She was talking in a high, wailing tone, making strange sucking sounds between frantic words. The street was blazing hot and so bright I had to stop under the awning of the office building and rub my eyes.

Baby was tucked into an alcove, holding her phone aloft and rambling to it. The sucking sound was her dragging deeply on a vape pen at the end of every sentence.

"I don't know what I'm gonna do." Baby sucked on the vape. "I don't know what full custody means. I still don't have access to my credit card. We've got eight hours to go. Stay tuned and I'll get you all updated as soon as I can."

"Who the hell are you talking to?" I asked.

"My followers." She used the phone's camera to fix her hair. "This is the worst day of my entire life. This is the worst day in the history of humankind."

"That's . . ." I shook my head. "That's a big statement. Not the least because your dad died three days ago. Our dad."

"He had it coming." Baby inhaled deeply in between sentences. "The guy had a twelve-pack of doughnuts for breakfast every day. What did he think was going to happen?"

I'd seen some tough-talking teenagers in my time, but Baby's performance was very convincing. I could almost believe she wasn't hurting at all over the loss of our father. I realized I was looking at a girl who had been raised by a hard, hard man. She spoke and stood and smoked the way I remembered he used to do, and she was looking at my eyes the same way, begging me to challenge her, just itching for an argument. Baby had her defenses up, her hackles raised. I knew I had a wild child on my hands here.

"Give me my credit card," Baby demanded.

"Let's just talk first, okay? What happened to your mom?"

"It doesn't matter," Baby said. She put her hands up. "I'm only gonna say this once, lady. You're not my mom. You're not my real sister. I don't care what Ira says about custody or legal charges . . . or whatever-whatever. I'm going to Milan."

"You're . . . going to Milan?"

"In eight hours." She glanced at her smartwatch. "I've had tickets to the Spellbex Music Festival there for months. My followers are expecting me to go. You're not stopping me."

"Barbara—"

"It's Baby. Baby Bird."

"Baby," I said carefully. "Your father just died. There's a woman here you've never met who's supposed to take care of you. Everything is upside down. I know you're scared—"

"I'm not scared."

"And upset. But let's slow down. I'm also kind of freaked, in case you were wondering. In eight hours, we're still going to be working this out, and that's going to be difficult if you're on a plane to Milan with . . . Who were you going with?"

"I'm going by myself."

"Wow," I said, incredulous.

"There's nothing *wow* about it. I go everywhere by myself. I just got back from Puerto Rico and the Fixy Life Festival. This is what I *do*. This is my *job*."

I held my head. "Your job? Baby, I can't even begin to explain what I think about a fifteen-year-old traveling the world by herself just to tell hundreds of strangers on the internet what she thinks of the live music scene."

"Hundreds? Excuse me?"

"Let's get in my car and—"

"Fine. Show me to your car." She flicked her hand at me. "I'll explain it to you while you drive me home so I can pack."

She stormed off importantly. I had to laugh, to stave off the urge to cry.

Jacob Kanular sat beside the hospital bed, listening to the bleeping of the machines monitoring his daughter. Jacob had sat in rooms like this before, looking over strangers in beds, a night shadow slipping in. Clients had hired Jacob to speed up the inheritance process, or to finish the job some amateur hit man had botched. Often all that was required was the simple blockage of a tube, the flipping of a switch. But now his ability to do the job remained in question.

He'd been ready to kill Ashton Willisee. But his first attempt at justice for Beaty had been a failure, which wasn't something Jacob had ever experienced on the job. He just didn't *do* failure. He didn't choose stupid locations. He wasn't caught out, as he had been the night before, by the coincidence of a police car pulling over a vehicle within eyesight of where he had planned to kill his mark.

Had he wanted to fail? Could he really kill again? Or had time, love, and family done away with the monster inside him?

Even as he wondered these things, holding his daughter's hand, his other hand held Ashton Willisee's phone, flipping through videos. He opened a folder entitled "Midnight Crew."

Ten videos. He clicked the newest, dated a few days earlier. He recognized the range hood in his own kitchen. The camera swept to the dining room, where the big kid with the golf club was lining up Neina's sculptures on the table. He saw his own figure slumped in a chair, unconscious, Neina bound beside him. He watched as the girl with the blond curl hanging from her hood forced a crying Beaty into another chair, winding tape around her chest.

"Please, please don't," Beaty cried on the video. "Mom! Mom!"

Jacob felt his lip twitch. It was the only outward sign of the searing rise of fury inside him. He rolled the video back. Ashton's main focus had been on his own activities in the kitchen. He'd only filmed a snippet of the girl tying his daughter to the chair. Jacob isolated the clip and played it again.

Please, please don't. Please don't. Please.

The phone screen went blank. An error message told him the phone had been remotely disabled. Jacob let the phone fall into a nearby trash can. He had what he needed.

I HAD to get the address for my father's office on South Alexandria Avenue in Koreatown from Abelman because Baby wanted to go home and would only give me her own address. The girl hunkered down in the passenger seat of my Buick, her long legs crammed against her chest, eyes behind huge round sunglasses, a scarf she'd extracted from her tiny handbag pulled over her head.

"This is so embarrassing. This car. This paint job. Worst day of anyone's life. Ever," she muttered to herself.

"This paint job was done by a very talented kid about your age," I said, "as payment for me fronting his bail money on a public exposure charge. I'm pretty fond of it."

"Why would you front some kid's bail money?"

"I'm a youth public defender back in Colorado."

"Oh, great. You're the law? That's just great."

I got the impression that Baby's reaction would have been the same even if I'd told her I was chief selfie appreciator at Instagram headquarters. She had recovered quickly from the horror of our meeting in Abelman's office and was now settling comfortably into angry denial, huffing and sighing.

"Help me out," I said. "Where did my—our—father die?"

"In his office," Baby said. "He was probably taking a phone call. He was always screaming down the phone."

"Who informed you of his death?"

"Ira."

"And who's been staying with you for the past three days?"

"Some kids from the beach."

"Which kids?"

"Oh, great. It's started already. *Who were you with? Which kids? Give me their names!*" Baby rummaged in her purse for her Juul. "Listen, lady, this interrogation stuff is *not* gonna fly."

"Interrogation!" I laughed. "Baby, if I was interrogating you, you'd know it. Are you telling me that after you were informed of your father's death you were allowed to go home alone to hang out with a bunch of other fifteen-year-olds? That can't be right. Who's had custody of you until now?"

"No one."

"This is insane! You're a minor! Why didn't Abelman take charge of you himself?"

"Ira knows not to mess with me." She gave a mean smile as she put the vape pen to her lips.

I reached over and flicked it out of her mouth. It sailed out the window into the wind. I had been flicking cigarettes, joints, and vapes out of kids' mouths for years and was right on target.

"Dammit!" she screeched.

"No vaping in the car," I said. "No vaping ever, in fact. You're *fifteen*. By the time you're twenty-five, you'll sound like Marlon Brando."

"Who?"

"Oh, jeez," I said.

"Look." She turned toward me. "Dad brought a hundred girlfriends around, and all of them tried to take a swing at being my mommy. So I'm gonna tell you what I always told them."

"Okay," I said.

"I haven't had a mother since I was two, because that's the last time I needed one. I take care of myself. I'm autominous."

"Autonomous?"

"That's what I said."

"Baby, you're a child. You're grieving."

"That's where you're wrong. I'm *not* a child. I have a job. I travel. My dad always gave me the credit card when I was going away or when he traveled, and I stayed at the house by myself. We had a system, and it worked," she said.

"Man." I shook my head. "When they were handing out sass in heaven, you loaded up a truck."

"Damn right." She took another vape pen from her purse.

"So what happened to your mom?" I asked. "Did she leave him?"

"They were never together. It was a one-night stand."

"What? Are you kidding?"

"I'm dead serious. She dumped me on his doorstep with a letter and a picture of the two of us."

Baby pulled out her phone and tapped to a grainy photo of a tall, attractive Black woman holding a baby.

"How old were you?" I gaped.

"Two." She exhaled a cloud of smoke. "I'm definitely Dad's, though. He got a DNA test."

"Oh, I bet he did," I said. "So what happened to your mom exactly?"

"She washed up on a beach in Papanoa three weeks later." The girl shrugged. "Somebody tied her to a cinder block."

"Oh, Baby. I'm sorry."

"I don't care." Baby snorted in the feigned nonchalant way I'd seen a thousand teenagers do before her.

"But—"

"He tried to find out who killed her, but he couldn't." Baby exhaled more smoke at the dashboard. "He found out everything about her, found some family and all, but he couldn't solve the crime. He had fun trying, though. He liked mysteries. It's why he started doing this job."

"What job?" I flicked the vape pen out the window.

"Dammit, bitch! You do that again and I'm gonna smack you, I swear."

"Dad gave up being an accountant?"

"An *accountant?*" Baby burst out laughing. I pulled into a parking lot in front of a strip mall. "He was an accountant?"

"Last time I saw him he was," I said.

"Well, when he got landed with me, he had a shop on Sunset that sold taxidermy."

"Oh, sure." I rolled my eyes. "Because that makes complete sense. So what was he doing lately?"

Baby gestured through the windshield. We were parked outside a small office door wedged between a busy nail salon and a crab boil restaurant. The stenciling on the door read EARLY BIRD PRIVATE INVESTIGATION—WE'LL GET THE WORM!

"'We'll get the worm' was my idea." Baby jutted her chin proudly. "When he started out, he was mainly just catching cheating husbands and bail jumpers. You know. Worms."

"Genius," I said.

I opened the office door, which led to a stairwell, and was hit with a wall of cigar stink. I walked up the rickety stairs as Baby followed behind me.

In a tiny office above the crab restaurant, my father's desk sagged under a pile of papers, books, and take-out containers, as well as gambling tickets and receipts, all sprinkled with cigar butts. Just as I had anticipated. The only difference from the office I remembered in Watkins two and a half decades earlier was the weapons. From the doorway I could see four knives—two big hunting knives lying on the desk, a penknife on a windowsill, and a kitchen knife stabbed into the wall by the window—plus a huge Magnum revolver on his battered leather chair.

I sighed and moved the gun, then sank into the chair. Baby shoved debris off an old sofa onto the floor with the familiarity of someone who had done it many times, and then reclined dramatically with an arm over her head, holding her phone aloft.

"The woman is trying to take over everything," Baby narrated to her followers. "She's ransacking my father's office now. I can tell she thinks she's my mom already. She says I'm not going to Milan, and she still hasn't given me my credit card. This is going to be a battle, people."

"Are you out of your mind?" I said. "Ransacking? I've touched one thing since I walked in!"

"The woman is trying to lecture me now," Baby narrated.

"I have a name. It's Rhonda."

Baby ignored me. I tried to shake off the annoyance creeping up between my shoulder blades. Baby had clearly hung out in this office a lot. My dad had spent enough time with her that she'd picked up some of his mannerisms—that aggressive hand flick and the jut of her chin at her own cleverness. She'd been dumped in his lap as a tiny toddler, and he'd chosen to raise her himself. There was no mistaking it.

I was deeply jealous of this girl.

My entire life, my dad had been aloof, stern, or completely absent. When I reached age thirteen, he'd had enough of me. What did Baby have that I didn't? What was wrong with me? I strummed my purple-painted fingernails on the desk.

"What was the lawyer getting at when he said I needed to secure this place?" I asked. "Both doors were locked."

Baby said nothing and tapped furiously on her phone. When she finished her post or whatever it was, she popped up again.

"I'm gonna go get a crab stick," she said. "I assume you want one. Maybe more than one."

"You assume right," I said, refusing to take offense. "Get me three. And if you try to run off to Milan, I will find you so fast it'll make Liam Neeson look like an amateur."

"Who's Liam Neeson?"

"What? Liam Neeson isn't even Marlon Brando old. He's current!"

"If you say so."

Baby didn't get far in the hall, it seemed. I heard her bump into someone, and I went to the door to listen in.

"I don't have time for this," I heard Baby say to the person. "I'm trying to make a run for it."

I put my hand on the knob but paused when I saw Baby's reflection in the mirrored surface of another door in the hall. She was standing with a teenage boy who looked tired and terrified. I froze where I stood, observing them.

"I need help." The boy swiped back his long, ragged hair. "Is your dad here?"

"He's dead."

"What?"

"What the hell do you need him for?" Baby folded her arms. "What's it been? Two years? I haven't seen you since . . ."

"The thing."

"Yeah." Baby stared at her feet. "The thing."

Both kids stood in the awkwardness, fidgeting with their clothes. Baby came out of it first. "You got tall," she said.

"You too." The boy wrung his hands. "I'm in trouble, and I can't go to the cops. I need your dad. What happened to him?"

"What happened to you?"

"I . . . I was abducted last night."

"What? What the hell does that even mean?"

"It means someone abducted me." The boy smoothed down his shirt. It was dirty and wrinkled. "Like, for real. Like, the guy tied me up and put me in a white van. He had a gun."

Even as the boy spoke, I could see his hands shaking.

"Are you high right now?" Baby asked.

"No, I'm not high." The boy's voice dropped. He took a step closer to Baby. "Look, your dad was always a cool dude, and he came through for us that time. I just thought maybe . . . Okay, look. It doesn't matter. I shouldn't have come here."

The boy turned.

I pulled open the door of the office and pointed at him. "Not one more step," I said.

Baby's eyes were full of terror. Not the physical kind. The social kind. Just opening the door and showing myself in all my aesthetic horror to someone she knew was clearly terrifying enough, but as I spoke, her eyes somehow got bigger. She was horrified that I might reveal who I was and make some kind of scene, which is exactly what I did.

"You two, get your butts in here." I pointed to the office.

Baby and the boy walked into my father's office. Baby's expression turned into a furious glare as she moved to the couch.

"What's your name, kid?" I asked the boy.

"Ashton Willisee."

"Ashton, is it true you were abducted?"

"Whoa!" Baby put her hands up. "Rhonda, you don't get to listen in on people's private conversations!"

"Yeah, I do." I shrugged. "When they involve crimes and the possible endangerment of the people around me, I do."

"I'm out of here." Ashton tried to get up.

"Sit down and tell me what happened to you," I said.

"Nothing happened." Ashton slithered down in his seat. He yawned, let his eyes drift half closed. I knew from my years of watching tapes of kids in police interrogations that adopting an overly relaxed stance was often a coping mechanism for kids in danger. I'd spent much of my professional life advocating for kids who appeared callous or indifferent during false confessions when really they were terrified.

"Nothing happened?" I pressed.

"Look, I just—" He gestured at Baby. "I know Baby from school. I was in the area, and I thought I'd see if she was here and . . . uh . . . pull a prank. Make up a story. I'm sorry, okay?"

"Ashton, I can help you," I said. "We can go to the police together. If there's a reason that you—"

"I've gotta go." The boy leaped to his feet. "It was just a prank, okay? That's all." He ran out the door.

"That was *so* uncool. I just . . ." Baby was shaking her head disgustedly at me. "I've got nothing. I'm, like, speechless."

I ignored her and went to the window, where I watched Ashton fast-walk to a Mercedes parked at the end of the lot. There was a bumper sticker on the back of the car. I had to squint to read it: PROUD PARENT OF A STANFORD-WEST ACADEMY STUDENT.

"Hey, Baby," I said. "What's the name of your high school?"

She snorted. "I'm too busy to go to school. I've been homeschooling myself since I was thirteen."

"Dad let you do that?" I sighed.

"People don't *let* me do things," Baby said. "I just do them."

I found a set of car keys on the windowsill. My father's car had to be out there in the lot somewhere. "So do you think Ashton was abducted?"

"Probably," she said. "But that's not the point. You can't eavesdrop on me and my friends."

"Baby, the abduction *is* the point," I said. "I know you're mortified to be around me. I get that. But you saw how obvious his body language was, didn't you? I mean, he was clearly telling the truth to you in the hall but lying when he was in here."

"I guess," she said. "I don't know about body language. But he had drag marks on the backs of his shoes. Fresh ones. There was still dirt on them. So I guess he *was* probably abducted."

"Really?" I was impressed. "You saw drag marks?"

"Yeah, right here." She touched the back of her heel. "I saw that once on one of Dad's cases. I was looking at the crime-scene photos of some chick who got killed in the woods up at Big Bear. Dad showed me the drag marks on her shoes like someone had dragged her unconscious body across concrete. You don't get marks like that if you're fighting and kicking."

"I can't believe Dad let you look at crime-scene photos," I said, fiddling with the car keys.

"You are so not listening to me." Baby turned to face the back of the couch. "I don't need anyone to *let* me do things."

I pointed the key fob at the window and clicked it. None of the cars in the lot flashed their lights. I hit the button again, looked around. Nothing. I clicked and clicked, until something behind me clicked in response under the desk. I turned and knelt, pressing the button on the key fob and listening for the responding click beneath the worn blue carpet.

I pulled up a corner of carpet that was curled against the bottom of the desk. Beneath it was a badly fitted wooden hatch set into the floor. The key fob disguised as a car key was clicking the lock on the hatch open and shut.

"Like Milan," Baby was saying from the couch, out of sight. "I'm going. I'm getting on that plane."

I opened the floor hatch to reveal a space filled almost entirely with a black duffel bag. I unzipped the bag.

Cash. Stacks of cash, bound with elastic bands. I pushed against the stacks of money, feeling for depth. A quick estimation told me there were millions here.

It was bad news. The mere sight raised the hairs on the back of my neck.

"In fact, we should go," Baby said. "I've got to pack."

"Yeah," I said, zipping the bag closed. "Let's go. I'll meet you at the car."

Chapter 4

VERA ARRIVED LATE. She always did. She liked to keep them waiting, give them an opportunity to talk about her. The more people talked about you while you weren't around, the more mythical you became. The more powerful.

She threw the keys to her convertible at the Soho House valet and wore her sunglasses all the way up the elegant white stairs to the restaurant, right to the table, so they wouldn't be able to tell whether or not she was pissed off at having been called to a meeting. Her crew were all watching her as she sat down. The tension was palpable.

The twins, Sean and Penny, were slumped in their chairs, looking bored. Ashton looked puny, dwarfed by Benzo beside him, whose muscles were barely contained in Hugo Boss.

No one spoke. A waitress came over, and Vera said, "Coffee, black," without looking up. She pushed her sunglasses up into her blond ringlets.

"You can explain," she finally said to Ashton.

Ashton sagged with relief. "There's not much more to add about what happened other than what I said in my text," Ashton began. "Guy grabbed me right outside the Playhouse. He let me go off the 405 near Mulholland. I wouldn't have escaped if it hadn't been for the cops driving by. He was gonna kill me."

"And why do you think this has something to do with our game?" Penny asked, idly perusing the menu.

"He knew who I was," Ashton said. "He knew my name. He was really angry. He was talking about what children deserve."

"What do you mean, what children deserve?" Benzo snorted.

"I don't know! He was like, 'Don't you know who I am? Don't you know what children deserve?' Something like that."

"Ashton, if this guy knows who we are, we're in trouble," Sean said. "Did you disable your phone?"

"Yeah," Ashton said. "It's dead."

"How long after he took you did you disable it? Could he have gotten all your contacts? Your videos?"

Ashton didn't answer.

"The guy doesn't know who *we* are," Vera said. "He knows who *Ashton* is."

The crew considered this.

"He grabbed you outside the Playhouse, right? You said he was waiting for you there," Vera said.

"Yeah." Ashton nodded.

"So he's been watching you onstage," Vera reasoned. "He sounds like some creep looking for a fresh young boy. He probably came snooping around a few months back, saw you doing the Romeo soliloquy or whatever the hell, and thought he'd wait for you after class. Give you what children deserve."

"I don't know," Ashton said. "I feel like it was connected to the game. Like someone figured it out."

"That's because you feel guilty. Funny, you weren't feeling so guilty when we hit your drunk uncle's house to teach him a lesson about smacking your aunt around. I seem to remember you enjoying that one. You were guilt free."

Vera's coffee came. Penny shut the menu in disgust and flung it on the floor. The waitress scooped it up.

"This guy, whoever he is, he isn't the threat," Vera said. "Ashton is. It's what Ash did that could get us all killed."

"What are you talking about?" Benzo leaned in.

"Ashton blabbed to a private investigator that he was abducted. He went crying to some—"

"I took it back," Ashton blurted. "I told them I was lying. They're not gonna—"

"Never interrupt me," Vera snapped. "Never."

"What did you say to these people?" Penny asked.

"I didn't tell them about the Midnight Crew," Ashton said. "I made like it was a prank. It's not going to go any further."

"It was stupid," Vera said. "Dangerous. If the cops find out about what we've been doing with the Midnight Crew game, we're all doing time. *Real* jail. With actual criminals."

"I know I'd be fine." Benzo flexed his pecs.

"Whoever the guy who grabbed you was, he wasn't one of our victims," Vera continued. "We've never hit anyone who wasn't a coward or a loser, and we've never really done anything bad enough to make people want to find us. We give them a scare, that's all."

"What about that kid?" Penny said. "She got pretty sick."

"She shouldn't have been there," Vera said. "She was supposed to be at a sleepover."

"Is she okay?" Ashton asked. "Did you che—"

"She's fine," Vera said. "I checked. It's not the sniveling old guy. No one could have found us that fast. It's not anyone we've hit. We're fine."

She took a notebook out of her bag and set it on the table.

"Now pay attention," she said. "Because we're hitting our next target tonight."

THE house in Manhattan Beach sat on the esplanade, a towering four-story white mass. The strip of concrete separating it from the beach, called the Strand, was toured by dog walkers and lookie-loos peering into the luxurious homes.

"This is not Earl's house," I said as we idled on the street.

"It isn't?" Baby raised her eyebrows at me.

"No," I said. "This is not the house of a former accountant, former taxidermy salesman, now-deceased gumshoe with an office above a crab shack."

"Well, I think I'd know where I live." Baby snorted. "Turn here. Park in the garage."

Baby had a small device in hand that was opening the double garage door, and I parked beside a black Maserati.

I wanted to scream at Baby that everything I'd seen that day was telling me Earl Bird had been a bad man and likely a dangerous criminal. But I reminded myself that she was a kid who'd just lost her father. Trying to adjust her perception of our father probably wasn't a good idea at the moment.

We passed through a door in the back of the garage and walked into the first floor of the house. It looked like there'd been a party held here last night: beer bottles on every surface, pizza boxes stacked on the landing of the stairs, discarded clothes piled in the corners of the rooms. But the dust over everything told me this was the result of months of neglect.

A teenage girl in a bikini lay sleeping on a couch in the first room we entered.

"Who is that?" I asked, pointing.

"Some girl," Baby said.

"You don't know her?"

"I told you, I invited a bunch of kids from the beach over when Dad died," Baby said. "Some of them are still here."

"I thought you meant friends, not random kids from the beach," I said. I went and roused the girl. "Hey. Hey. Excuse me? Honey, you've got to go."

"You can't kick her out," Baby snapped at me. "This is my house. My guests can stay as long as they like."

"You don't know these people."

"So?" Baby turned to go. "I'm going to go pack for Milan."

"Baby." I grabbed her wrist. "You are not going to Milan."

"It's so funny that—"

"I'm serious," I said. "Listen, I get it. Your dad is gone, and some woman who's only been in your life for five minutes starts bossing you around. You've had independence, and now a stranger thinks she can walk in and change that."

Baby glared at me.

"But you have to see where I'm coming from too," I said. "Dad created this situation, and we've got to deal with it. It's going to take more than a few hours to do that. You can't run off to Milan before we've straightened all this out."

Baby grabbed a beer bottle and flung it at the wall. It shattered, startling the girl on the couch and two other girls I hadn't noticed earlier, sleeping on blankets by the windows.

She pointed at the wall now dripping with beer. "Give me my credit card or next time that'll be your head."

"Baby, I've been visiting teenagers in juvenile detention since before you were born," I said. "If you think having a beer bottle thrown at me is the worst threat I've ever faced, you're dreaming. You're not getting the card. You're not going to Milan. End. Of. Discussion."

She stormed off. I did the same, internally raging at my father for having done this to us, and at myself for doing a terrible job of handling Baby so far. I didn't get her. She wasn't responding to sympathy, humor, or stern directives. I worried that eventually I would run out of my usual grab bag of strategies for dealing with teenagers in peril.

I went back into the garage and popped the trunk of my car, then hefted the duffel bag of cash out. I carried it upstairs and found my father's bedroom on the second floor. I could tell it was his from the cigar stink. In the en suite bathroom, I knelt and gave the block of wood under the cabinet doors an experimental push. It tilted out from its housing and toppled over.

Creature of habit, my father, just like me.

When I was a little kid, I discovered my father's hidey-hole in our home in Watkins. I walked in on him, his arm shoved into the space under the vanity in my parents' bathroom. Then I saw him pull out a jewelry case from the hidden space and place it on the floor. That's when he noticed me standing there and snapped with shocked rage, "What the hell are you doing?"

"Nothing!" I cowered. "What are you doing?"

"None of your business, kid." He shoved the case into his back pocket and pointed a finger in my face. "You tell your mommy about that box, or that little hole under the sink, and I'll gut every toy you own. You understand?"

I'd waited for the little jewelry case to turn up at my mother's birthday or at Christmas, but it never showed up.

Now I bent and looked into the darkness. It was clear items had been hidden in the space before, but nothing was there.

I unzipped the bag and took one last look at the money. A few stacks of bills had slid around, revealing a key on a yellow plastic tag near the top of the pile. The label on the tag was for a storage facility in Torrance. Trepidation washed over me. Whatever Dad was keeping out in Torrance must be as secret and full of malignant potential as the hidden cash itself. I took the key, secured the money under the vanity, then walked into the hall and saw Baby on a balcony overlooking the beach.

"We've got to go," I said.

"Where?" she asked. She swiped at her face to hide her tears.

"Torrance," I said. "Dad's got more surprises in store for us."

JACOB moved like smoke. It was a skill he'd learned in his time as a killer. Feather-footed despite his size, he wandered the second floor of Derek "Benzo" Benstein's house in the dark, overhearing the young man's voice as he talked loudly on the phone to a yacht broker in San Francisco.

"Well, that's just too bad. I need it sooner than that," he heard Benzo shout into the phone. "I told you I wanted the forty footer. I'm throwing a party on Sunday, Doug, and I need the yacht in the marina by that morning for the caterers."

Jacob went to the second-floor railing and looked down into the foyer in time to see Benzo smash the phone, scattering the fragments on the marble tiles.

Roid rage, Jacob guessed. His workup of Benzo had revealed just how much maintenance the son of Los Angeles's most successful film agent put into his appearance. Jacob had crept through Benzo's online bank accounts the way he was wandering through the boy's house now, noting his purchases of creatine, beta-alanine, and conjugated linoleic acid to build muscle.

Jacob snuck down the stairs and followed Benzo into the living room, standing just out of sight while Benzo flopped onto the big couch and flicked on the huge television screen.

Jacob lifted his gun and fired a bullet into the screen. The suppressor's *thunk* was overshadowed by the thunderous crack of the screen. Benzo leaped up and stared at the intruder.

No recognition. Jacob shook his head in disgust. Sure, he probably looked different, alert, dressed, unlike how Benzo had last seen him—gagged, bound, and helpless. Benzo looked at the gun, and all his muscles tensed.

"Dude, what the—"

Jacob lifted the gun and fired at the wall beside Benzo's head. The bullet whizzed past the boy's ear.

"Okay, okay, okay!" Benzo said, hands up. "Who are you? What do you want? Is this about my dad?"

"Look closely at me," Jacob said. "Think hard."

Benzo's breath quickened. "Oh, dude . . . Oh, crap. You're that Palos Verdes guy. The guy with the family."

"That's me." Jacob's fury almost choked off his words.

He held his pistol in one hand and used the other to pull a long, thin black rod from its holster on the back of his belt. He gave the cattle prod trigger a demonstrative pull and watched Benzo's eyes twitch as the end of the device sizzled.

"Man, it was nothing personal," Benzo said. "At least not for me. I didn't pick you. Someone else did. I don't even know what it was about. No one got hurt, right?"

Jacob fired a bullet into Benzo's thigh. The boy was tough. He screamed but didn't fall.

The pain seemed to give him courage. Benzo grabbed a lamp and flung it in Jacob's direction, using the distraction to make a limping run for the glass doors that looked out onto the yard. Jacob followed at a walk. He fired again and hit Benzo in the calf just as the boy reached the glass doors.

Benzo sank down, his legs useless.

Jacob walked forward, gripping the cattle prod in his hand.

Baby didn't speak to me the whole way to Torrance. She just sat there with her arms folded, her mouth in a pout. This was just a challenge, I assured myself. Baby wasn't distinctly different from any troubled teenager I'd dealt with before. She had the same wants, needs, fears. I just had to find a way in. I tried a different approach as we pulled into the all-hours storage yard emblazoned with a big green giraffe.

"Why would a kid lie about being abducted?" I wondered aloud, inviting anyone who might be within earshot to chip in.

"He said it was a prank."

"Weird prank," I said.

"I knew Ash at school. He and I had like a . . ." She shrugged. "I don't know. Somebody told me that he liked me, but I wasn't interested at the time. He was really short."

"That doesn't sound shallow at all, Baby."

"I'm talking epic short. Like Tom Cruise short."

"Ah, you know who Tom Cruise is." I breathed a sigh of relief. "So you're not irredeemable. Ashton said Dad came through for you two? What was that about?"

"It was stupid." Baby snorted. "We were all partying down on the beach, and Dad came down to hang out with us. Me and some of the kids had blow. The cops showed up, but Dad slipped them a couple of bucks and told them to hit the road."

"How old were you then?"

"Like, thirteen maybe?"

"So our dad bribed some cops to help you get away with snorting cocaine at age thirteen. Am I hearing you correctly?"

"This is Los Angeles, okay?" She shrugged. "You're not in Chicago anymore."

"I'm from Colorado."

"I don't know why Ash lied about not being abducted. Seems to me like he was scared out of his mind. If I had to put money on it, I'd say he was abducted but he didn't want you to know."

"Why not?"

"You're not trustworthy."

"What? How could he tell that just by looking at me?"

"You send mixed messages. The hair and the rock band T-shirt and the tattoos say *Look at me,* but everything else says you hate yourself and don't want to be looked at."

"What's everything else?"

Baby didn't answer.

"My weight?" I laughed. "You think I hate myself because I'm fat? Is that what you're saying?"

Baby shrugged again. "I don't know why you care about Ash anyway." She huffed. "Maybe he was looking for Dad because sometimes Dad would smack a guy around if you asked him to."

I massaged my brow, tired and torn between the desire to know more about my dad's life as a thug for hire and the instinct that the less I knew the better.

"Or maybe the guy's got something on Ash that Ash doesn't want the cops to know," Baby said.

"Like what?"

"What do I look like? A psychic?" She rolled her eyes.

"Well, you noticed the drag marks on Ashton's shoes," I said. "You've got instincts. Observational skills. I like bouncing ideas off you. You're smart."

"Stop buttering me up," she said. "I'm not a piece of toast."

I laughed. My dad had always said that when I was a kid, whenever he caught me sucking up to him for treats or attention. Hearing his words coming out of Baby's mouth tickled me.

My father's storage unit was number 66. I unlocked the door, bracing for more mysterious bags of cash or a bigger cache of weapons than the one I'd found at his office.

Instead, the storage unit seemed empty. In the center of the ceiling was a hook, and from the hook hung a chain. On the chain was another key. There was no label, no tag.

Baby yawned. "It's just a key. We can go now."

"This isn't good," I said.

"Why not?"

"Because the key to this unit was hidden," I said. "I found it tucked away among Dad's stuff in his office."

"So?"

"So Dad didn't want anyone to find *that* key. But on the off chance that someone did, he's got another unmarked key waiting here. Whatever he's hiding, in order to find it you'd have to find the first key to get all the way here, then figure out what this key is for to get all the way *there*. It's like a puzzle."

Baby yawned again. "Pretty stupid puzzle."

"Whatever this key unlocks, it can't be good," I said.

"Can we get nuggets on the way there?" she whined.

"We don't even know where 'there' is," I said.

"Well, obviously it's in the desert. Just go back and check out the navigation system to Dad's car, see where he's been lately. Try to find something, like, desert-y, I guess."

"How do you know it's in the desert?" I asked.

She pointed to the floor. There was a fine layer of sand scattered in a path from the door of the unit to the light, leading to the key in the center of the room. Baby let out a resigned sigh.

"He brought it in on his shoes," she said.

"Oh," I said. "Right."

"It's all about the shoes, this stuff," she said.

"Spoken like someone who's been running a successful detective agency for a decade, not a fifteen-year-old kid whose dad let her hang out with him on the job a couple of times."

"Well, maybe I'm just quick," Baby said. "Keep up, lady."

THE desert was alive at night. Our headlights picked up a dozen creeping, crawling things as we rolled down a long dirt track between low mountains, an hour and a half out of San Bernardino. Baby was in the passenger seat, her face lit by her phone screen as her thumbs danced over the glass.

In a shallow valley ringed by Joshua trees, a rusty shipping container sat lit by moonlight. I checked the navigation system we'd taken from my father's car and saw that the last route visited led directly to where we now sat.

I opened the glove box in front of Baby, taking out the Magnum revolver I'd confiscated from my father's office.

"Look," I said. "Technically I'm wading into hazy legal territory here. This is not my gun. It's not registered to me. Given the circumstances, I'm not even sure it's Dad's gun, but I—"

As I was speaking, Baby pulled a .25 Baby Browning pistol with a pink pearlite grip out of her handbag. "This isn't registered to me either," she said.

I just sat there with my mouth open. She flicked the safety off the gun with an expert motion. I took the weapon from her carefully, flicked the safety back on, and unloaded it. I slipped the magazine into my pocket and the gun into the glove box.

"Hey, I—"

"Just don't," I said.

She threw her hands up and huffed a huge sigh.

We both exited the car. The desert air was warm and heavy. Baby grabbed my arm as I fit Dad's key into a giant padlock on the front of the container.

"What's that?"

"What?"

"Listen!"

From inside the container came a long, regular grinding noise. The sound of snoring.

I UNLOCKED the container and threw open the door. A thin man on a narrow bunk snapped awake, sat upright. The movement rattled a long chain that ran from his ankle to a D ring bolted to the floor of the container.

"What? What? What is it? What time is it?" he stammered.

"Oh my God," I said. I walked into the container, completely forgetting Baby. Along the side of the container, a row of tables had been assembled. They were littered with huge steel canisters, glass flasks, beakers, tubes, and a series of machines I didn't recognize.

Everything not in that section of the container was devoted to the man on the bunk: his pile of clothes, his miniature refrigerator, a portable air conditioner, a small lamp by the bed. I looked up and saw a camera bolted to the ceiling.

"What is this, Rhonda?" Baby asked.

"It's a meth lab," I said. I went to the man on the bunk. "Sir? I'm sorry. I'm so, so sorry. Are you okay?"

"What's happening?" His bloodshot eyes followed me as I came to unlock his chain. "Are we moving?"

"You're moving the hell out of here," I said. I prayed silently that the key that unlocked the padlock on the door fit the one on his ankle chain. It did.

"Who are you ladies?" the man said. I was surprised when he didn't bolt as soon as the chain hit the floor.

"I'm Rhonda Bird. My father—"

"Is Earl." The man nodded. "You look just like him."

He started gathering his dirty clothes into a backpack. I looked at Baby, who shrugged. The man wasn't acting like someone who'd been held prisoner and forced to cook meth in a stinky shipping container in the middle of the desert. He glanced around. "Can you tell me the date?" he asked.

"Ah, sure, it's . . ." I looked at my watch. "It's the fifteenth?"

"Yes!" He pumped a fist. "Excellent. Five days to go."

"Until what?"

"Until the Miffy's Tornado Tower of Doom chocolate shake promotion is over," he said. "Could I trouble you to drop me at the Miffy's in San Bernardino? They're twenty-four hours."

He strolled out of the container, leaving Baby and me staring after him in bewilderment.

THE man was sitting in the back seat of my car, staring straight ahead, when I emerged from the container. Baby was in the front seat, playing with her phone. Under the table in the lab section I'd found six kilos of crystal meth, which I'd wrapped in a sheet and bundled into the back of the car. I'd add it to Dad's bathroom hidey-hole later.

"He's delirious," Baby told me as I slid into the driver's seat. "He hasn't stopped talking about that stupid chocolate shake."

"What's your name, sir?" I asked, starting the car. "Can you tell me how you got into that container?"

"I'm Dr. Perry Tuddy," he said. "Your father put me there."

"Bull!" Baby held up a hand. "Dad isn't a meth dealer who locks people up in the desert. This guy is crazy."

"The Miffy's in San Bernardino would be much appreciated," Dr. Tuddy reminded me.

"Look, Dr. Tuddy, you're not acting like someone who's just been freed from a pretty hellish situation," I ventured.

"I'm fine," the doctor said. "The situation you just relieved me of hasn't been that hellish."

Baby and I looked at each other.

"This isn't my first incarceration," he said. "The first time I was abducted, a cartel in Mexico City put me in a basement under a steelworks factory. I caught a foot fungus down there that took me three months to get rid of after I was released."

"How long were you down there?" Baby asked.

"Five months," he said. "It was my own fault. I kept resisting cooking the meth for them. Trying to escape every chance I got. Now I just do what I'm told. I usually get let out or sold to another cartel after a couple of weeks."

The car filled with silence. I drove on through the dark, trying to envision my father as a cartel man. I *had* just come from his inexplicably lavish dwelling on the sand in Manhattan Beach. My heart sank in my chest.

"He's telling the truth," Baby said, flashing her phone screen at me. "There are tons of missing person alerts on this guy. 'Dr. Perry Tuddy, last seen at Walmart in Studio City, missing two weeks.' 'Dr. Perry Tuddy missing three weeks . . .'"

"What makes you such hot cartel property, Dr. Tuddy?"

"Perry is fine." He was watching the desert roll by the windows. "They want me because while I was studying for my Ph.D. at Claremont I developed an alternative to methylamine, which is essential in the production of crystal meth. The cartels were having trouble getting hold of pseudoephedrine, so they started using methylamine because it's cheaper and easier to get. My alternative is even cheaper and easier than that.

"I was studying the effects of methylamine and some other chemicals on the brain in pursuit of a cure for Alzheimer's, not illicit drug production," Perry continued. "But the *LA Times* ran a story about my work and how pharmaceutical companies were bidding for the patent. I was abducted a week later."

"Why don't you hire a team of bodyguards?" Baby said.

"Because this is my life," Perry said. "I'm not going to go into hiding like a criminal just because I'm a genius."

I opened my mouth to reply, but I couldn't decide what to think of his comment about criminals and his own genius, and his acceptance of regularly being abducted because of it.

A purple chrome Subaru WRX roared past us on the highway, heading in the opposite direction. Cartel men? I quickly took the next exit before they could realize they'd just passed the women they saw on the shipping container camera liberating their captive genius.

At the Miffy's in San Bernardino, Dr. Tuddy wrangled his tall, gangly body from the back seat of my car and walked off toward the restaurant without saying goodbye or thanking us for releasing him. Baby shook her head in disbelief.

"Maybe he just likes being abducted," she said.

"You might be right, but those cartel guys don't mess around," I continued. "It's only a matter of time before they stop playing catch and release with the good doctor."

I rolled out of the parking lot and switched on the radio. A news broadcast was just beginning.

". . . of the eighteen-year-old has not yet been ruled a homicide, but LAPD officers have issued a call for witnesses who might have seen a white van in the area of Trousdale Estates."

"Trousdale Estates," Baby said. "That's in Beverly Hills."

"White van," I said, turning up the radio.

Chapter 5

Morning came too soon. At the Denny's on West El Segundo, I ordered the Grand Slam and sat making phone calls, dealing with my abandoned life back in Colorado and the present situation in Los Angeles. Baby ordered black coffee. She sat sipping it while I smothered my pancakes with maple syrup.

"You eat this kind of thing every day?" she asked.

"Only when I've had a hundred-twenty-pound orphan dumped on me."

"*Excuse* me?" She scoffed and looked around in case someone had heard my overestimation of her weight.

"I'm adjusting to my life as a mother," I continued, ignoring her. "I need the energy."

"You're not my mother," Baby said.

"I've got a piece of paper that basically says otherwise."

"If you skipped breakfast a few days a week, you'd lose weight," she said. "Intermittent fasting. Google it."

"Did you body-shame Dad, too, or am I just lucky?" I asked.

"That's different," Baby said. "It's okay for guys to be fat."

"Excuse me," I said to the server as she topped up my coffee. "Could you please tell me what year it is? My daughter here thinks it's 1959."

The two of us shared an eye roll.

"I'm not your daughter," Baby said after the server left.

"Look at this," I said, pushing a newspaper toward her. The Los Angeles *Daily News* had a little more on the murder of Derek Benstein than we had heard on the radio the night before. The eighteen-year-old had been shot dead in his home. Witnesses mentioned seeing a white van without plates parked two blocks from Benstein's house.

"Whoa." Baby sighed. "I knew that guy."

"Oh. I'm sorry."

"Not well. We were at school together. Never shared a class or anything."

"So we've got two eighteen-year-old rich kids targeted in the same week," I said. "White van at both incidents."

"Hmm."

"Do me a favor." I pointed to her phone on the edge of the table. "Find out if Derek Benstein and Ashton Willisee are friends on Facebook or Instagram or whatever the hell."

Baby fished around on her phone while I waited for her answer. It was clear that my curiosity was piqued over what had happened to the kid I had seen in my father's office. Why had he lied to protect someone who had apparently tried to abduct him? Was it the criminal investigator in me, my propensity to want to learn the truth and see justice done whenever I could manage it? Or was it just that I sensed this investigation was something Baby and I could do together, a project we could share that might bring us closer?

"Bingo," she said, showing me her phone screen.

I saw Ashton Willisee's picture beside an image of the brawny and taut-faced Derek Benstein.

In the parking lot, Baby stopped by my Buick, still playing on her phone.

"So thanks for the free breakfast and all, but I've got to roll," she said. "Places to go, people to see—you know how it is."

"First of all, that wasn't breakfast," I said. "You consumed exactly zero calories in there. We've still got Dad's funeral to organize, and I need your help with—"

"He always said he wanted a black carriage pulled by six black horses at his funeral," she said. "That's all I know."

"Are you kidding me?" I sighed. "A carriage and horses?"

"You'll figure it out. Call a movie set or something."

"I want to look into this Willisee and Benstein thing," I said. "There's something there."

"Not my problem," Baby said. "I gotta bounce."

I was about to tell her she wasn't going anywhere, but her retreat was halted by a force much more persuasive than mine. She turned and slammed into the chest of a thick-necked guy in a black shirt covered with roses. Three more men emerged from the purple Subaru, which I recognized from last night. They were all around us before I could form a plan of escape.

"Rhonda, right?" the big guy said. "We want to talk to you."

I pulled Baby backward, away from the huge lug in the ugly shirt. The four guys seemed to be attendees of some kind of bad shirt convention. Embroidered roses, lilies, and hibiscus flowers adorned lapels and cuffs all around us. And the guy closest to me had a gun tattooed on his right cheek.

"I'm Martin Vegas," the big one said. "We got a problem."

"You bet we do," I agreed. "Baby, get in the car."

"No way." She stuck close to me. Her voice dropped to a murmur. "I'm not leaving you alone with these guys."

"What are you gonna do?" I murmured back. "Unfriend them to death? Get in the car." She didn't budge.

"We can probably skip right to it," Vegas said. "We're friends of Earl's. Sorry to hear he passed."

"Yeah, you guys look real torn up about it," I said.

"We are torn up. About losing not only Earl but our talented cook too," Vegas said. "Tuddy was hard to obtain. He's very in demand. Your dad played a big part in bringing him in, and now the two of you have undone that arrangement."

I tried to stifle the dread running through me at the mention of *your dad*. If Vegas knew we were Earl's daughters, he probably knew everything. He would know I was staying at my father's house. He would know about my job in Colorado. He would know I was the only adult in Baby's life. And those were dangerous pieces of information for drug cartel guys to have.

"Well, we won't waste your time," I said, pulling Baby toward the car. "You must be anxious to find Tuddy. Good luck. Last time I saw him he was on a Greyhound bus to Seattle."

I stepped back. The assembly of men moved around us. One of the guys leaned on the passenger-side door of my Buick, preventing me from shoving Baby in.

"Tuddy will show up again," Vegas said. "What we're anxious about now is getting our money and product back."

"We don't have that stuff," Baby said.

"Yeah, we do," I corrected her. "I took the meth from the shipping container. And about three million bucks in cash from Dad's office in Koreatown."

"First, why the *hell* would you do that?" Baby slapped at me. "And second, why the hell would you admit that *right now?*"

"They'll figure it out eventually. They're rubbing at least two brain cells together, although probably not much more." I glanced around the circle of guys. "And I took that stuff because I didn't have a full grip on the situation yet."

"Well, now you've got a grip," Baby said. "So give the guy what he wants before his goons kill us."

"Goons?" the guy with the gun-mouth tattoo said.

"Sorry," Baby squeaked. "I meant, like, henchmen?"

"I could probably accept *henchmen,*" Gunmouth grumbled.

"Look," Vegas said. "We're businessmen, okay? We're practical people. So your father didn't brief you on what you were supposed to do when he died. That's okay." He waved a consoling hand. "Not your fault. Just give us our stuff, and we'll all move on from this."

"No," I said.

Vegas blinked in disbelief.

"I don't know what I'm going to do with the meth or the money. But I do know I'm not giving it to you."

All the air seemed to go out of Baby at once. She wavered a little by my side. I didn't. I held strong, because someone my size does that—stands steady and as immovable as a sea cliff.

Gunmouth moved first. But I wasn't far behind him.

Baby's headscarf was the perfect handle. Gunmouth went for it, grabbing it like the end of a rope. I covered his hand with mine. My hand was bigger; my fingers squeezed his like a mitt around a baseball.

Gunmouth's eyes widened as I increased the pressure on his hand. In less than a second, something in his hand made a dull pop sound. He screamed. I held on. Baby was wailing.

I kicked out as another guy came for me, a sideways kick to the side of his knee. Another crunch. His leg bent at an unnatural angle, and he released a scream. I squeezed Gunmouth's hand one last time, heard another pop, and let him go.

Two men on the ground, wailing, two standing looking unsure of themselves—Vegas and his only remaining henchman.

I knew they were thinking about drawing their guns, but the windows of the Denny's beside us were crowded with people, some filming on their phones or calling 911. We all knew the smartest thing for Vegas to do was make a hasty retreat.

"Get in the car, Baby," I said a final time. She slipped into the vehicle, and I got in after her. Vegas glared at us all the way out of the parking lot. I knew he would be back in our lives sooner rather than later.

"Sooooo," Baby said in the car. "Can we make a deal?"

"I'm listening," I said.

"Can you maybe tell me the next time you're going to break a guy's hand? Like, maybe give me some warning?"

"It's not something I usually spend a lot of time planning."

"Where's the money?" she asked.

I laughed.

She folded her arms and huffed. "What, you think I'm going to take it all, drive to Vegas, and have a wild time?" she asked.

"That does sounds like something you would do." I shrugged. "That or spend it all on teeny-tiny handbags."

"Seriously, though, you bust into my life all, like, *Hey, Baby, guess what? You can't do this. You can't do that. You're too young. You're too irresponsible.* Then you go and steal from a Mexican drug cartel?" She threw her hands up.

"I wouldn't say *steal*. I prefer *confiscate*."

"Those guys chop people's feet off," Baby said. "If you're not going to give the cartel their stuff back, what *are* you going to do with it?"

"I don't know yet."

"Why don't you give it to the police?"

"The police will want to know where I got it," I said. "And the answer will implicate our father in a criminal enterprise."

"So? What do you care?" she asked. "The guy's dead."

"How do you like the idea of being homeless?" I said. "If the police think Dad was a drug dealer, they can take the house. They can empty his bank accounts."

Baby just stared out the window.

I turned onto the 110, following the signs for downtown LA.

"Where are we going?" she asked.

"Back to school," I said. "I think some kids are being hunted."

Baby said nothing as I punched into the GPS the address for Stanford-West Academy, which I remembered from the out-of-place bumper sticker on Ashton Willisee's Mercedes.

The huge wrought-iron front gates looked impressively secure as we drove up—but all it took was some vague mumbling about being a lawyer, here to see Ashton Willisee, before the bored guard rolled back the gates without question.

I drove through the immaculate campus grounds toward large

cream buildings nestled among lush green trees. My lovingly restored 1972 Buick Skylark's leopard-print paint job stood out among all the high-end automobiles parked in the lot next to the school's administration building. I figured I'd have more trouble in the school office, but at the first mention of the word *attorney*, the receptionist simply pushed a button and asked someone on the other end of an intercom to track down Mr. Willisee. She let her eyes wander over me, but I couldn't tell if she was appreciating my System of a Down T-shirt or giving me the Fat Person Look-Over.

"A lot of lawyers come here?" I asked the receptionist.

"Sure do," she said with a yawn. "About five a day. Lawsuits mostly. These kids are always suing someone, or someone is suing them. School hours are the best time to meet with child clients. Can't pay the maid to listen in here."

Baby and I exchanged a look at the receptionist's candor.

Before long, Ashton came around the corner of a long hallway. He stopped short at the sight of Baby and me.

"Oh no." He shook his head. "Nope. We're not doing this."

"Five minutes," I said. "We're here to help you."

Ashton didn't even look at the receptionist as he gave the command, "Call security."

"You can give them five minutes," the receptionist shot back. "System of a Down fans are good people."

"Rock on." I flipped her the sign of the horns.

Ashton didn't put up much of a fight. He walked quickly to a café-like area off the administration building that was enclosed by walls of pink bougainvillea. Students were sitting in groups, ignoring one another as they tapped on phones or laptops, earbuds plugging their ears. The space was eerily quiet.

"I remember when a bunch of kids being together meant noise," I said, trying to lighten Ashton's mood. "All I hear now are computer keys."

"So you're old," the boy said, sliding onto a chair across from us. "Get over it."

"What happened to Derek Benstein?" I asked.

"Who?" Ashton folded his arms.

"Don't even try." Baby rolled her eyes. "The two of you are all over social media together. You guys posted about eating at Soho House, like, yesterday." Baby waved her phone.

I was silently thankful at young people's propensity to let the internet know what they were doing at all times.

"Okay, so?" Ashton snapped. "My friend was murdered. I don't know anything about it. What do you want from me?"

"So you're going to claim it had absolutely nothing to do with your abduction two nights ago?" I asked.

"I wasn't abducted!" Ashton took out his phone and fired off a text. "You're, like, obsessed with me, lady. Don't you have anything better to do than try to get all up in my life?"

"This is what I do." I could feel Baby's eyes on me. "Everything about you is screaming *I need help,* and it has been since the moment I laid eyes on you."

Both Ashton and Baby fell into silence.

"Look," Ashton finally said. "Benzo was a friend of mine, and what happened to him is, like, really messed up, but he was into a bunch of bad stuff, okay? He was using black-market steroids to get big. The kind of stuff you can only get from criminals. He probably tried to rip off his dealer and got shot."

My phone rang. I glanced at it, planning to ignore it, but the call was coming from my legal office back in Colorado. I excused myself and walked a few feet away to take the call, knowing I had cases that needed reassigning. Baby and Ashton sat sullenly in their chairs. When the call ended, I pretended to type out an email, my ears pricked for their conversation. I knew it was helpful to let them align with each other against me. I hoped they would get real with each other the way teenagers sometimes can without the presence of adults. I found myself smiling as Baby attempted to do just that.

"My life is crazy right now," Baby said. "I did *not* see it coming, Dad dying on me."

"Heart attack?"

"Yeah," Baby said. "Good guess."

"Wasn't hard. He was always yelling."

"I still pick up my phone and try to call him." Baby sounded sad.

"I tried to call him just this morning, all like, *Dude, you've got to help me. This crazy chick is trying to take over my life.*"

"Are you trying to relate to me right now because Benzo's dead?" Ashton asked. "You think that's going to work? I don't even know you anymore. And I don't know that bitch at all."

"Rhonda's pushy," Baby said. "I get it. Try spending days with her. I'm about ready to blow my brains out."

"What is she, like, your mom or something?"

"No way. Does she look like she could be my mom?"

"I don't know. Maybe."

"She's my sister," Baby conceded. "Kind of. Half sister. We have the same dad. She turned up when he died. She's here from, like, Chicago or something."

Or something, I thought, exhausted.

"Maybe she's exactly what you need right now, though," Baby said. "If there's nobody in your life who can help, maybe it's going to take someone from outside to save you."

"That is some Hallmark-level crap," a new voice said.

I turned and saw a girl with blond ringlets approaching the table. She was dressed in expensive black silk, leather ankle boots, and a handbag that was three times the cost of my car. She let the bag fall beneath the table like it was a sack of trash.

It's not often that I feel the wave of dizzying electricity that seems to come with purely bad people, but I felt it now as I stood before this girl. Every animalistic sense in my body went on alert. Big trouble had just arrived.

Something changed in Ashton. His spine seemed to stiffen.

"And what are you doing back here, Teacher's Pet?" the girl asked Baby.

"Don't." Baby turned and glanced at me, her eyes wild. "Just leave it, okay?"

"What's going on here?" I asked. I gestured to the new girl and Baby. "Do you guys know each other?"

"No," Baby said. "We don't. I think we're done here, Rhonda."

"Are you sure?" the girl asked. "Because what you've been doing is harassing my friend here about his buddy, who was brutally murdered yesterday. He's traumatized, and you're questioning him without warning, consent, or police presence. Minute by minute you're racking up millions in a civil lawsuit for emotional damage caused by you violently bursting in to interrogate him over his friend's murder."

"Fine," I said. "We're done here, Miss . . ."

"Miss Go Screw Yourself." She smiled.

Baby and I left the blonde with Ashton and headed back to the car, Baby sticking close behind me.

"Don't stop," she said, glancing back.

"If I'd known you were this twitchy, I'd have come here alone."

"Yeah, well, I didn't think anyone except Ashton would recognize me. I had braids then, and I'm about a foot and a half taller now, and my skin is so much clearer. Australian pink sand exfoliating scrub. You should get on that."

"Uh-huh."

"It's been two years. Things change so fast around here I figured everybody would have forgotten," she said.

"About what?"

"Just drop it, Rhonda."

"This is *the thing* you and Ash were talking about in the hallway outside Dad's office. You hadn't seen him since *the thing*. What happened?"

She didn't answer.

"I'll google it."

"Yeah, only if you're a nosy, invasive, obsessive bitch."

"I *am* a nosy, invasive, obsessive bitch." I shrugged.

Baby didn't respond. When we reached the car, I unlocked the doors and she silently slipped into the passenger seat.

I got in and turned the key in the ignition.

Sparks zinged along the base of the bench seat beneath us.

"Oh *no!*" I said as flames burst from the floor of the Skylark and began to coil around our ankles.

"WE'RE dead," Ashton said.

Vera yawned and took out her phone to text the twins. She and Ashton were the only Midnight Crew members who still attended high school. Penny and Sean had technically graduated, though their disregard for formal education had increased as the time until their trust funds kicked in dwindled. And Benzo had never been an academic. His parents had basically bribed his teachers to pass him every year since kindergarten.

"We're not dead, Ashton. We're fine."

Vera needed to rally her people. A meeting would be required with the entire posse over Benzo's murder. Excitement was coursing through her, but she needed to maintain a nonchalant air with Ashton, the most panicky of their number.

"I know a guy who lives across the street from Benzo." Ashton leaned in, gripping the tabletop with white knuckles. "He said they brought him out on a stretcher, and he could see marks on one of Benzo's legs. Like, weird bruises."

"Maybe he was tortured." Vera shrugged.

"How are you not losing your mind over this?"

"Because whoever we're dealing with is stupid," she said. "He came after the weakest members of the group. He should have gone right for the snake's head." She tapped her chest.

"So you're admitting that this is someone we've hit with the Midnight Crew and not just something random?" Ashton said. "It's someone who wants revenge."

Vera gave him a dangerous look. He sank back in his chair.

"Now that we know he's after us," she continued, "we'll be prepared."

"Right. So we'll get out of town." Ashton nodded. "We can go to my mom's place in Aruba, wait it out there. Penny and Sean's aunt is, like, in the FBI, I think. She can track this guy down, pin him with something that has nothing to do with us."

"You've been working on that little plan all morning, haven't you?" Vera reached over and gave Ashton a condescending stroke on the shoulder. "You must be tired."

"Come on, Vera."

"We're not running from this guy," she said. "My people don't run."

"Your people?" Ashton asked, but even as the words left his mouth, he seemed to want to snatch them back.

Vera's father, Evgeni Petrov, was thought to be somewhere in New Jersey, living under an assumed name, being protected by allied factions of the Russian and Armenian mobs. Vera wasn't stupid—she knew it looked to everyone like he'd run away from bad debts and underhanded deals inside the mob. But her father had done this before. He went underground, dug in. Then when things settled, he rose and attacked.

"We're going to find this guy ourselves." Vera lifted her bag and slung it over her shoulder. "We're not kids anymore. We deal with our own problems."

Ashton stepped in front of her, blocking her path. She was impressed with him for challenging her, holding her glare.

"This is getting out of control," Ashton said. "You said from the beginning, 'No one gets hurt.' You also said, 'If we ever get found out, we back away, go underground, come up with a smart plan.' This isn't smart, Vera. This is reckl—"

Vera grabbed Ashton's crotch and squeezed slowly. Ashton bent double as his mouth slammed shut.

"I'm saying something different now," Vera said. The people around them were all looking up from their screens, tugging earbuds from their ears. "And you better listen carefully, because I make the rules, and they've changed."

Chapter 6

I LUNGED SIDEWAYS and grabbed the handle of Baby's door. In one movement, I barreled us both out of the car in an awkward, painful roll just as the front of my car exploded.

I knew Baby was screaming, but I couldn't hear it. There was only ringing in my ears as we crawled into the middle of the parking lot, out of the reach of the flames.

As I dragged myself to my feet, Baby hung off me by her fingernails with one leg wrapped around my waist. I had to peel her off and place her on her feet, where she stood trembling and watching the car burn.

"What happened?" she wailed. "What happened? What happened, Rhonda? What did you do?"

"What did I do?" I brushed singed pieces of fabric off my shoulders. "I pissed off a Mexican drug cartel, that's what."

People were rushing out of the administration building. Where once they might have run toward us to assist, the sight of the burning car had everyone bolting in the other direction, disappearing back into the building. Unexpected and dangerous events on school grounds meant active shooters to these people. Baby and I stood watching the flames as sirens began to wail from the buildings around us.

"All right, listen up," I told Baby. "We've got to get our story straight."

By the time the SWAT team had evacuated the school and handed the parking lot crime scene over to the local police, it was sunset outside the Stanford-West Academy. Baby sat on the curb. Neither Ashton nor Miss Go Screw Yourself had been among the crowds that eventually came around to gawk.

I'd offered a range of explanations about the Buick Skylark's explosion to the officers who'd approached me as the hours passed. I'd feigned flat-out confusion. I'd claimed the car was possessed by an angry demon, or by the ghost of my deranged father. My words initially managed to shut down further explorations by the authorities of what had happened. The men and women who dealt with the scene seemed simply relieved that there had been no one seriously injured.

While I waited for another round of questioning, I stood in the corner of the lot and watched a forensic photographer unload equipment from his car. Sometimes it's the people on the sidelines who offer the most assistance when working an investigation—the photographers, cleanup crews, and junior officers who work crowd control. I had learned from years of experience looking for witnesses and new angles on my cases that these people were far more useful than the higher-ranking, more "important" people involved in solving a crime.

I approached as the photographer was clipping a lens to the front of the camera hanging around his neck. "Ma'am." He smiled, showing bright white teeth. "How many dead?"

"None," I said.

"Oh." He seemed a little disheartened.

"It's my car that exploded." I pointed. "So I'm having a terrible day. How do you like the idea of doing a favor for a woman who could use some cheering up?"

"Depends on what it is." The guy smirked.

"You must know some other crime-scene photographers in town, right?"

"Sure." He shrugged.

"Do you know who worked the shooting in Trousdale Estates last night? The teenager?"

"Maybe." He shrugged again. "Why?"

"I'm just interested in those pictures."

"You a journalist?" he asked.

"Maybe." I mimicked his shrug. I reached into my pocket and pulled out my wallet. I'd taken some cash from the three-million-dollar bundle of trouble hidden in my father's bathroom. I fanned them for the photographer. "Does it matter?"

"Nope." The photographer had the money and my business card inside his chest pocket in a flash. "I'll get in touch."

I headed back to the smoking wreck of my car. I knew I was in trouble when a new officer approached. He strode toward me across the lot in a pitch-black uniform that hugged his enormous muscular frame.

Officer Summerly's name badge gleamed in the setting sun, making me squint as he stood squarely in front of me. This didn't seem like a man who was going to be easily brushed off.

"Okay." Summerly took off his cap and wiped sweat from his temples with a black handkerchief. "Let me hear it."

"Ejector seat," I said.

"Excuse me?"

"The car is a retired stunt car," I lied. "It was mechanically altered in preparation for a small film that was supposed to be shot in Watkins, Colorado, in 1993. *The Adventures of Leopardo Smith*. You ever hear of it?"

"Wha— No." Summerly shook his head.

"Leopardo was a spy. The ejector seat was for if he was ever cornered by villains in his car," I said. "I bought the car off the lot when the film's funding was withdrawn. I guess after all these years the mechanism exploded." I shrugged helplessly.

Summerly breathed in deeply. "Lady," he said. "That's the most incredible thing I've ever heard."

"I know, right?" I laughed. "Lucky no one was injured."

"No, I don't mean incredible like amazing," Summerly said. "I mean *in-credible*. You expect me to believe that story?"

I didn't respond.

He pointed to the officers milling around behind him. "See that officer over there? Name badge says Hammond?"

"I see her," I said.

"She says you told her you ran over a can of gasoline."

"It's possible I said that." I nodded.

"That officer over there by the tree says you told him your car was possessed by a malevolent spirit." Summerly pointed.

"Mm-hmm." I nodded again. Baby was listening carefully from the curbside.

"And for me"—he gave a frustrated laugh, tapped his chest—"you come up with this . . . this *ejector seat* tale?"

"I saved the best for last," I said.

"What really happened, Miss . . ." He jutted his chin at me.

"Bird. Rhonda."

"Bird." He clicked the top of a shiny black pen, slipped a notebook from his chest pocket. "From the beginning."

"No comment," I said.

Summerly lifted his eyes. "Are you kidding me?"

"No," I said. "I have no comment. I don't have to make a

statement on what happened here today. I wasn't even legally obliged to give you my name. But I did, because I'm nice."

"Oh." Summerly deflated slightly. "A lawyer."

"That's right."

"Your car exploded in a school parking lot, Miss Bird," Summerly said. "You have to tell us what happened."

"No, I don't," I said.

"Yes, you—"

"Are you going to charge me with a crime?"

"Hell yeah, I am." He took a pair of handcuffs off his belt. "Unless you tell me who blew up your car, then, yes, I'll charge you. This is . . . uh. Well, it's public endangerment, at least. Child endangerment. It's lying to police."

"I haven't lied to the police."

"All of your stories are conflicting!"

"Well, how do you know I don't believe they're all true at the same time?" I shrugged. "I might be crazy. Concussed. You would have to prove my intent to purposefully deceive you in a court of law to make that charge stick, Officer Summerly."

Summerly shook his head and laughed. I liked the sound of his laughter. It was heavy and husky and strong.

"Miss Bird, when I examine this car—"

"You don't get to examine my car," I said. "I don't give you permission."

"You can't be serious. It's a piece of evidence."

"Only if there's a crime," I said. "So I'll ask you again. Are you going to charge me with a crime?"

Officer Summerly's eyes wandered over my face. He took a step closer and lowered his voice.

"You know what I think happened here?" he asked.

"Please tell me." I smiled.

"A couple of months ago," he murmured, "Danny Trejo and Benicio Del Toro, I think it was, were in this action movie where they played Mexican cartel guys. Their signature move was to rig explosives under the driver's seat in people's cars. I saw the movie. Good movie."

I waited, listening.

"Bombs in cars haven't ever been a cartel thing in real life," Summerly said. "But ever since that movie came out, there's been a rash of copycat car bombings all over the Southwest."

"Okay." I shrugged. "So what's that got to do with me?"

"Are you tied up with a cartel, Miss Bird?"

"No comment." I smiled.

Summerly took off his hat and fanned his face.

"Look, it has been a long, hot shift," he said. "My last stop was a dog stuck in a crawl space under an industrial oven in a bakery. I'm hot and tired. I just want to go home."

"So go home," I said. "There's no crime here."

Summerly gave up. He took a card from the back of the notebook and slapped it into my palm. DAVID SUMMERLY. "When you're ready to talk, call that number."

Baby appeared beside me as Summerly departed. She caught me checking out the officer's ass as he walked away.

"You were into that guy," Baby said as our Uber turned off onto the Pacific Coast Highway toward Manhattan Beach.

"Oh, please." I snorted. "I'm a lawyer. Any mystique or allure men in uniform might've had for me wore off years ago."

"Not *that* guy in uniform," she said.

"Don't be such a smart-ass."

"What? He was into you, too, I think," she said. "Anyway, he seemed nice. And he's a good size for you. You'd need a big guy. He was built like a tank. I clock you two."

"I'm going to ignore your incredibly rude comments about his physical size in comparison to mine, as though that means anything at all about our romantic compatibility," I said, "and instead ask what you mean by 'I clock you two'?"

"Like, I think it's a good idea, you two being together," she mused. "Clocking something means you like it. I don't know where it comes from. Maybe it's like 'It's time for that to happen.' You could say 'I clock this handbag' and mean 'It's time for me to own this handbag!'"

"'I clock this,'" I said. "I like it. I'm going to start using it."

"Don't. You're too old. And by the time you say it to anyone, it'll be over. People won't be saying it anymore, and you'll be even more lame."

I massaged my brow, trying to recover from being called fat, old, and lame within a single minute.

"Oh no." Baby sat bolt upright in her seat as we turned onto the street where my father's house sat in the row of luxury homes before the water. "There are people in the house!"

There were indeed people in the house. Inside and outside. In the upper window I could see a woman in a green uniform vacuuming. Three men were hauling trash toward the curb, where a row of twelve other garbage bags stood by the road.

Baby leaped from the car before it had even stopped rolling. "Who are they? What's happening?"

I got out of the car and chased her down. I put a hand on Baby's shoulder. "Relax. I hired a crew to come in and clean the house. The place looked like a bomb site."

Baby whirled around, her eyes filled with horror. Then she took off into the house. While I paid the cleaners and sent them on their way, she remained upstairs somewhere. I surveyed their work on the living room. My father's house had been rid of the stench of cigar smoke and now smelled of floral cleaning products. There were no nameless teens in sight. The enormous kitchen was gleaming. I heard Baby come down the stairs and found her trembling in the middle of the spotless foyer.

"Are you okay?" I asked.

"They went into my room," she said shakily. Her eyes were huge, brimming with rageful tears. Her teeth were locked. "*They cleaned my room*. How. Could. You. Do. This?"

"How could I . . ." I laughed, confused by her reaction. "Baby, the house was filthy. It was like something out of *Hoarders*. There was a pancake stuck to the wall of Dad's shower. A *pancake*. Normal people can't live like this."

"They touched my stuff," Baby said. "All my clothes—"

"Yeah, I saw your clothes," I said. "I glanced into your room. There was three feet of clothes on the floor in there."

"You *bitch!*" Baby barked.

"Whoa!"

"You don't touch my stuff," Baby screamed. "You—or your cleaners or anyone associated with you—you don't ever, ever, *ever* touch my stuff!"

She stormed out the back door. As she crossed the street away from the house, I stood stunned, looking after her. Then I climbed the stairs to her room. With the kind of reverence reserved for an ancient temple, I crossed the threshold and stood inside on the Hoover-tracked carpet. The closet stood open, overpacked with washed, folded, and hung clothes. There was a desk against the window that was neatly arranged with things the cleaners had had no clue what to do with: candle holders and notebooks, hair clips, old iPhones.

I looked around the room and tried to imagine what was so precious that Baby would flip out with the kind of panic she had failed to demonstrate when we were almost killed in a car bombing only hours earlier. When I saw nothing that answered my question, I left the room and closed the door with a strange sense of certainty that I would end up paying for what I had done to the teenage girl whether I understood it or not.

Ashton knew that Sean and Penny's driver was named Tom. The twins had been driven around by the same withered, white-haired man since Ashton first met them at some Brentwood mansion pool party, their parents getting drunk in cabanas while the kids were taken out for gelato by the help.

Ashton glanced through the darkened privacy screen of the Mercedes-Maybach S 650 Pullman. He wondered about Tom's life as a private driver to a pair of spoiled rich brats. He wondered if Tom questioned his existence, the fairness of Sean and Penny's place in the back of the vehicle and his in the front.

Ashton sure questioned it. As they drove to pick up Vera,

he questioned his own place with the two. He questioned the dangerous games they liked to play.

Ten minutes later, Vera slipped into the car and dropped her handbag onto the console beside her, tossing her shopping bags from boutique jewelry stores onto the floor. She threw a look around the limo's cabin.

"Benzo is dead, and there's some kind of sicko after us," Ashton said. "We need to be really careful right now."

"Don't talk like you're in charge here, Ashton." Vera gave a thin smile. "You sound like an idiot."

Ashton worked his jaw, letting seconds pass as he recovered his dignity. "So what do we do?"

"We hit another house," Vera said.

"What?" Ashton cried.

"Yes." Penny was nodding eagerly. "I was thinking the exact same thing, Vera."

"We set a trap, lure this guy out," said Vera.

"This is insane." Ashton shook his head.

"He's probably been following us from the moment he took Ashton's phone," said Vera. "He likely emptied the phone of everything he needed before you could shut it down. He'll know who we are, where we live. He'll have our videos. That's why we can't go to the police or to any lame private investigators." She gave Ashton a withering look. "Tomorrow morning, we split up and try to shake him off. Then we come together again and make sure he's following us to the next raid. While he thinks he's watching us, we can get a good look at him."

She took out her phone and tapped away.

"I'm sending you a list of suspects," Vera said. Ashton felt his phone buzz in his pocket. "This is every male victim we've had in the last year."

"What if it's not one of the guys we actually hit?" Ashton asked. "What if it's a relative of one of our victims? Or a friend? Or someone they hired?"

Everyone was looking at their phones. Ashton sighed at their silence.

"What is your plan, exactly?" he said. "Once we find out who's after us?"

"Simple. We grab him, make him tell us what he's got on us," said Vera. "Then we destroy everything, cover our tracks."

"And then what?" Ashton asked.

"We kill him, of course," Vera said.

Ashton laughed, but it sounded forced. He could see glitter dancing in the twins' eyes. They loved this kind of talk.

"We're not killing anyone," Ashton said. "That was never what this was about. The Midnight Crew is about having fun and blowing off steam, maybe scaring some people, messing with them. That's why *I* joined, anyway."

"You joined because you were angry," Vera said. "Your uncle made mincemeat of your aunt's overpriced nose job at Thanksgiving, and you wanted to feel like the big man for once. Now that you've righted things in your family, you're not as angry at life." She threw her hands up. "That doesn't mean you get to walk away from the Midnight Crew. That's desertion."

"Treason." Sean nodded. "Going AWOL. You do that in war and army guys will put you up against a wall and shoot you."

"Don't pretend you're some kind of hard-core military guy, Sean," Ashton said. "You spend a grand a month on pedicures."

"Who are we hitting?" Penny bounced in her seat. "I'm ready to go. This guy killed Benzo. We're going to find him."

"It doesn't matter who we hit," Vera said. "As long as we move fast."

She stopped to think for a moment, watching the downtown stores roll by the window. "There's a woman on my street with this dog. A little terrier. It barks at me every time I walk by. They'll do. We go tomorrow night."

Chapter 7

THAT NIGHT IN MY deceased father's house was a long, exhausting one. Still rattled from the fight with Baby, I'd spent hours texting her in vain. I'd lain awake until three a.m., when I heard her come in. She'd ignored me on her way to her bedroom, slamming the door in my face when I tried to talk to her.

In the morning, Baby's bedroom door was still shut. I wandered to the rooftop of the massive house and discovered a large swimming pool stretching over its expanse. To the right of the door opening onto the roof, by a row of weather-beaten lawn chairs, stood a rusty home gym draped with old towels.

I've been lifting weights since I was ten. My dad had set up a gym in our garage in Watkins with a treadmill and a set of dumbbells. I wandered in one morning and saw him struggling to bench fifty pounds. I rushed in and helped him get it up and into the rack. Like the idiot that he was, he was embarrassed and banished me from the garage. The banishment turned his gym into an alluring destination for a young and lonely me.

As I perused the free-weights rack, the sensation of being watched prickled over my skin. I looked over and noticed that on the roof of the adjacent house, a place that appeared to be under renovation, with scaffolding erected in the gap between the two homes, a group of tanned young men were crowded around their own gym equipment, keeping a careful eye on me.

I jutted my chin at them in what I intended as a friendly but tough manner. Three of the four didn't respond. The fourth put a foot up on the lip of the roof and glared at me. I guessed the fat chick playing with weights made a mockery of everything they stood for—health, strength, physical masculine beauty, pushing their bodies to the limit, like a bunch of modern warriors. I wasn't welcome here, even on my own rooftop.

One of the dudes loaded his bench press up with 220 pounds, glancing over at me as he made some comment to his bros. I went over to Dad's bench press and loaded it up with the same. As I sat on the bench, the guy lay back and pumped out five fast reps. I did the same. The bros laughed. One of them pushed his friend out of the way and loaded up another 80 pounds. I watched him work five slow, perfect reps. I loaded my weights up to 300 pounds and did the same.

Confusion hit on the opposite rooftop. The bros huddled.

The biggest of the bros began loading up the bench press bar. I stood and mimicked him, loading as he loaded. The numbers climbed: 360, 380, 400, then 440 pounds. The big guy struggled through three reps, his body trembling. I cracked my knuckles, but before I could lie down, one of the dudes came to the edge of the roof.

"Don't be stupid, lady!" he yelled. "You'll hurt yourself!"

"We'll see!" I yelled back. I went to my bench. I loaded on another 20 pounds. The guys gathered at the edge of the roof and folded their arms—concern for my safety, or their own reputations, written on their stern faces.

I pumped out five slow, careful reps. My arms trembled, the muscles straining. I pumped out a sixth rep and heard the guys erupt in moans of awe as I fit the bar back into the rack.

I don't know what else I expected. A round of applause, maybe. A smile. But I got none of that. The guys took in my display, then turned and left the rooftop without another word.

I was alone only a moment before Baby stepped out through the big glass door leading onto the roof.

"We need to talk," she said.

"I invaded your space," I said. "I totally get it."

"No, you don't get it. Because as far as I know, you've never had someone walk into your life and turn absolutely everything upside down, including your own bedroom!"

"It needed to be done. You and Dad were living like pigs. But I should have consulted you. Or given you a chance to—"

"Don't try to side with me," Baby seethed. "I'm pissed at you. So pissed I can hardly breathe."

I tried to stay silent, but the words bubbled up.

"You know what, Baby," I said. "I *have* had someone walk into my life and turn absolutely everything upside down. That person was you. I've never been a mother before—do you understand that? I have no idea what I'm doing here!"

"You are *not* my mother!"

"Well, I'm something." I shrugged. "You can't have nobody in your life taking care of you, Baby. You're a *child*."

"See, Rhonda, this is what you do," Baby sneered. "You fall back on that 'You're too young' crap whenever you're losing an argument."

"Well, it's true!" I said. "And I'm not losing this argument. It's not even an argument! You're just yelling at me!"

"You're yelling back!" she howled.

"I know!" I covered my eyes, took a breath. "Urgh. I know."

"I'm going to get you, Rhonda," Baby said. "I'm going to show you exactly how childish I can be."

She stormed off again. I saw her walking down the stairs with her phone in her hands, texting furiously.

My phone buzzed behind me on the workout bench. I picked it up. In my email, a message with no subject header was sitting in the in-box from a name I recognized. I opened the zipped file attachment in it, and a trail of photographs began downloading. In the first, I saw the twisted dead body of Derek Benstein lying beside a darkened glass door.

SANTA Monica Pier was crowded with people. Past the roller coaster and Ferris wheel, a huge, pink Styrofoam cup had been erected halfway down the pier. The cup towered over the crowd, and an enormous straw wavered in the gentle breeze.

I positioned myself on a bench by the pier rail between two sets of fishermen and watched the crowds looping slowly around the giant cup, receiving their free Miffy's Tornado Tower of Doom chocolate shakes. I analyzed every face. It was three hours before the right man came along.

Dr. Perry Tuddy was hiding from the blazing sun under a ball cap wedged onto a tattered blond wig that was tied in a ponytail. I sidled up to him, and he flinched at the sight of me.

"Oh, dear." He expelled a sigh. "Back to the container, is it?"

"That's all the fight you put up every time these guys come to abduct you?" I asked. "You're not even going to try to run?"

"How am I going to run without spilling my shake?" He gestured to the counter, three customers ahead of us. I tried to answer but couldn't begin to approach that kind of logic.

"I'm not here to stuff you into a van," I said. "I need your help with something else. Grab your shake and one for me, yeah? I'll meet you by the taco stand."

Tuddy got the shakes, and the two of us stood in the shade, watching the sea for a while. Jet Ski riders were trailing bright pink flares in promotion of the Miffy's giveaway.

"I know this is going to sound crazy," I told Tuddy, "but I think I'm on the trail of a killer."

I told Tuddy what I knew about Ashton Willisee, describing the chance meeting with the scared, obviously lying teenager in my father's office and the visit to Stanford-West Academy. I told Tuddy that I thought Ashton was hiding something. The fact that he would lie about his relationship with Derek Benstein had convinced me that the boy was trying to disguise possible knowledge of what had happened to his friend.

"Let me ask you a question," Tuddy said between sips of his shake. "What has this got to do with you?"

"Nothing," I admitted. "My only connection is that Ashton came seeking my father's help, and I stuck my nose in. But there's something in that kid's face. I feel like he needs help."

"How could you read him like that?" Tuddy asked.

"I guess because I've felt it myself." I shrugged. "When my father left, that's what it was like. I had my mother, my school friends. But I still felt like I was drowning, and there were a bunch of people on the shore who couldn't rescue me."

Tuddy and I watched the water. I used my long spoon to scoop chocolate chunks from the bottom of my shake.

"Okay." I sighed. "Maybe there's more to it. My little sister knows Ashton from school. I just met this girl, and we're not the best of friends yet. So maybe getting involved in this investigation, helping her friend, is something we can do together."

"Okay, so how can I help, then?" he asked. "I mean, why chase me down, of all people?"

I laughed, a little embarrassed. "Look, it's hard to explain, but . . . I think I saw your freak flag."

"My *freak flag?*"

"Yeah," I said. I showed him my tattooed arms, gestured to my pink hair. "I mean, look at me. You can spot me a mile away. I fly my freak flag proudly. But you—you're more subtle. You keep letting the cartel lock you up like an animal. And I think that's because a part of you enjoys it, and that's freaky."

He, too, toyed with the chocolate in the bottom of his cup. "I'm addicted," he confessed.

"Addicted to getting abducted? Who the hell enjoys being locked up?" I asked.

"Me," he answered. "Have you heard of dopamine fasting?"

"No," I said.

"Dopamine is an organic chemical produced by your body. It's a part of the catecholamine and phenethylamine families. It acts as a neurotransmitter so that—"

"You're losing me, Tuddy."

"It's your happy chemical," he said. "It's essential in helping you enjoy things. The taste of chocolate. The smell of sea air. When you're locked in a dark room for a whole day, with no stimulus to release your dopamine, your brain stores it up."

"Okay," I said.

"When I spend a month alone in a shipping container, it's like I shut down. I store up the dopamine in my brain. Then when I'm released, it's like I'm literally *walking on sunshine.*"

I watched him becoming more animated as he spoke.

"This, all this, it's like it sparkles." He gestured to the world around us. "I can smell everything. I can feel everything. I'm high for weeks after a release. It's like the high you get from heroin, you know? Only it lasts days, not hours."

I stared. Tuddy stood smiling at me.

"I wouldn't know what the high from heroin is like," I said. "Would you?"

"I spent eight years researching addictive chemicals," he said. "You think I didn't mess around with my own stock now and then?" He shook his head sadly. "That's why all those companies began bidding for the patent on my methylamine alternative. They wanted to buy the product from me even though it wasn't complete."

"Because you were a liability," I concluded. "Nobody wants to work with an addict."

"That's right," he said. "In other circumstances, they would have hired me to continue my research. But I was so deeply addicted to heroin at the time, I was damaged goods. It was only the months-long incarcerations with the cartel that got me clean. The first time, I had a guard watching me twenty-four hours a day. I couldn't touch a gram."

He turned to me, his eyes glittering.

"So, yes," he concluded. "Freak. Big freak. How can I help you, my freaky friend?"

I handed Tuddy my phone, then leaned over and flipped through the photographs of Derek Benstein's crime scene for him. I hadn't looked carefully at the images myself, only scrolled through them briefly, trying not to focus.

I paused at the photographs of Benstein's torso, which was covered in bruises and marks. The photographer had paid particular interest to purple marks on Benstein's thigh, visible at the hem of his boxer shorts.

"Huh," Tuddy said. "This young man has been tortured with some kind of electrical device. Probably a cattle prod. These are electrical burns," he said, pointing. "You see?"

I looked and immediately felt a little ill. "I see."

"You can also see he's been starved of oxygen," Tuddy said,

enlarging an image to focus on Benstein's face. "The capillaries in his eyeballs have burst, consistent with electrocution."

I walked away, went to the edge of the pier, and looked at the water, sucking in the sea air.

"Are you okay?"

"I don't spend a lot of time looking at pictures of dead bodies," I said.

"Neither do I." He shrugged. "But this young man is no longer in pain, if that's what's disturbing you."

"How do you know so much about electricity and the human body?" I asked.

"We did some experiments in my first residency with electroshock therapy. My professor was trying to develop a new therapy for depression. That's how I got into the study of narcotics and Alzheimer's."

"Okay," I said. "I think I have everything I need."

"Perhaps worth mentioning he was also shot." Tuddy thrust the phone at me. I winced, saw only red, torn flesh. "See here?"

I snatched the phone away.

"Thanks for the help," I said, closing the images. "If I need you again, where can I find you?"

"Hopefully inside a steel box, somewhere quiet, far away," he said. I took down Tuddy's phone number as he recited it, and then I walked into the crowd, leaving the doctor to his musings. There were darker things on my mind. I was sure now that someone was enacting revenge on Ashton Willisee and his friends. If I was going to stop him, I had to find out why.

Baby was waiting for me on the steps of our father's house when I arrived home in an Uber. She smiled sweetly as I approached. I should have listened to the niggling uneasy feeling in my belly as she tossed me a heavy set of keys.

"Let's roll," she said. "We'll take the Maz."

"Let's roll?" I asked. "Just like that?"

"Yeah." She turned and headed through the open garage door.

"I've got a lead on some people who are connected with both Ashton and Benzo. You still want to go messing around that whole, like, case thing. Right?"

"Right," I said. "But you seem to be forgetting you just about ripped my head off this morning about your room."

"I know." She flicked her big sunglasses down over her eyes. "I was being stupid. I checked out my room properly, and they didn't get to any of my private stuff. You were trying to do the right thing." Baby took a deep breath. "So I forgive you."

"Oh." I laughed. "How nice."

"Don't push your luck with me, Rhonda," she said. "You do not want to get on my bad side permanently."

"Whatever you say," I said. We climbed into Dad's Maserati. I was enveloped in his smell again, smoke and sweat, fried food, bad cologne. Despite Baby's cool exterior, I was feeling upbeat about repairing our relationship.

"Where are we going?"

"We're going to see some very important people," Baby said, plugging her phone into the car's system. A map appeared on the console. I could see texts pinging silently at the bottom of the screen, the number of unopened messages climbing steadily. Again the feeling pulsed through me that I was missing something. No teenager could possibly be so inundated by communication on any regular sort of day. I brushed off my uncertainty, thinking that some news in her social circle must have broken. I headed for the address on the screen in downtown Los Angeles as the garage door slid closed behind me.

The GPS led us to Santee Alley, the downtown fashion district. My father's Maserati was a smooth, humming, luxuriously awful ride compared to my Buick, and for the first time I had a moment to grieve my lost leopard-print lady. I stood by the window of a children's clothing store, gawking at a pair of eight-hundred-dollar shoes for toddlers.

Baby tapped away on her phone. She stopped to check her

reflection in the window of the store. She dropped a hip and pouted at herself as I stifled a laugh.

"We don't have an appointment," she said, stepping back to look at the next store over. "We'll have to beg our way in. So it's important that you stay out of sight."

"What is this place?" I looked up. The windows at the front of the other store were blackened. A single gold letter *U* was bolted above the black door. "*U?* What's that stand for?"

"It's not *U* like *You.*" She rolled her eyes. "It's *Ooo*—Ooo La La."

"What does it mean?"

"Nothing. It's, like, the most relevant emerging fashion boutique in the world." She huffed. "And that's how you say it."

"I thought you said we were coming to see very important people."

"We are," she said. "Sean and Penny Hanley are just . . . *everything.*"

"*'Everything'?*" I said, mimicking the reverence with which she had said the word. Baby didn't so much as crack a smile.

"Get out of the way, Rhonda." She waved me off to the side and pushed a pearl buzzer set in the wall. The door clicked as it unlocked, and I had to scramble to follow Baby into the store before the door shut on me.

The space inside was elaborate but confused. It seemed the store's designers hadn't known if they wanted to go for abandoned warehouse or haunted Edwardian mansion. Candelabras stood by crumbling faux brick walls, and diamond chandeliers hung on worn brown ropes from exposed pipes. There were two racks of clothes in a space that might have accommodated fifty. Behind a counter, a young woman with a blond bob was arranging paperwork. In a corner of the room, a young man, who so closely resembled her that they were clearly twins, was slumped in a plush velvet chair, scrolling on his phone. He lifted his eyes from the screen, looked me over, laughed, and went back to his scrolling. The young woman came out from behind the counter with a similar disdain.

"You don't have an appointment," she said to Baby. "And who are you?" She gestured to me.

"This is my fashion consultant, Eleanor Wave," Baby said. "I'm so sorry we didn't check in earlier. We just arrived from Paris."

The young woman gave Baby a full visual examination, then stood back like she'd been slapped awake. She put a hand to her chest with the kind of drama that made me want to giggle.

"I'm Penny Hanley." She offered her hand. "Oh, your cheekbones."

I waited for more. There was none. Baby nodded like someone accepting condolences at a funeral.

"Matte," Baby said. "Can we?"

"Please." Penny gestured to the racks. Baby went and shifted items of clothing along the nearest rail. Some pieces were so thin—mere strips of fabric—I assumed they were men's ties.

"Who's Matt?" I whispered, coming alongside her.

"My fashion name. Not Matt, like the man's name. Matte. With an *e* at the end. Like the finish."

"That's hilarious," I murmured.

"Don't touch the clothes. Just the hangers."

"Where are the prices?"

"There are no *prices*." Baby rolled her eyes.

"I didn't know you were into this kind of stuff," I said. I gestured to the filthy denim cutoffs Baby wore. "Those shorts look like you got them off a three-year-old hobo."

"They're supposed to look like that." Baby huffed. She turned and strolled over to Penny and her brother with one of the men's ties. Some kind of approval was given, and Baby slipped off her T-shirt. There was no dressing area to speak of. Once she had it on, it appeared that the garment was not a men's tie but a strip of black fabric meant to cover her breasts horizontally. Baby pouted in a mirror, posing in the top. Penny seemed to be on the edge of bursting out with words, holding herself back with difficulty. Finally, she gave in.

"I have to ask. Who are you repped by?"

"I'm independent," Baby said.

"Oh." Penny fanned herself like a southern belle. "Wow. *Wow*. Sean? She's independent."

Sean looked up, squinted at Baby, then gave a bored sigh. "Hire a time machine, because you're at least a year too old."

"WELL, those were just about the worst people I've ever met," I said when we were outside again. "But I think she *clocked* you, if that helps."

"That was Sean and Penny Hanley," Baby said.

"Yes, you said." I tried to keep up as she all but jogged away from the store. "They own the fashion label, do they?"

"No, they just work there," Baby said.

"They're *store clerks?*" I said. "Where do they get off having that kind of attitude?"

"They have very influential opinions in the fashion sphere," Baby said. "They only work at the store because their parents have, like, ideas about them holding real jobs, I guess. That's what I heard. Their dad's Michael Hanley, the lawyer."

"So they don't even have a background in fashion?"

"Why do you hate them so much?" Baby said. "Penny is beautiful, isn't she? Much more beautiful than she is online."

"They were a couple of stuck-up idiots," I said. "And I don't hate them. I don't even know them. But I hate this side of you. They looked at me like I was a walking ball of bacteria, yet here you are talking about them like they're royalty. They couldn't have been eighteen years old. You don't need to listen to people like that." I couldn't grasp what was making me so angry about Baby and her fawning over the Hanley twins. "Is that what you're into? Fashion? You want to be a model?"

"Obviously," she said. "And those two *are* royalty. They've made people's careers with a single Instagram post. If Sean says I look too old, believe me: It's a problem."

"Baby." I drew a long breath. "If you want to be a model, fine. That's great. But it's obvious to me that you have a talent for criminal investigation. You're observant and smart. You'd make a crack private investigator or a lawyer or a cop or—"

"Oh, come on. You don't even know me."

"That moron in there didn't know you!" I gestured back to the store.

"He knows what he's talking about."

"And I don't?" I rubbed my eyes. "This is so stupid. Why did you even subject me to that whole miserable experience?"

"Because Sean and Penny are another link between Ashton Willisee and Derek Benstein." She showed me her phone. I looked at pictures of the kids together. "The Hanleys used to check in regularly with Derek and Ashton all over town. Them and Vera Petrov."

"That's the girl from the school?" I pointed to a picture. "Miss Go Screw Yourself? The one who has some dirt on you that you won't tell me about."

"That's her," Baby said cautiously.

"Okay. So the Hanley twins are friends with our guys," I said. "And?"

"So two days ago, right after the murder, they scrubbed their social media of any ties to Derek," she said. "They weren't just friends; they're now *hiding* the fact that they were friends. Ashton didn't want us to know he was friends with Derek. Now the Hanleys don't either."

"How did you get all these pictures of them together, then?"

"I've screenshotted and saved, like, everything Penny has ever done online. I went back and checked my archive."

"Why were you saving all the stuff related to that pathetic little brat?"

"Because she's my hero. I want to be just like her."

"Oh, wow," I said. I resisted another tirade. Baby clearly had a lot to learn.

"It gets better. The Hanleys have also gone dark," she said. "They haven't posted on any of their accounts for the last forty-eight hours. That's a record. Something is happening here. Sean and Penny are involved with whatever's going on."

"I'm not entirely convinced," I said. "All this social media stuff—it's useful, but it's not concrete enough for me."

"That's because you're old and weird." She shrugged. The coldness was coming over her again. "I don't care. It's your stupid case."

"You're right. This is good work, Baby," I said. "Let's follow them. See what they do when they get off work. If you could possibly call it that."

Chapter 8

JACOB WALKED INTO Yellow Bar ten minutes after Vera and requested a seat at the counter, where he could watch the violent little princess in the mirror behind the rows of bottles along the bar. He ordered a vodka neat and perused the shelf of expensive bourbons.

Vera Petrov was a girl after his own heart, he had decided. The only real predator among the children calling themselves the Midnight Crew. Though his background check on her hadn't revealed any suspicious deaths around her, Jacob could tell it was only a matter of time before she killed for the first time. She had the instinct. It was a biological thing. Vera's was a brain that was always assessing others, measuring threats, looking for opportunities for herself. She'd probably inherited it from her gangster father.

Vera had spied an opportunity, Jacob could tell. He saw the object of her fancy. At an adjacent table, a party of middle-aged men were huddled together over a battered notebook, running through scribbled lines. Probably rappers, from the bling and the custom Nikes. On the corner of the table, a pair of leopard-print sunglasses rested unattended. Vera wanted them. He witnessed her desire in a single glance.

Jacob guessed Vera had been stealing all her life. He knew she liked trophies. One of his watches had gone missing the night his family was attacked. She probably had a stash of items at her home, tucked away safely in a box. Personal things—photographs, jewelry, handmade gifts.

He watched as Vera paid her tab in cash, dropped her handbag by the edge of the rappers' table, and then scooped the sunglasses into the pocket of her jacket on her way back up from bending to retrieve it. It was an artful move.

Jacob was in the parking lot only seconds behind her, observing the valet bringing her Porsche up from the garage as he slid into his own car. At the traffic lights they were side by side, Vera completely unaware of him as she disinfected her stolen glasses with an alcohol wipe and tried them on. She checked her reflection in the rearview mirror, smiled icily.

Jacob looked at the pistol lying on the passenger seat beside him, a .45 ACP he habitually took out of the glove box and lay beside him every time he drove. He imagined himself opening his door and popping Vera a few times through her window.

But he reminded himself this wasn't like one of his old jobs. This was personal. He needed to take it slow, like he had with Benzo. He had to make sure there was pain.

I WAS surprised by Sean and Penny Hanley's first destination when they left work: a Walmart. From a distance, Baby and I watched them tour the hardware aisle. Sean took a hammer off a rack, turned it, looked at the claw, and said something to his twin that made her laugh. While he twirled it, they went to the weapons section and played with a crossbow but didn't seem serious about buying it. In the end, they each bought a hammer.

While Baby had seemed very enthusiastic about the mystery surrounding Ashton Willisee and his dead friend, she lost interest halfway through our tour of the Walmart. She paid all her attention to her phone, which was dinging and buzzing with a frequency I had not yet witnessed. I was sure now that something was going on. In the parking lot, I watched Baby smiling at the screen while we walked back to the Maserati.

"Why would they buy two hammers?" I asked. "Even if they are building or repairing something by hand together, which I highly doubt, why wouldn't they just pass the hammer back and forth?" I continued. "Or if they're working on separate projects, what are the chances that—"

"I don't know, Rhonda. Jeez, give it a rest, will you?"

In the car, she took out eyeliner and started applying it.

"Aren't we just going home?" I asked.

"Uh-huh." She smiled knowingly.

"Baby, what have you done?" I watched her carefully. She shrugged. Her phone vibrated off the seat beside her and fell onto the floor. I drove home with a darkening sense of peril.

THERE were already crowds two blocks from the house. Young men and women getting out of cars or sailing down the streets on bikes, cell phone screens lit up in the gathering dark. I caught a glimpse of my father's house one street away from it and saw lights on inside.

"Oh, dear." I sighed. Baby let out a mean little laugh.

"You shouldn't have messed with my stuff," she said. "This is *my* house. Dad's house. You tried to put your stamp on it, and I'm here to show you that you can't do that."

"So let me get this straight," I said. "As revenge for me hiring strangers to come into the house and mess with your personal possessions . . . you've invited a thousand strangers to come into the house and mess with your personal possessions?" I asked.

"I barricaded my bedroom door." She grinned. "My stuff is safe. Yours? Well, I guess we'll just have to find out."

There were too many teenagers in the street outside the house for the Maserati to turn onto our road. I parked, then pushed through the crowd to the front door and intercepted a skinny teen boy heading out in what was obviously my Van Halen T-shirt, the fabric dripping to his knobby knees. The crowd was crammed into the living room, music thumping loud. The scent of alcohol and weed smoke hung over everything. My boots crunched on plastic cups and food wrappers.

I climbed the stairs to the spare room where I had been sleeping and found my suitcase torn open, empty. A bunch of girls were sitting in the corner watching a YouTube video on my laptop. I snatched the machine away to a chorus of whines and stowed it under a hutch in the hallway, and then went to check on the three million dollars of cartel money and drugs that I had hidden in my father's bathroom. A crew of boys was hanging out in there, apparently oblivious to the hidden space beneath the vanity. They were passing a bong, sitting around the bathtub.

Baby was dancing on the pool table in the first-floor lounge when I found her. The bar had been stripped of every bottle and every glass. I saw a girl going by with a bottle of Pappy Van Winkle bourbon and took it from her.

"Hey! That's mine!" she yelped.

"Honey, you couldn't possibly appreciate it," I said, walking on. I stood at the end of the pool table, drinking Pappy from the bottle and watching Baby dance until she noticed me. I was getting looks from all directions. They were all beautiful, sun-bronzed, and youthful. I was twice their age and three times their size. When Baby finally looked down at me, she had the same contempt on her features as they all did.

"Who's that?" a girl beside her asked.

"My sister!" Baby yelled. "Can you believe it?"

"Whoa, crazy! So if your dad was Early Bird, and you're Baby Bird, she's . . ." the girl said. They looked at me.

"Big Bird!" Baby said. They both cackled.

I stepped up to the edge of the pool table. "Enjoying the festivities?" I asked.

"Sure am." Baby grinned, crouching and leaning in so I could hear her. "This is what you get for messing with my stuff, Rhonda. You shouldn't mess with me—I'm the queen!"

I nodded. A stupid, childish, competitive spirit was twisting in me. *This is what it's like to have a sister,* I thought. I had the strange compulsion to throw Baby's iPhone in the pool.

"You know what's *hilarious?*" I asked.

"What?"

"I could make myself the queen of this whole party in ten minutes flat and you don't even know it."

"You think so?" She blurted out more laughter. The other kids were giving me laser-beam eyes. I was the loser big sister. The party crasher. The fun police. But not for long.

"Watch and learn, little girl," I told Baby. I turned and walked out of the house.

When the weight-lifting dudes' front door opened, the first thing I saw was a giant red logo on the wall. A flexed biceps, veiny and bulging, the word BRUH underneath. The long-haired, beefy dude who opened the door recognized me from the rooftop weight-lifting showdown. He seemed as surprised to see me as I was to see the long table of computers set up in the dining room behind him, monitors everywhere. His fellow muscle-bound friends were all staring at me.

"You're a tech company?" I said.

"Yeah." The beefcake glanced at his friends. "What? You think just because we lift that means we're idiots?"

"I lift." I shrugged. "I lift better than you."

"That's what you think." He puffed up. "That wasn't my best performance this morning. I'm recovering from bursitis."

"What's Bruh?" I asked, gesturing to the logo.

"It's an app. Tracks your protein intake, lifting schedule. Stuff like that. You can order supplements and share your progress with other bruhs." He spotted a troop of girls going into my father's house behind me. "Party at your place, huh?"

"Yeah," I said. "You and your bruhs are invited. But you have to bring something with you."

Baby was pouring cocktails in the kitchen when I arrived back at the house with my crew of meaty tech heads. I led them through the crowd without stopping to speak with her, pushing aside kids to make way for the steel poles they were carrying. A bunch of kids followed us up to the roof, where the bruhs dropped the poles and left to get some more.

There were about a hundred young people standing around the

pool, no one with so much as a toe in the water. I felt sad for them, for the simple fact that being the first one to jump in the water was social suicide to these kids. The weight-lifting coders had brought the painter's scaffolding from the side of their house up the stairs and to the edge of the pool and erected it within twenty minutes. Baby appeared beside me, inhaling from her vape pen. I resisted flicking it out of her mouth.

"You said ten minutes," she said.

"You can't get good help these days," I replied.

One of the dudes had climbed to the very top of the scaffold, tested its sturdiness by rocking it back and forth. He gave me the thumbs-up and climbed down. Even with her head swimming with booze, Baby soon caught on to what I was doing.

"You wouldn't," she sneered.

"Hold my drink." I grinned.

Height is relative. Twenty feet experienced while standing above thick landing pads, safety-harnessed under the watchful eye of professionals, feels like what it is: twenty feet. The same twenty feet experienced from the top of rickety scaffolding, standing above concrete and water and the watchful gaze of a hundred drunk teenagers feels like one hundred feet or more.

I climbed the scaffolding with difficulty, my legs trembling. The farther up I climbed, the deeper my regret stretched, until there I was: at the top.

The pool below blazed neon-blue with underwater lights, and as I stood there, I realized the crowd around the pool had just about tripled. It seemed like every kid got out their phone and started filming. Three hundred white lights. Even with the wind in my ears, I could hear individual jeers and insults.

"You won't do it!"

"Come on, fatty! Get down!"

"Thar she blows!"

I looked down and saw that Baby had folded her arms triumphantly, her head cocked, listening to the chants all around her. I took my hand off the rail and stepped to the edge of the scaffolding, my toes hanging over the gaping nothingness.

THEY STOOD BETWEEN TWO big properties in a dark alleyway that was overgrown with bougainvillea.

Vera, Ashton, Sean, and Penny were listening, waiting for the terrier on the other side of the gate to find the meatball they'd laced with diazepam and go off to nighty nights.

"What's to stop this guy from leaping out and mowing us all down right now?" Ashton asked, glancing into the street. He was imagining every shadow as a tall man with a big rifle.

"He's not like that," Vera said. "He messed around with Benzo. He wants to take his time. He'll watch us tonight and creep up on one of us when we're alone."

"Well, that's just awesome," Ashton said. "My parents flew out to New York this morning. I'm alone tonight."

"Go get a room at the Ritz." Penny was tucking her hair under her mask. "They have great smoked salmon at breakfast."

Vera pushed open the gate at the back of the house. The crew followed her through a lush garden, past the little terrier lying unconscious on its side on the terra-cotta tiles. Vera took out her lock-picking kit, knelt, and worked the doorknob. Ashton bet she had been picking locks since before she could walk.

They opened the door and shuffled inside. Ashton's eyes adjusted to the darkness after a moment. He smelled dog and wondered how the scruffy little thing they'd passed in the yard could infest the house with such an odor. Then he saw the rack bolted to the wall beside him. The hooks holding four leashes.

One small, thin pink one. And three heavy chain-link ones.

Ashton saw the dogs over Sean's shoulder. Three enormous figures emerged in the hallway before them, sharp ears pricked and luminescent eyes locked on the intruding teenagers.

A scramble, a crash. Vera, Sean, and Ashton backed up hard, crushing Penny, the last into the house, against the closed door. The dead bolt had clicked into place automatically, and it stuck slightly as Ashton grabbed at it over Penny's head. He heard a scatter of paws on tiles and gave up on the back door. He whirled around, followed the shadows before him into a room off the hall. The door slammed shut, and immediately there came the sound of huge paws scratching at it, wet, snapping barks coming through the wood loud and clear.

"Oh, crap! Oh, crap!"

"Turn on the light! Find a light!"

Ashton backed into a table. Sean found a light switch, revealing a spacious office, leather wingback chairs, and a U-shaped desk. Ashton caught a glimpse of his own reflection in the window to the street, the black skull mask hiding his tensed jaw and bulging eyes.

All at once the dogs fell silent.

A female voice called out from the hall. "Who's in there?"

"Nobody speak," Vera whispered. Ashton grabbed her arm.

"What the hell do we do? We're trapped!"

"Shut up." She pushed him off.

"Who's in there? Answer me!" the voice called.

Ashton heard a sound that made his throat constrict and his stomach lurch. A loud double crunch, metal grinding on metal.

Sean recognized the sound as well.

"That was a shotgun," Sean said. His voice steadily rose in pitch. "Vera! What do we—"

"I'm calling the police!" the voice said.

"You don't want to do that!" Vera shouted back.

"We're dead." Penny was at the window, looking down over the drop to the concrete below. "We're all dead."

"I'm dialing now!" the voice called. "Move a muscle and I'll fire through the door!"

"Put the phone down, lady!" Vera shouted. She was fishing in her pocket. As Ashton watched, she took out a small gold lighter and held it up to the door, flipped it open and ground the wheel.

"What are you doing?" he asked.

She ignored him. "You hear that, bitch?" Vera asked, flicking the lighter open and shut. "You hear that?"

Ashton, Sean, and Penny stood back as Vera went to the drapes, held the lighter to the bottom of one.

"I'm lighting this place up!" Vera called.

"You're going to kill us!" Sean said.

"Listen, woman!" Vera went to the door. Yellow flame was

creeping up the curtain. "You leave us in here and the room will burn. By the time the cops get here, you'll have four dead kids on your hands. You want to try to explain that? Smart thing to do is call off the dogs, let us go, and save your house before everything you own is toast and your ass is in jail."

Silence. Ashton watched black smoke coiling against the ceiling. Penny started coughing.

"It's getting hot in here!" Vera called.

The door opened. Ashton felt relief rush over him. Until he saw Vera reaching for the gun in the waistband of her jeans.

Chapter 9

I JUMPED.

Freeze-frame. Time locked into place.

The wind rushed past my ears. The blue surface of the pool soared up at me. For a long time it felt like I hung in midair, falling and yet not falling. A sound came up from the crowd, the sharp intake of three hundred gasps. My arms and legs were flung out, and my eyes were bulging as I descended.

Later, I would see footage of the fall. Like a great, round star, I descended over the pool, my belly rippling, my thighs jiggling. My stomach hit the surface of the water first, sent an undulating wave out in a perfect circle from the center of the pool. Then the rest of me hit. The pool spewed water, soaking everyone. The giant wave rolled out over the rooftop and flooded through the door to the house and down the stairs. I was swallowed whole beneath the surface of the pool.

Under the water, I heard nothing, saw nothing. When I broke the surface, my ear canals cleared, but there was no sound. I stood and wiped the water from my eyes, looking around. The silence seemed to hang. Then three hundred kids all raised their arms and let out the greatest, loudest cheer I had ever heard.

Fifty kids jumped into the pool with me in one united motion. They all just dropped their phones and jumped. Kids were all around me suddenly, whooping and splashing and trying to lift me. More kids piled into the pool. The rooftop was flooded again. Screaming and laughing and cheering filled the air.

My plan had worked. Like a thousand youth icons before me, I'd made a spectacular, dangerous, and stupid gesture, and in response the teenage mob had accepted me as their queen.

There was only one figure outside the pool who was standing still. Who was not grinning. That figure was Baby, and in the chaos and noise she soon disappeared.

VERA threw open the door. She knew she had lost touch with reality and that disconnecting in this way was a good thing. Disassociating. It would help her go into a fully instinctual mode to protect herself. She had already decided that it was fine if Ashton, Sean, and Penny didn't get out of this mess alive. She cared about only herself.

She pivoted, stepping into the hall and bringing the gun up in one smooth motion. A tall woman stood there in a robe with a pump-action shotgun held with the barrel pointing upward. Vera fired twice. Hit the woman in the stomach.

She blasted the dogs without really aiming. She hit one in the leg, and the others bolted, startled by the noise of her gun. Vera ran for the back door, twisted the dead bolt, and yanked it open, running out into the cold night air.

When she looked over her shoulder from two blocks away, she saw three masked figures behind her. Her crew had escaped. They all stopped in the dark outside some mansion.

"Well," she said. "That was unexpected."

"What was unexpected?" Sean's voice was low, dangerous. "The three attack dogs? The shotgun? Or the four of us now suddenly facing murder charges?"

"Attempted murder at best." Vera snorted. "She'll be fine. I hit her in the stomach. No need to get all dramatic."

Vera could smell smoke. In the distance, sirens wailed. She pulled off her mask and slipped the gun into her waistband.

"You're weirdly quiet," she said to Ashton.

"I have nothing to say," the boy said.

Vera waited, but he didn't continue. She looked at them all, felt the tide turning against her in their silence.

"Listen," she said. "If you guys think—"

Her words were cut off by a sound, a sharp pop on the sidewalk at their feet. Sparks. They all looked. Another pop and Penny collapsed like a folding chair.

"I've been shot!" she wailed. "Help, I've been—"

Vera didn't stay to hear the rest. She threw herself behind a car as more gunshots went off all around them.

I'D DONE three laps of the house, trying to find Baby, toured the Strand all the way to Hermosa Beach, my clothes drenched and heavy and my hair plastered to my skull. When my phone buzzed, I looked down at it. A Twitter account I hadn't used in six years was being tagged in a new post. The teens from the party had found me and were linking me to the video of my dive. It was going viral. A tweet attached to the video read:

Bell E Flopp just OWNED a house party at Manhattan Beach! EPIC!

I stood on the beach, feeling helpless. A couple of girls walking up the beach stopped and pointed at me.

"Yo, there she is!"

"It's her! It's Bell!"

I gave an awkward wave, politely refused selfies.

When I finally found Baby, she was sitting on the ramp of a lifeguard tower, vaping. She spotted me and stood.

"Don't run off again," I said. "My clothes are wet. I'm getting chafed like you wouldn't believe."

"You were right." She threw her hands up. "You're queen of the house. Queen of the internet. Queen of the world. You win, Rhonda. Now go away and leave me alone."

I was glad she was still angry and not crying. An angry teenage client had always been a lot easier to handle than a sad one. But nothing about Baby had adhered to the principles of managing teenagers that I had followed since I had been one myself. She was the one kid I couldn't possibly understand.

"I'm not trying to win anything against you, Baby," I said.

"Whatever."

I watched the waves crash and dissolve into the blackness.

"Here's the thing," I said. "I'm not going anywhere. You can push me, but I'm not going to go away. Dad's gone, and I'm here to stay. And those are two realities you have to deal with."

Baby didn't respond. She sucked hard on the vape.

"Have you even cried about him dying yet?"

"No," she said. She turned away, but I saw her lip tremble. "I'd rather cry about *you* being here."

I didn't take offense. Baby wouldn't meet my eyes.

"Have you cried about him dying yet?" she asked.

"I haven't," I admitted. "But losing him is harder for you than it is for me. You didn't have a proper mom. My mom was great. Is great. You probably feel like you're on your own in the world. But you're not. You've got me. I'm not the enemy."

Baby didn't respond.

"Do you want a hug?" I asked.

She seemed to consider it. "I don't want to hug you. You're all wet. And we haven't even figured out who you're supposed to be in my life. You're here trying to be my sister right now. But one minute you're trying to be cool and then you're telling me not to listen to the Hanley twins about my age. It's like you don't know if you're my friend or, like, my boss."

"It's going to be fine, Baby. When we get back to Colorado, you—"

"When I *what?*" Her head whipped around. "Colorado?"

"Well, yeah," I said. "You can't stay here by yourself, and I have a job. I have a condo. I have friends, and—"

"*I* have a job! *I* have friends!" Baby yowled. "I'm not going to Colorado. If you try to take me there, I'll run away and you'll *never* find me."

A punch of terror hit my chest. I knew her threat was real.

"Hey, hey, Bell!" someone called. I turned and saw two gangly boys jogging across the beach toward us.

"Are you Bell E Flopp?"

"I guess so," I said. "No selfies, guys."

"Some dudes are going through your stuff back at the house," one of the kids said.

"It's okay. Everybody's going through my stuff." I sighed.

"No, we mean, like, badass guys." The boy nearest me swept his long black hair behind his ears. "Like gangsters. They're old. Like, forty maybe? And they're really looking for something. They're breaking stuff and throwing things around. They pushed some girl down the stairs."

"Have they got flowers on their shirts?" I asked.

"Yeah. And real bad tattoos." The boy nodded.

Baby and I looked at each other. For once, we were instantly on the same team. She rose, and we ran toward the house.

PENNY, Sean, and Ashton were crouched behind one car with Vera behind another. Bullets skittered off the curb. Vera figured the shooter had to be in the trees on a nearby hillside.

"We're gonna die," Sean said. Penny moaned beside him.

Vera held her breath, crouched, and sprang forward, leaping the gap between the two cars to join the rest of the Midnight Crew. Sparks flew as a volley of shots popped into the bumpers of the cars beside her.

"Penny, you need to shut up," Vera said. "You sound like a dying cat." She examined her friend's ankle.

"It's shrapnel," Vera concluded.

"I've been shot," Penny whined. "He shot me. He shot me!"

"I said, it's shrapnel," Vera said. "Stop losing your mind."

"How would you know? Are you a gun expert?" Sean asked.

"I know because her foot is still attached," Vera growled. "He's not shooting at us with a BB gun."

The crew was silent. Vera needed to rally them.

"I've seen a gunshot wound before," Vera said, forcing herself to soften her tone. "My dad brought a guy home once who took a hit in a robbery. They had a deadbeat doctor treat him in our garage. That wound was from a 9-millimeter gun. Whatever he's shooting at us with, it's bigger than that."

"What the hell are we gonna do?" Sean asked. "If we break cover, he's going to kill us."

"If he wanted us dead, we'd be dead," Vera said. "He's playing with us. He just wants to watch us squirm. In a couple of minutes emergency services are going to be swarming all over this place, and we'll be trapped here like sitting ducks."

"I can't go to jail." Sean ripped his mask off, gripped his hair in both hands. "I'll kill myself before they put me in there."

"You're all being so dramatic." Vera laughed suddenly. She looked at Ashton, but he was still worryingly silent. Vera needed to make a gesture. Show them she was still in control.

She slowly rose. Then, with more confidence, she stepped out into the street between the cars. She could hear Penny screaming in protest. Sean begging her to come back. But the only sound that was important was the pocking of bullets at her feet. The window of the car behind her blew out, the bullet missing her shoulder by mere inches. Vera knew he could hit her if he wanted to, but she wasn't going to play his game. She lifted up her arms, her pistol in one hand, and smiled broadly in the direction where she guessed the shooter was hiding.

"Let's go!" she roared. "I'm right here!"

The sirens in the distance had grown much louder. Smoke was flooding the streets, smudging the streetlamps. She heard voices shouting. A bullet hit the car beside her.

"I'm coming for you!" she called.

Lights came on in the house next to where she had guessed the killer was hiding. The firing stopped. Vera smiled as dogs barked and people stirred in the properties nearby.

It was Ashton's hands that gripped her shoulders, turned her to go. She looked back into the darkness and fought the desire to run up there, to shoot wildly into the trees. Instead, she followed her crew as they disappeared into the night.

She knew the real confrontation wasn't too far away.

As soon as I stepped into my father's house, every kid in the building erupted into cheers. The sound carried upward through the levels to the rooftop. I noticed the Bruh guys walking out through the living room toward the front door carrying pieces of scaffolding. A smart choice. It wouldn't have been long before teen boys tried to top my dive with backflips and tumbles of their own.

Vegas and two of his guys had discovered the door to Baby's bedroom that she had hidden ingeniously behind a bookcase on the third floor. The bookcase lay on its side, books and trinkets spilled out onto the carpet. The door to my father's bedroom I'd passed on my way up the stairs had been closed.

Vegas was sitting on Baby's bed next to a nervous-looking teenage girl. His two thugs were leaning against the window, seemingly waiting for us to arrive. Vegas's boots were a startling fuchsia-dyed leather branded with patterns of violets.

"Jeez. What size shoe are you?" I said. "If I didn't know you were the world's most disgusting human being, I'd think of buying those gorgeous things right off your feet."

Vegas glanced down at his boots.

"We've finished messing around, Rhonda," he said. "It's time to transition our relationship into reduction mode."

"You're firing me? But I'm your key assets holder!"

"Very funny, Rhonda." Vegas smiled. He reached out with his arm and scooted the teenage girl closer to him. Her eyes were pleading with me. "I'm being serious now. I want to terminate our relationship, and the only way I can do that is if you tell me where my stuff is."

I looked the men in their eyes, each of them in turn. All I had to do was tell them where the cash and drugs were hidden. In seconds, they could retrieve what they wanted.

But if I let them do that, there would be no reason for them to keep Baby and me alive. There would be nothing to stop them from opening fire on us. On any of the kids in the house.

"You're a businessman," I said. "We can negotiate. But not under these conditions. Let the girl go and we—"

"You don't have any leverage in this situation," Vegas said. "You'll either give me what I want now, or you'll give me what I want after I've demonstrated what you have to lose."

I could see a revolver sticking out of his back pocket. I tried to think, but my brain was thrumming with panic.

"Let that girl come over here to me and we'll talk," I said.

The girl piped up. "I really would like to go."

"Quiet, honey." Vegas snuggled her closer. The girl wriggled, tried to lean away. "The adults are talking."

The cartel boss nodded at one of his men.

"Maybe I need to put a bit more pressure on the situation," Vegas said.

The goon went for Baby, as I knew he would. But she was ready. I hadn't noticed her hand creeping along the doorframe to a shelf on the wall, packed with loose items the cleaners had gathered there.

She grabbed a snow globe and smashed it into the goon's face. Her blow was quick, sharp, and true. The heavy wooden base of the globe pulverized his upper lip against his teeth.

It was clear to me in that instant that Baby had never been violent with anyone before. As soon as she'd landed the blow, the girl dropped her weapon, grabbed her own mouth, and howled in horror at what she had done. I stepped in, shoving the guy into the desk.

Vegas watched all this from the bed. His remaining goon watched from the window. Both had hard, unsurprised stares.

I waited for Vegas's second man to come for me, but before he could, something outside the window caught his attention, and he gave a frustrated sigh. The ceiling was lit by red and blue lights. Downstairs I heard kids screaming warnings, fleeing out the door to the Strand and the beach.

Vegas stood and slipped by me, glancing at me as he went, the promise of future violence clear in his eyes. As his goons followed him, one cupping his bleeding face and the other helping him along, the girl on the bed burst into tears.

I STOOD ON THE THRESHOLD of my father's house, watching the long arm of the law clear the Manhattan Beach streets.

The cops swept at the kids in rows. Every time they cornered some, others would billow out beyond reach and pool back together. The entire crowd was gone within fifteen minutes.

Officer David Summerly's approach was less intimidating this time. I missed his earlier commanding stride toward me. He walked up and stood on the stoop, his hands on his hips.

"I'm going to get you this time," he said. "You might have wriggled out of a charge for the exploding car, but you can't wriggle out of this. This party is disturbing the peace, plain and simple. There must have been five hundred kids in there."

"Five hundred?" I asked, reluctantly proud of Baby and her efforts. "You think?"

"I can charge you with disturbing the peace, and also charge you for every instance of illicit drug use on your property."

"I hate to break your heart, but you're not going to put the cuffs on me tonight, Summerly. At least not for a crime."

He rolled his eyes, waiting. I couldn't keep the grin off my face as I replied.

"The owner of this domicile is deceased," I said. "I haven't yet filed the paperwork to claim the property as my own. I don't know if I ever will. But until then, no one can authorize a search of the premises, and you can't do one yourself because you can't prove anything illegal happened inside."

"Yes, I can," he blurted. He gestured to the street. "All these kids came out of this house!"

"Have you got any proof of that? Photos or video maybe?"

"Probably. It's probably on the patrol cars' dashcams."

"Are you personally going to verify that footage in a court of law?" I asked. "Because the way I see it, all these kids showed up and caused a ruckus *around* this house. But you have no proof that any of them were inside or that these rambunctious youths have anything to do with me. I'm only as guilty as those people next door." I pointed to the Bruh house. At the houses across the street. "Or them. Or them."

"A party has clearly occurred on these premises." He waved an arm through the open door, at the beer cups and broken glass and pizza boxes everywhere.

"Maybe I just live like this." I shrugged.

Summerly gaped at me. "You just *live* like this?" he said. "Every morning you get up and throw glitter and pills everywhere? These . . ." He picked up an item lying at my feet. It was a huge pair of novelty sunglasses. "These are yours?"

I took the sunglasses and put them on. "They sure are," I said, smiling up at him.

Summerly burst out laughing. "Lady, if you really do live this way, I want to be a part of that life." He adjusted his belt, stretched his back. "There's probably enough stuff on the floor in there to cure my backache for the next twelve years."

We continued to smile at each other. I took the sunglasses off and thought about saying something further. But I didn't.

He stepped down to the sidewalk. When he turned back, I was sure he caught me checking out his butt again, but it didn't matter, because what he said blew apart any and all concern that might have existed before he opened his mouth.

"You know," he said, pointing at me, "I really like you."

My mouth fell open. I couldn't find the words to reply. I just stood there as he went back out onto the street.

When his driver arrived, Sean took the keys to the Pullman from him and told him to go away. The old man did. Good staff were like that. They did exactly as they were told, no questions asked. There were no weird looks about Penny sitting crying on the curb with her leg soaked in blood, the two of them dressed in black and obviously rattled.

"You can't drive," Penny wailed as her brother helped her into the front seat.

"I can drive," he said. "I drove to a bodega last year when the house lady was sick."

"Take me somewhere nice," Penny said. "I can't go to a regular emergency room. Call ahead and get us a private room."

"We're going home, and I'm calling you a vet," Sean said.

"What?"

"That's what you do when you get shot," Sean said. "We can't go to a hospital. The police will be involved."

"So call me a deadbeat doctor!" Penny said. "Like Vera's dad did with that guy."

"You think I have a list of dodgy doctors in my phone?" he snapped, pulling awkwardly out from the curb. "A vet will be cheaper. A vet we can buy, any vet at all. No problem."

"Ask Vera for—"

"She needs to know we can handle this ourselves," Sean said. "Now shut up. I'm trying to concentrate here."

It was on Sunset, outside the white walls of the Archer School for Girls, that they noticed the black BMW in their rearview mirror. The driver had stopped his vehicle close behind Sean and Penny. Uncomfortably close.

"It's not him." Sean put a hand on his sister's knee, a rare gesture of affection. "Vera said he would just watch us tonight. Too risky to come after us with all the chaos back there."

"Who is it, then?" She turned with difficulty in her seat, stared out the back window. "Is it . . . is it a gang?"

"Not in that car."

The light changed. He accelerated slowly, and the BMW stayed right behind them.

"Turn onto the 405. North on it, not south." Penny's voice was low, strangely calm. "Speed up. We'll outrun him."

For once, Sean did what she said. That's when he knew he was in real trouble. Penny was talking sense, and he was listening. With a white-knuckle grip on the wheel, he turned onto the freeway, eased his foot down on the accelerator.

Penny was right. He couldn't drive. He didn't look before he changed lanes, almost sending a Saab careening into the center divider. The Saab driver leaned on the horn. He heard shouts, felt humiliated. The BMW was right on their tail. The Pullman wasn't built for speed. It was built for gliding with style.

"We're going to be fine," Penny said. "We're going to get out of this."

"Call 911," Sean said.

"We can't," she said. "This was a bad idea. Turn off the freeway again. We'll lose him in the hills."

He did as she instructed, and after a while, the road narrowed, began to wind through the hills. Sean gained space between him and the black car, losing it again as he slowed hard for corners. The killer knew he couldn't drive. He was probably back there laughing at him.

"We shouldn't have come up here," Sean said.

"Shut up! Pay attention to what you're doing!"

"He brought Ashton up here. This is his hunting ground. We're falling into his trap. Call someone, Penny. Call anyone!"

"I've got no reception!" She looked up from her phone to him, her eyes wild. Then she spotted something on the road. "Stop, stop, stop!"

Sean swerved right toward a hill, but the tires slid in the gravel, fishtailing, hooking around the deer harmlessly as it stood frozen in the road like a marble statue. The Pullman was so long it ground over the edge of the road, up and over the low bank of vegetation marking the drop-off, rocks scraping the underbelly. Sean felt them gouging the surface beneath his feet. The gold, sparkling city below was suddenly right in front of them, and they were plunging absurdly toward it.

In the panic that gripped him as the car tumbled down the ravine, he realized that he wanted to scream but couldn't.

He must have blacked out, because when he woke, the car was crumpled against a tree, a branch piercing its roof. Hissing sounds were issuing from the car all around him. Penny crawled out through the windshield, stepping on him to get herself free from the wrecked vehicle.

She leaned through the squashed window on the passenger side. "Give me your hand."

Penny pulled him free. They held each other in the dimness, listening to their pursuer crunching through the shrubs and stones toward them.

"Go, go, go." He pushed at Penny, but she was rigid with terror, stumbling in the loose rocks. Sean thought about pulling her to the ground, trying to hide. But all his senses were telling him they needed to run, run, run.

A puttering sound filled the quiet ravine, like gloved hands clapping, and Penny screamed. Sean knew the killer had sprayed the brush around them with bullets, his suppressor dulling the sound from the houses below. He tried to keep Penny moving, but she went down clutching her side.

She was in too much pain to make a sound. He followed her hand to the hole just under her ribs on the right side. Warm, wet, drenching his wrist and arm in seconds. Sean had a choice to make now. Die with her or survive alone.

"Don . . ." she managed. "Sean, don't le . . ."

The footsteps were coming. Sean squeezed Penny's hand, already consoling himself about what he was going to do.

"I love you," he told Penny, because he supposed that might help. Then he turned and ran.

THE edge of the road lit up white, softly at first and then blazing as the car passed in the night. Sean watched it from where he hid in the bushes ten feet back from the asphalt, down an embankment on the hillside.

He had lost the killer while the man dealt with Penny. There had been a kind of yelp and gurgle on the wind, and then nothing. Sean had made his way sideways up along the edge of a ravine. Now all he had to do was get the attention of a passing motorist and he was home free. His Hublot, the glass now cracked, told him it was four a.m.

Sean crawled forward into the shelter of the next clump of bushes, closer to the edge of the road.

A truck rumbled along the ridge in the distance. He watched, ready to spring. When it was right next to him, he saw two Hispanic men sitting in the cab. Sean sank back into the bush. He didn't want to spend precious seconds of his escape trying to explain the need to step on the gas in broken Spanish. He watched the truck go by. The crunch of its tires on the road masked all but the final moments of the killer's approach.

Sean turned, just far enough to catch the blur of a big hand sweeping up to grab a hunk of his hair, the other gripping his shoulder hard. He was yanked backward, hitting the ground with a thunderous impact that knocked the wind out of him.

He opened his eyes and tried to suck in air. When he breathed, though, only one lung inflated, the air struggling through his lips, as thick as honey.

He reached up and gripped the tree branch protruding from the left side of his chest, sticking out from his smashed ribs by two feet or more. He thought about how, in movies, actors managed full conversations while impaled like this through the back, but he could move his lips only silently.

An old man stepped around Sean, stood in front of him.

In his dying moments, Sean watched the killer's face and tried to recognize him. But the old man seemed to be just an old man, like so many other indistinct, unimportant people who had fluttered in and out of Sean's life.

Chapter 10

It was five in the morning when the knock came at the door. I had been shifting around the house restlessly, gathering little baggies of drugs from among the party debris in a kind of grim treasure hunt and emptying their contents into the toilet.

At three a.m., Baby had appeared behind me in the kitchen, sniffing the air like a gopher just emerging from the earth. She had been sitting on the concrete wall at the edge of the Strand, drinking flavored vodkas with some remaining teens while I rattled around the house. I knew she was in for the hangover of her life, but I didn't go out there and call her in. She had taken on the strange new woman in her life for Queen of the Party and lost. Her bedroom had been invaded by commercial cleaners and drug lords, and her father was only a few days dead. She needed to get it out of her system.

"What is that smell?" She groaned.

"Spam." I showed her the pan I had been laboring over. Four thick slices of the tinned meat were bubbling in butter.

Baby gagged. "That's not right."

"It's right by me." I shrugged.

She slid onto a bench. "I'm feeling very emotional," she said after watching me cook for a while.

"You don't say?" I smiled.

"I hit a guy in the face with a snow globe." Her words were slurred. "I've never hit anyone. With anything. Ever."

I glanced over. Her lip was trembling.

"Rhonda, I didn't even know his name!"

I couldn't stifle a laugh. She started laughing with me.

"You want some Spam?"

"Hell no. Are you crazy?" She watched me start eating. "You're just going to eat it like that? No toast? No eggs?"

"I don't like anything to interfere with my Spam," I said.

She watched with a horrified look, then reached over and plucked a juicy slice from my plate. Within minutes, I was frying myself more Spam while Baby devoured the original batch.

The knock at the door came maybe fifteen minutes after Baby had slouched off to bed. I opened the front door and found Officer David Summerly standing there. His collar was unbuttoned, and he was tapping his hat against his thigh.

"You didn't say anything back," he said.

"When?"

"When I said I liked you."

"Oh." I tried to look nonchalant. "I guess I figured that was just an LA thing. Hollywood, you know. People get dramatic."

Summerly laughed. "Well, it's not an LA thing, Rhonda. I wasn't being dramatic. I was being real."

He stepped up from the front walkway, onto the stoop. I didn't budge from the doorway.

"I see a lot of crazy stuff," he said. "Nothing surprises me much anymore. But you talking your way out of both jams you got yourself into over the past couple of days, that was really something else. That was like verbal . . . legal . . . gymnastics."

"I'm pretty flexible," I said. "Why don't you get in here and I'll show you a couple more of my moves?"

We both laughed at the cheesiness of our banter, the silliness of needing to exchange words at all when our bodies were busy doing all the talking for us. He was advancing into the entryway. I was walking back, drawing him in, both our hands already restless, ready to grab at clothes, to explore the warm skin beneath. I closed the door behind him, and Officer Summerly's hand found mine as I led him toward the stairs.

Vera walked into her house from the back entrance, climbed the stairs, and quietly shut the door to her bedroom. She hadn't been explicitly told by her father to stay at home and care for her mother during his absence, but it was expected that the hens would huddle together for safety when the rooster was away. It was a ridiculous rule. Vera wasn't a frightened chicken but a lone wolf capable of hunting and surviving on her own. The light under her mother's bedroom door had told Vera that she was up, even at four a.m., probably watching religious programs.

She went to her laptop, pushed it open, and clicked on the app that controlled her hidden cameras. The day before, she had hidden a couple of cameras in trees along the street outside the property with the dogs. The feed was live, showing a cluster of fire and emergency-response vehicles currently jamming up traffic, the typical gathering of neighbors and gawkers outside the police tape.

She rolled the footage back to the start. She stopped and played the tape. The four of them arriving, slipping under the cover of the vines around the alleyway, mere minutes passing between their disappearance from view and the lights inside the house flicking on as the woman was alerted by her dogs.

As the action played out inside the house, a car rolled slowly down the street and disappeared. She rolled the footage back, took a screenshot of the car. An old, beaten-up panel van, dark blue or green, the back windows blocked with curtains.

No, that wasn't him. The man had used a white van to abduct Ashton. There was no need for two vans. And this vehicle was too distinct, too memorable.

Vera knew she should be looking for something that wouldn't look out of place in the neighborhood at night. He wouldn't bring his grab van. He'd bring his everyday car.

She rewound the footage back further, to just before they would appear onscreen. A car rolled by. Vera stopped the film and screenshot the image.

She knew a little about cars. If there was one status symbol among Russian mobsters, it was their mode of transportation. She googled some BMWs and found the model—the Gran Tourer. Jet-black. The website advertised that instead of a trunk, the car had a big cargo space for kids' scooters and sports bags, nets behind the front seats for their iPads and crap. A family man. A man with kids, killing kids. Vera smiled. This was very interesting.

She opened the list of Midnight Crew victims on her desktop and deleted all the childless couples. There were four men remaining. One of them had been the jerk from the mall who had stolen her and Ashton's parking spot. Vera sat back and thought. The mall guy was the same guy with the kid who had collapsed. Jacob Kanular. But she remembered his car from the mall: a blue sedan, whizzing into the space ahead of them. Not a BMW. She selected the Kanular family from the list and rested her finger on the Delete button. Then she stopped.

A white van. A blue sedan. Was there another car?

She remembered the Kanular guy glaring at her over the duct tape wound around his head, his black eyes strangely calm, calculating. She googled the Kanulars' address and selected Street View. Outside the house, Google had caught someone coming home, one door of the four-car garage rolled halfway down, a pair of legs, jeans, and boots, standing by the trunk of a vehicle.

She saw the BMW symbol on the trunk of the car and smiled.

Officer David Summerly lay beside me in the late-morning light and stared up at the ceiling. He was probably turning over the same idle things in his mind that I was. How he was going to get out of the house without running into Baby, who was clattering around in the kitchen below. Whether we would see each other again. How to discern if the morning's recent activities meant anything.

Something crashed in the kitchen, and we heard Baby's curse echo through the big house.

"Is there any more Spam?" she roared.

"I know that kid, you know," Summerly said.

"Really?"

"Yeah," he said. "I responded to the thing at the school a couple of years ago."

"What thing at the school?"

"Nobody told you?" He paused for a moment. "I shouldn't, then. But . . . if you're her guardian, maybe it's relevant."

I had told Summerly some of my situation with Baby in the hours since he'd shown up.

"What happened?" I asked, knowing even as I said it that I was betraying Baby's trust.

"She kissed a teacher," Summerly said. "She got confused, I guess. She was thirteen. She might have thought the guy was flirting with her or something, wanted to be her boyfriend. You know how teenage girls dream up these things sometimes."

I nodded. "How did it happen?"

"Story is, she was the teacher's pet. He'd kept her back on her own after class that day to compliment her on her work, and she just launched herself at him and kissed him."

"Whoa," I said. "Are you sure that's how it played out?"

"Yeah." Summerly nodded. "We looked into it. He did not, as it turned out, want to be her boyfriend. Not at all."

"And he didn't know it was coming?"

"No," Summerly said. "The whole thing took him by surprise. And she was so upset about having done it and been rejected that this male teacher thought, *Oh, dear. I better let the school authorities know*. Because he's thinking, next thing you know Baby'll be saying *he* kissed *her*."

"That's the way it usually goes."

"Mm-hmm," Summerly said. "So he made damned sure his boss heard his version of events first."

"I see," I said.

"So the school authorities brought the police in just to make sure everything was dealt with correctly. My superior officer handled it. I assisted. We questioned Baby and the teacher. They both said the same thing. She got confused. Tried to plant one on him in the classroom."

"Oh, Baby." I covered my eyes. I could feel my sister's hurt and humiliation. "How did our dad handle it?"

"You could tell he didn't know what to do. He sort of brushed it off, told her it was no big deal."

"How did the other kids find out?" I asked. "When we were at the school, another girl there seemed to know about it."

"You know how it is." Summerly shrugged. "People talk. Kids overhear them. How is she? Is she okay?"

"How does she seem?" I asked. As if on cue, the sound of glass smashing came from downstairs followed by more cursing from Baby. "It's a weird time with her dad gone and me being in her face, as old and lame and intrusive as I am."

With the room around us still trashed from the party, and Baby's activities downstairs becoming louder and louder, it seemed impossible to stay in bed. I got up and pulled on a T-shirt and boxers and threw Officer Summerly's shirt at him.

"I'll distract her while you sneak out the back," I told him.

"Who are the teenagers now?" He smirked. His phone bleeped, and he took it from the nightstand, checked the screen. "Will I meet you later for . . ."

"For what?" I asked. But he had become consumed by what he was reading. I threw his hat at him.

"I was going to say coffee, but I've got to go." He pulled his shirt on. "I've got a call out past Upper Canyonback."

"Where?"

"It's . . ." He waved vaguely north.

"What is your beat, exactly?" I asked. "First you turn up at Stanford-West Academy; then you're here in Manhattan Beach. Now you're getting called to a canyon?"

"I cover for a lot of guys," he said, slipping his shoes on quickly. "I've got to go."

He wouldn't meet my eyes as he headed for the stairs. I was left with the distinct sensation that I had just been lied to.

When I found Baby, she was trying to sweep up the broken pieces of a beer bottle on the kitchen floor, standing barefoot, surrounded by shards. I walked over and shooed her away.

"Let me handle this," I said.

"Was that the guy?" she said.

I looked up. Summerly was just disappearing up the Strand, as visible as any mountain-size man would be.

"What guy?"

"Oh, come on." Baby slapped me playfully. "You just had that cop in your room, didn't you? The one with the ass!"

"Baby." I sighed.

"This is so romantic!" Her eyes were dazzling with excitement. "You're perfect for each other! And if you're spending all your time with him, you won't be messing with my life."

"Who says I'm going to spend a minute more with that guy?" I asked, sweeping the glass into a dustpan.

"What, don't you like him?"

This was yet another unfamiliar side to the girl who had proved to be the most unpredictable teenager of my life. This sudden gushing fascination with my love life defied her usual surly, wizened outlook.

"Baby," I said, "despite what you might think about overweight and socially defunct women from the howling depths of Colorado, we are perfectly capable of sleeping with random guys without needing them to rescue us from crushing loneliness by getting romantically involved. Now go take a shower," I instructed. "I'll make coffee."

The doorbell rang. Baby tottered over in the bemused fashion of a girl only just coming to terms with the idea that I, of all people, was more sexually liberated than she was. She opened the door to Ashton Willisee. His exhausted, terrified face made me drop the dustpan into the trash can at my feet.

"I need help," Ashton said.

THE boy smelled of smoke. One of the knees of his black jeans was torn. Ashton walked in stiffly and went to the living room, numbly staring at the party junk on the couch as though he didn't know how to shove it aside to sit. Baby assisted.

"We killed someone," Ashton said.

"What the—" Baby's eyes got wide and locked on me.

I put a hand up as I sat down across from him. "Ashton, don't say another word," I said. "Whatever you've done, you don't need to make it worse by blurting out something that might count in court as a confession to people you barely know."

Baby's eyes grew even larger. "He just said he—"

"He's shell-shocked, panicked, maybe injured," I said to Baby. "He needs his parents and a legal representative on hand as soon as possible. Ashton, call your parents now and—"

"I don't have my phone," he said. "And I don't want a lawyer. Last night my friends and I broke into a house in Brentwood, and while we were there, we got trapped. We set the place on fire to escape. We killed the lady who lives there."

I held my head in my hands, my thoughts racing to find a way to contain the situation legally. Baby's phone was glowing as her thumbs danced over the screen.

"I'm going to jail," Ashton said.

"Well, not for murder," Baby said. We both looked at her. She scrolled one-handed. "'A home invasion in Brentwood has left a woman with multiple gunshot wounds and neighbors terrorized.' Looks like half her house burned down, but she's alive. She's in stable condition at Santa Monica Med Center."

All the air seemed to go out of Ashton. There was silence as Baby continued to scroll.

"You killed two dogs," she finally said. She looked up from the phone at the boy beside her. "You jackass."

"I didn't mean to kill or hurt anybody," he said. "And what happened last night wasn't my fault. When it started, when I got into all this, we were just trying to scare people."

"I'm really going to advise you to stop talking now," I said.

"I don't have any choice," Ashton said. "I have to tell someone because he's going to kill me."

ASHTON told us everything.

It had started with another excruciating Thanksgiving dinner. In the hours after sunset at his parents' vacation home in Carpinteria, Ashton stood on the balcony and watched his uncle Ray argue with his wife, Francine. Then his uncle smacked the side of Francine's head. When Ashton went downstairs to explain what he'd seen, the adults smirked and shrugged or wandered away, changing the subject the way they had with everything unpalatable he'd brought up over the years.

As Ashton spoke, I recognized a pain in him that I had witnessed many times across my career working with troubled youth. The unmistakable hurt of a child ignored, a child discovering that justice didn't always play out in the real world.

In that moment, Ashton had realized every story he'd ever been told in his life was a lie. Sometimes in life people didn't get what they deserved, and that ugly truth so rocked the boy's world that he began to obsess over the slap. It stopped being about Aunt Francine and Uncle Ray and started being about everything. The whole unfair, awful, stupid world.

Turning to Vera, Benzo, Sean, and Penny had been the natural move, he told us. Ashton thought of the crew as his "angry" friends. The members of the Midnight Crew were capable of hate. They *listened* to Ashton when he spoke about feeling alone, feeling like just another of his parents' accessories—a toy that had been fun to tote around when he was small and cute but eventually had grown tiresome as he got older. He was a troublesome boy. He wanted to talk about legal reform and taxes and poverty and things that made his parents and their guests very uncomfortable. They couldn't throw money at him and make him shut up. That was annoying.

Vera had texted their group, saying, *We should do something ourselves.*

Ashton had sent a laughing emoji, and for a while there had been silence. He'd got the feeling that the others were talking on a text thread without him. Then Vera had texted again.

Let's meet up. I can tell you about our game.

The game was everything Ashton had wanted. One big, loud, violent release. They called themselves the Midnight Crew.

The look on his uncle Ray's terrified face when he and his friends stormed into the bedroom in black skull masks and threw on the lights had given Ashton a deep pleasure. They locked his aunt in the bathroom and tied Uncle Ray to his desk, then taunted and belittled him, leaving him bloodied, sobbing and drooling onto his paperwork as they ransacked his house.

The righteous violence released his tense neck muscles so that the next day he was actually walking straighter. Thinking clearer. He was braver, smarter, fiercer. He felt tough. Capable. Ashton was finally the big man.

The next raids followed quickly. Ashton barely listened to the justifications for the victims they chose. Some guy had catcalled Penny outside a construction site. A woman had turned Vera away from a dance club. All he had to know was that these were bad people who didn't know their place.

As I sat listening to Ashton, my mind bounced between pity and fury at the child before me. A part of me wanted to scream at him that the "righteous anger" that had led him down his violent path was just the whining of a spoiled brat. But another part of me knew that it didn't matter how much money a kid had. If a parent ignored, abandoned, or abused their child, an angry seed was planted that could grow into a poisonous tree. The slap Ashton witnessed that had so outraged him wasn't as important as the parents who hadn't listened to that outrage.

"How did your little game get this out of control?" I asked when

Ashton had finished his story. He looked up at me, gripped the torn knees of his jeans.

"We messed with the wrong guy," he said.

I SAT thinking. Baby scrolled and tapped on her phone. I knew that even though she seemed distracted, she had been soaking up everything, probably confirming or discounting what Ashton said with searches online. He explained Derek Benstein's death and the terrifying encounter he had had with the killer outside the house in Brentwood the night before. It was a lot to take in.

Ashton was watching me hopefully. Even though I hadn't decided how best to help him, I needed to begin throwing ideas around just to ease the tension before it consumed him again.

"Whoever this guy is," I said, "he's on your list, and he's got a big-ass rifle. He's probably military or ex-military. So we look at the list of the houses you hit and find a military family."

"That's fine if he's one of our victims. But it doesn't help if the person we're looking for is a friend or associate of someone we targeted," Ashton said. "Or someone they hired."

"Excuse me for butting in." Baby put a hand up. "But isn't finding the guy who's hunting you a problem for the police?"

"Are you kidding, Baby?" Ashton turned to her in shock.

"Nope," she said.

"We go way back, you and me," he said.

"I go way back with the cute lacrosse player from school. This guy?" She gestured to him. "I don't know this guy at all."

"I didn't come here to hand myself in," Ashton said, turning to me. "I came here for your help. I'm sorry. You have no idea how sorry I am for everything we did. What we did was wrong. So wrong. But at the same time, I don't want to die for it."

"No, Ashton, you don't want to pay for it," Baby scoffed. "You don't want to do time, so you're hoping Rhonda will make this all go away. That's what rich kids do. Well, you should have thought about that before you *broke the law*."

I put my own hand up. "Baby, you don't get to lecture people about being spoiled when you're sitting on a twenty-thousand-dollar couch in your dad's fifteen-million-dollar house. And the party you hosted here last night shows you're much more Courtney Love than Mother Teresa."

"I don't know who either of those people are," Baby said. "But I do know that if someone busted in here, tied me to a chair, and broke all of my worldly possessions, I'd probably want to clamp a car battery to his nipples too."

"Baby, *outside,*" I snapped. She followed me in a huff as I got up and went to the Strand, slamming the door behind us.

As soon as we got outside, Baby took her phone out and started tapping on it.

"Put that away and look at me."

"In a second."

"What are you doing? Are you googling Courtney Love?"

"No." Baby scrolled. "She seems cool, though."

"Derek Benstein didn't have a car battery clamped to his nipples," I said, pushing her phone down. "He was tortured with a cattle prod and then shot to death."

"How was I supposed to know that?" Baby took out her vape pen and put it to her lips. "Online it just said he was electrocuted. He's dead. What's the difference?"

"The difference is that I've seen those crime-scene photographs," I said. "And his death was horrific."

"How did you—"

"Never mind." I grabbed the vape and threw it into a nearby bush. "What I'm telling you is that Ashton has come to us admitting he's done terrible things and saying he's sorry. He's asking for help. When a person asks for help turning things around, you've got to set aside everything that happened before that moment and try to start fresh."

"You're nice," Baby said, plucking the vape from the ground and bringing it to her lips. "I guess you've probably had some nasty kids come to you wanting you to go into the ring for them in the courtroom."

"I have," I said.

"Rapists and killers and stuff."

"That's right."

"And how did you know which ones really were sorry and which ones were just playing you for a sap?" Baby asked.

I tried to answer, but no words would come.

"I don't trust this guy." She nodded toward the house. "Yeah, I knew him back when we were kids, but this is some heavy stuff right here."

"You're still a kid," I said. "And news flash! You don't trust anyone. You don't trust me, and I'm your flesh and blood."

"Well, what does that even mean?" she asked.

I stepped back and exhaled, reminded myself that I was trying to talk about family trust and loyalty to a child whose mother had dumped her on her uninterested father's doorstep.

"Let's just not call the police yet," I said.

Baby got some kind of alert on her phone. Something was going on in her internet world.

"Let's get more information and see what kind of danger we would be putting Ashton in if we did that. We don't know if this guy is watching him right now. If he senses Ashton's about to be locked up, out of reach, he might make a move."

"I'd say you're right," Baby said. "He'll probably move on Ashton next."

"What? Why?"

"Because Sean and Penny Hanley are dead," Baby said. She turned her phone toward me. I saw a car crushed against a tree, the hood streaked with blood. "Only Ashton and Vera are left."

VERA walked up the cobblestone driveway, smiling her best girl-next-door smile. Jacob Kanular's house seemed smaller in the daylight. The dark hours created long shadows and yawning spaces that frightened children. Vera wondered if Jacob's daughter had been scared of the dark. If she ever would be again.

It was the wife's social media profile that had given Vera everything she needed. Jacob was a vacant space online. Neina, whose sculpture page on Instagram had tens of thousands of followers, had posted a brief note about Beaty's condition the day after Vera and her crew invaded the house.

Pray for us. Beaty in hospital after severe asthma attack. All shipments/commissions postponed until further notice.

An earlier Instagram post about participating in an upcoming exhibition at the Palos Verdes Art Center had given Vera the ruse she needed to get through the gates. She tucked her clipboard under her arm and went to the front door, the same door she had run through with her crew only a few nights before. She tried to look eager when Neina opened the door.

"Annabelle Cetes." Vera put out a hand.

"Is this going to take long?" Neina asked. "I'm busy here."

"I just need a couple of snaps of the pieces you planned to exhibit for the program and the online marketing scheme." Vera brandished the little camera hanging around her neck.

"This was too awkward to explain through the intercom." Neina leaned in the doorway, sighed. "But the pieces I put together for the exhibition were destroyed. There was . . . an accident here at the house. I won't be participating in the exhibit. I explained all this to—"

"Oh, I'm so sorry," Vera gushed. She pulled out the clipboard and flipped the pages on it. "This is so weird. You're still on my list. I should have been told about this. I'm so sorry."

Vera squinted in the sunlight, wiped invisible sweat from her temple. *Take the hint, lady,* she thought.

But the killer's wife didn't budge from the doorway.

"Hoo!" Vera said. "A real hot one today, isn't it?"

"Was there anything else?" Neina asked.

"Do you think I could come in for a moment and make a call back to the office, see what's going on? It's so hot out here."

Neina looked back into the house. Vera smiled sweetly again. She knew Jacob wasn't home. She'd watched the house from the hillside for half an hour for any sign of him before approaching but had only seen Neina through the windows.

It seemed now that the woman was reluctant to be alone in the big house with a stranger. Vera positively beamed innocence while fanning her cheeks in the heat.

"Can't you—" Neina began.

"I'll only be a moment," Vera said.

She stepped back reluctantly as Vera followed her into the foyer.

The Kanular house had been cleaned since the Midnight Crew's rampage. The only indications left of their presence were bare shelves and the smell of fresh paint in the air.

Vera followed Neina into the big living room. There was a suitcase spread open on the couch, another standing in the hall leading to the bedrooms. Neina was leaving. Vera guessed a husband running around enacting his grisly revenge on a bunch of teenagers when he should have been sitting beside their dying child would put a strain on any marriage. That's assuming Neina knew what was going on. How smart was she?

Vera settled on the arm of the couch and made a fake call on her phone. She huffed as it wasn't answered.

"Could I trouble you for a glass of water?" she asked.

Neina seemed to stifle a sigh but went to the kitchen. Vera followed. When Neina took a glass from the cupboard and then to the sink, Vera let her hand wander across the counter toward the knife block.

"Oh, sorry." She laughed. "Uh, a cold one? Do you mind?"

Neina rolled her eyes and went to the fridge, turning her back on her visitor.

Something about the hospital room felt different as soon as Jacob walked in. Though the flowers and cards at his daughter's bedside were the same, he sensed a shift in the air. Jacob knew the smell of death, and he also knew the scent of life. He went to the bedside and took Beaty's limp fingers in his.

There was blood under Jacob's nails. He noticed a splinter, probably from the tree branch he had used to impale Sean Hanley, embedded in one of his knuckles. He picked at it and almost missed Beaty's fingers moving in his. Her hand gripped his for an instant—no more than a flutter, but the movement shot a bolt of painful energy through Jacob. He looked at her passive face and saw no signs of wakefulness.

Finally, finally, some of his work out there in the world, hunting down the ones who had done this, was bringing some life back into his little girl. Three of them were gone, and their passing was bringing Beaty home one step at a time.

He stood and brushed off the legs of his dirty jeans. He'd walked into the hospital looking like he'd been scrabbling up rocky ravines, but his appearance hadn't raised eyebrows. The halls were full of people who looked bedraggled and worn.

He had to find someone, tell them Beaty was coming back. He would get them to order more brain scans. He kissed Beaty and walked into the hall, grabbed his phone as it buzzed in his pocket. Neina's name flashed on the screen.

"She moved," he said before his wife could speak. "I felt Beaty's hand move."

"Can you come back to the house, please?" Neina's voice was tight, strangely low. "The police are here."

"What?" Jacob stopped walking.

"There was another home invasion last night in Brentwood. A woman got shot. The police know what happened to us."

A painful prickling was creeping out from the center of Jacob's chest. His old instincts warning him.

"Do they know . . ." he said. Neina was silent for a long time, and his thoughts screamed words he could never say out loud.

Do they know what I've been doing?

"Just come here," Neina said. "Now, Jacob."

"I'm on my way," he said.

He hung up. The old Jacob, the hit man for hire, said one word to him: *Run*. Beaty would be okay, or she wouldn't. Neina would be okay, or she wouldn't. If he decided to go into the ether again, there would be no coming back, no dropping in now and then. He either abandoned them completely now or stayed to fight through whatever implications his revenge would have on his existence as a father and a husband.

He tapped the phone against his leg.

Could he have his vengeance *and* go back to the life he had built himself here with Neina and Beaty? Or was having both of those things simply too much to hope for?

Jacob decided he had not lost hope yet.

He turned and headed for the parking lot.

NEINA Kanular put the phone down on the tiles beside her face and stifled a scream. She was pressed facedown on the floor of the kitchen, the teenage girl's boot heel pressing into her shoulder blades. Neina rolled onto her side and clutched at the deep slash wound the girl had cut across her chest. She scrambled into the corner of the kitchen.

"Jacob's coming," she said. "It's him you want, right?"

The girl didn't answer. She was using the knife to flick photographs stuck to the refrigerator door onto the floor. Beaty and her friends. Beaty and Jacob at the helm of a small sailboat.

"If he comes and sees there are no cop cars out front, he'll know something is up," Neina said. "You'll need me to get him in the door."

"I don't need you for anything," the girl said. She shifted the knife in her grip. "You've served your purpose."

She advanced toward the older woman. Neina dragged herself to her feet, backed against the wall, an animal cornered.

"Now, don't scream," the girl said.

Chapter 11

At a gas station off the 405 heading north, I kept Ashton in my sights as he walked into the main building to buy some snacks. I filled up the orange Jeep I had borrowed from the Bruhs. The huge biceps logo on the side of the vehicle wasn't the most subtle thing in the world. But I'd turned the keys in the car knowing it was unlikely to explode on us, which was more than I could say for my father's Maserati.

I watched the teenage boy inside the gas station. He guzzled a bottle of water and shoveled the contents of a bag of Cheetos into his mouth as he walked to the counter to pay for an armful of snacks. It had been a big night.

Baby leaned against the car beside me, her eyes hidden behind her huge sunglasses. I knew she was nervous. She rubbed her shoulders, trying to ease some of the tension as I pumped the gas.

"This is the worst idea I ever heard of," Baby said finally.

"When the heat is on, you go underground," I said. "We've got a Mexican drug cartel after us *and* a revenge-bent psycho after Ashton. Neither of those parties is going to pursue us all the way to Colorado, or if they do, we'll have time to lose them and form a plan to keep ourselves safe when we get there."

"Yeah, that'll be easy to do with us driving around in an orange car with a giant armpit printed on it." Baby gazed at the freeway. "Let's assume we get there safely. Then what? We, like, hide out in your crappy condo until this all blows over? Just crawl under the beds with your thousands of cats pawing at our faces? Get real, Rhonda. This isn't going to blow over."

"Okay, first of all, my condo is awesome. And what's with the cats? Why would you think I have thousands of cats?"

Baby shook her head.

"Oh, I see. I keep cats because I'm so fat and lonely I just sit at home waiting for a man to come along and marry me?"

"You're missing the point," she said.

"Look, Vegas is a businessman. Or so he keeps telling us. Hopefully, if he's weighing risk versus reward, he'll find it far more rewarding to go back to the beach house and try to find the money and drugs there while we're gone rather than come after us," I said. "He might even be successful after a while."

"So you did hide it in the house," Baby said.

"The search will keep them entertained," I continued. "Those guys want their stuff more than they want us. So we set them up to get busted while they're searching. One problem solved. As for whoever is after Ashton and his friends, without him in the picture, the killer will have only Vera to focus on. We can call the police and negotiate Ashton's surrender, and we tell them this guy is going to be watching Vera, and—"

My words were cut off by a wail of sirens. Two squad cars and an unmarked sedan pulled into the gas station, surrounding us, the last to arrive screeching to a halt only feet from Ashton as he exited the building. He dropped his armful of snacks.

Officer Summerly was the last person I expected to see exit the lead unmarked vehicle and walk toward me. He took a pair of cuffs from his belt and snapped one onto my wrist.

"Rhonda Bird," he said, "you're under arrest."

Jacob was rusty. He had made mistakes, and the biggest of them was falling in love, building a family. As he drove through the streets of Palos Verdes, slamming his foot on the accelerator of the BMW, he scolded himself.

When Jacob had been a killer for hire, he'd loved no one, nothing. He had obeyed the rules of men like him. Keep your back to the wall and your gun loaded. Always have a backup plan, a bug-out bag, a safe house.

Jacob had abandoned all of it when he met Neina, told himself he wasn't that man anymore. But that man would never die. The old rules should have been obeyed.

Jacob crested the hill and pulled over, looked down at the house perched on the cliffs looking over the sea. The sun was low over the horizon, making the windows of the house blaze pink. Jacob was glad he couldn't see inside. He knew that there were no officers sitting around Neina. The gate to the property was open, and there were no cars in the driveway.

Which meant Neina was dead.

Rusty. Stupid. He'd allowed himself to be lured away from the only thing in the world more precious to him than his wife.

Jacob stepped on the gas and headed back to the hospital.

ONE of the patrol cops was trying to grab Baby, with Ashton surely next, while Summerly shoved me toward his sedan.

"What the hell is this?" I yelled as he shoved me into the back seat. I waited while he walked around the car and got in. "Are you kidding me? You're arresting me for what?"

"I can hear you, Rhonda. You don't have to shout."

"Where are you taking those kids?"

"Just calm down." Summerly turned the wheel and headed out of the lot. "We're all going to the West LA station."

"What the hell is going on?"

"I've been lying to you, Rhonda," Summerly said. "I'm not a patrol cop. I'm a detective. Gang and Narcotics Division."

"Well, congratulations!" I sneered, the new threat of danger creeping up my spine. "What has that got to do with me?"

"Oh, I don't know," Summerly said. "Do you happen to know someone around here who might have millions of dollars of cartel cash and drugs in their possession somewhere?"

I bit my lip.

"You're not under arrest for possession." Summerly watched me in the rearview mirror with his warm brown eyes. "But I gotta tell ya, if I didn't like you so much I'd be tempted."

"Well, what am I under arrest for?"

"Nothing," he said. "We were making a show of taking you into custody so that the guy working for Martin Vegas who was sitting in the yellow Camaro at the gas station where we picked you up would know you guys were off-limits."

"You . . ." I tried to think. "What guy? There was a guy?"

"You didn't notice?" he said. "The car was bright yellow."

I felt strangely deflated. Stupid and gullible. Since I arrived in Los Angeles, I had been playing with the big bad kids, and I'd just been revealed as the odd one out. I'd thought I was putting the pieces of the puzzle together, and all this time it had been shifting around me as I stumbled along.

"So you've been onto me since the car bombing?" I asked.

"No, we've been onto you since Earl died," Summerly replied. "Rhonda, your dad was working for us."

VERA felt numb. She had always wondered what her first real kill would feel like, whether she would work through it mechanically, like her father, or whether she would connect with what she was doing emotionally. But killing Neina Kanular had been like smacking a mosquito. Vera felt a little ripple of satisfaction and nothing more.

She had the mind for it. She really was Daddy's girl.

Vera walked now through the hospital halls and took the elevator to the fifth floor. Neina hadn't given up any further information on her daughter's location, but Vera knew the girl wouldn't be hard to find.

She walked confidently onto the ward and turned left into the first room as though she knew exactly where she was going. She shoved back a curtain to reveal an old man with a neurosurgery scar sleeping with his mouth open.

Three more rooms revealed nothing more. Vera pretended to read a chart on the wall about visitation hours while she thumbed the safety off the pistol inside her bag. She knew that if Jacob returned earlier than she expected, she would need to be ready. Her hope was to slip in and out, leaving the kid for her father to find, lifeless in the bed, still warm to the touch.

She turned into the next room and found a cabinet crowded with cards and flowers, the bay where the bed should be sitting empty. She snatched up a card: *Dear Beaty, We hope you . . .*

Vera threw the card on the floor.

Outside the room, an orderly in a blue uniform was cleaning off a whiteboard with a cloth and spray.

"I'm looking for my sister." Vera smiled, her hand on the gun in her bag. "Could you please help me?"

Ashton saw Rhonda Bird being driven away in an unmarked cop car, then stood and looked around. Baby was standing beside the open door of the second squad car while a silver-haired officer tried to corral her into the vehicle.

Two things struck him. The first was that everybody seemed to have forgotten his existence. This meant that whatever Rhonda and Baby were being arrested for, it had nothing to do with the Midnight Crew. The second was that the officer at the front of the remaining squad car had slid into the vehicle, leaving her partner alone to deal with getting Baby into the car, and the old patrol cop was struggling with the outraged teen.

Ashton gathered up his pile of snacks. He walked up behind the older officer and gave him a nudge.

"Hey, man."

The officer turned.

"Catch this."

Ashton threw all his snacks at the officer at once. Two bags of Ruffles, a Hot Pocket, a can of nuts, and two doughnuts. He didn't need to tell Baby what to do. While the old man struggled to catch the treats, the teenagers bolted.

I sat quietly for a moment. My father, an undercover operative?

"My dad was—"

"Not a hero," Summerly said. "He was not working with the police out of a sense of honor and justice."

"Oh."

"We had a tracker planted in a shipment of drugs from Mexico, and your dad received it," he said. "We got him dead to rights. He agreed to work with us in a sting on Martin Vegas. All he wanted was to stay out of jail, so we cut him a deal."

Anger was boiling up inside me. "Is Perry Tuddy in on all this?"

"Of course," Summerly said.

"So all his crap about enjoying being locked up by the cartel was just a lie?"

"No. That guy is a genuine nutcase. He gets himself locked up by the cartel because he enjoys it. But we approached him after he was last released and asked him if he wouldn't mind us placing a tracker on him, too, to see where the cartel took him. And, yeah, even though he likes being locked up, I felt conflicted about it. What kind of jerk lets a guy rot in a shipping container in the desert just to make a case?"

"I don't know. The same kind of guy who would sleep with a woman just to make a case?"

Summerly jerked the wheel and slammed on the brakes. He turned and stared at me.

"You can't honestly believe that's what I did."

"I don't know." I shrugged. "It's hard to believe you have any genuine feelings for me while I'm cuffed in the back of your police car, Dave."

"You're only back there for show," he said. "How would it look to Vegas's guys if I tossed you the keys and we both swung through Miffy's for a shake?"

"Just about as bad as it does for us to be sitting here by the side of the road having a heart-to-heart."

"I don't care." Summerly snorted and locked eyes on me. "Rhonda, I haven't met a person like you in . . . all my life."

"How romantic. I've lost feeling in my fingers, and I really need to pee. Can we get moving?"

"I was kind of hoping you felt the same."

"I don't know how I feel about you. For me, it was just something that happened. I haven't thought about it yet."

"Oh, so it's okay for it to have been just something that happened for you, but not for me?" He smirked. "Nice."

"I don't care what kind of something happened, as long as it wasn't something for the sake of searching my house for Vegas's drugs and money while I was asleep."

"Well, it wasn't." Summerly huffed.

"Well, good," I snapped.

We sat in silence.

The yellow Camaro drove by us on the freeway, the driver's head swiveling toward us as he passed. "That was him. He saw us. Vegas's guy will report back that Baby and I are locked up and out of reach. You can let me go now."

"Not until you tell us where Vegas's drugs and money are."

I sighed. "If I do that, I'll be admitting that I have it."

"Tuddy says you took the meth from the shipping container," Summerly said.

"Yeah, well you've only got his word on that."

"Rhonda, I'm not going to charge you with possession of the drugs and cash." Summerly looked me right in the eyes. "But if you don't tell me where it is, I can't protect you from Vegas."

"And you can't catch him either," I said.

Summerly didn't reply. He was asking me to trust him. Not only about the hours we had shared together but also about my future, about whether or not I would spend it behind bars.

Baby would go into foster care without a legal guardian to care for her. I tried to imagine her arriving on the doorstep of a crowded group home packed with teenage runaways.

"Take me to the station," I said. "I want to speak to Baby."

"Rhonda, I need you to tell me where—"

"I've done enough talking," I said.

VERA followed the signs to the children's ward on the second floor. She gripped the gun in her handbag and went from room to room, peering in to look for bed 29. She wondered if Jacob had called ahead and requested that Beatty be moved.

If that was the case, it meant that Jacob had found his wife in a pool of blood on the kitchen floor, and he would be on his way back now, so she didn't have much time. Trying to hide his daughter instead of calling the police meant Jacob had not alerted the authorities of her plan. It meant he wanted to fight.

She smiled. She wanted that too.

Vera found the girl in an empty room. There was a dullness and a sunken quality to her features that told Vera the girl wasn't out of the coma yet.

Vera climbed onto the bed, straddled the girl, and wrapped her fingers around Beaty's thin neck.

The machines started ticking and singing around her. A part of Vera's mind knew that killing her this way would bring nurses and doctors, and she'd have to dispense with them too. But she had to take Beaty. Then Jacob.

The girl bucked underneath her, the gagging, jerking dance of the unconscious body deprived of air. Vera held on.

Two nurses burst in, their squeals of horror making Vera retract her hands from the girl's throat. She leaned over and fumbled in the handbag she had thrown on the table beside the bed while Beaty coughed and spluttered. Vera grabbed her gun and fired twice, hitting a nurse with each bullet. They lay still on the ground.

Outside the door, chaos was growing. People had heard the gunshots and were shouting. Vera heard footsteps, alarms beginning to sound. But as she focused back on strangling the girl, all she was really listening to was the sound of Beaty's final gasps for air as the life drained out of her.

And then he was there. Jacob came into the room silently and quickly. He wrapped an arm around Vera's neck, dragged her backward, and threw her against the wall. The gun clattered onto the floor between the two dead nurses. Vera righted herself and locked eyes with the man.

The two teenagers ran through the streets. They didn't talk.

Eventually they stopped on a street corner to lean against a fence, huffing with effort. The sweat on Baby's forehead shone like a mist of diamonds.

"We need a plan," Baby said. "You've got an assassin after you. I've got the police and a cartel on my tail."

"I can't believe this is happening." Ashton tried to suck in air. "It was never meant to be like this. I'm not this person."

"You can have a mental breakdown about it later." Baby held a hand up. "Right now, we've got to get off the streets."

"Can you call Rhonda?" Ashton asked. "She knew what to do. She can tell us what to do."

"The police would have taken her phone, probably," Baby said. "It's just us now."

"But Rhonda—"

"She can't help us," Baby snapped. "Her big plan was to go to Colorado and hide. She was right about one thing. We need to get out of the city." The girl wheeled around on Ashton. "You're rich. We go to a bank and you get as much cash out as possible. We go to an airport and hire a pilot to take us to, like, Bermuda. Maybe a private jet. Have you got a private jet?"

"No," Ashton said. "And I'm not as rich as you think. I've got access to a thousand bucks or so, but that's it."

"What? Are you kidding me?"

"I overspent a while back." Ashton could feel his neck and jaw becoming hot. "My parents put me on lockdown. I get two thou a week spending money. That's it."

Baby shook her head in disgust.

"I might know where we can get three million bucks," she said. "That should keep us safe for a while."

"Jeez," Ashton said. "You think? We could buy a boutique hotel to hole up in. Maybe a passable yacht."

"Getting the cash will be dangerous, though," Baby said, his attempt at humor shot down with a single glance. She grabbed his hand. "Come on," she said. "This way."

"DAMMIT." Summerly yanked the wheel again. We had been driving along in stony silence when his phone rang. He'd listened to the call and then thrown the phone down. "Baby got away."

"What?" I sat up. "Got away how? Where is she?"

"I don't know." Summerly flicked the sirens on. "They were putting her in the car at the gas station when some kid came up and got in the middle of everything. The two ran off together."

"Ashton," I said.

"Who?"

"Never mind. We've got to go back and find her."

"I'm trying." Summerly leaned on the horn as drivers ahead of him tried to get out of his way.

I didn't know Baby completely, but I thought I knew how she would act under duress. I felt confident that she would go back to the house for the drug cartel money. There'd been a sharpness in her eyes at the gas station when she realized that I'd given her a clue to the whereabouts of the cash.

So you did hide it in the house, she'd said.

Baby and possibly Ashton would almost certainly head to the house. Vegas and his guys were probably heading there, too, now that he knew I was under arrest and out of the picture.

I almost told Summerly. But my trust had been ground down to nothing. If I sent the police back to my father's house, I risked surrounding Baby with cops just as she left the premises with a bag full of cash and possibly the cartel drugs, since I'd stuffed the meth into the duffel too.

Maybe the best thing I could do would be to help Baby get in and out of the house quickly, before Vegas turned up. The longer Baby and Ashton searched for the money, the longer they would be in danger. I had to tell them where to find it.

I worked my phone out of my back pocket and tossed it onto the seat beside me. In the front of the car, Summerly's phone rang again and he reached for it and answered.

"What? Where? How many?"

He was distracted. I shuffled sideways and lay down on the seat, my mouth to the phone.

"Hey, Siri," I murmured.

"*Yes?*" the robotic female voice answered.

"Text Baby."

"What do you want to say?"

"Under vanity."

"Your text says, 'Under vanity.' Would you like to send it?"

"Oh my God," Summerly said from the front seat. He swung the wheel, cutting through traffic and off an exit ramp.

"Where are we going?" I asked.

"Change of plans," he said. "Baby's gonna have to wait. There's an active shooter on the loose."

THE blond girl, Vera, launched herself at Jacob. She hit him in the stomach with her shoulder but didn't even knock the wind out of him.

Jacob twisted and threw her against the other wall of the little room. They scrambled together, knocking a vase of flowers off the bedside table and onto the floor.

Vera screamed with rage and pain as Jacob picked her up again and threw her into the hallway. He took a moment to roll his shoulders, flex his triceps. He was going to take his time.

Vera scrambled away up the hall, her hand bleeding. Jacob walked up, tried to straddle her, but she slashed at his leg with something sharp, a piece of glass from the broken vase. He bent and punched at her face, missed, hit the floor, felt her nails gouge across the side of his head and into his eye.

Jacob grabbed Vera's wrist and bashed it against the linoleum until the shard of glass came free. She wriggled out of his grip and ran around a corner and down a short hall, scattering terrified hospital staff and visitors. Jacob followed. He drew his gun and blasted three times into a door, one bullet hitting an inch from her shoulder as she barged through.

Jacob pushed through the doors and found himself in a huge operating theater. On the operating table a man lay unconscious, his chest spread open. Thc surgical staff cowered as Vera snatched a scalpel off the tray table. She brandished the scalpel in one hand and beckoned Jacob with the other.

Jacob ran at her. He batted the scalpel away, taking a deep cut across the palm of his hand. Her other hand was coming at his face with some kind of steel hook, another instrument she had snatched. He slammed her into the steel cupboards, felt the *thunk* of the hook as she embedded it in his shoulder. She scrambled out of his hands, slipping out into the hall again.

He followed her, drawing his gun. A chair swung out of nowhere into his field of vision. He lifted an arm and blocked it. The attacker was some civilian hero in a pink shirt hoping to save the day. He reached out, grabbed the guy by his lapel, and landed a punch in his stomach that folded him in half.

Screams came from behind a door marked as a nurses lounge. Jacob went inside and found Vera there, clutching a plump woman in scrubs around the throat. Vera pushed a cutlery fork against the woman's neck, jutting her chin at Jacob defiantly as she backed her hostage away.

"Think about it," Vera said. "Stop and think about it. You won't kill an innocent woman just to get to me."

"Don't be so sure, little girl," Jacob said. He shot an orderly in the chest. Vera dropped her hostage as Jacob surged forward to fire again. The bullet entered Vera in the arm, sending her flying back. Jacob might have grabbed her then, but a pair of nurses who had been behind a table made a run for it, cutting between them, giving Vera the seconds she needed to shoulder her way through the lounge's other door, back into the hallway.

Chapter 12

THE PARKING LOT OF the hospital was in chaos. Summerly's sedan nosed its way in between the vehicles of staff and visitors trying to flee the scene. I could see patients and civilians standing at windows inside the hospital, watching the activity.

Summerly's phone had continued to ring as he drove, but he left it wailing alone on the seat beside him. The radio crackled with updates, which he now and then responded to.

"Unit Five at the scene. We're getting reports on the identities of the shooters," a voice on the radio said. *"Two suspects. One male, fifties. Female, late teens. Male has been identified as Jacob Kanular. He's local. Has a kid in critical care. Over."*

"This is Summerly. Who's the girl? Over."

"A witness recognized her as one Vera Petrov."

"Oh my God," I said. "He found her."

"You say something?" Summerly looked at me.

"I know the girl," I said. "Vera. Well, I mean, I don't know her. But I'm pretty sure I know why Kanular is after her."

"You know why they're shooting at people?" he asked.

"They're not after random people. Kanular is after Vera."

"That doesn't make any sense. Witnesses are saying they're both shooters," Summerly said. "People inside the hospital have told officers on the scene that the girl killed two nurses."

I shook my head. Terror and dread washed over me.

"I don't get it." Summerly put the car into park. "How do you know the shooters, Rhonda? What's your link to all this?"

"Never mind," I said. "I don't have time to explain. Uncuff me, and let's get inside."

"You're not going anywhere." Summerly pulled his gun from a shoulder holster. "You're not a cop. Stay in the car."

Summerly got out and ran toward the hospital. I growled with frustration. I knew there was a spare handcuff key in the glove box of every squad car in Colorado. I hoped LAPD detectives had the same rules. I struggled forward and kicked as hard as I could at the inside of the door.

"WHAT's 'vanity'?" Baby asked. She stood in the kitchen of the Manhattan Beach house, the cupboards all around her emptied of pots and pans, plates and glasses, all of it now mixed with the party debris on the floor. Ashton was in the hall nearby, going through a cabinet of silverware.

"It's, like, your self-esteem, I guess?"

Baby looked at her phone. "I got this text from Rhonda that just says, 'Under vanity.' It's probably autocorrect. Unless she's trying to tell me that I'm too full of myself?"

Ashton's eyes widened. "The bathrooms. Come on!"

The teens ran to the stairs. Halfway up, they heard the front door burst open. Baby shoved Ashton down, and the two huddled, listening. They crept back down a couple of steps and peered around the banister at what they could see of the foyer.

A single boot appeared. Blue ostrich skin with a skull-shaped cap on the toe. Martin Vegas dropped the twisted and bent handle of the front door on the tiles at his feet.

"Go." Baby pushed at Ashton to head upstairs. "Go, go, go."

Ashton and Baby slipped into the guest bathroom on the third floor and shut the door as quietly as they could. Baby's shaking hands fluttered over the sink.

"*Under* vanity," she breathed, ripping open the doors under the sink. "This thing is called a vanity. But it's not here. It's not here. I don't see anything."

"How many bathrooms does your place have?"

"Six. But this is the room Rhonda has been sleeping in."

"Doesn't mean it's the vanity she was talking about."

"Damn," Baby said. "But I know it's not in my bathroom."

"Where are the others?"

"There're two on the ground floor. We can't go down there now." As though to confirm her words, they heard a crash from the lower floor as one of the gang members smashed something. "There's one on the roof, next to the pool. And my dad's bedroom is on the next floor down."

Baby ran to the door, slipped silently out into the bedroom. Ashton followed closely behind her, marveling at her fearlessness. She peeked out into the hall and crept down the staircase before even glancing back to make sure he was behind her.

She's one of those girls, Ashton thought. *The ones who just assume you'll follow.* The ones who walked ahead of him into parties like they hadn't arrived in the same limo. The ones who tossed their handbags at him at the airport and expected him to catch. He was following Baby as though on a string. He was so distracted by his self-reflections that he didn't even see the cartel guy with a cast on his hand and a gun tattoo on his face turn into the second-floor hall as Ashton reached the lower landing.

Ashton and Gunmouth faced each other, the cartel henchman so stunned he didn't even lift the gun he carried at his hip.

"Hey!" the man said, raising the hand strapped tightly into a dirty fiberglass cast. Ashton leaped across the hall and threw himself into the bedroom with Baby, slamming the door shut.

"They're here!" Gunmouth shouted. *"Ellos están aquí!"*

A HOSPITAL is a busy place. So when I walked in to find the hospital seemingly empty, a sense of unreality gripped me. People had dropped bags and other belongings as they ran—a coffee spilled here, a teddy bear discarded there, telltale signs of panic. I followed the empty hall until I found two police officers, who swiveled and pointed their guns at me.

"Get down! Get down! Get down!"

"She's with me." Summerly appeared beside me, a troop of officers at his side. He was trying to strap a bulletproof vest to his thick chest. "I told you to wait outside."

"You did," I said.

"But you're here. Which means somebody let you out or you ripped my car open like a sardine can."

"I'm sure it's fixable," I lied. The detective's car door had collapsed under my boot by the fourth kick. "Where are they?"

"We think they're in the cafeteria, in a seating area above it," he said. "But look, this is not your scene."

"I want to help."

"I know you do." He nodded tersely. "You're that kind of person. I get it. But Rhonda, you don't just get to pick and choose which situations to insert yourself into."

"Yeah, I do," I said. "And I've picked this one because there's a teenage girl up there who needs help, and that's what I do and I'm good at it. And I'm not just *inserting* myself into this situation. I'm *barging* in. Because I'm good at that too."

I shoved past him, waiting to hear him order his officers after me. But those words didn't come. When I turned and looked after a few seconds, I realized Detective Dave Summerly was beside me, marching toward the double doors at the end of the hall that led into the cafeteria.

"You're crazy," he said. I thought I saw a flicker of a smile at the corner of his lips. "Damn crazy woman."

ASHTON threw himself against the door. The handle rattled, and after a few seconds a thump came against the wood as Gunmouth heaved himself against the opposite side of the door. Baby joined Ashton, throwing all her weight against their side. After a few moments of silence, they heard a click.

"Get down!" Baby shouted.

Four bullets smashed through the door, a second after Ashton had hit the carpet. He barely managed to keep the door shut as the man in the hall threw himself against it again. Baby ran to a bedside table and shoved it sideways against the door. Ashton dragged over the dresser.

"Dar la vuelta al lado!"

"They're going around the side!" Baby cried. "Go, Ashton!"

Ashton dove into the bathroom, throwing open the doors of the cabinet beneath the sink. Deodorant cans, cologne bottles, face-cloths, soap packets. Nothing else.

"It's not here!" As he rose and turned, he knocked the wooden façade at the bottom of the cabinet with his toe. It tilted inward, one corner popping out. He wrenched the wood away, then shoved his hand into the dark space and felt fabric.

He dragged the bag out from beneath the vanity and ran into the bedroom in time to hear gunshots. He saw Baby cowering against the pile of furniture they had shoved against the door.

"Come on!" He grabbed her hand. They shoved open the bedroom's large window together. Beneath part of it was a huge bougainvillea bush. Ashton looked down the side of the house and saw Vegas and two of his guys clambering over the fence separating the back half of the property from the front.

"I can't do it," Baby said. She gripped his hand, backing toward the door of the bedroom, where the man with the gun tattoo was shouldering through the door, splintering it slowly.

"I've got you," Ashton said. He gathered her up and helped her climb onto the window casing.

They closed their eyes, held hands, and jumped.

They hit the ground hard, the duffel bag buffering them from the thorns of the bougainvillea, but Ashton struggled to maintain consciousness after his head smacked the ground. A few seconds passed before the screaming pain. Then Baby dragged him up, Ashton's feet pounding the pavement crookedly as they sprinted for the front of the house.

He was wide-awake now, hearing the hum of the garage door opening remotely—Baby's doing. He ducked under the rising door and then jumped into the Maserati beside her. She squeezed her eyes shut as she turned the key in the ignition; then when the car started, she threw it into reverse.

The still-moving garage door scraped along the length of the roof as they backed out and turned into the street. The tires screeched, and the back window collapsed in a shower of glass shards as bullets zinged off the frame of the car.

"Hold on," Baby said as she slammed her foot down on the accelerator.

Jacob and Vera were alone together in the wide mezzanine seating area perched above the cafeteria. Vera knew this was the place where one of them would die. As she'd hoped, Jacob put his gun down on the nearest tabletop and smiled at her.

She wanted it to be equal. Two killers coming together, discovering who was the strongest, using only their hands.

"You've been doing this awhile, haven't you?" she said. "You're not just some dad who's pissed. There were others before Benzo and Sean and Penny."

"I've been doing it since before you were born."

"What are the chances?" Vera asked. "We choose some ass from a mall parking lot and he turns out to be a real psycho."

"We're more common than people think," he said.

She went to him. He grabbed her throat and squeezed. She kicked the wound she'd given him earlier, ground her heel into the glass cut in his thigh while she grabbed at his head. They wrestled, knocked over a table. She reached for a weapon, something, all thoughts of fighting it out with him bare-handed abandoned as Jacob continued to grip her throat.

Then he slipped.

There must have been something on the floor. Coffee, it smelled like. His leg slid out, and Vera's feet touched the floor for the first time in seconds. She felt her adversary falling, and she went with it. They crashed into the glass barrier of the mezzanine, shattering a pane of it. Vera dug her heels into the floor, pushing Jacob out over the edge as he gripped the floor with his bloody hands, glass grinding under his palms.

Vera pulled herself to her feet, stood above him. He'd been so frightening. Now he was just an old man hanging from a ledge by his bloody fingers. She lifted her boot and placed it on top of his knuckles as Jacob's wide eyes looked up at her.

"WAIT!" I cried.

Vera looked at me. Beneath her, Jacob Kanular gripped wildly at the edge of the mezzanine with his free hand. Vera's bright blond curls were matted with blood. Unknown emotions crossed her face as she took in the sight of me and Dave Summerly standing at the edge of the huge dining area.

Officers began spreading out around the room with guns drawn, aiming where the other shooter hung, one hand now loosely wrapped around a barrier pole with the other beneath Vera's boot. A female officer was slowly climbing the open stairs leading to the mezzanine, on Vera's right, her pistol drawn, blocking the girl's exit on that side. But there was no one yet at Vera's back, still leaving her an escape through the hallway doors behind her. I had to delay the girl until she was completely surrounded.

Vera stood watching me, stunned, but in mere seconds the shock dissolved, and I saw her calculating how to manage the new situation. My presence and what it meant. I put my hands up and stepped forward cautiously.

"Vera," I said. "I—"

"Don't even start." Vera held up a finger. I saw a flash of something in her. Confident and cutting and sure of herself. "Don't say my name like you know me. You don't know anything about me."

"I don't have to know you to know what this is," I said.

"Oh, yeah? What is this?"

"This is a terrible situation that's going to get worse if we're not careful. You've got time to think this through."

"No, I don't. I'm not going to fall for your delaying tactics. We both know the door is closing. This is goodbye."

"Vera," I said, "I care about what happens here."

She laughed hard, shuffling her feet, making Jacob grind his teeth as he kept clinging to the very edge of the mezzanine.

I felt Summerly's hand on my shoulder, pushing me forward a little. "Keep at it," he murmured. "You're doing great."

"I care about you, Vera," I said.

"Are you kidding me?" She snorted. "You met me once!"

"Nope," I said. I shook my head, and I meant it. "I've met you a thousand times before. You're every kid I've ever walked into a courtroom with. You're every boy and girl I've sat with in interview rooms, in bedrooms, in prison cells. I've met so many kids like you, Vera. Kids who found themselves in the kind of mess that can't be gotten out of. This is a pretty good mess you've made—don't get me wrong. Spectacular. But you can get out of it. All you have to do is take the help I'm offering you right now."

Vera looked down at the man hanging from the mezzanine. I saw her weight shift so that she crushed his fingers harder. Jacob yowled. Vera seemed to be considering her options.

The female cop to her right was five feet closer now, her gun leveled at Vera's head. I didn't expect what happened next.

The girl smiled sweetly. A little sadly. Like she was giving in.

"Okay." Vera nodded. She lifted her boot and eased back a step. I watched her raise her hands. "I'll take the help."

I rushed forward. The female cop did too. Behind me, I heard

Summerly's footsteps as we all ran toward the falling man who had let go. For an instant, we completely forgot about Vera.

It was exactly what she'd planned.

I reached Jacob first. I fell as he fell, clipping me with his weight. We both sprawled on the floor, with him draped over my thighs. I leaned sideways and dragged myself out from under him. It was the only thing that saved my life. Because Vera had backed up not to escape but to grab a gun from somewhere behind her. She first fired into the shoulder of the female cop on her right but immediately then leaned over the edge of the mezzanine and fired at Kanular.

She fired twice. The first bullet whizzed between our heads and pounded into the linoleum floor. The second shot was on target. I saw his head buck and a hole appear in his forehead.

Jacob's body went limp. I heard footsteps running, officers coming to assist the female officer on the stairs, quickly carry her out, as Jacob slipped away. I hung my head over him, too scared to look up in case Vera decided to fire again.

I heard doors swinging open and shut as she ran through them. The footsteps of officers in pursuit. But I knew there was no point in running after her. I had seen in Vera's falsely sweet smile the confidence of a girl with a plan. I'd thought it was relief that I had given her, a sense that she was going to be taken care of now. But it was just the grin of a spider watching the last group of insects step into its trap.

When I dragged myself to my feet, I was alone. The cafeteria sprawled around me, broken glass and blood on the floor. The killer named Jacob Kanular stared up at me, unseeing. I felt the failure of being unable to save him, or Vera, reach deep inside me, into my bones, and carve its mark.

Chapter 13

THEY FLED. BABY GRIPPED the wheel, and Ashton hung on to his seat belt with gritted teeth as Baby took the car through the streets, blasting through red lights.

It was only on the 110 heading north that Baby finally eased off the accelerator. Ashton unclenched his jaw. In silence they rode, glancing now and then at the rearview mirror.

"I think we lost them," Ashton said.

"Don't jinx it," Baby said.

Ten minutes passed. Fifteen. None of the cartel guys seemed to be following them.

"I think we lost them," Ashton repeated. The teens looked at each other. Ashton felt laughs ripple up his throat, and suddenly they both were laughing hard, swiping at tears, banging their fists on the dashboard and whooping.

"Well? Get the bag, man. Show me the money," Baby said.

"Show me the moneyyyyyy!" Ashton cried. He dragged the bag into his lap and pulled out a stack of bills. He ripped the elastic band from the stack and threw it up, letting the cash rain down all over the two of them in the car.

Baby laughed. He loved the sound of it, low and smoky, a cool girl's laugh. He remembered that laugh from school. Back when everything was uncomplicated, pure, wonderful.

"What are we gonna do now?" Baby said.

A silence descended on them. Ashton gathered up some money, began stacking the bills back together. He pulled one of the packages of meth out of the bag and turned it over in his hands, tossed it onto the back seat.

"The smart thing for us to do is find Rhonda," Baby said. "Ask her where to go. We use some of the money to keep ourselves safe for now. We hole up in a hotel. We buy some phones to call her and wait for her to come get us. She comes, helps us negotiate your surrender, and then packs me up to live with her and her cats forever in some loser town in Loserville."

Baby eased out a long sigh. Ashton kept stacking the cash.

"That's the smart thing to do," he agreed.

They drove in silence for a while.

"I don't feel like being smart right now, though," Baby said eventually.

"Neither do I."

"This might be, like, my last night of freedom," she said. "And yours literally."

"Yeah, like, *literally*."

"I don't *feel like* going to Colorado." Baby looked at him. "And I'm sure you don't *feel like* going to jail."

They smiled at each other.

"Vegas?" Baby asked.

"Vegas, Baby!" Ashton laughed.

Baby floored it. The engine thrummed. They didn't look in the rearview mirror again.

Dave Summerly found me at his car, dialing and redialing Baby, my hands sweaty and my heart racing.

"The Bruhs just called me," I said without looking up.

"Who?"

"The Bruhs!" I snapped.

"I don't know what you're say—"

"My neighbors at the Manhattan Beach house, Dave," I said, trying to regulate my breathing. "They said they heard gunshots inside and saw Baby and Ashton flee in my dad's Maserati. They're on the run out there somewhere, and they probably have three million dollars on them."

"They *what?* She knew where the money was?"

"I told her."

"Rhonda!"

"I knew she'd go for the money. When she escaped at the gas station, I thought she'd go home and collect it, and I was right. It's a good thing I told her where the money was, or she would have been caught trying to find it by the cartel guys."

"You just *knew* she'd do that?" Summerly asked.

"She's my sister," I said. "We've got to find her."

"Well, if you think you've got this sister-sister ESP thing going on with her, you figure out where she is now, and we'll try to snatch her up before the cartel does," he said.

"Don't you have to try to catch Vera Petrov?"

"The pursuit has been taken off my hands." His shrug was labored. "I've been stood down, for now. Seems I let a civilian lawyer into the danger zone around an active shooter and she got an inch and a half away from having her head blown off."

"Oh, Dave. I'm sorry."

"Doesn't matter." He gripped my shoulder. "You almost had her, Rhonda. I saw it in her eyes. She thought about coming with you. If we ever had a chance of connecting with Petrov, that was the moment. I think you did good, and I'll defend my decision to let you help."

I leaned into him a little. His hand ran along the back of my arm, a small, swift gesture.

"I'm coming with you," he said. "We're gonna find these kids. Where do two reckless kids with nothing to lose go with three million bucks and a Maserati?"

Baby's voice traveled back to me from a couple of days earlier, the first time she'd asked about the money's location.

You think I'm going to take it all, drive to Vegas, and have a wild time?

Dave seemed to know what I was thinking.

"Rhonda, they wouldn't," he said.

"Don't bet on it," I said. "Ashton thinks he's going to jail for the rest of his life, and Baby thinks I'm going to abduct her and lock her in my cattery of social doom."

"Your what?"

"Never mind."

Night had fallen. I looked helplessly at the lamps as they sprang to life all over the parking lot. I thought of Baby driving through the night with the cartel behind her. If they were clever, Martin Vegas and his guys would let Baby and Ashton get a little ahead of them. Hang back, so the kids would think they'd gotten away. Vegas and his boys would wait for the teens to relax, before pouncing when the opportunity arose.

I saw it as the obvious strategy, but I was older and savvier than the kids. I knew Baby and Ashton would fall for it.

"How do we catch them?" I said. "They have a head start."

"I might know a way," Summerly said.

At night, from three thousand feet above the desert, the I-15 from Los Angeles to Las Vegas looked like the ocean. There were long stretches of nothingness, bare roads; then here and there clusters of gold lights floated in the blackness like little meetings of fishermen. Streams of slow-traveling red dots wound gently through the desert basin, the taillights of people leaving the coast for the city of cards and dice.

Summerly hunched over his phone in the seat in front of me as he connected it to a cable in his headset, punching in a call before he'd secured the unit over his ears again. "I need CHP keeping an eye on 15 near Barstow, at the turnoff for route 127, and at the state border, just before Primm," he yelled as the helicopter blades thumped outside our windows. Then, once his headset was in place, he continued in a quieter tone. "Yes, that's what I said. No, you don't need his approval. You've got mine. It's two kids in a black Maserati!"

My headset clicked as Dr. Tuddy was patched through from his seat next to the helicopter's pilot. I saw his shaggy brown hair shift as he tilted his head back toward me.

"Beautiful night for an air pursuit!" he said, his voice barely audible through the headset.

"You're so good to loan us your chopper!" I said.

"This is one of many toys I bought with the patent money," he said. "It's not the best of my collection. I also have a Bell 47G from 1946. It still runs! I'd have suggested we take that one, but it wouldn't cope with our collective weight."

"There's also no way I'm getting into a seventy-five-year-old helicopter!" I yelled. "Are you nuts?"

Dave ended his call and sat back.

"Vera's gone," he said. I had the awful feeling that we would hear from her again. Vera had gotten a taste for blood, and wherever she ended up next, people would start to disappear.

"We weren't dealing with a kid there," Summerly said, as though he could read my thoughts. "She wasn't a child making a mistake. She was a killer with training wheels."

"And now they're off," I agreed.

He nodded.

"I'm sorry," I said. "I should have—"

"You couldn't have known, Rhonda. You did your best, and that was pretty amazing, even if it didn't work out."

He reached into his pocket and took out a handkerchief. I wasn't crying but took it anyway. Only when I looked down did I realize it was for the blood still on my hands, on my face.

"They said Jacob Kanular had a kid in the hospital?" I asked.

Summerly nodded. "His ten-year-old daughter came in after a severe asthma attack. She's been in a coma. A unit went to the house and found her mom dead. Knife wounds."

"If that poor little girl wakes up, they're going to have to tell her that both her parents are dead," I said.

"She's awake," Summerly said. He was scrolling through his phone. "She's on her way to another hospital. I've got a report here that says she's cooperating with police as best she can."

I looked out the window. Summerly reached over and rubbed my knee.

"You can't save them all, Rhonda," he said.

"I know," I said. "But I like to try. It feels like I'm helping some version of me when I was that age. In some stupid way it's almost like if I help enough of them, I'll get back there, through time, to myself. I'll be able to undo all the pain."

"That's a nice thought." He smiled at me. But I didn't have the strength to return it. Baby and Ashton were down there somewhere in the dark, and our hopes of finding them seemed to be ticking away.

Baby took her right hand off the wheel and reached out to grab Ashton's arm, shaking him awake. The hypnotic shadows of rocky terrain drifting by had taken him deep into slumber.

"Police," she said.

"Oh, man." Ashton sat up. In the distance, a cluster of California Highway Patrol vehicles sat on the wide median between the two lanes of the freeway heading in each direction, but all of them were pointed toward their eastbound lanes. The taillights of cars ahead brightened as they slowed on approach.

"Is it a roadblock?"

"Whatever it is, it's for us. It's gotta be."

"I'm getting off the road." Baby swung the wheel at an exit and made a couple of turns to get her to the opposite side of the interstate, where the CHP weren't watching. She doused the headlights and rolled unseen. Abruptly, the front wheels began to shudder over rocks.

"This thing wasn't designed for off-roading, Baby!"

"Hang on."

They crept through the blackness more slowly.

"There are ravines out here. Crevasses!"

"Shut up, Ashton. Don't be such a wimp," Baby said. "It's a crevasse or a jail cell. Which would you prefer?"

In time, Ashton looked back to see a single pair of headlights behind them, blinking out too.

"It's them. It's them. They're back there. Speed up!"

Together they felt the rocks, shrubs, and stumps of Joshua trees thump under the vehicle. Ashton watched the lights of the slowed vehicles on the highway disappear when a huge pair of headlights flicked on only feet behind their vehicle.

Baby screamed. The sound was strangled out by terror as the car behind smashed into their rear bumper, shoving the car sideways. Desert dust coiled and spun in the blinding light.

"Get ready to run!" Baby cried.

Ashton looked ahead. A torn and rotting billboard loomed into view and then collapsed, folding around the car as they plowed through it, bringing the Maserati to a crunching halt.

Ashton barely had time to read the sunbaked lettering: ROCK-A-HOOLA WATERPARK.

THEY crawled from the wreckage. Ashton's blood was rushing so hard that new injuries did not register in his mind—a nail scraping along his arm from the billboard frame, a sharp stone slicing his ankle as he stumbled in the dark. He grabbed Baby's hand, and they raced over the cracked concrete of what had once been a wide walkway between the attractions of the water park. Ashton followed her through the doorway of a crumbling building under a broken sign that read TICKETS.

"What is this place?" Ashton breathed.

"It's an old water park. Abandoned. I used to come out here with some skater boys."

"You would hang out here?" Ashton scoffed. The darkness inside the building made it impossible to see the room around him, but he could smell its contents: stagnant water, urine, old beer. He kicked a blanket out from under his feet and crouched behind the counter, holding the rusted frame of an empty fridge. "Who hangs out at a haunted water park for kicks?"

"The pools make great skate ramps." Baby shoved at him. "Keep your head down."

They waited. Sure enough, in the moonlight, they made out the shapes of four men emerging from behind where the Maserati was nestled in the collapsed billboard. They were walking. *Bad men always walk,* Ashton thought. They didn't need to run. All Vegas and his crew had to do was hunt them from building to building until they locked them down.

A voice drifted toward them from the group of shadows. Baby and Ashton gripped each other in the cool darkness.

"We just want our stuff!"

It was Vegas who had spoken. His deep voice was calm. Ashton almost felt like going to him. He sounded safe.

"It's in the car!" Baby yelled.

"Shhh! Are you crazy?"

"The sound will bounce off the buildings," Baby said. She was right. Vegas's men shifted at the sound of her words but didn't turn toward the ticket kiosk. There was a pause; then one of them turned and walked back toward the Maserati.

"They'll go now," Baby said. "You watch. They'll leave us alone. They don't want to hurt two stupid kids."

"We're too much trouble," Ashton agreed, shuddering with fear. "Not smart. Not worth the effort."

They waited. The man returned from the car with the duffel bag. In the dim moonlight, the cartel men checked the bag; then one of them shouldered it.

Then the men fanned out across the park.

Ashton could see it clearly. He was going to die out here in the desert. When he was gone, there would be reports of his involvement in the Midnight Crew. They would sit uncomfortably next to photographs of him on the Stanford-West Academy lacrosse team and the honor roll. Eventually it would all prove so unpalatable that his family and friends would stop talking about him altogether, and that would be it. He would exist as a family myth shared by distant cousins about their relative who was murdered by members of a drug cartel.

"We can't let this happen," Ashton said to Baby, crouched shivering beside him. "It can't all end like this."

Ashton's words seemed to give her strength. She nodded, and they ran through the back doors of the kiosk.

Baby climbed through a shattered fence, and they ran through a kiddie pool overgrown with razor-sharp desert plants. Ahead of them, the gentle curves of a roller coaster rose from behind a pool ringed by giant concrete elephants.

"Listen." Ashton dragged Baby to a stop. "They're going to search for us building by building. We have to think smart. Go somewhere unexpected."

He pointed up at the roller coaster. A single train, three cars long, was stuck on the tracks twenty feet from the ground. Baby nodded. They turned and ran.

"Hey!"

From the battered, graffitied remains of a hot dog hut, a figure cloaked in a blanket emerged in the moonlight.

"You little jerks, keep it down!"

"Shhh!" Baby waved at the vagrant. "Go back insi—"

The night erupted with white light. Ashton hadn't realized there were members of Vegas's crew so close behind them. The homeless man in the blanket bucked and twisted as the bullets tore through him, his body falling in a heap.

Ashton grabbed Baby's wrist to hold her back as she instinctively leaped forward to help the victim.

"Come on! Come on!"

A scent of fire was on the breeze. Vegas and his guys were going to smoke them out. Ashton and Baby rounded a corner and were confronted by the sight of an ancient carousel set alight, flames climbing up candy-cane poles. Beyond the carousel, another hot dog stand was just catching fire.

They raced along a line of palm trees, climbing onto the roller-coaster platform.

"We'll climb up there." Ashton pointed up the steep rise, to a row of carriages stuck on the track. "They'll never look for us up there."

He put a hand out and found Baby frozen. "I can't do it."

"Yes, you can! Come on! We've got to go!"

"They're going to light the whole place up." Baby stammered, "L-look. There's fire on the other side. They're going to trap us!" Her shirt clung to her body with sweat. "We don't have a gun. We don't have anything!"

"Baby, I've got you." Ashton climbed up off the tracks and onto the platform. He had his arms open to hold her when the bullets cut him down.

The first shot hit Ashton in the lower back. Baby watched him arch backward, his eyes wide. The second bullet seemed to shove him forward, slamming into his shoulder from behind. He fell into her, and they went down on the rotting wood. Baby held him, expecting the next shots to take her, for it all to end in a burst of pain as a bullet cleaved its way into her skull.

But it didn't.

The gunfire kept coming, but it was from behind her now.

Baby saw Officer Summerly step up onto the platform, taking cover behind the driver's control desk as he shot at the cartel guy who'd appeared at the other end of the platform. Baby squeezed her eyes shut against the white light popping at the corners of her vision. Ashton didn't seem to be breathing. She told herself she needed to let go of him, but her fingers wouldn't unlock from around his arms and shoulders.

She came to herself eventually, forcing her legs to move. She dragged Ashton down off the platform, onto the ancient detritus in the dirt: cigarette butts, flattened paper cups. While more gunshots zinged over their heads, she held Ashton's face and yelled at him to wake up. That it couldn't end this way.

She pressed her fingers into his neck.

He was gone.

Baby was aware of movement. Two cartel guys were trying to advance toward Summerly. Silence then drifted out over the roller-coaster platform, and Baby lifted her head in time to see the police officer pursuing Gunmouth into the dark.

Another of the cartel guys lay flopped on the stairs up to the roller coaster, his mouth open and leaking blood, the height restriction sign hanging above him on a rusty chain.

The sound of footsteps made Baby turn and look over her shoulder. Martin Vegas stepped onto the tracks twenty feet behind her. His footfalls were soft, measured, the casual stroll of someone completely assured of his situation. Yet they seemed to shake the entire structure.

Vegas had a silver revolver in his hand, hanging by his thigh.

"It doesn't have to go this way, you know," he called out to Baby. "I'm always on the lookout for girls like you."

Baby couldn't say anything. Her skin prickled.

"You've got that look," Vegas said. "It's very marketable. Young. Fresh. Put a California girl like you in a Mercedes convertible, maybe a surfer dude in the passenger seat, and I can move mountains. You'd get a cut of everything we make."

"Screw you," Baby snarled.

"This isn't clever," Vegas said. "Look at your situation. It's win-lose. If you choose to lose, you don't get to play again."

He drew the hammer back on the revolver. Baby refused to look at the weapon. It didn't matter how big the gun was, how sickening the sound was of the cylinder turning. If she was going to die, it would be between the two of them in those very last seconds. Baby watched Vegas drawing them out, savoring them, the way he had probably dozens of times before.

It was this indulgence that cost him his life.

I'D SCALED the structure behind the roller-coaster platform as quietly as possible in the darkness, but with every inch I advanced, I was sure Baby or Vegas was going to hear me. The rotting wooden beams creaked under my weight. As I hauled myself up onto the tracks, I felt the whole wooden frame rock back and forth in its fittings thirty feet below. I swung a leg over into the first car of the roller-coaster train and tumbled in, throwing my weight forward. Nothing happened. I saw below me, in the moonlight, Vegas aiming a gun at Baby.

I could only hope Baby would get out of the way in time. I leaned back, threw myself forward again, felt the carriage's rusty wheels grind on the track. Another shove and something snapped.

The train screamed down the tracks. My stomach lurched. I gripped the silver lap bar and yowled as the looming figure of Martin Vegas twisted around, spotting me soaring toward him in the car without time to leap out of the way.

A heavy, thundering crunch and Vegas disappeared under the coaster wheels, shoving the car upward and to the side, throwing me onto the platform with enough force to tear the skin from my forearms and rip holes in the knees of my jeans.

I rolled and crawled to the edge of the platform. I didn't look back at the twisted body of the gangster for long. A shattered arm poking out from under the car was all I needed to confirm that Vegas was at least too broken to do any more harm to us.

The car had stopped an inch from where Baby was cowering over the body of Ashton Willisee. I reached down, and with difficulty, she let go of her friend and let me haul her up.

We held each other, two sisters bloodied and bruised and shaking. In the distance, I saw Dave Summerly and Dr. Tuddy coming together, the big cop embracing the thin scientist with smiling relief now that the fight had ended.

As SHE had done the night before, Vera crept into her house in Brentwood and walked past her mother's bedroom. There was no telltale white light shining under the door this time. Her mother was in the first-floor living room being questioned by police officers.

Vera had come home to find the house surrounded. The police had been waiting in the shadows beneath trees, waiting for Vera to return. Stupid. If they knew anything about her father, they'd have known that having a discreet way of entering and exiting the family home was the first priority of any Russian gangster worth his—or her—salt.

Vera had slipped onto her neighbor's property, unlatched the gate that led under the decking of his aboveground pool, and walked in a crouch through the crawl space, past the pool filter, and into the space under the decking of her own home's pool. From there she had accessed the basement through a hidden panel and quietly climbed the stairs.

She went to her bedroom, opened the closet, and brought down an empty backpack. Vera didn't know what her life would be like by the time the sun rose. All she knew was that her day had been filled with killing, and she'd never felt more exhilarated than she did now, packing her passport, wallet, and gun into the bag. She wanted more days like this one.

Vera went to the hall, looked down over the banister at the officers standing in the kitchen doorway drinking coffee. One of them was using her father's favorite mug. Vera thought about shooting him where he stood. It was an easy shot. But now was the time to be smart and slip away into the dark.

She'd be back, when the time was right.

Chapter 14

I DRESSED FOR MY FATHER's funeral in an Opeth T-shirt with a peacock on the front, worn over jeans with a nice blazer. Baby's partygoer friends had left me little to choose from, and I hadn't had time to hunt down formal clothing options in a city full of people a third of my size. Baby descended the stairs in a little black dress that was so short it made me choke on my coffee, but I decided it wasn't the day to come down on her about her fashion choices.

She looked older. It had been only days since Ashton was shot dead right in front of her, a shock to her system that came only moments before she also witnessed the gruesome death of Martin Vegas. For a kid who had lost so much already, the week had stripped away her innocence.

We hadn't talked much since the night at the water park, let alone about whether her future lay in Colorado or Manhattan Beach. She snapped her little handbag closed and checked herself in the hall mirror, eyeing the makeup she'd layered on over a deep gash carved high on her cheekbone.

I had passed her bedroom a couple of times a night and peeked in, saw her lying on her side scrolling the same news sites I was scrolling in my own bed. The world was just beginning to learn what Ashton and his friends had been up to in their spare time, and videos of their activities were surfacing on the dark web. The hunt for Vera was continuing without success, and a hidden room in Jacob Kanular's house, revealed during a search, was leading investigators down a long, dark path to discover just how many times the mysterious father had gone on the hunt before.

The doorbell rang.

"That'll be our ride," I said.

Short of any functioning vehicle, I had hired a limo to take us to the Hollywood Forever Cemetery, but I had the driver leave us outside the wrought-iron entrance gates. When Baby stepped out of the limo beside me, she stopped dead at the sight before her. Six black stallions stood harnessed to a gleaming black carriage, its top-hatted driver waving at us from the front bench seat. My father's coffin was visible in the back of the carriage, surrounded by red roses. Baby and I climbed up into the front of the carriage to sit on either side of the driver.

"Where the *hell* did you get this?" Baby blurted.

"Warner Bros. is doing another *Dracula* reboot," I said.

As Baby and I stood by the grave, we looked around us. I'd invited a short list of people from my father's address book to the funeral, but somehow the word had spread. Among the neighbors and legitimate business associates were others with whom he'd clearly had more illegitimate dealings: tattooed bikers huddled under a tree, sly-looking mafioso types in pinstriped suits, guys in sports jackets with suspicious bulges at their hips and ankles, and a smattering of what were clearly undercover cops there to eavesdrop on any criminal whisperings. A few women, maybe girlfriends or mistresses, cried loudly and elbowed one another for space close to the grave.

A few of these attendees—gangsters, hit men, loan sharks, or whatever the hell they were—gave Baby their condolences as the priest readied himself for the service, some pushing thick envelopes of cash into her hands, which she secreted into her handbag. I pretended not to notice. When the priest began speaking, I leaned in to Baby.

"I know about the kiss," I whispered.

"What?" She wheeled on me. "Are you kidding me?"

"No, I'm not."

"You're telling me this *now?*"

"When the hell was I supposed to tell you?" I said. "When Martin Vegas was shoving a gun in your face? When you were in your room crying about Ashton? Over cupcakes at the wake while we try to decide which one of these guys the undercover cops are after?"

"I don't know," Baby said. "How about three weeks from now, when I've had a chance to get over this." She gestured at our father's grave.

"I'm telling you now because I think it'll help you get over this." I looked at the grave before us. "What happened between you and that teacher was a mistake made by a confused kid."

"I can't believe this," Baby muttered, folding her arms.

"I'm trying to tell you that those times, when you're feeling confused and alone and you do stupid things, are going to keep coming. And while Dad's not here to help you through them anymore"—I pointed at our father's coffin—"I am."

Baby sighed, but it was unreadable to me. It could have been exhaustion or solace—I didn't know.

"Look," I began, "I know I annoy the crap out of you—"

"You don't annoy me, Rhonda," she said. "You're cool."

"I'm cool?" I laughed. "Me? Of all people?"

"Sometimes." She smirked. "You're kind of exciting and weird. That's cool."

"How's this for cool?" I said. "I quit my job this morning."

"You *what?*" Baby gasped. People turned to look at us. The priest kept speaking, oblivious.

"We're staying here," I said. "I'll take the bar exam and any other tests to get licensed in California. Try to get some local defense gigs, I guess. I don't know. I'll work it out. But the truth is, cleaning up after Dad is going to be hard. I've got to shut down his office. Make sure there are no more little criminal surprises hiding under the floorboards. We'll probably have to fend off legal action against the house. The police will want to know if it was acquired with drug money."

"Sounds hard," she said.

"Too hard to do from Colorado." I nodded.

She sighed again. This time I could hear the relief in it.

THERE were indeed more criminal secrets hidden in my father's office. Beneath the stacks of paperwork, I found what looked like a human thigh bone, a half-constructed ransom letter made from cut-out pieces of magazines, and a golf club spattered with blood. It took three weeks to get the office tidy enough for a person to walk around in it. Baby spent most of this time lying on the couch playing with her phone or napping.

I was scrubbing ancient coffee stains and water marks from the surface of the bare desk when a man in a suit knocked on the half-open door. His hair was slicked back neatly, and he wore a leather shoulder bag across his chest. Baby looked up for long enough to calculate the types of things that interested her about men—whether the bag went with the suit, whether his stubble was deliberate, whether his eyes were the right shade of sapphire blue—and then she went back to her phone.

"Is this the office of Earl Bird?" the guy asked.

"It was," I said. "But he's no longer here."

"I'm actually here to see Rhonda Bird," he said.

I felt a little prickle of pain in my chest, the same bodily warning bells that told me that my life was about to change, without any sense of whether it would be good or bad.

"That's me," I said.

"A guy named Summerly sent me." The man glanced around the room. "Said you might be able to help me with a private investigative matter."

I hadn't seen Dave Summerly in person since the night at the water park. But we had texted. A lot. I was keeping him in the wings of my life until I sorted out exactly what my new life in California would look like. I'd told Dave I needed time to get into step with Baby, to figure out just how much control and influence I could or should have on my new charge. He'd respected my wishes, and I liked that. But this new development was a bolt out of the blue.

"Dave said what?" I sputtered. "I . . . I'm not . . ."

"She'll meet you downstairs at the crab shack in ten minutes," Baby said, popping up from the couch. "Get a booth at the back."

Once the guy was gone, I shook my head at Baby.

"I'm not a private investigator," I said.

"Summerly seems to think you are." She shrugged. "Or at least that you could be. I do too."

"Well, that's just too bad," I said. "Because I don't know if that's the kind of job I want to take on."

"So let's go and find out." Baby smiled. I watched her for a moment, saw the excitement brimming in her eyes, and remembered that part of what came next for us would be working out a new life not only for Baby but for myself too. I needed to be open to experiments and mistakes.

"Okay," I said. "Let's give it a shot."

Baby clapped her hands in triumph and bumped my hip with hers, and for a moment I felt like a terrific mother. Or sister.

Whatever.

Then Baby said, "Maybe we should start a detective agency."

I laughed. "That's the worst idea I've ever heard."

After*Words*

James Patterson holds the title in the *Guinness Book of World Records* for the most number one *New York Times* bestsellers. His books have sold more than three hundred million copies, and he has created several beloved series, including Alex Cross, Women's Murder Club, Michael Bennett, and NYPD Red, to name a few.

Patterson is passionate about getting kids to enjoy reading. When his son was twelve, Patterson realized he was a lukewarm reader. When asked why, the boy complained that there was nothing good to read. Thus Patterson embarked not only on a quest to find books that interested his own child, but to write stories that would hopefully get other kids reading as well. This led to numerous young adult books, such as the very popular Maximum Ride series.

However, Patterson has not achieved this success alone. He has partnered with a variety of co-authors, often helping jump-start their careers. Australian writer Candice Fox, who co-authored *2 Sisters Detective Agency,* is an ideal example.

Fox had been a popular thriller writer Down Under, but when she first partnered with Patterson in 2015 on *Never Never,* she reached a whole new audience when the book became a bestseller. She and Patterson collaborated on several more books after that. Since *2 Sisters Detective Agency* debuts a new series, we can expect more terrific collaborations to follow.

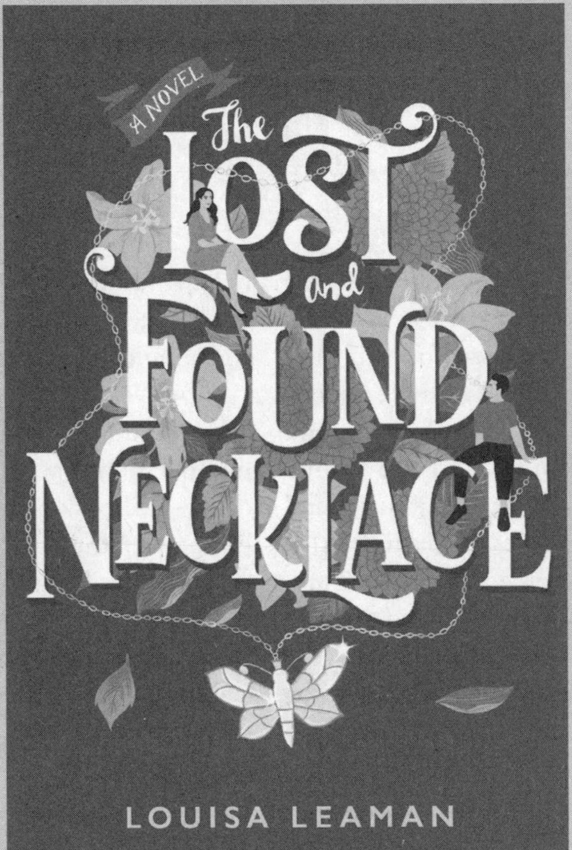
A NOVEL
The Lost and Found Necklace
LOUISA LEAMAN

Chapter 1

Behind the heavy oak doors of Hutchins Auctioneers lies a necklace in a glass cabinet, waiting for the touch of warm skin and the eyes that will admire it in its next cycle of life. Like all good heirloom jewelry, this art nouveau beauty holds more energy than its small, exquisite form would suggest. Jess Taylor, nearing thirty and frequently fearful of her expanding quarter-life crisis, has little idea what the necklace might do for her, but nevertheless feels rather sentimental as she stares at the glossy auction catalog photo and its accompanying description:

> An emblematic art nouveau design comprising a silver neck chain with a central butterfly pendant and moonstone. The wings are a fine example of the "plique-à-jour" enameling technique, embellished with mother-of-pearl and set within a delicate silver frame. A combination of twentieth-century craftsmanship and the allure of one of nature's most enchanting creatures make this a perfect addition to any collection or an ideal gift for a loved one.

She spins back to the one childhood memory in which the necklace features: herself in her mother's bedroom, maybe five years old; the pine dressing table with its three-way mirror, hair straighteners, a bottle of CK One perfume. In the drawers, the lipsticks, the hair-spray cans, the homemade Mother's Day card from Jess and her sister, Aggie—and best of all, the velvet jewelry box.

This, Jess remembers vividly: the allure of the box; her pudgy hands hovering over the lid, her anticipation as it lifts. Silver chain links running through her fingers; the candy-like beads and gems. And then the butterfly necklace, the iridescent wonder of its plump moonstone; the enamel of its wings glowing emerald green.

Jess remembers her mother warning her not to touch the wings, saying "very old" and "art nouveau" with a smile and a faux French accent. Jess looks once more at the catalog photo, imagines the actual necklace in her hand; how it will feel to have it resting in her palm again, so light and delicate, as though it could flutter away at any moment—rather like her mother did.

"Is IT usually this rowdy?" Aggie asks, snatching Jess back to the moment. "Feels more like a boxing ring than an auction."

The room is hot, made worse by the number of people spilling in, coughing, fidgeting, flapping their catalogs, talking loudly.

"Just wait," says Jess. "Some dealers play dirty. I've seen fistfights before."

Aggie eyes her.

"Not me. There's an unspoken etiquette. When someone else clearly wants an item, don't deliberately bid it up to make them pay more and *definitely* don't cut in at the last moment."

Aggie nods, then looks at the catalog photo. "It's pretty," she says, "but I'd struggle to find something to wear it with."

Of course Aggie would struggle, thinks Jess. She's a functional dresser. Jess, by contrast, plans her clothing around jewelry, sometimes plans her days around it.

"It's too stylized."

"It's typical art nouveau, Aggie, which is all about flowing, sensuous lines and whiplash curves."

"Okay, expert, so what exactly is the art nouveau?"

"A short-lived but influential design movement," Jess explains.

Having trained as an art teacher, then built an online jewelry business, she knows her way around Edwardian filigree and art deco geometry; but it's this, art nouveau, that she loves most of all.

"It lasted from around 1898 to the start of World War One. Essentially it was about good design and craftsmanship, an attempt to backpedal away from the growing taste for mass-produced goods."

"Why a butterfly?"

"Nature was a hot theme, lots of flowers, insects, and birds. And women, either as sexy, naked nymphs or . . . something scarier."

"Very Freudian. Designed by men, no doubt."

"Well, here's the thing," says Jess, eyes glinting. "Not our necklace. Apparently this one was designed and made by our great-great-grandmother, Minnie Philomene Taylor. Cool, huh? I mean, back then, female jewelry designers were a rarity."

"Very cool," says Aggie, somewhat unconvinced, "but that dangly moonstone will break off in seconds."

She tenses her shoulders, furrows her brow.

"Jess, are we really going through with this? A thousand pounds for something you'll never dare wear because it's too flimsy?"

"It's survived a century so far," Jess argues, knowing she'll pay five thousand if she has to. "I have faith." She shuts the catalog. "Besides, it's not for me, is it? We're doing this for Nancy."

"Oh yes, dear, sweet grandma Nancy."

"Whatever you think of her," says Jess, eyeing her sister, "she's our only remaining family on Mum's side. This necklace means something to her. If getting it back into her hands is the one thing I can do, then I'll know I've done my duty."

"Okay, but just so we're clear about the limit . . ."

Jess rolls her eyes. How is it, she wonders, that she and Aggie always slip so readily into their little and big sister contours?

"Since the necklace has a reserve price of one thousand, we go no further than that, agreed? Ed wants a skiing trip next February. Steph's broken her phone screen, and Marcus is demanding every game console under the sun. If I blow the contents of my rainy day jar on a piece of unwearable costume jewelry—"

"Heirloom jewelry. A piece of heirloom jewelry that represents our family's heritage, Aggie. These things matter."

"Not as much as my desire for the Mercedes S-Class."

"You are so shallow."

"And you are so . . . nostalgic!"

The man in the row behind them leans forward and berates the sisters with a sharp "Shh!," causing them to fall together and giggle like schoolgirls. When they've recovered, they realize the auction team—the caller and the lead men—are gathering at the front.

"I need the toilet!" says Jess, rising, a rush of nerves aggravating her bladder. "I'll be back in a second."

"But—"

"Save my seat."

Jess starts to move off, but as her left leg trails, she is reminded that the journey to the lobby and back will not be as speedy as she'd like, as it used to be. With big sister sovereignty, Aggie passes Jess her walking cane, watching protectively as Jess leans heavily into the pole, wincing with pain.

The bidders in the front row take care to clear the path of bags and coffee cups. They smile as Jess passes—and out of politeness she smiles back, but inside, she would rather not play the game of pity tennis. She knows people mean well, but concerned looks are a painful reminder of her how her life has changed. Because before that *dreadful* day, she'd had no need for help or pain medication. She'd been independent, self-assured, full of spirit and curiosity.

The lobby, like the auction room itself, has a certain classical elegance. Its mint-green walls are adorned with stucco plasterwork and gilt-framed oil paintings. Jess makes her way to the toilets, and once she's done, she dials her grandmother Nancy on FaceTime. After a minute, the eighty-two-year-old Nancy is there, looming into the screen with her thin white hair and papery skin.

"Hello, you," says Jess warmly.

"Jessy!"

"How are you feeling?"

"Oh, you know, so-so. Went in the gardens, did some digging. Damn foxes have been soiling the lawn again."

"Those foxes! Listen, Grandma, I'm here to get your necklace."

"You are?"

Her eyes brighten, the "Nancy twinkle."

"I'm at the auction. Aggie is here too. Front row. Don't worry. We'll get it for you. I caught a glimpse of it in the catalog. It's so beautiful! And you really think it was made by my great—what is it?—great-great-grandmother?"

"Minnie Philomene Taylor. A trailblazer, Jessy, just like you."

Jess smiles. "I'd like to hear more about Minnie."

"I have a photo of her in my bureau. I'll show you when you next visit. There's lots I want to tell you, Jessy. Minnie's necklace binds us all. If it wasn't for"—she sighs, half closes her eyes—"for all those years we were without it."

"Yes, I've been dying to ask, what happened to it, Grandma? Why did it leave the Taylor family?"

"Never mind the why," Nancy says sharply. "The important thing is *you're* now bringing it home. And how are you feeling? How are your legs?"

Jess nods, realizing she'll have to pick her moment if she's to unearth the family gossip. Nancy has always been prickly around talk of the past. In her spritely days, she had a few anecdotes: her boast about being "born in Hollywood," her travels as a punk rock fan, and her pride in the fact that following convention had never been the "Taylor way." There'd been the occasional reminiscence from Jess's estranged father, Richard, but he'd never welcomed questions. In fact, he'd never really welcomed the Taylors, period. Jess had learned to live with a certain thinness of heritage.

"I saw a specialist last week," she explains, indulging Nancy's change of subject, "who thinks he can get rid of the worst of my back pain. With an epidural, like they give women in childbirth."

The phone crackles.

"Childbirth?"

"Sorry, Grandma. Signal's terrible."

"Are you telling me you're pregnant? With that Tim?"

"No, Grandma. No babies. Not yet. Tim and I are happy as we are. Anyway, I better go because they're about to start the auction. Wish me luck. I promise I'll make it happen. Love you."

"You too, Jessy."

As Jess hobbles back to the action, she is shocked to see the room is now full. The doorway is crowded with hawk-eyes, arms folded, acting casual. She knows the sort: the Rolex-wearing old guard, a club of retired men in their sixties who do this for sport.

Jess moves past them uneasily, praying their interests lie in the array of Victorian hair brooches and model trains that precede item 22, the necklace. She doesn't want a bidding war. Unease, however, is not a good mix with a dodgy back and a walking aid. She places the tip of her cane awkwardly, feels her leg buckle as she stumbles into the person in front of her.

"Sorry . . . so sorry!"

The person, a man, unexpectedly youthful for this auction room, helps her steady herself. Their eyes meet fleetingly. His dark sparkle, beneath hooded lids and a mop of chestnut curls, startles her. Immediately she is drawn to the rest of his face, to his arched nose and full lips. She goes for a smile, but then she spots it, the spark-killing pity gaze as he glances at her cane.

Then, smooth as silk, he leans toward her, whispers in her ear. "That's one accessory I could make use of right now."

She blinks.

"To help me fend off these tyrants," he says, nodding toward the hawk-eyes. "Lend it to me. So I can pin their thieving arms to their bodies, and stop them from bidding up everyone else's items."

He grins, and Jess realizes she had him wrong. He's not a pity person at all. He's a life force. A thrill rushes through her limbs.

"Certainly it has its uses," she says, matching the glint in his eye with her own before plowing a path back to the front.

"Good afternoon," says the auctioneer, once Jess is settled back in her chair. "We have a packed event for you, a veritable cornucopia of items big and small. Starting with lot number one . . ."

The sisters sit back as a set of mother-of-pearl cuff links is paraded around the stage. The room is slow to get going, which Jess takes as an encouraging sign. They sit through a complete model railway, a crystal decanter, and two rare watches.

Half an hour in, the necklace is next. Jess's palms start to sweat. Aggie fusses over the bidding card.

"You know our rule," she hisses. "Stick to the limit."

"Yes, yes," Jess replies, eyes fixed on the auctioneer, waiting.

"Item twenty-two," the auctioneer bellows, "this exquisite art nouveau butterfly necklace, constructed with enamel, silver, and moonstone. Its exact origins are unknown, but our experts have suggested it bears some resemblance to the work of French designer René Lalique. With a reserve of one thousand pounds, I open the floor at six hundred. Any advance on six hundred?"

Her breath held tight, Jess shoots her hand up.

"That's six fifty. I have six fifty. Any advance on six fifty? Thank you, sir, seven hundred."

The sisters spin around to see who has dared bid against them, but the bids come so fast the auctioneer's call bounces around the room like a ping-pong ball. There is no way to see where it has landed or where it will go next.

"Seven fifty . . . eight hundred . . . eight fifty. Do I see nine?"

Jess thrusts her bidding card out, desperate to catch the wave.

"Nine hundred, to the brunette lady in the front."

She grins, triumphant that she has reclaimed control, only to have it snatched away immediately.

"Nine fifty . . . one thousand . . . one thousand fifty . . . one thousand one hundred . . . that's one thousand one fifty. Ladies and gentlemen, this is a very special item. Do I have one two?"

Jess lifts her card again, her teeth clenched tight.

"We said no more than one thousand," Aggie warns.

"But we can't stop here. It's only just cooling down. We need to keep control of the bidding until it slows completely, then—"

"One thousand," Aggie asserts. "That was the limit."

"One thousand two fifty . . . one three . . . one three fifty . . ."

Jess bites down on her thumbnail, then shoots the card up. Aggie clamps it back down. They glare at each other.

"It's just a silly bit of costume jewelry, Jess."

"It's Nancy's. Don't you care?"

"Jess, she's barely with it these days. You'll get it for her, and she won't remember what it is."

"That's not true. Sometimes she is with it. She was just now."

The bids continue. One four. One four fifty. One five. One five fifty. Jess's heart thuds. Aggie bows her head despairingly.

"Not with my money," she presses.

"Fine," says Jess. "Then I'll do this alone."

She thrusts the card out, holding the auctioneer's gaze.

"One six, right here," he says, smiling. "Excellent choice. Any advance on one six?"

The room is silent. A whirl of emotions fills Jess's body. The necklace is about to become hers, back in Taylor hands forever, where it should be. But six hundred pounds more than she said she would spend! She sickens at the thought of the money.

"Last time," says the auctioneer, "or it goes for one six to the brunette lady at the front."

Jess screws her eyes shut, waits for the hammer to fall, fingers crossed, brow furrowed . . .

Another bid slips past.

"One six fifty," the auctioneer calls, surprise in his voice. "I now have one six fifty. Madam, can you advance on one six fifty?"

Lost in her torment, Jess doesn't hear, doesn't open her eyes, doesn't respond. What was it Nancy said? *Minnie's necklace binds us all.* It has to come back. It needs to come back, where it belongs.

"Once . . . twice . . . Okay," says the auctioneer. The hammer falls hard. "One six fifty to the gentleman at the back."

"Wha—?"

Jess's eyes ping open. The gentleman at the back?

The room relaxes into a chorus of chatter and coughing.

"Who?" says Jess in outrage. "*What* gentleman at the back?"

"The gentleman that's just been your savior," says Aggie, arms folded. "Honestly, Jess, that was ridiculous."

Jess blinks, shakes her head.

"Why didn't you tell me? Some jerk bid over me, and you just let him get away with it! You knew I hadn't noticed, didn't you? You could have nudged me, given me the chance to bid against him! Now it's gone! Our chance has gone! Our necklace . . ."

The shock and disappointment cascade over her.

"It should be ours," she says, disbelieving. "It was loved by our family forever. It's not for some stranger who doesn't care."

Aggie rearranges the collar of her shirt.

"Once again, Jess, you're over-romanticizing things. Clearly it hasn't been loved by our family forever, because . . . why would it be here, being sold in some musty auction room?"

Jess just stares into nothing, incredulous that the Taylor necklace has been snatched away, right under her nose.

"Who got it?" she pesters. "Did you see?"

"Behind you," says Aggie. "Mister Smug Face over there. He's getting up. . . . He's going to collect the necklace!"

Half covering her eyes, Jess turns to look. As she focuses on the distant figure working its way up the side aisle, she gasps.

"Oh no! It's him! It's . . . the curly, sparkly cane guy!"

"The who?"

"Oh, never mind. Just . . . what a scoundrel! He implied he plays fair, said he wanted to stop the hawk-eyes from nicking other people's bids. And now he's done the exact same thing to me!"

She stares in fury as the curly-haired, sparkly-eyed man strides up the steps and is handed a purple box, presumably with the necklace inside. Her heart feels as though it's tearing in two.

"He's stolen from us," she snarls. "Therefore he's going to hear my wrath."

"Jess! He bid on it fair and square. Besides, the price was out of your league and you know it. Let's call it a day, go drink a bottle of merlot or something. I'll break the news to Nancy if you can't."

Jess crumbles, buries her head in her hands.

"Oh, Nancy." She sniffs. "No. I'll tell her. This was our thing."

As Jess sulks, Aggie checks her phone for messages.

"Three voice mails," she moans, clamping the handset to her ear. "Scratch the wine," she says, teeth gritted as she listens. "It's Steph's school. She's been skipping class with the Vegan again. Why? *Why* does she do this to me?"

"Because she's sixteen," says Jess. "And you're her mother."

"I have to go," says Aggie. "The high school wants a meeting. Honestly, I never skipped class when I was her age. You did. But I was always on point. My daughter should take after me. Not her rogue aunt. Are you coming?"

Jess sighs. "You go. Get Steph sorted out. I might hang about for a bit, see if I can waste my money on some other silly piece of costume jewelry. I'll see you later."

"But how will you—?"

"Aggie, please. I'm not completely incapable. I can handle an hour on public transport."

"All right, all right. I'll see you at home."

"Good luck. And . . . don't be too hard on Steph."

Jess sits out the rest of the auction, barely aware of the lots that come and go. As the auction comes to a close and the hall starts to empty, the compulsion—perhaps her true motive for staying behind—comes to the fore. Curly-Sparkle is one of the last to leave.

As he makes for the door, Jess staggers after. By the time she catches up with him, he's in the street hailing a taxicab, the boxed necklace tucked under his arm. As a cab pulls up, she knows it's her only chance—now or never.

"Wait!" she cries.

He doesn't hear but climbs into the back of the cab and starts giving the driver instructions. Jess slams herself forward, ignoring the pain, then blocks the door with her stick. Now he looks up.

"Oh, hello again."

"We need to talk."

"We do?"

"Yes." She eyes the purple box. "About that."

"You mean my necklace?"

"My necklace," Jess corrects.

"Er?" Curly-Sparkle gives her a puzzled smile.

"That necklace," says Jess, brow furrowed into a deep V, "is my family's heirloom. I came here to get it back for my eighty-two-year-old grandmother. I had my handle on the auction the entire time, and then just as the hammer was about to drop on my final bid, *someone* decided to throw out a chippy little one-six-fifty offer."

Curly-Sparkle shrugs.

"Some you win, some you lose."

"Oh, come on. I deserved that bid, and you know it."

The cab driver coughs. "Do you want this ride, mate?"

"Yes," says Curly-Sparkle. "Just . . . give me a moment."

He turns back to Jess.

"Look, I'm sorry how things turned out, but ultimately my bid won. You took your eye off the ball. What can I say?"

Their gazes lock together. Jess tries her best to glare him into submission, but his confidence doesn't waver.

"Perhaps I could give you a lift somewhere?" he suggests. "And on the way maybe we can resolve the matter. Or you could just scold me some more, whatever helps. Either way, can we come to some kind of peace? I like to sleep easy at night and"—he grins—"you're strangely endearing."

Jess snorts her outrage.

"No, thank you," she asserts.

He smiles, unfazed. "Suit yourself."

He shuts the door. Jess hobbles on. As she walks, however, a small torment bores into her soul: the thought that Nancy's necklace is about to disappear once more. Tears stream down her cheeks. *It's just a necklace,* she tells herself. But then . . .

The cab slows beside her. The passenger window comes down. Curly-Sparkle leans out.

"Are you sure?" he says. "I'm heading for Portobello. I can drop you where you like . . ."

He holds out the purple box as though trying to tempt her with it. She takes a breath. He's trouble, of that she's certain, but the necklace . . . she *can't* let it go. She stops, turns to face him.

"Are you open to deals?"

"I might be."

The door opens. Jess climbs in.

"WELL, here we are. I'm Guy, by the way, and you are?"

"Jess."

"Nice to meet you, Jess. First, where are you headed?"

"The Central line is good. Queensway or Lancaster Gate."

"Hear that, driver? A drop-off at Queensway Tube. Thanks."

He turns back to Jess, brushes a hand through his curls. Immediately she notices a large and unusual gold leopard's-head ring on his middle finger.

Bold, she thinks, staring at the leopard ring; someone who's not afraid of standing out, who dares to take risks. Someone who lives to be happy. Her gaze drops to the purple box.

"So, what of this necklace?" he says, watching her. "You say it's a family heirloom. What else can you tell me?"

"If I tell you, will you sell it to me?"

He shakes his head.

"Will you at least let me look at it?"

"I don't want to tease you, give you hope then let you down."

"Which is a roundabout way of saying you've got no intention of selling it to me. I'm wasting my time?"

Guy sighs. "If I could sell it to you, I would. But I have my reasons for wanting it too. I have . . . a responsibility. Anyway, how can you be sure it's your family's exact necklace?"

"I'd know it anywhere. I used to play with it when I was little, in my mother's jewelry box. It disappeared after she died."

Guy lowers his eyes. "Sorry about that."

"It's okay," says Jess, racing through the sentiment. "All a long time ago. The thing is, recently my grandmother's started asking for it. I've been keeping an eye on auction sites, not thinking I'd ever find it. And then, well, it turned up. Almost as though . . . it was meant to. But then you came along and ruined it."

Outside, the traffic slows to a standstill. The warm evening descends into the streets, and long shadows of smartly dressed pedestrians pattern the pavements. Suddenly a trio of drag queens march out of a side street, followed by a pair of stilt walkers.

"Overspill from Pride," says the cab driver. "Half the streets in central London are gridlocked."

"Looks like we're going nowhere fast," says Guy, sinking into his seat. "You're stuck with me a little longer. If you can bear it."

Jess gives a noncommittal nod, hiding the fact that she feels curiously glad. She winds down the window, sits back.

"Is that Versace, circa 1976?" says Guy, leaning over to share her view of the drag queens and their assortment of costume jewelry. The colors are kaleidoscopic: plum, turquoise, citrine.

"I love those paste brooches," he says as the queens strut past. "It's like they're telling the world: You think we're super frivolous, but we're epic enough to rock vintage Versace."

Jess grins. "That's how I think about people, through their jewelry. No one *has* to wear jewelry. Earrings, brooches, bracelets—none of it's necessary, not in the way clothing and footwear are."

"The ultimate extra," says Guy, smiling.

Intrigued, she momentarily shuts her eyes. When she looks again, her attention returns to the gold leopard ring on Guy's left hand. He twists it, revealing the ring's emerald eyes.

"It's a favorite," he explains. "It's sacred to me."

"Your own family heirloom?"

"Kind of."

"And what does a golden leopard head say about Guy . . . ?"

"Van der Meer. The full hit is Guy Arlo van der Meer."

"That's quite a name."

"My ancestors were big in the Dutch diamond industry."

Jess nods, cautiously impressed.

"Okay, Guy Arlo van der Meer, what does your choice of finger adornment say about you?"

"I think *you* should answer that," says Guy. "We both know that the optimal way to appreciate jewelry is to see it on another person's body."

He lifts his ringed hand, offers it to her for closer inspection. She takes it, thrilled to touch his warm skin.

"Very playful," she says, "but I can see that it's fine. Good gold, carefully worked. An heirloom, you say?"

"That's right."

"Then I'm going to assume you're not entirely shallow. And that you're desperate to tell me your life story, something about your grandmother's great-aunt who smuggled the ring on a cruise liner, tucked in her corset, so it wouldn't get pinched by the riffraff."

He laughs. "How did you guess?"

"There's always a cruise liner and a corset involved," she replies, taking in his face with a flick of her eyelids. Those chestnut curls . . . What would he do, she wonders, if she swept those luscious loops from his face, brought her lips to his . . . and . . .

Oh, Jess! she berates herself sharply. *No!*

She folds her arms. Just because he looks like her type and acts like her type doesn't make him her type. If life—and Aggie—has taught her anything, the lesson is definitely: stay away from "her type." Besides, she has Tim. She has matured and found Tim, who is lovely and, best of all, a fully functional human being.

"Look," she says, dropping Guy's hand, "you outbid me and won. I accept your victory. I just need you to understand that this necklace means more to my grandmother than you could begin to imagine. I told her I was getting it for her. I made a promise."

"Never promise."

"Too late. The bottom line is, I'd do anything—"

"Anything?" says Guy, his left eyebrow scaling his forehead.

"I'll give you the money that you paid the auction house."

Guy shrugs. "I was thinking more along the lines of dinner?"

"No, thank you," she replies. "I'm spoken for."

"Spoken for?"

"I have a boyfriend."

Guy shrugs. "So is this boyfriend the love of your life?"

"Quite possibly," says Jess as she fixes her thoughts on Tim.

Tim, who is so utterly handsome with his solid, square jaw and sweet brown eyes. A proper grown-up with a steady soul.

"I'm here for the necklace, that's all," she asserts. "If you'll sell me the necklace, then we can go our separate ways."

"And if I don't?"

Silence bulges as the cab moves forward, crawling to the next set of traffic lights. On the pavement ahead, a crowd has gathered in front of a shop window.

"What are they looking at?" says Jess, hoping a more neutral conversation will defeat the tension.

"I'm not sure," says Guy. "Some kind of sale. Let's see—"

Before she can react, he opens the door of the cab.

"I'll be right back!" he calls, dashing toward the crowd.

Jess blinks. Curiosity has fueled her since childhood. The places she's never been, the things she's never done—they shimmer in her thoughts like unopened gifts. But she's never joined a random crowd just to see what the fuss is about. She looks at her watch, then realizes the purple box is now there on the seat unguarded.

Her heart thuds. The necklace. No barriers. She creeps her fingers toward the lid, then opens the box, peeps inside.

"Oh!" she gasps, drawing a hand to her mouth.

It is more beautiful in real life than she'd remembered. Immediately it speaks to her, its little, fat moonstone glinting in the sun. She lifts it out of the box, cradles it in her palm. She turns the pendant over, and there, carved on its base, is one simple word: *OUI*.

She looks up, feels a lightning strike of emotion in her soul.

With no sign of Guy, she knows she has her chance to take the necklace. She could tuck it in her pocket, walk away. But . . . she can't. She places the necklace back in its box, snaps it shut.

"Doughnuts!"

Guy is at the window, holding a tray of chocolaty doughnuts.

"They were selling doughnuts. That's what the crowd was for. I bought us some. You okay? You look a little . . . startled?"

"I'm good," she squeaks, smiling. "Look at those bad boys!"

"Have one."

He shoves the tray in front of her, grins like a schoolboy.

She accepts one of the smallest on the tray. They eat in silence, licking the sugar from their lips. The traffic opens up, and a few minutes later, the cab pulls in front of Queensway Tube station.

"Well," says Guy. "This has been a pleasure."

"Thank you for the doughnut," says Jess. "And . . . if you should change your mind about selling the necklace . . ."

"I'll stalk you on Instagram."

"Promise."

"Never promise. But for the record, yes, you'll be the first person I go to . . . if I change my mind, that is. By the way, the dinner invitation is still very much open."

"Right. Thanks. In that case, I'll be sure to stalk you too . . . if I change *my* mind, that is."

"Oh, you'll change your mind," he says, holding her gaze, an infuriatingly cocky fix in his sparkling dark eyes.

She half smiles, opens her door, takes longer than necessary to back away. Then finally they part, the necklace between them—craftily, quietly playing its part.

Chapter 2

THE AROMAS OF SUNDAY LUNCH—succulent meat, crispy potatoes, buttery carrots—fill the airy kitchen–dining room extension. Every weekend since its installation, the marble-topped island unit has hosted meals of various origins, from Malay to Cajun, all prepared with Aggie's signature precision.

"Open-plan living, lesson number one," says Aggie, fanning the oven, "the smells get everywhere. Fine when you're baking sourdough. Not fine when you're roasting half a cow."

She then turns to her husband, Ed, flaps her hands, and is bemused when he doesn't immediately understand that the gesture means "Open the bifolds." Eventually he shuffles to the doors and heaves them apart. A bolt of cool air blows in. Everyone seats themselves, and the dishes are shared and served.

"Wine?"

"Yes, please," says Jess.

"Me too," says Steph, eyeing the bottle of Picpoul.

"I think not," says Aggie, snatching her daughter's glass away. "And don't start with 'All my friends' parents let them,' because I know your friends' parents and they all feel the same way I do."

Steph scowls, while Marcus, her younger brother, smirks at her from behind his floppy bangs. The exchange isn't lost on Jess, who, having lived at her sister's for the past eleven months, has grown close to her niece and nephew. She gives Steph a bolstering wink, then casts her eyes to Tim, hopes he's ready for this hefty slice of domestic life. But, of course, he's easy with it, complimenting Aggie on her potatoes, smiling at the Hoppit children, and chatting bikes with Ed.

Once the plates are loaded and the glasses are poured, he gives a little cough, the educator in him that likes a captive audience.

"So," he says. "I got short-listed. I'm in contention for the deputy head post."

Ed cheers. "Great news, mate!"

"Excellent," says Aggie. "That school is lucky to have you."

"Well," says Tim modestly, "the post's not mine yet. The interview is next week and—"

"He'll get it," says Jess with a rush of pride.

Jess can see Aggie from the corner of her eye, looking pleased. Although Aggie has never admitted it, Jess knows it was she who set them up, asking Ed to pinpoint the most eligible man in his cycling club, then somehow have him "drop in" one Friday evening just as Jess and Aggie were mixing gin and tonics.

That evening, everything changed. The way Tim presented himself, so solid, so sorted out. They talked all evening. The next morning, he phoned to ask her to dinner. He took her to a steak house, and they swapped stories about families and books and the challenges of working with young people. She noticed he wore a good-quality watch and a single copper bracelet, which, when quizzed, was apparently to ward off arthritis.

"But you're still the good side of forty?" said Jess.

"It's preventive," he explained. "I'm shoring myself up for the future."

Honest from the start, he explained he'd been married before. It had shattered him, but now he was over it and excited for what was next. Jess was thrown by this candor. Thrown and charmed.

When the first date led to a second, then a third and fourth, Jess had to check herself: an attentive, grounded boyfriend with a steady job! What was happening to her? All her exes had been passionate, live-for-the-moment types. But really, who needed romance so intense it hurt? All that pain for nothing.

"What about you, Jess?" says Ed. "Had any more thoughts about what you'd like to do next? More teaching? I know you've got your jewelry business, but that's just a sideline, right?"

There's little point in saying the truth—that she's happy with her "sideline" jewelry business—because they won't believe it. The Ed/Aggie manual contains an exacting plan: earn money, spend money, earn more money, spend more money.

"I've told Jess she should go part-time at Baxter Academy," says Tim, emptying the last of the gravy on his plate. "In fact, the Creative Department is looking for another teacher right now. She'd be great." He looks at Jess. "*You'd* be great."

"Hmm," says Jess, quietly dissenting, "there's only so much teen action I can handle."

"But you're very good with them," says Aggie. "I mean, Steph tells *you* things she never tells me—"

"Because Aunty Jess is the only sane person in this family," growls Steph.

Silence ensues, and little brother Marcus spots an opportunity: "Callum Arnold says he saw Steph and Vegan Jared kissing behind the cricket pavilion, when they were supposed to be in study group. And did you hear Jared got arrested for smoking—"

"Oh, shut up!" Steph hisses. "No one gets arrested for smoking."

"No," says Aggie, "they just die of lung cancer."

Ed sighs, catches Tim's eye. "Fancy a pint later, Tim?"

"Would love to, mate, but Jess and I have got plans."

Jess blinks. "We have?"

This is news. In the nine months they've been dating, Tim has shown a consistent preference for spending Sunday evenings preparing for the school week. She catches his eye.

"So . . . what are we doing?"

"You'll find out," he says teasingly.

She smiles and wonders, digs into her beef. Twin sensations of excitement and apprehension grip her—the possibility of a ring in a box. Surely not. They're not *there* yet.

"So," says Ed, refilling everyone's wine. "I hear you ladies had fun and games at the auction on Friday."

"Stress, more like," says Aggie, cutting Jess a frown. "But all's well that ends well. We haven't, thankfully, blown one and a half grand on a necklace . . ."

Steph's eyes widen. Marcus gasps.

"One and a half grand? I could buy a top-of-the-line virtual reality kit for that," he rails.

"Yeah, but why would you?" says Steph, baiting.

"What would you spend it on? Rizla rolling papers for your *boyfriend?*"

"Oh, go away!"

"No, you go away!"

Aggie hammers the table with her fists. "Steph! Marcus! Just stop!" She turns to Jess. "How did Nancy take the news, by the way?" she asks.

Jess bows her head, stares into her plate.

"You haven't told her yet?"

"I just . . . didn't want to do it over the phone. I'll go and see her. I thought I'd take the train one day next week."

"I'm sure she'll appreciate it," says Aggie. "I'd join, but . . ."

"You're working."

"What's for dessert?" Marcus demands.

"Trifle!" exclaim Jess and Aggie, both knowing that at the end of every fragmented Sunday lunch, cold custard pulls the loose ends together.

"You two," says Tim, nodding between the sisters, "you're so different, and yet . . . you're peas in a pod."

Jess feels a fierce rush of love for the sister who, in one moment, can rile her with her patronizing remarks and, in the next, make her feel like there's no one in the world she'd fight harder for.

After lunch, Jess and Steph clear the table. As they rinse and stack Aggie's prize earthenware plates, Steph is thoughtful.

"Mum says that before you met Tim, you went for bad boys."

Jess throws her head back and laughs.

"Mavericks," she corrects. "I like to say 'mavericks.' And what your mum doesn't realize is that while, yes, some of them were a little flaky, they were also lots of fun to hang out with."

"Tell me more."

"I'm not sure your mum would approve of my kind of relationship advice."

"Well, it's got to be better than hers. She's never even *met* Jared, and all she can say is vegan this, vegan that, like, what's the big deal about being vegan? She heard one bad story about him—"

"Um, I think she's heard a few stories actually. The skipping class, the smoking, the snogs behind the cricket pavilion. Your mum, she . . . she just wants the best for you."

"Best for *her*," Steph says. "So who were these maverick exes?"

"Okay," says Jess. "First there was Brian the artist—although, really, he was just a high school senior with paint on his trousers. Then there was Andrew, who ran his own music night. He turned out to be a total control freak. Then there was a musician from Ireland. Unfortunately, he had some, um, bad habits. And then . . . I fell in love with a skydiver from South Africa—"

"He was a choice pick, wasn't he?" says Aggie, sweeping in. "Steph, don't believe anything Aunty Jess tells you. They were bad boys. But now—hallelujah—now there is Tim Dukas. Which means there is hope. *Jess.*" She spins to face her sister. "He's getting ready to leave. Go get your coat."

From the smile on her face, Jess senses Aggie knows something.

"What?" she quizzes. "What's going on?"

"Go!" says Aggie. "Go follow your Prince Charming."

"Any ideas?" Tim asks as he leads Jess across the lawn.

Brimming with excitement, he looks across at her and smiles. It's like a second life. When things first fell apart with his ex-wife, Cassidy, he was in a spiral. Everything he thought he'd have at that point in his life—a happy marriage, young kids, a home—had been suddenly whipped out of his grasp.

All he'd wanted to understand was what he'd done wrong.

Up until the day Cassidy had told him she was leaving, his life's mission had been to make her happy. Everything she'd asked for: a new car, a five-star all-inclusive fortnight in the Canaries, ballroom dance classes. But with the divorce now done and dusted, he realizes his mistake. He should never have given his soul to someone as needy and self-centered as Cassidy.

He sighs, shakes her off. Because now he has Jess.

The two women couldn't be more different. Jess is everything Cassidy wasn't. She is thoughtful, fun, imaginative, and independent. Will she love what he's done for her? He hopes so.

He can see in her eyes she is intrigued, wondering what they're doing in Stratford's Queen Elizabeth Park.

"Any idea?" he teases.

"Not a clue," she says.

He hooks one hand over her eyes and the other around her walking cane, gently guides her forward. "Don't look, don't look!"

"Where are you taking me?"

"Through here . . ."

He leads her toward the newest of the rows of apartment blocks, the expanse of sleek glass and wooden cladding towering over them. He leans against the entrance door, types in a key code, and ushers Jess into the atrium. Her eyes still covered, she waves her hands into the space. He presses a small object into her right palm.

"Open your eyes," he says.

Before she can fully comprehend what she's seeing, he turns her toward an orange door bearing a number 3. She looks at the door, then at the object in her palm. It's a key.

"Is this—"

"Our new front door," he says, the smile bursting out of his face.

STUNNED, Jess inserts the key in the lock and twists: a brand-new apartment, open-plan, real hardwood floors, fully furnished. Dazzled by the shapes and surfaces surrounding her, she steps forward. It's ready to live in, ready-designed—a corner sofa, designer dining chairs, and a balcony with city views.

"This is just the show flat," says Tim, "but you get the idea. We can choose a different kitchen, any colors we want on the walls."

"For real?"

He nods. "I've paid a deposit. Obviously the block's still being finished, but one of these units is ours. In the very near future."

"Ours?"

"My house is under offer. Your flat can be rented out. But this place . . . *This* can be ours. Come see."

He leads her across the room.

"Oh, Tim!"

She sways and blinks, the enormity of the idea overwhelming her. It's a happy enormity, of that she is certain, but an enormity nonetheless. Not a ring—but a huge step toward a ring.

"Look," says Tim, "you can see the park from the balcony, and there's Stratford station and . . . Well, what do you think?"

"I think it's amazing. You're . . . This . . . It's just . . . *amazing*."

He smiles, relieved, then opens his arms. With bewildered exaltation, Jess falls into them.

"I know it's a big deal," he whispers, "but you'll struggle going back to your old flat. And it's pretty claustrophobic at your sister's. This is the answer, right? Our own place."

The thought of the old flat gives Jess a twinge. Her first grown-up purchase, it had been her home up until last year. The third floor of a yellow-brick Victorian terrace with high ceilings and cast-iron fireplaces, original tiles in the hallway, so much history in those walls. But Tim is right—there's no way she'll be able to negotiate the three flights of narrow stairs. It will never be home again.

"You've . . . you've totally surprised me," she says.

"You have your sister to thank for that. I asked her advice, and she told me to keep you on your toes."

"Did she now?"

"She was just trying to help," says Tim. "Personally, I wasn't sure if you were ready. I mean, sometimes you're, you know . . ."

"What?"

"A bit . . . faraway. I can't always tell what's going on in your head. Your cues confuse me."

Jess frowns. "Sorry."

"Don't be. It's fine. I'm in. You're in. It's celebration time!"

Tim goes to the pristine kitchen and starts opening a bottle of champagne. Two flutes rest expectantly on the countertop.

"I arranged this with the woman at the property office. She suggested the champagne. Sweet, huh?"

"Very sweet," says Jess, accepting her glass, still absorbing the shock of it all.

They sip their champagne on the balcony and admire the view—the urban patchwork of Stratford, East London's hub of hipsters and young professionals.

"I'm sure you don't want to live in a flat forever," says Tim, taking Jess's hand in his, "but this is a start. There's shops, cafés, bars . . . everything we need."

"Can we afford it? What's the cost?"

"Don't worry about that. My salary will more than cover it."

"But we'll go halves, right?"

"If you really want . . ."

Yes, I want, thinks Jess, instinctively urged to keep things equal. She's never relied on a man before, has no intention to start now.

"No pressure," he says. "Take a few days to think it through, but this is me telling you that I'm buying this flat and I want you to live here with me. I love you, Jessica Taylor."

He pulls her toward him, kisses the top of her head. She shuts her eyes, safe in his circle, feels his arms enveloping her.

"You're a diamond," she whispers.

How lucky has she been? When they first met, she was just starting to emerge from the lowest place she'd ever been. She'd lost her job, her physical freedom, her confidence. She'd never imagined that, in less than a year, she'd be standing on the threshold of a healthy relationship, with a man who not only said the right things but *did* them too.

"Jess," he says with utter sincerity. "You make me so happy. I can see it all ahead of us. Kids . . . maybe two, three? A dog?"

"Sounds perfect," says Jess, pressing her head to Tim's chest.

Then her eyes spring wide.

"Tim," she says, gripped by impulse. "Before all of this comes together, you need to meet my grandmother."

"Your grandmother . . . Nancy? The one with the necklace?"

"Yes. Come with me this week. It would mean a lot to me."

"Consider it done."

Chapter 3

Wednesday, a bright, clear day, Jess and Tim take the train to Sydenham. Tim has cleared the afternoon for interview prep, but dutifully agrees to squeeze in the requested grandmother visit.

Nancy's care home is a 1960s monolith on a hill. She'd insisted on being in the shadow of the Crystal Palace, even though there is little of the palace left, save for the overgrown garden colonnades and a few tired stone sphinxes.

"Brace yourself," says Jess as they push through the double doors. "Her lucid moments are rare now, and she's prone to the odd sweary outburst, so don't expect instant approval."

Tim grins. "I need her *approval?*"

"Don't worry. It's not a deal-breaker. Anyhow, Aggie has most definitely given you the thumbs-up, so . . ."

"I'm going in the right direction."

"You totally are."

Holding hands, they walk down the corridor together. After signing in at reception, they proceed to Nancy's room. The sterility of the beige walls and rubber floor saddens Jess. It is hardly the realm of a woman who, in her sixties, moved to a plot of woodland in the wilds of Snowdonia, where she built her own log cabin. Now she requires round-the-clock care, but . . . she is Nancy still. As soon as she sees Jess, she sits up.

"Jessy!" she croaks.

"Hello, Grandma," says Jess tenderly, kissing her cheek. "Look, I've brought someone to meet you. This is Tim."

Nancy scans Tim's features with her small, sharp eyes.

"Hi," says Tim, offering his hand. When the effort is ignored, he grins, not sure where to put himself.

"Good news," says Jess in an attempt to bolster the introductions. "We're moving in together."

Nancy tips her head back. "Why do that?" she sneers.

"Grandma—"

"You used to be a true Taylor, Jessy. Doing your own thing, always going to new places. What's happened? Lost your spirit?"

Jess winces. "I'm *fine.* Sure, I've had to slow down a bit"—she waves her cane—"but I'm still me. I've just . . . matured."

Jess glances at Tim, gives him an eye roll of solidarity.

"It's not maturing," Nancy mutters. "It's shrinking. Did you see those foxes have been tearing up my lawn again?"

Always the foxes. Except Nancy hasn't seen her lawn in a year.

"Okay, Grandma," says Jess, resigned. "Let's get you comfy."

She fluffs Nancy's cushions, then turns back to Tim.

"At least she hasn't sworn at you," she whispers. "That's good. Have a seat. And . . . sorry."

Tim squeaks into a plastic-coated armchair while Jess arranges her gift of bananas and puzzle magazines, but she can see Nancy twitching, looking . . . looking for the necklace.

"Where is it, Jessy?"

Jess sighs, shakes her head.

"I'm sorry, Grandma. It went to someone else. I tried, but there was this guy—called Guy, as it goes—and he swooped in at the end of the bidding and cinched it. I did everything I could. I even chased him down Kensington High Street, hijacked his cab, sat and pleaded with him for an hour while we waited in traffic."

She sees Tim flinch.

"I told him how much the necklace meant to you, thinking he might have the heart to sell it to me, but unfortunately, he wouldn't play ball."

"Bastard!"

"He really was—"

Suddenly Nancy grips Jess's hand, digs in her nails, and speaks with utter authority. *"Find him,"* she insists. "Get the necklace."

And then she is silent.

Jess and Tim exchange glances. The wall clock ticks. Tim picks up a puzzle book, pretends to read it.

"You didn't tell me you got in a cab with that *Guy* person," he says, a crease in his brow.

"I—I didn't think it was relevant." Jess shrugs. "I mean, the man nicked my bid, wasted my time, then refused to sell. That's that."

Turning from Tim, she tries to distract Nancy with a sip of water, pressing the straw to her lips. Nancy just spits it away.

"What about a walk then, Grandma? It's beautiful out. We could go to your favorite place, like always."

"Not today," says Nancy.

The clock ticks on. Jess sighs. She knew the news of the necklace's loss would cause upset, but the intensity of Nancy's despondence is bruising. She straightens the bedsheets, remembering the day her grandmother left for Snowdonia. She and Aggie were still teenagers. One autumn afternoon, among packed boxes, Nancy waved goodbye to her urban street, gave each of her granddaughters a brisk hug, then took off in her tatty red car.

"But the girls need you here," Jess's father, Richard, had complained, having been reliant on Nancy since their mother's death.

"Don't be ridiculous," Nancy had countered. "They're all grown up. They need life, not some old sack like me getting in the way."

Just then, as though a switch has been flicked, Nancy opens her eyes, sits up, pushes off her blanket, and brightens.

"Oh yes," she exclaims. "Could you take me out? I would dearly like a turn around the Great Shalimar."

"The what?" says Tim.

"It's her name for the Crystal Palace," Jess explains. "Every time I visit, that's where she asks to go. We wheel around the concrete, check out the stone sphinxes, and then she asks for a cup of tea and we come back. It's sweet, if a little repetitive."

"You know the glass is really something," says Nancy.

"Was," says Jess, kindly but firmly. "The palace isn't there anymore, Grandma. It burned down in 1936. It's just a ruin now, but we can go and take a look, can't we?"

She smiles and squeezes Nancy's hand, relieved that if she can't deliver the necklace, she can at least do this for her grandma.

The sun shines, dispersing the few clouds that dare to intrude on the June afternoon. As Jess pushes Nancy's wheelchair, they approach the first of the stone sphinxes, which flank a tattered staircase and a vista of nettle-filled scrubland.

"Built for the Great Exhibition of 1851," says Nancy, mechanically recounting as she always does. "First in Hyde Park, then moved here. I never saw this happening, of course."

"No." Jess laughs gently. "You weren't born."

"Nor was my mother, Anna. And nor was Minnie."

"Oh yes, tell me about Minnie."

"Minnie Philomene Taylor, born in 1881. She was your great-great-grandmother. She made a necklace."

Jess winces. "Yes, *the* necklace."

"My mother once called it the True Love Necklace. She gave it to me when I was seventeen. Oh, I'd so like it back."

"I know," says Jess regretfully.

Moving on, Jess turns Nancy's chair toward where the palace entrance would have been. Nancy's eyes widen, as though she is seeing the crystalline marvel as it was—the cast-iron structure towering above, the sheen of the glass, the fountains, the elegant Italianate gardens, people everywhere.

"It was the world's first theme park," Tim reads from his phone, "known as 'the Palace of the People.' Apparently it housed sports matches, festivals, and concerts. Even had a roller coaster."

"How does *he* know?" says Nancy scathingly.

"Wikipedia," whispers Jess. "He likes looking up facts."

Nancy snorts. "Our Minnie," she says, "didn't need the Wikipedia. The Great Shalimar was her playground."

"It was?"

"In her teens she would go for walks, often to here," Nancy replied. "Minnie loved to sit at the foot of the stone sphinx near the entrance, where she could admire the ladies. She liked to look at their finery—their bustles and shawls and brooches."

Jess smiles. "This place must have made an impression on her."

"Yes, but what really opened her eyes was Paris."

"Paris?" Jess blinks. "When did she go to *Paris?*"

"Enough now," says Nancy, suddenly prickly. "I've had enough. I want to go back."

"Sure," says Jess, flustered. "We can do that. Of course."

Back at the care home, a quietness engulfs them. Tim sets to work on one of the puzzle books, periodically checking his watch. Nancy remains agitated. She rocks in her chair, rubbing her arms.

"Grandma, what's the matter?" says Jess.

Nancy scrunches her eyes shut.

"I want to show you something," she says.

She nods to the top of the bureau, to a folder that looks like it hasn't been touched since the '70s. Jess fetches it. With trembling hands, Nancy fumbles in the file, then pulls out a pair of photographs. She then straightens the first one and hands it over: a Victorian family portrait. Within the crumpled sepia Jess sees a woman in a dark dress standing beside a mustached man. On their laps are a young boy in a sailor suit and a baby in a lace gown.

"These are my ancestors?" says Jess, wide-eyed.

"Yes. This is Minnie with her parents."

"She's the baby?"

"Yes."

"And the boy . . . her brother?"

"Died young," says Nancy. "Burst appendix."

"Oh."

Jess holds the photo close, awed by her connection with these long-dead figures. A handwritten date on the back says "1882."

"How do you know all this?" she asks Nancy.

"My mother told me stories."

"You mean Anna?"

Jess processes the name. Anna Taylor. Suddenly it sinks in, that as well as being Nancy's mother and her great-grandmother, Anna Taylor was also Minnie's daughter.

"Yes," says Nancy, smiling. "Anna told me stories, about her life, about Minnie's life. Stories kept her going. We lived in such squalor when we left Hollywood, but Anna's sparkling stories elevated her. And I enjoyed hearing about Minnie's life."

"Tell me," says Jess, leaning forward.

"Her parents—your great-great-*great*-grandparents—were upright people from Sydenham," Nancy explains. "He did accounts, earned enough to afford a house on Hammond Road with two servants. She was an accomplished viola player, very musical."

"Was Minnie musical too?"

"I believe not. She was given lessons in everything from pianoforte to watercolor painting but showed a lack of application. She was easily distracted. Rambunctious, one might say."

Jess smiles. "Now *that* I can relate to."

"Her instinct for jewelry began in childhood. She took an interest in the trades on the high street, wanted to understand how craftsmen worked. She once went 'missing' for hours, until her uncle found her, filthy, down at the local blacksmiths', watching them firing up their furnaces. Her parents were horrified. Their antidote was to find a suitor. In 1899, Minnie was persuaded to marry Robert Belsing, a junior accounts clerk at her father's firm."

"You say 'persuaded'?"

"Well, it wasn't for love—not on Minnie's part—but in her parents' view, it was a good match. That's how marriages were in those days, Jessy. After the wedding, Robert Belsing applied for an overseas office. In 1900, he and Minnie relocated to Paris."

"Aha, Paris."

"Yes. They arrived just in time for the Exposition Universelle."

"Nineteen hundred! France's world fair! I know it," says Jess delightedly. "It's where art nouveau came to prominence. Did Minnie go?"

"I believe Robert agreed to take her after some coaxing. It was there that she found her purpose: All she wanted was to make jewelry. You see, out of all of the wonders at the Exposition, what enchanted Minnie most was the Palace of Decorative Arts and, in particular, the jewelry boutique of René Lalique."

"Yes!" Jess beams. Lalique, famous for his art nouveau jewelry, was one of the most influential designers of the period.

"So Lalique's jewelry inspired Minnie to make our necklace?"

"No. Lalique's designs gave her the language, but her inspiration—the true *heart* of her intent—was her discovery of true love."

"How sweet. With her husband, Robert?"

Nancy stiffens. "Absolutely not."

"Oh."

"After the Exposition, Minnie began keeping a sketchbook of ideas," Nancy explains. "In secret. She begged Robert to let her inquire about training at Lalique's workshop in Paris, but he wouldn't allow it, couldn't accept such a modern ambition for his wife. Back then, jewelry was very much 'man's work.'"

"So how did she manage to make the butterfly necklace?"

"According to Anna, when Robert discovered the sketchbook, stuffed down the side of Minnie's daybed, he flew into a rage. He locked her in their apartment, feeding her little more than bread and water. When she tried to escape, the fool used his fist."

Jess shudders, looks to Tim, and feels very grateful.

"Quickly Minnie realized that if she was to survive she would have to play along. As Robert's ire faded and he allowed her some basic freedoms again, she squeezed herself into his vision: the modest, decorative, obedient wife. But then . . ."

Nancy sighs, shuts her eyes, clearly starting to tire.

"What?" begs Jess, anxious, knowing Nancy's focus will only hold for so long before confusion consumes it. "What then?"

"She ran away," whispers Nancy. "With the little money she'd managed to sneak from Robert's desk, the dress she was wearing, and a hunk of dry bread, she ran from him. She knew that there was no going back, that if Robert ever found her, he'd destroy her, that her parents would disown her. But still, Minnie ran."

"Where did she go?"

"Be patient," Nancy snaps. "I'll show you."

With a shaky hand she holds the second photograph toward Jess. It's a portrait of Minnie as a young woman.

"Oh!" Jess exclaims. "She's wearing the necklace! There it is!"

The butterfly shines like an emblem above Minnie's chest, wings ready to fly. Minnie, meanwhile, sits upon a garden wall, the natural light suggesting a summer afternoon.

"That photograph was taken at Pel Tawr," says Nancy.

"Pel Tawr?"

The name resonates, the pine-forested estate in Snowdonia where Nancy's log cabin stands. Jess sits back, scours her memory. She recalls the big, old Arts and Crafts house on the top of the hill above the cabin, the sign at the gateposts: Pel Tawr.

"Grandma," she presses, "is that the same Pel Tawr where your cabin is? Why did Minnie go there?"

"To *be,*" Nancy whispers. "You see, just before she ran away from Robert, she found an article in an English newspaper about an artistic community in the Welsh mountains. The owners, the Floyd family, had thrown open the doors of their Arts and Crafts house to *all* who shared their values of design and community—young, old, male, female. When she read about this, Minnie realized she had to find her strength and *go*—"

"To live her best life," Jess concurs. "So did Minnie make the necklace there at Pel Tawr?"

"Yes," says Nancy. "With Emery."

"Emery?"

"Emery Floyd."

Nancy then takes Jess's hand, pulls it tight to her chest.

"We called it the True Love Necklace," she strains, barely audible. "Because everyone who wore it found their soul mate. First Minnie. Then Anna. Then me. Then your mother."

"So who'll be next?" says Jess, half joking, before realizing the significance of the answer. "Oh, Grandma," she says, scorched with emotion, "I'm so sorry I didn't get your necklace."

She goes to stroke Nancy's face, but Nancy pulls away. Sleepy from exhaustion, she closes her papery lids over her gray eyes.

"Well," Jess says quietly, to herself more than anyone, "I may not have the necklace, but I certainly have my soul mate."

She glances at Tim. He looks up and smiles, eyes full of warmth.

"You okay?" he says.

"Yes," she says.

Jess kisses Nancy goodbye, then goes to him: her savior, who makes her feel loved, who'll never hurt her or make her feel like his property. As Tim rises from his chair, it's the least she can do to kiss his cheek and tell him how lucky she feels.

In their local restaurant that evening, Jess feels closer to Tim than ever and is distracted by the pleasure of his broad shoulders and neat jaw as they eat sticky ribs and sweet potato fries. She smiles to herself and sips her gin and tonic.

"You know," says Tim, between mouthfuls of charred corn, "she wasn't as scary as I thought, your grandmother."

"Ah, she's mellowed with age, but she used to be a spitfire. It's strange to see her dependent on nurses and carers. Sometimes I wonder if she'd have been happier if we'd left her to it."

Jess shuts her eyes, recalls Nancy's cabin in Wales—the smoky smell of the wood burner, the rough-cut beams, the dust on the floor. Then her mind wanders to the house on the hill, to Pel Tawr, to Minnie Taylor and her necklace, the "*OUI*" engraved on the back. Why is it there? What does it mean? She knows it translates as "yes," but yes to what? To life? To love?

"I should go there," she says, jolted, "to check on the place."

"Wha—?"

"To the cabin. I should go to Nancy's cabin."

Tim nods, having not quite followed Jess's train of thought. "Right. Sure."

"This week?" she suggests. "You could come with me?"

Tim twitches. "Um . . . work. It might be tricky. I can't just—"

"Of course. I'll go by myself. I'll get a train down and—"

"Really?" Tim stares at her. "On your own?"

Jess tenses. True, she hasn't done anything of significant independence since her accident. A trip to Wales by herself would be a big step, but she feels a lift in her heart as she thinks of it—that Taylor spirit perhaps? The "*OUI*" effect?

Tim shakes his head, his brow furrowed with concern.

"I'm not sure, Jess. How will you cope? I'd be worried. With your back and hip, you're . . . more vulnerable than most."

"Vulnerable?"

"I don't mean . . . What I'm trying to say is that you might need help at some point. If I'm there, I can carry your bags, help you on the stairs. Hell, if it comes to it, Jess, I can carry you."

Jess knows he's referring to the epic piggyback, when her hip seized from too much sitting on low grass at a picnic, and he had to carry her all the way from Victoria Park to Hackney station.

"I love helping you, Jess," he says brightly. "I mean, my mum always told me I was the nurturing type."

Jess stiffens. "That's like you're saying you're with me just because you can *nurture* me."

"No, Jess, I'm with you because I love you, because you make me happy . . . because . . . because having both had our ups and downs with relationships, we want the same things. We're ready to settle and grow together. Our lives can grow."

She softens. "I know what you mean. You know, I actually love that you're a nurturer. I've had my share of bad boys."

"I *know*. When I asked your sister if she thought it would be a good idea to invite you to move in with me, I got the talk of doom, about how you're prone to rash decisions, and that you've picked some wrong 'uns. She actually recounted a list of your exes."

"The joker, the philanderer, the man-child, the escape artist?"

"Those. The escape artist wasn't so fun, was he?"

Jess looks down. "No, he wasn't."

"Your type?"

"Not anymore," she says with an emphatic smile.

"We're a good team."

"We so are."

THERE'S a sale coming, thinks Guy. He can feel it. As Stella gazes at the sea-green butterfly wings, her expression says it all.

"It's luscious," she says, stroking the opalescent moonstone. "Oh, Guy, it's just what I've been looking for. How old is it?"

"It's art nouveau, early 1900s, so you're looking at well over a century. Are you interested?"

"Assuming there'll be a nice friend's discount?"

"For my best client, of course. I bought it for one six, but I reckon it'll be worth way more in a few years. Art nouveau jewelry is due a resurgence."

"Then I'll have to lead the way. Will you put it on me?"

She turns, lifts her hair, revealing the tanned nape of her

neck—holiday leftover from a week in Saint-Tropez. He places the necklace around her shoulders, then turns her toward the mirror.

"Love it," she says.

Guy nods. As long as Stella's happy, the world is at peace. But then he pauses, puzzled. The necklace is such a vivacious piece, yet somehow on Stella it looks dead. He daren't say this, of course; he needs Stella to love it. Every time she's photographed wearing one of his finds, Guy van der Meer Jewelry gets a boost.

He blinks, flashbacks of childhood briefly zipping to the surface: all those years of disappointment, no one present in his life long enough to notice his quick mind and artistic eye. So many empty days, wasted and broke. In the circles he'd grown up in, it hadn't been cool or "manly" to be creative. No one gave a damn about jewelry, unless they were nicking it out of other people's drawers. And school hadn't added much to the proceedings. That troublemaker label had followed him everywhere—four expulsions and an addiction to smart remarks had meant his teachers had known of his reputation before they'd even met him, dismissing him as "destined to fail."

Here in Stella Weston's high-ceilinged Chelsea hallway, fears for what his life might have been start to loom. But then Guy catches his bright reflection in the mirror, a sentinel next to Stella—the fashion media superstar who trusts his opinion and knows nothing of his frowzy past—and is reminded that he has built this incredible life for himself, relying on little more than his natural affability and eye for design. Okay, so he's told a few fibs along the way, but the high-end jewelry trade is a closed group. A good name is everything. With a sigh, he focuses on the gains.

A prize antique necklace for Stella. It's a dream deal.

Yet as he gazes at those tiny plique-à-jour cells, the discomfort of the pairing grates. The fact is it doesn't look right on Stella. The shape of the butterfly clashes with her pointed face; the color dulls her skin. There is something else too, an awkwardness, a *resistance,* almost as though the necklace doesn't want to be there.

A thought strikes his soul. The woman who accosted him in his taxi—Jess—she'd laid claim to this butterfly with such fire. All that stuff about it being her family's heirloom . . . At first he'd shrugged it off, but what if the necklace knows better?

He thinks of Jess, with her cupid lips and bright eyes, the rightful bearer of the butterfly. Looking back, he realizes he had a sense about her the moment she fell into him in the auction room, nearly taking him out with her walking cane. He smiles, eyes sparkling.

"What are you so merry about?" Stella probes.

"Nothing," he says, pushing the smile back inside.

Jealousy doesn't rub well between him and Stella. He knows the deal. Stella shares the spoils of her lifestyle, introduces him to useful people. In return, he decorates her with the best of his treasure and gives her his undivided attention.

MEANWHILE, on the other side of London, having said goodnight to Tim, Jess sips a cup of tea in the Hoppit kitchen and thinks about Aggie. Aggie was always a perfectionist at school, on time, hard-working, worrying about exam grades. These days her happiness seems to be intrinsically bound to other people's admiration of her things: her big house, her glossy hair, her clever children.

But really, who is Jess to judge? A pang of guilt rises at memories of how Aggie took care of her, how she negotiated with doctors, chased the insurance company, paid a bunch of medical bills and never asked for the money back. But before that, even, how she picked up the pieces whenever Jess had a new broken heart. And before *that*, when they were children, growing up motherless, with a disinterested father and a difficult grandmother, how Aggie had been the surrogate parent, taking care, making things right, ever patient whenever Jess was in trouble at school.

A twinge in her hip forces Jess to stand, and with searing sharpness, a memory comes back: that moment at the airport, waving goodbye to the Hoppits. *Just a quick trip,* she'd said. A knot of regret fills her. *Why* did she do it? What motivated her to quit her teaching job and buy a one-way ticket to Mexico City?

Why didn't she see it then? The infamous Taylor "spirit" reconfigured as a load of old nonsense. How about a simple, straightforward life like everyone else, with a good man and a sound job and a nice home and maybe . . . maybe a child? *Why* didn't she see it then, that a normal life could be just as rewarding as a wild one?

Those nights in hospital. The sensation of Aggie's hand on her forehead, gently stroking the hair from her eyes.

"Maybe it's time to stay in the quiet lane, Jessy," she'd whispered.

And in that soft light, unable to move, unable to speak, machines beeping all around her, Jess had made a silent pledge. From now on, she would make better choices. She would stay in one country, live one life, get one job and stick to it. She would avoid all men owning more than one mobile phone. And make a conscious effort to replace the words *spontaneous, thrill-seeking,* and *adventurous* with *erratic, unreliable,* and *fraud.* She would rebuild her life, and in time, she would make her sister proud.

Mission refreshed, Jess empties the dregs of her tea and goes to turn out the light. Just then, however, she hears her phone buzz. Out of habit, she checks it, then blinks. It's a friend request from Guy Arlo van der Meer. She checks out his account and sees what she thought she'd see: a photographic carnival of glamorous parties, gallery openings, and film premieres. In his profile he describes himself as a treasure hunter. She laughs heartily.

"What kind of overblown job title is that? What a nob!"

She laughs some more. Then, annoyed that he wouldn't sell her the necklace, she denies the request and shuts off her phone.

Chapter 4

Jess spends Friday afternoon preparing shipments for customers. A quirky 1950s rhinestone brooch in the shape of retro sunglasses is going to Kent; a 1980s statement necklace with coral cabochons is traveling to Japan. Carefully she wraps the necklace in tissue paper, ties the package with a ribbon, and adds one of her gold stickers: MISS TAYLOR'S RETRO AND VINTAGE COSTUME JEWELRY.

Jess's one-stop online shop—specializing in vintage jewelry from the '40s to the '80s—is starting to grow. She hand-selects every piece, sourcing them from auctions, estate sales, and flea markets. It's not as stable as teaching, but it feels more joyous.

As she clears away the day's work, her phone buzzes. Tim's number flashes on the screen. She grabs it, eager to hear the news.

"So?"

"So . . . I got it!"

"You did? Woo-hoo! Does this mean I'm officially moving in with a deputy head teacher? We should celebrate."

"Got it covered. My workmates have organized drinks. The Star Tavern. Eight o'clock. And . . . maybe we should announce we're moving in together as well. Make the night extra special."

"That's a lovely idea. Although shouldn't we go somewhere more exciting than the Star? Change it up a bit?"

"Nah. It's got to be the Star. Friday night tradition. We'll have fun, promise. Right, I better get back to work. Love you."

"Love you too. And . . . well done."

Jess smiles, then climbs the stairs to her bedroom—formerly the Hoppits' guest suite—and starts plundering her wardrobe. She selects a black sundress, pairing it with a turquoise scarab-beetle bib necklace: a classic example of twentieth-century Egyptian revival, inspired by the discovery of Tutankhamen's tomb in 1922.

She jumps in the shower, brushes her teeth, then starts drying her hair. Through the noise of the dryer she doesn't hear the door when Aggie comes home, doesn't hear her calling, doesn't notice her in the doorway. Finally, she shuts off the dryer and grins.

"Hey, Aggie, how was your day? Help me get my hair right, will you? We're celebrating. Tim got the job."

"Jess—"

"I'm now officially the girlfriend of a deputy head teacher! Can you believe it?"

"*Jess.* It's Nancy." Aggie pauses to breathe and frown. "The care home called on my way home from work. I'm sorry, Jess. They think she's really deteriorated."

Jess shudders. "But I only saw her a few days ago . . ."

"Her stats are all over the place. Her heart rate keeps slowing. They said days, weeks maybe, if we're lucky."

Jess sinks to the floor, swamped with sorrow. Aggie goes over and pulls her into an embrace.

"It's the natural way of things," Aggie whispers. "She's had a long life, Jess. Eighty-two. That's really something."

Jess can barely hear her sister's platitudes. All she can think of is the sadness on Nancy's face when she told her she'd failed to reclaim the necklace. Through her tears she thinks of Nancy's words: *We called it the True Love Necklace.*

"I—I have to go," she says. "There's something I have to do."

She checks her watch. There is time—just about.

"Do what you have to," says Aggie, kissing Jess on the cheek. "And it's great news about Tim's job. Nancy would be thrilled to know you've finally sorted yourself out and bagged a good one."

"Uh . . . yeah," says Jess, sniffing, wiping her tears, a little less convinced of this than Aggie.

When Aggie has gone, Jess picks up her phone and scrolls through her feed to find Guy van der Meer's friend request. She clicks Accept, then starts typing:

> *Please. I need the necklace. Buy/borrow. It's urgent. Can we meet in an hour? Will explain then. From one "treasure hunter" to another, thanks. Jess (of the doughnuts)*

If he will meet her, in central London somewhere, and if it's a quick transaction, she can get the necklace and still be back in time to toast with Tim. She drums her fingers on the dressing table.

Her phone buzzes. She grabs it and reads his reply.

> *Jess (of the doughnuts). How you intrigue me. Meet me in the jewelry galleries of the Victoria and Albert Museum. In front of the best stuff. One hour. Guy*

She smiles. The best stuff? What would that be? And how is it that he's chosen her favorite place in London—the jewelry galleries.

Why does he have to . . . *get it right?* She ruffles her hair, adds a dab of color to her lips, then dons the black dress and scarab necklace. Finally, she checks herself in the mirror and is surprised to see something like exhilaration gazing back at her.

"Only for the necklace," she tells herself. "For Nancy. Get the necklace and go. That's all."

THE Victoria and Albert Museum in South Kensington houses five thousand years of human creativity. Jess knows her way through the grand entrance, down the marble stairs, along the corridor, to the two-tiered cavern of the jewelry gallery, where exhibits range from Celtic breastplates to plastic punk chokers.

He is not here.

The gallery is quiet, save for a few fashion students sketching medieval torques. The best stuff? She scans her eyes across the gallery. Instinctively she is drawn to the twentieth-century cabinet, where she seeks out her long-time favorites: an art nouveau hair ornament in the shape of an orchid and a Lalique pendant in the form of a female head with tentacles curling out of the hair.

Suddenly she hears a voice behind her.

"You chose well."

Guy is reflected in the glass, eyes glinting, framed by those telltale curls. As he steps toward her, a flutter fills her stomach.

"So the art nouveau is your best stuff too?" she asks.

"Close but not quite."

He takes a seat beside her and points to the glowing case of Queen Victoria's sapphire and diamond coronet.

"That," he says emphatically, "is the best stuff. You don't wear a headpiece like that and get ignored. You rule an empire."

They face each other. Jess feels her pulse quickening.

"Thanks for coming," she says. *Stick to business.*

"You had me at treasure hunting. So what's the deal?"

"Do you have it?"

"Have what?"

"The necklace," she says, exasperated. "I *need* the necklace. This wasn't just a ruse to get you to hang out with me again."

"No?" he says. "You've made an effort with the Cleopatra affair though. Definitely a notice-me piece."

Jess reaches her hand to the shield of turquoise beetles.

"Scarabs were a symbol for good luck in ancient Egypt." She shrugs. "Soldiers wore them into battle."

"Ah, so you've come to do battle?"

"I've *come* for the necklace," Jess urges. "My grandmother . . . Her health is bad. We had a call from her care home, and it's not great news. I just want her to see the necklace before she . . ."

She shuts her eyes, but tears trickle down her cheeks anyway. Then her composure crumples entirely and the tears turn into sobs.

"Oh," says Guy, mouth open, sparkle shadowing.

Tentatively he wraps an arm around her, pulls her toward him.

"I get it," he whispers softly. "You want the necklace for her. For family. Family is everything, right?"

But Jess barely hears his words. She sobs into his shoulder. Thoughts of Nancy tangle themselves up with thoughts of her long-deceased mother, Carmen, and all of it is overwhelming.

After a minute, she sits up and apologizes for her outburst.

"It's fine," says Guy. "Happens all the time."

"Does it?"

"Well, no, but—"

He smiles, and she can't help but smile back.

"So . . . you're a treasure hunter too?" he finally asks.

Jess sniggers.

"Why is that funny?"

"Because I saw it on your profile. It's the most ridiculous and overblown job title I've ever heard."

"I wouldn't take it too seriously, Jess. But in a roundabout way, I'd say treasure hunting describes what I do. I deal in antique jewelry. My clients come to me looking for something special."

Jess's insides somersault. He deals in antique jewelry. Of course he does! Why does it feel like the universe is making him more and more attractive to her, when all she needs is the necklace?

"So who are these clients?" she quizzes.

"London's wealthy, money to burn. Last month I had to find a gothic ring for an international rock star. Yesterday I reunited a war veteran with his beloved art deco fob watch. That's what I really like doing, helping people find items they've lost."

"So you like a quest?"

"I do. You'd be amazed the lengths people will go to in order to be reunited with something they treasure."

"Not at all amazed," she says pointedly.

His phone buzzes, a pester in the quiet space. He shuts it off.

"I'd love to tell you more about it," he says, "and hear more about *your* treasure hunting. How about that dinner, later?"

Jess lowers her eyelids, thinks of Tim, their big night.

"Not today," she says.

"Well, that's an improvement on outright no. A cup of tea then? The café's just down the corridor."

One cup of tea. She checks her watch, nerves churning.

"Okay," she says, dropping her shoulders. "A quick cup of tea, just so we can sort out the necklace, then I *have* to go."

In the café, Guy nudges Jess to a table next to the grand piano, then goes to order. Jess takes a seat and prays Aggie isn't watching over her with some undisclosed crystal ball. Guy's presence feels like a deceit. In his company—she can't help it—she just seems to *glow*. She swallows her guilt.

Guy returns with a tray of tea and mounds of cake, including pecan pie, lemon drizzle, and scones with clotted cream.

"Wow, you have a sweet tooth!" she exclaims.

"One of many weaknesses," he confesses, "but life's too short for alfalfa."

He hands Jess a spoon, then dives into the fruity, creamy, cakey jumble. Jess eyes him, the way he eats with gusto.

"So tell me more about your jewelry business," says Guy, leaning forward as though keen to know every detail.

"It's called Miss Taylor's Vintage and Retro Jewelry. My mission," she says, "is to smash the throwaway culture that has us reaching for two-for-one mass-produced supermarket charm bracelets sooner than we'd buy something preloved."

"Quality, design, fine craftsmanship, and the magic of past adventures captured within," adds Guy.

Jess's eyes widen. How he *gets* her! She hands him her business card. "I'd like to grow it," she says, "reach more people."

"Of course," he says. "You know, if you need any contacts—"

"Thanks, but to be honest, I'm thinking of going back to teaching this September. Design and technology for rogue fifteen-year-olds. There's a post available. Apparently their last teacher quit suddenly after an incident with a jigsaw blade—"

"Yikes! Are you sure about this?"

"It's a grown-up job," she says. "And I'm trying to be grown-up. Besides, the soon-to-be deputy head is my, um, boyfriend."

"The boyfriend who speaks for you. How's that working out?"

"Great, actually."

"What jewelry does he wear?"

"A smart watch and a copper band for warding off arthritis."

"That's not jewelry. That's artless timekeeping and quack medicine."

Jess bristles, her gaze catching on Guy's leopard ring.

"We can't all be diamond magnates," she says. "So tell me about your jewelry business and your family, the van der Meers? Are you close? Did they inspire you?"

"Something like that," he says evasively.

The way he brushes his hand through his curls, jiggles his knee, she senses he'd prefer to avoid the topic. She moves on.

"So, with all this cake in your life, do you ever go to the gym?"

"No! *Bor*ing! I like dancing—that's exercise, right? And I once tried horse riding, but that was a big mistake. You?"

"I used to do all sorts," say Jess ruefully.

Guy casts his gaze to her walking cane.

"So what happened?" he says.

She shuts her eyes at the question she dreads. At least he's blunt about it. Shc takes a breath, readies herself to dive into the past.

"A year ago . . . I fell out of an airplane."

"What?"

"It wasn't intentional. I did a skydive in Mexico. My parachute failed to open."

His eyes widen. *"Whoa!"*

"I hit a tree branch, then a bush, then a field full of alpacas. The flora damaged me, but at the same time it broke my fall and saved my life. If I'd hit the ground directly, I'd have been jam."

Guy blinks, open-mouthed. "Do you . . . do you remember it?"

Jess lowers her eyelids and smiles. "You mean you want to know what it's like," she says, leaning close, "at six thousand feet in the air, to have your mortality rush to meet you?"

"I do," he says, leaning closer.

"The din of white sky, the loom of the green fields, and the eerie serenity that engulfs you when you realize . . . death is real and it's coming. And all you can think is: Have I done it right? Have I lived my life the way I was meant to?"

Guy leans closer still. She can smell his aftershave.

"If it's not impertinent of me to ask," he says, holding her gaze, "have you? *Have* you lived the way you were meant to?"

Jess dips her gaze, tunes into the ache in her back.

"I thought I had," she says. "I used to be very carefree, but . . . my outlook is changing. I'm *growing*. Like, I can see myself as a mother, sort of. Or, at least, as someone who gets married and goes on one holiday a year rather than ten. You know, normal stuff."

"Rrrright. Good luck with that."

"Do I detect sarcasm?"

Guy shrugs. "Leopards," he says, flashing his ring. "Some say the spots never change."

Jess shakes her head. "Nah. I've had my fingers burned and learned the lesson. From now on, I want a calm, simple life."

"So what were your injuries?"

"I fractured my spine and smashed my pelvis. I was airlifted to Mexico City in a helicopter, but by then I'd lost consciousness. I woke up in hospital a week later. Four operations and seven titanium plates to piece me back together. After that, I spent two months in a rehab center, where I healed and found a new way to walk. And then I flew home to the U.K."—she takes a breath—"and now I'm trying to find a new way to live."

"But you *do* live. And you *can* walk."

"And it's getting better every day," says Jess, brightening.

"What were you doing in Mexico?"

"Looking for silver."

"There we go, treasure hunting!"

"It was to help start my jewelry business," she explains. "Before I went to Mexico, I was a struggling trainee teacher. I mean, I liked the idea of it, but my head of faculty kept telling me I had to follow a specific curriculum and use certain kinds of vocabulary. I was fed up and wanted a change, and someone told me the silver in Taxco was good, and then I saw a cheap flight and . . . went for it."

"So where did it go wrong?"

"I made the mistake of falling in love. Matteus from South Africa. For six months we lived the backpacker dream. We hiked through rain forests, lazed in hammocks, explored secret Mayan temples. Lots of quesadillas and *lots* of tequila."

"Was Matteus into silver too?"

"Nope." Jess sucks her breath. "He was an extreme sports instructor. He took jobs around Central America, teaching zip-lining, rappelling, canyoning, and"—she pauses—"skydiving."

"Oh—"

"That day . . . he packed my parachute."

Guy blinks, half horrified, half captivated.

"*Your boyfriend packed your parachute, and it failed to open?* Jeez! Was he *trying* to bump you off? Was he after your silver?"

Jess forces a laugh. "He'd packed a thousand parachutes before. The authorities investigated, said the issue was technical. No foul play, just a snagged string. One of those things."

"But *still,* he's got to be blamed for something?"

Jess hangs her head. "It's complicated. I don't blame him for my accident, but . . . after . . ."

She shuts her eyes, exhales, feels the sting anew.

"At first he really cared for me. He was there every day at the hospital. My sister flew out, and he helped her too, made sure she had a decent hotel, assisted with the Spanish. And while I was trapped in that hospital bed, utterly immobile, he told me everything I needed to hear. We made plans, mapped out the rest of our lives. It was the thing that got me through, the thought of getting back to London with Matteus and making a life together.

"And then, just as I was coming around from my fourth surgery, he sent a text saying he was very sorry, but he just 'couldn't do it anymore.' Said he was going fly-fishing in Guatemala or something. Although judging by his Instagram account, it was pretty clear he'd met someone else. I don't know. We've lost touch."

"Oh, Jess! You need to improve your taste in men!"

"Noted. And I have. I mean, Tim is lovely. He's nothing like Matteus. Total opposite."

"Glad to hear it."

Jess sits back, relieved to have shared the story. She has rarely felt comfortable talking about it, yet now that it's out there, a wall has come down. She takes a mouthful of pastry and cream.

"So where are you now with your recovery?" asks Guy.

"My extreme sports days are numbered, but I'm good. I've been well looked after, staying with my sister and her family. And now I'm ready to get my independence back. In fact—"

She pauses, suddenly self-conscious about revealing that she and Tim are moving in together. A nearby phone alarm beeps, reminding her of time passing, time she hasn't got.

"Anyway, about my necklace," she urges.

Guy stretches, scratches his belly, releases a slow exhale.

"I assume," she asserts, "that it has no real meaning to you, not in the way it does for me, so if we can make a deal right now—"

Guy winces.

"It would mean so much to me," she persists. "And obviously it would mean the world to my grandmother."

"I get that, Jess, but—"

"*Please*. At least, if you won't sell it to me, maybe I could borrow it for a day? That's all I ask. Lend it to me for just one day."

Guy shakes his head. "I'm sorry. If I could, I would, but it's no longer mine to lend. It's in the hands of my client now."

"Your *client?*" Jess cringes. "Who . . . who is this client?"

"Stella Weston."

"The supermodel?"

"Ex-supermodel turned influencer. She has a thing about butterflies. She's planning to wear the necklace to the Capital Gala. She's been negotiating with dress designers all week. That necklace is hopefully going to get her hashtag trending for days."

Jess glowers, pained at the idea of her necklace now reduced to a mere fashion accessory for an Instagram post.

"But would it hurt to swap it for something else?" she pleads. "I could find her an equally lovely butterfly necklace, for free."

"Ah, Jess, there's no way she'll pass it up now. She's consulting with her media team as we speak. In fact, that was her phoning. I expect she wants me to take her to her favorite sushi place and feed her seaweed."

"How romantic. Well, enjoy that, won't you?"

"Jess, I'm not her boyfriend."

"But you run around after her, do whatever she tells you?"

"We're good friends."

Jess huffs.

His phone buzzes again, and his head drops. Suddenly he looks exhausted, as though being "good friends" with Stella Weston is more an effort than a joy. He checks the screen, shuts his eyes.

"She wants me now."

"Oh, does she? Well, off you trot, then—"

Jess gets up to leave.

"Wait," he says.

He grasps her hand. His touch makes her shiver.

"The gala is coming up. Once she's worn the necklace, it'll go in the closet, and she won't look at it again. If your grandma can hang on, once Stella's had her moment, I'll get it for you."

"*If* she hangs on . . ."

"I'll do what I can," says Guy. "Don't worry. I'm a pro at these sorts of shenanigans."

"I bet you are," says Jess as she walks away.

As she shoves herself through the revolving doors, a kernel of panic rises. No necklace for Nancy, and now she's running late for Tim—his big night, *their* big night. She checks her watch and hobbles headlong through the rain to the Tube station.

THROUGH THE COZY LIGHT OF the bar Jess sees him. He is in the Baxter Academy huddle, the trestle table at the window—the same one as always. She can see in his face that he's a little forlorn. And she knows, arriving an hour later than promised, that she has done this to him. She steels herself, smiles, and waves.

"Jess—"

"I'm *so* sorry," she says, diving to kiss him, breathless with guilt. "I—I just got . . . *caught up*."

Tim makes room for her on the bench.

"Hey, everyone," she says, extending a wave around the group.

They all smile, say hi, take a moment to ogle the scarab necklace, then return to their conversations.

"I messaged you twice," says Tim, mildly accusatory.

"I know. I'm so sorry. I was on the Tube."

"The Tube? Why were you on the Tube?"

Jess hesitates. "I—I wanted to look at some sparkles," she says, instinct ordering her to go easy with the truth, "so I went to Kensington, to the Victoria and Albert Museum, just to browse."

She holds her breath, straightens her scarabs, knees twitching. Tim stares at her as though trying to read the thoughts in her head.

"You and your sparkles," he says eventually. "You're here now. That's the main thing."

He kisses her softly, and everything shifts back into position. Relieved, Jess steals a sip of his pint and snuggles into him.

"Have you told them? About us moving in together?"

"I was waiting for you."

"Ah, yes." Jess looks at her lap. "Sorry again."

"Oh, come on," says Tim, jostling her. "Shall we?"

He clears his throat, tings his door key on his beer glass.

"People. We have an announcement."

They stop immediately, look toward him.

Tim grins. "We wanted to tell you all . . . we're moving in together."

"Oh wow!"

"About time!" Everyone jumps in with hugs and handshakes.

Colette, one of the math teachers, kisses Jess on the cheek.

"Congratulations. I was hoping things would move on

between you two. I've known Tim for years. You make him happy."

"Thanks," says Jess. "He makes me happy too."

"Good," Colette says, nodding profusely, grin fixed, giving Jess the distinct feeling she's being second-guessed.

Do they know? About Jess meeting Guy again and allowing herself, for just an hour, to enjoy his company? *Get a grip,* she tells herself. She tenses, makes her excuses, and escapes to the toilet.

The cubicles are quiet, and Jess is grateful for the peace. She runs a tap to rinse her hands, despairing at her ability to throw the pieces up in the air just when everything was falling into place.

"Oh, Jessy," she sighs. "What are you *doing?*" Disloyalty is not her style. And Guy van der Meer is not her type.

Anymore.

Because any man can look good on the spot, say the right things, make a girl feel special. But kudos to Tim, who'll soon be helping her box up her things, carrying her forward into a future that works. Happiness secured: new home, good jobs, nice life.

But—is this really what she wants?

One word plays over in her head: "*OUI.*" She thinks of Nancy with her cabin in the woods. Of Minnie, fleeing her marriage. And Anna, the Hollywood dreamer. In their own ways they were all risk-takers, but were there happy endings for each of them?

She makes a silent pledge to find out all she can about the lives and loves of the women who made her, hoping that somehow their stories, their journeys, will lead her to clarity.

Chapter 5

The North Welsh countryside is green upon green: low pastures, a backdrop of heather-clad mountains, and the jagged outline of pine trees. As the taxi pulls up to the entrance of the

Pel Tawr estate, Jess leans out and smiles. She has one night booked in a nearby guesthouse. Aggie couldn't—wouldn't—join her. Tim couldn't get the time off work at the last minute. But maybe time alone is what she needs right now; time to think. She pays the taxi driver, and with a wince she clambers out of the cab.

Jess makes her way down the hill, through the trees. There ahead, in a shaft of sunlight, is Nancy's cabin. Jess stops to pay her respects to the sheer feat of its existence. The logs in its walls came from the woods. And although Nancy had help with the heavy work, the details had all been down to her and her handsaw.

Since Nancy took ill, it has been standing empty. Jess can see evidence of its neglect. The overhanging roof is rotting; the porch is threatening collapse. Possibly it isn't structurally sound. Possibly it never was, not that Nancy would have cared.

The door shudders open. There was never a lock, typical Nancy. Inside, the air is dank, but the interior still has its hobbit-hole charm. Jess wanders inside, wiping the dust off surfaces. Wood pigeons have built a nest on the shelf above the bed. The bed itself is strewn with a hand-knit patchwork throw, just as Nancy left it.

With a sigh, Jess straightens the blanket and plumps the pillow. She then goes to the drawing desk, still cluttered with ink pots and sketches of leaves and acorns—the remnants of Nancy's final artistic musing before she was carted off to institutional perdition. She'd been an illustrator, specialized in natural forms.

Jess sifts through the desk, opens the drawers. They are filled with piles of used cartridge paper, a menagerie of flower and beetle sketches. Beneath all of this, a large yellowed envelope. She tugs it free and dips a hand in: thick glossy paper, like photographs. She empties them onto the desk, and her mouth drops open.

The photos are all images of a teenage Nancy posing against a brick wall. The distinctive butterfly necklace dangles against a circle dress with a full skirt, hallmarks of '50s fashion. In some of the images Nancy is beside a street sign: Denmark Street. A known London landmark, it was the center of the music industry in the '50s and '60s, housing numerous recording studios.

Jess turns one of the photographs over and sees a small gold sticker in the corner: PAUL ANGEL PHOTOGRAPHY, 1954.

She searches her memory. Paul Angel? It doesn't catch.

"Oh, Nancy," she whispers, "look at you!"

Apart from the born-in-Hollywood brag, she knew that Nancy had traveled, that she'd spent a year in Berlin being "punk," that she'd trained as a furniture restorer, then an illustrator. But there was never any mention of her modeling. Jess laughs, delighted that even in her twilight Nancy still has the capacity to surprise.

Satisfied the cabin is at peace, Jess tucks the photos into her bag, then goes outside and looks up to the big house on the hill. Pel Tawr. Fueled by curiosity, she follows the remnants of a path.

Eventually she reaches the house. It is huge, at least seven bedrooms, and unmistakably Arts and Crafts with its notional medieval beams, Gothic turrets, multiple chimneys, and carved stone.

Suddenly a mound of golden fur comes bowling into her.

"Oh! Who are you? Where did you come from?"

The fur mound—a lively but genial golden retriever—is then overshadowed by its owner, a tall, elderly man in a wax jacket.

"Are you lost?" he says with relieving kindness.

"Um, not exactly," she says. "I was just—"

As the man steps into her sight line, he stares at her. "Well!" he says. "If I didn't know better, I'd say you were a Taylor."

Jess blinks, nods. "You . . . you know me?"

"I know that look. Those round cheeks, those huge green eyes. So you *are* a Taylor?"

"I am. My name is Jess. I'm—"

"Nancy's granddaughter."

"Yes!"

"She told me all about you. How's she doing, old girl? We've missed her terribly, Rufus and I." He ruffles the collar of the dog, which Jess assumes to be Rufus. "We used to trek down to her cabin every week, have a cup of tea with her, make sure she was okay. It was me that found her in that terrible state—"

"Oh, of course."

"I spoke to someone . . . not you?"

"That would have been my sister, Aggie. She's everyone's emergency contact. Thank you for making that call. If you hadn't checked, who knows how long she'd have been that way."

"Well, I never liked to interfere. Nancy liked her space. She made that clear when she approached us to buy the land."

"She approached you?"

"Yes. We hadn't considered selling any of our land before, but when she inquired, well, we realized it would be an ideal way to raise funds for the upkeep of the house and grounds."

Jess nods, intrigued. She'd always been puzzled by Nancy's random relocation to Snowdonia, but now she sees that it wasn't random at all. Maybe it was because of Minnie.

"How is she now?"

"Not so well, I'm afraid. She's being well looked after, but . . ." A prickle of emotion catches in Jess's throat.

The man nods sadly. Rufus whines and brushes his legs.

"Introductions," he says. "I'm Bevan. Bevan Floyd."

Floyd? Jess recalls Nancy's description of how Minnie had "made the necklace there with Emery *Floyd*." Before she can say anything, Bevan starts ushering her across the lawn.

"Grand old girl," he says, gesticulating to the house. "She's been in the family for generations. My wife and I took her over in the late '80s. But originally, she was built as a country retreat, overrun by deep thinkers and artists. We had furniture makers, weavers, potters. It was the Arts and Crafts movement—"

Jess laughs, delighted.

"This interests you?"

"So much."

"Then perhaps you'd care for a tour?"

Jess grins. "I would *love* a tour."

The smell of oiled oak hangs in the air. *It is the smell of age,* thinks Jess as she steps inside the vestibule, picturing all the artists and thinkers who have passed through this space. The interior is immaculately kept. Even the wallpapers are original, their colored botanical designs swirling across the walls.

"Are they William Morris?" asks Jess, awed.

"They are. A little faded in parts, but we won't be replacing them. They're the character of the house."

The vestibule opens into a large double-height space, surrounded by nooks and fireplaces, doors leading into other rooms, corridors into rooms, corridors into corridors.

"So," Jess ventures, "I'm dying to ask, but are you any relation to Emery Floyd?"

"Why yes, he was my great-uncle. He had the run of the place in the early 1900s. How do you know of him?"

"Nancy mentioned him. Briefly."

Bevan smiles warmly. "So she told you about Minnie?"

"She told me a little, but not enough. I guess it's why I'm here. I know snippets, but not the full story. I gather Minnie and Emery were close. Nancy referred to Emery as Minnie's soul mate."

"Yes, I believe they were happy together."

"In that case, do you know anything about a butterfly necklace that might have been made here?"

Bevan muses. "With a drop moonstone? Glassy wings?"

"Yes."

"Come with me."

Jess's heart quickens. She follows Bevan through a maze of corridors into a sun-filled white room that looks out across the lawn. He plucks a framed photo from a cabinet and hands it to her.

"This is the necklace you described, I think."

Jess gazes at the image. There is Minnie, in wide-legged trousers, the butterfly at her neck, standing next to a tanned and ruggedly handsome mustached man, his shirtsleeves pushed up so that his sinewy forearms are on show, ready for work.

"Oh yes!" she says with a surge of excitement. "This is Minnie! And this is the necklace! This is it!"

"How remarkable," says Bevan. "How did you know about it?"

"Nancy asked me to find it for her. She told me Minnie had made it here. It was then passed down through the generations, and at some point it went missing. She called it the True Love Necklace."

Jess stares at its image, hanging from its creator's neck. She absorbs its details, her hotline to the past. The allure of Emery Floyd is not hard to see—his brawny physique and smiling eyes suggest an appetite for life. The True Love Necklace chose well!

"So they were a couple, right?"

"Yes, although they never married. I gather Minnie had a difficult ex-husband who refused to grant a divorce."

Robert Belsing, thinks Jess. Whatever became of *him?*

"She never used his name," Bevan explains. "She was always known to our family as Taylor. I should also show you these . . ."

He opens a drawer, and in it there is a selection of metal tools: files, pliers, a small hammer, and a chisel.

"You'll see they've been engraved with an 'M. T.,' which we took to stand for Minnie Taylor."

Jess gasps. They are aged but perfect; the very tools her great-great-grandmother used to scrape and craft. Her personal set.

"May I touch them?"

"Of course."

She lifts out the chisel, trying to imagine the way Minnie would have worked it in tiny movements, refining, beautifying.

"Do you have much of her stuff here?"

"Just these, I'm afraid. We found them in the workshops when we were clearing out. There is, of course, the sketchbook."

Jess's eyes light up. "Minnie's?"

Bevan shrugs. "It's just a few drawings, some memoirs. Been left on the bookshelf for years, gathering dust. Useful to you?"

"Hugely."

"Then I'll fetch it."

He shuffles to the corner, to a library nook with rows of books and thick, green curtains. After a minute's search, he pulls a battered leather-bound tome from the top and presents it to Jess.

"Here, you might as well have it," he says, smiling.

"Oh, thank you," says Jess, hugging the sketchbook to her chest.

"So did Minnie stay here a long time?" she asks curiously.

"Well, yes. Pel Tawr was considered her home. She and Emery

had a daughter, the famously audacious Anna, but of course you probably know all about Anna."

"I know the name," says Jess. "Nancy was always sparing with the Taylor family history. She never liked to dwell on the past."

"Yes, of course," says Bevan. "We talked about lots of things, her and me, but there were certainly a few topics that were off-limits. She'd never let me ask about her daughter, Carmen."

"My late mum."

"Yes. I gather she died young?"

"She did. She had a stroke."

"You poor dear."

Jess shrugs. "It's okay," she says breezily. "All a long time ago." She hugs the sketchbook tighter.

"Tell me more about Anna, will you? From the little I know, she lived quite a life."

"Well, yes, she was known for her vivacity. She moved to Hollywood in the '30s. Like many young women of the time, she was seduced by the glamour of the silver screen."

"So the story about Nancy being born in Hollywood is true!"

"Indeed. Like her mother, Minnie, Anna had a passion for jewelry. She became a film-set jewelry designer, worked in various studio costume departments, worked on some big movies."

Jess gasps. She'd largely assumed the Hollywood claim to be something of a fantasy, but the truth is more extraordinary.

"How old was she when she left?" she asks.

"Nineteen, maybe twenty. It was just after her mother—after Minnie—died. Typhoid. It swept through the area. I suppose this loss left Anna with a certain sense that she should now go forth and follow her dreams. A month later, she took passage on Cunard-White Star's newest liner, the *Queen Mary*. Four days from Southampton to New York, then a train right across the states. Quite a journey for a young solitary woman."

He thinks for a moment. "Jossop's," he adds. "That's the name of the jewelry company she went to work for. Nancy once mentioned it. Jossop's of Hollywood. And there was a producer, a man Anna got engaged to, a Christopher . . . Christopher Roderick."

"Wow!" says Jess, overwhelmed. "There's so much to figure out, so much to discover. All thanks to the butterfly necklace."

"Well, isn't that the wonder of heirlooms? They keep us connected to the people who've gone, yet to whom we owe so much."

"Yes," says Jess. "They really do."

She sighs, then looks to the window. On the terrace outside she spies a stone sculpture of a peacock.

"That's Percy. He roamed the estate for decades. Emery made the sculpture of him just before . . ." He pauses, shrugs. "Well, why not come outside and see it up close."

He throws open the patio doors, leads Jess out. The smell of fresh-cut grass hangs in the air.

"Here he is," says Bevan, patting the stone peacock.

Jess places a hand on the peacock's back. She realizes there is something achingly sad about the way Percy looks out across the valley. Like he's forever waiting. She turns to Bevan.

"They *were* happy together, weren't they?"

"Oh yes," he says, "they had some very halcyon years together, a decade in fact, before . . ."

He stalls, casts his eyes down. Jess senses what's coming.

"The war?" she guesses.

"Yes," says Bevan. "Emery joined the Welsh Fusiliers, sailed out in May 1917, taking his sketchbooks with him. He was killed five weeks later. Drowned, of all things."

"Oh no," says Jess.

"And that, I'm afraid, was where Minnie and Emery's love story ended, like so many of that era, all too briefly."

A wedge of sorrow catches in her throat.

"But they were *soul mates,*" she protests. "That's what Nancy told me. The necklace brought them together."

"Ah," says Bevan, "there is a philosophy that the way of soul mates is to come into our lives to challenge us, move us forward. It's not the job of a soul mate to accompany us through our entire life or share every detail of our being. Once its purpose has been fulfilled, the soul mate is free to disappear."

Jess nods, wide-eyed.

"Like Emery," she whispers. "He restored Minnie's joy after a bad marriage. He made her happy, gave her a child, and then . . . he fluttered away."

"Like a butterfly."

Jess stares at the sky, then turns to Bevan. "Thank you so much for your time," she says, tucking Minnie's sketchbook into her bag. "And for sharing your home with me. It's wonderful."

Bevan smiles. "Consider it your home too."

"Yes," says Jess. "Yes, I suppose it is in a way. Thank you."

Jess hobbles down the lane, toward the village of Beddgelert. She finds her guesthouse on the main street, a traditional stone cottage with log fires and the promise of sausages and fresh eggs for breakfast. She checks in and manages the final push upstairs to her bedroom, where she flops onto the ruched satin bedspread.

As the sun sinks behind the trees, Jess places her haul of Taylor memorabilia beside her on the bed and turns her attention to Minnie's sketchbook. At the back there are a dozen pages of writing, presented like a memoir. Marveling at the sight of her ancestor's elegant, looped script, Jess softens into her pillow and reads:

> I arrived full of anxiety, having made my way alone, by train, then boat, then another train. I was greeted on the lawn by the youngest of the Floyd children, who seemed merely amused by my sudden appearance. I believe they were rather used to sudden arrivals and departures, such was the bohemian way of their home.
>
> I was then brought to the kitchen and given some soup and asked about my background. I said little, other than that I wanted to join the artists. They were kind to me. A bed was made, and I slept nonstop for thirty-two hours. When I awoke, the sky was blue, the birds were singing, and a lightness came over me.
>
> In the parlor, I met Emery Floyd, the young gentleman of the house. As he talked, I could not help but be inspired by his mind. He confided he had once wished to study Eastern philosophy and medieval literature, but that wordy ideas were not

his forte. He said he believed his true gift was in his eyes and hands, their ability to communicate with each other, and this I wholly understood.

In the weeks that followed, I noticed him watching me as I wandered alone on the grounds. The house was not without its social routines, but I walked alone and spoke little. It's almost as though the shock of my transition had wiped out my character.

I think Emery could sense this. He gave me the space I needed, but didn't quite let me slip away. He brought me things—an unusual flower or piece of embroidery, hopeful that it might ignite an opinion or comment. He introduced me to Percy, the resident peacock, who ruled the place. Emery's calm attentiveness softened my nerves, and as the spring rains eased, my confidence returned.

I took an interest in the flower gardens, where Madame Floyd grew dahlias, euphorbias, and lilies. I started sketching again, first the flowers themselves, then the birds and insects that inhabited them. The butterflies in particular drew my attention.

"The *Callophrys rubi,*" said Emery one day, observing my sketch of a vivid green-blue butterfly. "This part of Wales is known for them, where they mate and breed."

He told me that far away in Japan butterflies had great symbolic value. They were thought to be the souls of humans, representing joy, longevity, womanhood, even marital happiness.

As he spoke, one of the same green-blue butterflies landed on my thigh and a deep reasoning burrowed into my mind that this force of beauty should be the subject of my first jewelry creation.

As though reading my thought, Emery took my hand and led me to his workshop, where he furnished me with tools and taught me the basics of silversmithing and stone setting. He never once saw outrage in my desire to make jewelry. He just saw magic.

We grew closer every day. When my butterfly pendant was finally finished, he handed me an engraving tool.

"You must mark your work."

"Mark it?"

"With your name, your insignia, so that the world knows that you, Minnie Taylor, created it."

For a moment I considered whether to attempt my signature or just my initials, but then it came to me—a word in my head, somehow more meaningful, more potent than any other. *Oui!*

Yes to art. Yes to freedom. Yes to love.

Overcome, I struggled to fit the clasp, so he fixed it for me and placed it gently around my neck. As his fingertips caressed my skin, I knew he wanted so much to kiss me. And I wanted him to, but my tender heart trembled at the thought and I cowered.

That evening we took a boat out on the lake. As we rested in the middle, I could not resist leaning over to admire myself in my necklace. Gazing at my reflection, I tipped too far forward and hit the water with a splash. Emery screamed to me.

"Minnie!"

I couldn't stay above the surface. I felt the life leave my lungs, and I knew I was drowning. Then I saw him diving forward, seizing my arms, and pulling me to the air. He heaved me back onto the boat, where I gasped and stared, awestruck, into his eyes.

No longer holding back, he leaned down and kissed me, and it was a kiss of such intensity that all my demons were vanquished in that instant—a kiss of true love. I reached for my necklace, felt it there against my heart, and suddenly it seemed like the loves and lives of the whole world were bound within its form.

Minnie Philomene Taylor. Pel Tawr, 1918.

Jess reads it again, herself in awe: the incarnation of the True Love Necklace explained by Minnie herself. Jess finds a sense of closeness to Minnie; the fact that they both had a brush with mortality intrigues her. A hundred years apart, and the life lesson is the same: Never take happiness for granted.

And Minnie's happiness clearly lay with Emery. It was *their* necklace. Jess thinks of all the design masterpieces she's seen in galleries around the world. To what extent does a creator's intent become imbued in the creation itself? Can the quest for a soul mate really be *bound within its form?* Such a lovely idea.

"If only it were true," she whispers, shutting the book.

Chapter 6

In Aggie's kitchen, over a plate of gluten-free macaroons and kombucha tea, Jess shares the spoils of her trip to Wales.

"Is that really Nancy?" asks Steph as she paws over the Denmark Street photos. "And is that the necklace?"

"It is."

"It's lush. *Why* didn't you buy it?"

"You know why," says Aggie. "It was too much money. Plus we were pipped to the post by a most *unfortunate* human."

"Who do you think Paul Angel Photography is?" asks Steph.

"I'd love to know," says Jess. "I'd ask Nancy, but—"

"Oh, Jess, I meant to say, while you were away, the hospital called. Thcy said Nancy's picked up a bit. The old bird's clinging on. For what, I don't know."

For the necklace, thinks Jess.

"Perhaps I should speak to our dad?" she says, thinking out loud. "Maybe he'll be able to fill in a few details. I should call him."

"Ugh, really?" says Aggie. "The last time I spoke to our darling father, all he wanted to talk about was Eileen and her cruises. He didn't ask a single question about me. Or you, for that matter."

Jess nods. On this, she and Aggie agree. Their relationship with their father, Richard Barrow, has rarely borne fruit. There was no dramatic falling-out, just a slow disintegration of the bond. It didn't help that, a decade ago, he met Eileen, remarried, moved to Kettering, and had two more children, twins, Rosie and Ben. He'd come to Jess's bedside after her accident, but as soon as he'd realized she was going to survive, he'd sloped back to his Other Family shadow world, despite promises to visit every week.

Jess sighs. "Maybe you're right."

Between sips of tea, she talks on. Aggie is only vaguely impressed to learn that there's truth in Nancy's Hollywood claim, but Steph is chuffed at the prospect of being related to a movie mogul.

"I never heard the name," says Aggie dismissively. "Christopher Roderick? Doesn't ring any bells. Probably made B movies."

Jess is about to suggest they look him up when Steph, two steps ahead, waves her phone and presents his Wikipedia entry.

"'Christopher Roderick, 1904 to 1972,'" she reads. "'Hollywood movie producer, best known for the box office flop *Descent of the Sun*. Roderick went on to direct a series of low-budget horror films in the late 1930s, but postwar, his career went into decline.'"

"Does it say anything about his personal life?" asks Jess.

"Just that he died of lung disease and that he lived with his partner . . . Bernard."

"Bernard?"

"Bernard Almer. That's what it says."

"Okay," says Jess, her mind ticking.

"Oh, and there's this," Steph continues, "'Roderick's mansion on Hollywood Boulevard has recently been acquired by the Golden Age Restoration Trust and is now open to the public.'"

Jess's eyes pop wide.

"How cool is that! We have to go! We have to see it!"

"Can we?" Steph grins. "Mum? Can we go?"

"Oh, *please*," says Aggie. "No one is going anywhere. For all we know, it's a bunch of nonsense that our great-grandmother was engaged to a movie producer. I never heard the name Christopher Roderick before. And if he and Anna *were* together, one can only wonder what kind of relationship it actually was."

"Maybe he identified as bi?" says Steph.

Aggie rolls her eyes. "I'm not sure they used that term back then. Anyway, why are we even discussing this? Think about the here and now. What about your new flat, Jess? Your kitchen plans? You'll need a decent coffee machine. And a KitchenAid."

Jess is saved by the clatter of the letter box.

Aggie fetches the pile of letters, hands one to Jess. Casually Jess accepts, expecting another hospital bill, then sees a handwritten address and unfamiliar lettering. With a rush, she lifts the seal, peeks inside, and spies the stiff, gilded edge of an invite.

"What is it, Aunty?"

"Oh, nothing."

Aggie eyes her suspiciously.

"I better go," says Jess, "get on with some jewelry post."

She hastens to her room, the envelope pressed against her chest. An invite. Guy van der Meer has sent her an invite to the Capital Gala. Her heart starts to race. What is his game? Is this about the necklace . . . or about her? She checks the date of the event: Saturday, August 6. Nearly two weeks away.

Thank you for the invite. Am I expected? Jess (of D-nuts)

Well, obviously. That's the point of an invitation :) Guy

I'll think about it.

How is she anyway, your Big G? Hanging in there?

She's okay, thanks. For now.

Wanna hunt?

Hunt?

Hunt for treasure. Then have coffee. And cake. Come to Portobello. I'll take you to my favorite jewelry shops.

Presumptuous.

Just get on the Tube, will you? It'll be fun.

Jess chews her lip, stares at the clock. Tim won't finish work until six; then he'll have cycling and then he'll probably want to grab a pint at the Star. He won't even have to know.

Okay, she replies.

Message sent, she cups her mouth with her hand. That's it. She has crossed a line. She has agreed to a non-necklace-related meetup with Guy, almost qualifying as a date. She knows she should be ashamed of herself, but while she's scared of the lie that this is starting to become, deep down she realizes she is more scared of the thought that, perhaps, with Tim, she is *living* a lie.

Portobello Road—with its bohemian street market a mix of food, antiques, curios, fashions, and trinkets—thrives in the sunshine. Three centuries ago, it was a country lane leading to a farm, which then became a network of elegant crescents and terraces, which were crowned in 1864 by the arrival of Ladbroke Grove railway station. Which is where Jess meets Guy.

He gives her a peck on the cheek; then, paying no regard to her cane, he strides off through the stalls. At first indignant, she struggles to keep pace. She then realizes her leg can move faster than she'd thought. She has grown so used to the people in her sphere slowing down. But now she wonders if she can in fact do more.

"So you like art nouveau?" says Guy as she catches up.

"I do."

"Me too. I like that it's ornamental, yet deeply earthy. Hard to define, but if it was a Shakespeare play, it would definitely be—"

"A Midsummer Night's Dream?" says Jess. "Magic, love, and a hint of the macabre?"

"Exactly."

They walk on, past the rows of colorful Georgian terraces and the shops selling vintage shoes, old vinyl, military memorabilia.

"I love living in Portobello," says Guy. "There's always something random to look at."

"Can't be cheap. Do you rent?"

He smiles, a little shamefacedly.

"Not really . . . I, um, occupy Stella Weston's mews house."

"Rrrright."

"I know how it sounds, but she needed a tenant, someone she

could rely on, and I needed a roof. Stella has several properties around the world. She flits between them."

"Just friends?"

"Just friends. If you must know, Stella's main romantic interest is a Greek dot-com billionaire whom she sees twice a year. They sunbathe on his yacht in Mykonos, and she thinks it's love."

"Sounds a bit sad," says Jess.

"It is. I mean, beauty and fortune have given Stella everything, yet she's one of the neediest people I know."

"You care about her, don't you?" Jess ventures.

"I do. She's been good to me. Stella and I are close, but we're not romantic close. She's lonely. She wants a little loyalty in her life, so I do my best to be there for her."

"In exchange for status and a crash pad in Ladbroke Grove?"

"You say it like you think I'm using her, but Stella knows the score. She's all for helping me network and build my profile. It's a mutual thing." He huffs, folds his arms. "We all have to play the game at some point. That's just how it goes. So there."

"Okay, okay," says Jess, surprised by this sudden turn of defensiveness. "If you say so."

"I do," he says curtly.

They come to a churros stall. The smell of hot, sweet batter and melting chocolate is intoxicating, and it breaks the mood.

"Rude not to," says Guy jovially, before ordering a large portion with extra cinnamon sugar.

"So what of the other Taylor women?" he asks as they walk on through the sunny air. "Explain what I'm getting into here."

"Getting into?"

"Well, clearly I enjoy your company—"

"Steady," she whispers, a flush brightening the apples of her cheeks. "Save the schmooze for someone who'll buy it."

Guy shrugs, unperturbed.

"Since you ask," she says, pausing to admire a china figurine, "I've embarked on a mission to find out what I can about where the necklace came from. At first I just wanted to understand why Nancy was so desperate for it, but now it's given me a heap of questions about my family. I'd like to know more, because . . . sometimes I feel like a stranger to myself. Does that make sense?"

Guy nods wistfully. "Yeah, it kind of does."

"My mother died young, when I was only six," she says. "She was an illustrator like Nancy, worked for a publishing company. Carmen Victoria Barrow, née Taylor. I took the Taylor name back when I fell out with my dad."

"Do you remember her well?"

Jess smiles.

"Only in my dreams. I think of her now as this beautiful dark-haired princess with green eyes and perfect teeth. I remember her showing me the necklace—"

"*The* necklace?"

"The very one," she says, holding his gaze. "I also just found out I'm possibly related to a golden age Hollywood producer—"

"*Hollywood?* So why are you here? Why aren't you drinking wheatgrass in Beverly Hills?"

"I don't like wheatgrass . . . but I'll visit one day. I'd love to find out more about my great-grandmother, Anna, about her life there. She made jewelry for the movies apparently. I think maybe she's the ancestor responsible for my adventurous streak."

"Adventurous streak? If you have an adventurous streak, then get on a plane and get yourself to Hollywood."

"What? Just like that? Just go?"

"Ah, sorry, maybe you're not such a fan of planes—"

"No, it's just . . . spontaneity isn't really my thing anymore."

"Nonsense."

She hangs her head. "Look at me. I can't simply jump on a plane and go here and go there. Everything's an effort. Everything takes planning. And sometimes . . . everything just *hurts!*"

If Tim were at her side right now, he'd smother her with hugs, tell her she's safe. Guy, meanwhile, gives a nonchalant shrug.

"Can't?" he says. "Or won't?"

Jess tenses, caught by his judgment.

"Seriously," he continues, cajoling. "Hollywood's not as far away as it sometimes seems. I go to L.A. all the time. Stella has a house there. She likes to throw parties. It's in the hills, got a great pool."

"Lucky you. Nice perk."

"What I'm trying to say is, if you ever want a traveling companion, someone who knows Hollywood, I'd be happy to oblige. In fact, what I'd do," he says, "is take you to *Old Hollywood*."

"Old Hollywood?"

"So many stories. *So* much decadence. Musso's. I'd take you to Musso's. It's this restaurant on the Boulevard, near the old Egyptian Theatre, called the Musso and Frank Grill. I tell you, Jess, it hasn't changed in *seventy* years. It's like stepping back in time."

"Sounds amazing," she says. "And I will go. Eventually."

"Ah, stop the excuses. Go now. There's no time like now."

"Yeah, yeah," she says drily, aware that while a stroll down Portobello Road with Guy van de Meer is an inappropriate flirtation, a rendezvous on another continent is at a whole other level.

NANCY looks thinner than ever. Her breathing is shallow, but her eyes still twinkle. At the side of the bed, Jess has the envelope of Nancy's Denmark Street photographs in her hand, hopeful they might ignite a reaction. She scatters them on Nancy's blanket.

"Look," Jess whispers. "This is you. This is *you,* Grandma, as a young woman wearing the necklace!"

She flips one of the photos to reveal the sticker on the back.

"'Paul Angel Photography, 1954,'" she reads. "Who is Paul Angel, Grandma? Do you remember when these were taken?"

Nancy's gaze is fixed to the ceiling.

"I've been squirreling around," Jess persists, "seeing what I can find out about our Taylor women. I went to Wales and discovered these photographs at the cabin. Bevan Floyd showed me around Pel Tawr and told me about Minnie and Emery and the making of the necklace. And he talked about your mother, Anna, about her going off to America. So it's true? You *were* born in Hollywood."

She pats Nancy's hand. Suddenly Nancy springs into verbosity.

"Oh yes, on good days, my mother was impeccable," she exclaims. "She'd set her hair, arrange her jewelry—earrings, brooches, hairpins, bangles. On bad days, though, she'd just lie on the sofa, drinking sweet sherry, endlessly lamenting her beloved Zedora . . ."

"Zedora?"

"Yes, Jessy, with the gilded toilet handle that Lucille Ball was rumored to have broken."

Jess laughs. "What on earth is a Zedora?"

Nancy looks pensive.

"It's all gone now."

"What?" say Jess, tensing. "What's gone, Grandma?"

Nancy sighs. "Her life. My mother's glamorous life. All her stories . . . They became nothing more than stories, from a world we'd never get back. *Move on,* I used to think. I knew better than to join her in the shadows of nostalgia, Jessy, because while those stories always began with jubilance . . . they finished with tears."

"What happened, Grandma, to make her so regretful?"

Nancy scowls. "That's Anna's business."

"But—"

"We came back to London and lived in a terrible place."

"Are you talking about the tenement block?" says Jess, remembering how Nancy had sometimes talked of a grimy flat in Poplar, where she'd spent her early teens.

"That place," she frowns. "The surrounding streets were still pitted with bomb damage. No running water, never a clean sheet."

"So what on earth happened to Hollywood?"

Nancy looks vacantly around her, her focus starting to drift.

"'You should marry the grocer's son,'" she says with a twisted Welsh American accent, which Jess assumes to be an impression of Anna's. "'The grocer's son has something about him. Choose your suitor well, my girl. Don't make the mistakes I made.'"

Nancy leans toward her photo, taps the necklace with a fingertip.

"My mother thought our butterfly would attract the grocer's son," she recounts. "With all her dramatics, she pressed it into my palm and said it would be in my interest to try it out on him."

"And did you?" says Jess, gripped.

"Absolutely not. I hated that dolt."

Jess picks up a few more of the Paul Angel photographs.

"So what about these images, Grandma? You're wearing the

necklace in them. What are you here . . . fifteen . . . sixteen maybe?"

Nancy grins impishly.

"Yes, I skipped school," she whispers. "I wore my best dress so that no one would know I was a student and took a Routemaster to the center of London."

"To Denmark Street? Did you want to be a musician?"

"Goodness no," says Nancy. "I was looking for a pawnbroker."

"A *pawnbroker?*"

"My mother was reckless with our finances, wasted everything on nail polish, sherry, and cigarillos. I wanted money she wouldn't know about so that I could buy food and stockings. I'd heard about the pawnbrokers from neighbors, places you could get quick cash. So when she gave me the necklace, I took it—"

"*You* pawned the necklace?"

"Not quite."

Jess puzzles. "Then . . . ?"

"I jumped off the bus at the first shop I saw, on the corner of Denmark Street, only to discover I was too early. The shop wouldn't open for another hour, so I took the necklace out of my bag, clipped it around my neck, and"—she smiles suddenly—"as I crossed the street, I noticed I was being admired."

Now there is a fulsome twinkle in her eyes.

"He was there in a trilby hat," she whispers, "hunched over his camera. He called after me, said he liked my necklace, asked if he could take a photo of me wearing it. So I took it off, pushed it into his hands, and told him: 'My mother wouldn't want you to take my picture, sir, but if you like my necklace, I'll sell it to you.'"

"And did that work?"

"He pushed it back to me and I clipped it back on. But then he noticed my malnourished limbs and offered to take me to Gideon's Café to buy me a breakfast. He promised he wasn't a sleaze, said I could ask anyone on the street. They all knew him. He said he photographed musicians, and that some of them had come from the United States, like Little Richard and Nat King Cole. So I told him"—she puffs out her chest—"that *I* was born in Hollywood. He said I'd have to tell him all about it over a fried-egg sandwich.

"As he spoke, he lifted his camera. And I started posing. I shut my eyes and began thinking about how outraged my mother would be, only to realize I didn't care. When I opened my eyes again, Paul had lowered his camera and was gazing straight at me. It made me feel quite peculiar, like everything in my soul was leaping. Then as he gazed at me, Jessy, his eyes, huge and blue with long, dusky lashes, I sensed them scanning the necklace at my neck . . . and that . . . that, I think, was where the magic happened."

Jess sighs, entranced.

"So it was Paul Angel," she whispers. "*He* was your soul mate."

Nancy smiles, an inner radiance shining through.

"What happened to him, Grandma? Did it work out?"

At this, Nancy snaps her eyes shut. She turns away, leaving Jess with the feeling she has just acquired more questions than answers.

Chapter 7

THE TRAVEL AGENT raises his brow.

"Tomorrow?" he asks.

"If possible," says Jess, crossing her fingers.

The agent taps his computer keyboard. Meanwhile Jess floats through the moment. The impulse that has carried her here, to Abbotts Travel, hums in her chest. She yearns to find out more about Anna, to uncover more Taylor secrets while Nancy is still able—just about—to fill in the missing details. She can almost hear Nancy's voice in her head: *You're a Taylor! Get on that plane!*

"Okay." The agent strokes his beard. "Leaving what time?"

"Hmm," says Jess, her thoughts drawn to the Capital Gala at the end of next week. "I'm on a time limit. Maybe . . . first thing?"

"Spur of the moment, eh? Good for you."

They both grin, and the hunt for a deal begins.

AN HOUR LATER, TIM matches the travel agent's surprise.

"Tomorrow?" he says. "Los Angeles? *Tomorrow?*"

"Real cheap flights," says Jess, beaming. "I reserved two. The agent can hold them for an hour. I just thought—"

Tim scratches his head, gives a confounded sigh.

"I'm not sure you did think, Jessy. Otherwise, you'd have considered the fact that I simply can't drop everything and go off for a random week of jollity."

"But the school holidays have started. Why not have a surprise break? Besides, it's not a week, just a few days."

"All that way for a few days?"

"Loads of people do it," she says. "The flights were a bargain, and we can stay in a hostel."

Tim balks. "I'm forty. I don't want to stay in a hostel."

"Oh, come on, it'll be an adventure."

Jess sighs. This hasn't gone the way she'd hoped. Meanwhile Tim paces the floor until he manages to find something nice to say.

"Thank you for the thought. I do love your spirit, Jess, but you know what I'm like. I need a plan. I need routines."

Jess twitches.

"If you really want a holiday, maybe we could go away at the end of the summer, late August? Do something that'll be easier on your hip? After all, you're supposed to be resting and healing."

Jess glowers. "I don't want to rest and heal. I want to live. I want to do it all and go *crazy*. Think about it . . . Hollywood!"

"Jess, I *can't*." Now he is churlish. "And to be honest, this sudden adventure-seeking spirit of yours is frankly rather maverick."

"As you wish," says Jess, "but I'm taking that flight."

"On your own?"

"On my own."

And so they part, neither side winning, neither side losing, but with a distinct sense of disconnect wedged between them.

At the airport, among the holiday crowds and families, Jess finds a seat and eats sushi alone. It occurs to her that this is the first time she has flown since her unhappy return from Mexico. It's a big, wild step. But somehow, she understands, it's a step she needs to take, a little bit of her old self returning, reminding her that she is still Jess Taylor.

"Well, cheers to that," she says as she glugs from her water bottle, before feeling her phone buzz, a message from Guy.

So that dinner? How about tomorrow? G.

He's certainly persistent. She thinks for a moment, then replies.

Can't. I've taken your advice. J.

She attaches a photo of her boarding pass, and knows—*hopes*—it will incite a different response from Tim's. Indeed, Guy sends a page of emojis, expressing various states of shock and delight.

These little fellas are trying to say GOOD FOR YOU. G.

Jess smiles, about to shut off her phone when he messages again.

So yes to dinner? Musso's. Saturday, seven o'clock? G

She replies:

Ha-ha. J.

As she scoops up her backpack, he messages one more time.

May you find what you're looking for. G. x

Out of nowhere, the sentiment of this, or maybe the laden addition of the kiss, makes her burst into tears.

THE heat gets her first, then the brilliant blue sky, brightening the hills and streets. How much it must have changed since Anna arrived in the 1930s. Yet, everywhere Jess looks, there are remnants of that history in the streamlined curves of the deco buildings and the elegant villas. As she walks the length of the Strip, she feels them around her, the ghost whispers of Anna Taylor's life.

Jess has made a list for her time in L.A.: First she will seek out Christopher Roderick's mansion. Then she will hunt for evidence of Jossop's Jewelry, the company she was told Anna worked for. With whatever time is left, she will embrace the standard touristy things: the Egyptian Theatre, the Walk of Fame, Rodeo Drive.

After a hearty brunch, Jess grabs brochures from the coffee-shop window. Her attention is drawn to a leaflet for a house tour, bearing the logo of the Golden Age Restoration Foundation. The main image features a Spanish mansion with castellated turrets and pink walls. At the top is a word that strikes her heart: "Zedora."

Her beloved Zedora.

Zedora must have been the Hollywood house where Anna lived. With her heart in her mouth, she reads every word of the leaflet: "See Zedora, a historic mansion in danger of being pulled down for development. Former home of golden age movie mogul Christopher Roderick. Tours every day."

She stares, the pieces of the puzzle slotting into place. *This is it,* she thinks. She checks the time of the tour. Midday. Perfect.

AWAY from the tourist-mobbed landmarks, Jess finds herself among rows of gritty streets where art galleries and strip malls hide bistros and tattoo parlors, then on steep, sleepy lanes with elegant homes in traditional styles. Following the map on the leaflet, she takes another turn; then at the top of the hill she sees a turret.

At the gates—rusted filigree ironwork, bearing the name Zedora—Jess is greeted by the Restoration Foundation tour guide.

"Welcome," he says with an unexpected monotone, pointing to the name on his pin badge: JACKSON.

Jess and Jackson are soon joined by a group of Korean students and an elderly couple from Alabama. Jackson ushers them into Zedora's scrubby, overgrown grounds and clears his throat.

"With so many prestige mansions within a few miles," he says as though reading from a script, "you might wonder why you've arrived here. Hollywood has its share of ultramodern palaces with every amenity. But rewind for a minute and follow me. The true prestige is in the past. This is where the long-gone stars of the silver screen had their feuds, their affairs, and their fun."

They proceed to the front porch, and the oak door is heaved open. Inside, a swirling marble staircase graces an enormous hall, flanked with sculptures of gilded cherubs. Beyond the hall Jess sees a living room with mirrored walls. There has been some attempt to furnish the rooms: Italianate velvet sofas, a console crowned with a vase of ostrich feathers, a sunburst wall clock.

Suddenly the air seems alive. Anna is with her, she is certain.

"Excuse me," she says, pestering Jackson, "can you tell me anything about Zedora's occupants? I'm especially interested to know about a couple called Anna Taylor and Christopher Roderick. They would have lived here in the 1930s."

"You've been doing your homework," says Jackson. "The house was built by the Roderick family in 1926. Christopher Roderick remained here until his death in the early '70s."

"And he was a movie producer, successful by the looks of this place?"

"Debatable. He is best known for the 1936 swashbuckling blockbuster *Descent of the Sun*, which, in some circles, is considered to be one of Hollywood's most overblown follies. But fortunately for Christopher, the Roderick dynasty was wealthy enough to absorb a flop. Nonetheless, in Christopher's final decade he was a reclusive figure. He lived here alone with his long-term life partner, the celebrated choreographer Bernard Almer."

"Ah, yes . . . on that matter, do you know how things finished up with his wife, Anna Taylor? She made jewelry for the movies."

Jackson hesitates. "Christopher never married."

"Oh." She shrinks back. "But . . . he was engaged once . . . ?"

Jackson shrugs. "It wasn't unheard of for gay men in Hollywood to conduct relations with women in order to conceal their sexuality, so maybe, but there's no official record of this. There is, however, an unconfirmed rumor that he fathered a child. You'd have to look at birth records to be certain."

Jess brightens. Could this child be Nancy? As the tour group files to the next room, she lingers at the window, absorbing every detail. An engagement that never resulted in a marriage, an illegitimate daughter, and Roderick's subsequent commitment to another man. All said and done, Jess can only wonder whether Anna's life at Zedora was as rose-tinted as its walls.

Eager to uncover the next piece of her puzzle, Jess escapes the house tour and searches "Jossop's" online. She is amazed to find that the company is still trading as a jewelry business, and its headquarters are now a store on Rodeo Drive. Tired of the walking, Jess hails a cab. From the window she spots the famous Egyptian Theatre, with its pyramid frontage and lofty palms; then a nearby restaurant sign snags her attention: MUSSO & FRANK GRILL.

She puzzles for a moment, then remembers that it's the name of the restaurant Guy described. She winds down her window, leans out with her phone, and takes a photograph. Before she can question herself, she sends it to Guy with a message.

Tempted? J x

Immediately she regrets her action, realizing such a gesture cannot be construed as anything other than flirtatious. She shoves her phone back in her bag, berates herself. Thankfully Guy doesn't respond, bringing the flirtation to a sensible dead end.

JOSSOP'S of Rodeo Drive. The window displays say it all. The kind of jewelry that makes her shudder—big, blinding bling, favored by ladies who lunch and host charity balls. Jess pushes open the door, expecting to be wafted with a you're-not-our-typical-client vibe, but is greeted pleasantly by an elderly woman wearing a sharp suit dress and an edgy plastic choker.

"Hello, dear. How can I help?"

Jess smiles, wondering where to start. "I—I'm afraid I'm not here to buy jewelry. I'm on something of a mission."

"A mission? Well, that does sound exciting."

"I believe my great-grandmother may have once worked for this company, back when it made costume jewelry for movies."

"Ah, we certainly made jewelry for the movies. All the studios used us. From 1925 right through to the early '50s."

"You don't anymore?"

"Sadly, no. Other companies got in the way, doing things on the cheap. When producers would no longer pay for our high standards, we started to focus on retail. I'm Ellen. Marti Jossop, our founder, was my grandfather."

Jess feels an instant kinship with this woman.

"How lovely to meet you. I'm Jess Taylor."

"Pleased to meet you, Miss Jess Taylor. So tell me about this great-grandmother of yours."

"Her name was Anna Taylor. I believe she worked at Jossop's in the 1930s. She came from Wales originally. I don't suppose you'd remember? She got engaged to a movie producer. You might know of him . . . Christopher Roderick."

Ellen nods.

"I do indeed. Christopher produced *Descent of the Sun,* which was Jossop's biggest-ever project. We made nearly four thousand items for that movie. Back then, we weren't the high-class jewelry shop you're standing in now. We had a warehouse on the Boulevard. When I took over in the '70s, we came to Rodeo Drive. Do you like jewelry, dear?"

"I love all kinds of jewelry."

"So you take after Anna."

"Then you know about her?"

"I know *of* her. I know she played a part in Jossop's success. Wait a second. I have something that might interest you."

She disappears to the back of the shop, then returns with a box.

"This is a bunch of keepsakes that we took from the old premises when we moved. Take a look."

She pries off the lid of the box, revealing piles of invoices, pamphlets, and a few black-and-white photos. She sifts through them with her manicured red talons.

"Here," she says, removing one of the photographs and presenting it to Jess. "This might tell you something."

Anna! It's clearly Anna—those unmistakable Taylor cheeks. Jess grins; her great-grandmother, suddenly vivid in front of her, all the way from the 1930s. She draws the photograph closer, observing that Anna appears to be at work, fitting a faux bronze cuff to a sweaty-looking actress in a gold lamé playsuit.

"That's on set, preparation for thc 'pirate slave' scene," Ellen explains. "Marti used to say Anna was the darling of the costume department. She was liked by the cast too."

Jess's attention is drawn to a young, suited man standing behind them, slightly in shadow.

"Who's that?"

"That, dear girl, is Christopher Roderick. No doubt wading in, about to insist those bangles are fitted tight." Ellen rolls her eyes. "That man," she says, "was the bane of Marti's life."

"Was he a good producer?"

"He was uptight and snappy-tempered," says Ellen. "Didn't stop his popularity with the young women of the chorus and crew, however. They'd collapse into giggles whenever he came near. But not Anna. She was a shrewd one. She listened and watched and got to understand everything she could about Christopher Roderick; then slowly, surely, she positioned herself in his sight line."

"You think she engineered it?" says Jess.

"Put it this way," says Ellen, "Anna joined *Descent* as a costume junior, but by the time the movie wrapped, she had a ring on her finger. A nice one too, Marti told me. Got coverage in all the gossip columns. They celebrated at the Trocadero. Here . . ."

Ellen passes Jess another photo, this one of the famous Café Trocadero with its Italianate roof tiles and red-carpet welcome.

"In its day, it was *the* place. Fred Astaire went there. Cary Grant. Lucille Ball. Christopher was friends with all of them."

Jess beams, recalling Nancy's seemingly arbitrary flourish: *the gilded toilet handle that Lucille Ball was rumored to have broken.* Then she remembers the melancholy that followed.

"So . . . although they got engaged, they never actually married," Jess says. "Perhaps it was something of a lavender relationship? I heard Christopher ended up with a man called Bernard Almer."

Ellen shrugs. "Ah, Bernard, yes, lovely man. You're right. I expect the engagement had little substance behind it. Christopher clearly felt obligated to maintain a straight image. As for Anna, whether she understood what she was getting into or not, the engagement certainly gave her the opportunity to quit working and languish in all the nicest boutiques and restaurants."

Jess sighs, unsatisfied. Surely Anna would have wanted more than a mere illusion of love. Her eye then catches on a film script, or more specifically, on a doodle scribbled across its back cover: written in pencil, outlined in a heart, the initials A. T. and A. J.

"A. T.?" says Jess, delighted. "Could that be Anna?"

Ellen picks the script out of the box.

"Hmm. It's from *Descent*. Could well be Anna."

"So who's A. J.? Did Christopher Roderick have a nickname?"

Ellen ponders this, looks thoughtful.

"A. J.? My guess is that stands for Archie Jossop, Marti's nephew. He hung around here in the '30s, helped Marti out. Perhaps he had a crush on Anna? Nice fellow, but not in Christopher Roderick's league. Archie's parents were corn farmers."

"I see," says Jess, curious.

"Dear Archie," says Ellen. "He went to Europe to fight during the Second World War, and we never heard what became of him. But take the script if you like. Take the whole box. There are a few bits of Archie's in there, letters and such. Marti kept them aside, in case the boy ever returned, but . . . sadly it wasn't to be."

"Thanks," says Jess, accepting the box eagerly, thinking only of rushing back to her hostel room and pawing through its contents.

THE hostel is quiet as the afternoon sun streams through the slatted blinds. Jess places Ellen's box in front of her and pries off the lid.

Most of the items are paraphernalia from Jossop's: receipts and invoices. At the bottom of the box, however, Jess finds a pair of handwritten airmail envelopes, yellowed with age, addressed to Archie at Jossop's. The handwriting on both envelopes is the same, although the postal dates are more than a decade apart: June 1949 and February 1961. The envelopes are still sealed.

"Come on, Archie," she whispers, digging her nail beneath the seal of the earliest of the two. "What have you got for me?"

She unfolds the thin sheets of paper inside and reads:

> 24th June 1949
> My dearest Archie,
>
> I hope you remember me. Our time together was brief, but it has stayed alive in my thoughts, so I'm writing to jog your memory and see if you might perhaps reply. My name is Anna Taylor. We met in Hollywood before the war, August 1936. You might

remember a terrible pirate movie we both worked on called *Descent of the Sun?* I'd just joined Jossop's costume department, and your uncle Marti, the owner, introduced us. He called me "Miss Anna."

Do you remember? You were sitting beneath a studio lamp, eating a baloney sandwich, when he told you to take me to the set and show me how it all worked. You stood and gave me the warmest smile I'd ever seen.

"So, Miss Anna," you said, "we're doing a pirate movie. It's a mess, but the studio brass has it in their heads that if the costumes look good and the leading lady sparkles, no one will notice their crummy script. You see, we aren't just making movies. We're making trends. You interested?"

Oh, Archie, I loved your accent, your constant patter.

You walked me around the set, and I could feel my heart beating madly with the excitement of it all. I remember you asking, "You wanna be an actress?"

"No," I said. "Why does everyone assume I want to be in front of the camera?"

"Because they all wanna be in front of the camera," you said.

"But I'm not them. I'm me."

You turned to me with that grin of yours. "So you are," you said, before stumbling into a four-foot fake anchor.

"Who left that there?" you said, laughing.

Then your eyes dropped to the necklace at my neck, took in every curve and line. Do you remember that necklace? A sea-green enamel butterfly with a moonstone?

"Well, that's the prettiest thing I ever saw," you said. "You don't see that no more."

You asked me where I got it, so I explained my mother had given it to me moments before succumbing to typhoid fever, that she called it the True Love Necklace. And you looked at me and you said: "Is that so?" And it was a full minute before we managed to shake off the buzz.

Jess pauses. So *this* was Anna's soul-mate moment—the necklace, like a charm, pulling them into each other's spheres.

Do you remember our first date, Archie? Well, yes, it was our ONLY date, but what a night! I'll never forget the bumbling way you asked, sweetly tripping over your words.

"I don't want to be forward or nothing," you said to me, "but there's this new diner called the Casa Casanova. It does this brisket, and everyone's raving about it. And you know, on my wage I can just about afford the fries at Hamburger Jack's, but for a really special girl, I always thought I'd take her to the Casa Casanova. Except . . . I never met this girl. So here I was, thinking I'd never get to taste the brisket everyone's so hot about, and then"—you looked at me then—"I did! I met her! And now I'm gonna take her to the Casa Casanova! And the brisket's gonna be a knockout, and the whole world's gonna be butterflies from now on."

And I just stared at you, mouth open.

"So," you said, "how about it, Miss Anna? Can we eat brisket together? Tonight?"

"Yes," I said.

You picked me up at seven, and in the back of the taxi, you talked. And you talked. About the streets, the hills, the movies, the jobless, the president, and the farm in Maryland where you were raised. And then, at the dinner table, where the brisket was indeed succulent, you talked even more.

When you finally tired of talking, you downed your martini and told me it was my turn. So I told you all about my upbringing in North Wales and my home, Pel Tawr. About my father, Emery Floyd, who'd drowned in the Great War. And about my mother, Minnie, who'd never been able to marry Emery because she was still married to a mean man from Paris who'd locked her in a bedroom for weeks.

After dessert, as the band struck up, you grabbed my hand and pulled me onto the dance floor. And as we jigged and spun, I felt joy like I'd never known.

At the end of the evening, you walked me back to my boardinghouse and wasted no time taking hold of my hand. At the front door, we kissed. It was my first kiss, and it was soft and sweet and everything I'd wanted. I went to bed with the memory of it and the swell of happiness in my stomach.

The next morning, with a near skip, I took the streetcar to work. I kept a lookout all day, but you were nowhere on set. Eventually I found the courage to ask Marti, who just shrugged and nudged a camera cable with his shoe.

"He had to leave, Anna, first train this morning. His pa's taken sick, dying sick. He's gone back to Maryland."

I just stood there and felt it inside, that the best thing ever had just become the best thing that never happened.

It broke my heart, Archie. Sure I've met other men. I've even been engaged. But you know what, I stopped wearing my necklace after you left. It didn't seem right, so I wrapped it in a silk handkerchief and kept it in my dressing table.

Oh, Archie, you may think I'm silly to be pining for you like this, a decade later, but it would mean so much if you'd just reply. So that, one way or another, I can stop pestering myself with the thought of what could have been.

With fondest feeling,

Anna Elizabeth Taylor

Jess folds the letter, heartbroken for Anna. So what happened to Archie? Clearly he never returned to Jossop's or received his mail. She reaches for the second letter, postmarked 1961. She presses it between her fingertips, prays that it holds a happy ending.

14th February 1961

Dearest Archie,

I write you again, my Valentine, in the thin hope that this letter will reach you. Since you never replied to my previous letter, I'm at a loss. The fact is I still think of you. So much has happened since I knew you, and sometimes I feel quite despairing of it all. I torment myself that if I'd done something more to keep you, then I'd be good. Ah, hindsight.

You know at Jossop's I made the scrappiest bit of nickel shine. These days I don't get the chance to make things. I had to move to London. Here, all I do is try to soothe my boredom with television soaps, but then I just end up shouting at the screen, outraged by all the cheap wigs and ridiculous earrings. At least my creations looked authentic.

It hurt me, Archie, to walk away from my life in Hollywood. I guess that's why I still think and talk of it, to keep it alive. Memories are my comfort. The other women where I live mock me. They think I brag. But if they had witnessed the sight of Clark Gable eating shrimp in my dining room, they'd put their sneers away.

You see, after you left—don't be mad—I caught the eye of Christopher Roderick, the producer from *Descent of the Sun*. The moment he asked me to marry him was one of the most elevating experiences of my life. Little Welsh Anna engaged to a Hollywood producer!

Our engagement party, open bar at his mansion Zedora, was the talk of the town for months. An orchestra played in the lobby. We had a full dance floor in the courtyard. The fountain overflowed with pink champagne!

All of it, Archie. I had all of it. Then I walked away. Because there's one thing I now know: You can't fake true love. That giddy, swooping feeling I had the night I ate brisket at the Casa Casanova with you—not a single second with Christopher ever felt like that. The truth is, my engagement to Christopher was a sham. He wasn't in love with me. He delayed and delayed our wedding plans, avoided all talk of it. In the end, I stopped asking. Our one romantic clinch had been awkward and clinical. The fact that it produced our daughter, Nancy, has been nothing short of remarkable. After that, he hardly touched me.

Well, it wouldn't surprise you to know that Christopher showed as little interest in our daughter as he did in me. At the end of the fall, 1948, after weeks of arguing, I made the decision to seek something better. With Nancy only eight years old, I began to pack our things.

At first I thought I'd go back to the mountains, to Pel Tawr, but as I sat out the five-day transatlantic boat ride, Nancy at my side, a sense of shame got to me. I'd left the mountains for a reason. I couldn't return to rural life.

The capital appealed, where the fashionable lived. London, surely, needed costume jewelry designers of distinction! But, goodness me, Britain after the war was a shock. I soon learned there was limited appetite for well-crafted pot-paste bangles, not when a loaf of stale bread was being hailed as a miracle. With no more money and no obvious way of making money, the true calamity of my decision to leave Zedora rained down on me. But it was a calamity I had to live with. For my dignity. For my daughter.

I've now come to understand that with Christopher, I was merely a foil. He prefers the company of men. This, in itself, doesn't bother me. I guess it's the fact that for years he strung me along when I could have been—oh, Archie!—I could have been so happy with you!

So here I am. Sometimes, during these long days alone, the only thing that settles my nerves is thoughts of us. Perhaps you've forgotten me completely. But perhaps—just perhaps—you still think of me sometimes? I do hope so.

Forever yours,

Anna Elizabeth Taylor

Jess sits back, absorbing every detail of what she's just read. Where, she wonders, has Archie been all this time? But then she thinks back to what Ellen said about him disappearing after going to fight in the Second World War, and the thought rises inside her that Archie met a similar fate to poor Emery Floyd, another casualty of another war, in some unmarked grave in Belgium.

She sighs. "Oh, Anna."

All that pining in vain.

On the last day of her L.A. exodus, Jess takes a final amble down the Boulevard, absorbing the sights and sounds of the buskers, the street artists, the party crowds. She is reminded of her early twenties, when she traveled extensively, welded to the buzz of new destinations. Could Tim ever understand this? What would L.A. with him have been like anyway? A riot of spontaneity and adventure, or a teacher's timetable?

In her rumination, she loses track of her steps and ends up at the Egyptian Theatre. In front of her is Musso's, and she thinks fondly of Guy's praise for it. Curious, she decides to get a closer view.

The interior drips with old-school glamour: high ceilings, dark wood paneling, and upholstered leather booths. A waiter in a bolero jacket shimmies past, holding aloft a tray of prime rib. She hastens to leave before facing the embarrassment of being asked for a reservation she doesn't have. But just as she's pulling open the door, a familiar voice bears down on her.

"Jess Taylor! What are you walking out for?"

She blinks and spins around, only to see Guy Arlo van der Meer, in the flesh, wearing a vintage Hawaiian shirt and slacks.

"I told you," he says, with a tone that suggests it's perfectly normal she should find him here, "this is *the* greatest place to eat in the whole of Hollywood. Come, sit down. I got us the best table."

She is speechless. Her feet don't move. Meanwhile Guy gives the waiter a nod.

"Two house martinis please, Sergio," he says, beckoning her forward. "And, Jess, don't look so freaked out. We made a date."

"We did?"

"Come *on,*" he says, ushering her into a seat. "Seven o'clock, Saturday night. I told you . . . we'd do dinner."

"But I thought you were joking."

"I sort of was, but then you sent me that photo and . . . it was *very* tempting. And I always follow temptation."

Jess just blinks, her thoughts cascading.

"It was a bit of a gamble to hop on a flight," he continues, "but as it turns out, you've honored the date, only twenty minutes late."

"Except I didn't," says Jess. "I just happened to be passing."

She bursts into laughter. How is it they are both here together? With her mouth still agape, she claws her way to reason.

"I cannot believe you came all the way here, just to take a chance on meeting me for dinner. You made all this effort . . . for *me?*"

Guy smiles. "Doesn't seem like an effort. It seems . . . I don't know . . . *fun*. You wanted me to, right?"

He holds her gaze, those eyes sparkling, making her feel like she is the only woman in the world, the only one that matters. It's intoxicating.

"You are good," she says, wagging her finger at him. "*So* good. I mean, *this* is a gesture. There aren't many of my species who wouldn't be flattered, but . . ."

"Too much?"

"It's too much for someone who already has a boyfriend, which I do," she asserts, determined to keep her loyalties intact.

Guy nods.

"I hear you, Jess. I haven't forgotten about Education Tim, but I really like your company, so . . . can we at least settle on friends?"

Jess smiles. "Okay," she says. "Okay. Friends it is."

Guy looks at her and beams.

"Great," he says. "Let's order, shall we?"

THE rest of the evening passes in a glorious, if slightly surreal, bubble of elation. They eat chops and fettuccine, washed down with martinis. They talk boundlessly about Hollywood costumes, the trickery of the camera, fake beards, and cleavage brooches.

"So how is my necklace?" says Jess as dessert is finally served.

"It's doing fine. More to the point, how's your grandma?"

"She's okay. She's hanging in there. Tough old girl."

"I bet. Tell me about her."

"Well, she had a certain passion in her. She traveled a lot, eventually settling in North Wales, where she built her own log cabin and lived liked a hermit. I went to check on it, and you know what? It turns out that's where it all began . . ."

Jess opens up about Pel Tawr and Bevan Floyd and Minnie's diary and the story of the necklace's creation. She then explains everything she's discovered about Anna in Hollywood. When she's finished, Guy gives a long sigh.

"Oh, Jess, talk about the wonder of lost and found jewelry. That's incredible. No wonder you're on such a mission to get your necklace back." He lowers his eyelids, looks into his lap. "Just so you know," he adds, "I deeply regret selling it to Stella."

"Well, I'm glad you understand," says Jess. "It's not just a piece of jewelry to me."

"No," says Guy. "It's your history."

Her eyes drop to his leopard-head ring. She would like to ask him about it, but when he senses her looking, he cups it, a warning not to probe. So instead she dives into her slice of dessert.

"I have to ask," she says between mouthfuls of cheesecake, "is this normal for you, jetting across the world for an evening?"

"Normal-ish. Can't say I do it weekly, but spontaneity is in my nature. I like to get on a boat or a plane or a kayak . . . and just *go*. Arms wide open to whatever I find."

"Arms wide open," she repeats thoughtfully. "I like that."

When it is time to leave, they are both joyous and drunk.

"You know what we should do?" Guy slurs, his curls flopping. "Go to the sign. Since it's your first visit and all."

"The Hollywood sign?"

Jess stares at her legs, just about sober enough to appreciate that alcohol, night hikes, and walking canes are never a good mix.

"I can't," she says.

"Can," he argues, then swoops her up in his arms. "I'll carry you there if I have to."

"Stop!" she shrieks, giggling. "I'm heavier than I look!"

He flings her over his shoulder, his strength thrilling her.

"Don't make me go!" she cries. "I heard there's snakes there!"

They get a few yards up the path, and then, exhausted, he drops her to her feet.

"You win," he says, heaving a breath. "It's a tacky trip anyway."

"This entire place is tacky."

"Not Musso's."

"Definitely not Musso's. I'll always remember Musso's."

Her words trail off as, suddenly, she realizes where this is heading. He grasps her hand, and his warm fingers wrap around hers. Every cell in her body wakens, desire shooting to her soul. Silent now, he stares at her. This is it. He's about to kiss her. And she would *really* like him to. But . . .

She pulls away, inwardly berating herself for her recklessness.

"I'm sorry," she says. "I love your company, Guy, but I have to think of Tim."

His eyes roll. "Of course. Education Tim."

"I won't betray him," she asserts. "Thank you for surprising me and making me feel brilliant, but you have to understand it can't go anywhere. Really, I—I should get back to my hostel."

Guy sighs.

"Come on," he says, resigned. "Let's get you a taxi."

Chapter 8

"WHAT THE HELL? Where have *you* been?" The inquisition, courtesy of Aggie, begins the moment Jess walks through the door. "You look *rough*."

Jess groans and shivers—the dehydrated aftermath of the worst hangover, coupled with a ten-hour sleepless flight.

"I feel rough, thanks," she says.

"So?" says Aggie.

"Don't ask. It was some kind of lost-weekend thing."

"Lost weekend? Really? Tim told me you suddenly demanded a trip to Hollywood."

"I didn't demand. I invited him. He said it wasn't convenient, so I went alone. It was just a mini-break, a few days abroad."

Aggie gives a haughty sniff.

"Tim says—and I agree—that there is something amiss."

"What? Because I decided to have a last-minute holiday?"

"Because you're being all mysterious and you keep covering your phone up and—"

"Aggie, you're overthinking," says Jess, with an ache in her forehead. "I'm fine. I'm just reminding myself to live again."

But not too much, she thinks, still reeling from the sting of what her phone had shown her postflight. As soon as she'd landed, she'd switched it on and looked up Guy's profile. She'd found a dozen images of him partying, shirtless, around a neon-lit pool, with several young women and, in particular, Stella Weston. So much for flying out just for her! For all she knew, he'd had the trip planned all along, one of his Stella Weston jet-set perks.

"Don't worry. I'll call Tim," she says, yearning to be back in the nook, safe and secure, her head against his comforting chest.

"Yes," says Aggie, clapping her hands together. "That's a start."

LATER that evening, Jess makes her way down to the kitchen for something to eat. At the TV room door she overhears Aggie and Ed talking quietly between themselves.

"What is it, you think?" says Ed. "I mean, she jokes about having a quarter-life crisis, but this is getting out of hand."

Immediately Jess knows they're talking about her. With a wince, she lingers, listens in.

"Oh, I don't know," says Aggie. "Really, she needs to be getting her act together, not running off to random corners of the world on a whim. Things were going so well with Tim, but—"

"Talk to her," Ed says. "If she'll listen to anyone, Aggie, it'll be you. Just keep steering her in the right direction."

The right direction? Jess bristles. *According to whom?* She is not their puppet. She can make decisions for herself. She retreats, resolving that the quicker she can move out, the better.

Overwhelmed by the need to hear Tim's voice, she calls him. All she wants is comfort, the reassurance of his soft, kind tones.

"Tim?"

"Jess!"

"Oh, Tim, it's so nice to hear your voice. Listen, I'm really sorry I left like that, with an atmosphere between us. Did you get my pictures? I should have sent more, but I thought . . . Anyway . . . now I'm back . . . and . . . are we okay?"

"Jess, we're *fine*. I was a bit sore at first, I'll admit, but then I thought, yeah, I'm being a boring middle-aged person. I should have gone with you. I'm sorry too. I missed you."

Relief washes over her. "Can we hang out?"

"Of course."

"And can we move in together quick?"

"Definitely."

She smiles into the handset. Guy Arlo van der Meer can party in Los Angeles all he likes. He can also sweep her off her feet, and even dare to fire her passions by nearly kissing her. But he can't, and she's pretty certain of this, ever make her feel secure.

On the morning of the Capital Gala, Jess visits Nancy. When she enters the room, a team of nurses is around the bed.

"It's okay," says her favorite nurse. "We've finished our checks now. Go ahead, spend some quality time together."

As she says this, she lightly touches Jess's arm. Jess understands what the gesture means: The time is coming. She catches the nurse outside the door.

"How long?" she says, realizing there's no other way to ask.

"We estimate around forty-eight hours," says the nurse. "Maybe a little less. Maybe more. We'll keep you updated, so if you want to be with her at the end you can."

Jess swallows, stops herself from tearing up. With a sigh, she goes to Nancy's bedside, takes her hand.

"I took a leaf out of your book, Grandma," she says, her voice tremulous. "I went on another trip. Last minute, I booked myself three nights in Hollywood. I went to Zedora, Grandma."

She pauses, wipes her eyes.

"I also went to Jossop's," she says, rummaging in her bag, pulling out the *Descent of the Sun* script. "The owner gave me this. Look, it's Anna's initials on the back of Christopher Roderick's movie script. Did she ever talk about someone called Archie with you? I think he was the man she was *really* in love with."

Nancy lowers her eyelids.

After twenty minutes of silence, Jess concedes defeat and kisses her grandmother goodbye. Just as she's leaving, however, she hears a murmur from Nancy's lips.

"My necklace," she whispers. "Did you get it? Paul is waiting."

"Not yet," says Jess, heavyhearted. "But I will. Hold on, Nancy, and I *will* get it for you."

In a daze, Jess takes a cab to Denmark Street. As the cab pulls in, the ciphers of urban development surround her. But she is pleased to find hints of the street's rock-and-roll past still humming from the few remaining rare and vintage guitar shops.

She walks up the street, then halfway along sees the remnants of a shop sign, the words ANGEL and PHOTOGRAPHY just about visible. She rushes to the window, but the UNDER DEVELOPMENT posters give nothing away. She backs away, then stumbles into a man walking the other direction.

"Oh, sorry!"

"No worries, love."

Jess's attention catches on the man's steampunk skull pendant. She takes in the rest of him: late sixties, leather jeans, band T-shirt. As he moves on and enters Gary's Guitars opposite, she pauses.

"Excuse me," she calls. "Do you work here?"

He nods.

"Do you know much about *this* place?"

She points to the empty shop.

"You looking for somewhere to rent?"

"No, I—I'm curious about the sign. Paul Angel Photography."

"Ah, that's well old. Paul went out of business decades ago."

"You knew him?"

"Sure, he and my old man went way back. They were mates."

Jess brightens.

"Really? It's just I'm doing some research, family stuff."

"Well, come in the shop," the man says affably. "Have a brew. I'll tell you what I can."

She obliges with a smile. Inside, the shop is a tatty but dedicated space for musicians and amp enthusiasts.

"Are you Gary?" Jess asks.

"I'm Nick. Gary was my dad. He started the shop back in 1958, on the crest of the music boom. I took it all on when he died, the guitars, the lifestyle . . . everything."

He passes her a tea in a chipped mug.

"Paul was already in business when my dad set up on the street. Music photographer, one of the best. Old school."

Jess takes out a few of Nancy's photos and shows them to Nick.

"Could you tell me anything about this woman? She's my grandmother, Nancy Taylor. Paul Angel's label is on the back."

Nick studies the images. "Well, I never! That's his girl. That's Nancy! They were inseparable."

Jess blinks. For as long as she can remember, Nancy had lived alone. That she'd ever had a romantic life seems extraordinary.

"Looking young there," says Nick. "I only knew her when she was older. Is she . . . ?"

"She's really poorly. She's dying."

"Oh, I'm sorry."

"Eighty-two."

"Good innings, at least. Did she find someone else?"

"No. No, she didn't."

"Such a shame," says Nick solemnly. "Five decades. That's a long time to be a widow."

"Oh no," says Jess, heart sinking. "What happened?"

"Heart attack. One hot May morning in 1969. His funeral was something. Heck of a turnout, testament to how much Paul was loved by his industry. But for Nancy, it was too soon."

"I bet it was. So what were they like? Do you remember?"

"Always together. The age gap was close to fifteen years, but it seemed to work perfectly for them. They ran Paul Angel Photography together. 'Gentleman Paul,' as he was known, became one of the most well-respected music photographers of his day. They had a daughter, Carmen, named after the opera."

"Yes," says Jess, beaming. "She was my mother."

"Of course," says Nick. "Paul was a doting father."

"Aw, that's nice to hear."

"Fancy a strum?" he says, gesturing toward a rack of guitars.

"Thank you," says Jess, distracted by the last thing Nancy said to her: *Paul is waiting.* "But I need to get going."

She thanks him again and makes for the door. Halfway down

Denmark Street she stops, takes out her phone, and calls Guy's number. They haven't spoken since Hollywood, since he sneaked off to party at Stella's L.A. pad, making her feel like a gullible fool.

"Hello," she says, voice clipped.

"Jess," he says, with cheer, "of the Doughnuts. Funnily enough, I was about to call you. Recovered from L.A.?"

"Yes, thank you."

"We had a lovely time, right?"

"I suppose."

"What does 'I suppose' mean?"

"It means I'm not in the mood for small talk. I'm calling because, once and for all, I need to get the necklace."

"Er, yes, but you do realize it's the Capital Gala *today?* Stella is primed for the red carpet, very much loving that butterfly—"

"Good for her," says Jess, "but I need my necklace."

Her emotions bubble. She doesn't want to cry again, not to him.

"It's happening," she says. "The nurse told me she reckons forty-eight hours. This is the one thing I can do for Nancy to send her off in peace. You *have* to get that necklace for me."

She can hear Guy sighing, under pressure.

"Look," he says, "maybe there's a way we can speed things up. Come to the gala. I sent you a ticket. We'll let Stella have her showcase moment; then we'll get the necklace off her immediately after. I'll say it needs repairing or something; then you can steal it into the night, Cinderella-style, get it to your grandmother."

Jess brightens. "Will you honestly do that?"

"Jess, I'll do whatever I can."

Jess sniffs, restores herself.

"Somerset House, the Strand," says Guy. "Stella will be on the red carpet about five thirty. Let her get a few snaps; then it'll be yours. And until then, just keep giving Grandma the elixir."

"Okay."

"And . . . since I'll be rocking a tuxedo, don't forget your best dress. It'll help the mission if you blend in."

Jess blinks, caught by the idea of Guy in a tuxedo, realizing that, despite the desperation of it all, some deep, inscrutable, shameful part of her cannot wait to see him again.

Tim stands at Jess's bedroom door, waits for her to notice him. She appears to be reorganizing her wardrobe, all her best things strewn across the floor. There is redness in her eyes, a hint that she's been crying. This grandmother stuff is crushing her. He grips the gift-wrapped box behind his back, gives a little cough.

Jess looks up.

"Tim? Oh, hi. I—I didn't think I was seeing you until later."

"You weren't, but I thought I'd call by anyway to see my love. So what's all this?" he quizzes. "Decluttering?"

"No, I—I was just . . ."

She pauses, shrugs, stares down at the ensemble of pale blue organza beneath her feet. There it is again, that faraway look in her eyes, that mystery distance that creeps between them.

"I have something for you," he says, keen to reclaim her focus.

He presents her with the box. She gazes at it and smiles.

"What's this?"

"Just a gift, knowing that you've been missing a certain butterfly necklace. Open it," he encourages.

Hopefully, the box lid says it all. She'll know from the brand name of the jewelers what's coming next. He holds his breath.

"*Ah,*" she says.

The way her eyes sail across the bright silver butterfly charm pendant within, she is . . . astounded.

"Do you like it?" he urges. "It's to make up for the one you didn't get."

"It's . . . it's . . ."

Jess really *is* astounded. She doesn't know what to say. He grins and breathes deeply.

"It's . . . so *sweet.*"

He takes it from the box and places it around her neck, turns her to the mirror, and they both admire her reflection.

"The shop assistant told me it's sterling silver, with something called cubic zirconia. But . . . you know more about this stuff than

I do. I just thought a nice piece of jewelry, to make you smile."

He tickles her ribs, and she squirms and turns and buries her face in his arms. That's more like it. Somewhere in the back of his head, he hears his mother reminding him to treat women well.

He was good to Cassidy, and she screwed him over.

But he won't pass it on. He'll be good to Jess.

Because Jess is deserving. Jess is everything.

It's sweet, thinks Jess. *It* is *sweet.*

So very sweet. But *awful.*

It's so new. So crudely designed. And so very shiny. It could never compare to Minnie's True Love Necklace, the ions and atoms of four women's lives absorbed into its links and curves.

But still, she appreciates Tim's gesture. It's only a necklace. She shouldn't be ungrateful. Yes, he bought her bad jewelry, but doesn't every partner make that mistake once in a while? Except, how *can* he be so out of touch with her taste in jewelry? When it is pretty much the reason she jumps out of bed in the morning.

"Aunty Jess!" Steph bowls in. "You said you wanted a second opinion about what to wear to the . . . uh . . . gala—"

She stops in her tracks, stares hard at Tim.

"Hello, Stephanie," he says.

Jess can tell by his voice that he'd like Steph to disappear fast—and that the word *gala* has caught in his throat like glue. Meanwhile Steph stares down at the pale blue organza effort.

"Is that what you're thinking of? It's gorge!"

Jess winces, glances back and forth between the two of them.

"But it's only games night at the Star?" says Tim, eyebrow raised. "No need for the prom gown."

"Yes, but . . . as Steph mentioned—I was about to tell you—I *am* coming to the Star . . . but first I'm attending a gala. In town."

His eyes narrow, and immediately she feels villainous. Steph, either oblivious or superbly astute, nods at Jess, then backs away.

"What *gala?*" says Tim, hands now clamped on his hips.

"It's the Capital Gala," says Jess, lowering herself to the bed to rest her hip. "Not my thing but . . . it's . . . a jewelry event."

"Oh. And who are you going with?"

"Just . . . a mate." She hates lying. She can't lie. "The truth is, I'm going to get the necklace back. *The* necklace—"

"You mean you're going to meet that Guy person?"

She exhales, drops her chin. "Yes."

"Right." The coldness in his voice says it all.

"I just want the necklace. For Nancy."

He clenches his jaw, stares at the ceiling.

"Whatever," he growls, grabbing his jacket and marching out.

Somerset House, the Thames-side venue for the Capital Gala, its neoclassical magnificence buzzing with paparazzi, is red-carpet ready. Jess approaches the entrance, shows her invite to security, and is welcomed through the gates.

She glances around, but there is no sign of Guy. With a despondent sigh, she checks her watch. Maybe he has other plans? Should she be surprised, given his antics in L.A.? She clenches her fists, her frustration for the necklace escalating, and then . . .

He emerges from the shadows of the colonnade, gorgeous in his formfitting tuxedo, a fluster in his eyes as he looks into the crowds. Against her better judgment, her chest fills with lightness.

She waves, calls out. "Guy! Over here!"

"Jess!" He waves at her. "Wait! I'll come over!"

Her mind fills with thoughts of their night at Musso's, their laughter, their near kiss . . . then the sting of those pool-party photographs. *Don't!* she warns herself. *Don't be fooled!*

When she looks again, she sees he is flanked by two glamorous women in red dresses and Cartier. And there behind him, looking the other way, is Stella Weston. The supermodel turned influencer, tall and willowy, olive-skinned, with straight chestnut hair. Her flowing white gown makes her look like a Grecian goddess.

"Jess!" says Guy, swooping her into a two-peck greeting, holding her gaze. "You look lovely."

"Thank you," she replies, urging herself to remain annoyed.

"Let me introduce you," says Guy, leading her toward Stella.

As Stella approaches, the first thing her eyes land on is the necklace. All that Taylor energy bound in its sea-green wings, now on the skin of a stranger! It looks wrong, unbearably wrong!

Jess sighs, takes a breath. Guy taps Stella on the shoulder.

"Hey," he says. "I have someone I'd like you to meet. This is Jess Taylor. She's a jewelry dealer. Like me. She has a business selling vintage and retro pieces. I tell you, she's got a great eye."

Stella graces her with an air kiss. Her focus is all over the place, constantly monitoring who else is out there.

"Lovely to meet you," says Jess. "What a perfect evening."

"Yes," says Stella, distracted.

"And—what an extraordinary necklace!"

"Thanks." Stella raises her fingers to the tips of the butterfly wings. *Don't you dare break it,* thinks Jess.

"Out of curiosity, do you know when it was made?"

"Uh . . . it's vintage."

"Of course. It looks vintage. I wonder what era."

She can feel Guy's eyes boring into her.

"Uh . . . an olden-day era."

"She means it's from the early twentieth century," says Guy, maneuvering himself between the two women and taking Jess by the hand. "*Jess,* why don't we get you a drink?"

"Great idea."

They walk toward the hall. The sound of a harp drifts up to the painted ceiling, a fairy echo above the fizzy chat. From the nearest waiter Guy takes two Bellinis, hands one to her.

"So . . . are galas your day-to-day thing?" Jess asks, leaning back against a fluted pillar.

"Nah," he says, the angles of his body mirroring hers. "They're my weekend thing. Day-to-day, I'm on my yacht in Monaco."

They both laugh, and Jess can feel the annoyance eroding. They huddle so close that their bodies almost touch. She can smell his aftershave, the scent of musk and vanilla. The urge to run her hands through his hair, pull him close, draw him in . . .

Suddenly a woman with a black bob and glittering diamond choker is in their sphere.

"My favorite jewelry dealer," the woman drools, showering Guy with intruder kisses, completely ignoring Jess. "Guy, darling, there's someone I'd like you to meet."

Jess inwardly cringes. How does he stand it?

"Have you heard of General Phillips?" the woman continues. "He's been looking into the whereabouts of his great-grandmother's brooch. He thinks he's traced it to Cape Verde, but he could use your help. First though, darling, you owe me a dance."

Within seconds, Guy is in this woman's arms, twirling onto the dance floor. A triple cocktail of disappointment, envy, and anxiety prickles through Jess's body. Guy seems so immersed in the dance, it's as if he's forgotten her existence.

As he turns, however, through the swirling lights, he catches her eye and smiles. And it feels like a truthful smile. So she allows herself this concession: that his devotion to this woman is perhaps purely business, a schmooze with a client. That his truth is not in this room, but somewhere else, somewhere . . . with her.

When the song ends, he breaks away and, much to the bobbed vulture's vexation, he returns to *their* pillar.

"Another drink?" he asks.

"Shouldn't you be schmoozing?"

"I *am* schmoozing."

Jess grins. "So now that Stella's had her fashionista moment, can we get *my* heirloom please?"

"Sure. What's your plan?"

"I thought *you* had a plan."

"I did. And it's worked."

She stares at him.

"I'm here for the necklace," she asserts. "Nothing else."

"Well, I was thinking I could tell Stella that the catch at the back appears broken, and that rather than risk losing it, I'll 'look after' it for her. I'll smother her with compliments, reassure her that she doesn't need bling to shine." He shifts, looks a little uneasy.

"Thank you," says Jess. "You're not nervous, are you?"

"Of course. It's Stella . . . and I'm lying to her."

"A small lie, for a good cause," she says.

"Okay, okay. Mission engaged. But I can't promise Stella will fall for it. If she senses I'm messing her about, I'll have to pull the plug."

"Oh, stop pandering to her," Jess scolds. "Just do it!"

Guy weaves into the crowd, and Jess aches with the pull and push of her feelings. She watches Guy approach Stella, whisper something in her ear. They both giggle, then disappear together. Tense, she goes to the bar and orders another Bellini. Ten minutes later, the Bellini downed, Guy is nowhere to be seen.

Her unease escalates. What are they up to? Where is the necklace? Steeling herself, she messages Tim to say that she'll be at the Star soon, and then she circuits the hall, past the throngs of hedonists and glitter cannons. She checks the lobby and then heads to the balcony, where the lights of the Thames sparkle. If she doesn't get the necklace tonight, what will the consequence be? The thought of Nancy denied her final wish squeezes her heart . . .

Suddenly a warm breath tickles the back of her neck. She stills and gasps as a pair of hands emerge beside her.

"Shh!" he whispers, softly slipping the butterfly necklace over her shoulders, his fingertips scintillating the cool of her skin.

He turns her toward him, and their eyes meet.

"Happy now?" he whispers.

"Oh yes," she says breathlessly, reaching for her butterfly.

The necklace, the Taylor legacy, *finally* around her neck—and through it she can feel the past in her blood, four generations of her family coursing into her veins: Minnie, Anna, Nancy, and Carmen. They are all here, whispering their wisdoms.

"Thank you," she says.

And then, on impulse, engulfed by gratitude, she leans up on tiptoes and plants a thank-you kiss. Just a thank-you kiss, but it unintentionally misses the cheek it's intended for and lands straight on Guy's lips. The moment shocks. They both fall away.

"Sorry," she gasps, her walking cane clattering to the floor.

Before she has a chance to pick it up, Guy lowers his gaze to the necklace, to that fat moonstone, where it rests against her milky skin. He stares, mesmerized, then looks up at Jess. This is it. No matter how risky, how wrong, *this* is how soul mates feel.

Jess shuts her eyes and gives in to the fervor. Her fingers entwine with Guy's. Her heart is on fire, her breath so fast it's dizzying. And as she leans toward him, in the space where their lips hover, desperate to touch, everything feels suspended: every star, every cell, every hope . . . *everything* hangs in this moment.

So she dissolves into the pleasure of kissing Guy Arlo van der Meer. All at once everything comes to life, the truth of her heart colliding into his, the bond between the wearer and the watcher, a tightening knot, declaring itself: undeniable, indelible.

Then the magic is broken by a vibration between their bodies.

"My phone," says Jess, hurtling back to reality.

She doesn't need to look at the screen to know that it's Tim. She shudders from her bliss, shocked, appalled at herself.

"Oh . . . I don't know what came over me . . . I shouldn't have . . . I'm sorry, really sorry."

Guy grips her hands.

"Sorry?" he says. "Why be sorry? You went with your instincts. We both did. We could do it again. And again. And again."

He pulls her toward him, cups her cheeks with his hands, and she wants *so much* to let him, but the thought that she's building a life with Tim, one that she needs, is bigger than this. *Get real, Jess.*

"I'm sorry," she says again; then she hastens away.

Reeling, Jess hails a taxicab. Her first thought is to direct the driver to Nancy's care home in Sydenham, but then she remembers it's past nine o'clock. The care home will now be closed to visitors.

Jess sits back, puts her hand to the necklace, and breathes. She could—*should*—go to the Star, catch last call, focus on Tim.

"Head to Wanstead," she says to the driver.

When she arrives at the Star, she immediately sees Tim over by the window, being "the Man."

"You made it!" he says cheerily, a few pints into drunk.

Jess hugs him tight, desperate to right her wrong.

"So did you get it?" he asks.

"Yes," she says cautiously.

"Show me."

His gaze drops to the sea-green butterfly at her neck. She waits for his reaction. But his face hardly changes; then he shrugs.

"That's it?" he says. "*That's* what all this fuss has been about?"

"You don't like it?"

She eyes him, wills him to be at least a little impassioned.

"It's . . . elaborate," he says. "I mean, it's certainly fussier than the one I got you. Here, have a drink."

He scoops her into a hug, hands her his pint. And despite the silent confusion snaking through her mind, she smiles and accepts and does her level best to join in. *Familiar*, she reassures herself. Not boring. Just familiar. And familiar is good. Familiar is secure.

An hour later, they return to Jess's room in the Hoppit household. Tim is drunker than Jess and in a buoyant mood.

"I need to ravish you," he says, pulling her toward him.

She wants to feel closeness. So she flicks off her shoes, loosens the straps of her dress, determined to conjure the spark. Tim kisses her, but then retreats to the en suite bathroom. She hears him rooting around at the sink. He then pokes his head around the door.

"Forgotten my dental floss," he says. "Do you have any?"

It crosses her mind that, barely a year into their relationship, they should be obsessed with each other, rolling across the bed with throw-it-in-the-air passion.

"I don't care about dental floss," she says.

"You should. Better than brushing—"

"I mean, I don't care about dental floss right now," she says, layering her words with seductive suggestion.

"Patience, Jess. Let me get a glass of water and put my phone on charge. I'll be with you in a second."

She flops back, wilting into the ordinary.

Five minutes later, Tim reappears. He undresses and slips into the bed beside her, but beer and tiredness have got the better of him and he is soon asleep. With a sigh, Jess curls up against him. After a moment, however, she feels something digging into her neck—she is still wearing the necklace. She unclips it, runs a finger across its chain links. Her thoughts surge: the way he gazed at the necklace, then spun her into his arms, the way they kissed.

It was a *"OUI"* moment.

And a *"OUI"* moment can't be minimized or dismissed. Nor can it be defined by a yearning for security or the avoidance of a "type." If it's there, it's there. She resolves to find a way out of this mess, a way to end things with Tim. There's no point settling for the familiar when your heart, in truth, wants something else.

Chapter 9

THE NEXT MORNING, having slept little, Jess is awake early. She dresses, tucks the butterfly necklace in her bag, and takes the first train to Nancy's care home. As she approaches the reception, the staff are extra welcoming. *Ominous,* she thinks.

"Come along," says a nurse, ushering Jess along the corridor. "It's good that you're here. We were just about to call you."

"You mean . . . it's time?"

The nurse nods, holding the door open for her.

"Right, okay," says Jess, gulping, as she enters the room.

Nancy is peaceful, her eyes slightly open. Jess goes to the bedside, takes out the necklace, holds it to the light.

"I got it," she whispers. "Finally, Grandma, I got it for you."

Nancy stirs.

"Oh, Jessy, my lovely Jessy," she whispers, barely audible.

Jess takes her hand, places the necklace in her grandmother's palm, and closes her cold, frail fingers around it. Nancy tries to speak again, but it comes out as a gasp. Jess leans closer.

"What is it, Grandma?"

"Paul," she whispers. "My Paul. He's waiting for me."

"He is," says Jess, eyes slick with tears.

"He was my true love, Jessy."

"I know."

Shakily, Nancy draws the necklace to her chest.

"Minnie," she explains, straining to get her words out, "Minnie poured everything she had into making our necklace. All her hopes, her dreams . . . her *soul* went into it. Now it lingers inside."

With a sudden surge in her thin arms, she thrusts it toward Jess.

"You . . . you want *me* to have it?"

"Oui," gasps Nancy, before collapsing back to her pillow.

Awed, Jess cups the necklace's delicate enamel and metalwork. The wings feel so *alive* in her hands. And through their energy a thought starts to pester, that Nancy's desperation for the necklace was not for her sake but for Jess's.

"Nancy . . ." she begs, so many questions to ask.

But Nancy is silent.

"Oh, Nancy," Jess cries, her voice a siren in the quiet. "Not yet, Nancy. We've got some fun to have yet, you and me."

At this, Nancy smiles with half her mouth. It is enough to show Jess that she isn't sad. She is at peace.

Silently, softly, the air changes. After a moment, Jess looks to the window and is struck by the sight of a butterfly landing on the ledge. A small tortoiseshell, it sits perfectly still, then opens its wings and flutters off through the bright blue sky, entirely unaware that the soul of Nancy Maria Taylor has just left the earth.

In the days that follow, a new family landscape emerges. Aggie cuddles her children in a way she doesn't usually. Tim comes to the Hoppit house with flowers for both sisters. He sees Jess's teary face and, without a word, pulls her into an embrace. In his arms, it feels safe to release, to let it all out.

Jess wears the necklace all the time, because something of Nancy's energy seems to remain within it. Aggie occupies herself with arrangements for the funeral. On Thursday afternoon, she summons Jess to the kitchen on the pretext of choosing buffet options for the wake. Once that business is out of the way, she slaps her hands on her knees, clearly poised to say something deep.

"Anyway . . ."

Jess watches with caution, sensing an incoming lecture.

"Tim's been a star throughout all of this, hasn't he?"

Jess murmurs.

"All good between you two?"

"Yes."

"Because . . ."

Here we go.

"I've been doing some research." She gives Jess a meaningful stare. "On your new 'friend.' Guy van der . . . *whatever* . . ."

Jess bristles. She's been at the mercy of her sister's "research" in the past. Aggie's discovery that Andrew the band promoter had a serious gambling habit, or that Mac the Irish musician had many, many baby mamas. All to show Jess what she seems so ignorant of herself: that the men she's attracted to are riddled with issues.

Jess sighs. "Aggie, I really don't think it's necessary for you to go giving him the third degree. You're wasting your time."

"Except . . . you met him in L.A., didn't you? I saw it on your phone. And then this gala you went to? You've been acting weird. My hunch is you've been avidly interacting with him—"

"It was to get the *necklace*."

"Oh, Jess, you can't tell me it was simply about the necklace, because . . . I'm your sister. I *know* there's something between you two." She sighs. "But what *you* need to know is . . ."

She pauses.

Jess bows her head.

"He's not who you think he is."

Aggie pushes her tablet in front of Jess and scrolls through her Pinterest board of "evidence."

"For a start, his name is not Guy van der Meer. He's not from a Dutch diamond dynasty, as various gossip columns imply. His name is Guy Davis. He went to school in *Ramsgate,* had a Saturday job in a chip shop, and got zero qualifications. So whatever elaborate backstory he's been telling you, it's a load of old crock."

Jess's mouth drops open.

"So . . . he changed his name," she reasons. "Big deal. People do that all the time."

"The point is, Jess, if he's lying about his name and his family background, what else is he lying about? I've looked through his profile. He thinks he's some kind of international treasure-hunting playboy, living the jet-set dream. Look at this . . ."

She scrolls through photo after photo, Guy posing and partying, always surrounded by exotic locations, sophisticated people.

"As exciting as he might seem, Jess, you can see he's just a show-boater. I won't let you risk your future happiness."

Taut with frustration, Jess throws up her hands.

"Well, it really doesn't matter," she says, "because, as I've told you, there is *nothing* romantic going on between me and Guy van der . . . Davis . . . or whatever! So just . . . drop it, will you!"

She storms away, Aggie's revelation spinning in her head. The warning is immovable: He really is a liar. Another one.

Of course it shouldn't matter. The passion she'd felt with Guy was an anomaly. A mistake. How could she ever doubt Tim? Tim who at every turn has shown himself to be loyal and mature. Tim who doesn't play games or sneak off to L.A. after-parties.

But still . . . that kiss at the gala, it burns in her heart; that kiss was a "yes" moment.

As Guy lazes in the young grass of Green Park, hands clasped behind his head, Jess is in his thoughts. Her bright eyes and quick mind, the way they kissed when he slipped her the necklace.

He has thought about little else for days, but has kept the reverie to himself, Stella being ultra-insecure this week. Here she comes with two water bottles, after aborting her attempt to Rollerblade. It has been a week of "doing things" with Stella, feeding her ego, keeping her distracted from the news about her dot-com billionaire, Yannis, who has reportedly proposed to a swimwear model.

"Why the constant smiling?" Stella demands, thrusting a bottle into his hand.

"I'm thinking about someonc."

"Who? Tell me. Come on. It's time you spilled the beans."

"If you must know, it's Jess," he says. "Jess Taylor. I introduced you to her at the Capital Gala."

"Jess? I don't remember any Jess. Is she worth remembering?"

He sighs. "She is to me."

"And where did you meet her?" Stella asks.

Guy hesitates, unsure whether to mention the necklace. It has been a sore point between them since he smuggled it to Jess at the Gala. He had hoped Stella would forget about it, but . . . she has been unusually picky. The night she had to give up the necklace for "repairs" was the night she also learned of Yannis's indiscretion. And now she keeps pestering for the necklace, almost as though she's convinced that the two events are interlinked.

"Well?" she presses.

"Let's just say we met in a haze of time," he explains.

"You like her?"

"We have a connection. And it's a connection I've never had with anyone else."

"Oh, please, spare me, Guy. You're the Connection Casanova."

Guy laughs, then shakes his head.

"I'm telling you, Stella, this is different. This is real. It's real and it's messy and . . . suddenly I don't know what to do with myself. Because I like her. I *really* like her."

"Sounds like infatuation to me. Not healthy, Guy. Lust/love. They're not the same thing, you know. Something tells me you'll obsess about her until the shine wears off, then you'll dump her and move on to the next. So just don't. Go. There."

Guy cogitates on this, then climbs to his feet.

"No!" he says, suddenly animated. "*No.* I like her. I really, truly like her. In fact, sorry, Stella, but I think I'm in love with her."

Stella glares at him, open-mouthed.

She'll never tolerate him being in love with someone else. He can see in her eyes that she fears losing him, her most loyal, doting best friend forever, who tells her the truth and does as he's told. He knows, deep down, that theirs is not a balanced friendship, but where would he be without her?

"She has something to do with my necklace, doesn't she?" Stella demands, eyes narrowed. "I *want* that necklace back, Guy. You said it was with the repairman, but it must be fixed by now."

Guy sighs.

"I paid for it," she asserts. "So it's mine. Get it for me."

"All right, all right," he says.

He hates the way he feels like her puppet. His role has been to keep her amused for the forty-five weeks of the year that she hasn't been with Yannis. In return, he gets a rent-free home, trips to L.A., and an open door to London's rich list. He's built his business on reputation. They like him. They *believe* him. But at what cost?

He paces, the tendrils of his past threatening to creep to the surface, reminding him of the life he's escaped, of those sad kids in that care home in Kent where he grew up.

No. He's gotten away from all that. He's become a success.

So just keep rolling the dice, keep in the game.

"You'll have it back by the end of the day," he says.

Stella plants a kiss on his cheek. "Thank you," she coos. "Now, I'm thinking, what about Cannes this autumn? Should we go?"

He grins. *Yeah. Why not?*

Wary of the reason behind Guy's request to meet, Jess hobbles toward his suggested venue: Hatton Garden, London's diamond center. Her hackles are up. She can only assume he chose the venue to fit in with his "van der Meer" diamond family charade. She steels herself, resolves to be more annoyed than ever before.

There he is, leaning against a lamppost beside a glittering window display, in a moss-green shirt and jeans, oozing confidence.

"Ta-da! Another jewelry-themed destination," he says as she approaches.

His attention immediately falls to the butterfly necklace. The sense of his gaze both thrills and enrages her.

"So I suppose you picked this location because it's familiar territory?" she snarls.

He shrugs.

"Diamonds?" she nudges. "The van der Meer family legacy?"

"Oh yes, sure"—he catches her eye, maintains the conceit—"although my family specialized in raw diamonds. A lot of the ice around here is synthetic. Not so good."

Raw diamonds? *Really,* Mr. Davis? She glares back at him.

"So," she snaps. "What was so urgent we needed to meet?"

"Well. I thought we could get a coffee or maybe lunch—"

"Can't," says Jess. "I've got things to do."

"Oh."

His disappointment is palpable. That face, eyelids half-lowered, an unexpected hint of vulnerability, it feels—or at least it *seems*—genuine. She blinks, holds her breath, emotions surging.

Stay firm, Jess, she tells herself. *Don't fall for it.*

"Please," she says, determined to sever the occasion, "if there's nothing else you want from me, I have to get on."

"Why do I get the feeling you're being funny with me, Jess?" Guy stares at her. "Is it Tim?"

Jess sighs, lowers her head.

"I have a question for you," he says. "You say you're committed, but what if it's the wrong relationship? What if the person you're really meant to be with is standing right in front of you?"

"You're just a diversion," she says.

"Brilliant. Great. What's not to love about diversions? Although I could be the main journey, if you like. Really, try me. Watch me become an excellent main journey—"

"*No!*" Jess asserts. "We're not a thing. We can't be."

"Well, if that's the case," he says, recoiling like a scolded animal, "I might as well put it out there . . . I need the necklace back. Stella wants it. You've had your favor, so now, please"—he holds out his hand—"let me return it to its legal owner."

Jess glowers. She hasn't yet told him of Nancy's death. Fair enough, but still, it's as if it's not just the necklace he's asking for, but the very memory of Nancy, so raw and unprocessed.

"I'll give you the money for it," she implores, barely able to look at him. "I'll go straight to a cash machine now."

"It's not about the money, Jess. Stella wants her necklace. She's nagging. My neck's on the line."

"But you said . . . *you said* she wouldn't miss it."

"Well, she has, and that's that. My loyalty's to Stella. I mean, she's someone I'm actually *enough* for."

"Nancy's gone," Jess says. "She died on Sunday morning."

Immediately Guy softens, comes toward her.

"Oh, Jess, I'm so sorry. I didn't know. I—"

He pulls her into a hug, whether she wants him to or not. She can't deny that there is comfort in his arms. But then—perhaps she's being paranoid, just imagining it—then she becomes aware of his fingers at the back of her neck. And it feels as though they're working their way toward the necklace clasp. She backs away.

"You were about to undo it!" she accuses.

"*No.* I was just comforting you. Oh, for heaven's sake. I can't win, no matter what I do. But you know what? Out of all of this, Jess, legally the necklace is Stella's. She paid for it."

"This isn't about legality," Jess rages. "This necklace"—she hastens it from her neck—"is about my life! And now you're demanding it back like you really don't get it! Just take it," she hisses, pushing against him in anger. "Take it back to Ramsgate!"

Guy flinches.

"Yes, that's right," she says. "I've seen through the 'diamond family' crap. You're nothing but a lying fake, Guy *Davis*."

He stares at her, mouth open. But before he can argue, she is away, wielding her cane as though it's more a weapon than an aid.

Chapter 10

THE BREAD IS DRY around the edges. In her scrutiny of the buffet, Aggie is underwhelmed. They should have known to cut the loaves last. No one likes a stale egg sandwich.

It was a somber service, and now this wake, in the oldest of Shoreditch's pubs, promises to be quietly excruciating. The guests are few. Jess will cite Nancy's old age and singular lifestyle as the cause of such a small crowd, far too forgiving to acknowledge that a certain disagreeableness of character drove everyone away.

Aggie looks cautiously over at her sister. She's is no longer wearing *that* necklace, but it's hard to tell whether this is a good or bad thing. She hasn't spoken much this week.

Hooray for Tim, who patiently fusses over her. Thank goodness that the discussion regarding that "other" male distraction seems to have sunk in. Once the grief is out of the way, hopefully things will fall into place: Jess and Tim, happy in their new home.

The family piles their plates with chicken wings, then gathers at one of the wooden tables. Just as Aggie is finishing her first glass of wine, a specter appears in the doorway: their dad, Richard Barrow. They have spoken little in the last two years and seen each other even less. Richard has gained weight. He has also, Aggie notices, lost a few more hairs. Overall, it is not a cheering sight.

"Hello, girls," says Richard with a sort of shuffling warmth.

"Hello, Dad," says Aggie, smoothing the way.

"This looks cozy . . . nice spread . . . Am I too late?"

"You missed the service, but you're in time for the buffet."

Looks are passed around the table. Jess breaks into a startled smile, then shuffles along the bench, making space for him to sit.

"Eileen and the twins send their condolences," says Richard. "They couldn't make it, what with school and everything—"

"Sure," says Aggie crisply.

"I've got to ask, did she . . . did she go quietly?"

"She did," says Jess. "I was there."

"Oh, Jessy," says Richard, eyeing her with some vague attempt at fatherly concern. "I hope you aren't too sad. After all, you were always her favorite."

Classic, thinks Aggie, *rub it in.* Jess: the favorite. They sit in silence while Marcus wriggles and makes the table rattle.

"We weren't expecting you to come," says Jess eventually.

"For all our differences," says Richard, "I had a soft spot for the old girl. She picked up the pieces when your mother passed."

His eyes dart from daughter to daughter. Aggie struggles to give him anything other than a hard-glazed glare, so he lingers on Jess.

"How are you doing, Jess?"

"I'm okay, thank you. Overall the hip's much better."

"And your jewelry? Last time you said you were setting up some kind of online jewel business. Is that . . . ?"

He gestures to the butterfly charm pendant, which Jess has layered over a plain black shift dress. Aggie is so glad she's finally taken to it, such a sweet gesture from Tim. Okay, it's a little indistinct, not Jess's usual style, but it's the thought that counts.

Tim holds Jess's knee, urged to protect her. He knows the last time Jess spoke with her father wasn't pretty. There was some argument about how he'd stopped visiting her when she was broken in the hospital. His own daughter! Suddenly Tim feels glad for the stability of his own upbringing. He'll be there for Jess. Always.

She's got his necklace on. It's a good sign. She'll never admit it, but it suits her. A more sedate look—perhaps it will help the world take her a bit more seriously. Whatever. He's just glad she's wearing it. For a moment it seemed like he was losing her. Perhaps it was the stress of losing her grandmother? He must be patient. And he *must* get her to apply for that teaching post. A proper focus might help curb her restlessness.

The cycle of life, he thinks. With every ending, there's a beginning. Nancy is gone, but the future is theirs. He digs out his phone and makes a note to speak to Aggie about ring ideas.

Obviously he should start by introducing himself to Jess's father, man to man.

"Mr. Barrow," he says, aiming for sleek geniality. "I'm Tim."

"Call me Richard."

"It's excellent to meet you at last, in spite of these sad circumstances. You're probably already aware, but I'm dating Jess. Perhaps we should sit down, have a chat some time? Share a pint?"

He's not quite the in-law Tim imagined—golfing days, family lunches, walks in the forest. But there you go. Jess is the important one. Keep things upbeat, pull these tenuous family ties together.

"So." Tim stands up. "Another round, everyone?"

"No, no," says Richard. "Allow me."

"No, please, my turn," Tim insists.

"Honestly, it's my turn," says Richard.

"Yes," say Jess and Aggie. "It's definitely your turn, Dad."

Guy paces, stares at the pub door. Jess is in there. He has to get her on the spot, grab her attention, and open her eyes. They could be great together. He knows it. And he's pretty certain that she knows it too. He sighs, takes a breath. What is this? *Butterflies?* For the first time since childhood, he actually has butterflies. She—Jess of the Doughnuts—is giving him butterflies.

He sighs again; then with a now-or-never push, he makes his way into the pub, spies her through the crowd.

Jess is weary. Her father, her sister, Tim . . . *all* of them seem hell-bent on crowding her today. She knows they mean well, but she needs space, time to breathe. She gets up, heads for the toilets; then halfway across the pub floor, she is stopped in her tracks.

Guy stands square in front of her, takes hold of her arms.

"Jess," he says, eyes more sparkly than ever, that impish, impulsive smile bursting from his face.

"Wha-what are you *doing* here?"

"Don't talk," he says, still smiling. "Just listen."

She glances around her, aware that everyone in the room is now looking in their direction.

"I'm really sorry about Nancy," he says. "I realize what she meant to you. Is that your family?" He nods to the table, the opened mouths. "They look like a good bunch." Then he lowers his voice. "Except for your sister, with the judgy eyes. Not convinced she's a fan, but . . . the thing is, Jess, what I've come to say is this."

He fumbles in his pocket, pulls out a purple box. He stares at it, then offers it to her.

"Of course, if you'd rather stick with high street replacements . . ." he says, scrutinizing the silver charm necklace dangling from her neck. "I mean, really, Jess, please tell me you're only wearing that because your niece and nephew gave it to you."

"It was Tim, actually," she says. "Tim gave it to me."

Guy gives her a look, then blows a rush of air through his mouth.

"The thing is," he says, fingers trembling as he opens the box, "I made a mistake. I got all petulant and demanded the necklace back when I shouldn't have, because what I truly understand now is that this butterfly is meant for you."

He removes the necklace from its insert and offers it out. Jess's mouth falls open. The necklace, back where it belongs.

"I've sorted things out with Stella," Guy explains. "I've told her I'm done, quitting the trap I've been in. I gave her back the money for the necklace. She's pretty pissed off, but if that's what it takes to prove that I want to start something—"

"Start something?" Jess blinks. "What do you mean?"

"I want to start an adventure. With *you,* Jess."

Before she can articulate a response, he cups her cheeks in his hands, takes his lips to hers, and kisses her with such passion that her eyes are forced shut and her body feels weightless. The rest of the room blurs. She melts into his touch, unable and unwilling to resist. His lips are so soft, his body warmth so soothing, but . . .

"Stop!" she cries, shaking her head. "You can't just turn up here with all this . . . fanfare. You can't come at a person, out of the blue, kiss them in the middle of their grandmother's wake, with all their family watching, and their boyfriend and—"

"Is that the bit that bothers you?" says Guy. "That your family is watching, because—"

"Oh, there is so much about this that bothers me, Guy. Don't you get it? I don't trust you. You're not the trustworthy type. And that's no good for me. We can have all the sparkly, doughnut-based moments we like, but if the foundation isn't there—"

Guy throws his head back, exasperated, but *still* smiling.

"Why are you so determined to shove me into a 'type,' Jess? I'm just . . . *me.* Sure, I'm kind of flawed. And, yes, I've got some questions to answer, but give me a chance. I can't make assurances that we'll spend the next twenty years setting ourselves up with a mortgage, marriage, mini-mes, and life insurance, but what I can tell you is this . . . From the moment we met, something clicked in my head. And I think it clicked in yours too. Am I right?"

"I—I—"

Her instincts curl and coil—that fear in her soul, so deep and primal, telling her she cannot, must not be fooled again.

"I am indeed Guy Davis. Which is a bland, crappy name that I decided I didn't want, but that doesn't mean I'm not capable of being truthful. The fact is, I started calling myself Guy van der Meer because it gave me confidence. With a name like that, I became important. I *felt* important. Suddenly I was a diamond heir with a rich history, rather than Guy Davis from Ramsgate."

He holds up his leopard ring.

"It's not an heirloom, Jess. I bought it in a junk shop six years ago. My parents were nasty, penniless screwups, so I grew up in foster homes. By the time I was sixteen, I'd had fourteen different addresses, six different schools, and no qualifications. But I wanted better, so I moved to London and I made it work. I bought this ring with my first decent paycheck; then I made up a whole story about how it had been left to me by my wonderful father."

He stares at it and laughs.

"Silly, really, but you know what? Sometimes when I look at it, I almost *believe* in that father."

He looks at Jess, eyes pained.

"I promise I'll tell you the truth about my life, about the games I've played, the mistakes I've made, and the ways in which I've risen above them, if you'll just give me the time. Because you're the one, Jess. You're the one I can be myself with."

She senses he's about to kiss her again. But there is Tim, lurching toward them with the most furious glower on his face.

"Mate," he says, coming between them.

Guy steps back.

"She's had enough, all right? I'm not sure what you think you're playing at here, but—"

"Oh, I'm not playing," says Guy. "I'm deadly serious."

"Wise guy, are you?" Tim sneers.

"Just Guy, actually."

Guy offers a handshake. Tim puffs out his chest, plays for dignity, but refuses the shake. After a moment, Guy retracts.

Tim looks to Jess. "Are you okay? Do you need me to get someone to escort this . . . desperado out of the pub?"

"Desperado?" says Guy. "What . . . you can't take a bit of healthy competition, my quote-unquote 'mate'?"

Tim inhales, eyes bulging.

"You're hardly competition," he growls. "She's with me. She isn't interested. You've teased her with her grandmother's necklace for weeks, and now you've got the cheek to barge into her family wake and act like you're some kind of jumped-up heroic Romeo. But my instinct is that you're merely a freeloader. Always were, always will be. Leopards don't change."

At this, a veil of anger shadows Guy's face. His whole body tenses. Tim stares him down.

Don't fight, Jess wills them. *Anything but that.*

Too late. Guy attempts to put Tim in his place with a dismissive flick of the hand. Tim flies back at him, fists in the air. But being unaccustomed to pub brawls, he misses and stumbles into a stack of chairs. He gets up, wipes his brow, has a second go. On both sides, there is some shoving, scrapping, a definite attempt to tug hair. Then they stumble apart, breathless and messy. And then, just in time, Jess's dad returns with a tray of frothing amber pints.

"So." He grins, oblivious. "How are we getting on? Here you go, Tim. Get this down you and—"

Suddenly he spies the necklace in Jess's hands. The color drains out of his face, and he drops the entire tray of drinks to the floor.

"Where . . . where did you get that?"

"From Nancy," says Jess. "She made me find it before she died."

"How?" He looks aghast. "How could she? I made sure—"

Jess cocks her head.

"You knew about it?"

"Of course I bloody knew about it!" he yells, and then without a goodbye, he storms out of the pub.

"Well," says Aggie, smarting in the corner, her red lips pursed, "*this* has all gone how I hoped it would."

Meanwhile, regardless of what Tim would like to do to Guy, the bar staff save him the pleasure. They pick Guy up by the scruff of his shirt and walk him toward the door.

"You need some fresh air, mate."

"I'm not your mate," Guy protests, but the staff are unmoved.

As he's carried away, he calls to Jess: "Let's have an adventure, you and me! Arms wide open!"

And then he is gone. And the pub is silent. And Jess feels like crawling into the biggest hole she can find and never coming out.

But first she has to face Aggie, whose big-sister scowl says: *Jessica Taylor, you've got some explaining to do*. And Ed, who has leaped into brotherhood mode, ushering Tim back to the family table, telling him to stay cool. And Marcus, who is giggling uncontrollably into his games console. And then of course Steph, unlikely to ever take her aunt's romantic advice seriously again.

Jess looks across at Tim, and their eyes meet. He gives her a withering look and mouths *I love you*. He'll be apologetic later, mortally embarrassed. He'll have the good sense to admit he acted rashly, but he'll also tell her he'd do the same again if it means protecting their relationship. He'll always be loyal.

Yet her heart screams to check on Guy. She owes him that.

She finds him in the street. He is pacing, looking out for a cab. His lip is bloody.

"Wait!" she cries. "Oh! Is your mouth okay?"

"Bah, it's nothing," he says with dented pride.

"I'm sorry," she whispers. "Tim isn't normally like that . . ."

Guy, smiling, runs a hand through his curls. "To be honest, Jess, I'd do it again. I've got an idea for us, you see. I was thinking—"

Jess sighs. Here he goes again.

"One last shot," he says. "I'm going away—and I think you should come with me. That tip-off I got at the Capital Gala was about an antique ruby brooch in Cape Verde. For a good old boy who wants it for his sick wife. I'm taking the seven twenty ship from Southampton two weeks from Saturday. I thought you might prefer a ship to a plane. We'll travel old school. Treasure hunter's way."

Jess shuts her eyes. Somewhere in her mind there is space for this, a space that says YES! But it's not a space she can venture to right now. Guy nods, as though the action will persuade her.

"I know there's Education Tim to think of," he continues. "He's obviously a nice person—despite calling me a desperado and trying to punch me, but"—he gives her a wink—"he's not the guy for you. *I'm* the Guy. Hey, did you hear what I did there?"

"Everything's a joke to you," says Jess, exasperated.

"But you like a joke."

"Guy, you have to leave me alone. I feel secure with Tim. We have plans. We have a future. Meeting you, I kind of think it's been a test, to see whether Tim and I really are meant to work out—"

"A test? Jess, I think about you all the time. And . . . you're trying to tell me you think it's just a test. Are you kidding?"

Jess looks down. "And we passed," she says solemnly. "I know what I need in life, and I'm sorry, Guy, but it's not you."

He frowns, the hurt etched into his face.

"What, Jess, what is it about me that you're so afraid of?"

She shrugs, holds up her walking cane.

"This," she says, suddenly teary. "Going through all this again. You said it yourself. You're not able to give me guarantees. But Tim is. So if you really care about me, then you'll leave me alone."

A cab pulls up. Guy opens the door, hopeful that she'll change her mind. But Jess stands resolute. Eventually he climbs in, then slams the door and looks ahead. The cab moves away. And this time Jess doesn't attempt to chase after it.

Chapter 11

JESS PUTS THE NECKLACE in its purple box and tucks it away in a drawer. The next day, she adds the boat ticket Guy has sent her, passage to Cape Verde. His presumptuousness is both his allure and his downfall, she thinks. He messages her, asking if she received it. She doesn't respond, and he doesn't message again.

In anticipation of the move, Jess starts packing up her things. With every filled box, she feels a step closer to the rest of her life, and it feels . . . good. She even contemplates the teaching post.

Any lingering enthusiasm for the "charming thrills" end of the boyfriend spectrum is quashed completely when Steph comes home early one afternoon in a flood of tears.

"He's dumped me and gone off with Lina Bird, just because she volunteers for Greenpeace, and—"

"Jared? What a rat! He doesn't deserve you, Stephanie Hoppit!"

"But he's my one. Always. I'll *never* stop loving him."

"You will," says Jess softly. "One day, really soon. You'll meet someone else, and they'll show you a different kind of love. And it'll be a better love. Or maybe it will be worse. But either way, it will teach what you *do* want in life and what you don't."

Steph wipes her tears with her sleeve.

"Thanks," sniffs Steph. "But don't tell my mum, will you? She'll only say 'told you so.'"

"I won't. But I think *you* should. Your mum can actually be great in a heartache. She's nursed me through a few, and never once has she said 'I told you so.' Well, once or twice, maybe, but—"

"What about that man at Nancy's funeral? You know, the one you kissed in front of everyone."

Jess winces. "We had a bit of chemistry between us . . . a lot of chemistry, in fact . . . but . . . in the end, it wasn't to be."

"But you got the feels?"

"Yes. No. Look, if you must know, a few years ago, yes, I would have totally 'got the feels' for someone like that. But now I want something different. I want to feel grounded."

"Oh." Steph looks disappointed. "It's just . . . That kiss, Aunty, it was . . . proper."

"No," Jess says with a sigh. "It was a show. Some men like to put on a show. That doesn't mean we should applaud."

LATER that afternoon, when she's packing jewelry, her heart weary, Jess's father calls. She resists the urge to answer, but then he calls a second time and then a third. Finally, her curiosity caves.

"Hello?"

"Jess, oh Jess, you answered. I didn't know if you—"

"What do you want?"

"I realize I may have some explaining to do. I'm sorry I left the wake like that. It wasn't my plan to. Could . . . could we meet?"

Jess exhales, stares at the wall clock.

"When?"

"I'm your way this afternoon. I thought, maybe, we could lay some flowers on Nancy's grave, if . . . if you're up for it?"

"Yes," says Jess, too tired to battle. "Yes, okay."

THEY meet at the entrance gates of Abney Park Cemetery, both with bunches of flowers. Jess has assembled some wildflowers and bracken, knowing they were Nancy's favorites. He smiles at her; then his attention catches on the necklace.

"Looks nice on you, Jessy," he forces himself to say. "Do you wear it a lot?"

"Yes. It makes me feel close to Nancy."

"So where exactly did you find it?" he says, eyeing her.

"At auction. Nancy described this necklace to me in detail. She was passionate about it. So for months I kept my eye out, and then one day it popped up on my screen and I knew straightaway it was the one. Coming home to us. Like it was meant to."

"Because I have to tell you, Jess, when I sold it, I never for a second thought I'd see it again. Honestly, I took it to the most obscure backstreet dealer I could find."

Jess narrows her eyes.

"So it was you? You're the reason it came out of our family."

"Yes."

"But it was my mother's heirloom," she quarrels. "All that history . . . It was never yours to sell."

"No," he says limply. "You're right. It wasn't."

They walk through the graves, row after row of headstones.

"So why *did* you sell it?" she asks after a moment.

"You know your mother believed it was charmed," he says, "that it had mystical power. She had some idea that it lured me to her. Some French nonsense. There's a word on the back, right?"

"Yes," says Jess. "It just says '*OUI.*'"

"That's right. She used to say she finally understood the meaning of the word the day she met me, that I made her come out of herself. Carmen was a shy one, you see. But I gave her confidence. Believe it or not, Jess, I was once a social dynamo."

"Hmm."

"The thing is she'd had a funny old upbringing, Carmen, after her dad died—"

"Paul?"

"Yes, that's right. He died when she was young, and soon after, Nancy went off to do her own thing, so Carmen was left in the care of her grandmother, Anna."

They walk on, the birdsong following them.

"Anna had a lot of opinions about how Carmen should be. Quite a snob, hell-bent on marrying Carmen off to the nearest available banker. But two days after Carmen's fifteenth birthday, Nancy came back, very different from how Carmen said she remembered her. Apparently her hair was spiked and dyed purple."

That's Nancy, thinks Jess.

"One thing hadn't changed," says Richard. "Nancy was still wearing the necklace. That night, she gave the necklace to Carmen, said it was *her* turn, made her promise to wear it."

"And did she?"

"Not straightaway. Under Anna's influence she was busy with a secretarial course. Then the following summer she enrolled in art college, much more her thing, where she befriended two punks with shaved hair. They took her to a music festival, told her to dress wild. Since the butterfly necklace was the wildest thing she owned, with a pair of jeans and a cardigan, that's what she wore."

"What festival?"

"Glastonbury, 1982."

Jess blinks. "Glastonbury?"

"The mud was biblical, Jess. I don't think Carmen had seen anything like it. Within an hour she'd lost track of her college friends, so she forced herself through her shyness, bought a pint of cider, and trudged across the mudscape. She came to the main stage, where Jackson Browne was performing—one of the last musicians her father had photographed before he died.

"As the crowds danced and cheered, she was happy. It didn't matter that she was freezing, soaked, and *way* out of her depth. She was just so happy. Then someone fell into her, caked from head to toe in gray sludge. Carmen gasped and backed away; then, through the filth, she saw the shine of his piercing green eyes, which then fell to the wings of the necklace. 'I'm Richard,' he said, and their faces lit up with smiles."

"You?" says Jess, amazed. "You met at Glastonbury?"

She can't help but smile, the thought of her frumpy, fusty father in a field full of rock music and chai tents.

"Oh yeah. We were right in the thick of it. Me with my mud suit, and your mum with her necklace. And that was it for me. In all that rain and mud, there she was, my Carmen, a jewel in the dirt."

"But if the necklace brought you together," Jess presses, her bitterness resurfacing, "why get rid of it the minute she's dead?"

Richard bows his head, folds his arms.

"Perhaps its magic wore off," he says, shoving his hands in his pockets. "Because it didn't remind me of our union in the end. It reminded me of what went wrong. I loved her, Jess, but—"

"Don't tell me. She met someone else."

"Why do you say that?"

"Because that's what all the women in my family have done when in possession of the necklace. They've run off and found happiness with some random other man."

"No, Jess. It wasn't your mother who met someone else. It was *me*. With Eileen. You have to understand . . . Your mother and I, we were in love, but we grew apart. Having you girls changed me. I stopped being the fun, zany guy. I started working all the time, worrying about money, taking it out on her, yelling and sulking."

"That still doesn't explain why you sold off her necklace."

He stops again, breathes slowly. *He looks beaten,* she thinks.

"After her death," he says, "I felt so angry. Angry at the world. Angry at myself. Angry at Nancy, who clearly blamed me, not for your mother's stroke, but . . . Her final year, it wasn't a happy one. We were arguing a lot. I'd started my thing with Eileen. Honestly, it's a miracle you girls turned out so well—"

"That's debatable," says Jess solemnly.

He sighs. "Anyway, after your mother died, that necklace sat in the house, and it was as if it were glaring at me, some kind of cruel souvenir of what we'd had, what *I* had thrown away. Eventually I couldn't take it anymore, so I took it to a dealer on the Commercial Road. Got twenty quid for it, which I drank away in a weekend."

"Dad! Do you know how much it's now worth?"

He shrugs.

"When Nancy discovered I'd sold it, we had a crazy, crazy argument. Nancy called me a coward, and I told her she was a coldhearted madwoman who'd failed her daughter. And that was it, the fault line in our relationship. We were never friendly again."

"No," says Jess. "I saw that."

"She really resented Eileen and the twins, but . . . For me, that was my chance to put the mistakes behind me, get things right, even if it meant"—he looks down—"failing you girls."

As he says this, he steps back, stalled by regret. She breathes hard; then she leans forward on the tips of her toes and kisses him once, on the cheek—because in spite of it all, he was, is, and always will be her father. And he has a tear in his eye. And she now knows that he is sorry, truly, deeply sorry.

A few steps on, they find Nancy in the sun. The earth is still fresh. Jess kneels down and places her flowers at the stone.

"In spite of everything," her father says, "there was something about the old girl I admired. I mean . . . she was a one."

"Yes," says Jess, "she really was."

They walk on together, take the long path around to the exit.

"Oh, look," says Richard as they pass the final row of graves. "Talking of the past, there is your great-grandmother's headstone. Anna Elizabeth Taylor. Like the film actress."

Jess blinks. "That's *her?* That's Anna?"

"What? You mean, you didn't know? I thought that's why you chose Abney Park Cemetery."

"We didn't," says Jess. "It was stipulated in Nancy's will. So . . . do you really think that's our Anna?"

"Oh yes, your mother brought me here when we were dating. She said it gave her peace to be here. I only knew Anna briefly, but as I said, she was quite a force. Once engaged to a movie producer. And did you know Nancy was—"

"Born in Hollywood," they both say together, smiling.

Before they move on, Jess kneels beside Anna's grave.

"Anna Elizabeth Taylor," she reads, "1913 to 1982."

Then her gaze catches on the headstone beside it.

"Archie Marshall Jossop, 1914 to 1983. Beloved to Anna."

She gasps. Anna and Archie, so they *were* reunited.

"Oh my," she says. "Right here. There's a love story right here."

"There certainly is," says her dad. "Archie was an old boy Anna knew from her Hollywood days. Your mum was rather fond, said he made Anna happy."

"Tell me," says Jess.

"From what I gather, it happened out of nowhere. Carmen had been out, back to Denmark Street to sign paperwork for her late father's business premises. That afternoon she returned to the house with a guest. I remember the moment . . . the way he walked in beside her. 'Well, I'll be damned!' he said. 'If it isn't Anna Taylor!' An old boy, he was, face lined, salt-and-pepper gray. But how he smiled! 'Oh, Anna,' he said, 'you're not gonna believe this, but there I was, making my way down Denmark Street!'

"He claimed he was in the market for a new guitar, that he'd been browsing the shops when he bumped into Carmen. He'd had to look twice because he recognized her face, but couldn't get the age right in his head. Then he spotted the necklace. He ran straight after her, asked outright: 'You're not related to an Anna Taylor, are you?' 'Well, sure,' said Carmen. 'She's my grandmother!'"

Jess smiles, delighted. "So what happened then?"

"He came back with Carmen and joined us for tea. 'Oh, Anna,' he said, 'have I had a life!' He told us all about how he'd taken off from his family farm when the war needed Americans, that he thought he'd be fighting for glory, then found himself running for his life. He said it had messed with his head, and for a while he'd lost his way. When all that nonsense was over, he decided to stay in England, try his luck in the music industry."

"So?" says Jess.

"He was tone deaf. Anyway, he got on with life, got himself a little business, wholesale belts and handbags. Did all right, five warehouses and a nice place in Holland Park. Do you know, he'd lived in London for twenty-two years before bumping into Carmen? Married once. Divorced once. Three grown kids. But the way he looked at Anna . . . even I felt it. He talked to her about brisket, had a lot to say about brisket. But all I could see was Anna smiling, flinging her bony, seventy-year-old arms around his shoulders and saying: 'Archie Jossop, I've been waiting for you!'"

"Oh wow!" Jess sniffs, wipes her tears—happy tears. "So the necklace finally brought them back together!"

"Yes, I suppose it did," says her dad. "He certainly became a fixture after that. He and Anna were inseparable."

"Do you have more stories?"

"Plenty."

"Then maybe we should talk more," she says.

"Yes," says her dad kindly, "maybe we should. Perhaps . . . in a few weeks you could come over, you and Aggie, come for lunch. And bring . . . whatshisname?"

"Tim."

"That's it, Tim."

"Did you like him? You know we're moving in together."

"He was . . . pleasant. But I kind of liked that other fellow, the bounder with the kiss. Now *that* one had something about him."

Jess sighs. "Oh, please. Not you as well."

"The thing is, Jessy, I learned the hard way. I ignored my heart and followed my head. And I messed up the thing that mattered most. Your mother was the love of my life. And I blew it because I was so fussed about being sensible and keeping control. Don't make the same mistake I did. Listen to your heart." He pauses, then adds, "Do you know what your mum would have said?"

"What?"

"Trust the necklace."

Chapter 12

Tim is alone in his classroom, scheduling staff for the forthcoming school year. He sees Jess approach and smiles.

"A lunchtime surprise! To what do I owe this pleasure?"

But immediately he senses something's different.

There is a tightness in her brow. She is wearing that old-fashioned butterfly necklace again, and somehow, the fact of this feels significant. It wallops him in the chest, the sense of what's coming, what he has known would come all along.

"Hmm," he says, rocking back on his chair. "Something's up?"

Jess smiles, but there are telltale signs of old tears in her eyes.

"I've been doing some thinking," she says.

"Sounds ominous."

She clutches her hands in front of her. She looks so delicate, and he wants to put his arms around her, to protect her, but . . . this is not what she wants. He understands that now.

"I get the feeling I know what you've come here to say," he says as gently as he can. It's hurting her to do this, and so it should, but he'll make it easy. He'll be a gentleman.

"Come here," he says, taking her hand, pulling her close.

A tear trickles down her cheek. He wipes it with his fingertip.

"You've given me so much," she whispers. "You've restored my confidence. You've made me feel loved when I was lost. But, above all, you've showed me that there really are smart, kind, mature men who can cope with conversations about babies and house buying.

But"—the tears flow freely now—"as much as I'd like to share all of that with you, in my heart, I know I can't. I'm not ready. I might never be ready. I'm not . . . *wired* that way."

"It's okay," he says, squeezing her hand. "It's okay. I knew. I *knew* it was coming. I've denied it for ages. I could tell you were always edging away. And that's what you have to do. I get it."

She sniffs, reaches into her bag, takes out the key to the Stratford apartment. "This is yours," she says, pressing it into his hand.

It's a sting to the soul, but he braces himself, smiles through it.

"Thanks," he says. "So what now?"

"I'm thinking of going on a trip," she says.

"With *him?*"

"Maybe," she says after a pause. "I'm really sorry."

He groans, the leaden truth hammering into him.

"The fact is, Jess, that day at your grandmother's wake, when he stormed in and kissed you . . . as mad as I was, deep down, I *knew*. I could never kiss you like that, with so much *pizzazz*. It's not my way. But it's *your* way. So . . . I understand."

Now she sobs.

"You're *so* good! And one day really soon you'll meet someone who's perfect for you and you'll blow them away." She gives a wry little laugh. "Is it right that I already feel jealous of them?"

"No, it's not," says Tim, more bitterly than intended, "because you've made your choice, but . . . thanks for the compliment."

She sighs, frowns, then kisses him lightly and walks away.

JESS hastens to the exit, sorrow like a rock in her throat. In her wretchedness, she can only question her judgment. Has she just taken a pass on the best option she might ever have?

But as she reaches the door, she catches sight of the "who's who" staff photographs in the lobby, spots three new starters beaming out. One of them is an attractive fortysomething woman with auburn waves and an open smile. She is wearing a shiny charm necklace, not dissimilar to the one that Tim bought Jess; and beneath her photo, her interests are listed as history, cricket, and cycling. Jess smiles, feels the bud of hope returning. There is someone for everyone. As she exits, a second wave of emotion washes over her, and this one is elation. Elation mixed with clarity.

She finds the ticket in the drawer where she hid it, trying to forget its presence. With a rush of adrenaline, realizes there are only four hours until the boat leaves. She messages Guy.

Are you still sailing? Doughnuts x

No reply. In haste, she throws her favorite dresses and jewels into her backpack. A toothbrush. Sandals. Swimsuit. What else? What is this trip all about? How long will it last? Where will it lead? All these questions—and she doesn't want the answers. The not knowing is the thrill, a reminder of what it is to go chasing into the unknown, hunting for treasure, whatever that may be.

As she drags her backpack down the stairs, clattering her cane against the banisters, she hears the front door click. Aggie flusters through, takes one look at Jess's baggage, and balks.

"What? You're not moving already, are you? I thought the flat wasn't finished until October?"

Jess sighs, braces herself.

"Actually, I'm not moving into the flat."

"Oh?"

"Actually, I broke up with Tim."

"You . . . *broke up?*"

Aggie's mouth drops open.

"Oh, come on, Aggie. You know me better than anyone."

"But . . . *Tim!* Perfect Tim, with his really good job." She blinks, the horror building as she processes. "You can't. You . . . *can't.* What are you going to do? How are you going to live?"

Jess sighs. "I'm going away for a while. Guy bought me a boat ticket. To Cape Verde. To find a long-lost ruby for an old general."

Now Aggie is incredulous.

"You cannot be serious, Jess? This is madness. Besides, I thought . . . I thought we were *done* with all of that—"

"No, Aggie, *you* were done. I was always . . . confused. I've listened to you enough, too much probably. I value your opinion, and I love you to the ends of the earth, but you need to understand that I'm different than you. I want different things from life, and that doesn't make me better off or worse off. Just different."

"Oh, Jessy . . ."

Her ire now turns to tears. Jess softens, takes her hands.

"Aggie, this is about me. Not what you want for me. But what *I* want for me."

"But can you trust that man? You hardly know him."

"I realize it's nuts, but it's making me feel *alive* again. I don't think I want a settled life. I don't even know if I want children. I adore yours, but nothing in me seems to want my own. I can't funnel myself into the wrong-shaped life just because the world assumes it of me. Please, you have to understand—"

"Oh, Jess," Aggie sobs, "why do I feel like my nexus of control is collapsing?"

She squeezes her sister super tight.

"I love you to the ends of the earth too," Aggie whispers. "And I'm proud of you. And . . . maybe, deep down, maybe I wish I was more like you. Because believe it or not, sometimes . . . sometimes *I* wish I could let go and do something out there too."

Jess brushes the teary waves of hair from her sister's face.

"Aggie," she says, smiling, "you can do whatever you want to do. You're a Taylor."

She catches sight of the time.

"Oh no. If I don't leave now, I won't make it. Oh —"

She dithers. She hasn't thought this through.

"Where are you headed?"

"Southampton dock."

"Give me your bag," says Aggie. "I'll drive you."

"Really?" Jess beams at her sister.

"I've been looking for an excuse to go flat out in the Merc. Ed doesn't allow me to go over sixty."

And with matching grins, they exit the house, jump into the car, and take off, almost literally, leaving Ed, who is just wheeling his bike up the street, to blink and wonder.

"There. It's *there,*" says Jess, pointing at the sign for the passenger terminal.

Aggie swings the car right.

"Shall I drop you? Shall I park? Is there time?"

Jess checks her phone. Half an hour to spare. But Guy still hasn't replied to her message. The thought dawns on her that all this go-get-your-man exhilaration might be for nothing.

"I don't know, Aggie. I think, drop me. I'll figure it out."

"Okay," says Aggie, "but if you need me . . . I won't drive home just yet. And you'll call when you get there? And you'll send us lots of pictures? And when you get back—"

"We'll come for Hoppit Sunday lunch."

"Promise."

"Of course," says Jess. "And . . . one more thing . . . I had a chat with Steph last week. I think she and Jared have had a wobble—"

"Hooray!" cries Aggie.

"Just go gently with her, won't you?"

Aggie growls.

"Aggie, perspective! When we were young, Dad had to worry about whether our boyfriends were sneaking us into illegal raves. If all you've got to worry about is whether Jared is going to lecture you that eggs Benedict is a sin, then count yourself lucky."

"But I want her to have options—"

"Aggie! Steph is only *sixteen*. Let her go on her journey."

Jess smiles at her sister, then kisses her cheek.

"Thank you," she says.

"Thank *you,*" says Aggie.

And with that, the Taylor sisters part.

With her backpack and her cane, Jess marches through the terminal. Her legs feel good. The discomfort in her hip is distinctly diminished. Perhaps, she thinks, the pain is starting to become a lesser feature of her daily life. At the kiosk, she hands over her ticket and her passport, all the while furtively looking around her, looking for *him*. She breathes slowly, tries to still her nerves.

"Oh boy," she reassures herself. "It'll be fine. Whatever happens in the next ten minutes, it will be *fine!*"

"You all right?" says the man in the ticket office.

"Oh yes," she says, grinning to mask her spiraling apprehension.

"You've only got twenty minutes. If you hurry down there, you'll find the foot passenger entrance. That'll get you straight on deck; then someone will show you to your cabin."

"Thank you," she says.

But then a thought catches. Jess raises her hand to her neck, feels the pulse of the necklace, its wings beating the rhythm of her heart.

"Excuse me," she asks, "how do I get back to visitor parking?"

The man shrugs. "At the other end of the terminal, but . . . you'll struggle to make it there and back before—"

"I'll chance it," says Jess, staggering away as fast as her crooked hip will allow.

She pulls out her phone, calls Aggie, who answers immediately.

"What? Is everything okay?"

"There's something I forgot. Where are you parked?"

"Next to a yellow bollard. . . . I can see you . . . I'm waving."

Jess spots Aggie in the distance and works up to a run—the first since the accident. She arrives panting, flustered, a little overawed, then hastily removes the necklace and hands it to Aggie.

Aggie blinks. "No offense," she says, "but I don't want this. It's really not my style."

"Not you, Aggie. It's for Steph. Give it to Steph. Tell her . . . when the time is right . . . It just might help."

Jess gives her sister a final hug, then runs/hobbles back to the terminal. She reaches the boarding gate, shoves through it just in time, joy blooming within her. She looks around the deck, but he isn't anywhere. A crew member offers to show her to her cabin. Perhaps he'll be waiting inside or has left some hint of his presence . . .

But the cabin is undisturbed, pristine. Ah well.

Jess flops back on the bed and stares at the ceiling. What was it Bevan Floyd told her about soul mates . . . they fly into your life for a reason, then they leave. Certainly, it happened to Minnie and Emery. Then Anna had a long time without her Archie. Nancy lost

Paul. Carmen lost herself. And now . . . Jess is here and Guy is not. Could it be that he brought her to this point, then fluttered away?

She gets up again, goes to the outdoor deck. The sun is just starting to set, a smear of peach and pink. She leans over the balustrade, faces the breeze. It will be okay, she tells herself. She is a Taylor, and it will be okay. Guy played his part—a soul mate's way—helping her move forward in her life. Maybe that's enough?

She blinks back her tears, takes a bolstering breath.

But then she feels a hand slide beside hers. She looks down, sees two emerald leopard eyes gazing up at her.

"You're here!" she gasps.

"So are you," says Guy.

"Oui," she says with an enormous smile.

He takes hold of her shoulders, then scans her neck, concern on his face. "But . . . you're not wearing your butterfly?"

"I passed it on. I think . . . I think it served its purpose for me."

And, sure enough, as she takes in the glow of Guy's face, she realizes the vibrancy between them is there regardless, necklace or otherwise. Her heart beats so fast, it's as if a billion plique-à-jour butterflies have taken it over. And they are all with her, she thinks, agreeing with her: Minnie, Anna, Nancy. And Carmen.

The boat sounds its horn. The fresh sea air whips up.

"So," says Guy, "are you ready for an adventure, Doughnuts?"

Her eyes flash with the thrill.

"I couldn't be more ready," she replies.

Then they curve together, laughing and kissing, the entire world ahead of them, the sunset in their eyes—and the love between them now ready to fly.

After*Words*

When Louisa Leaman set out to become an author, the last thing she expected to write was romantic fiction. She penned children's books, nonfiction guides, and even fantasy—but never romance. "I didn't consider myself a romantic kind of person," she says, "at least not in the conventional way."

However, given how well romance was selling, she figured she'd give it a try. She was worried she'd find the usual tropes—the meet-cutes, the happily ever afters—too restrictive, but she found the process surprisingly enjoyable. "What I've learned," she explains, "is that, at its core, romantic fiction is about human interaction."

Now, with several romance novels under her belt, Leaman finds genuine satisfaction in portraying the emotional intimacy between two characters. "I want to show on the page my belief that the best kind of romance, the most meaningful kind," she says, "happens when two people are willing to let their guards down and be vulnerable." According to Leaman, this is the idea behind *The Lost and Found Necklace*—that opening your heart can help move you forward, "not just in your relationship, but within yourself."

Leaman was born and raised in Epping Forest, Essex, England. In addition to publishing novels, she also writes for the Victoria and Albert Museum. She currently lives in Woodford Green, England, with her husband and three children.

GIRL
IN
ICE
A NOVEL
ERICA FERENCIK
AUTHOR OF INTO THE JUNGLE AND THE RIVER AT NIGHT

Chapter 1

Seeing the name "Wyatt Speeks" in my in-box hit me like a physical blow. Everything rushed back: the devastating phone call, the disbelief, the image of my brother's frozen body in the Arctic wasteland.

I shut my laptop, pasted a weak smile on my face. There would be no tears at school. Grief was for after hours, for the nightly bottle of merlot, for my dark apartment, for waking on the couch at dawn, the blue light of the TV caressing my aching flesh.

No, at the moment my job was to focus on the fresh, eager face of my graduate student as she petitioned for a semester in Tibet, a project in a village deep in the Himalayas accessible only via mountain passes on foot and maybe llama, all to decipher a newly discovered language. As I listened to her impassioned plea—trying to harness my racing heart—an old shame suffused me.

The truth was, I'd never embarked into the field anyplace more frightening than a local graveyard to suss out a bit of Old English carved into a crumbling stone marker. Never had my curiosity about a place or a language and its people overridden my *Just say no* reflex. I'd declined a plum semester-long gig in the Andean mountains of Peru to study quipu, or "talking knots"—cotton strings of differing lengths tied to a cord carried from village to village by runners, each variation in the string signaling municipal facts: taxes paid or owed; births and deaths; notices of famine, drought, crop failure, and so on. I'd even passed on the once-in-a-lifetime chance to deconstruct a language carved into the two-thousand-year-old Longyou caves in Quzhou, China.

Why?

Anxiety: the crippling kind. I'm tethered to the familiar, the safe. I function normally in only a handful of locations: my apartment, places on campus—excluding the football stadium, too much open space—the grocery store, my father's nursing home.

Ironically, I was the one with the power to give or withhold the stamp of approval for my students' research trips, as if I were any judge of risk and character. Watching the glistening eyes of the young woman before me, one of my favorite students, I stalled a few moments as I attempted to soak up her magic normalcy. No such luck. I signed off on her trip to Tibet, wondering, *How does she see me, really?* I swear I caught a glint of pity in her eyes, of disdain. It was like she knew my secret. Her teacher was a fraud.

I'm a linguist. I can get by in German and most Romance tongues, and I've got a soft spot for dead languages: Latin, Sanskrit, ancient Greek. But it's the extinct tongues—Old Norse and Old Danish—that enrapture me.

Languages reveal what it is to be human. This desire to make ourselves understood is primal. We make marks on paper, babble snippets of sound—then agree, by way of miracle, that these scribblings or syllables actually mean something, all so we can touch each other in some precise way. Sanskrit has ninety-six words for love, from the love of a new mother for her baby to one for unrequited romantic love, but it has twice as many for grief. My favorite is *sokaparayana,* which means "wholly given up to sorrow." A strange balm of a word, gentle coming off my tongue.

Though words came easily for me, I tended to miss the patterns that were staring me in the face. The fact that my ex genuinely wanted out didn't hit me until divorce papers were served. The fact of my father passing from just old to genuinely ill with lung cancer and not-here-for-much-longer didn't sink in until I was packing up the family home and found myself on my knees in tears, taken down by *dolor repentino,* a fit of sudden pain. The stark realization that my twin brother, Andy—the closest person in the world to me—had been pulling away for months came to me only after his death and at the very worst times: lecturing in a packed auditorium, conversing with the dean in the hallway. When it happened, these vicious, sudden, psychic stabs, I'd close my eyes and repeat to myself: *sokaparayana, sokaparayana,* until I could speak again.

I felt safest in my office, with my books, charts, runic symbols, and old texts; and when I deciphered a chunk of language—even a word!—a thrill of understanding juddered up my spine. The distance between me and another human being, for that moment, was erased. It was as if someone were speaking to me, and me alone.

For two decades, these glimmers of connection had been enough to sustain me, but over time, they began to lose their shine. I yearned to be drawn closer to the human heart. Not through words, however telling or ingenious, but in the living world.

At precisely eight o'clock that night—the end of office hours—I got up and locked the door. Squared my shoulders, smoothed my skirt, and sat back down. Outside my window, remorseless late August sun cast long shadows across the quad.

I clicked open my email. I was in no mood to hear from Professor Speeks about my brother, his fond recollections of mentoring Andy through the rigors of grad school, or even some funny thing Andy had said during their year together on the ice.

I considered deleting the message without reading it, but a tingling buzzed my fingers. Something said: *Don't.* So I opened it.

From: Wyatt.Speeks@ArcticGreenlandScience.org
To: VChesterfield@Brookview.edu

Hey Val, hope you're doing well, all things considered. Something's happened out here. We found a body in the ice out on Glacier 35A. A young girl. We were able to cut through the ice and bring her back to the compound. Val, she thawed out alive. Don't ask me to explain it, I can't. She's eight, nine years old, I'm guessing. And she's talking pretty much nonstop, but in a language I've never heard before. Even Pitak, our supply runner from Qaanaaq, had no idea, and he speaks Inuktun. Jeanne's stumped too, so we're both just keeping the girl fed and nodding our heads a lot and trying to figure out what to do next.

I've pasted here one of her vocalizations. Maybe you can figure out what she's saying? You're the expert. Give it a try, then call me. And please don't tell anyone about this.

Wyatt

The girl *thawed out alive?*

Sweat bloomed on my brow, even though the air conditioner was blasting. I got up, walked to my window, sat back down. Checked the time: too early for a pill. I rattled open my file drawer, extracted a bottle of Amaretto, and filled my coffee mug halfway. The sweet, warm alcohol hit my empty stomach fast.

I thought about all the times I'd let Andy's voice play in my head these past five months, how he was still so alive for me in this way. Memories of us as kids chasing each other through the lake house in upstate New York, T-shirts still damp from swimming. Or cozied up with our beloved mutt Frida, playing cards.

Little by little I'd pored over the photos, letting myself "feel everything," as my shrink instructed. Mourning every shirt and shoe, I gave away or got rid of his clothes and belongings; though I couldn't part with his drawings. The only other place he lived on was in my phone: a dozen saved messages remained.

Now, on my screen, the forward arrow on the voice clip Wyatt had sent throbbed red. My finger pushed the PLAY button.

The first slam to my gut was the panic in this high, sweet girl voice that—even if you didn't understand a word she said—made you want to reach out and wrap her in a hug. The tremulous ache in her utterly foreign words only intensified in the twenty-eight-second clip, as if she was pleading. I tried to picture this child trapped in the ice, to imagine what horrors had brought her there.

I played it again. *What language is this?*

Of course, West Greenlandic was my first guess, but I heard no correlation. Greenland had been settled by Danes—but no, this was Danish put through a blender and mixed with what, *Finnish?* Not quite that either. The vowels were too long, the accent on the last syllable. It wasn't Norwegian, clearly, and it was too clipped and choppy to be Swedish. I pulled up some Old Norse, the language of the Vikings, and listened alongside the girl's quavering voice. The cadences were similar in places, but I couldn't match up a single word. This language was completely new to me.

I was lost.

I sat back. Tried to recall all I knew linguistically about where Wyatt was—where Andy had died.

Three main dialects of Greenlandic were spoken in Greenland: West Greenlandic, East Greenlandic, and Inuktun, which had only about a thousand native speakers. In grad school, I'd been fascinated by this culture built from animal skin, sinew, bone, stone, snow, and ice, but in the end, I became more of a generalist. I deciphered languages quickly, given enough context and clues.

I got up and paced, holding my drink. The reality was, I didn't *have* to do anything. I *could* pretend I never opened the email. Ignore Wyatt's calls. All I wanted was to crawl back home and hide with my booze and my misery and never come out.

If only I hadn't heard her voice! I could have forgotten the whole thing. But even after the clip stopped playing, I could still hear her, feel the sound, a high thrum in my jaw. Talking to Wyatt brought back all the horror with Andy, but *who was this girl?*

It's just a phone call, Val, I thought. *You can do this.*

I knocked back the rest of my Amaretto and picked up the landline to dial Wyatt halfway around the world at his climate research station on Tarrarmiut Island, translated "land of shadows," off Greenland's northwest coast. Already my palm was slick with sweat as I listened to the odd *dud-dud-dud* of the international call. If it wasn't too cloudy, and the antennae hadn't been ripped away by the near constant fifty-mile-per-hour winds, the satellite call would go through, and there would be simply no going back.

The next day, I pushed through the doors of my father's nursing home, wondering how many more Saturday mornings I would spend with him—out of a sense of obligation, or some fantasy that one day he might like me. Or, more practically, how many more Saturday mornings he would be here on earth.

I signed in on a clipboard at the nursing station counter.

"Hey, Val," said Carla, the head nurse. "How's it going?"

She knew about Andy and was a good person, but I plastered on a fake smile because I just didn't feel like sharing for one second how it was actually going. "How's my dad today?" I asked.

"He's good," she said. "Hates the new activity schedule. Skipped breakfast again." She glanced at a form she'd been filling out when I walked in, before looking back up at me. "He's in the lounge."

"Thanks," I said, now fully anticipating a dad storm cloud and suddenly glad to be sneaking in a box of caramels, which were his favorite, though forbidden on his diabetic diet.

A rehabbed hotel built in the twenties, the home retained the tang of disinfectant, air barely cooler than the heat-blasted day. Sad zebra fish mouthed dully against the glass of an aquarium.

My ninety-one-year-old dad, Dr. Joseph Chesterfield, climate scientist, once a strapping six-foot-four hard charger with a fierce intellect and fiercer temper, the terror of climate research stations around the world, sat motionless, sunk deep in the belly of his favorite wingback chair. His knobby knees jutted up higher than its arms, with several inches of hairless shin on display. He'd dragged the chair to the window for a view of the outside world, a place I knew he missed desperately.

He was fast asleep. I considered my options. I could catch up on some grading back at the office, ride the stationary bike in my bedroom for precisely three miles—

He opened one aquamarine eye. "You said ten o'clock."

"I lost track of—"

"It's ten past eleven," he stated firmly. He hitched himself up, swept back cottony wisps of hair, and gestured to a matching chair. "Sit," he said. "Contemplate the universe with me."

I dutifully lugged the chair toward where he sat in the sun.

"So, why aren't you eating, Dad?" As if I ate like a normal human being anymore either.

"I don't eat when I'm not hungry."

I handed over the caramels. Side-eyeing the staff, he tore off the clear plastic wrapping and popped a piece of candy in his mouth, almost reluctantly holding out the box in my direction.

"No, thanks."

"Watching your figure?" His eyebrows waved, as if he thought this might be a good idea.

"They're for you, Dad."

He chewed aggressively, jaw muscles flexing and dancing. Then he blew his nose into a soggy handkerchief, taking me in with watery eyes. "What have you got to say for yourself?"

"I talked to Wyatt last night."

His eyes widened. "Some kind of what . . ." His voice quavered as he cleared his throat. "New information?"

"Not about Andy." I considered not telling him a thing. "Dad, have you heard of someone thawing out alive after being frozen?"

He glared at me, then blurted, "Is this a joke?" Several nurses and residents glanced over at us.

"No," I said softly, hoping he would mimic my tone.

"Is Wyatt losing his mind out there? I know I would, after what happened with Andy and wintering over the year before. Jerk didn't even come home for the funeral."

"He couldn't leave . . . the research, remember?"

"I never liked him." He tossed the box of caramels on a nearby table. "Who called who? He called you?"

"I called him, because he sent me an email about finding a girl frozen in the ice." I leaned a little closer to him. "She woke up alive, Dad. She's speaking, talking all the time, but Wyatt can't understand what she's saying; neither can Jeanne—"

"Jeanne? That tough old bird's still out there?"

"Dad, he sent me an audio clip. I can't understand a word of it."

"Even *you* can't sort it out?"

"It's like nothing I've ever heard before."

"Let's put aside for now this thawing out alive. Where did he say he found this girl?"

"Glacier 35A—"

"He's hundreds of miles from anything. There is no indigenous population there. Never has been."

"Dad, Wyatt's not crazy. He's a lot of things, but he's not that."

My father leaned forward in his chair. "We only had his story, Val, you know? Anything could have happened out there."

"He wants me to come up. Try to talk to the girl. He'll pay my expenses, any loss of income. He wants me to come right away."

"Greenland? The Arctic Circle? *You?*" he snorted. "You've never been out of Massachusetts."

I felt helpless and sad. What good did it do to tell him I had been on a plane a few times—miserable and zonked out—but showing up for exactly one wedding and one funeral before scuttling back home like a hermit crab to its shell? No one had to remind me of my shortcomings, especially my father. I knew which twin had been the favorite, the most charming, funny, brave.

But I was the one left alive.

"Dad, I'm just telling you what he said. Of course I can't go. I've got school, and I've got . . ." I trailed off pitifully. What *did* I have? No husband, no children, just my father. Work was weird too—a sabbatical freed me next year to translate a series of books of Aramaic poetry. It had lit me up when I applied for the gig months before Andy's death; now, spending six months dragging meaning from the texts that tilted heavy on love poems felt tedious.

Dad sank deeper in his chair. "Something's going on."

"Yeah, well, clearly—"

"No, Val, listen to me." His voice grew deep. "Wyatt is up to something, and it has to do with your brother. He's a wily son of a bitch." He levered himself to his feet and grabbed his walker.

This resentment over Wyatt's closeness with Andy was not a new theme with my dad. Andy's prof had relentlessly mentored him until, one fine day, Andy earned a doctorate in climate science. Everyone at his graduation dinner could feel their affection for each other. Teacher and student acted like father and son.

Which was the problem.

"Come on." My father's face grew rigid with determination. "We're going for a walk."

At the door, he turned to me and—even though I wanted to—I couldn't look away. For just a moment, all the rage, grief, and despair I couldn't bear to feel was etched into his once handsome face. His son, his heart—the boy who melted him in ways I never could—had taken his own life, and only I was left.

I grabbed my purse and matched his halting pace down the hallway and out the double doors into Boston's summertime heat.

"You know, Val, that I don't believe your brother killed himself."

"Yes, Dad. But what are you saying?"

He banged his walker on the concrete. "Your brother," he said, "was not depressed. He was not the type—"

"Dad? Of course he was depressed. He'd been depressed for years. You didn't know him—"

"I knew him!" he shouted, spitting droplets into the air. His eyes grew wet. "He would never, ever, do something like that."

"Dad." My voice verged on a whisper. "Maybe we don't talk about this now." Sometimes I thought his grief would strike him down, take his last strength, and I wouldn't be able to survive it.

"Let me talk." He leaned heavily on his walker. "Your brother. He was sad about what we're doing to the planet, but he loved it. He—he would *never* . . ."

He wobbled, the walker's rubber tips catching on the pavement. I caught his heartbreakingly thin arm. "Dad, take a second. Sit."

I held him gently, and he let gravity sink him onto a nearby bench. "Listen, kiddo, if I wasn't such a decaying old heap of garbage, I'd be on that plane today to pay Dr. Speeks a little visit. *Right this second,* do you hear me? And *dammit* if I wouldn't get the truth," he said, searching for his handkerchief.

His paranoia about Wyatt's role in Andy's death made no sense to me. But what good would it have done to remind him that, after what was described as a normal March evening at the Tarrarmiut Arctic Science Station, where the temperature hovered at twenty below with fifty-five-below-zero wind gusts, Andy was found outside at dawn, curled up on his side, barefoot, wearing only boxer shorts. Frozen to death. No signs of a struggle.

"It's hard to accept, Dad, but—"

"But you, Val. You're young. You're strong, even though you're wasting your life pretending you're not. And you've got that break coming up at school. Whatever you call it."

"Sabbatical—"

"You *go,* understand? He's even gonna pay your way. And you know why? Because he knows you'll be able to figure out what that girl—wherever he found her—is trying to say, because *that's what you do.*" His voice caught. "That's what you've spent twenty years of your life getting good at."

Sweating in my too-heavy cotton shirt and skirt, I realized that the reason I'd even told him about the call was because I *wanted* him to change my mind. Talk some smack to the stuck person who clung to her routine of rigid control: up at six, never in bed later than ten after a *Columbo* rerun, only to stare into the dark, wondering, *Why am I so afraid, and what, exactly, am I afraid of?*

I could feel my dad watching me. He wasn't concerned about my safety or happiness. I was an implement of justice only.

"Go, Val," my father said, gripping the handles of his walker, veins bulging. "Or don't bother coming to see me anymore."

THAT night, I lost count of how many times I played the twenty-eight-second clip. Slowing the girl's voice down, speeding it up, trying to sync it with every known language in the world. *What is she saying; what does she want; what has happened to her?*

As I got drunker and more exhausted, the lines blurred and she became me as a little girl, hidden behind a brother I adored and resented in equal measure, giving inchoate voice to my own anguish. I got so drunk I finally played Andy's voice mails. I may as well have stabbed myself with a pair of scissors.

But the next morning, I awoke sober and clear. Over coffee, I played each voice mail again, erasing them as I went. I would never see Andy again. But this girl was alive. The pleading in her voice unmistakable, her suffering clear. And Wyatt had a temper—a couple of hair-raising stories Andy had shared jumped to mind. How was he with little kids? Jittery, I opened my bottle of pills and dumped them on the counter. Two weeks' worth. I'd need enough for a month, maybe more. Double doses for the plane. It could be done.

I pulled down the thick notebook of Aramaic poetry I'd committed to translating during my sabbatical. Opening to the ancient words, I felt my eyes glaze over. How could I possibly stay here, knowing I might hold the key to unlocking a living human child's desperate needs, tragedies, secrets?

I showered, dressed, and, just before leaving for class, wrote to Wyatt to ask about arrangements to get to Greenland.

He booked me on the next plane.

It left in eight days.

Chapter 2

After a ridiculous series of security checks at four in the morning, I stood swaying under the harsh lighting of the military waiting area of the airport, a bleary, semi-destroyed version of myself. Smacked down by Ativan, I reminded myself over and over that I only had to do one thing: *Get on the plane.* I rubbed salve on my hands—my skin always a bellwether of my sanity—though no amount of lotion seemed to touch this eczema.

A monstrous black cargo plane brooded on the rain-slick runway. Workers loaded crates of machinery and supplies through a two-story-high cargo door. *How will this beast lift itself from the earth?*

The flight to Thule, Greenland, the U.S. Air Force's northernmost base, was only the first leg to Wyatt's frozen island eight hundred miles north of the Arctic Circle. I'd scrolled up and down Wyatt's email that spelled out flight details; no return trip was scheduled. He mentioned wanting to be off island by the last week of October, when the sun set and didn't rise again until February. As to getting home, we were at the mercy of these military flights.

The day after I agreed to come, my government-issued polar gear arrived in the mail: quilted overalls; high-tech leggings and long-sleeved shirts; an orange parka, vest, hat, and giant orange boots. Immense Gore-Tex gloves came most of the way to my elbows. I shivered to think I would need all of it just to survive.

"Hey," came a lilting female voice behind me.

I turned, nearly smacking my knapsack into a young woman.

"Are you by any chance Valerie Chesterfield?" she asked in a sparkling British accent.

"Yes," I said, reaching out to shake the hand she offered me.

"I'm Nora, and this is Raj." A slight, handsome man with a ropy sort of strength under his Polartec sweater held out his hand with a bright smile. He wore round gold-wire spectacles that emphasized the intelligence in his deep-set brown eyes.

Nora was slender and hazel-eyed, with a wide, somewhat crooked smile and beautiful teeth under a slightly hooked nose. Shining black hair fell past her shoulders in natural waves—a real beauty in a charmingly imperfect way.

In a last-minute email, Wyatt had informed me I'd be meeting married polar marine scientists Nora and Rajeev Chandra-Revard at the gate before our flight. This news helped normalize the situation slightly: It wouldn't just be me, Wyatt, the girl, and Jeanne—the mechanic—with whom I'd be living for seven weeks out in the middle of nowhere.

"So, this is all quite thrilling, isn't it?" Nora said. She fizzed with energy and excitement. I did my best to mirror it back.

"A little, yeah."

She laughed, eyebrows knitting slightly. "Just a little?"

"Won't this be an incredible opportunity for you?" Raj said in an equally charming British cadence. "To decipher some unknown language? Wyatt told us you were quite the expert."

Nora cast him a sidelong look. "Come on, darling, best not to discuss that here, remember?"

Maybe they'd signed the same government contract I had: It

stipulated keeping mum about the girl anywhere except on-site.

"What about you? Are you excited?" I asked.

"Well, of course we are!" Nora said. "This is huge for us. Competition is brutal for any assignment in the Arctic. We're all killing ourselves to be chosen, you know?"

"Being in the lab all the time gets tiresome," Raj said. "I'm jumping out of my skin half the time."

"Same for you, right?" she asked brightly. "Don't you leap on the chance to study languages in the field?"

"Absolutely."

"Boarding for Group A," a voice droned over the loudspeaker. I looked at my ticket: Group A. My last chance to escape back to life as I knew it. As Nora and Raj turned toward the gate, I told myself, *Take deep breaths. Just follow them—along with dozens of others who are clearly not the least bit afraid to board this plane.*

The small digital recorder where I had downloaded the girl's twenty-eight-second vocalization rested in my jacket pocket. With every step, I told myself, *This is why you're going to keep on walking: this girl needs your help.*

Steep stairs led to a vast, poorly lit space, like a hollow whale made of steel. A domed ceiling soared above. Berths fitted out with army cots bolted to the floor flanked mountains of gear. Nora and Raj grabbed a berth; I snagged the one next to them. A few passengers got down to the business of sleeping; others lay with their heads propped up on one elbow, reading. I wondered what their reasons were for traveling halfway around the earth.

We blasted off into the night. Without windows, it felt surreal, as if we were in a rocket ship hurtling to Mars. I bit an Ativan in half and chewed it like candy.

As Nora and Raj curled up together on their cot under a sleeping bag, I freed my cartoon-orange parka from my pack, balled it up, and stuffed it under my head for a pillow. A symphony of snorers held sleep at bay, as did the grinding roar of the engine.

Hot in my hand was a quarter-size, heart-shaped piece of lead, formed in the gizzard of a loon in the lake where Andy and I spent our childhood summers. Loons ate fishing sinkers thinking they were fish, dying as a result. He'd found this one in the skeletal remains of a loon along the shore. He gave it to me for my birthday—our birthday, really—when we were ten. At the time, I said it was a weird, sad present, but he told me that everyone loved loons and that the heart shape was a sign that it was time for us to love them back. I've carried it with me ever since.

As I began to pore over my language books, I was reminded of the complexity of West Greenlandic. Most words in this language are composed of multiple elements called "morphemes," word parts that often create "sentence-words"—the longest of which is over 200 letters long. Nouns are inflected for one of eight cases and for possession. Eight moods as well as the number and gender of both the sentence's subject and object inflect every verb. Subdialects spring like weeds. Sure, I had all my downloaded dictionaries, but in all honesty, the learning curve seemed impossibly steep.

Fresh cracks on my fingers throbbed. The thin red lines looked like nothing much, but often woke me at night with pain. I rummaged for my salve, which gave me a few moments of relief.

To distract myself, I scrolled through images of tiny West Greenland coastal towns—barren, rocky hillsides dotted with small, brightly painted wooden houses, the great Greenland ice sheet in the distance. In the past, delicacies included fermented meat or fish and fermented seal oil, which apparently tasted like blue cheese. Seal eyes were a treat. People still hunted and fished to survive: caribou, musk ox, seal, polar bear, and narwhal.

The culture teemed with myths, but as usual, the language told me more than any single fact. It even betrayed a wry sense of humor: the island with a name that meant "not enough moss to wipe your ass with." *Taimagiakaman* referred to the "great necessity": that of having to take the lives of animals to feed people and their dogs. The word in Inuktun for climate change translates to "a friend acting strangely"—what a personal and beautiful way of describing a relationship to the natural world.

The legendary plethora of words for snow is no myth, but the number of words for ice—topping 170—taught me more. There were words for dense, old ice: ice that was safe for a hunter and his sled and dogs to cross; words for grease ice, water in its earliest stage of freezing, which won't support a person but will allow seals to break through and breathe. Perhaps inspired by the necessity of knowing what kind of ice you were dealing with, there were a dozen words for fear, because even seasoned hunters could die in a flash if the ice gave way. Among these flavors of fear were words for being at sea in a puny sealskin kayak as a storm barrels down, the fear of calamitous violence as when facing death, and a fear of someone who must be avoided at all costs.

The words that stopped me cold, though, were *nuna unganartoq*, which meant "an overwhelming affection and spiritual attachment to the land and nature." Something as simple as the warm feel of a rock face baking in the sun, to an emotion as ineffable as the sense of infinity when witnessing a heart-stoppingly beautiful vista. *Nuna unganartoq* was something I had never experienced, but I knew where I'd seen those words before.

It was how Andy had signed all his letters.

The last time I'd seen my brother, just over a year ago, I'd been working late correcting summer-session papers in my office. In a swirl of whiskey-smelling air, Andy barreled in. Even drunk and distraught, Andy was so much more handsome than I would ever be beautiful. Burly and strong, but with an athlete's grace. A solid six-footer, he had hair that grew wavy and thick, a rich auburn; mine was thin and fine. His features were well-defined: full lips, aquiline nose, deep-set, haunted eyes; without makeup I was washed-out, thin-lipped, snub-nosed, and tiny-eyed. So why did I feel like I was looking at myself when I looked at him? Was it because he possessed so many of the qualities I could only dream of?

That evening he wore baggy khaki shorts I recognized from high school days and a filthy cotton madras shirt. His skin glistened, as if he'd been running. The tang of Andy sweat, Andy panic, filled the tight space. Eyes red-rimmed and wild, he perched on a chair.

He said, "Am I interrupting anything?"

It was the manic Andy who'd come to see me that night; it put me on guard and exhausted me. "What's up?"

"You know it's over, right?"

I exhaled and began to pack up my papers for the night.

"We've passed the tipping point. It's already too late."

"Please, Andy—" It's not that I wasn't freaked out about what was happening to the planet—I was—but I'd heard this rant countless times, and there was no stopping him once he started.

As he went on about how hopeless things were, about the millions of animals that were going to die, catastrophic flooding, hurricanes like no one's seen before, I finally stood and zipped my briefcase shut. He slipped a can of Red Bull from his shorts pocket and gunned it down with a shaky hand, saying, "Because even if we fix everything that's broken, Val, which we *can't,* the problem is, no one can fix human nature. We're greedy, selfish, stupid, and shortsighted by *nature.* And that's what's going to kill us all. Hopefully."

I snapped off my lamp. "What do you want me to do about it?"

He chewed on a fingernail, assessed me. Scratched a bug bite on his leg; a constellation of red marks covered one thigh. *Has he been sleeping outside?* He asked, "Can I stay with you tonight?"

I sagged a bit. "Well—why? Can't you go home?" He lived with his fiancée, Sasha.

Andy's eye twitched. "Sasha kicked me out."

"Oh, no—"

"You know what, Val? I will *not* bring children into this world." He jabbed his finger in my direction as if I'd been badgering him about this. "I will not do it. Sasha's been riding me on this for months." He then crossed an ankle over a knee, waggling his big Teva'd foot crazily. "I've got a better plan anyway."

"You're tapping my last nerve, Andy."

"Come on, Val. Hear me out."

I sat back down, my overstuffed leather chair giving a little *poof* of defeat beneath me. This was bad. Andy plus "a better plan" *always* equaled sirens and flashing red lights. We both drank too much; the difference was he did it in public.

I propped my chin in my hands. "What's the plan?"

Frenzied hope took over his face. "It's about Wyatt."

I raised an eyebrow: *Go on.*

"He's stationed in Tarrarmiut. It's an uninhabited island off the northwest coast of Greenland. He's still doing his climate change study, getting some of the oldest ice core samples of anybody up there, but he's discovered something amazing. Something to do with his pet mouse. I wish I could tell you more, but I can't. Val, this is going to change everything. You've heard about the ice winds, haven't you? Those three hikers in the White Mountains in New Hampshire who froze to death instantly? One minute it was forty degrees near the top of Mount Washington, the next it was thirty-five below zero, and they didn't have a chance."

I pictured the press photo of the hikers. Two men and a woman frozen to death in the act of climbing, the woman with her arm mid-reach, about to grasp at a tree branch along the trail.

"That was some kind of freak thing."

"It was *not* a freak thing, Val. It's starting to happen all over. Look, katabatic winds are a temperature gradient thing. In Greenland, they're called piteraqs. They come down off the glaciers, hurricane strength, unbelievably cold, but no one lives on the glaciers, so not a lot of people know about them. Now, with climate change, they're starting to happen all over the world—"

"I haven't heard—"

"They're covering it up because they don't know how to stop it and they don't want people to panic!"

"*'They'?*"

"I'm not paranoid, Val." He ran a trembling hand through untamed hair.

"What does Wyatt want from you?"

"Another scientist in the room. Someone to verify his findings."

"He has Jeanne. Isn't she a researcher too?"

"Jeanne's a grunt, not a scientist. She keeps the snowcat going."

"How long will you be there?"

"As long as it takes to get the proof we need."

I started to feel queasy. "But Andy, in a few weeks it's going to be nearly impossible to get out of there. Remember when that happened to Dad when we were kids? He went to Antarctica, and the weather turned and—"

"This is the Arctic; it's different."

"He had to winter over. Eighty degrees below zero and dark for six months. Andy, don't do this."

"Dad wants me to go."

"Fine. Did you tell *him* what this is really about? You know, everything you're not telling me?"

Andy shrugged. "He trusts me when I say this is going to make a difference for mankind."

Of course Dad approved of the trip. Some groundbreaking scientific discovery might make the Chesterfield name go down in history after all. "I gotta go home," I said, getting to my feet again.

He looked up at me hopefully, almost puppyish.

"Go home," I said. "Apologize to Sasha. Get a grip."

He got up, his face blank. "Cool. I get it. I'll figure it out."

Before I could stop him, he was out the door and down the stairs, banging through the doors of the lobby to the quad. I watched him from my window as he crossed the soccer field at a clip, almost running. I stepped outside my office into the hallway.

In my current fantasy, the one where I let him stay with me—just a small, sisterly act of kindness—everything would have turned out differently, but that night a horrible emptiness echoed in the shadowy corridors. My heart was lodged in my throat with dread, and it was all I could do to take a full breath.

Nine long, sleepless hours later, Nora, Raj, and I stood among dozens of others dressed to our teeth facing the cargo door, packs at our sides. People looked tired, even bored. *How could they be?* The hatch unmeshed from the floor and hauled itself upward.

A gray dome of sky met a flat expanse of snow and ice an incalculable distance away. To the west, a pure white, flat-topped mountain rose starkly out of a navy-blue sea. A dozen or so squat buildings sat arranged in intersecting rows like words on a Scrabble board. The Thule base. Nothing else man-made in sight.

The three of us stepped out into a world of white. Drugs long worn off, I focused my eyes on my giant orange boots. *You are still on the earth,* I told myself, *just a different part of it.*

An unsmiling marine manned a set of scales next to the door that led to the runway for our second flight, our final leg to Tarrarmiut, another three hundred miles north. Our four-seater ski-plane idled in the frigid air. In the cockpit sat Pitak, the local pilot from Qaanaaq whom I recognized right away from Wyatt's description. We were handed a hot wrap—our lunch, fried eggs rolled in pancake-thin bread—and instructed to pare down to no more than forty-three pounds of personal belongings.

Altogether my bags weighed fifty-one pounds; I reddened as I dragged them off the scale and to one corner to do my culling.

Nora, whose bag clocked in at a sleek thirty-nine pounds, approached my mess. "Need some help?" Nodding, I scrambled to contain a sheaf of drawings that had spilled from my bag. Nora picked them up. "Wow, did you make these?"

I reached to take them back, but she was already leafing through them. "No, my brother Andy drew those."

Small, gorgeous watercolors of nature alternated with unnervingly accurate pencil portraits of our father and other relatives. He even drew himself in caricature. I had boxes of them at home but wanted to bring some with me, for luck, to keep him nearby.

Nora held up one of the drawings. "What an amazing artist he is! This one should be in a gallery or something."

My heart ached when I saw which one she was admiring. Once, when Andy'd been hospitalized, he'd assured me he would never do such a stupid thing as take his own life. Told me he was more worried about what *I'd* do on one of my bad days. So we made a pact: We would never hurt ourselves. A few days after I spoke to him, I received the drawing Nora held now.

In colored pencil: Andy, sporting a silly grin, held a gun to his temple. Apparently he'd fired, because out the other side of his head flowered a lush cornucopia of beautiful things: a strutting peacock, an elegantly wrought elephant, ripely blooming peonies. I snatched the paper from Nora just as she was turning it over to the other side, where the billowing contents of his head continued but darker: gargoyles, a blackened forest, the earth in flames . . .

"He's not around anymore, I'm afraid, my brother," I said, tucking the drawing under the others. "We were twins."

"Oh dear, Val. I'm so sorry to hear that."

She looked genuinely shocked. So I told her the story, or at least what I thought was the story. "Wyatt didn't tell you?"

"No, nothing." She glanced at the crew readying the plane. "So, this is going to be hard for you—being where it happened."

"It's hard no matter where I am." I tucked the drawing in my bag.

"Well, the drawings are light, so they shouldn't be an issue," she said with a touch of relief. At least this was a solvable problem.

I hefted a stack of picture books. "It's these books, for the girl . . . it kills me to leave them behind."

"Let's put them in my carry-on," she said with a bright smile.

"Thank you, and the drawing pad and the markers too, if you really don't mind. I've got to have those."

She complied, loading her bag with the books and supplies. "So, do you think you'll be able to suss out what she's saying?"

"I have no idea."

Nora tucked her hair under her hat, a wool one with the braided strings hanging down on either side that looked adorable on her. "Well, I think you'll be brilliant. I just hope Raj and I can get our work done before we have to get out of here. We have three months of work to do and half that much time to do it." She glanced outside. Raj stood next to the plane, waving at us. "I guess it's time to get out of here. They're waiting for us."

Quickly I grokked the particular terror of small planes: the lawn mower engine, the thin metal skin the only thing between you and your erasure once the earth yawns beneath you. Across an infinite horizon, in countless shades of blue and white, land became indistinguishable from sky. We were in it now: what I privately referred to as *the Enormity,* an emotional or physical place so overwhelming I couldn't face it without drugs or alcohol. We buzzed like a tiny silver bee over a backbone of slate-black massifs. Stomach-dropping cliffs plummeted to indigo fjords dotted with icebergs.

Beneath us, a wedge of brown darkened a massive promontory of sea ice. Nora tapped Pitak on the shoulder. We veered away.

"What's wrong?" I called out over the deafening engine.

"Walrus," Nora yelled back to me. "Big herd. Thousands probably. They spook at any loud sound and stampede. The young ones get trampled. It can get pretty bad."

I nodded, in no mood to pursue details.

An hour and a half later, we dropped down through sleety bands of clouds, skidding onto rough ice before shuddering to stillness in a cloud of snow. Three yellow buildings huddled together several dozen yards away. Out on the bay on sea ice, a bright yellow dome-shaped structure flashed between blasts of snow.

A figure burst from the orange door of the longest building—two industrial trailers joined end to end—and made its way toward us. I'd only seen him maybe a half-dozen times, but I knew that slightly bowlegged gait, that hurry-up-and-get-it-done stride. Wyatt leaned into the wind dragging a metal sled behind him, his unzipped parka flapping over quilted overalls and a thermal shirt. Behind him, the orange door banged open again, and another figure emerged in a parka. Nora, Raj, and I got ourselves out of the plane, a bitter gust buffeting us as we tried to get our bearings.

Wyatt engulfed me in a quick hug; even that brief intimacy startled and disturbed me, perhaps because he was probably the last person to see Andy alive. I exhaled, tried to smile.

"You look good, Val, you look good. You okay? Trip okay?"

"It was long. We're pretty wiped out—"

"Nora? Rajeev?" He shook their mittened hands, lingering a bit on Nora, as if he wasn't expecting such a beautiful woman.

"Call me Raj," her husband said, one arm slipping around Nora: a statement, for sure. We all introduced ourselves to Jeanne, a heavyset woman hard in her forties, ruddy-cheeked and moon-faced, brown, silver-streaked hair escaping her hood and whipping in the breeze. She mumbled her hellos, staring at each of us in turn as if her eyes were ravenous for new faces.

"You guys hungry?" Wyatt gestured at the ugly yellow building. "Jeanne's been working her magic all afternoon."

"I think we could all use some food," Raj said, heaving a box of supplies onto the sled. "The eggs back in Thule were a joke."

Jeanne's forehead furrowed. "You're not a vegetarian, are you?"

"Why, do I look like one?" he said with a smile.

"You'd starve to death around here if you were," she said without a shred of humor. She bent down to help Pitak unload a case of canned goods from the belly of the plane. He moved at twice her pace, all the while trying to jolly her up. Her smiles were rare.

"So, this weather! Crazy, right?" Pitak called to Wyatt. "Summer forgot Greenland this year."

"It was bizarre!" Wyatt said. "Two weeks in the fifties, a little melt, then boom, back to this."

Pitak's face grew serious. "The girl is okay?"

Wyatt nodded. "My friend Val here's going to help us out."

"She a doctor? From America?"

"Sort of," Wyatt said, clearly interested in changing the subject. He sidled up to Pitak. "So, did you get them?"

"Oh, man, I almost forgot." Pitak hopped back up into the cabin of the plane. Grinning, he tossed Wyatt a plastic bag tied at the top. Wyatt caught it and tore at the sack. Three avocados, perhaps the only green objects in hundreds of miles, fell onto his boots.

Wyatt dove down, stuffing them in his pockets as if they were bricks of heroin and we were the DEA. "Man," he said, laughing, "I owe you my life, Pitak."

Smiling, the pilot climbed back into the plane. "Eat them slowly, friend. See you in seven weeks."

Seven weeks.

Wyatt, Jeanne, Nora, and Raj headed toward the bleak buildings, all of them banana yellow, doors painted orange, like children's toys dropped in a sea of white. Andy had told me the bright colors made the buildings easier to spot during a blizzard. I wondered which orange door he'd come out of that terribly cold night just five months ago. Would we be walking across the hallowed ground where he'd taken his last breath, hopefully past all pain?

The wind froze tears to my cheeks; I headed toward the blur of yellow and orange and the sound of human voices.

Chapter 3

WYATT CRACKED OPEN the door, motioning for me to hurry up, so I slipped in behind everyone else. For a minute or two we all crowded together awkwardly in the drab hallway, shedding our parkas and stomping the snow off our boots.

Powerfully built through the shoulders and arms and well over six feet, Wyatt towered over all of us, but his gait—a tendency to walk along the outer edges of his feet—brought an odd delicacy to how he entered a room. According to Andy, most of the little toes on each foot had been lost to frostbite during an assignment manning a weather station in Antarctica. Still, he wore the ruggedly handsome face of a man who had spent most of his six decades outside; he was bearded, black hair salted with white, dark eyes under heavy brows, a strong chin, and a good set of teeth.

"Let me give you the nickel tour so you can settle in," he said. At the first room on the right, the largest in the building, he gestured at one corner, where a few old Macs as well as a sleek new PC battled for space on a long table strewn with files and papers. "This is where I try to get work done," he said. Metal cabinets flanked another beat-up wooden table crowded with microscopes, Bunsen burners, and test tubes. The room's one long picture window looked over an inlet packed with drift ice as tall as ships.

"And this is where we chill," he said. A chocolate-brown L-shaped couch took up most of the rest of the room. In the air: onions, sweat, chicken soup, and a sulfuric smell—*formaldehyde?* Above us, tube-shaped fluorescent lights buzzed and snapped. An ancient television slouched under a well-used dartboard. A plastic bowl of Cheez-Its teetered on the TV stand next to an empty Wild Turkey bottle. So, there was alcohol here: *Thank goodness for that.*

The floors were covered with cheap rugs, the walls a noxious green.

"You've been here how long, Wyatt, a year?" Raj asked.

"Closer to two." He turned toward the hall. "Let's keep our voices down. The girl is sleeping."

We all nodded and followed along behind him like ducklings, except for Jeanne, who clomped off to the kitchen, its floor-to-ceiling open shelves crammed with all manner of food. Wyatt's room was first: dark paneling; bed unmade; books, notebooks, papers, and magazines in teetering piles.

He knelt down. Peered at a pure white arctic mouse in a wire cage. "Here's a guy you all need to meet. This is Odin."

"Like the Norse god?" Raj said.

Narrow-eyed, Wyatt tilted his head up toward Raj. "What are you, some kind of wiseass?"

For a few seconds, no one said a word. Then Wyatt burst out a sudden, forced-sounding laugh. "Kidding, my friend. But for the others here, Odin was the god who killed himself to gain knowledge about the realm of the dead." He reached into the cage and lifted up the mouse. After a bit of scrabbling, the creature cuddled in his palm. "When I found this guy, over a year ago now, he was in the Dome, frozen solid. But now look at him."

"Well, *that's* impossible," Raj said with an exasperated exhale.

"Really?" Wyatt said.

"Cells burst when they freeze—"

Nora took his arm and tugged at it. "Come on, darling, he said it happened." She took off her hat; her shining hair fell all around her shoulders. "Look, we're all exhausted—"

"Who do you think is sleeping in the other room?" Wyatt said.

Raj lifted his hands in an appeal for a truce. "You know what? Fine. I'm here to do my research and go home."

"That was my understanding too." Wyatt settled Odin back into his cage with great gentleness. Without another word, Wyatt stepped between us, and we trailed him past another open door.

"Jeanne's room is here."

Jeanne's narrow bed was neatly made with a faded handmade quilt. Half a dozen grubby dolls sat propped against the pillows;

next to them a couple of disturbingly real-looking doll babies in doll diapers cuddled one another. We all paused, Nora and Raj exchanging *What the hell* glances, but Wyatt kept the tour on a clip and motioned us to the bathroom: a sad, beige affair with a beige porcelain toilet and plastic shower, narrow as a coffin.

"Facilities," he said. "No tub, I'm afraid, but otherwise she flushes up to thirty below outside. Colder than that, we make other arrangements. But you'll all be long gone before then."

Wyatt gestured at a door across from the bathroom. "The girl's room." Shivering, I could hear her vocalizations in my mind.

He paused at the door across from Jeanne's room. "Val, this is your little piece of paradise."

The room was the same dreary shade as the hallway, but a mural covered one wall. A trio of badly drawn palm trees sulked over what I guessed was a tropical beach. Wyatt clicked on a tube light, illuminating a twin bed with a red sleeping bag unzipped over it under a small window. A table with a reading lamp cozied up to the bed; next to that, a simple bureau, desk, and chair. The rest of the room was stacked floor to ceiling with boxes.

"We had to improvise a little with the girl here and all, sorry. Your room's also the storeroom—well, one of them."

"It's fine," I said. "Which was Andy's room?"

Wyatt looked uncomfortable. "I took it over. I figured—"

"I just wanted to know. I'm fine here."

He gave me an efficient nod. "Now, Nora and Raj, I thought you could crash on the couch tonight, since it's too late to get you settled in the Dome, okay?"

They agreed, and we all shadowed Wyatt back to the office/living room. Outside, the wind whipped the snow sideways. It stuttered rat-a-tat at the wide picture window. "So, we're in the main building now, which we call the Shack. Jeanne does her repair work in the Shed. We heat it, but not as much as home base here. Behind the Shed is the Cube, where we store the snowcat and snowmobile, like a garage. Out in the bay is the Dome, but you knew that. Now, some ground rules." Wyatt paused near a whiteboard scribbled over with calculations. "Anyone, that includes me and Jeanne, goes *anywhere,* you sign here on this log sheet." He held out a clipboard chained to the wall, tapping it with a Sharpie as he spoke. "Mark the time you go out and why. Bring your walkie-talkie everywhere when you're out there, got it?"

He handed each of us one of the blocky, old-fashioned things. "Super simple to use. It's your responsibility to make sure the batteries are working. Jeanne can give you new ones; just ask her.

"I've rated the storms one, two, and three. Level one: up to twenty-five-mile-per-hour winds, windchill to twenty below. You go outside with my permission only. Level two: twenty-five- to thirty-five-mile-per-hour winds, windchills to minus thirty. Raj, Nora: The Dome can't handle that in terms of heat, so we all work and sleep here. Permission to leave granted from me on an emergency basis only. Level three storm: thirty-five-plus-mile-per-hour winds, windchills minus thirty or below, no one leaves under any circumstances. You'll find that there are ropes connecting all the buildings. Crucial for getting from place to place if you're caught in a whiteout. Look, I know all this sounds like common sense: Who would go out in a blizzard with thirty-below winds? But these are close quarters. Storms can last for days. It gets boring when we can't do our work—for me too. So, the temptation is to push the limits and go out anyway, but that won't work here.

"All right, then," he said, glancing at each of us as though we were a set of problems it was his job to solve. "Let's eat."

In the center of the table sat a bowl of peaches, apples, oranges, and grapes, all fresh from the plane. Wyatt snatched up an orange and inhaled it, smiling. The avocados were nowhere in sight.

Cornstarch-thick beef stew and white bread—cut thickly and spread with margarine that tasted a little off. Jelly-jar glasses of boxed wine that I deeply appreciated. Everyone chatted about their work, the strange weather, the trip, as if there weren't a young girl in the other room who had thawed from the ice alive. The lunacy of what I'd done—traveled a thousand miles from my safe apartment to a frozen wasteland with a bunch of near strangers—hit me just as I felt my meds slack off. My hands shook as I buttered a slice of bread; Wyatt noticed, and I flushed. He had a certain appeal, even at twenty years my senior, but more than that,

I wanted him to like me, admire me, as much as he'd liked Andy.

Jeanne, who hadn't taken her eyes off Nora since she sat down, said, "So, how will you two be keeping busy out in the Dome?"

"I'll be diving quite a lot," Nora said, finishing up her bowl of stew. "On the lookout for fin whale and humpback, narwhal, beluga. Tracking how the changing sea ice here has affected their range and communication. Darling?"

Raj said, "And I'll be sampling various kelps for changes since the last survey was done a couple of years ago: health, type, range. But who cares about that?" He turned to Wyatt. "What I want to know is where you *really* found this girl." He eyed Nora and me in turn, as if seeking backup. "Sure you didn't just fly her over from the mainland as some sort of stunt?"

Wyatt paused, stew-laden spoon in the air, to consider Raj. "Maybe you should stick with seaweed."

Raj made a small noise of exasperation, picked up his plate, and headed to the sink. Nora followed suit, Wyatt side-eyeing her. She rinsed their dishes and leaned against the kitchen counter. "Okay, so tell us. The day you found her, what was that like?"

Wyatt kept at his stew. "Not sure this is the right time—"

"It was just a regular day," Jeanne said, her voice dreamy thick. Head tilted, a barrette holding back her shoulder-length hair, she seemed to address the center of the table. "We were headed out to Glacier 35B to get the rest of the samples. Remember, Wyatt?"

"Two weeks ago," Wyatt added quietly.

Jeanne said, "Five months after Andy passed, to the day."

I stiffened. We all did. Raj and Nora stood silently by the sink.

Wyatt pushed his food away, face weary. "We'd finished drilling cores in the northeast quadrant, and we were heading back across the ice lake—what we call the section of the glacier near the Osvald Fjord. Overnight a fissure had opened halfway across, maybe thirty yards long, split sheer down a thousand feet. We saw it from the snowcat, and we started going real slow parallel to it. That's when something caught my eye a couple of yards down the far wall of the crevasse. This crescent-shaped flesh-colored thing. It was a child's foot, from the side, from the heel down to the little toe. It was like,

I don't know, seeing a tarantula in my cereal bowl. Totally crazy. It was getting late, so we had to come back the next day with equipment. Jeanne did this ingenious setup with a pulley and a ladder and a swing, got me down there to have a look." Jeanne cast her eyes down, stirring her stew. Was she blushing? "I'm dangling over this bottomless pit, trying to make out if she was standing, or lying down, or what. It took a while to figure it out."

"So, was she standing?" Raj asked.

"It looked like she was running."

"Was she alone?" Nora asked.

"As far as we could tell," he said with a sigh. "We took a day or two to scope out a big area, nothing we could see. So we went back with this battery-powered saw and carefully cut around her and hitched the block of ice to the cat. Towed it back."

"But this island has never been inhabited," Raj said. "The literature, the history, all the charts say—"

"Look, here's the going theory," Wyatt said, lifting his eyes to Raj. "Last year, there was a major caribou migration change. A couple families pulled up stakes down south and came out here for the hunting season. We got a lot of sleet that year, and it coated the lichen, encased it in an inch of ice. The theory is the caribou starved to death. No one ever heard from the families again."

"Why not just return the girl to her village," Raj said, "if that's where you think she's from?"

"It'll happen soon enough."

Raj shook his head. "So what does Pitak think of all this?"

"Remind me, Raj, why that is your concern?"

Raj took off his glasses and wiped them on his flannel shirt. "Child of color, taken by a white man, it's not like it's a new—"

"Aren't you listening? Nobody *took* her, we *found* her."

Raj looped the wires of his glasses over his ears, face hardening. Nora leaned into him with her shoulder, but he ignored her. "It's not right to keep the girl from her community—"

Wyatt raised his voice a notch. "Nothing's been proven. If she was with her family, then where are they? They would have fallen down the same crevasse, been nearby."

"They could be anywhere—"

"People from this village, if that's even where she's from, speak the same dialect as Pitak, but he couldn't understand any of the sound bites I played for him. Why is that? We just don't know her story." He took a big bite of a brownie and chewed.

Everyone stayed quiet. The cold violet light of the Arctic sunset poured over us. My head pounded with exhaustion.

"What's she like?" I asked quietly.

"What's she like?" Wyatt shook his head. "The first day, all she did was scream. She was terrified of us, of everything. She smashed plates, lamps, dumped out all the kitchen drawers, but now, now . . . it's like all the air's gone out of her. We try, but truth is, she's freaked-out and confused. Inconsolable."

"You've got your work cut out for you," Nora said to me.

I nodded, my heart thrumming in my chest. *Inconsolable. How can* I *possibly comfort her?*

Jeanne fingered a saltshaker shaped like a happy cartoon whale. "I heard her crying outside my window all winter long. I kept telling Wyatt—I don't know how many times—but he just said—"

The color rose in Wyatt's face. "Not now, Jeanne."

"That voice . . . it was like I knew her all along—"

Wyatt shoved himself from the table. "Knock it off, Jeanne," he hissed under his breath. "We've talked and talked about this."

Jeanne looked around, and her gaze rested on me. Wide-set and gray, her eyes contained a chilling emptiness. "She was calling for help, but Wyatt, he wouldn't let me go out and let her in—"

"I'm supposed to let you head out for a stroll when it's seventy degrees below zero?" Wyatt said. "To chase some phantom?"

She smiled eerily at me. "Well, she's here now, isn't she?"

Wyatt got to his feet, slammed his chair into the table.

I felt a presence in the doorway and turned to look. A pitifully small Inuit girl hovered in the shadows. High, wide cheekbones under bottomless black eyes, ruddy skin that glowed with the heat of the room. Her ink-black hair looked as if a mad person had cut it. Her body was lost in an enormous Christmas sweater featuring Santa's sleigh and eight reindeer flying up over one shoulder. Its hem swept the floor—it had to be Jeanne's or Wyatt's. As she scanned the room, taking in the three newcomers, her eyebrows met in an upside-down V of concern. Slowly I got to my feet and said, "Hello, I'm Val," in West Greenlandic.

The girl screamed, pivoted, and bulleted down the hallway.

A cold light filtered through my frost-rimmed window at just past six, bringing the weird palm trees into focus. Already I missed my cramped, lonely apartment. I couldn't imagine Andy or anyone else loving this brutal, desolate place, but he had.

The smell of coffee drew me from my room. Jeanne's door stood ajar, bed made tight, creepy dolls neatly arranged sitting against the pillows. Raj and Nora were nowhere to be seen.

Bearded like a pirate, salt-and-pepper hair escaping his skullcap, Wyatt hunched over his computer, a map on the screen.

"Right there," he said as I approached with my coffee, pointing to a tiny black dot on a vast glacier. "That's where we found her."

It looked impossible. A little girl alone, frozen in place ten feet down the wall of a crevasse. To truly understand her—the realization hit me viscerally—I had to go to this place, no matter how doped up I needed to be. "I'd like you to take me there. Can you?"

"Your job is to be with the girl. It's not like we have time—"

"My job is to figure out her language, but part of that is knowing as much as possible about her. Seeing where she came from."

He took a bite of a waffle. "I'll think about it."

"What about those caribou hunters who disappeared?"

He looked relieved by the change of topic. "I am honestly mystified. I'm not sure I believe the story. It's a good twenty miles to the mainland. Would they really come here for some caribou? And why would they bring their families? Why wouldn't just the men go?" He dosed his coffee with a splash of fresh cream. "But, you know, crazier things have happened here, that's for sure. I haven't had the chance to go out there and really search."

He zoomed in to the featureless expanse, as if by staring long enough the mystery of the girl in the glacier would reveal itself.

"When did she eat last?"

"Yesterday morning, and it wasn't much. Maybe she's on a food strike to get what she wants. She likes fish and beef, especially raw hamburger." He went to a refrigerator in the kitchen, unwrapped a package of ground meat, spooned some into a cereal bowl, and gave it to me. "She uses her hands."

I took the bowl and a glass of water to her door. "Hello, girl," I said in Danish. "I'm not here to hurt you. I'm here to help you."

The thud of a bed shoved against the door.

"I have food," I said in West Greenlandic, a language I didn't know as well by a long shot. The word for "meat" escaped me. I grabbed the doorknob and turned. The thump of her small body against the hollow door. "Be calm, young girl. Here is beef, and a glass of water, right here, here for you." I rolled my eyes at my pitiful command of the language as I set down the food and water.

Silence.

Wyatt lingered, a watchful presence. "Is that her language?"

"No idea. Does she use the toilet?"

"She's terrified of it. She puts her waste in a coffee can I gave her. Makes sure to leave that out for me every morning."

"What was she wearing when you found her?"

"Caribou skin coat, polar bear pants, and one sealskin boot. The usual outfit for indigenous folks around here in super-remote settlements, as far as I know. Don't know why only the one boot."

"Where are they, the clothes?"

"We had to cut them off of her. I threw them away. But I asked Pitak to send me some girls' clothes with the supplies we got in yesterday." He gestured at a cardboard box near the door.

"What's with the Christmas sweater?"

"We gave her a pile of our clothes, and she grabbed that. Hasn't taken it off since she laid eyes on it."

I walked by him to sort through the box. Felt his eyes on me.

"I'll leave you to it," he said finally, wandering off toward the kitchen in his odd shuffle walk.

I exhaled.

For two hours I sat on the floor and talked through the door, occasionally nudging it open a crack, but she wasn't having it. Still,

I could feel her just behind it, listening. Wyatt paced, until something seemed to snap in him. He rapped hard on the door.

"Hey, girl," he said. "You know, we're trying to help you."

"Please watch your tone of voice," I said from the floor.

So he poured on the honey. "Come on, sweetie pie, you gotta be starving by now. How come you don't like old Wyatt?"

I got to my feet, faced him. He towered over me; I took a step back, said, "Maybe you could leave us alone for a while?"

"I didn't do anything to her, you know. Never once raised my voice. She smashed half my test tubes, and I was cool as a cuke."

"I'm sure you were."

He gave me a look I couldn't parse, but there was no warmth in it. "Enjoy your girl talk. See you in a couple hours." He threw on his parka, pulled his hat down over his ears, and left.

When I turned back to the girl's door, the hamburger and glass of water were gone. In its place was a coffee can half filled with urine. I carried it to the bathroom and flushed the contents.

As I passed Jeanne's room, I detoured to her bed, grabbed a doll, and returned to the girl's room. An empty bowl and water glass were set outside the door. I didn't know the Greenlandic word for "doll." I slid down to my usual position and said, "I have little baby for you. Want to see it?" I leaned into the door, and it gave enough for me to slide the doll in. The door slammed shut.

Seconds later, it was wrenched open and the doll sailed over my head, its ceramic face shattering in pieces on the floor.

Guess she didn't like the doll.

In a salad of languages including Old Norse, I chattered through her door about anything I could think of: how I wished she could have met Andy, the things I liked to do when I was her age, even Greenlandic history. I asked her what had happened to her, who her family was, what was the last thing she remembered.

Maybe it was only to get me to stop talking, but after an hour, the door creaked open. A rank, acrid taste—unwashed hair and skin, the memory of leather—filled my mouth. Her clotted breath came rough in her throat as if her nose was stuffed up. Had she been crying? It all broke my heart a little bit. She stood inches from me, a small, somber-faced child backlit by morning sun.

She whispered, *"Stahndala,"* and again, *"stahndala."*

I pointed at her. "Are you Stahndala?" I said in English. "My name is Val. *Val.*"

Her face screwed up in confusion.

I motioned for her to come out. Fear in her eyes, wild black hair sticking up every which way, she took a few steps into the hall. Santa's reindeer led by Rudolph, his nose a puffy red ball sewn onto the loose knit, flew diagonally up the sweater. Her tiny toes, blackened with grime, poked from under the ragged hem.

"Stahndala," she whispered hoarsely.

She looked at me with such pleading in her dark eyes; I simply wasn't ready for it. The frank reality of her, this girl from ice. *Who are you, dear child?* I drew in a sharp breath. *What should I do?*

Bit by bit, so as not to startle her, I reached down toward the pile of her new clothes, holding them up one by one, but tears welled up, with little gasps for air as she began to sob. I upended the box, praying Wyatt had snagged some toys too. Of course not. I tossed some deerskin boots on the floor.

She stopped crying and said something. Three words.

"The boots?" I whispered. They were real deerskin, not the fake awful crap. "You want the *kamiks?*" The Inuit word for "skin boots." I held them up.

She took a few steps toward me, then ripped them out of my hands before fleeing to her room. But she did not slam her door.

Cautiously I approached her room.

She faced her window wearing the boots, shoulders shaking, hands flat against the icy pane.

"Hey." I sat down on her bed. "It's going to be all right."

She whipped around and spouted several long sentences, each word polysyllabic and complex. *What is this language?* It was so eerie and beautiful it gave me chills; it was more like Greenlandic Norse than anything, but with a modulation, like Mandarin. She plopped down on the tattered rug and stretched the cheap sweater over her knees, sullenly playing with Rudolph's red nose.

I approached her with slow, measured movements. She stiffened but didn't run. With zero plan at the ready, I sat down cross-legged in front of her. She watched my every move, scooting back toward the wall behind her. I made small noises of comfort.

When she had settled, I pointed to myself and said, "Val."

Then I pointed at her. She narrowed her eyes but said nothing.

"Val," I said, more forcefully, then gestured at her again.

She screwed up her face, backing away from my finger.

I reached out my hand, gingerly touched one of the reindeer on her sweater. In English, I said, "Reindeer."

She repeated the word in her lilting cadence. "Rane-dar?"

I thrilled at the sound of English from her. "Yes, *reindeer*."

She shook her head and stuck her finger square in the reindeer's face. *"Kannisiak."* She stabbed her finger at each reindeer in turn. *"Kannisiak."* She seemed to silently count the rest, before announcing, *"Venseeth kannisiak."*

Caribou. Eight caribou.

Of course that was why she loved that sweater.

I laughed and had to stop myself from hugging her. *Eight numbers and a noun in just one session! What had I been so worried about?* I sat back, grinning goofily at her. At that pace, I'd have the basics of her language mapped out in a week.

Chapter 4

Eyes obscured by mirrored glacier glasses, Wyatt shifted the snowcat into neutral. We faced a final white wall: the tongue of the glacier that split the mountain range.

A panorama aches to be seen, so I let myself look, take in the Enormity, willing myself not to throw up in the cat.

"You okay?" Wyatt asked.

"Yeah. Doing good."

"Have to say," he said, chewing a thick wad of spearmint gum, the cloying smell filling the small space, "I'm still not clear on how this little trek is going to help you with the girl."

"I need to see where she came from," I managed to say, squeezing Andy's lead heart, hot in the palm of my right glove.

He shifted gears, and we crawled across the ice for several minutes of awkward silence until he turned to me with a blazing smile, white teeth flashing. "So, Val, how are you with secrets?"

"Depends on the secret."

"Wow." He grinned. "Complicated lady."

Was he flirting? "Why don't you just try me?"

"Here's the deal," he said as he cut the motor, and we slid to a stop. "You could learn a lot of important information out here, with that girl. Sensitive stuff. And whatever you learn, you need to share with me and only me. We're partners, understand?"

"Of course. Sure." My voice a touch too high.

He sighed and turned back to the ice. Perhaps feigning a stretch to get closer, or perhaps he genuinely needed to move in the cramped space, he eased his arm around the back of my seat. I half closed my eyes and took in a narrow band of silver-blue lake.

"You're so much like me, Val. Passionate about what you do. You've cracked the code on languages no one's been able to before. You've got a rare sort of mind. Your brother was in awe of you."

At the mention of Andy, we both quieted a moment.

"He told me everything about you, Val."

Everything? "I'm glad he had a mentor like you."

"Look, it's been a few days with the girl. Learn anything yet?"

"Not a word." Did my face betray my lie? I looked down.

"We've only got a matter of weeks here. It's the middle of September. We lose an hour of sunlight every couple of days. True night—polar night—is coming. By the end of October, it's dark twenty-fours a day, for four months. Temps get to sixty below."

"My dad once stayed too long, in Antarctica."

Wyatt's arm stiffened behind me; he removed it. "How's your dad doing? Such a brilliant guy. I still reference his work."

His change of tone knocked me off balance. I suddenly felt claustrophobic, the air thick and too warm in the close cabin.

"He was fascinated by the story of the girl."

"Thought we agreed we keep quiet about all that."

Sweat prickled me. "I left out the part about thawing out alive."

"You sure, Val?"

"He would never have believed it anyway. He thought coming here would be great for my career." Above us, dozens of big white birds with black-and-orange beaks circled, shrieking. Thankful for the distraction, I said, "What are those birds?"

"Arctic tern." He peered up at them. "We're on their turf. Actually, they consider the entire Arctic their turf." He folded his arms. "What's life like for you back home? Anyone else missing you right now besides your dad?"

I turned to him, his face still too close to mine. "Can you show me where you found the girl now?"

"It's your party, Val," he said, starting up the cat. "But I'm telling you, you're not going to learn a thing."

Bit by bit, a deep blue line came into focus, zigzagging across the ice and out of sight. We came within a dozen yards of it before Wyatt turned off the machine. He leaned his forearms on the wheel, as if remembering. Silence filled the space between us.

Then he hooked his rifle over one shoulder, creaked open the door, and hopped out. Bitter cold filled the cabin in seconds.

"Coming?"

The temperature gauge on the control panel read ten below. I willed my gloved hand toward the door, observed myself step out and down. Wyatt hadn't waited—already he was yards away. I cinched my hood tight over my face as I followed him, and took small bites of frigid air into my lungs. Eyes still lowered, I walked a bit past him, until the brilliant blue fissure came into view.

"Val, that's close enough."

Stance rigid, arms tight to my sides, I peered over the edge. The fissure was shockingly wide, close to fifteen feet across, the inner slopes pale blue, intensifying to turquoise, indigo, then black as a grave down and down to unspeakable depths. An eight-by-ten-foot block of ice had been cut cleanly out of the wall opposite.

The girl had been trapped in this? How was it possible?

"What do you think she was running from?"

"Don't know, but whatever it was, she was plenty scared. Her expression, man, it was like she was running for her life."

I got down to my knees, took off my glove, and placed my hand on the ice. I had a feeling we were in a sacred place, that we were being watched, that there was more life around us than we knew.

"What are you doing?"

"I don't know." I wrestled my glove back on. Turned and faced him. "So, what's the deal with Jeanne and those dolls?"

He shifted his weight, squinted into the sun. "She lost her husband and daughter in a car crash. Daughter was only seven. Those were her daughter's dolls. Jeanne's a good person. A good worker, knows what she's doing. Anyway, we should get back."

I followed him to the cat. My legs heavy, my big orange boots kicking up little tornados of snow with every step.

Wyatt opened my door for me. "I'm sure it's pretty obvious by now. Nobody normal comes here. This place is just natural selection for people who want to leap off the edge of the world."

THE sun had dipped behind the mountains by the time the cluster of yellow buildings came into view. Wyatt toured me through the Cube and the Shed, all the while droning on about Jeanne's prowess repairing you name it and how she could practically throw a cake together out of cocoa powder and dust. I couldn't concentrate on a word of it.

I stopped a few yards from the Shack, the questions I'd been yearning to ask tunneling up my throat. Above us hung a nearly full moon, luminous among beating stars.

"Which door did Andy leave from that night, do you think?"

Wyatt looked exhausted, even a touch annoyed by my question. "You really want to get into that right now, Val?"

"Where did you find his body?"

"Come on." Shoulders slumped, he rounded the building, stopping at a nondescript hillock of snow and ice. "Here."

"Was he on his back? His front?"

"Val," he said quietly. He couldn't seem to look at me. "Don't make me . . . you saw the pictures."

"Tell me how you found him."

"He was on his side, sort of curled up."

In my mind, there he was, clear as day. A bear of a man made childish in striped boxers, his big feet frozen solid. On his side, knees up, arms folded against his chest as if to keep himself warm. I looked away from his glowing afterimage and back to Wyatt.

"Which door?"

"How could I know that, Val?"

I approached the closest one, and was about to turn away when something caught my eye. A series of scratches.

"What are these?"

Wyatt approached. "Those've been there for a couple of years."

I rattled the doorknob, pretended I was my brother.

"We think a polar bear did it. They're starving, you know."

"A *polar bear?*" I turned to face him.

"Why do you think I've got a rifle with me every second I'm outside?" He placed his hand over the scratches and widened his fingers. "Look. No man's hand is that big."

I brushed his hand away and placed mine there, stretching my fingers far apart. It was true; the spread of the scratches was huge.

"Val, I'm sorry, but who knows?" Wyatt shivered. "Maybe he changed his mind."

I blinked, gutted by this new possibility of suffering. Rattling the handle, I yelled, "Let me in, let me in, *let me in!*" Dizzy, I rested my forehead against the freezing metal, then went at the door again, banging and calling.

Wyatt stood away from me, hugging himself, as if ashamed.

Jeanne appeared around the side of the building clutching a length of pipe. "What's going on? Is everything all right? Wyatt?"

"Yeah, Jeanne," Wyatt said. "We're just . . . it's fine."

She gave me a dark look, searched Wyatt's face.

I wrenched myself around. "You're telling me you wouldn't have heard my brother beating at the door to get back in, Wyatt?" My voice cracked. *"Did you hear him?"* I knew I was accusing him of something horrendous, but at that moment I would have done anything for a story other than the one I still couldn't accept.

He took me by my shoulders and shook me quiet. "No, Val. I heard nothing that night. I wish I had. I'd have come, kiddo."

My breath was ragged, and I could feel the hate and blame in my face, but his expression was surprisingly kind. It disarmed and confused me. He reached out to hug me, and I let him.

"Come on, Val," he said gently as we pulled away from each other, both of us looking slightly sheepish. "I know it's hard, I do. I just process it the way I process it. And you have to do the same, I can see that." He took a step back. "But you don't want to scare the girl, do you? So let's go inside. It's been a long day."

We turned back to the main door. In the deepening dusk, Jeanne stood staring at us, lead pipe dangling from one hand.

I GOT my wish: two uninterrupted days with the girl. The problem was she turned away from me each time I tried to speak to her, as if she'd given up on me, as if I had already failed her.

All day long she planted herself on Wyatt's desk under the picture window, tracing circle after circle on the sweating pane as she chanted some lilting song. She drew three rows of eight rings: *Why eight?* The last circle she rubbed hard with her palm, as if trying to obliterate something. When I pushed her to move on to basics—my name, hers, simple nouns—she banged at the shining rings until I thought the glass would shatter, then ran to her room to bury herself under her bed in her fortress of blankets.

The hours-long twilights set me on edge: days that wouldn't quite end; true darkness that refused to arrive. Thunderous crashes of icebergs calving in the bay—Wyatt called it Arctic white noise—rendered me jittery and anxious. I began to tap a fifth of vodka from the fridge during the day, watering it down to cover it up, like I was a teenager. I had to parse out my pills; I had enough to last until I was home—not one day more.

I barely saw Raj or Nora except for meals; they ate quickly, as if anxious to get out of the stifling, steamy kitchen and back out to the Dome on the frozen bay. I envied their privacy, their ability to move around, the fact that they were making progress with their projects while I was nearly stalled with mine. Except mine was no project; she was a living, breathing, miraculous girl.

FOUR thirty in the morning. Small, hard fists banged on my door, blasting me from sleep. I flung open the door. The girl stood in her boots, drowning in a sweater of Jeanne's over her Christmas sweater, my hat engulfing her small skull, Wyatt's muffler that said ICE ROCKS wrapped around her neck. Only her burning black eyes showed. She stole my hand and yanked me down the hall to rattle the front door, shouting in her language.

"Hey, calm down," I said in West Greenlandic. She pushed me away, her hysteria rising as she pummeled the door.

Ignoring our skirmish, Jeanne padded past us in her men's wool robe and stockinged feet. She lit the range and started the coffee.

"It's not safe out there," I said to the girl in English.

"She wants to go home," Jeanne said, reaching into the fridge.

The girl slid down into a teary puddle, repeating one word over and over. *Tahtaksah.*

What did it mean? Was this the word for "mother"? Or "father"?

"Tahtaksah," I repeated to her. *"Tahtaksah?"* Frustration filled her face. I'd gotten it wrong. Again. She wailed.

Wyatt's door flew open. He thundered out of his room, pounding down the hallway. "What the hell's going on out here?"

"She's having a meltdown," I said.

"Sometimes I think being in the ice messed with her brain."

"You're not right in the head till you have some coffee, Wyatt, ever think of that?" Jeanne said, setting a mug on his desk.

He muttered and jammed his stockinged feet into slippers, pulled a sweatshirt over his long johns, and tapped his PC alive.

Jeanne and I exchanged a glance, but I couldn't read her. I'd told her days ago I was sorry about the doll, but even though she'd accepted my apology, she still seemed miffed.

"My God . . ." Wyatt hissed. "You been reading about these ice winds? Two more tourists died in Nova Scotia yesterday. Froze to death in seconds. It's like these piteraqs—which are normal here—are starting to show up around the world. On steroids."

"The temperature gradients, do you think?" Jeanne said.

"Absolutely. These massive jumps and drops . . ."

"Piteraq," I said, finally recognizing the term. "That's Inuit for 'that which will attack you.'"

"Sure will," Wyatt said. "Years ago, one was clocked at close to two hundred miles an hour in Tasiilaq. In East Greenland."

The girl continued to sob, but softer now, as if wrung out. I sat next to her on the floor, clueless and wretched.

Wyatt's chair squealed as he swiveled around to face me. "So, kiddo, what's the deal with you guys? Any progress?"

I kept my eyes on the girl's back, listening to her gasps for breath as she sleep-cried. "It's slow going. Maybe she needs to feel safer before learning even feels important to her."

Jeanne brought over a plate of eggs and bacon to Wyatt, who nodded his thanks. "Have you learned any more of her language? Or has she learned any English?"

"No," I sighed. *Why am I continuing to lie about this?* Some bone-deep instinct told me to, but it didn't come naturally, and my stomach jumped every time I did it. *Better keep track* . . .

"Seriously? Val, you've had almost a week with the kid."

"Look, I've been trying. It's just that . . ." I shifted on the floor, my body aching. "I don't even know the syntax I'm dealing with. Is it like English, subject-verb-object, or a dialect of Greenlandic, where the word order is more complex, or something else?"

"You're the pro, Val."

"But there's more to it than that. I can feel it. I don't know what's happened to her, what her culture is like, her family . . ."

"Maybe you're just not a kid person."

"Hey," I said, "I don't deserve that."

He burst out laughing. "Val, I'm just joking, come on."

I reddened. Wyatt switched from collegial to cruel faster than I could clock. "I've been trying."

He got up, finished with breakfast. "Well, you need to try a little harder, my friend. We're running out of time."

SCRIBBLING NOTES IN MY journal two mornings later, I paused to gaze out my lone window at a carpet of drift ice that clogged the bay. Then a white sheet of notebook paper that had been slipped under my door caught my eye. In Wyatt's sideways scrawl: "Had to get an early start. Nora and Raj at the Dome. Jeanne with me. Good luck with the kid. See you at dinner."

I wandered to the living room, nearly tripping over a pile of blankets at the front door, which turned out to be the girl's second night of hibernating there. I sipped my coffee, determination crystallizing. We—this girl and I—were going to have a breakthrough *today*. Already the ten hours of daylight we enjoyed the day I arrived had slipped to just under seven and was dropping fast.

I bent down and said in my sweetest voice, "Good morning, time to get up." No movement. "Hello," I said to the clump of blankets. "I've got fish here. Meat. Whatever you want."

She poked her head out—expression comically cranky—evicted her blankets, and got to her feet, my unknowable girl in her fraying sweater-dress. She flew down the hallway and returned with her special coffee can, now half-full, handing it to me with zero embarrassment. After emptying the contents, I found her sitting cross-legged on Wyatt's desk, chewing on a piece of raw halibut. She'd obviously figured out the refrigerator. I cleared a space on the desk and spread out the picture books, paper, markers.

"So, let's try this again." I pointed to myself. "My name is Val." I pointed at her. "You are . . ."

She crammed the remaining halibut in her mouth. That's when I saw her molars; they were almost completely worn down. My breath caught in my throat. From what I'd read, starting girls early in the tradition of chewing caribou hides to soften them enough to cut and sew for clothes was archaic, a custom no longer practiced except perhaps in isolated villages.

She swallowed the last piece and reached up toward the picture window. She squeaked clear a circle with her finger. I clicked on my recorder I kept in my shirt pocket. She drew another circle, each time saying what might have been a number. Two rows of eight rings, the third row only seven, the last of which she rubbed out hard. *Is it the act of counting that's important, the circles themselves, the rubbing out of the last one, or all of it?*

I noisily dumped out the markers and crayons, flipped open the picture books. "Okay, look at me, honey." As gently as I could, I took hold of her narrow shoulders and turned her toward me.

She tore out of my grip, punching down with her fishy hands, scattering the books and toys to the floor while shrieking.

A flame of fury and frustration shot through me. *Why won't she just try? What is wrong with me that she won't respond at all?*

I went to the front door, banged on it once. "You want to go outside? Say it: *outside*. Or you're not going anywhere."

Her eyes widened. She slid her legs off the desk and let them dangle there. I never grew tired of looking at her: this child who had lived a life worlds apart from mine. Her expressive face, capable of conveying humor, sarcasm, pain, delight, fear, and maybe even love, her miles-long words and sentences, her bursts of laughter, even her fits of tears were as much a wonder to me as her refusal to learn confounded me.

"Do you want to go outside?" I gestured at the door.

She nodded, not taking her eyes off me.

"Say 'outside.' *Outside*."

"Ou-sigh . . ." She slid her agile body to the floor with a thud and padded over to me. She reached up and rattled the doorknob, brow furrowed as she burned a *You promised* look into me.

What was I doing? Was this insane? Maybe not. I'd been running around after her for a week up and down the halls of this place; surely I could keep up with her outdoors for a few minutes.

Every article of clothing I laid before her she dutifully put on. Soon we stood at the door, parka'd, snow-panted, mittened, and mufflered. It never occurred to me to sign the log. "Ready?"

She nodded, pulling her hat down halfway over her eyes.

"Say 'outside.'"

She smiled a little. "Ou-sigh."

"Are you going to stay with me? Be a good girl?"

She nodded *yesyesyes*.

"Do you love me?" I asked, smiling.

She actually smiled back. Nodded once more. Of course it wasn't real, but it felt good all the same.

Gripping her hand tightly in mine, I opened the door.

She jerked her hand free and charged away from me like a scruffy little rocket, sending me tripping and stumbling forward onto hard-packed snow, the air bitter in my lungs. Behind us, the rime-powdered beach. Black seal heads bobbed in the water. Before us, the glacier that led to the ice lake snaked up the mountainside, disappearing in the pass that cut through the peaks.

Which is where she was headed. Quickly she grew smaller and smaller in all the terrible white. I still clutched her mitten.

I ran screaming for her to come back, my eyes tearing. My oversized snow pants and parka slowed me, binding my limbs. The slope steepened. Undaunted, the girl flew higher and higher.

"Girl! *Girl, come back!*"

The dot turned to look at me, then went back to running, but began to lose steam, alternating brief rests with short spurts up the slope. She was like a train chugging up a track, whipping up billowing snow clouds that obscured, then revealed her red parka.

"Stop!" I pleaded. "You've got to *stop!*"

She slowed to a walk, and I began to close the gap between us. I cursed my stupidity, the huge risk I had taken. Remembered what Wyatt had said about polar bears: *Why do you think I've got a rifle with me every second I'm outside?*

The girl scrambled along the lip of the glacier as if looking for a foothold, then disappeared into a funnel of snow. My heart spun in my chest. Had she fallen into a crevasse?

Wind swept the ice clean; she had dropped to her knees.

I pitched toward her, collapsing next to her, her tiny form lost in Jeanne's spare parka. "Girl, are you all right? *Girl?*"

"*Tahtaksah,*" she cried as she gazed up at the break between the cliffs. She reached up her one bare hand—purple with cold—moaning two words over and over. They sounded vaguely like West Greenlandic for "mother" and "father," but—*tahtaksah*—the word felt like pure emotion. *Does it mean longing? Grief?*

"Come on. We can't do this alone; we have to go back."

She wrenched herself around to look at me. That face: forlorn, bereft, but also determined—I'll never forget it—so much older than her age. I reached down for her bare hand, but she pulled it away and began a run-walk down the hill in the direction of the Shack. Soon, though, it was clear she was headed to the beach.

I broke into a trot. Desk-size floes lined the shore, creaking as they ground into each other. Long, shallow waves rolled under them, nudging them forward. A hundred yards out on a larger floe, a half-dozen harp seals luxuriated in the sunshine.

The girl casually picked her way along the shore as if we were out for a stroll. She turned and shot me a mischievous grin, before hopping onto one of the icy rafts, squatting as if it were a surfboard. Her weight had no effect; the disk of ice continued its ebb and flow until the waves subtly picked up speed and might and—bit by bit—floated her farther out, past the first line of bergs.

"No! No, get back here!" I jogged alongside her little craft—only a yard or so from me, but utterly out of reach. As I speed-walked alongside her, begging, "Please, come back here," she laughed.

The waves lifted her, lowered her, with slow, peaceful movements. She looked calm, happier than I'd ever seen her. One of the scals wriggled across its berg and slipped into the water.

The girl pointed to herself and said, "Sigrid."

Stunned, I stopped short. "*Sigrid?* Your name is Sigrid?"

"Sigrid." She patted her chest. She pointed at me. "Bahl."

"Yes!" I said, joyous even as I huffed along again. "I'm Val."

"Bahl," she said, as if correcting me. She stood up, perfectly at ease on her raft.

"Sigrid, get off the ice, will you?"

She laughed and jumped to another berg a bit farther out; it rocked slightly under her weight, but her balance was faultless. She motioned for me to join her. "Bahl, Bahl-y Bahllalala, Bahl."

A disk of ice twice the size of hers sailed onto shore, delivered there by a rogue wave. I considered it, then stepped onto it, falling immediately to my knees. A wave bloomed beneath me, lifting, then belching me forward. Like a slow, sick carnival ride, it sucked me away from shore, grinding its way among the smaller disks. I clawed my gloved hands into the ice and held on.

Sigrid laughed, clapping and hopping all around me on the neighboring disks, until even she realized we were drifting steadily away from shore. I remained in the same crouch I'd landed in; I couldn't bring myself to sit, or stand, or move. Chatting away, she leaped onto my little island, briefly patting my back—was this a game of tag?—before hopping berg to berg to shore.

"Bahl!" Sigrid called from the bank. But I just floated, paralyzed, stomach heaving with every roll of the sea.

"Bahl," she cried, alarm tinging her voice.

"Sigrid, go get help, please!" I tore one hand off the ice to point at the Dome.

For a long, terrible minute she ran along the bank as I had done, calling my name, until finally she bulleted off toward the Dome.

A choppy sea rocked the loose floes around me. I was just twenty feet from shore, but it may as well have been a mile. I began to lose feeling in my hands and feet. *Where are my words,* I thought. *Which one can save me?* Blinking tears into my eyes so they wouldn't freeze open, I conjured the Japanese word *zanshin,* a state of relaxed mental alertness martial artists strive for when facing an opponent.

As the floe rocked beneath me, I breathed *zanshin* until ice and sea disappeared and only the word remained.

Chapter 5

IT TOOK ALL OF thirty seconds for Nora to tow me to shore.

Sigrid had been able to communicate my distress—so she *could* make herself understood if she wanted to—and Nora had come running from the Dome and tossed me a rope. Now we sat inside on a wooden bench under the sunshiny glow of saffron canvas, Sigrid bundled in a fur blanket drinking hot chocolate cooled by ice chips.

Nora squatted near the four-by-eight-foot hole in the ice floor where she and Raj set off for their dives into the polar sea. The temperature inside the Dome hovered at forty degrees.

"He should be up any second," she said, checking a gauge.

"Thanks for getting me. I'd still be out there . . ." I shivered.

"It's okay," she said, her concentration full on the slushy blue hole. Raj was swimming somewhere under us, submerged in freezing water.

Suspended from one of the curved metal struts that held up the Dome and kept its shape, like the ribs of a whale, was a laminated placard entitled DIVING CHECKLIST, a twenty-five-step agenda to be checked off in preparation for a dive. A spare diving suit hung like a dead man from a large hook over the specimen table.

Nora paced in front of the hole, eyeing the timer as it clicked from fifty-nine minutes to an hour. "Okay, Raj, any time now would be good—"

Raj fairly exploded out of the water, his tank and gear clanking against the icy walls of the diving hole.

In alarm and surprise, Sigrid flung her cup of chocolate up in the air. She looked equally fearful, bewildered, and strangely delighted, repeating the same two words over and over.

Nora seized Raj by his armpits, heaving him up and out of the hole and onto his stomach. He slid a yard or so across the floor. Rolled over and yanked out his mouth gear, shuddering.

Nora laughed as she helped him wrestle off his tight-fitting neoprene headgear. "Poor girl's freaking out! Could she think he's some kind of seal-man?" Smiling, she handed him his spectacles.

Maybe that's what she's saying, I thought. *Seal man.*

"This is Sigrid," I said, escorting her over to Raj.

He sat up and smiled, held out his hand. "Nice to meet you, Sigrid. I'm Raj. I mean, Seal Man."

She didn't take his hand but, grinning with astonishment, reached up to touch his forehead gently, then his rubber-encased shoulder. Said, "Seal Man."

"How was it, darling?" Nora asked as she helped unzip his suit.

"Perfect. I was able to plant it about forty feet down. Got the coordinate, took a shot of it. We're good, I think."

"Brilliant," Nora said, freeing him from the rest of his suit. Shivering, he hopped into layers of clothing that had been laid out for him across the table. Sigrid couldn't take her eyes off him.

Nora poured Raj some chocolate, which he took gladly.

"How's it been going with her?" Nora asked, turning to me.

"Slow, I said. "She's probably speaking some West Greenlandic dialect. I'm not sure yet."

"Wyatt pushing you?"

"Every day," I said. "How is it out here for you? Cold?"

"We're used to it. We love the quiet."

"She does," Raj said. "I'm not sure I like it. Sometimes it's so quiet I can hear my own heart beating. Spooks me."

"Some days I forget we're standing on the sea," Nora said. "That there are seals and humpbacks and belugas floating under us, giving birth, fighting, dying . . ."

"Do you want to listen to them?" Raj asked me. "We have a very low-tech way."

"Sure." Sigrid's hand in mine, we followed Nora and Raj out of the Dome. Stood together in the rigid pristine air as endless twilight burnished the sky. Our footsteps squeaking along the ice was the only sound. I drew Sigrid to me and said, "You stay with me, understand? No running. Okay, Sigrid?"

She shook her head solemnly, said, "No."

Sigrid, *no*, *mother*, *father*, *seal man*. Six words in one day.

A few yards from the Dome, Nora got to her hands and knees on the ice, then lay down on her side, her ear pressed to it. Raj did the same. "Come on," he said. "Listen."

I copied them, holding my ear a centimeter from the ice. Sigrid, watching us, lay down next to me, her face inches from mine.

Right away, I heard it—a Martian language of clicks, pings, squcaks, pocks, chirps, and staccato thumps. Even though I was losing feeling in my ear, I didn't want to stop listening. I would have given anything to understand this language, or languages: a seal calling to her pup, warning of a polar bear nearby? A fin whale singing to his mate?

Nora sat up, brushed herself off. "We can also make or record sounds into a hydrophone. Come on, I'll show you."

Back in the Dome, she found a digital recorder and two microphones with cords. One she dropped into the hole, feeding it several yards down; the other she flipped on and spoke into. Her voice filled the Dome.

"Hello down there, brilliant sea creatures."

Sigrid reached up for the microphone.

"Should I give it to her?" Nora asked me. But Sigrid had already swiped it from Nora's grip. She made noises into the machine, similar to the squeaks and chirps we'd heard on the ice.

"Listen to that," Raj said. "She's quite good."

Sigrid squatted at the edge of the hole, keeping up her calls.

A long white spear poked out. *What in hell?* The adults jumped back from the hole as the spear thrashed at the ice, rapping at the glassy sides of the opening. Sigrid didn't budge; a proud smile stretched across her face as she glanced at each of us. Then she drew a breath and renewed her uncanny whistling and clicking.

"Holy crap," Raj breathed. "It's a narwhal."

The length of twisted bone lifted eerily higher, then turned toward us as if sensing us there. Two more horns broke the surface, each approaching six feet, each fighting for room in the narrow space. One of the creatures lifted its dark gray head from the water. A blast of fishy-smelling air burst from its blowhole as the muscular flap opened and closed.

"She's called them—those are male narwhals," Nora said.

Sigrid was reaching across species, across worlds! *She* was the linguist. Never had I felt such wonder.

"Get the camera—Raj?" Nora said in a whisper, unable to take her eyes off the rubbery gray heads and waving spears.

But he couldn't look away either. "It's in the dry bag."

Cursing, she scrambled in the bag and pulled out her phone.

The unicorn tusks waved—*What is this place?*—before clacking together one last time and sinking down and out of sight. The steel-blue water in the hole closed over them.

Now silent, Sigrid sat back, as if spent.

"Did you record that, Nora?" Raj said in a hushed voice.

"It happened too fast. I've never seen anything like it."

"That was . . . that was *yūgen*," I said.

"Yūgen?"

"It's a Japanese word for something that gives rise to feelings there are no words for . . ."

"That was *yūgen* all right," Raj said. "Just incredible."

We watched the water settle, waiting for another appearance of these fantastical creatures. But this moment was over forever.

"If I were an opportunist of the Wyatt variety, I'd say *this* is the road to fame and big bucks. Forget the thawed girl fairy tale."

"Raj, come on," Nora said. "Wyatt doesn't deserve that."

"Oh, no? Honestly, Nora, you *believe* him?"

She tilted her head. "Of course not—"

"He found her wandering on the ice somewhere, her family fallen into a crevasse or through thin ice, or who knows, maybe they're out there looking for her? Look, we both know he hasn't written a research piece in years. And have you checked out who's been assigned to head the new Arctic research base? The one they're going to build after they tear this place down next year? It's not him. He's not even on staff."

"Andy was being considered for that post, wasn't he?" I asked.

"He was, Val, but . . . well, I wasn't going to mention it."

"It's okay, Raj." I hugged myself, now feeling the frigid air.

"Raj," Nora said, "we're not here to investigate Wyatt."

"Someday I'd like to peek at that journal he's always scribbling in. Or those slides he's got locked away like they're state secrets."

"Slides?" I asked.

"The ones he can't stop staring at in the specimen fridge."

"Listen, Val," Nora said. "Maybe it is a good idea we keep this, um, narwhal thing to ourselves. Sound good?"

"Sure. I'm here to learn her language," I said. "That's it." I felt my stomach twist. Another secret to keep from Wyatt. On top of that, I wasn't exactly being straight with Nora. Of course I wanted to decipher Sigrid's language, but more than anything I wanted the truth about Andy, and now, Sigrid.

I had to find that journal.

It was just past three in the morning. Swathed in a veil of silver twilight, I hovered in the hallway, just outside Wyatt's room. Inhaling slow, measured breaths, I listened. Just the sound of Wyatt's snoring, the whine of the wind.

I tiptoed to the kitchen. A cone of light shone down from the hood of the oven; the rest of the room malingered shadowy and vague. I crept into the main room. Every inch of Wyatt's desk swam with files and papers, but I knew what Raj had been talking about. A ragged, eggplant-colored leather journal, held together by thick black elastic. Centimeter by centimeter—listening for his snoring—I carefully creaked open the drawers of his desk. Old calendars, batteries, rusted razors, junk. No journal.

I was about to slink back to bed, defeated, when I noticed that the specimen fridge, just a small cube plugged in behind his PC, was unlocked. *Slides . . . locked away like they're state secrets . . .* I froze, every cell on high alert. Still he rumbled on.

The fridge opened with a little pop of suction.

On the left side, a dozen metal rings held test tubes filled with what looked like blood, each vial and its corresponding ring labeled in Wyatt's slanted scrawl. One metal ring was empty. On the right side, several dozen slides were stacked in wire racks. Each was labeled, but there wasn't enough light to read them. Slowly I turned the little fridge toward the garish light from the window. With trembling hands, I removed a stack of slides.

The first one read ODIN, MUSCLE.

Then: ODIN, BLOOD.

Three more slides were labeled ODIN, STOMACH.

The sixth one said *GYNAEPHORA GROENLANDICA.* Latin for Arctic woolly bear moth. Again: MUSCLE, BLOOD, STOMACH.

I froze. *What am I doing here?* I didn't even know what I was looking for. Blood like a rush of wind in my ears.

The tinkling of an alarm, distant.

The snoring stopped.

My hand shook. I stopped breathing. Listened.

Just the buzz of the light over the stove, the malevolent silence from the boundless waste outside the window.

Head pounding, sweating in the chilly room, I put the slides back in reverse order, praying I'd gotten it right. My hand hovered over the test tubes of blood—*That empty ring*—I couldn't quite think straight—*had I removed a test tube and put it somewhere?*

Closing my eyes, I mentally sequenced what I'd just done, praying it was right. Shut the fridge. Padded down the hall, pausing in the shadow of Wyatt's door. Caught in a triangle of light cast by his lamp, wearing a ragged T-shirt and sweats, Wyatt sat on his bed facing his window, one arm tied off with a length of rubber cord. Poised at the crook of his elbow he held a needle, plunger ready. Perhaps he sensed me there, because his leonine head had begun to turn just as I slipped away and out of sight.

SPARKS flew between Jeanne's hands as she welded two pieces of metal shelving together, unaware I had come in until the wintry blast from the open door of the Shed hit her. She cut the power and flipped back the face guard of her helmet. She didn't smile.

"Where's the kid?" She slipped off her welding gloves.

"Sleeping. Is this a good time to do this?"

"Good as any. Just about done repairing these shelves," she added with a touch of pride as she stashed her tools in cubbies. A floor-to-ceiling walk-in freezer took up nearly a third of the space, its door padlocked. *Why lock a freezer?* I knew the ice cores were stored there, but what else might be?

The thought occurred to me—unbidden—that I had never seen Andy's body. I'd been too upset to identify it. Dad had taken care of that horrific task. Andy had been cremated, because he'd always told me he wanted his ashes to be scattered over the ocean.

My breath bloomed white in the frosted air. I was there because of Wyatt's latest dictum: Everyone on-site needed to know how to use all the vehicles. That morning he had run me through the basics of operating the snowmobile, but directed Jeanne to school me on the ins and outs of the snowcat.

And I was praying for a quick lesson. Jeanne put me on edge; something about her was a cautionary tale I hadn't yet deciphered. The chronic anxiety in her face, her downcast eyes, as if some

Sisyphean task consumed her. First to rise, last in bed, she was forever cooking, cleaning, sweeping, hauling, repairing gear, clearing snow. She'd even repaired the doll Sigrid had smashed, gluing together every ceramic shard of its flush-cheeked face.

We headed outside, and I climbed into the snowcat. Jeanne creaked open the passenger door and heaved herself up next to me. A brisk wind rattled the machine as we sat on the glinting ice field. Once I got the hang of remembering to raise and lower the ice blade and rev the motor just so, I had us—after a few clumsy fits and starts—rolling across the tundra toward the frozen bay.

"What brought you here, Jeanne?" I asked after a few nearly companionable minutes.

She didn't answer right away, and I began to wonder just how awkward this trip would get. She withdrew a flask from under her seat and took a pull. "Whiskey?"

"Sure, thanks." I hated whiskey, but not enough not to drink it.

"You asked why I came here. My husband and daughter were killed by a drunk driver a couple years ago. Wyatt tell you?"

"Just that it happened. I'm sorry."

She nodded but kept her eyes on the glistening ice field. "Adam and Frances. Everything I was living for—gone, just like that." She flipped the flask up, took a long swallow. "Best not to linger on it. Few months later, I see this ad for a cook-slash-mechanic way up north, middle of nowhere, and I think—that's for me. I can fix anything, cook anything, and I love the cold."

"And you have Wyatt, so you're not totally alone."

She shrugged. "He's my boss. Had tons of them, some better, some worse. He's not perfect, but he leaves me alone in the ways I need to be left alone." She gestured with the bottle at the blip of yellow on the stretch of luminous sea ice before us. "Why don't you head over to the Dome? We can do a circle around it and head on back." I did as she asked. The machine juddered as I made the turn—too sharp—then fell into the task.

She shifted in her seat, offered me another sip from the flask. "So, the girl, uh, Sigrid—got her figured out yet?"

"Not exactly."

She turned to me, unsmiling. "Wish I could have been the one to help with the girl, but I guess high school dropouts don't fit the bill. Wyatt wanted you up here in the worst way."

I could feel the whiskey joining forces with my meds, making me brave. "Can you tell me what it was like, thawing her out?"

"That day, that was something," Jeanne said almost wistfully. She freed a beat-up pack of Marlboros from the pocket of her parka, lit one. "First of all, day we found her, there was no doubt we were gonna cut her out, bring her back. Wyatt'd already froze and thawed out Odin a couple times, and he had some confidence in that regard. Anyway, the first couple days we kept her in the Shed. The ice around her was more'n a couple feet thick in places. But when it got close, maybe a couple inches or so, we brought her into the Shack. Laid her out on a tarp on the kitchen table and just blasted the heat and never left her. Put towels around her to soak up the melt. It started to smell weird in there, like sulfur, but also like flesh, or rotted leather, or mud. I thought of my daughter in the morgue, you know, and I almost couldn't take it, another dead girl in front of me. I even said to Wyatt, 'Why are we doing this? I can't go through with this,' especially after everything that happened with Andy. I mean, a mouse is one thing, but a girl . . ."

I felt her watching me but kept my eyes on the yellow Dome, solitary in the dead white vista. We crept along in the lowest gear.

"But Wyatt, he always has things under control. Like I said, he's been a good boss, and I felt like I owed him a little faith, you know? So we watched her till most of the ice was gone. And she became—she was just a little girl lying on the table in a rotted caribou anorak and polar bear pants and one boot, eyes open, and she looked so scared. Then we cut off her clothes real slow, real careful. You think she's dirty now, but so much of that is stain from those wet skins. We covered her with blankets, like she was sleeping. It was crazy, what we were doing. I couldn't believe we were disrespecting a body like this, a body that had been at peace in the ice."

She blew a lungful of smoke out a crack in the window. We sat just beyond the Dome in a world of white. "Why don't you cut the motor? You need to practice starting her up anyways."

Nodding, I turned off the ignition, cutting the heat, stilling the shaking joystick. Vicious cold slipped through every window.

"Then her left hand twitched under the blanket. We both yelped and jumped back. After a while, I thought we both imagined it. But then her jaw dropped, and her mouth opened and closed, so we checked for a heartbeat—nothing. So: boom—right away, Wyatt was on her with the defibrillator. Just about bounced her off the table she's so small, but he did it again and nothing. I begged him in Frances's honor to *stop*. I said, 'Wyatt, maybe this is some rigor mortis thing setting in; just leave her be.'"

Her voice had broken a little. I didn't dare start the machine and break the spell. Icy air encircled my legs and feet in a frigid vise.

"I smelled flesh burning, but he kept at it. I was in the corner sobbing, 'Oh, I'm so sorry, forgive us this unholy thing,' to whatever gods this girl prayed to. I was begging him, *begging* him to stop, Val, you understand? But Wyatt *willed* that girl alive."

I nodded, but she wasn't looking at me; she was gazing out at all the white, deep in thrall of the Enormity. "Must have been the tenth try, something changed. You could feel it in the room; this crackling energy filled it up. He was looking down at her, smiling. From where I sat, I saw her hand shoot up and sort of smack his arm, and I screamed and ran over. The girl was coughing and gagging, but she was breathing! *She was breathing*. Wyatt had this look of rapture. And I felt like, in a weird way, we were her parents, or her second set of parents, you know? I mean, he started her little heart, but we worked together to bring her out of the ice, to bring her alive. Think about that." She turned to me. "Pitak thinks God saved Sigrid because killing all her family and all the hunters who were going after those herds of caribou was too much of a punishment. It was this act of mercy, you know?"

"Could be."

"I'm sorry you were punished, Val. To lose your twin like that."

My fingers stiffened with cold; I forced myself to move them. "Tell me what it was like, Jeanne, to find my brother that day." The gates seemed open, so I had to try.

She took another sip of whiskey; her face closed down. "Wyatt found him, not me. He must have told you everything by now."

"He told me his version."

"Well, I don't know what you're getting at," she said testily. "There's only one version." She pushed herself up in her seat, capped the flask. "But all right, if you need to hear about it so bad. Him and Wyatt had some contest going on for months about trying to find out what made Odin thaw out alive. They messed around with everything: shellfish, moss, lichens, flowers, even pollen. That night they were drinking, laughing a lot. Or maybe they were arguing; it was none of my business. They were the best of friends; they didn't need me around." She flicked her half-smoked cigarette out the window. "Well, that's half true. Wyatt still needed me for day-to-day stuff 'cause Andy wasn't great at the nitty-gritty, you know. Don't get me wrong, I liked him; he was a good man—"

"He was a dreamer, I know."

"Right, scattered. Point is, he made things a little more complicated. Times it felt like Wyatt'd forget the important stuff, like how he still needed good ole Jeanne around to get him in and out of a crevasse alive because she brings along the right ropes. I mean, those two could yabber on about science till the cows came home, but talk won't save you out there." She sighed mightily. "Anyway, that night I left them to their carousing and headed off to the Shed. Had an ice drill to fix. Went to bed after that—assumed they had too. Woke up the next morning, and he'd found Andy. Wyatt was destroyed. Never seen him like that. I felt sick about it."

I clutched the wheel. "Just tell me one thing, Jeanne. Were all the doors locked the morning Wyatt found him?"

"Locked?" She grimaced, leaning over me to turn the cat's key. "Have a look around. No locks on any of the outside doors. Locks freeze out here; they're a pain in the ass. Besides, who would we be locking out? Polar bears can't turn doorknobs. Look, Andy went out there, who knows why, but he could have come back in if he wanted to. Whatever he did, Val, he did it on purpose."

It was nearly midnight. We'd all stayed up drinking wine, getting into heated theories about Sigrid, before Jeanne turned in and Nora and Raj trudged off to the Dome in haunted blue twilight.

"So, Wyatt," I asked, "what's next for you, after this place?" I sat on the rug with Sigrid, who—newly entranced with markers—scribbled on drawing paper. She'd refused to go to sleep that night, hadn't eaten much, and had barely spoken all day.

He tossed the dregs of his wine in the sink, whipped around to face me. "Ah, come on, Val," he said with derision. "Don't be coy. You must have googled me by now."

I reddened. "Guess I missed something."

He exhaled. "I was"—finger quotes—"*inappropriate* with a student back home. Grad student. She came at me, she was all over me, it was . . . mutual. Then she blew the whistle. The powers that be are letting me finish my time here." He tugged at his beard. "So this is my last dance. Who knows where I'll end up after this."

"I have a feeling you'll land on your feet."

He strolled over to me, reached down, and traced his rough finger along the side of my face. I was stunned, but didn't stop him. When was the last time a man had touched me? Still, the flip from aggression to seduction unnerved me, and I felt my expression tightening. Sigrid had stopped drawing and watched him.

"You think less of me now, don't you?" He stroked my hair.

Shivering, I drew back, and he pulled away. "Look, Wyatt, it's none of my business how you deal with—"

"Val, I mean well. That's what people don't understand. Yeah, I've made bad decisions. Done things out of passion that aren't right." He gave me a searching look. "Here's the thing. I'm not the worst guy. I call my mom—she's ninety—every Wednesday morning, nine o'clock sharp. Right here, on the sat phone. And hey, I've got some arthritis, but I'm not completely washed-up. I'm sixty-one, which is a crime in America, to be over thirty . . ."

I laughed and nodded, and he finally smiled. I thought about the exquisite Japanese word *shibui,* the beauty of aging, a concept that doesn't exist in American culture in any real way.

Wyatt got comfortable at his desk; Sigrid returned to her scribbling. "I've never been more passionate about what I'm doing." He leaned forward, his face half in shadow. "I'm not just curious about stuff. I *have to know*. Those odd striations a mile down in the ice, what's the explanation? *How does the world work?*"

He lowered his voice. "And Val, listen. I loved Andy—you know that—but I care about all my students. So many of them are going to go on to change the world. They're doing it now. I'm very proud . . ." He rubbed his forehead, exhaustion plain in the deep creases of his face. "So what's left? I've got these cores, this fifteen-year body of work, which I'm damned proud of. But now, *now?* It's the girl. The girl is everything. The reality of her, the science of her, the *why* of her. Let me show you something."

He lifted the top off a long, low freezer in the kitchen. A fog of dry ice billowed into the stale air of the room. Slipping on canvas gloves, he reached in and gingerly lifted out a tube of ice four inches in diameter and a yard long: an ice core.

"See this? Pulled it out of Glacier 27G this morning. I've got dozens of these. This is going in the walk-in freezer in the Shed tonight. I've sent hundreds of these back to the States, which is, in total, hundreds of thousands of years of data." He held up the steaming rod. It glistened in the window light. "You're looking at a couple decades of climate information—hydrogen and oxygen isotopes, levels of CO_2—all compressed into a few centimeters a year. I could spend years reading all of these, trying to understand what was happening during different time periods. It's like a puzzle with a million pieces. The difficulty is seeing the whole thing, the patterns among all the clues about temperature, precipitation, volcanic activity. It all drives me crazy some days, you know?" He slipped on a pair of magnifying-lens glasses to peer at the core. "Is that what it's like with Sigrid, Val? Too many puzzle pieces?"

I looked for Sigrid, but she'd finally gone to bed. I sipped at the dregs of my red wine, dreading my answer. "Her language isn't rooted in any known language. Certain words are similar enough to West Greenlandic to be loanwords—"

"It's been close to three weeks." His tone shifted, chilled.

"Look, I'm making progress." My hand trembled, the skin painfully cracked and raw. "She's coming along."

But I was lying. Again. Sigrid was clamming up, wanting only to wander around outside, watch Nora and Raj do their dives, sit on the counter as Jeanne cooked or hang out with her in the Shed. She was fretful, fidgety, and distracted. Something felt off.

Feeling his eyes burn into me, I stood. "I'm going to talk to her."

I FOUND Sigrid sitting on top of her bed, facing the window, bare legs dangling, a pad of paper on her lap. She drew by lamplight with great concentration.

"Hey," I said softly as I approached her.

On the page, outlined in black, emerged what looked like strips of seaweed, or like snakes or worms, sometimes separate, at others in squiggly piles. A wide-winged bird soared over the odd shapes. She carefully colored the seaweed strips dark purple; the bird—very simply drawn—stayed white with a black head and long red beak. When she was done, she spread it across my lap.

"Thanks, Sigrid."

She put her hand on my arm and looked up at me with trust in her eyes. I clicked on the recorder hidden in my pocket. Pointed at her drawings. "What are these? Can you tell me about them?"

For several minutes she spoke to me in the strangest way: patiently, as if I'd better pay attention because *this was important*.

She began most sentences with one of seven words—I'd been tracking this much at least. But now she spun off into some kind of explanation, gesturing, pointing at the bird, then the squiggly lines, back to the bird. I repeated the words she used back to her, *"Sahndaluuk, kahdayglu,"* and she got very excited.

She jabbed her dirt-encrusted nail over and over at the snake and bird, then carefully tore the piece of paper from the pad. Folding it into the smallest possible square, she tucked it in my palm, closing my fingers around it. She reached up with both hands for my face; I lowered my head to hers, and she rubbed her forehead on mine, like a benediction. I wanted to ask more questions, but she dropped to the floor and disappeared in her hideout.

Later, I crawled into my own bed and unfolded the drawing under the glow of my desk lamp. *What the hell is she trying to tell me?* Squiggly lines and birds; clearly, these things were both meaningful and a secret. I played back her speech. *If this girl is Greenlandic, why doesn't she speak any of the dialects?*

The seven words that preceded each sentence, phonetically, were *stahndala, tahtaksah, oosahmtara, mahkeensaht, sahsahnaht, neneesaht,* and *verohnsaht.*

The mystery haunted me. *What in the world are there seven of that she needs to refer to each time she speaks?* Days of the week, the seven deadly sins, the seven seas, wonders of the world—none made any sense at all.

Chapter 6

THE SECOND WEEK OF October, a blizzard swept down off the mountains so fast and so fierce, no one was prepared for it. Blinded by the whiteout, Nora and Raj had to use the rope—hand over hand—to battle their way from the Dome to the Shack. Wyatt raced back from the glacier, shaken. Only Sigrid, Jeanne, and I had been safely in the Shack when the storm hit.

Two days later, the blizzard showed no signs of letting up. It became hard to imagine any reality other than howling, snow-filled darkness. We'd gone through most of the card and board games, and a good deal of alcohol. I felt walled in, jumpy.

As the credits rolled on yet another old science fiction DVD, Raj wrangled himself to his stockinged feet. Bored to distraction, he wandered to Wyatt's desk. Sigrid sat on the desk with her sweater stretched over her knees, rocking as she stared out the picture window, the view like living inside a thunderhead. Odin rustled in his wood shavings, his nose pushing through the cage.

"How's the research going?" Raj asked.

Wyatt shifted in his seat. "I'll get there. It's a matter of time."

"What have you tried?"

"I've worked with arctic char, cod, flounder—they can all survive temps below freezing—all kinds of arctic shellfish, some amphibians, lichens, moss. You know there are lichens that stay frozen for years and thaw out just fine?"

"But how do you study the why and how of all this?"

Wyatt considered Raj, said, "I test for cryoproteins, or other cryoprotectants, isolate them, then try them on their own, or combine them in every possible way."

Raj listlessly plopped down on the couch, glasses flashing in the dim light. "What do you mean, 'try them'?"

"Raj," Nora said from a sprawled-out position on the rug. "Can you get me some tea?"

"In a minute."

Wyatt said, "I worked with lemmings at first. Put them on special diets, injected them, froze them, but so far . . ."

"Just a bunch of dead lemmings?"

Wyatt drained his can of beer. "I think I need to be working with larger mammalian subjects. You up for it?"

Raj scoffed, got up and poured himself some wine, Nora her tea, and sat on the floor next to her. "With all due respect, Wyatt, this is crackpot science. You know it, and I know it."

Wyatt crushed the beer can and tossed it in the trash. "Tell you what I know. Odin exists. Three times he's thawed alive."

"Where'd you find him?"

"In the Dome. What difference does it make? Sigrid's alive. And people all over the world are freezing to death in these ice winds. Five, six, a dozen people at a time, wiped out. And it's going to get a lot worse. You think knowing what kept Sigrid from dying won't help the human race?"

Sigrid turned to Raj from her perch on Wyatt's desk, a smile dimpling her cheeks. She said, "Seal Man."

"That's me, darling," Raj said to Sigrid with pride. "Seal Man." He hopped to his feet and went to give her a hug, but she withdrew, smile fading. He took a good look at her. "You know, she looks a little peaked. Can we at least try to give her a bath?"

"We heat up the water," I said, "but she won't go near it."

"So, Raj, you two seem tight," Wyatt said. "She say anything else to you besides 'Seal Man'?"

"Oh, for sure. We chat all day long, don't we, Sigrid? She's told Seal Man all her secrets, every last one of them."

"I see." Wyatt got up, brushing past Raj on his way to the kitchen, where he extracted another beer from the fridge. "You know what I'd like to do? Get a blood sample from her."

Sigrid drew her circles in the condensation on the window, one after the other in neat rows, before rubbing them away.

"Bad idea," Raj said.

"Why would you do that?" Nora pushed herself up.

I sat forward on the couch. "Wyatt, come on. You can't do that to her. You're just going to ruin any progress I've made."

"Any *progress* you've made?" Wyatt snorted. He kept his eyes on me, then said, "Hey, Jeanne, got a second?"

Jeanne set aside some bread dough she'd been working and dutifully came into the living room.

"So, guys, it's simple. I need a blood sample. Raj is right, look at her. Something's up with her."

Sigrid, reading the room, dropped down off Wyatt's desk and wandered over to me, her sweater fanning out on the rug.

"Nora?" Wyatt said. "Help me out?"

She turned to Raj. "Maybe it is a good idea. Poor kid. She can't tell us how she's feeling."

Raj paced. "I can't be a part of this. She won't understand."

Wyatt rooted around in a drawer, pulled out a box with a red cross on it. "It'll just take a second. She may need antibiotics. Val, come on, help us out. Explain it to her somehow."

All eyes drilled into me.

My knees went wobbly as weakness flooded me. In my effort to conserve my stash, I'd gone a few days without a pill. I rued that decision as heat flashed up my neck and shoulders.

"Can you just give me a minute?"

"Of course," Raj said.

"You stay with Seal Man and Nora," I said to Sigrid. "I'll be right back."

I ran to the bathroom and threw up. The walls rippled and throbbed as they closed in. *I just need a pill,* I thought. *Then I'll be able to deal with this.* I staggered down the hall toward my bedroom, chiding myself for needing the chemical balm.

I jerked open my sock drawer. Nothing. Only socks.

My heart did its fight-or-flight dance. I wrenched out the drawer and dumped the contents onto my bed. Just socks, a couple of pairs of underwear, a scarf. A safety pin.

Where are my pills?

I emptied each drawer on the bed. Nothing. Someone had taken them. *Or am I just losing my mind?* I sat on my piles of clothes on my saggy bed, quaking. How would I ever go out on the ice again? How would I ever get home? *No pills, no pills.*

Screams from the living room shocked me to my feet. I bolted down the hallway. Their faces ghostly by the TV's shifting light, Jeanne held Sigrid down while Wyatt took vial after vial of blood from her arm. Nora and Raj stood back while Sigrid shrieked, her eyes never leaving mine.

I ran at them. "Get off of her—let her *go!*"

"Stand back!" Wyatt growled. "Or she's going to get hurt."

Wyatt was right. All I could do was watch as the tubes filled with Sigrid's dark blood, until Jeanne finally released her and she ran caterwauling by me to her room.

The storm ended at dawn. We all took shifts shoveling out the main door, heads down, exchanging minimal good-mornings, as if each of us—in our own way—was the guilty party. I felt sick at heart about what had happened, furious at Wyatt and Jeanne, frustrated that we—me, Raj, and Nora—seemed to constantly bend under Wyatt's will. *What was wrong with us?*

Around noon, I ventured outside to relieve Raj. I found an eerie and terrifying sight. Snow flowed over the tops of the buildings, the Dome now just a blip of yellow in the alabaster bay. We'd practically been erased from the landscape.

Raj was chopping out the snowcat abandoned in the storm by Wyatt. Its cabin was encased in snow and ice.

"How's it going?"

He gave me a look, like, *Really?* and kept on banging at the ice with a hammer and chisel. "How's Sigrid?" he asked.

"Hard to tell. She's doing her old push-the-bed-against-the-door thing."

"Look, Val, I feel terrible about last night. They had her pinned and that needle in before either of us could move."

"Hey, I abandoned her too."

He started to speak, stopped himself. "Maybe it's a good thing. He's got his sample. It's over."

"You really believe that?"

"I believe we have to get through the next couple weeks the best we can. Let's just survive it." He went back to chopping.

That afternoon, as our meager light began to fade into velvet black, Sigrid still refused to leave her room. I left a dinner of fried fish and canned black beans—her new favorite—outside her door.

The next morning, the dish sat cold and untouched.

"Hey, Sigrid." I stood outside her room sipping a cup of coffee. Knocked a few times. "It's me, Bahl. I'm coming in."

The door was unlocked, bed back under the window that faced the Dome. Sketch pad on her lap, Sigrid sat cross-legged on the floor, her slight back bent, a child island in a sea of drawings. The air tasted static with her manic energy, her helter-skelter tufts of wild blue-black hair tipped by lush morning light. It hit me in the chest how much I cared about this child, and how dangerous caring was, because of how quickly people can be taken away. I took a breath and tried not to spin off into dread.

I knelt to examine her drawings, expecting squiggles and birds, but no. Each was the same: She'd traced seven circles per sheet of paper. Every circle drawn with a black marker and left blank in the middle except for the very last one. On the first few drawings she'd neatly filled the final ring with red ink, but with each subsequent drawing her work on the last circle turned more and more frantic, until agitated red marks burst through its boundaries.

"Sigrid."

She looked up at me, fist clutching the marker midair. Bald fear in her eyes. Clearly I'd interrupted some nightmarish reverie. She grabbed my leg, pulled me toward her, whispering, "Bahl, Bahl."

"Yes, I'm coming." I sat cross-legged beside her.

As if she were afraid my attention might lag, she raced through another drawing, each circle more sloppily drawn, until she came to the last one. Tossing the black marker aside, she seized the red one and attacked the final circle with it, tearing through the paper, crying in a helpless way before hurling the marker at the wall.

"Hey, Sigrid, hey." I reached out and touched her shoulder, but she swatted my hand away. Jumped up and whirled around to face me. A crescent-shaped knife glinted in her fist. "Whoa, put that down," I choked out. "I'm not going to hurt you."

She circled me, knife held high. Through choking cries of rage and disappointment, she rambled on in her language, "Bahl" interspersed between phrases.

"I'm so sorry I let that happen to you. Never again."

She stood behind me now, crying and talking at the same time, the knife hovering at my neck. I braced for the pain, for blood to pour down my back. I could have reached back and grabbed the knife but would have been too late to stop her from cutting me.

"Sigrid . . ." I breathed.

She began to sob. Slowly I turned to face her.

I whispered the seven words that prefaced her sentences: "*Stahndala, tahtaksah, oosahmluru, muhkeensaht, sahsahnaht, neneesaht, verohnsaht . . .*"

She lowered her arm and hiccupped, her face breaking into a confused smile. I repeated the words as I reached to take the knife.

"Can I have the knife, Sigrid?" I made a slicing motion. "Jeanne'll be looking for it. It's not safe for you to have it."

Cheeks ruddy with emotion, she gazed at me with the oldest eyes in the world, as if not understanding why I still didn't understand. *Keep the knife,* I thought, *if it makes you feel better.*

The drawings frightened me more than the fact that she was collecting knives. I picked up her final one. I sighed, running my fingers over the bloodred hole she'd made. "What are these circles?" I asked in Danish, West Greenlandic, English.

She gathered up all the peculiar drawings and piled them in my lap. Maybe because I'd been listening to her cry, I began to quietly cry myself as she took my hand and pressed it on the gouged-out drawing. Her efforts felt so full of her own urgent needs.

I searched her dark eyes. "You haven't eaten in a couple of days. Aren't you hungry?" I pointed at her, rubbed my belly.

With a cry of frustration, she swept the drawings off my lap and disappeared under her bed. I dove down onto my belly.

"Come on, Sigrid, don't do this. Everyone is sorry." For several minutes I rattled on about nothing, trying every bribe word imaginable to get her to come out. No effect. Then I remembered her joy when she watched Raj burst out of the water after his dive.

"What about going to the Dome? We can watch Seal Man."

From her pillows came Sigrid's faint voice, "Seal Man?"

"They're doing a dive today." I went to the door. Made sure I made a lot of noise opening it. "See you outside for Seal Man."

Watching Raj prepare to dive was like witnessing a holy ritual. With solemn quiet, he unhooked the red-and-black dry suit that hung from the ceiling, its alien-like red gloves dangling from the sleeves. He sat on a folding chair, flopping the suit out in front of him. Starting with the legs, he worked the rubber fabric over two layers of long underwear. Though clearly he and Nora had memorized each step, Nora consulted the bulleted checklist. She whispered her way through every zip and valve, each adjustment and setting. Raj may as well have been on his way to the moon.

Bug-eyed, Sigrid sat next to me on a bench watching the transformation. Suited up for the most part, Raj paused in his preparation and excused himself, crossing to a corner of the Dome where a towel-size, colorful mat had been laid out. Facing away from us, he got down on his knees and prayed quietly to himself.

Nora laid out the rest of the gear on a rubber mat: air tank, weight belt, fins, goggles, headgear, knife, flashlight. Satisfied with her work, she lifted a kettle off a Coleman stove. "Want some cocoa?" She glanced over at Sigrid, who nodded.

Sigrid chugged the chocolate, handing Nora back the cup as if fully expecting a refill. Nora laughed and gave her one.

Raj finished his prayers and poured himself some cocoa.

Sigrid wiped her mouth, said, "Seal Man." She jumped from her seat and led me over to one of the remaining two dry suits suspended from hooks. She placed my hand on one of the sleeves.

Nora smiled. "That spare suit would fit you perfectly."

"No," I said to Sigrid. "*Seal Man*. Not Seal Bahl."

She shook her head and reached into one of her mittens, unfolding a scrap of paper; she had torn the snake image from one of her drawings. She squirreled it into my hand and squeezed my fingers tight around the paper, saying, "*Taimagiakaman*."

I knew this word. . . . I gasped and got down to my knees to be at her eye level. "Say that word again, please, Sigrid."

Face full of anticipation, she whispered the word to me again, syllable by syllable as if to say, *Really, you finally understand?* Pointed at the beat-up image on the paper.

Translated literally, the word meant "the necessity of understanding nature—in all its complexity—to stay alive," but it was also shorthand for "Let's find the things we need to stay alive," or "These are the sacrifices we need to make to stay alive."

Somehow this Inuit word was a part of her lexicon. I felt like a person emerging from a dark cave, granted a glimpse of sun.

"You need this to stay alive"—I pointed at the paper—"this seaweedy thing, is that right?"

She gestured at the spare suit.

"You want me to . . ." I glanced at the hole. She nodded.

"You guys ready?" Nora called over to us. "He's all set."

I knelt and looked at Sigrid's sweet face glowing with excitement. "Let's go watch Seal Man." She looked disappointed but followed me to the hole. Slushy water sluiced against its sides.

"How cold is it?" I asked.

"Barely above freezing." Raj shook out his arms, quivered his legs. "Quick dives, always keep moving, that's the key."

"Darling, are you ready?" Nora said with quiet intimacy.

Below us, the dull cry of the ice, the screech of the Dome's supporting poles as they scraped against it. The place felt so barren—just folding chairs, a few tables, a heater, and a couple of cots pushed together. I suddenly missed trees.

"All set," Raj said. "I love you."

"I love you too," Nora said.

He got down to the rubber mats and scooted over to the hole. Wasting no time, he folded his arms across his chest and slipped in with a small splash. He fit in his mouthpiece, gave Nora a thumbs-up, and dropped down into the cold blue eye.

"How long will he . . ."

"This is an eight-minute dive," Nora said, staring after him.

"It's not possible that I would ever do this," I said.

"The worst part is going to oxygen," she said thoughtfully. "After that, the biggest danger is getting so blown away by the weirdness of everything down there you lose track of time."

A kitchen timer with a big second hand ticked off the numbers on the dial. Nora clicked on the mic. "Raj, how's it going?"

His voice was garbled. "Good. Twenty-three feet. Murky. Out."

"Roger that," she said into the mic.

A thud. Sigrid had climbed to the table from a chair and knocked the heavy diving suit from its hook. She grabbed the suit by one creepy red glove and hitched it bit by bit across the mats. Dropped the cumbersome pile of rubber at my feet.

"Guess she wants you to dive," Nora said with a laugh.

I stepped away from the suit. "Sigrid. I'm no seal woman. No."

"Maybe just put it on," Nora said. "Make her happy. You don't have to dive, but we can go through the steps for fun."

"If I dive, will you take a bath?" I motioned washing myself.

She nodded. It was fun asking her questions when she was in this mood, knowing she would say yes.

"Is she doing okay?" Nora helped Sigrid ease a leg of the suit over my pants. "That was rough with Wyatt."

"I think so." Warmed by Sigrid's smile, I felt like a parent who would do anything to make her child happy. "Do you guys want kids someday?"

Nora yanked a zipper across my thigh a little too hard. She

took a few seconds to answer. "We had a son, but he died. It's all we want—or it's all *I* want anyway—to try again, but it's been a year and, you know, nothing." Her face was pale against her dark hair, her features tight. "We've already done five steps on the checklist."

The clock read three minutes, thirty-three seconds.

"I'm so sorry."

She clicked on the mic. "Raj, darling, how's it going?"

"Fine. Forty-three feet. Clearer now. Out."

"Roger that."

She clicked off the mic. "His name was Charlie. He was only two months old. He was born with a heart defect. They tried surgery, but he died during the operation. Can you imagine? Seven doctors huddled around our baby, and none of them could . . ."

She glanced at the clock. Four minutes, twenty seconds.

"You don't have to do this," I said. "Get me geared up, I mean."

"It's okay, I want to. Sigrid looks so happy, watching us," Nora said with a wistful smile. She worked the hood over my head, showed us on the checklist where we were: step fifteen.

I stretched my arms so she could jigger the sleeves up to my shoulders. She said, "Raj hasn't been able to put himself back together at all, really. Sometimes I think grief affects everything."

She hauled the big zipper across my chest and took a step back. "Look at that, you're already at step eighteen, see?"

I felt like a sausage in the dry suit, which reeked of old rubber.

She turned back to the clock. Six minutes had passed.

"How many times has he been down there?"

"Oh, we've dived hundreds of times. All kinds of conditions." She clicked on the mic. "Raj, how's it going?"

His mic snapped on, but only static came through.

"Bloody thing," she said. We sat on stools next to the slushy blue pit, watching the second hand tick into seven minutes. Sigrid sat cross-legged next to me on the floor, occasionally grinning up at me or hugging my rubber-encased calves.

Nora got up and paced around the hole, then back the other way, never taking her eyes off it.

The second hand swept cruelly around the face of the clock. We were soon staring down nine minutes.

Nora clicked on the mic. "Raj, are you on your way up? Over."

Continuous static grated the air, spitting and crackling.

Nine minutes, fifty-seven seconds.

"Raj, can you confirm—"

He exploded from the water, shards of ice flowing off his black-hooded head. I nearly fell backward off my stool, while Sigrid clapped and laughed. He bobbed for a moment; then Nora, with shocking strength, hauled him out of the water. She got down on the ice and helped him sit up.

"Couldn't you hear me?" he sputtered.

"Something's up with the mics." She cradled him, one hand over his heart. "All we heard was static for the last five minutes."

He coughed a bit, shook his head, and peeled off his rubber hood with a wet smack. He looked me up and down in the spare suit and laughed. "So, you're going to give it a try?"

Which is when I made my decision. I could at least drop in with my head above water—show Sigrid the suit wasn't for nothing.

"Just going for a quick dip." Making sure Sigrid had her eyes on me, I scooted over to the hole, dropped one finned foot in, then the other. Snakes of cold encircled my calves.

"Val, that's brilliant!" Nora said. "She'll love you for it."

"We got you," Raj said. They gathered around, took me under the arms, and helped lower me down. Sigrid did a little happy dance, clapping her hands and chattering away. I focused on her as cold swept up my legs, shocking my torso and chest. I thought I'd lasted a good minute, but later Raj broke it to me that it had been only fifteen seconds before they hauled me out.

When it became clear I wasn't actually going to dive, Sigrid turned away, refusing to look at me. Dripping, I apologized as I unpeeled the gear. Shc kept repeating that word, about the snake being necessary for her to stay alive. It cut me to feel the limits of what I could do for her—for anyone, including myself—just as it began to register with a flash of joy that I had, in fact—unmedicated—dangled my body in the great polar Enormity.

Steaming water sloshed in the massive pot as Jeanne heaved it from the stove and poured it into the metal tub. I'd scared up a few slivers of lavender soap, laid them on a clean washcloth next to the tub. Anything to tempt Sigrid into taking a bath.

"What do you think, Sigrid? Give it a try?" I called over to her.

She got up from the couch with her chin high, gave me a look that said, *You chickened out on the dive, so no bath for me,* and ambled down the hallway toward her bedroom.

"Sigrid's stubborn," Jeanne said, folding her arms across her gray sweatshirt. "She's got her own mind. Just like my Frances did." Her face was puffy and red after several early-evening glasses of wine. I thought, *She's me, in some fun-house way. How close am I to this?*

We both watched the water settle in the basin.

"Listen, Jeanne, I was wondering . . . I've misplaced some of my medicine, these pills I take. Have you seen an orange bottle?"

On her cutting board, Jeanne arranged a shank of red caribou meat. "Check all your pants pockets?"

"Yes."

She brought a cleaver down on the shank, cutting cleanly through the shattered rib. The wine-red meat glistened under the sterile lights. "They should be in there. Found them when I was washing up. Put 'em back when your pants were dry."

"But I've checked all my pockets—coats, shirts, everything."

She peeled off a stray knot of gristle, flicked it in the trash.

"Well, to be honest, I wouldn't put it past Wyatt to chuck them." She arranged the slab of meat for another hit of her knife. Gave me a sidelong glance. "He's very antidrug, you know." *Whack.* "Or have you asked Raj or Nora? Raj seems to be having a bit of a rough time, if you ask me—"

I took a step closer to her. "So, you read the label."

She waved the cleaver. "Well, they were right in front of me."

"You should have just found me and handed them to me."

Jeanne wiped the sweat off her forehead. "What am I, your servant? You were somewhere with the girl. Making her your best friend." She stuck the cleaver into the meat. "Listen, I got enough I gotta take care of, never mind making sure you got your pills."

"Okay, I believe you. Never mind." But I didn't believe her. I would never put my pills in my pocket, for one thing.

She worked the cleaver free, laid it down on the cutting board with a strange reverence. "You know, everything was so peaceful here before Andy came. Wyatt and me, we had these long, quiet days, just getting work done. None of this high drama."

"I'll expect my pills back by breakfast," I said, my voice higher than I'd intended. "In my room. No questions asked."

"Val, I didn't take your precious pills." She turned to face me, wiping her meat-stained hands on a rag. "And speaking of missing things, I'm down a knife. My crescent knife. Have you seen it?"

"No," I said, my face hot.

She opened the oven door; the aroma of baking corn bread flowed out. Suddenly I was dizzy with hunger. "You know," she said, "Andy lost things all the time."

The mention of his name was a shot of pain between my eyes.

She took out the hot bread and set it on the rack. "Every day, we're looking for his spikes, his headlamp, his knife, his gloves."

"I don't misplace things. People assume twins are the same—"

"He was a pretty mellow guy, when he was in a good mood. He played practical jokes on us all the time. Used to put Wyatt's frozen specimens—you know, lemmings and so on—in his bed. Wyatt freaked out. But they were like brothers. Never saw anybody crack Wyatt up like Andy could with his silly drawings and whatnot. And the way they talked? Couldn't get a word in edgewise."

I was quiet, hungry for more, but she misinterpreted me.

"I'm sorry for yapping on. Can't imagine how you must feel."

"It's okay."

"I mean, sometimes I get depressed too. What's left in this world for me, besides fixing the next thing that breaks, and the next, and the next? Guess I'm a stubborn old broad. I just hang on." She raised her mug of wine to me, drank it down, and set it on the counter with a flourish. "See you in an hour for supper?"

"Sure," I said, unable to repress an image of the cleaver tomahawking into my back as I walked away.

"Jeanne and I are headed back to Glacier 35A tomorrow," Wyatt announced as he sliced into his caribou steak. "We'll be back pretty late, so you're all on your own for dinner."

"Brilliant," Nora said, winking at Raj. "We'll get a curry."

Raj's face stayed serious. "Why are you going back there?"

"Just feel like there's more to learn about the girl out there."

I took a swallow of wine. "If it's about Sigrid, I need to go."

"Not a good idea." Wyatt's voice was flat. "This is serious work. We can't be worrying about you—"

"I won't even leave the snowcat."

He served himself some rice, not meeting my eye. "You need to watch the girl. Make some actual progress."

Just the sound of knives slicing across plates, glasses clinking.

"Sigrid can hang out with us," Nora said cautiously. "Seal Man would love it, right?"

Raj shrugged a yes. "Sure. We'll keep an eye on her."

"We can talk about this in the morning," Wyatt said.

"We don't have to talk," I said. "What time should I be ready?"

Jeanne and Wyatt exchanged a glance I couldn't decipher.

"Maybe Val needs a little break, Wyatt," Nora said. "What she's doing with Sigrid isn't easy—"

A long, guttural ringtone purred from Wyatt's desk. We all jumped. I'd never heard the sound before.

"The sat phone," Jeanne said, vaulting from the table, but Wyatt had already sprinted to his desk and begun sweeping away papers, magazines, books. Two more rings, and he found it.

"Wyatt Speeks, Tarrarmiut Station." He stared at me as he listened. "I'm good, sir. We're all good. How are you?" *Who is he sir-ing? Is he in trouble?* ". . . Yes, she's right here." He held the phone in my direction. "It's for you. It's your father."

As I took the phone, I was gut-punched by my last image of my father: his stooped back as he turned away from me that broiling summer afternoon he dared me to come to this place.

"Hey, Dad."

"Val, what's going on?"

I glanced around the room. Everyone was watching me.

"Nothing. I mean, I'm fine," I said as quietly as I could. I took a walk around the cluttered room. The second I stepped beyond a five-foot radius around Wyatt's desk, static roared in my ears.

"Can you talk privately?"

"Not really."

He sighed heavily. "Hadn't heard from you. I was getting concerned. So I'll ask the questions, you say yes or no. Do you think Wyatt killed your brother?"

I sat on the edge of the desk, gazing out at the skyline of majestic bergs in the bay. "I don't have an answer for that."

"Are you safe there now?"

"Pretty much."

"Answer me."

"Is anyone really safe?" I said louder than I'd intended.

"Val, I want you to get out of there."

"Why?"

"You know why," he growled. "Look, I'm going to make some calls. Get cash to the right people, whatever it takes. What happened to Andy happened. But I can't lose you too."

I pictured Sigrid's eager, trusting face as she whispered the word for "Let's find the things we need to stay alive."

"That's not a good idea, Dad."

"I shouldn't have pushed you to go. You're not up to the task."

Odin lumbered around his cage on Wyatt's desk. These days the mouse was logy, not even climbing on his wheel for a spin.

"That's a crappy thing to say to me, Dad. I'm already here."

The phone crackled and buzzed, and for a moment I thought he'd hung up, but then his voice blasted through loud and clear. "Listen to me. You're going to lose the sun pretty soon. I've got connections in Thule. I'll wire some money over, and they'll get a plane out to you in two days, weather permitting."

Raj and Nora set the last dish in the rack, Nora laughing at something he'd said.

"I won't get on it."

"Don't do this to me, Val."

"Dad, I'm doing what you wanted me to do."

A long pause. "You're not Andy, Val. I forgive you for that."

"Thanks a lot."

"There's no shame in coming home."

"I'm not leaving until I finish what I started. Take care—"

"Don't you hang up on me, Val—"

"I'm saying goodbye, not hanging up. There's a difference."

A frustrated silence. "The fact is, I'm—I'm fresh out of caramels. Can't get my hands on any sweets around here. You've got to get back here soon and bring me some, is that a deal?"

"Sure, Dad, I promise. Boxes of them."

"Goodbye, Val. Stay safe." A clumsy clunking sound as he hung up, then the vaguely disturbing, high-pitched dial tone.

Was I mistaken, or had I felt him wanting to say he loved me? It wasn't a word we'd ever exchanged, as far as I could remember. But right then, I decided to stop protecting my heart, to take my chances next time and be the first to say the word "love."

Chapter 7

I WOKE WITH A JOLT. My battery-powered alarm clock had died, and I could tell it was late. The air brimmed with the smell of coffee. Muffled conversation, the stomp of boots down the hall.

I dove into my clothes, brushing my hair as I hurried down the hallway. A pallid light leaked into the main room.

Wyatt stood at the front door. "Sleeping Beauty awakes."

"Where is everyone?"

"Girl's asleep. Jeanne's helping Nora and Raj fix some piece of dive equipment in the Dome. You're lucky for that. Otherwise we'd've been long gone." He zipped his parka and flipped the hood. "I've got to de-ice the cat. Soon as Jeanne's back, we leave."

"Fine," I said, gulping lukewarm coffee.

He left, a frosty blast of air in his wake.

I sat on the couch considering my options. I needed alcohol, something, anything to take the edge off. I viscerally craved the surge of calm from my daily pill. But it wasn't to be.

Drug-free, I felt the ghosts of everyone in the room, could smell Wyatt's, Raj's, Nora's, Jeanne's sorrows, angers, their griefs, their regrets—all so viciously raw. I couldn't last here like this.

I had to move. Find some alcohol. A pathetic Band-Aid, but a necessary one. I checked around the kitchen. The boxes of red and white wine had been drained the night before. Listening for Wyatt's footsteps, I tiptoed to the low freezer on the kitchen floor and opened it. Just frozen food, no booze.

Damn. I had to try the Shed.

I slipped on my boots, threw on my parka, and left the building. As I fumbled with the rope that connected the Shack and the Shed, I prayed that Jeanne was still tied up at the Dome. I reached the Shed and pushed open the heavy door.

"Jeanne? It's Val." My voice cracked in the thin, frigid air.

No answer. I snapped on the overhead bulb. As always, the place made me want to run. The stench of crankcase oil; the circular saw hulking over the far end of the table. Gaskets, tubing, plastic jugs of mysterious liquids. The place vibrated with a latent violence.

A cursory check revealed no boxed wine, *damn*. The walk-in freezer was a remote possibility; it had a combination lock. I gave it a tug, hoping Jeanne had forgotten to spin the dial. No luck. Got down to my knees next to the smaller freezer. I yanked on the combination lock; its two teeth disengaged from the round barrel.

She hadn't spun the dial.

The lid of the freezer resisted at first, then let go with a snap of suction. Through the mist I blinked at the outline of an animal. I'd only seen them in photos, but it had to be an arctic fox. It was curled up as if sleeping. I touched its black nose: a frozen marble.

Next to it, tucked into ziplock bags: several frozen arctic lemmings; an antediluvian-looking fish with wide, flat eyes; and a puffin, its cartoon-orange beak and webbed feet bright even under the plastic. All in perfect condition, icebound.

I slowly slipped my hands under the fox. A filigree of ice crackled free, tinkling into the box. Underneath him, the mother lode. Three full fifths of Smirnoff vodka. I laid the fox on the sawdust-covered floor, picked up a bottle, unscrewed the cap, and drank.

Two swallows later, a wave of self-loathing crashed over me. *Why not do it? Why not just take Dad's offer and get out—*

The sputter of an engine firing up outside the Shed startled me. My head swam. *I'm a mess, but I'm all Sigrid's got.* Heart smashing against my rib cage, I tucked the bottle of vodka in my parka, wiped my mouth, and ran to the door. Wyatt and Jeanne were just turning the snowcat to face the glacier. I took off as fast as I could across the field of ice toward the idling machine.

Buffeted by winds lashing down from the glacier, the snowcat rocked on the ice lake, its American flag on the hood snapping crazily. I sat buckled in the back seat like a child left in a car waiting for her parents to finish shopping. I watched Wyatt and Jeanne drill ice core after ice core, loading the gray tubes on a metal sled.

Through slitted eyes I took in the sun, a sizzling fat ovoid resting on the horizon. I reached out my gloved finger, tracing its perimeter on the steamy glass, just as I'd seen Sigrid do countless times. Traced another, and another, until I'd drawn a row of circles. My finger hesitated. *The circles were suns! Days!*

My hand fell from the window. Sigrid drew a picture of suns every day, each day with one less sun. *She was counting down.*

With a blast of icy air, Wyatt lifted himself into the driver's seat. A few yards from the cat, Jeanne knelt on the ice, struggling to free a core from the corer with a plunger. "Last chance to see the crevasse up close," Wyatt said. "You change your mind?"

"I'm coming."

I flipped up my hood, tightened the drawstring around my face. Climbed down onto the ice, following Wyatt's wide red back as he crunched across the snow in his rocking gait.

We stood only ten feet from the abyss. The fissure had widened; the sharp edges around the block that had imprisoned Sigrid now softened from exposure to the sun; the deep blue of the ice had soaked in the heat. Now it looked hard and glassy.

"Why are you taking samples from here?" I called to him.

"Question is, why did it take me so long to think of it?"

Jeanne, a smudge of red and black behind veils of fine falling snow, yanked at a cord on a small yellow engine. It started up like a lawn mower. She and Wyatt hoisted a twelve-foot pole, the last five feet or so a bright red screw-shaped device. It was already turning fast. They struggled to keep the pole going straight down into the ice, then hauled it up bit by bit. Working full tilt, they laid the corer down, bumping out into a wooden trough a perfectly cylindrical, yards-long ice core that glistened blue and silver gray. Finally, they loaded the core and equipment on the sled we'd towed from the Shack. I couldn't help admiring their coordination, this dance in which each knew precisely what steps to take and when.

The entire panorama—snowcat, Jeanne, Wyatt, sled—disappeared and reappeared through curtains of snow and fog. I had a sense of unreality. The crevasse, a jagged blue wound, beckoned me. I crunched a few steps closer. How far would I fall? It would be easy, so much easier than everything I'd been trying and failing at: discovering the truth about Andy, deciphering Sigrid, battling my grief and fear. For several long, frigid seconds, I was lost.

Wyatt approached me, and, painfully, I slammed back into my body. Sobriety edging closer, I extracted my bottle of vodka from an inside pocket and took a long pull. Instead of the soft release a pill usually granted me, the booze spun me off to a rageful, dark place: How much had Andy suffered that dreadful night?

"What are you doing, Val?" Wyatt gestured away from the crevasse, at the cat. "Come on, we have to get out of here." He'd seen me drinking; he knew I had raided the Shed. I didn't care.

"Why don't you tell me what really happened that night with Andy? You have nothing to lose by telling me the truth."

He stomped his boot on the ice and groaned. "Unbelievable."

"You haven't told me a damned thing—"

"Of course I have. Many times. Are you . . ."

Drunk? Crazy? "Not blow by blow, you haven't."

His mouth thinned into a grim line. "Okay, Val. Let's go over it again. Andy and me were working on our separate projects. I was cataloguing the cores. He was . . . experimenting with different ideas about Odin. But he was depressed. Nothing was working for him. He was a gloom-and-doom kind of guy a lot of the time. Look . . ."

My voice rose to a fever pitch. "Jeanne said she heard you laughing, that you guys were having a great time. Such a great time she went off to work in the Shed, and—"

"Val, you've got to calm down, okay? You need to take a few steps away from that thing. Come on, a few steps toward me . . ."

"I'm fine where I am."

He paced closer, arm outstretched. "Just take my hand, okay?"

My body felt wooden with cold, molten with vodka and fury.

He let his hand drop to his side. "Val, no matter how badly you may want it to, my story's not going to change. It's going to be the same horrible, sad, tragic story, I'm sorry to say. It could have been something as stupid as Andy going out for his chocolate. He was always hiding his stash from me. Maybe he got turned around out there somehow, we'll never know."

"Andy hated frozen chocolate." I tried to feel my frozen fingers in my gloves, to feel the contours of Andy's lead heart.

"I got him to like it." Wyatt took a step toward me, closing the gap. One push, and I would go careening into hell. "You're an enigma to me, Val. I haul you up here to do a job, something I was under the impression you were uniquely good at, by the way, and Andy's all you've been thinking about. No wonder you've got nothing on the girl." His countenance took on an ugliness, as if he were making some terrible calculation. He glanced at Jeanne, nodded. *A signal?* She turned away, busied herself with the sled.

Wyatt stood legs spread apart. "Enlighten me, Val," he said. "What do you want from me? Do you want to go home? Because I can arrange that. I can get Pitak here in a day and a half—"

"I want to stay," I said, my voice barely audible.

"I think—no, I *know* you know more than you're telling me about the girl. You keeping secrets from me concerns me."

I took a step away from the abyss and toward him. He didn't budge.

"I know this, Wyatt. You have zero chance with Sigrid without me."

Jeanne fired up the cat. Without a word, Wyatt turned and trudged across the bleak stretch of ice. Each of his steps left me more alone in the Enormity. He did not look back as he climbed into the cat. All pride erased, I broke into a run, crying out to the both of them to wait for me, begging not to be left behind.

WYATT ordered all of us to gather in the living room that evening at seven sharp. No word why. Sigrid had gone to bed early, but the rest of us were there.

"I've had a chance to look at the cores we drilled today," he said as he blew into the room, a yard-long ice core encased in a wooden tube under one arm. He glanced at Jeanne, then at each of us, as if to say, *Pay attention*. He lifted the wooden lid from the core. Hundreds of slim bands of alternating pale blue, gray-white, and murky storm-cloud colors glistened. At about the midway point, a thin, coal-black ring encircled the tube.

"Here," he said, pointing with the blade of a hunting knife. "Around the seven-hundred-year mark. See it?" We all leaned forward to get a better look. "Human remains."

"Oh," Nora breathed.

Raj asked, "How do you know they're human?"

"I looked at the cells. Human bone cells are shaped differently from those of other mammals. They're like concentric rings. Want to have a look?" He gestured at the microscope behind him.

Raj didn't take his eyes off the black ring. "No."

Wyatt continued. "I don't believe Sigrid was encased in ice a few months ago, with her family chasing caribou. I think something happened to her between 1300 and 1400 or so, around the Little Ice Age. I think she's ancient."

We were all silenced, but the rightness of Wyatt's words slammed me in my gut. This was why everything—from markers to beds to snowmobiles to heat flowing from a box—fascinated her. This was why modern Greenlandic was mostly noise to her.

"What's the Little Ice Age?" I asked, breaking the silence.

"A cataclysmic, compressed, natural climate change event from around A.D. 1300 to 1800," he said. "Here's my theory. Sigrid could have been caught in some naturally occurring piteraq in 1300, similar to what we're calling 'ice winds' today. Think about it. Around 1250, there's evidence that pack ice in Greenland had grown beyond what anyone had ever seen. Summers disappeared. Temperature fluctuations were crazy fast."

"This has nothing to do with—" Raj said.

"Just listen!" Wyatt snapped. "These katabatic winds—these piteraqs shooting down off the glaciers—they can easily kick past a hundred miles an hour, hit seventy, eighty degrees below zero—the question is, are these being roiled up by insane temperature swings happening around the world right now?"

Raj folded his arms over his chest. "You've gone from human remains in a core to some wacko theory about ice winds then and now? Tying it in with the whole Sigrid fantasy? This is *not* science—I don't know what it is, but it's not—"

"Last week." Stone-faced, Wyatt clicked his PC alive. "Saint-Eustache in Canada. Small town north of Montreal. Temperatures bouncing all week from fifty, sixty degrees to zero or below. Friday? Boat ride on the Saint Lawrence. Four people freeze to death. Why? How?" He clicked some more. "The week before. Amsterdam, ten p.m. A woman's walking her dog along the seacoast. Both found dead the next morning, frozen solid. You think what I'm doing here with the girl isn't important? It might be the most important science on earth right now."

Raj said quietly, "Why didn't you film Sigrid thawing out?"

"What?" Sweat popped on Wyatt's brow. "We just didn't. We were too caught up in what was happening."

"You're telling me you weren't interested in proof?"

"All I'm asking is for you to listen, dammit!" Wyatt said, face dark. We watched him pick up the core with great care and place it in the low kitchen freezer. "The Little Ice Age did terrible things to people's lives. Decimated their food sources. Pitted them against each other for resources. And those winds must have been nuts. People's number one priority—besides finding food—must have been protecting themselves from those piteraqs."

A tinny, mechanical sound quieted him. A windup walking polar bear marched into view from the hallway.

I jumped up. "Sigrid?"

No answer.

I sprinted down the hall. She sat slouched with her back against her door. Listlessly she fidgeted with Rudolph's nose, now just a few red strings. "Bahl." She looked up at me with exhausted eyes.

I put my hand on her forehead—hot—and carried her into the living room. She turned her head away from the concerned faces.

Raj approached her. "Hey, honey, it's Seal Man." At the sound of his voice, she turned toward him, her face brightening a bit. His gentleness moved me. "Not feeling so great, huh. Okay for me to just touch your forehead for a second?"

She nodded. He laid his hand on her temple. "Wow, oh wow. She's on fire. We've got to get her to the mainland right away."

"Let me have a look at her," Wyatt said behind me. To my surprise, she allowed him to touch her as well, even let him hold a thermometer briefly against her forehead. "She's just shy of one hundred. Poor kid. We can crush antibiotics up in her food."

"You need to get her out of here, Wyatt." Raj faced him.

"She has the flu. Or some kind of bug. She'll be fine. Jeanne, get me some hamburger, and we'll—"

"And what if she's not?" Nora said, gathering up their gear.

"If there's no improvement by morning, I'll make a call, okay?"

As I carried Sigrid back down the hallway, I paused as she deposited a balled-up slip of paper in my hand. Felt her intense gaze as I opened the drawing: six circles, the last slashed red.

"Okay, Sigrid," I said. "I think I understand." With a soft whimper, she hugged me so tightly I could barely breathe.

I SPENT most of the night awake—*in thrall*—feeling, *knowing*, that Sigrid was ancient. Realizing that the Inuit words in her speech borrowed from *her* centuries-old language, not the other way around, and they were mostly concerned with elements of survival. A small, tantalizing window into the distant past.

The next morning, still lost in wonder, I passed Wyatt's desk, pausing by Odin's cage. He lay on his side in a sea of food pellets, his breathing rapid. I set down my coffee and had a closer look.

Wyatt whistled as he flipped pancakes in the kitchen.

"Your mouse doesn't seem to be feeling too well."

"Ah, he's fine," Wyatt said. "You check on the girl?"

The girl. As if she didn't have a name. "Still sleeping." I'd gotten her to drink an antibiotic-laced cup of cocoa the night before.

Wyatt was stacking pancakes on a plate as I began to suit up. "I'm heading over to the Dome while Sigrid's still asleep," I said.

"Why?"

"Just a change from my room. I've got some books on Thule culture I want to show Nora and Raj—"

"That girl knows exactly how to survive the ice. You get that, don't you?" His affect had changed: whistling gone.

I looked for my gloves. "It's logical that she would."

He laughed. "These people *survive,* Val. And that girl? She's *seen* things." He came toward me. "She's playing us."

Heart racing, I pulled on my snow pants, big orange boots, vest. "What do you want me to do, Wyatt?" I jammed on my hat.

"What can you say in her language? Tell me."

"Man, woman, seal man, outside, caribou, numbers—"

He waved me away. "She understands far more than that. *Far* more. She doesn't seem to like me. Is that the problem?"

"I—"

"Make me the bad guy. Tell her it's a secret between you two, what she did, what she took. Whatever you have to do." He folded two sticks of spearmint gum in his mouth, chewed with vigor. "We have days left here, not weeks."

I turned toward the door. "I'll be back in a couple of hours."

He expelled an exasperated sigh and held out the clipboard. I took it and wrote in my destination and when I was headed back, even though I thought it was ridiculous. He snatched it back.

"You think you're special, Val? You think you're safe from the ice winds? You think any of us is safe?"

He stood too close to me, blocking the door, his breath stinking of maple syrup, stale coffee, spearmint. Seconds passed.

"Look, your anger is a bit much for me sometimes, Wyatt. There isn't much light left. . . . Can I get by, please?"

He stepped back with a melodramatic *After you* gesture.

I opened the door. Cold rushed me.

"Listen."

I turned to him.

"Jeanne's been working on something to help us out at the site. We're headed back tomorrow, first thing. All of us. I need all hands on deck. The girl comes too."

He closed the door, and I turned to face the glittering expanse. Step by step, I made my way toward the Dome, eyes on the ice beneath my feet, rope gripped tight. Stared straight down.

A snorting, scuffling sound to either side of me brought me to a halt. I tried to quiet my banging heart. A shadow broke the sun on my face; hooves crunched brittle ice. I looked up.

A herd of caribou—a couple dozen at least—surrounded me, their breath snorting out dragon puffs through flared nostrils. Heavy gray flanks over spindly legs that clicked as they walked, shining brown eyes set deep in inky faces. They swayed their huge necks toward one another and back at me as if confirming, *She is nothing, no danger, keep moving.* In a casual gallop, they threaded around me, leaving me in their wake.

I burst into the Dome, full of the story of the caribou. Nora and Raj made me hot tea, settling me in the corner of the Dome nearest the heater. I tried not to look at the dark blue hole in the ice opposite us. After a few sips of tea, I brought out Sigrid's drawings of squiggles and birds, spreading them out on their worktable.

Raj glanced at Nora as he pulled up a chair. "We should tell you, Sigrid's been giving us these drawings as well."

"Mostly she gives them to Seal Man," Nora added.

I sat back, faintly hurt. "What do you think of them?"

Raj drew his finger thoughtfully along the squiggly lines. "These could be a kind of seaweed, don't know. But that bird does look like an arctic tern."

I retrieved the drawings of "suns" I kept in one of my Greenland books. Flattened them on the desk. "What do these look like to you? Could they be suns, do you think? Or moons?"

"I guess . . ." Raj said.

"Think about it. This is what she draws. *Why?* She's drawing squiggles, birds, and then circles, the last one red, and look how she colors it, see? Like it's, I don't know . . ."

"Like it's what, Val?" Nora asked gently.

"Like those suns indicate days." My voice quavered. I extracted one of the earlier drawings. "Look. Fifteen suns, the last one blotted out with red Magic Marker." I scrambled in my pocket, hands shaking as I unfolded her latest drawing. "This one is from last night. *Five circles.* The last one, look what she did to it."

The red marker had torn the paper nearly in half.

"She's trying to tell us she has five days to live. Don't you see? She has *five days* unless we find her this snake and this tern. Otherwise she'll die." Hysteria rose in my chest.

Nora and Raj exchanged a glance.

"Val," Nora said. "Would you fancy a little drink, maybe?"

"A *drink* drink? You have *alcohol* here?"

Raj laughed. "All we have is this revolting Icelandic liqueur."

"I'd love some."

Raj poured a shot of brown liquid into a metal coffee cup. "You know, we've been a little worried about you, Val."

"Why?" The liqueur tasted like actual mud, but sweet.

"You seem somewhat strung out. Have you been sleeping?"

"I was up all night reading books on ancient Inuit culture."

"Too stimulating," Raj said. He tossed me a copy of their diving checklist. "Read this. You need something boring and tedious."

I stuffed the checklist in my pocket. "Can we talk about Sigrid now, please? Do you realize how old this girl is? These people hunted seal, narwhal, walrus—even whales!—from flimsy sealskin boats. They made sleds out of whale jaws. They spoke some ancestral language, which evolved into Greenlandic but is incomprehensible to me." I dropped my head in my hands. "And I'm terrified, because we've only got these five days. . . ."

Raj set his drink down. "That's one interpretation, Val. I can see that. But do you really believe she thawed from the ice alive? Much less that she's hundreds of years old?" Face drawn tight, he leaned forward. "I think this girl has been *taken* from somewhere, and—mark my words—Wyatt is going to pay for this. We're going to get Sigrid back to her home, and he is going to bloody pay."

"I agree with Raj, Val," Nora said. "When we first got here, all I said was let's report this, but now—and probably this is selfish—we want to stay and finish our study here. It won't be long. We never dreamed she'd get sick."

"But her language," I said. "It isn't a living language. I've checked her vocalizations against every conceivable dialect database. Her language, to me, is proof that—"

"Look, Val," Raj said, regarding me with thin patience. "The minute I believe that girl woke up alive from seven-hundred-year-old ice will be the minute I believe she's trying to tell us she's dying. Otherwise, to me, she's just some confused kid stolen from her family by some greedy guy trying to game the system."

"I know your research is important," I said. "And I'm sure it's easier to think Wyatt found her on the ice. But nothing points to that, not the clothing she was found in, not her behavior, not her language, not her ground-down molars—have I told you about that?"

"Plenty of Inuit still work skins with their teeth."

"Actually, that's completely false." I tossed my books on Greelandic history on the table. "Just look at these, will you, please?"

"Sure," Nora said with a polite smile, but I wasn't convinced. "You want company going back?"

"No," I said, suiting up. "I'll be fine."

Once outside the Dome, I practically ran back to the Shack, head down against the bracing wind. I was furious and sad I hadn't been able to convince them of what I knew in my heart: Time was running out for Sigrid. And if I was alone in helping her, so be it. Alone was a place I knew well.

Chapter 8

Two in the morning, and I still felt three cups of coffee awake.

According to the book on ancient Nordic cultures balanced on my lap, the Dorset people dominated the north coast of Greenland from around 600 B.C. to A.D. 1300 but were decimated when the Thule arrived around A.D. 1200. Only a hundred years to wipe out a people. I had to wonder: Did the arrival of the Little Ice Age play a role in the friction between the Thule and the Dorset?

The human remains Wyatt found in the core dated to around A.D. 1300. *Was Sigrid Thule or Dorset?*

I began reading about all the brilliant ways Arctic people had innovated with what few materials they had.

"Arctic rabbit skins were used for periods. Small bird skins turned inside out made baby booties. People lived on the knife edge of survival. Starvation was . . . not uncommon."

I thought of how Sigrid ate—so fast I thought she would choke, as if there would never be any more food.

I paused at a 1901 photo of an Inuit hunter wearing a cavernous sealskin parka, so big he could squat in it—the idea being he could light a fire inside it to keep warm while waiting on the ice for a seal to emerge from a breathing hole. It reminded me of Sigrid and her obsession with the Christmas sweater.

According to the text about hunting, narwhals were the filet mignon of sea mammals. I thought of how Sigrid had called the narwhals up from the depths with her own voice.

I skipped to the pages on the role of women.

"Women were tasked with preparing the dead for burial. They closed the mouth and eyes of the deceased, washed them, dressed them in a clean, new skin. Encircled their own eyes with soot to indicate mourning. Just one day was reserved for grieving. After that, people were expected to get back to the business of survival."

I stopped cold at the photo of an *ulu,* known as a "woman's knife." My stomach flipped. This ancient, crescent-shaped knife was the same size and shape as the one that Sigrid had chosen to steal.

Brain on overdrive, I forced myself to close the book. I went to the kitchen in search of wine. Mid-pour, I heard a dull thud.

I knew every creak and groan the building made. This was different. A living being made this dull *thump, thump, thump.*

After checking that everyone in the Shack was asleep, I scanned the moonlit ice field from the window. Nothing moved. I pictured the animals hunkering down in the dark. Then I heard it: a high, keening whine that could have been the wind, but wasn't.

Another cry—high-pitched, sinewy, sad. Clearly from outside the Shack. *What is out there?* I heard a long, drawn-out whimper. So very, very faint. *Am I imagining it?*

I heard it again. It sounded human. Raj or Nora? I tugged on boots, threw on my parka and gloves, yanked on my hat.

Feeling as if I'd lost my mind, I unlatched the front door. A *thud-thud-thud,* a scraping sound. A bang. It sounded like it was coming from the Shed. I stepped out into the ferocious cold, pulling the door closed behind me. Blinking to keep moisture in my eyes, I felt along the wall of the Shack for the rope that joined the two buildings. From the Shed, a dull pounding, a mewl.

Someone was dying.

I walked faster, achieving a clumsy trot.

Inside the Shed was barely warmer than outside, my footfalls heavy on the creaking slats. I clicked on the overhead lamp. Shadows leaped across the room. The air snapped with quiet.

"Hello?" I turned in a slow, frightened circle. "Is anyone here?"

I thought: *I've got the wrong building. The sounds must have come from the Cube—*

Behind me, a dull scraping sound. Spine rigid, I turned around.

Nothing. Just the walk-in freezer where the ice cores were stored. The floor-to-ceiling steel door leached its own chilled fog.

"Hello?" I said, my voice thin and wheezy. "Is someone in there?" I pressed my gloved palm flat on the steaming surface.

Nothing.

"Answer me!" I banged on the door, kicked at it.

A dull scratching from inside. Andy was trapped in there, too cold to speak, and I was about to let him die all over again. I grabbed the combination lock, spun the dial, tugged at it.

"Who's in there?"

A terrible lowing sound, from something in unimaginable pain.

I spun around. Wrenches, saws, hammers. *Hammers.* I snatched up a heavy sledgehammer and turned toward the door.

I could barely lift it over my head, and I brought it down full force but out of control. *Bang.* I missed the lock completely.

A kicking sound, a howl.

"Hold on, I'm coming!" I tore off my gloves and wound up again, coming at the lock sideways like a club. A colossal clang, and the lock was damaged now. Breath ragged, I whispered Sigrid's seven words like an incantation. Spun a hard circle and came slamming at the lock from underneath. It broke off with a metal scream. I found a smaller hammer and banged at the remaining metal until it bent just enough for me to slip it off.

From behind the door: utter quiet.

I was too late.

I lifted the latch; the door opened wide with a smack of suction.

Ice smoke rolled out, obscuring my view, until, as if from a dream, I saw a massive caribou on the freezer floor. One side of his elegant antlers had broken off and lay in pieces on the floor.

"Come on," I choked out. "Get up! You have to get up." I ran to the door of the Shed and flung it wide. "See? You can go. *Go!*"

But he lay like a broken statue, ice knitting around his closed eyes, cockeyed antlers motionless. I ran back to the freezer, stepped up onto the raised floor. Without thinking, I reached down to touch his long muzzle. He lifted his tremendous head with a snarl. I jumped backward and climbed out of the freezer.

Still collapsed on the floor, the creature snorted, huffing the night air, reading freedom. He lifted one front hoof and scraped it along the corrugated metal again and again, seeking traction of any kind. For long, terrible moments he stayed front half up, bottom half glued to the floor, until, with a harrowing cry, he unlocked his haunches and lifted himself all the way up to standing. He trembled so hard and so long in the steam of his cage, I thought for sure he would fall to his knees again and simply die.

I heard voices.

Framed by the open door, the figures of Wyatt and Jeanne began to make their way up the hill toward the Shed.

"Come on," I said. "You've got to run." I backed up into the shadows of the room, trying to give the animal space.

With a clop, the caribou tendered a leg out and down on the floor of the freezer. Took a wobbly, jerky step. Panted, snorted, shook his lopsided head. Commanding his body forward, he scrambled clear of the freezer and clattered down to the wooden floor of the Shed. Took a few confused steps—a half circle toward me, a half circle away, as if he'd lost the scent of the way out.

"Bah!" I screamed, waving my arms, anything so he would move. I breathed the musky tang of his thick fur.

He skittered back, then pivoted—hooves screeching—toward the doorway, his big body and one antler filling it. Tilting his head sideways, he negotiated the opening, then launched himself full throttle across the snow. Jeanne and Wyatt, just yards from the door, reared back and out of his way, watching him leap toward the glacier as if witnessing something of the divine.

"That's unforgiveable." From her seat on the floor, Nora nudged a breakfast of fried fish closer to Sigrid's bed, no doubt hoping hunger would lure her out. "What did they say to you?"

My head pounded from lack of sleep, adrenaline from the night before still pulsing through me. "That it was none of my business. That it was *science*. Said I was getting in the way."

Nora shook her head. "Look, Val, I would let it go. A few more days, and we're out of here, all of us. We just have to hang on."

Sigrid crawled out from her lair and gave us both a shy smile; in no time she was tearing through her plate of food.

"She seems better," Nora said with a little laugh.

"Her fever's gone, but have you seen her eye? Wyatt says it's pink eye."

Nora walked around the bed for a closer look. The outer corner of Sigrid's left eye drooped and was tearing up. "That's not pink eye. Maybe a palsy that goes away when the cold goes away—"

"You really believe that, Nora?"

She sighed. "I don't know what to believe anymore."

Sigrid's door swung open; Wyatt's haggard face appeared. "Raj and Jeanne and me are ready to go. Cats are loaded up. Think you can get her suited up in a couple of minutes?"

I said, "She's not well enough to go, Wyatt."

"We discussed this last night, and we agreed, remember? I need all of you to help out. She can't stay here alone."

"Why don't I stay back—" Nora started.

"Her fever's gone," he said. "She won't even have to leave the cat. I've got blankets, hot chocolate. She'll be like a bug in a rug."

Neither of us said a word.

"Get her dressed," he said, pulling the door shut behind him.

Outside a few minutes later, the sun was a smear of yellow paste between the pearl-gray worlds of land and sky. The still air nipped at the flesh. Sigrid and I settled into the back of the cat, with Jeanne riding shotgun. Wyatt, inscrutable behind his mirrored glasses, motored along the rough ice toward the glacier that undulated over the mountain pass. Nora and Raj followed in their snow machine. To our left, the land sloped down to the beach.

Wrapped in Jeanne's old red parka, Sigrid sat next to me drumming her fingers on the window. Behind us, we towed a Dr. Seussian contraption Jeanne had built—a circular plate as big as a garbage can lid she'd hooked up to a motor.

As we crawled up the glacier between gleaming ice cliffs, Sigrid broke out of her odd funk. She squirmed into the front seat and sat on Jeanne's lap, eking a rare laugh out of her. Jeanne's device clanking and banging, we coasted a few yards across the ice side by side toward the glacial lake, until we stopped and all was silent. Already the shadows of the two snowcats stretched nearly halfway across the lake as the sun flattened on the horizon.

Wyatt broke the silence. "Val, you and Sigrid stay in the cat." He unlatched the door and jumped out onto the ice, Jeanne right behind him. But there was no keeping Sigrid in that cab. She grabbed the door handle and swung herself out.

"Bahl," she said, reaching toward me. *"Bahl."*

"Coming." I stepped down to the ice as she raced to the crevasse, which had widened by several yards.

"I said stay in the cat," Wyatt called over.

"Sigrid," I shouted, holding out my hand. "You're too close!"

Chin thrust out, she marched along the fissure, arriving at the gouged-out place where she had been freed from the ice. She paused there but said nothing. Some decision made, Sigrid spun on her heel and jogged toward the mountains.

I caught up with her as she stopped and squinted at the snow-swept, barren peaks. She said in her language, "Mother, father."

"Your mother and father are here?"

She nodded. Behind us, Nora, Raj, Wyatt, and Jeanne, now toy-size figures on the ice, struggled to drag the strange contraption across the frozen lake.

I knelt down. Her eye looked worse, red, oozing, sagging down in one corner. It hurt to look at. "We have to go back, Sigrid."

She pointed to the mountains. "Mother, father," she pleaded.

"We can't—"

A gunshot split the air. Wyatt was making his way toward us, shouting and waving his arms. He was pissed. I didn't blame him.

"We've got to head back, honey. I'm so sorry. I promise we'll come back for mother, father, okay?"

Sigrid's face crumpled with disappointment. She looked on the verge of bolting, but I took hold of her arm, half dragging her at first until she realized I meant business and kept pace with me.

As we joined the others, Nora knelt on the ice, arms wrapped around the bright yellow motor that whined and vibrated as if it wanted to dance away with her. The cord looped across a few yards of ice to Wyatt and Jeanne, who gripped either side of the T of the ice-core-drilling machine, its massive screw replaced with the heated metal plate that spun against the ice. Raj leaned into the plate, using his body weight to try to guide it across the surface, but it wouldn't budge.

"Turn it off!" Wyatt called over the motor.

Nora shut it down.

Wyatt pushed the plate aside in disgust. It had burned a circular hole a yard across and a few inches deep. A light snow had begun, quickly covering the perfect circle of polished ice.

Raj got up. "Are you sure this is where you took the cores?"

"Of course I'm sure," Wyatt said.

"We're going to have to do this a little at a time," Jeanne said, circumnavigating her invention. "It's a pain, but we can't slide it. We're going to have to keep making circles."

She got down to her knees, casually brushing snow off the ice ring. Her gloved hand froze mid-sweep. She sat back on her haunches. "Wyatt," she breathed. "Nora, Raj. You have to see this. Val, keep Sigrid back in the cat."

ONCE they got the hang of it, they worked fast, burnishing contiguous rings until they'd covered an area the circumference of a good-sized room, all the while gesticulating, talking animatedly to each other. Sigrid had nodded off as soon as we settled in the cat. *What had they discovered that Sigrid wasn't allowed to see?*

She woke as soon as Wyatt opened the door, squinting at him.

He looked stricken. "Val, come and see this. Leave her here."

But Sigrid had already vaulted from the cab. I jumped out after her as she sprinted toward the weird pattern of shining circles that gleamed like giant ice lily pads. Raj knelt with his camera, snapping shot after shot. In a rare moment of stillness, Jeanne rested against her ice-polishing invention, staring down into the depths. Nora sat back on her heels next to a gleaming ring.

When Nora caught sight of Sigrid, she sprang to her feet, caught her and swung her up in her arms, facing her away from the site. Then Nora lost control of her, and Sigrid slipped free. Wyatt made a grab for her, but she shot her arms up fast and twisted cunningly out of his grasp, bulleting toward the shining ice.

She came to a halt at the edge. Snow lightly patterned Sigrid's slouching hat and baggy coat. *What is she looking at? Why is everyone so quiet, their faces turned away?* I wanted to run back to the cat, to anywhere that felt safe, but how could I not bear witness? The cold air an ache in my lungs, I made my feet move to stand next to her.

She didn't budge. She was a child in a state of wonder, of horror, of understanding.

Beneath us, a scene of utter devastation. A couple of yards under our boots, a ghastly diorama: several dozen Inuit people frozen in place in the midst of fighting, spears and knives drawn. Dressed in polar bear leggings, sealskin anoraks and boots. Many had terrible wounds, their necks gashed or arms severed. Men, women, children. Some were twisted in impossible positions; others looked stunned into icy suspended animation. A half-dozen sled dogs were caught on their hind legs, snarling, paws mid-churn.

Sigrid dropped to her hands and knees and began to crawl, clawing at the ice with bare hands. She stopped directly over a woman—a few yards beneath the ice—who had collapsed facedown across a man who lay on his back. A knife jutted from her lower back. Crying, Sigrid repeated one of her seven words, "*Tahtaksah,*" then, in her language, "Mother, father."

Wyatt walked the perimeter of the polished ice, eyes never leaving Sigrid.

"Why did you bring her here . . . ?" Nora murmured.

"I didn't know it would be like this . . ." Wyatt's voice trailed off.

I got down on my knees next to Sigrid. "You're sad," I said. "For your mother, and for your father. I'm so sorry." And that's when I understood, kneeling with Sigrid just yards above the seven-hundred-year-old bodies of her parents, that *tahtaksah* meant "sad, grief-stricken." Seven words used constantly . . . Where had I read about the seven basic emotions? *The Book of Rites,* a first-century Chinese encyclopedia, named the "feelings of men": fear, sadness, contempt, surprise, disgust, anger, and joy.

I finally understood: In her language, every sentence began with an emotion. What a compassionate, gentle way to communicate: prioritizing feelings over facts.

"What is she saying to you?" Wyatt crouched a few yards away.

"That she's sad. That her mother and father are beneath us."

"Let's get out of here," Nora said. "What good is this doing?"

Raj wandered to the far side of the cleared area as if scouting a better angle for photos. He came to a halt, knelt, and set aside his camera. Polishing one of the circles with a gloved hand, he said, "Guys, you have to come see this."

Nora knelt beside her husband. A strangled yelp escaped her. Wyatt and Jeanne quickly made their way to stand behind them.

Wyatt let out a low whistle. "Better get over here, Val."

Sigrid had sunk into a state of melancholy. I'm not sure she felt or noticed the kiss I placed on her head before joining the others.

I gazed down into the dim, blue otherworld. A baby boy, perfectly preserved, floated a few feet below the surface, his body partially wrapped in a dun-colored rag that seemed to flutter in an eternal wind. His dark eyes were open, and he looked alert, one chubby hand reaching out as if to touch his mother's face.

"My God, Raj," Nora breathed. "Look at him."

He gripped her arm, consumed by the sight.

Nora said, "Why is he so far away from all the others?"

Wyatt knelt next to her. "Maybe he was swept up in the same gust that took Sigrid? She was found just yards from here."

We all squinted at the azure depression on the other side of the crevasse, piecing together the weirdly plausible explanation.

"Perhaps they tried to place the children away from danger," Raj said softly. "But the wind had other plans."

"He looks just like Charlie, doesn't he?" Nora hugged herself. "Look at him. His smile, his eyes . . ."

Raj wrapped his arm around her waist and pulled her to her feet, tried to lead her away. "Come on. This isn't good for you—"

She brushed him aside. *"Just let me look at him!"*

"I say we cut him out of there," Wyatt said. "He looks in good shape, not like the rest of them."

Raj snatched up his camera. "You've finally lost your mind."

Wyatt smiled and tipped his head to Jeanne, who was already on her way back to the sled and the ice saw.

Raj got up into Wyatt's face. "This sick little sideshow cannot go on," he growled. "I will not let it. Your game with Sigrid. This place"—he gesticulated at the shining circles beneath us, the vast lake with its jagged blue scar, the peaks beyond—"is sacred. This is a gravesite. We should leave these poor people in peace."

"Maybe we should take a vote," said Wyatt. "Nora?"

"I . . ." She wiped her eyes, looked at her husband imploringly. "I— *Look at him.* I can't just leave him. Not if . . . Raj, I'm sorry."

He said, "Then what about everybody else down there? Why don't we thaw out the whole lot? What have we got to lose?"

"Look at them, Raj," Nora said. "They're all—"

"Dead?"

She dropped her head. "Maybe. But we can start with the boy."

Wyatt turned to me. "Val?"

Raj stepped away from the cleared ice. I got on all fours to look as Jeanne returned to lay down the ice saw at Wyatt's feet. Would this baby be the final clue to understanding how to survive the ice winds? *Andy, what would you do?* I got closer, peering at the boy's flushed cheeks, bow lips, toothless smile. *Darling boy, is your little heart ready to beat again?* How could I know?

"Val, your vote?"

Sigrid tugged at my pant leg, nudging me away from my position over the boy. I stood up, feeling a hundred years old. "Okay."

"Cut him out?"

I nodded.

Sigrid rubbed her hot palms on the ice, making it clear as glass. Her face somber as she looked at each of us in turn. She seized the handle of the ice saw and began to drag it toward the cat.

"What's the problem?" Wyatt said.

"Looks like we've got a 'no' vote," Raj said.

I ran after her and turned her toward me. She dropped the ice saw, and I hugged her tight. "We're going to leave your mother and father," I whispered. She winced at the words "mother," "father." "We're going to cut the baby free." I pointed to where he lay.

"Stahndala," she said, her face shining with tears.

By now, I knew this word.

It meant "fear."

THAT night, Sigrid seemed to have just one goal, and that was to drag from under the sink the giant metal basin Jeanne used to make her vats of stew. "Really?" I made scrubbing motions. "You want to take a bath?"

She nodded. Jeanne went off to heat up some more water.

We had just finished a remarkably congenial dinner of arctic char, reconstituted dried potatoes, and peas, an event made surreal by the proximity of a baby frozen in a trunk-size slab of ice on the counter. Wyatt and Jeanne had cut ample space around him, over a foot on all sides, so it wasn't clear how long the thawing process would take. Nora stood next to the block, occasionally sliding her fingers across the ice, as if she could already touch the boy. Raj gazed up at her, eyes blazing with love and worry.

Wyatt gestured at the block of ice with his cup of wine. "Without Jeanne's crazy brilliant ice-polishing gizmo, we'd have come home with nothing today." He gave her a brief round of applause, and we joined in. Up to her elbows in dishwater, Jeanne—blushing hard—nodded her acknowledgment, but by the time she gave Wyatt a shy smile, he'd turned away and was on to other things. "So, I'd like to declare tomorrow a day of celebration. We've all been working hard, and besides, tomorrow is a certain person's birthday." Wyatt smiled at Nora, who rolled her eyes and laughed.

"Yes, I'm turning twenty-one," she said. "Or wait, maybe it's more like . . . thirty-three."

"Forecast for tomorrow is actually pretty balmy for late October," Wyatt told us. "Three hours of sunshine, three hours of twilight on either side, highs in the teens. I'm thinking a tropical theme up on the roof. Hawaiian shirts. Fruity drinks. Anybody? Raj?"

Raj caught Nora's eye; she nodded, smiling.

A thud, another thud. Two small boots landing across the room.

Sigrid stood naked next to the tub, arms by her sides. A mirage of a girl from another age. She was even slighter than she'd seemed, delicate ribs visible above her taut belly, little knobs for knees, impossibly tiny hips. She looked at us as if to say, *When are you going to stop talking and pour my hot water?*

It took an hour of soaking and scrubbing to make any progress on the grime. We replaced the water at least twice. She eventually had had enough and climbed out of the tub. I'd laid out some clean clothes, but she opted for her filthy leggings and Christmas sweater, now missing half a sleeve as well as Rudolph's nose.

When I approached with a comb, she climbed on a chair—all obedience—and sat facing the block of ice. In front of us, the baby flew sideways through the ice, a cherub escaped from Michelangelo's ceiling. The ice made dull popping sounds as it melted. After I was done, she headed to the living room where I kept the picture books, paper, and markers and gathered them all up in her arms. She tromped down the hallway to my room. I followed.

She heaved everything helter-skelter on my bed. Opened one of the picture books and pointed at a bird.

"Bird," I said.

"Bird." She reached up into the air as if grabbing a bird.

"You need a bird. You want a bird. *Sigrid want bird?*"

She said, "Sigrid want bird. Sigrid want bird." She flipped madly through the book; then, frustrated, she shoved it to the floor.

I had an idea. "Wait here, please, Sigrid." I ran to the kitchen, got a glass of water and a piece of ice, brought them back. Set the ice a few inches from the water on a sheet of notebook paper on my desk. Curious, she slipped out of bed, stood next to the desk.

"Ice," I said, touching the chip.

She repeated, "Ice."

I pointed to the glass. "Water."

"Water."

Giddy with excitement, I drew a line on the paper with little arrows from the ice chip to the water and said, slowly, "Thaw."

She let me take her finger and touch the ice, trace the arrows, then touch the glass of water. "Thaw," I repeated.

She smiled and said, "Taw."

"Yes! Now watch." I drew another line with arrows, this time from the water to the ice. "Freeze," I said. With her finger I touched the items one by one. "Water, freeze, ice. Ice, thaw, water. Now you do it."

"Ice. Taw. *Wah*ter. *Wah*ter. Feeze. Ice. *Feeze!*" She giggled.

"Good job, Sigrid."

She learned so fast. Through repetition, goofy pantomime, picture books, and drawing, she mastered *yes, no, freeze, thaw, girl, baby, eat, drink, hungry, wake, sleep, walk, fish, dog, talk, hair, eye, snow, water, ice, ice bear, seal, walrus, dead, alive,* and *fly*.

I was so thrilled by her progress I hugged her, surprising her. Then I let her go and hugged myself, an enraptured expression on my face. Pointed at her. "Val loves Sigrid."

She thought this was hilarious. She hugged herself, saying, "Love, love, love Sigrid," before bursting into her own language.

How would I ever grasp her stream of consciousness answers?

She reached for the Inuit picture book—the real one, not the kiddie version—pointed at a photo of a hunter next to a woman.

"Mother, father," I said in her language, then in English.

"Mother, father," she repeated in English. She uncapped a red marker and crossed out their faces, then their bodies.

"Dead," I whispered.

"Dead," she said, solemn-faced. "Mother, father, dead." She pointed at herself, said, "Sigrid, dead."

"No, Sigrid is *alive*." I pointed to myself. "Val is *alive*."

"A*ligh*," she said.

"Yes, *alive*."

Gesturing at herself, she said, *"Stahndala."* Afraid. Then, slowly, "Sigrid dead a*ligh*." She indicated the baby in the photo, a small face peering out from a papoose on the mother's back.

"Baby," I said.

"Baby," she said thoughtfully.

"Is baby dead alive, Sigrid?"

She looked at me soulfully, said, *"Stahndala."* Afraid. She put her forehead on mine and breathed me in, and I breathed her in: ivory soap, strawberry shampoo, a little-girl smell, snow. She pulled away, said, "Joy, Val, seals, many, love, want, joy." It reminded me of an old Inuit saying, "May your life be rich in seals." Is this what she was saying to me, a kind of blessing?

Looking into her eyes, I said, "Joy, Sigrid, seals, many, love, want, joy." She smiled, eyes nearly closing above her high cheekbones, and backed her body up into mine, a tiny hot ball.

She was asleep in seconds.

JEANNE bustled around me as I rinsed my coffee cup in the sink, her sweatshirt dusted with flour and powdered sugar. Above us, a clattering of boots on the roof, muted laughter, the tinny twang of canned Jimmy Buffett. Nora's party was already in full swing at eleven in the morning, just before the break of "day."

"Sure I can't help, Jeanne?" I asked.

"You can grab those crackers and cheese," she said, lugging a six-pack of beer out the door.

"Got it," I said to her departing figure. The tray of crackers and steaming cheese dip sat next to the block of ice, now covered by Raj's beautiful prayer rug. I gently drew back the rug and saw that overnight the block had shrunk to half its original size. The baby's body was clearer than ever: the tiny fingers, his wide, flat nose, the eyebrows just a brush of fine black hair.

After checking on Sigrid—she'd shown little interest in getting out of bed that morning—I suited up and headed outdoors with the cheese dip. The sun was a yellow sheen at the horizon.

Up on the roof, Wyatt strummed an unplugged electric guitar as he belted out "Margaritaville." Under his down vest, he wore a Hawaiian shirt, skullcap cockeyed on his head. He sat on one of several blankets spread out over the roof. Nearby, Jeanne struggled to balance a few glasses on a tray. A ladder led the way to the party.

Wyatt gestured at the spread. "Join us, won't you?"

Balancing my tray, I started up the ladder. Nora and Raj sat next to Wyatt on some couch cushions. I set the cheese next to the drinks tray, where a bottle of tequila cozied up to a pitcher of Kool-Aid. I made myself a strong one.

Wyatt turned to Jeanne, who handed him a "margarita." Taking the drink, he said, "Why, thank you, Jeanne, for arranging this lovely party. I'm sure Nora will remember it forever."

"You're very welcome."

Nora let out a rapturous sigh. "Yes, what a brilliant way to spend a birthday," she said. "Sunbathing in the Arctic. And now, this amazing thing is happening inside our kitchen, this miraculous moment is coming. . . ."

Raj put his arm around her. "Nora, take it easy."

She smiled, but shrank from his touch. "What good does it do to be negative? I've been praying for him since the second I saw him."

"So have I, love."

"I see no reason why we shouldn't be hopeful," Wyatt stated. "It happened once. It can happen again." He turned in my direction. "Tell us, Val, how's the young lady doing this morning?"

"She's got a bad headache. Otherwise, she's better. No fever."

"Could have sworn I heard you two talking last night," Jeanne said. "You guys making progress?"

I swirled my drink in my cup. "Here and there. I was listening to recordings. Old Norse, West Greenlandic. That sort of thing."

Wyatt set his guitar aside. Picked up the tequila bottle. "You seem like best buds to me these days. No new words to report?"

Heat flushed up my neck. "No, sorry to say."

"Well, *there's* a terrible shame, don't you think? For me, for you"—he swung the bottle around—"for all of us. But, hey, you know, it doesn't matter. Because—that little boy in the kitchen? He's the missing piece, as far as I'm concerned."

"I'm going to go check on Sigrid," I said.

Nora said, "I'll come with you."

THE lump under the blankets didn't move. In the air, an acidic, greasy tang. Nora knelt down to a small, glistening pile.

"Looks like the poor thing's been sick."

"Oh, no." I gently folded the covers back; Sigrid yanked them over her head with a growl.

Nora went to the kitchen, returned with a wet towel, and began cleaning up the mess. "That was you talking last night, wasn't it?"

"Yes," I said, relieved to spill the truth. "Last night she completely turned around with me, Nora. She wanted to communicate. She learned a couple dozen words, easily!"

"That's brilliant, Val."

"But why now? Why did it take weeks for her to open up?"

Nora shrugged. "Maybe she realizes her family really is all gone. You're it for her now."

Why hadn't that occurred to me? "Nora, you've got to keep this on the down-low, okay? That she's finally talking to me?"

Jeanne rapped on the open door, startling us. "Hey, birthday girl," she said to Nora, unsmiling. "Mind going up to wait for your cake?" Not waiting for an answer, she disappeared from view.

Nora returned to the roof, and I joined Jeanne in the kitchen. I watched her rifle through a drawer next to a tall, round cake, extracting a beat-up box of birthday candles and matches. From beyond the open door we could hear peals of laughter from Wyatt mingled with the muffled sounds of Nora and Raj talking.

"You have birthday candles here?" I asked her.

"People have birthdays in the Arctic." She poked a few candles on the cake. "Mine was last week."

"Why didn't you tell us?"

She waved me away, concentrating on her decorations. "Never liked my birthday. Happens to fall on a really bad anniversary, if you want the truth about it. Wyatt never remembers it anyway."

I opened the front door wider in preparation to march outside with the cake. Jeanne struck a match and lit the first candle.

We could hear Wyatt speaking in a stage whisper. "Well, you'd think that after a year I'd screw anything . . ."

Her hand shaking slightly, Jeanne moved to the next candle.

". . . and then I think, Jeanne's not *that* bad. . . . I mean, she is female . . ."

Something clattered on the roof, a plate or silverware, maybe. A bitter gust shunted down into the kitchen from the open door, sucking all warmth from the room. Jeanne struck another match.

". . . but then the same thing always happens. I have a really good look at her . . . and forget it."

Jeanne's hand shook badly now as she lit the final candle.

"Ready?" she said, her face pinched and hard and sad, before picking up the cake and starting for the door. I felt punched in the gut—as if he'd been talking about me instead of Jeanne—but cleared my throat to try to belt out my best "Happy Birthday."

Chapter 9

It was just past four o'clock in the morning. Under blinking fluorescent lights, we all crowded around the industrial-sized sink, bleary-eyed. After a long day of thawing, the baby, with his inscrutable smile, soft rise of belly, and fat-dimpled knees, rested in a shallow lake of warm water. Though stiff as a statue, he had nearly melted free of his ice block. From the window the black polar night gazed down on us, stars sparking with their unspeakable knowing. Sigrid, hair mussed with sleep, stood on a chair next to me clutching the rim of the sink. The mood was reverent.

We'd prepared the defibrillator, dialed down to its lowest charge; the syringes of atropine and adrenaline filled to the proper dosage placed side by side; blankets set out. But like any birth, there came the time when all anybody could do was wait.

Raj, face haggard, broke away from the group, wandering into the living room. Instinctively, we closed ranks tight around the baby, listening to Raj pray, a low muttering chant.

"Okay, let's get started," Wyatt said. "Like we talked about."

I was the first to touch him. I was terrified but slid my hands into the lukewarm water and under his tiny buttocks and shoulder blades as instructed and held him. His skin softened slightly at my touch as I gently settled him back down. Jeanne poured more warm water into the tub as Nora, cooing, massaged his shoulders, arms, and fingers, cracking off what was now just a patina of ice from his tender baby flesh. The rag that had partially covered him, perhaps the remains of some ancient diaper, disintegrated in our hands. Wyatt, in wonder, stroked the baby's face.

"Jeanne, are you ready to turn him to clear his lungs?"

"I can turn him," Nora said.

"No," he said gruffly. "Stick to the plan."

Raj's prayers grew louder, more insistent.

"Raj, get in here, man!"

Raj quieted and came to stand between Nora and me. "What do you need me to do?" he said.

"Give him some love," Wyatt said. "Like we talked about."

With his long, graceful fingers, Raj reached into the sink and stroked the child's stomach. I rubbed my thumb along the child's nose and across his forehead. Flecks of ice slid off his fat cheeks.

His flesh had real give now, though it was still so terribly cold. Nora tenderly laid her thumbs on the two petite frozen ponds over his eyes; in moments they slid away. Wyatt reached into his mouth, swiped it with his little finger. The baby's jaw dropped down—we all gasped—and Wyatt held it open and peered down his throat with a flashlight. "His throat is clear."

Supporting his head, Wyatt lifted the baby out of the water, his arms and legs hanging limply. Jeanne drained the sink and poured in new bathwater. Wyatt gently laid the baby back down.

"Come on, guys, it's time," he said. "Jeanne, take him."

Jeanne lifted up the child and carefully turned him over so he lay facedown along her arm, which rested on her thigh. With the heel of her hand, she rapped him on his back. His arms juddered forward with the force of her blow.

He lay motionless as if he had fallen from a great height. She gave him another firm rap. Nothing.

"Again, Jeanne, come *on!*"

She clapped him a third time, a fourth; we all leaned toward them, listening for the cough, the grab for breath, the miraculous cry. Each time his body jumped at her touch, then stilled. I had to remind myself to breathe. Sigrid, her face solemn, broke away from the scene, drifting into the living room. We all felt the loss of her spirit in the room.

"Bring him here," Wyatt said, his face dark. Jeanne settled him on a bed of towels piled on the kitchen table. "Nora, ready?"

She nodded, positioning herself at the baby's head. With two fingers, Wyatt pushed rapidly down on the baby's chest, pausing for Nora as she put her mouth over the baby's nose and mouth and exhaled two short breaths. Each time, the little chest rose and fell. He looked like a doll, his skin losing, not gaining color.

"Raj, the injections."

Raj flicked the needle, and a drop rolled out. Angled it down and punctured the skin, injecting into the child's heart.

We waited. No sound, no movement. Unbearable stillness.

Nora cried out but covered her mouth.

"Jeanne," Wyatt said. "Come on, get him ready."

She brought over two small pads that had been cut down from the adult size and spaced them diagonally across his tiny chest. Wyatt flipped on the machine, said, "Stand back."

We did.

His small frame bucked with the shock.

Wyatt checked for signs of life.

Nothing.

Another shock. A third.

"Nora, *let's go!*"

Eyes shining, Nora tilted the baby's head back and blew into him. I felt numb. Helpless. I thought of Sigrid's small body enduring all of this, but there she was, doodling on the sketch pad on the living room floor.

After three more rounds of compressions and rescue breathing, the baby lay inert on his pallet of towels.

Jeanne readied the defibrillator and zapped his little body once, twice, three times. Wyatt stood by, ready for a fourth round.

Raj staggered back from the table. "He's gone. Let's stop this."

"Nora, come on, the CPR," said Wyatt.

"But Wyatt, nothing's . . ." She turned away and stumbled out of the kitchen. Raj followed her, wrapped his arms around her.

"His lungs are clear!" Wyatt roared. Nobody moved. "Are you all insane? Jeanne, help me."

Jeanne dutifully tilted the child's head back. For close to five more minutes, they tried to breathe life into that tiny body, into lungs that rose and fell with Jeanne's breath. But there was no independent movement, no pulse, no heartbeat.

No child's cries. No exultations. No miracles.

Nora extracted herself from Raj's embrace and lurched back to the kitchen. She went to the baby, who was bathed in moonglow, elfin arms splayed, perfect fingers fixed in a curl. Cradling his head, she gathered him up and swaddled him in a towel.

"Wyatt, please, you did it with *her*." She nodded in Sigrid's direction. "Why couldn't you make it work for him? You told us you knew what you were doing." Her voice broke into a sob.

"Nora, please." He turned away. "We're all disappointed."

"Disappointed?" she cried with reddened eyes. "I'm holding a dead baby. *Disappointed* . . ." She paced. "You're the one who said you knew how. You're the one who said he would *live*—"

"Guess you weren't listening very well, Nora. That wasn't—"

Raj approached her, reached out for her. "Come on, darling—"

"Don't touch me." She backed up against the far wall under the hanging pots, eyes flashing. Held her nose to the baby's head and inhaled his scent. "Oh God, why does he smell so good? That shouldn't be. He smells like he's alive. Are you sure he's gone?"

Raj got a little closer. She allowed it. Sigrid shoved aside her drawing and wandered into the kitchen to Nora's side.

"He died seven hundred years ago, sweetheart," Raj said.

Rocking him in her arms, Nora collapsed into the child, sobbing. Sigrid stretched upward and wrapped her arms around Nora's waist. Momentarily startled out of her hell, Nora reached down and stroked Sigrid's hair.

Wyatt held his arms out to Nora. "Give him to me."

She gripped the baby tighter, broke away from Sigrid, and darted into the living room. "Oh, no. You've had your chance with him. You're not fit to touch him again."

Wyatt followed her in his awkward, yet eerily fast, stocking-footed gait. "He's dead, Nora. Maybe . . . if I take some samples, I can understand why Sigrid lived and he didn't. Find out what he ate . . ." He reached out again; she slapped him away.

"You keep your filthy hands off this baby."

His face turned hard. "Nora, do you know how many people froze to death in an ice wind off the Oregon coast yesterday?" he hissed. "*Fifty-seven.* Fifty-seven people who—if they'd had access to whatever protected Sigrid—would be alive right now. And you—*a fellow scientist*—stand there telling me to look away, to *squander* clues that are literally in our lap?"

Raj stepped between them. "Let's calm down. Why don't we take the baby to the Dome for the night? Talk in the morning."

"Fine," Wyatt said. "But the baby stays here. In fact, it's too late to go to the Dome. No one's going anywhere tonight."

In the dream, a woman cried, *My baby, where is my baby?* As she lunged at my ankles, jagged ice tore at my face as I tumbled into a pit. . . . I jolted awake, the laminated dive instructions I'd used to fall asleep cutting into my cheek. It was eight a.m, two hours since we'd gone to bed.

Go back to sleep, I told myself. But something felt off.

I slipped on my clothes and padded down the hall. The night before, after we'd all agreed to do nothing with the baby for the moment, we left him where he was for the night: on the kitchen table, covered by a towel. As I shuffled into the kitchen, I kept my eyes averted from the table as I made my coffee, then settled on the couch near the picture window.

Eyes glazed with fatigue, I scanned the snowfield, luminous under turquoise skies. *What was that?* I slammed my coffee cup down. Bolted to the window. A red dot bobbed along the icy slope, advancing steadily down to the brash ice at the shore.

Sigrid. *What the hell was she doing?*

I whipped around, scouring the kitchen. Yelped.

The baby was gone. Even the towels were gone. I glanced back out the window. Sigrid was a red speck now. I suited up fast and woke Nora and Raj as quietly as I could.

The three of us were soon plunging through the violet half-light. Even as I ran, I wondered, *What is different?* The air felt above freezing, full of moisture, even with the winds off the glacier. Our boots sank into the snow. Along the beach, dozens of walruses dozed, a wide brown wedge along the line of foaming surf.

We called out to Sigrid. She ignored us. In the middle distance, she paused at a small, dun-colored lump, knelt down briefly as if to examine it, then tore off again toward the beach.

Nora and Raj approached it, slowed, stopped. From a few yards away I realized it was a baby walrus, whimpering and pulling itself along by its flippers. I ventured closer.

"Val, stay back," Nora said. "He's probably sick."

Sigrid stopped at a relatively calm stretch of beach. Exchanging looks, we slowed as we approached so as not to spook her. Finally, she turned to look at us. Nora uttered a little gasp. Sigrid had blackened the area around her eyes—she must have used the charcoal pencils from my box of markers and crayons. Her droopy eye looked terrible, its inflammation emphasized by the black.

"Tahtaksah," she said. Sad. "Baby dead."

She removed the knapsack—mine, I realized—and eased out the towel-swathed body of the boy. He wore a pink doll's hat.

Raj got down to help her, but she pushed him away.

"Don't take it personally," I said to him. "Women are the last to touch a body in her culture."

Several yards from us, a thousand-pound bull walrus grunted and barked, eyes bulging from his regal head.

"Keep your voice down," Nora whispered. "You don't want to startle them. Any loud noise, and they'll charge."

Stumbling slightly, Sigrid made her way to the nearest floe and lay the baby down facing the great purple dome of sky. In his pale green towel and pink hat, the child looked like a doll that had fallen from the sky. In seconds, a strong wave lifted and swept him out several dozen yards. No one could reach him now. We all stepped back as though the ocean might take us too.

On his floe, the baby drifted and twirled. Then he dipped down and out of sight, and all was a wash of blue and white again.

Without a word, Sigrid trudged toward the baby walrus, which had stopped moving. We rushed to join her. It had rolled onto its side, closed eyes black slits, mud-colored flesh motionless.

Sigrid dropped to her knees, excavated her crescent knife from deep inside her parka, and without hesitation sliced open the walrus's belly. Stunned, we only watched as she plunged her bare hands into the steaming cavity and removed the purple slab of liver, tossing it onto the snow. Shrieking, an arctic tern shot down out of the sky and snatched it up, flying away with his prize, while a dozen more circled above, screaming and cawing.

While we adults stood silently, Sigrid cut deeper into the walrus's abdomen, carving out chunks of meat and blubber and throwing them onto the snow. She took off her parka. When three birds dive-bombed at once, battling over the last shreds, she pounced over them using her coat as a net. Two escaped easily, but she lay on top of the third struggling under the parka. She reached down under the hood; the snap of its neck a dull reality.

We all exhaled, none of us with a clue as to what she might do next. She held out the dead bird to me, saying, "Sigrid want bird."

I knelt, eye to eye with her and the limp creature in her arms. There was no mistaking her pride and satisfaction. "You finally got your bird, Sigrid. *Verohnsaht.*" Joy.

She said, "Sigrid want *sahndaluuk.*" She looked from Nora to Raj and back to me. "*Sahndaluuk.*"

"The drawings," Nora said. "Of the snakes and birds. I just thought of something. Let's go to the Dome, and I'll show you."

Sigrid crouched on the floor of the Dome with the dead tern. Charcoal-saddened eyes intent, she studiously severed one of its wings. Picking two of the hollow, straw-like feathers clean, she sliced one of them on the diagonal, creating a sharp point, inserting the thinner feather into the larger one, like a plunger.

Meanwhile, Nora grabbed a magazine called *Marine Invertebrates* and flipped it open to a spread featuring different kinds of eels. Brought it to Sigrid. "Here, sweetheart. Have a look at this."

Crying out excitedly, Sigrid dropped the feathers and wrested the magazine from Nora's grip. She pointed to one of the eels.

"That's an ice eel," Raj said.

Sigrid ran to me with the magazine, pointing and talking fast.

I said, "*Sahndaluuk?*"

Yes, she nodded. *Yesyesyes.*

Of course, the word meant "eel"!

"They're not as common as they used to be," Nora said. "But—Raj, we haven't sorted through yesterday's specimen bucket."

Raj hauled a sloshing plastic bucket from the far end of the Dome. "This was at ten meters down," he said.

Sigrid peered into the bucket. In the seawater wriggled a baby octopus, a bright jellyfish, several small slender fish, and a nearly transparent eel about a foot long. "Bahl," she said, pointing at it.

"Get it out of the bucket, Raj, can you?" I said.

He reached in with a sieve-like tool. He lay the sieve on the floor, and the eel zigzagged out onto the ice.

Sigrid brought her knife down, slicing its head off neatly. As black blood spurted from the headless creature, Sigrid held the tip of her hollow, sharpened feather at the artery, where lines of blood mapped the eel's translucent length. She shoved the sleeve of her parka up her arm and inserted the sharp tip into the crook of her elbow, working the tapered feather into the larger one, injecting herself until what little eel blood the feather held was gone. Uttering something unintelligible, she stumbled a few paces, then scrambled along the ice as she tried to catch the eel. Even headless, it wriggled with eerie vitality, its blood quickly draining out. Practically transparent except for its black veins, it nearly disappeared where it lay on the ice, lifeless.

"That's what she's been asking us for all this time," I said. "A bird and an eel, not a snake. Not seaweed."

Sigrid scrambled to her feet. *"Sahndaluuk,"* she moaned.

"Are there any more?"

Nora dumped the bucket over; the contents sluiced out. The little octopus slid into the diving hole. But there were no more eels.

Stricken, Sigrid squatted at the hole, said, "Sigrid ice alive." As if coming to terms with the fact of just the one eel, she wandered back to me and held out her arms. *"Taimagiakaman."*

"What is she saying?" Raj asked.

I lifted her onto my lap. "It's an Inuit word that means the necessity of staying alive through knowledge of the natural world. For her, surviving the ice winds by injecting blood from this eel." Sigrid burrowed into me, moaning the word for eel. "But look at her. This eel isn't enough. How can we get more?"

"They used to be a very common species." Nora knelt next to us, stroking Sigrid's hair. "But the climate's probably pushed them farther north. They hung out just under the ice, but now?" She turned to Raj. "Could be they're near the ocean floor."

"We don't have the equipment to dive that deep," Raj said.

"But maybe we could drop the traps much deeper," Nora said.

"We'd have to dive down and anchor them." He shook his head.

Sigrid excavated from the pocket of her parka a balled-up piece of paper, took my hand and wrapped my fingers around it.

"What's this, Sigrid?" I smoothed the picture out over my knee.

"She was drawing that while we were with the baby," Raj said.

I could make out a rough depiction of two sets of stick figures, facing each other and holding arrows. A child's rendition of what we'd all seen in the flesh from the surface of the ice lake. Between the two groups she'd drawn a vertical line, dividing them.

"Sigrid, are you in this picture somewhere?" I pointed at the drawing. "Where is Sigrid?"

She put her finger on a diminutive figure in the crowd on the left side. "Sigrid," she said softly.

I traced my finger across the figures on the left side of the vertical line. "Is this your village? Your family? Mother, father?"

She nodded.

"And the baby? Where is the *baby* in the picture, Sigrid?"

She moved her finger to an oval shape near the feet of the people on the right side of the picture. A look like shame passed over her face, and she snatched the sketch from me.

"What, Sigrid?" I stretched out my arm. "Sigrid? Please?"

With a good deal of reluctance, she handed it back, resting her finger on a squiggly shape just above the drawing of herself. The same snakelike image she'd been churning out. An ice eel.

"So your family, *you, Sigrid,* and your mother, father, here," I said, touching the people to the left of the line, "had the ice eels, had *sahndaluuk,* but these people"—I ran my fingers over the stick-drawn figures on the right—"had no *sahndaluuk?*"

"*Tahtaksah.*" Sad. "No ice alive."

"My God," Raj said. "People were killing each other for eels."

Nora sat down heavily next to us. "And the other village didn't have the eels, which is why the baby died in the ice wind, and why we couldn't revive him." She reached for the magazine with the spread featuring eels of the Arctic. "Maybe there was some secret about where the ice eels were, or how to get them."

I turned Sigrid's face to mine. Already her eye was drooping less severely. I said, "Ice alive. *Tukisilitainnaqtuq.*" The word meant "the sensation of understanding a thing for the first time."

Smiling, she repeated the word back to me. My heart fell open. Here was another loanword, an expression from her language that had persisted across all these centuries.

Sigrid slid off my lap, went to the table, and turned her drawing over. Drew two circles. Scribbled over the second one.

I said, "She has two days, maybe just one."

The walkie-talkie on the table crackled to life. Wyatt's voice was raw. "You need to get back here right now."

We all looked at one another. Then Raj said, "Nora and me—we're going to get cracking on these traps. Figure out how to get them as far down as we can."

A surge of hope rang through my body as I suited up to head back to the Shack, a sense of being so much closer to understanding how to save Sigrid. I prayed she felt this as well, but all kinds of exhaustion had flooded back into her face, and her hand felt limp and lifeless in mine as we made our way across the ice.

In the spectral gloom of the Arctic twilight, Wyatt sat hunched over his desk, the beam of his headlamp lasering a spotlight into Odin's dissected body. The mouse lay spread-eagled on his back.

I slipped off my parka. Sigrid took one look at Wyatt and the dead mouse and vanished down the hall.

"You let this happen," Wyatt said, not looking up.

I dropped onto the couch. "By the time I saw she was gone—"

"You're telling me you couldn't catch up with an eight-year-old?"

He spun around; I squinted into the burning light. "Why couldn't you bring the body back?"

I pictured the tiny boy, a dash of pink and green floating in an incomprehensible Enormity, under towering ice arches and bergs.

"It was impossible. She'd already put him on the floe."

"I see."

He kept the blinding light in my face until I dropped my gaze. "It's what she wanted to do, Wyatt."

He turned back to his work. With a needle-nose tweezer, he draped something grisly over a slide. "Some polar bear's having himself a tasty snack right about now, I'll bet."

My shoulders slumped. "I'm going to get some sleep."

"Where are the lovebirds?"

"They've got things to do. What happened to Odin?"

He flipped the light up on his head, rubbed his eyes. "He died last night. Must have happened while we were busy with the boy."

"He wasn't looking too well, I noticed."

Wyatt tossed his headlamp on the desk. "His eye was drooping, and he was starting to stumble around. He was just a mouse, but he was my pet too. Loved the little guy."

What was I supposed to say—*sorry for your loss?* I gathered myself to leave. In full view were the contents of his small refrigerator; slides and test tubes covered every available space. A few slides had been turned over, revealing a date scrawled on the other side.

The door burst open; Jeanne blustered through. "You ready to head out?"

"What's going on?" I asked.

"Something's wacko with the weather equipment," Jeanne said. "We got some real weird readings, these really high temps. Then no readings at all." She poured herself a glass of juice. "I think a bear took it down, but I don't know. We've got to check it out."

Quickly Wyatt assembled the slides and tubes back into the fridge and began suiting up, signing off in the log with a flourish. "We might be a while. I wouldn't wait up."

I nearly crawled back to my room, the lack of sleep finally taking over. Sigrid, still in her hat and parka, sat in bed surrounded by drawing pads and books on ancient Greenlandic cultures. She moved over to let me in. Took my hand—ravaged by eczema—and turned it over in hers. From the pocket of her parka she removed a fist-size gray cube of walrus blubber she'd secreted away and warmed it between her palms. Chanting "Bahl" in her singsongy way, she rubbed the greasy cube into the skin of my hands, wrists, and forearms. The smell wasn't bad, like almonds or walnuts.

"Thank you. *Verohnsaht,*" I said. Happy. "But Sigrid." I took the block of fat from her, set it on the night table. Her face was wiped clean of the charcoal, but her eye drooped again, worse than ever. She wore a look of indelible sadness, as if she knew she was going to die, that it was simply too late. It devastated me.

"Where are the ice eels, Sigrid?" With a Sharpie I drew my best ice eel on the sketch pad. "Your family knew. *Ice alive.*"

She stilled my hand; then, her movements deliberate, she tore off a clean sheet of paper. The perspective flat but recognizable, she traced the particular outline of the mountain range, the glacial lake where she'd been found, a zigzag line for the crevasse. She looked up at me, eyes pleading, *Do you understand?*

"Yes, I know what you're drawing. Keep going, Sigrid."

She traced smaller circles—footprints?—stepping off the ice lake and marching over what looked like another mountain range. Then she began to lose me. She drew three piles of flattened circles, connecting them with lines. From the last cluster of circles, she drew her little tracks to a set of waves—a beach?—and with great concentration, a pile of ice eels.

"What are these, Sigrid?" I pointed to the squashed circles.

She gazed up at me as if to say, *How much more do I have to explain to you?* She looked so weary. I flipped through the Greenland book to the thick section of photographs in the middle. We pored over pages and pages of them. On the last page, Sigrid slammed her hand down, yelped with excitement. She pointed to a picture of cairns. *Inuksuit.* Piles of rocks, seven, ten feet high, created as graves or to mark good hunting grounds. Sometimes vaguely in the shape of humans, often used as silent messengers.

I struggled to understand how Sigrid's three cairns were related to one another. *Why can't I just go straight to the ice eels that—according to her drawing—are at a beach?* And what about distances? We couldn't seem to get anywhere with how close the cairns were to one another, much less how far away the eels were.

We both had to give up on it after a while. She could barely keep her eyes open. I folded the drawing and zipped it into the side pocket of my sweater for safekeeping. Even as I hugged her good night, she began to doze. In minutes I followed suit. It was during those odd, between-worlds minutes of drifting off, brain cycling through images of the day, when I saw the numbers flicker by.

The month, day, and year I knew so well.

I sat up as if a demon were hurtling toward me from the dark corner of the room. Sigrid barely budged.

Where had I seen them?

Gently I peeled off the heavy sleeping bag and crept down the hall to the main room. *Are Wyatt and Jeanne still outside?* I heard no snoring. They had to be gone.

Indigo light draped across the room. A bloated moon ogled the glittering landscape.

Wyatt's specimen fridge opened with a soft popping sound. I slid out the first few racks. Ran shaking fingers across the slides and tubes: mosses, pollens, shellfish, seaweeds, each with its Latin name and—on the reverse—the date the sample was taken.

I had to move faster. I had to find the date I'd seen—*unless I'd imagined it*—when Wyatt was dissecting Odin. Forced myself to concentrate as I scanned every specimen. Listened for the snowmobile. All the dates meaningless.

Until I saw them. Two test tubes, one filled only halfway: BLOOD. Two slides: MUSCLE, STOMACH. All marked 3/21/23.

The date of Andy's death.

I flipped over the slides, turned the test tubes. Read: *"Dilectus meus discipulus."* "My beloved student."

I picked up the full test tube of cold blood. As if rejecting the knowledge of what they held, my fingers opened. The vial dropped from my hand, shattering on the desk. Blood spattered everywhere—the specimens, the rug, my shirt, Wyatt's keyboard.

The next few minutes are fuzzy. I know I went to the kitchen—hands slick with my brother's blood. Drained down what was left of the box of red wine. Slid down onto the tile floor and curled into a quivering ball. Began to hyperventilate. Repeated Sigrid's words for emotions: *contempt, fear, sadness, disgust, anger,* until the distant but unmistakable buzz of the snowmobile entered my consciousness.

Heart thumping, I forced myself upright, jumped to my feet. Flipped on the overhead lights. *How could just one test tube of blood end up everywhere?* Terrorized, I frantically got to work, even as I knew it would be impossible to clean every stain.

Chapter 10

MINUTES LATER, HEAVY BOOTS clattered on the roof. Above us, Jeanne's and Wyatt's unintelligible shouts. I rested my fingers on Sigrid's forehead. Too hot. Her pulse pounded in her velvet temples, her breath shallow and fast.

Fully suited up, I bent down. "Sigrid, you have to get up."

She spun away, tunneling into the sleeping bag.

"Let's watch Seal Man and Nora look for ice eels. *Sahndaluuk.*"

With a moan, she rolled toward me. "Bahl," she said, eyes still closed. *"Stahndala."* Fear.

"I know you're afraid, Sigrid."

She patted her forehead, said, "Pain, pain."

"I know your head hurts, but I need you to wake up."

"No, Bahl," she groaned. Said, *"Ionanut."*

The Inuit word for "It cannot be helped."

"No, we're going to get you ice eels, no *ionanut!*"

"Sigrid dead. Sorry."

"No, no, Sigrid *alive.*" I gently but firmly pulled her to a seated position. "Seal Man. Ice eels. Sigrid alive, come on, now." Head lolling forward, she mumbled nonsense words as I dressed her.

Above us, the whir of an electric drill.

"Sigrid, can you walk?" I lifted her off the bed, and she wobbled, pitching forward and landing on her hands and knees.

"You can't. It's okay." Crouching down, I said, "Climb on my back. I'll give you a ride. It'll be fun." I grabbed her arms, looped them around my neck, and stood. She wrapped her legs around me, and I huffed her up a bit higher on my back. She barely weighed anything. As I passed Wyatt's desk, I stole one of his syringes, zipping it into an inner pocket of my parka.

I stepped outside. Twilight. On the roof facing away from us, the cottony silhouettes of Wyatt and Jeanne as they bickered about the best way to repair the satellite dish that had toppled over.

Clutching the rope that joined the two buildings, I took off toward the bay and the Dome. Chilly vapor snaked off the crusty snow. It had to be close to sixty degrees. I unzipped my jacket and took up an awkward run. Sigrid's arms stayed tight around my neck, her small body bouncing against my back.

I unzipped the heavy canvas of the Dome and burst inside.

Curly hair sticking up crazily, Raj faced the diving hole as he struggled to work his diving suit up his arms with shaking hands.

He whipped around to face me. "Val, help me with this!"

A sick, electric panic vibrated in the moisture-laden air. I slid Sigrid into a chair, tossed a blanket over her, and ran to Raj.

"Where's Nora?"

"Oh God, Val! We built this special weighted trap and sent it down—the line broke, so she dove down to check on it. Her line's been cut, or it's caught on something. She's not answering—*help me with this!*"

I wrestled with the main zipper; it was tangled in the fabric. With a yelp, I freed it, then zipped it across his chest. He grabbed his hood. "Put on the emergency suit, Val, I'll need—"

"I can't dive—"

"Put it on!" He clutched my arm, fixed me with bloodshot eyes. He jammed on his flippers with two loud thwaps. "You don't have

to dive, just get the suit on. I need someone to shine a light for me when I'm down there. Keep your head above water."

"Why don't I just shine the light—"

"Nora's going to die, do you understand?" He unhooked the suit from the struts and threw it to the floor. *"Put it on!"*

Feet first, I battled with the bottom half of the suit, reciting the diving steps as each was completed, methodically and too slowly, until Raj took over and we raced through them, ending with the heavy tank, which nearly knocked me backward. For a moment, we stared at each other, absolute terror in his eyes. I felt numb.

He dropped into the hole, then bobbed up, reaching to grab a blocky flashlight that emitted a strong beam of blinking red light. "There's just forty minutes left in the tanks. Watch my safety line. As soon as I go under, get in and hold this light down as deep as you can. Don't move until I get back."

He sank down into the fizzing blue hole. His safety line, a neon orange rubber cord, jerked from slack to taut. I fit the regulator in my mouth and practiced breathing through it as I watched the seconds tick down. Removed it.

I sat at the edge of the hole, legs dangling in the icy slush. Gave Sigrid one last glance—and pushed off.

Instant oblivion.

Weighed down by the tank, my head and shoulders dropped underwater—not my plan. My legs were like two logs as I tried to kick my way to the surface. I caught hold of Raj's line and popped my head and shoulders clear of the water with a shout.

Scrambling for the blinking flashlight, I plunged it into the depths and held it as steady as I could, now fighting my own buoyancy. Cold crawled up my arms, crushed my chest.

At the three-minute-and-twenty-second mark, Raj's safety line suddenly took on a life of its own, snapping from one side of the hole to the other as if it were a fishing line hooked with an immense fish. As if something had gotten hold of him.

I screamed his name.

Back and forth his line lurched. *What is happening to him? What is pulling him away?* The stretched-thin cord set in motion the heavy box of diving equipment it was tied to, dragging the box across the ice toward me. It gathered momentum, sliding across the ice floor as I watched. With a boom, it butted up against one of the struts that supported the building, just a yard from my head.

The strut bent but held.

Bobbing in the slushy blue hole, I closed my eyes, prayed.

Raj's line slackened. I couldn't tell which was worse—the taut line or the alarmingly flaccid one. I had to see what was going on. I was useless just dangling there like fish bait.

I fit the goggles tighter over my eyes, the regulator in my mouth, and dropped my face in the brine. It was as if I'd plunged it into a bowl of ice shards.

I sucked in a mouthful of manufactured oxygen. It tasted like rubber, but I filled my lungs with it and consciously blew it out. My diving watch showed already nearly five minutes had ticked by. Arm aching, I shone the blinking flashlight down into the depths, following Raj's orange line—tight again—until it disappeared in the murk. The light gave up at around ten feet down.

Raj's line jumped again. Danced across my sleeve, then slid to the sharp edge of the ice hole, as if whatever had him changed direction, the line so stressed it trembled like a guitar string until it snapped loose, its new tail fluttering in the violet beam.

I swept the flashing light in an arc. A zebra-striped fish eyed me. No Raj. I had to stay calm. Again and again, I shone the light across the gloom, until it lit up a human shape. A dark silhouette.

Nora floated facedown in the shadows, her arms out to either side like an angel's, body undulating in the current. Her bright yellow tank glowed neon in the light. A diving rope tied around her waist kept her in place, as if she were a kite maneuvered by a sea creature on the ocean floor. I screamed into my mask.

I lifted my head out of the water, popped out my regulator, and gasped for air. Snatched up Raj's line. It had been cut at an angle, clean and straight across. *What could have done this?* Twenty-nine minutes of air remained. Raj was not in my sights, but I could still help Nora. I angled the regulator back in my mouth. Again, dropped my head down beneath the slurry of ice and brine, flipping my headlamp on as I had seen Raj do. I left the flashlight behind.

My body colder than it had ever been, I swam down to Nora and then beneath her as if I were flying in slow motion. Now I could see: A makeshift trap rested on the seafloor between two sharp-edged rocks. *Could her safety line have been cut as she'd tried to pull it up? Was Raj's line slashed as he tried to free her?* I seized her arm; she was limp. Her beautiful face glowed alabaster, but her eyes were closed, mouth open. She looked dead. I untied the rope around her waist, meaning to bring her up, but she shot up, banging into me. Her body turned with the current, traveling sideways.

I kicked out after her, caught hold of her flipper but couldn't keep my grip, and she slipped free. Her body rotated with dream-slowness, the black of her suit meshing with the fathomless void that was sucking her away, until only the bright yellow tank glowed, and in seconds that was gone too.

Watching Nora fade into the shadows, I couldn't muster the will to move. I almost abandoned myself. I almost pulled out my regulator and drank my fill. But I couldn't. Didn't.

The numbers on my dive watch pulsed—nineteen minutes, eleven seconds of oxygen left—but that fact did not set me in motion. Above my listless body the ice ceiling dripped with blue and green stalactites. Forget above the ice, *this is the Enormity,* the underbelly of dreams, the inverse mountain, all of it unbearably exquisite and strange. I couldn't take my eyes off it. In my head Nora's voice: *The biggest danger is getting so blown away by the weirdness of everything down there you lose track of time.*

A muffled explosion as a berg split and crashed nearby. My ears banged; water shuddered around me. A ringing silence followed; had I lost my hearing? I kicked and waved my arms, rotating my body in the murk until I had no idea which way was up.

Seven minutes, twenty-five seconds of oxygen left.

I couldn't let go of the thought, *I have to swim after Nora.*

Precious time passed, indecision paralyzing me. But of course I knew: Nora was gone. I had to get the eels, or Sigrid would be gone too. I focused on the trap.

Kicked down to it. Trapped behind the slats of the box and fine red netting: a boiling knot of eels. The bone white rope drifted in the current. I caught it, tied it around my waist as it had been around Nora's. Sand and grit had drifted into the trap, weighing it down. I clawed it loose from the seabed, a cloud of swirling sand.

Two minutes, thirty-five seconds.

I charged upward. Still roped to me, the trap popped free from the seafloor, its drag like a body chained behind me.

Frantically I flashed my dim headlight up toward the underbelly of the ice. Green rings glowed everywhere.

But which is the diving hole?

I pictured it: a long oval shape, like a bathtub. Caught sight of it. Clawing at the water, scissoring sluggish legs, I made slow progress toward the glimmering beacon as the trap jerked along beneath me. Finally, I reached it and thrust my hand up, expecting air. Solid ice greeted me. *Had it frozen over? Impossible . . .*

This wasn't the hole! The trap bumped up against my back, then floated past my face, eels churning.

Fifty-nine seconds.

Pushing up against the solid ice, I sent myself back down a yard or so. Had to see the geography of my underworld. I twisted my neck, trying to comprehend what I was looking at.

There were dozens of these glowing circles, these false holes. It was only then that it hit me. The ice sheet above me was slowly creeping along, like a sky full of clouds in a swift wind.

That explosion was no calving berg. The Dome had broken away on its own ice floe. And it was moving.

I kicked myself down, dragging the wretched crate behind me like everything I'd ever dragged in my life, the great weight of my fears and phobias and grief and all I could not solve.

Forty seconds.

What makes the diving hole different from all these other rings of thinning ice, Val? What?

I scanned the rippling ceiling of ice for some sort of clue. Shockingly far away, a faint lavender light blinked on and off.

The flashlight I'd abandoned near the edge of the hole.

I thought, *It's too far away. I'm going to die down here.*

I kicked off toward the smudge of winking purple, the horrendous trap jerking me back half a stroke for each one I took.

You have to let it go, Val. Untie yourself and let it go.

Twenty-seven seconds.

Could I make it to the hole with this trap chained to me? I pictured Nora's lifeless body rolling in the blue hell, Raj's corpse butted up against the soapy underbelly of some pitiless berg.

I had to let the eels go.

Sigrid will die without them.

I will die with them.

Thirteen seconds.

My clumsy rubber fingers grappled at the knot, but to my horror the force of my swimming had tightened it to something I didn't have the strength, dexterity, or time to loosen.

Two seconds. One.

Blinking red zeros.

With a low hiss, the pump of oxygen slowed. My head felt gaseous, like a balloon. I stopped fighting the rope and became still. I felt high. Then the purple beam swept across my retina, jump-starting some primal life force. Sipping at the wisp of air that remained, I pictured my body free of anchors and slim as a knife. What did it mean, this bright pulsing marvel above me, this tender neon angel? Oxygen-starved weakness rippled through me, ironing me flat. All I knew was to go up, to touch that sweet glow. I was aquatic; I was a sea creature; I was something about light.

What is it? I'm supposed to want light.

Want light.

I SHUDDERED awake. Among the clink of dishes and scrape of silverware, Wyatt and Jeanne spoke in hushed tones. I squeezed my eyes shut. Could still feel their rough grip as they hoisted me from the freezing water, hear my oxygen tank bang against the sides of the hole, taste my first sweet shot of heavenly air.

I inhaled the odors of brewing coffee, fried fish, wet wool steaming over the heater, musty couch stink as I gathered blankets tighter around my shoulders. Every muscle and bone of my body ached, my mouth sandpaper dry. I hazarded a peek at the rug—I'd done a fair job cleaning the bloodstains, but how soon would he learn about the broken test tube; *did he already know?*

I recoiled at the screech of Wyatt's chair as he dragged it close. Jeanne bustled around, then landed in the blown-out recliner next to him. Deep blue twilight lent their faces a deathly pallor.

"Where's Sigrid?" I managed.

"She's fine," Wyatt said. "She's sleeping."

I shed the blankets. Sat up. Remembered; saw everything. My gut hollow as I choked out a sob. "Raj, he—then Nora . . ."

They let me cry for quite a while before saying a word; I thought that was strange even as it was happening.

"What happened out there, Val?" Wyatt said calmly.

I took a deep breath, tried to oxygenate my brain, keep my cool. "You two were up on the roof fixing something. Sigrid wanted to see Raj, see Seal Man, you know, so we went out there—"

"I saw you. I called. You didn't answer."

"Raj—he was about to dive because Nora . . . was in trouble."

"What were they diving for, Val?"

"Specimens . . ."

"What kind of specimens?"

I drew a blanket back over my lap, suddenly cold again. "How should I know? Raj asked me to suit up, so I did. He dove to look for her, then I dove to look for him, but then his line—"

"How do you know how to dive, Val?"

"I read the dive checklist when I can't sleep. I memorized it. And I've watched them dive a bunch of times."

He leaned back. "So many talents I knew nothing about."

Jeanne poured a cup of coffee and brought it to me. I thanked her with a nod. "What time is it? How long have I been asleep?"

"Around seven. Eighteen hours or so," said Wyatt. "Temps have gone way down. It's about five degrees out there now. Snow's supposed to quit soon, but it's going to blow pretty bad out there all night. Jeanne's radioed for help, but we're stuck here. No one's coming till the wind dies down."

I turned to face them. "How did you get to the Dome?"

"The floe it sits on broke away, but it butted up against that long spit of land that juts out. Otherwise you'd be out in the middle of the ocean by now. You're a lucky woman."

I flashed on Nora and Raj, forever entombed in the haunted blue grottoes under the ice. "Have you reached their families?"

"No." He got up and paced in his floppy-toed socks. "Haven't tried. Wanted to talk to you first."

"Well, they should know. You should try. I'll talk to them."

"Relax. Eat something."

Jeanne brought me a plate of fried fish. I didn't touch it. "What about the crate?" I asked.

He leaned back against the kitchen table, the light casting circles under his eyes. "We have it. Why do you want to know?"

"Because it had . . . it had their specimens." My hands balled into fists, fingernails cutting me.

Wyatt popped a fried potato into his mouth. "No, it didn't."

"Of course it did. I was hauling it up and it—"

"The trap was empty, Val. The netting was torn when we pulled it up. Maybe you have something to tell me about that crate?"

"Who cares about the crate? Nora and Raj—"

"I care about the crate. I care *a lot* about the crate. Clearly, so do you. So does Jeanne, don't you, Jeanne?"

Jeanne gazed out at the snow. "Gotta say, I'm curious about it."

"Yeah, *curious*. About what Nora and Raj were so frantically searching for. Wondering why you risked your life to bring it up."

I set my coffee down, tightened the blanket around my shoulders, and stood. "I'm going to go see Sigrid."

"Don't be rude," Wyatt said. "Answer the question."

The hair on the back of my neck stood up. The words *Dilectus meus discipulus, My beloved student* paraded across my mind.

Wyatt watched me closely. "We want to save that girl as badly as you do, don't you get it, Val? What good to us is she dead?"

We're stuck here. No one's coming till the wind dies down.

I threw up my hands. Let the blanket fall to the floor. "Ice eels." I looked from Wyatt to Jeanne, both poker-faced. "That's how she survived the ice. She needs the blood of ice eels to live.

Periodic injections. She used a hollow bird feather to inject herself—"

"Oh, come on, Val, why are you feeding me this crap?" Wyatt massaged his forehead. "You're gonna make me do something I don't want to do. And the irony is, I like you, Val."

I clutched the back of his chair, suddenly dizzy with fear. "There were no eels in the crate?"

Wyatt poured himself a jelly jar of wine. "Did you know that I'm dying, Val? I've got cancer. Just a few people know." He sipped his drink, set it down. "Jeanne knows."

Jeanne reddened, kept her eyes on the carpet.

"Make a dying man happy. Tell me the truth about the crate."

"It was full of ice eels—they must have gotten out—"

"*There was nothing in the crate!* But it doesn't matter, does it? Because that's the wrong answer, Val. *That's the wrong answer.*"

Sweat needled my brow. "I *saw* her—"

"Ice eels were the *first* thing I tried! Who knows how long ago. Had to be before Andy got here, over a year now. Complete waste of time. Kind of like asking you to come here and talk to the kid." He sought out another chunk of potato, chewed it thoughtfully. "So that's it, Val? That's your final answer?"

"Final answer?"

"She's dying, Val."

"Look, Wyatt, I can prove it—"

"Jeanne?" Wyatt said. She turned to him. "Let's get this done."

Jeanne tossed my parka and snow pants next to me. "Put these on." Her tone set every fiber of my being on edge. She turned away to slip on her own gear, as if ashamed.

"Why, Jeanne?"

But she wouldn't look at me. She unhooked the rifle from the wall and slung it over her shoulder. "Questions later."

I dropped my gaze, focusing on the task of pulling on my snow gear as slowly as possible while my mind lunged for some sort of plan. *But what's theirs? Is the rifle for protection or for something else?* Wyatt scuffled down the dim hallway, returning moments later half dragging Sigrid. Her appearance shocked me. Both her eyes drooped. She limped along, whimpering with every step.

He gave her a mean little shove toward me. "Get her dressed."

"Sleep," she moaned as I pulled her close. "Sleep, Bahl."

"I know, Sigrid wants sleep, but first we have to get dressed." I worked her snow pants over her leggings, then put on her parka.

With effort, Sigrid lifted her head to Wyatt's dark face, read it, and whispered, "*Stahndala.*" Fear. She crawled into my lap.

"What did she say?"

"That she's afraid."

Wyatt ambled into the kitchen, extricated a caribou steak from the freezer, and dropped it in a pan already sizzling with oil. "I don't get any satisfaction from this, I really don't."

"Wyatt, what are you talking about?"

Jeanne hovered at the door, hood cinched tight, gloved hand on the knob. "Let's get moving, you two."

Carrying Sigrid, I plowed through knee-deep snow to the Shed, Jeanne at my heels. She knocked the door open with the butt of her rifle. Clomping around the dimly lit room, she took down some dusty jelly-jar glasses from a high shelf.

"What's going on, Jeanne?"

She held her palm out flat toward me as if my voice or my question pained her. Popping open the lid of the low freezer, she liberated a bottle of vodka and filled the two glasses, sliding one toward me. "Sorry," she said. "Don't have anything for the girl. Been meaning to get some kind of hot plate in here for cocoa."

I drank the vodka down in a few gulps. Suddenly restless, Sigrid pushed herself away from me, and I set her down.

"What did he ask you to do, Jeanne?"

She smiled crookedly. "Well, how did he put it?" She chuckled. "He's got a way with words. 'The girl will have to thaw out at a more convenient time.' Something like that." She knocked back the rest of her vodka, shook her head, set the glass down hard. "Gotta say, it's harder than I thought. Then again, everything's harder than you expect. Don't you think?"

"Jeanne, I don't know what we're doing here."

She poured us out two more shots and capped the bottle before approaching the walk-in freezer. "Good thing I had a spare lock for this puppy. You sure beat the hell out of the last one." She spun the dial, mumbling as she peered down at the numbers. Quietly I lifted a ball-peen hammer from a hook on the wall and dropped it in a roomy inside pocket of my coat. The tumblers aligned; she swung the door wide. Frost smoke rolled out.

Jeanne crossed to the table, snatched up the rifle, and shouldered it. "Get in. Both of you."

"You can't be serious."

She tilted her head. "If you'd actually done what Wyatt brought you up here to do, learn Sigrid's language and such, we wouldn't be standing here like this. He'd have the answer. We could save her. Now, what choice do we have? She's dying."

"She needs the ice eels, I've told you. And even if— Jeanne, *look at her!* She's so weak, she'll never thaw out alive again—"

Sigrid reached her arms up to me; I swept her up.

Jeanne said, "I thought you liked this girl, even *loved* her—"

"I *do* love her!" I clutched Sigrid closer to me. "And so do you."

She shifted the gun. Jerked it toward the freezer. "Get in."

"You're insane." I set Sigrid down, unzipped my coat, lifted her up again, and zipped her in close to my body.

"It'll take ten minutes. The pain goes away fast, and then you're warm." She raised the gun. "Get in the damn freezer."

"No!" I faced Jeanne and the long muzzle of the gun. "First tell me what happened to Andy."

"Good try. You know all that."

"I found the blood samples Wyatt took from Andy's body."

She lowered the gun, looked me in the eye. Blinked. "He was already dead. It was all for . . . science."

"Jeanne, I'm going to die in there. You have nothing to lose." I shook so hard I feared Sigrid would fall, but she held tight.

The gun dipped to the floor. "Okay, I'm going to tell you this only 'cause I got brothers back home and I get it." Jeanne looked down and away from me. "Andy, he wanted to make this discovery in the worst way, bad as Wyatt. What Odin took or whatever to thaw out alive. So one night they fought pretty bad. Next morning, me and Wyatt found Andy outside, frozen. He'd left us a note, said, 'Thaw me out' in so many words. And so we did, and well, he woke up alive. Man, he had it figured, whatever it was."

"He *woke up alive?*"

Jeanne shifted her weight, set the gun down on her worktable—still aimed at us—and sat on a stool. "Yeah."

I took a step toward her. Clutched the handle of the hammer. *Hit her hit her hit her.* But I had to know. "How did he die?"

"You stay back," she hissed, fingering the trigger.

I complied.

"It was like this," she said, entering a kind of reverie. "Wyatt grilled him hard, but Andy? He just flat-out refused to say what he injected. Your brother, he . . . he really got it wrong. Wyatt's temper, I mean. He should have just spilled the beans. I mean, Andy was real weak when he came out of it—and Wyatt hurt him, he—he *cut* him, but your brother, he just smiled and smiled."

I took a step toward her, the hammer half out of my pocket.

She seized the gun, and I stumbled backward, the hammer dropping into the recesses of my coat as I struggled to keep Sigrid in my grip. *"You get back!"* she cried, her voice hoarse with emotion. She waved the rifle in my face. "Everything happened so fast. I couldn't stop him. I tried, but he—he grabbed a cushion and held it over Andy's face, and I couldn't—and then he put him back outside, just like we found him. Only he was really dead then. Wyatt said I was part of the whole thing, that I was guilty too."

"That makes no sense."

"But it does." She wiped away tears of rage or shame. "When Andy thawed out alive, Wyatt said to get out. Leave them alone. But I wouldn't do it, I refused, because I had a bad feeling about what Wyatt was gonna do, and I was right, so you see, if I'd left like he asked me to, maybe he wouldn't have—"

"Wyatt murders my brother, and you do his dirty business out here with us. Why's that, Jeanne?"

"Enough." She shook off any emotional residue and lifted the gun. "You, you get the hell in there."

"Just let us go, Jeanne."

"Go?" she snorted. "Where ya gonna go? This is for the best."

"We could try to find the eels." I eyed the keys to the snowmobile hanging on the wall. "You could help us! Or just let us—"

"Shut your trap."

"Doesn't matter what Wyatt asks you to do, you just do it—"

"Get in the freezer!"

Every shred of humanity leached from her face as she charged me, poking the barrel of the gun into my belly. I staggered backward, stepping up onto the steel platform of the walk-in, Sigrid's arms so tight around my neck I was close to choking. The ice cores in their neat rows glittered in the bleached light. Before I could draw a breath, the heavy door slammed shut.

Chapter 11

Complete and utter darkness.

Unfathomable cold. Hell.

Instinctually, I narrowed my eyes, blinking fast to keep them from freezing open or shut. Blindly, I unzipped my jacket and peeled Sigrid's arms and legs from me, forcing her to the floor of the freezer. She cried out pitifully.

"Sigrid." I bent down to her in the blackness, both of us gasping at the stinging air. "Brave girl, strong girl. Stay by the door."

I stepped away from her, into the center of the terrible cold black box. "Bahl!" she cried. I heard her crawling toward me.

"No, Sigrid, no!" I half dragged her back to the door. "Don't move. *Taimagiakaman,* okay? *Taimagiakaman.*" The necessity of staying alive. "Sigrid. Wait for me. Here."

I could barely move my fingers anymore, my blood a frozen sludge, mind congealing. I couldn't waste another second. I pulled the ball-peen hammer from the pocket of my parka, wound up, and swung at the ice cores. Again and again I pounded at a thousand years of Arctic climate history. Ice daggers stabbed me in the cheek. I didn't stop. I might have been screaming.

The door swung wide open. Sigrid, who had been leaning against it, tumbled out onto the floor of the Shed just as the light in the freezer snapped on, catching me half-crazed, mid-swing.

I stood in a sea of shattered cores and wooden cradles.

Jeanne leaped up into the freezer with the gun. "How dare you!"

She lunged for me. Lost her footing on a chunk of ice, smacking headlong into the wall of battered cores. The gun skittered away. I jumped over her and out of the icebox, slamming the door shut behind me. I scooped up Sigrid, scraped the keys from the wall, and sprinted to the door.

The snowmobile roared to life, and we charged out into the polar night. Even by moonlight, the way to the frozen lake was unmistakable. Adrenaline surged through me. Tucked inside my coat, hooded head down against the vicious wind, Sigrid nestled close as we climbed steadily upward, snow churning behind us.

I paused at the apex of the pass and cut the motor; I had to stop and think. I gathered Sigrid closer, but she barely moved and made no sound. We were nothing in the terrible blue expanse. The wind swept us clean, then covered us in sheets of crystalline snow.

All I could see was Jeanne frozen to death in the walk-in, but I couldn't face it. *It'll take ten minutes. The pain goes away fast, and then you're warm.* My mind blocked the image. I hadn't meant to kill her. *Don't think about it now, or we will die too. . . .*

The vodka had already burned through me; my mind was as clear as the night sky, achingly sharp. I forced myself to look at my surroundings. Car-size chunks of tumbled ice jutted up at odd intervals across the sparkling tundra.

"Sigrid," I whispered. I lifted her, turned her to face me. Her eyes at half-mast under the slouchy hat, arms wet-noodle limp. "The cairns, Sigrid. *Inuksuit.*" In her language, I said, "Rocks, many, ice eels, dead alive, paper, drawing, Bahl, want." No idea where I'd put the map. *How could I lose such an important thing?*

Her mittened hand crept up the side of my sweater under my coat. *Of course, that's where I put it, so I wouldn't lose it!* I took off my gloves and rescued the piece of paper. My heart sank when I looked at it. *Good Lord, where are we? Where are we going?*

Sigrid pointed to a craggy set of low mountains in the distance.

"That way? Are you sure?"

She turned the paper over, where the crude crayon drawing continued. Jabbed her finger at the three cairns.

I tucked her back into the folds of my coat and started the engine. As we threaded between waist-high and taller ice formations, I was always listening for another motor, the only other motor in hundreds of miles. The snowcat.

But we were alone.

We banged and growled up through the narrow pass. Descending over ridges of rough, uneven ice, we rocked so hard I was sure the machine would break apart beneath us.

Spread out before us, a snow-swept plain met the black bowl of night an untold distance away. I jammed the machine into neutral. "Where now, Sigrid?" My hands felt frozen on the controls.

She peered up at me as if to say, *Can't you see?* Her cheeks red, her smile like a Cheshire cat. She said, *"Verohnsaht."* Joy.

I scanned the desolate landscape. "Sigrid, I don't . . ." *But—there!* There was something. Between snow-filled blasts gusting across the plain, a pea size black form took shape in the distance.

I shifted into gear and tore off. Quickly the mass grew taller. In minutes, I kicked off the motor. We glided the last several yards in white silence. The rock creature loomed over us, one stone "arm" raised as if in judgment. Wide-set pillars served as stumpy legs, a thick slab capping them like a pelvis, a mammoth block as a torso. Two long, flat stones rested on top—its shoulder girdle—a roundish boulder set squarely in the middle. A stone man who towered close to twelve feet tall. How long had this craggy monster existed, condemning everything that passed? A hundred years? Thousands?

I climbed out of the machine and carried Sigrid to the beast. Grabbing on to the ledge that was the shoulder stone, she pulled us closer to it, speaking a few words lost to the wind.

Sigrid pointed to my eye, then toward a triangle-shaped hole created by the two shoulder rocks.

She said, "Eye. See."

I huffed her up higher in my arms, squinting through the fist-size hole. Perfectly framed, perhaps miles away, there it was. Another blocky, vaguely man-shaped form.

The second cairn.

I gunned the snowmobile across ridges of snow and ice to the next rock man. This one stood even taller, but cockeyed, one rock arm jauntily pointing skyward, the other down, like it was disco dancing. Four stacked oblong blocks made up its torso; the one placed where the belly might be curled inward like the fossil of a snail shell, breaking through to the other side in a perfect quarter-size peephole. I peered through the hole and sighted the third cairn, again perfectly framed by the opening. We were off.

We flew across rough, tumbled ice. The next cairn seemed to reach a rocky, beseeching hand to us. Up and over a shining blue hillock we sailed—I wasn't looking down—and landed hard. Belching out an ugly blast of diesel, the motor breathed its last. We coasted across the slick surface in silence, until we stopped.

Were we one, five, ten miles away? Impossible to tell.

I smacked the side of the machine, kicked at the pedals, screamed into the void. Tried the key again: *tick, tick, tick . . .*

Silence.

Or was it?

A motor. Faint, but real. The snowcat. I would know it anywhere. *How long has it been tailing us?*

"Sigrid." I shook her. "Do you hear? They're coming."

Her eyes glimmered open, and she nodded, exhausted, sad.

"We have to move, okay? We have to walk."

She closed her eyes and melted into me.

I got out of the machine. Set her down on the windswept ice. I ransacked the snowmobile in vain for anything we might use. By the time I raised my head from the guts of the machine, she had already commenced a stumbling walk in the direction of the cairn.

"Sigrid, wait!" I ran toward her, heartsick to leave the machine.

We were really in it now. I walked on feet I no longer felt. Looming in the distance, the last cairn cut a jagged black hole into a velvet sky matted with stars. I no longer felt the wind.

Sigrid tripped, fell forward, and didn't get up. I picked her up. She didn't have enough life in her to hold on to my back, so I carried her in my arms. I don't know how far I walked. The whine of the motor grew neither louder nor fainter, but stayed a steady buzz in my head. *Have I lost my mind? Is it just the wind?*

But if it is them, can they see us? I thrust my limbs forward, robotic. We were freezing to death.

I spoke to Sigrid using all the words I knew in her language, about a hundred by then, to try to keep her awake and with me, but there was no answer. How useless was all this—was *I*—if I lost her? *I can't lose her.* But the Enormity didn't care what I wanted; it just stretched out and out, beyond all human understanding.

I careened toward what looked like a snow-dusted boulder. The massive body of a musk ox lay on its side. It was gutted. Just a shell articulated by a huge set of ribs, yet a thin film of vapor rose off it, and its nose still glistened. Crouching, I stepped inside its oil drum–size body cavity. It occurred to me to wonder, *Where is the animal that did this?* Bloody footprints next to mine said polar bear: dinner-plate size, five claw marks, and deep.

I didn't care. It had to be twenty degrees warmer inside the tent of ribs and skin. I smelled meat, hide, blood, and offal. Under a shoulder blade the size of a snow shovel, a wedge of flesh still steamed. I lay Sigrid on the bloody snow, wrenched off my gloves, and clawed my hands between bone and skin, yelping as my blood turned from sludge back to liquid, from death back to life. With shaking fingers I yanked Sigrid's mittens off her terrifyingly stiff hands and worked them into the hot tendon. Her eyes banged open, then fluttered closed.

"You have to tell me what to do at the third cairn, Sigrid. Stones. Help, eels, dead alive, *alive,* please, now."

Sigrid mumbled what sounded like an incantation. "Love, happy, Bahl. Walrus, bone, ice eels, dead alive, dead alive."

Then she pulled her hands free, eyes slipping into the back of her head. I rubbed her hands and stuffed them in her mittens. Gathered her up and abandoned our shelter in a run.

As I crossed the ice with her, I could feel my energy waning as if a hole had been drilled into me. But I was pure intention, pure will. I threw myself toward that petrified third monolith like it was everything I'd ever wanted in this brief and miserable life.

I fell to my knees at the base of the rock beast, a penitent. This one—taller than the others—looked the most human, one rock foot slightly forward of the other as if it were in the midst of taking a step. It had a mouth, an ear-to-chin gash in the stone, as if it were trying to speak, snarl, or curse. It had only one stone arm, about five feet long, that narrowed off like an attenuated hand, pointing to something it had been pointing to for millennia.

Holding the child close, wind battering us, I circled the creature as I searched for a hole. Nothing to look through. My heart broke.

The sound of the motor ramped up, a dull, constant roar, not my imagination. A loaded gun aimed at us.

"Sigrid," I yelled through the wind. "There's no peephole. . . ."

I pushed back her hair. Spoke her name. But she was still.

From beneath us: grunts, barks, snorts, an appalling fishy smell.

What is this?

Only then did I look down, along the sight line of the stone arm. The ice field descended sharply. Low tide revealed a magnificent natural arch of ice over a pebbled beach. From the dark water the lusty blow of a fin whale. On the far flank of the inlet, an immense herd of walruses, perhaps thousands.

The stone arm commanding me, I half fell down the steep slope toward the beach, glancing back at the immobile face of the cairn. Its leering mouth seemed to say, *Just look, what you're searching for is right there, I cannot be more clear.*

Something snapped under my boot, turning my ankle. I looked around. A thousand white walrus jaws—interlocking chevrons—had been arranged in a semicircle, a demarcation of something precious. Holding Sigrid, I picked my way past the ring of walrus jaws, toward the dark beach. Which seemed to be moving.

Love, happy, Bahl. Walrus, bone, ice eels, dead alive.

Filling the shallow bay, countless gleaming ice eels twined around each other. The mat of twisting ropes shone under the moonlight, eminently peaceful, as if this was their homecoming under the ice arch, like salmon that have battled untold miles upstream to spawn and die where they were born.

A trace of diesel tainted the air.

The eel I stole from its brothers with my bare, bloodstained hands did not resist me; as if accepting its fate, it hardly moved as I prepared to cut off its head and gather the curative blood.

On the beach, just beyond the ice arch, the walruses grunted and snorted, flapping their flippers with a wet sound. The earth beneath us shook as they rolled and smacked against one another. I dropped down on the snow with the precious syringe, cradling Sigrid. I shook her, yelled her name. Her head lolled, mouth slack; I thought, *She's already dead, what's the use?* I laid bare her thin arm. Found a tiny blue vein and did my best to inject her there. Drew her close, prayed out loud in her language, "Hope, love, Sigrid, alive, wake up, wake up, wake up," as the rock hand pointed down at us. Even as I held her there, the tide sneaked in a few feet.

As the snowcat charged to the crest of the hill, she began to stir in my arms. Slowly, then with the vigor of a child wresting herself from nightmare. A surge of joy warmed me; if death came for me at that moment, how could there be sorrow? There could be no better thing I would do than what I had just done.

MINUTES later, I heard the slam of the snowcat doors—first the driver's, then the passenger side. It seemed to strike me bodily. Sigrid's eyes still looked terrible, but her voice was strong. "Bahl, *verohnsaht!*" Joy. "Love, thank, eel, ice alive, more, please—"

From the crest of the hill: low conversation, the crunch of boots.

"Okay, Sigrid," I whispered. "We'll do that later, I promise."

"Bahl, *stahndala.*" Fear. "Sea, wave, eat, eels, no!"

"The tide is coming in, I know. We'll gather the eels soon."

"Bahl," she said, worrying my sleeve, unconvinced.

Two human shapes, Wyatt and Jeanne, stood framed between the stone monster's legs. Sigrid wriggled out of my arms and dropped to the snow.

"Get up here," Wyatt said, his silhouette a black hole.

Behind us, the herd of walruses had begun to move. They raised their yellow scimitar tusks and bellied along the edge of the inlet, their great bodies obscuring the bay of eels.

"What did you do to her?" Wyatt said.

"It's the ice eels. They're down here, on the beach."

He shrugged his rifle off his shoulder. Aimed it at us. "No more, Val. Tell me what you gave her, and she lives. It's simple."

"I told you! They're here. . . ." I gestured at the crescent of black eels, but even from where we stood, it was impossible to make them out. "There must be millions of them."

Jeanne stood as mute and still as the rock pile behind her.

"I injected her, and look at her, she's *better*—"

"I can see that. We can both see that, right, Jeanne?"

She shifted her weight. "Sure can."

"Go! Go look for yourself." I nudged Sigrid behind my legs.

Gun still trained on us, he said, "Jeanne, go down there and see what the hell they're talking about."

But Jeanne just gazed out at the sparkling midnight water. As if working out some sort of dispute, the noisy gang of walruses broke into two distinct groups, now flanking the nest of eels.

"Jeanne?"

"No."

Annoyed, he half turned to her. "What the hell is wrong with you. Get down there." He jerked his gun toward the ice arch.

She stepped out of the shadow of the cairn. Moonlight cast a blue pall on her face; she looked oddly younger. "I don't need to go down there. They're telling the truth."

"What are you talking about?" Spittle flew from his mouth. "Jeanne, she tried to kill you."

"Wyatt, why would she lie to you?"

"Why *wouldn't* she?" he fumed. "How do you know it's the eels, Jeanne? How are you so sure—"

"Because I know."

He turned to her. "You've been running your own trials in the shed, is that it? *Betraying me?*"

"No, Wyatt," she said, as if placating a child. "I wasn't running my own trials." She drew in a long breath. "I was only . . . screwing up yours. Every single one of them," she added with a touch of pride. "I guess you call them double-blind, isn't that the term?"

Wyatt hurled the gun down. "What the hell is wrong with you?"

"It was pretty easy. I'm not stupid, you know. It's all just chemistry. It's like baking. You add an extra egg, a few more tablespoons of butter, and you've changed your cake."

"You and your damned cakes."

"And Odin. You found him in the Dome after those other polar divers left. The ones before Nora and Raj. They brought up a ton of spec buckets. Dumped 'em out all over the place." She puffed up a bit. "What do you think that mouse was eating in there?"

"But you were sabotaging my work! How would I know . . ." He injected calm into his voice. "Look, I thought we were friends, a team. Why in hell did you do this thing to me?"

I could barely make out her reply over the walruses' snorts. "Because . . . I didn't want you to leave this place. Leave me . . ."

Wyatt panted as if he'd been running. "No. Tell me *no*."

"Those times we— I know. It was different for you, but I . . ." Her voice broke, and she became unintelligible.

His shoulders sagged, and he gazed up at the answerless moon. "Oh, *please* tell me this isn't happening." He spun around to face her. "So what *did* you actually learn? Something you can prove. Because I think that's the very least you owe me after all of this—"

She squared her shoulders. "Honestly, Wyatt? We're even."

I didn't see it coming, what he did next. The explosion of sheer violence. He snatched up the gun and whipped the butt across her face. Knocked sideways, Jeanne collapsed onto the ice, moaning as blood spurted from her nose and mouth.

"That's just a taste," Wyatt said, wiping the gun on his thigh. "A tiny taste of what's coming to you." He came a couple of steps toward us. "Both of you. Get up here and stay here. Wait for me."

I began clambering up the hill, dragging Sigrid behind me.

But Wyatt didn't wait. He sprinted past us like a mad bat, hurtling down toward the ice arch and pool of eels beneath.

Jeanne was now so still on the snow I thought she was dead, until I saw her parka rise and fall. Tipsily, she rose up, coughed some blood, and turned toward me, her face a calamity. Her front teeth gone, bottom lip split. She reeled away from us, staggering a few paces, only to crumple back down to her knees. I ran to her, grabbed her around the middle to steady her. She lurched to her feet, knees wobbling.

"Are you all right, Jeanne?"

She pushed me away with a grunt. With a couple of spastic steps, she listed toward the ridge as if following Wyatt down to the eels, but stopped. As his form threaded through the two bands of walruses, the mood seemed to shift among them. Rumblings rippled through the two broods, snorts exchanged. The mob of walruses started merging back together. Only Wyatt's head was visible beyond the herd as he crossed under the arch.

Still hunched over, Jeanne watched the roiling mass of flesh and blubber. In her face, I read longing, fear, then—something else. Her eyes hardened. She stomped past us to the cat, animated by whatever possessed her. Wrenched open the door, climbed in, and started the engine. Slammed it into gear.

Halfway down the hill, she banged the machine into neutral. Revved it hard again, the engine noise echoing down the slope.

She didn't need to do more, because the walruses had been on the move the moment the snowcat blasted to life. It wasn't like they steamrolled over Wyatt; their crushing charge didn't seem intentional. There was just no place for him to go as they climbed over one another in their stampede to reach the sea and safety, flippers smacking, whiskered faces shuddering with terror. They crushed their own infants in their exodus as they filled the bay en masse, Wyatt's cries barely audible over their grunts.

I pulled Sigrid toward me. I didn't dare take my eyes off Jeanne.

For close to a minute, she sat unmoving in the snowcat, then reached down and switched off the motor. Just walruses bellowing; no more sounds from Wyatt. She fumbled at the door and climbed out of the machine. Took a few wobbly steps.

She dropped to her knees, crying Wyatt's name. The grief in her voice stunned me, this raw pain loosed from some place inside her. I thought to comfort her but couldn't seem to move my limbs. After a minute, her chin dropped down. She seemed cried out, drained.

I assumed she would stay there, wedged in the snow like that, but no. Gravity helping, she found her footing. Bolted with stunning agility down the bank toward the undulating mass of walrus flesh. Two big noisy females turned to her, shocked quiet at the sight of this woman jumping into their midst. Jeanne climbed onto one of their backs, teetered crazily as she tried to leap from there, but lost her balance and slipped down between them. She screamed once and was silenced.

THERE was nothing Sigrid and I could do for anyone except ourselves. We gathered the dregs of the eels that remained in the bay—no trace of Wyatt or Jeanne—and drove the snowcat from cairn to cairn, back to the empty Shack. My first call was to Pitak, who told me the winds would be calm enough the next day for him to safely fly out to the station and bring us to Thule.

A few tries later, I reached my dad on the sat phone. At first there was only dead air as I spoke that terrifying word "love" to him; in fact, he was quiet for some moments after I'd finished telling him all that had happened.

When he finally spoke, his voice was full of so much tenderness, I hardly knew him.

"You've been through hell, Val. How can I express my . . ."

"It's okay, Dad. Are you doing all right?"

"Don't change the subject. I wish . . . I wish your brother could know somehow what you've done. That I could have taken Wyatt's life with my own hands . . . that I could have spoken with Andy one more time. Fantasies, all of them."

"I have them too, Dad."

"Mostly I wish I could tell you to come home right now with Sigrid. Order you to come back and see your old man."

"I can't say what I'm going to—"

"I understand. You've got to see this through in your own way. But promise me one thing."

"Name it."

"When you do come back, I hope you'll tell me about yourself.

Let me just be a dad for a little bit, for the time I'm here. It's like I hardly know you, Val, and that's my fault, I know. Here you are, bringing me my favorite candy every time you visit, and I—I haven't the faintest clue what you like."

"I like strawberry licorice."

He laughed. "I'll get my hands on some. And I'll shut up and listen this time. Just let me get to know you. That would be a gift."

Chapter 12

In the rock-strewn yards of simple, brightly painted wooden homes, caribou antlers lie in tangled heaps. Strips of drying fish flutter in the wind as sled dogs yip and howl. Polar bear pelts hang over porch railings, black claws grazing the frozen turf.

Nearly two months have passed since Sigrid and I flew from Thule to the town of Qaanaaq, population 627, on the northwest coast of Greenland.

We live in sixteen hours of hard dark followed by eight hours of twilight; the sun won't return until February. But we're finding our way. Already Sigrid has friends her age who understand her well enough to sit on the swings together overlooking the bay. Pitak offered us the cozy in-law apartment attached to his home; he seems glad to have us here. Sigrid is learning the alphabet, working on writing down what she calls "talk marks." She can't quite grasp that paper comes from trees—she's never seen living ones!—and wonders why I won't tell her what animal-skin paper is made from.

There's talk of me staying and teaching the kids English, and I'm thinking about that. These days I feel less awkward around children. I think it has to do with feeling better about myself.

It's not that I'm planning to stay, it's just that I haven't left yet.

Dad and I talk a few times a week, and I feel the pull to go home, but I think, *How can I possibly leave her?*

The official story was that Sigrid was the only person found of the families who had trekked from the remote village to the island in search of caribou; that we at the research station had found her traumatized and were trying to bring her back to health when the tragedies occurred. She had no living relatives.

Meanwhile, the eels are being harvested and studied; much has been learned already. This particular ice eel cryoprotein was unknown until now, but it's a simple compound, one that can be made synthetically for pennies a dose. No need to eradicate the population of ice eels. Though cheap and easy to produce, it is—like any medicine—challenging to distribute, and the ice winds are hitting everywhere now. They're unstoppable. I know the story of these eels and how they'll change the world isn't over; it's just the end of my part in it, for now.

A COUPLE of times in my life, I have felt transcendence. Once, years ago, when I was witness to a baby being born, and last night, with Sigrid. She insisted we watch the Northern Lights together.

It was past midnight when she waited at the door, dressed in her parka and boots. I'd put her off most of the evening, because, you know, *the Enormity*. It had been months since I'd taken a pill, much less had one to take, and alcohol was scarce here. So, there I was. Sober, but not as steady as I wanted to be.

"Bahl?" she said, clearly losing her patience.

"*Stahndala,*" I said. Fear. "Big sky, night, dark, cold."

She said, with sarcasm, "Okay, come on, let's go," a phrase she'd heard me say countless times by this point—she knew it cracked me up coming from her—then marched over to our bureau, where she scrambled through the sock drawer. Grabbed Andy's heart-shaped lead piece, plopped it in my hand. "Joy! Bahl, Sigrid, safe, night, magic, warm."

Bathed in moonlight, we lay under caribou skins on the rickety dock. Across the entire dome of night, the Northern Lights rippled green and purple, yellow and orange, each display morphing in the space of a breath. I'd never seen anything more beautiful.

Sigrid held my hand tight, said, "Excitement! Lights, sky, story, father, mother, child, true, Bahl, want?"

Pretty sure she was asking me if I wanted to hear some story about the Northern Lights. "Yes. Tell me. Bahl want story."

She said, "Childrens, dead, spirits, play, dance, sky, alive."

So there they were: eons of children's spirits swirling in ecstasy across the night sky. *"Tahtaksah,"* I said. Sad. "Children, dead."

She got on one elbow, eyes sparking in the dark. "Come on, let's go, *verohnsaht!*" Joy. "Dance, play, children, baby, spirit, always, mother see, father see, safe, night, love. Always. Okay?"

I understood. The spirits of the children were dancing happily, and their mothers and fathers would always be able to see them.

I smiled, said, "Bahl, love, story, dancing, children, sky, night."

And so I dwelt in the Enormity and did not fall up into the sky, nor was I erased by my grief; I was wrapped in the arms of the world and the night and a precious girl.

Just before bed that night, I talked to Sigrid about the ice winds around the world, and my worries that humans were destroying the earth. An adult conversation, but she could handle it. I lost my way when I tried to explain the word "hope." But she told me about a word in her language for a particular kind of hope: the feeling a hunter has when he's waited all day at a breathing hole for a seal and one comes up but he misses with his harpoon, and even though the sun is going down and he's hungry and cold, he knows he'll try again tomorrow, and tomorrow he'll be successful. He has no doubt.

I love that word.

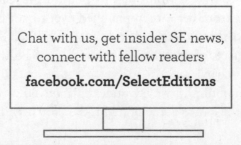

After*Words*

There's little that author Erica Ferencik won't do for a good story. To research her past novels, she's trekked deep into the Allagash wilderness in northern Maine and rafted the Amazon River in the Peruvian jungle. For her latest novel, *Girl in Ice,* the author spent three weeks exploring Greenland's remote, iceberg-packed fjords.

Ferencik admits this research isn't always easy, and her nerves sometimes get to her when it's time to climb into a canoe or board a helicopter. "But," she says, "my desire to research the books—to bring the reader the real sights, sounds, smells, the real feels of a place—always trumped my fear."

The initial idea for *Girl in Ice* was inspired by a much simpler trip: an outing to her local woods. While walking in the forest, she came upon what looked like painted turtles frozen in the ice of a pond. "They didn't look alive, but they didn't look dead either," she recalls. "It turns out that there are some animals and plants that have this freezing-and-coming-back-to-life thing down." From there, the author had a vision of a young girl frozen in an Arctic glacier, and a new plot was born—along with a new research adventure.

In addition to thirty-five years of writing, Ferencik's background includes stand-up and sketch comedy and a brief stint as a filmmaker. She currently lives in Boston with her husband and Maine Coon cat.

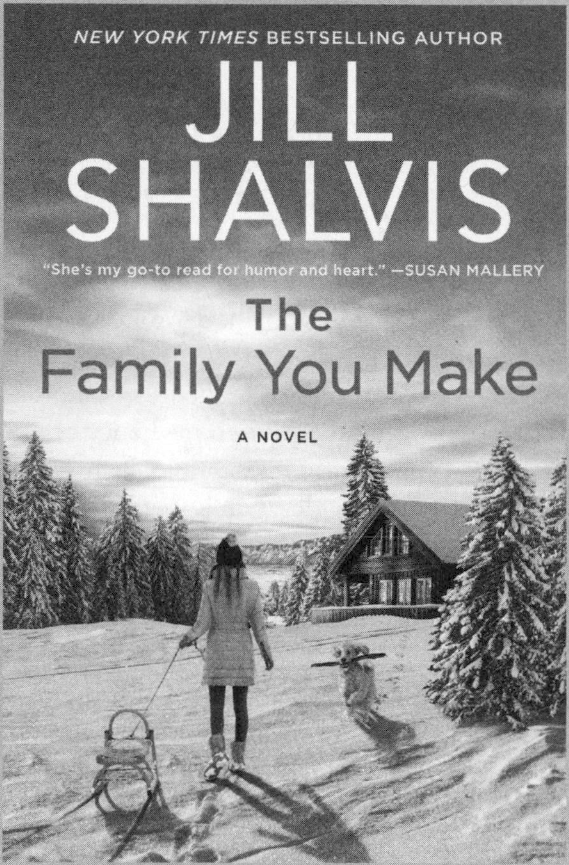
NEW YORK TIMES BESTSELLING AUTHOR
JILL
SHALVIS
"She's my go-to read for humor and heart." —SUSAN MALLERY
The
Family You Make
A NOVEL

Chapter 1

It wasn't often that Levi Cutler came within a hair's width of dying. But if he'd known biting the dust was on today's agenda, he might've done things differently, like called the waitress who'd tucked her number into his pocket the other night or learned to brew his own beer.

Forgive himself for his past mistakes . . .

Sitting back on the gondola bench, he looked out the window at the afternoon winter wonderland of North Diamond Ski Resort. The sky had been clear when he'd arrived, but now snow came down like white fire and brimstone, leaving visibility at zero. He knew what he'd see if it'd been clear—jagged snow-covered mountain peaks as far as the eye could see and a glimpse of Lake Tahoe due east, its waters so blue, so deep and pure, you could see a dinner plate three hundred feet beneath its surface.

A gust of wind jostled the gondola. The storm that no one had seen coming was kicking into gear. He'd hoped to get a few runs in before having to face the reason he was back in Tahoe, but that wasn't seeming likely. The gondola rose past pine trees coated in powdery snow, resembling two-hundred-foot-tall ghosts.

The gondola, built for sturdiness, swayed with the trees, giving him a quick stomach-dropping vertigo. But being in the business of knowing risks and algorithms, he knew the chances of dying in a gondola were nearly nil.

On the other hand, the risk of dying while skiing was a different game altogether. The smart decision would be to turn around at the top and go back down the mountain. Especially since the snow kept coming, harder and faster now, slanting sideways thanks to the strong headwind. The gondola did the same. He might spend most of his time on a computer these days, creating tech solutions to fix supposedly unfixable problems, but he'd grown up here. He'd spent his teen years working on this very mountain. As he knew all too well, anything could happen in a blink of an eye.

The gondola slowed toward the end of the ride. A lift operator, maybe seventeen, opened the door. He gave Levi a *Stay seated* gesture. "Sorry, sir, but we just got word, right after you boarded."

"No problem." Levi had been there, with his job on the line as he told belligerent tourists that no, they couldn't risk their lives on the mountain. "Need any help clearing people out?"

The kid shook his head. "The gondolas in front of you are empty. We're just waiting on one more employee. After she loads, I'll be right behind you on a snowmobile."

A woman appeared in the doorway. She nodded at the kid, then stared down at the one-inch gap between the platform she stood on and the tram floor. With an audible gulp, she clasped her necklace in a fist and hopped over the gap.

The woman darted past him to the opposite bench, close to the window. She closed her eyes and mumbled to herself something about how ironic it was to have "survived a whole bunch of crap only to die in a tin can hanging by a hook on a mountainside."

The gondola bounced, and she gasped, flinging her hands out like a cat trying to gain traction on linoleum. She was covered in heavy winter gear, the only thing visible being the long strands of her wavy dark red hair sticking out from under her ski cap.

As the gondola began heading down the mountain, she brought her legs up on the bench and dropped her head to her knees.

"You okay?" Levi asked.

"Just very busy having a freak-out here," she said to her knees.

"About?"

"About leaving my lunch in my locker back there. I don't want to die on an empty stomach."

"We're not going to die. At least not today."

Not lifting her head, she made a snort of disbelief.

Okay, he could admit the storm might be terrifying. "It's actually far less scary if you watch."

"I'll take your word on that. We're a million feet up."

"Five hundred and fifty."

"What?"

"We're five hundred and fifty feet aboveground. Approximately the same as five and a half stories—"

Her head jerked up, hitting him with some seriously green eyes. *"Why would you tell me that?"*

"Sometimes if you're afraid, knowing all the facts helps."

Her spine snapped ramrod straight. "Do I look like I'm afraid of heights?" she asked, just as the gondola jerked so hard that she gasped and grabbed the bars on the side closest to her.

"Right," Levi said. "You're clearly not afraid of heights at all."

She glared at him. "It's not heights that get me. It's tight, enclosed spaces swinging five and a half stories aboveground."

"Shift to the middle of the bench," he said. "Away from the windows. You'll feel better."

This got him a vehement shake of her head. "I've got to be at the window so I don't miss the crash." She grimaced.

The next gust hit hard. Everything flew to one side, including his companion. He caught her and pulled her down onto the bench at his side, keeping ahold of her for a minute. "You okay?"

"No! Not even close! We're an inch from falling and dying, and I don't know about you, but I had things to do today. Like *live*."

"A gondola fall is extremely unlikely. Maybe one in a million."

They rocked again, and she drew a shaky breath. "You know what I need? Silence. So if you could just stop talking, that'd be great."

The next gust hit violently, knocking them both off the bench and into each other on the floor. On their knees, they turned in unison to look out the window just in time to see . . .

The gondola in front of them fall, vanishing from view.

She gasped in horror. "Oh my God! Did that gondola just . . . ?"

"Yeah. Hold on," he said grimly. Their gondola came to a stuttering halt, swinging wildly, flinging both of them *and* all their stuff far and wide. Levi ended up face-planted against the window.

His companion hit him in the back. She scrambled clear to stare out the window at the gaping chasm where the previous gondola used to be. "Ohmigod," she whispered. "Was anyone in it?"

"The lift operator told me the cars in front of us were empty."

She leveled him with those amazing eyes, narrowed now. "So much for a gondola fall being one in a million!" She yanked out her phone and stared down at it. "Dammit. I forgot it's dead."

"They'll know what happened at base. They'll come for us."

The truth was her fears were valid. He didn't know what had caused the gondola in front of them to fall, but if theirs did the same, the odds of them walking away were slim to none. First up was getting them to stop swinging so freely, and he began to calculate the balance and weight needed to stabilize the car. "Hey, do you think you can get all the way into that back corner there?"

She blinked but didn't question him, just did as he asked, crawling to where he pointed while he moved into the opposite corner.

"You do realize this only works if we weigh the same," she said.

"We'll use our gear to even things out." His backpack was at his feet. "What have you got with you?"

She lifted her hands out to her sides. "Just what you see."

"You came up on the mountain with nothing on you—no snacks, no water, no emergency gear or equipment?"

"Didn't say that." She emptied out her many pockets. Steel water bottle, a bag of beef jerky, a pack of gum, and . . . a small first aid kit, which she held up for Levi to see. "Safety first, right?"

He noticed the medical patch on her jacket. "Ski patrol?"

"RN," she said. "I'm a traveling nurse, working a rotation at each of the five urgent care medical clinics in the area." She once again waved her first aid kit. "I'm qualified to save people's lives—even if I can't manage to get my own together."

He started to smile, but another hard gust of wind hit and they spun like a toy. There was a sound of metal giving way—the shelf above his head for passenger belongings—and Levi lunged to shield her body with his.

Everything flew in the air, and for a single heartbeat, gravity seemed to vanish. Levi wrapped himself tight around his companion, her head tucked into his chest when something hit his head.

And then it was lights out.

When the gondola finally stopped moving, Jane couldn't breathe. Something was on top of her, something heavy.

No, not a something, a some*one.* The guy who'd been steadfast in the face of her panic, and he was a dead weight. Carefully, she crawled out from beneath him. "Hey." She leaned over him and checked his pulse. Thready, but he was alive. "Can you hear me?"

Not so much as a twinge.

Mr. Talkative was out cold, leaking blood from a dangerous-looking two-inch cut that sliced through his right eyebrow and along his temple. She let out a string of oaths. Now what?

It was still snowing, but the wind had calmed and the gondola was now swinging gently. The floor looked like a garage sale gone wrong, their stuff scattered everywhere. On top of everything lay the steel shelving rod that had hit Mr. Talkative in the head.

This was bad. "Come on, Sleeping Beauty, rise and shine." The guy had lunged across the gondola to tuck her into him, saving her from getting hit. *What was that?* She was a perfect stranger.

She looked around for her phone before remembering it was dead. And anyway, who was she going to call? She knew security at the base would be working their way toward them for extraction.

The man still hadn't moved. Not good. She checked for other injuries. Nothing broken, but when she turned him onto his side, beneath his jacket she found his shirt sticky with blood. Shoving his layers up, she found two slashes across his back and shoulders.

Well, hell. "You had to play the hero." She shrugged off her jacket to stuff it beneath his head as a pillow. She stripped off her scrubs top and the thermal she had on beneath, using the former against the scratches on his back. The thermal she pressed carefully against his head wound to slow the bleeding. "Okay, seriously, no fair letting me be the only one awake when we die."

Nothing.

Stripping further, she pulled off her outer gear ski pants, which she rolled and used to prop him up on his side so he didn't lie on his wounds. Then she checked herself over. She looked like a horror flick victim, but she was pretty sure the blood was all his. She'd been through a lot in her life, and almost all of it she'd dealt with on her own. But today wasn't a day where she wanted to be alone.

"Come on," she cajoled. "If I have to be the one in a million to die in a gondola, you have to wake up to die with me."

Not even a flicker. So . . . she pinched him, right on the ass.

He let out a grunt, and she nearly collapsed in relief. "That's it," she murmured. "Now open those pretty gray eyes of yours and tell me once again how we're going to be just fine."

He groaned, sounding rough. "How long was I out?"

"A few minutes."

Still not opening his eyes, he gave a small smile. "You think my eyes are pretty. *And* you touched my ass. Admit it, you want me."

Maybe she'd hit her head too. "Why did you use yourself as a shield for me? That was so stupid."

"*Always* save the person with the first aid kit."

Leaning over him, she pulled back the shirt to check his head. Blood welled up. She quickly put it back.

"I didn't want you to get hurt," he said quietly, sucking in a breath when she applied pressure.

She honestly couldn't remember when anyone had done such a thing for her. Then she realized his color had gone green. "Breathe in through your nose. Hold, then slowly let it out." She breathed with him. "For the record, I'd have been fine on my own."

"Most people might say thank you."

"Yeah, well, I'm not most people." He *still* hadn't opened his eyes, pretty or not. "Are you dizzy?"

"I'm fine." Guy speak for yeah, he was dizzy as hell.

"It's my mom's fault," he murmured.

Great, he was delirious. "Your mom?"

"She taught me to protect others, always."

The blood was soaking through her shirt, so she deepened the pressure. He tried to sit up, but she held him still.

When she'd first noticed him sprawled out on the bench opposite of her as she'd boarded, she'd done her best to ignore him, distracted by her hatred of small, enclosed spaces. But it was impossible to ignore him now, on her knees and snugged into the curve of his long, broad-shouldered body, his blood on her hands.

Closest you've been to a man in a long time, came the entirely inappropriate thought, which vanished at the grinding sound of metal. She gasped and clutched at his arm. "What was that?"

She expected him to come up with some smart-ass answer, but he didn't speak at all. "No. Hell, no, don't you dare. *Stay with me.*"

He groaned, and she almost burst into grateful tears. "What's your name?" she demanded. "Mine's Jane."

His voice was barely audible. "You Jane, me Tarzan."

She laughed. "I don't know whether to worry that you're hallucinating or that you're an imbecile."

"Imbecile," he said. "At least according to my older sister."

Keep him talking . . . "Well, for future knowledge, it's Jane Parks, not Tarzan's Jane. You're close with your family?"

"Unfortunately. I'm also the black sheep."

"Is that because you tell stupid jokes?"

His lips quirked, but other than that, he didn't move, and worry crept into her voice. "Open your eyes, Tarzan. I mean it."

"Bossy." But he cracked open one slate, bloodshot eye.

"*Both* eyes."

It made him go green again, but he managed.

"Are you dizzy? Nauseous? Is there a ringing in your ears?"

"Yeah."

She took one of his hands and directed it to hold the compress on his head. "Now track my finger. *Tarzan!* Pay attention."

"*Levi.* My name is Levi."

"Well, Levi, are you watching my finger?"

"Yep. All twenty of them."

Oh crap, his pupils weren't tracking either.

"That bad?"

She pasted on her sweet nurse smile. "No. Not bad at all."

A very faint laugh escaped him as he closed his eyes again. "Don't ever play poker, Red."

"Jane." And she *did* play poker. The skill had come in handy in college. Especially since she had a fondness for having food in her belly and a roof over her head. After growing up a tumbleweed in the wind, she'd never needed more than the minimum to get by.

Levi had closed his eyes again.

"Hey. Hey, Levi, stay with me. Where did you grow up?"

"Here." He swallowed hard, like he was trying not to throw up. "Tahoe. Not the gondola."

She smiled. "Funny guy."

"I try. Where did you grow up?"

"I didn't. Not yet." It was her automatic, don't-give-too-much-of-herself-away answer, and she usually got away with it.

But Levi opened his eyes, then reached out and touched her cheek. His fingers came away with blood on them. "You're hurt," he said. She watched as he took in the fact that she was crouching over him in just her bra, but his gaze was brisk and methodical.

"It's *your* blood." She caught his hand. "Levi, I'm fine."

He gave a nod so slight she almost missed it. "You are," he agreed. "And brave." Then he closed his eyes and lay very still.

She checked his pulse again.

"My ribs are bruised but not broken," he murmured. "And you know head wounds always look worse than they are. I'm fine."

"Yeah? Then maybe you could put all those well-honed muscles to use and pry us out of this tin can."

That got a very small smirk out of him.

"Oh please, like you don't know that you look like an *Outside* magazine cover. Let me guess. You're a wildland firefighter."

His small smile widened a bit. "Data . . . scientist. Consultant."

"Sounds very . . . cerebral."

His smirk remained in place. "You think scientists can't have . . . what did you call them . . . well-honed muscles . . . ?"

He was fading, and panic surged anew. "What does a data scientist consultant do?" she asked desperately.

"I . . . extract and design data modeling . . . processes . . ."

He was clearly having trouble finding words. He needed X-rays. An MRI. "What else does a data scientist consultant do?"

"Create algorithms and predictive models . . ."

She looked around for the first aid kit that had to be here somewhere. Yes, there it was in the corner. She hooked it with her foot and opened it up. "Could you create an algorithm to tell me which fast-food joint is most likely to give me a stomachache when I'm inhaling food after a twelve-hour shift?"

"All of them. How about I feed you real food after this?"

She snorted. "Are you flirting with me right now?"

The man managed a small smile, sexy as hell. "I'm stuck in a gondola with a beautiful woman who took off her clothes. The least I can do is make her laugh."

She did just that as she found the antiseptic and gauze and doctored up his head. "This isn't exactly a laughable situation."

Another huge gust of wind hit them like a battering ram.

Jane crouched over him to keep anything else from hitting him. "Wonder how many gondolas have fallen at this resort," she asked with what she wanted to be a calm voice.

Levi covered her hands with his. "Until tonight? Zero."

She realized their faces were inches apart. Pulling back, she began going through the stuff littered around them, finding a bottle of water. "Are you allergic to acetaminophen?" she asked.

"No."

She handed over two pills from her first aid kit. He swallowed them before she got the water bottle open, then closed his eyes again.

"What else do you need?" she asked.

"Can you reach into my front pocket?"

"Not even in your dreams."

That got her another almost smile. "To get my phone."

"Oh." Right. She pulled out his phone and handed it over. He sent out a quick text, getting an even quicker response. "A friend on the search-and-rescue team says there's already a team in place, but they're being held up at base because there's zero visibility." He gave a very tense smile. "He said to hang tight."

Jane swallowed hard. She'd done a lot of dangerous things in her lifetime. For instance, the time she and other medical workers had been flown to a remote village in the Philippines that had caught fire while they were there. But this. Hanging by a thread, facing a fall that she knew neither of them could survive . . .

Levi reached for her hand. "We're going to be okay."

She stared down at his fingers. "That would be more believable if you weren't gripping me hard enough to make my fingers cramp. You think we're going to die, don't you."

"How about we don't put it out there into the universe that we're going to die, okay? Let's put it out there that we're going to make it, that there's no alternative."

Looking into his eyes, she almost believed him. Then he flashed a small smile. "Besides, you haven't thanked me for saving your life yet. Can't die before that." He held out his phone.

She stared at it. "What do you want me to do with that?"

"Call your family," he said quietly. To say goodbye, he meant.

Suddenly her heart was in her throat again.

She stared down at the cell phone, then glanced to the windows again. Snow blowing sideways, still zero visibility, still absolute chaos, but in here it was oddly quiet, insulated.

Levi was patiently waiting for her to make a call.

"My cat can't answer a phone," she said. "It's an opposable thumbs thing."

His lips quirked. She hadn't been trying to be funny, but rather distract from the truth—she had no family to call.

"Your parents?" he asked.

Her mom and dad had been troubled teens when she'd come along. By the time she'd been born, her dad had peaced out and her mom had left Jane with her grandparents. Eventually her mom had settled down, gotten a new family, and hadn't spoken to her in years. "They're not in my life."

His eyes softened, but she cut him off before he could speak, handing him back the phone. "Hurry, your battery's nearly dead."

Not moving anything but his finger, he activated a call on speaker. A female voice answered with a joyous-sounding "Levi!"

He closed his eyes. "Hey, Mom. Listen—"

"Oh, honey, I'm so glad you called! I didn't get a chance to ask what you'd like for dinner. I mean, it's so rare you get up here from San Francisco— Hold on a second. *Jasper!*" she yelled. "*Stop that!* He's digging in the yard. The gophers are making holes again, and Jasper fell into one and nearly broke his leg."

Jane looked at Levi in concern.

Levi put a thumb over the microphone. "Jasper's her dog. Trust me, he's indestructible." He pulled his thumb away.

His mom was still talking.

"Yesterday at my yoga class there was a woman whose son created a system with a camera that lets her know if there's a gopher in her yard. He's going to sell it and get rich."

"Mom, anyone can buy a security camera—"

"Sure, but you could make something like it and get rich."

"I'll get right on that," he said on a barely-there sigh that made Jane smile. "But about why I'm calling—"

"I mean as long as it didn't take any time from your personal life," his mom interrupted. "You need a personal life, Levi. You work too much. You haven't even made time to date since—"

"*Mom.*" Levi ran a hand over his face.

A blizzard and possible death hadn't rattled him, but this clearly did. And now Jane wanted to know what the *since* meant.

"Mom, I'm trying to tell you something."

"Oh, I'm sorry, honey. What?"

"I'm"—he locked eyes with Jane—"going to be late picking up Peyton from her after-school dance program."

Jane would bet that hadn't been what he'd planned on saying.

"Oh no," his mom said. "Levi, you promised. Peyton told everyone in her class you were going to show them that magic trick."

Levi looked pained, and Jane couldn't help it: a laugh escaped.

"Who was that?" his mom asked, apparently possessing bat-like ultrasonic hearing. "I heard a laugh. You're with a woman? *That's* why you can't pick up your darling niece? *Levi!*"

Jane winced for him, thinking he was about to get yelled at.

"How wonderful! I want to meet her. Put her on the phone."

Jane went from laughing to miming *no-no-no* with her hands.

"Mom, I'm not putting Jane on the phone."

"Jane! Is she nice? Does she look after you? Not that you need it, but you're thirty and all you do is . . ." She paused. "I'm sorry. I always forget what exactly you do. It's something with data."

Before Levi could answer, they were slammed by another gust of wind and heard the unmistakable sound of metal straining. Jane covered her mouth with her hand to keep her scream to herself.

"Levi, what was that?" his mom asked, sounding tinny.

His phone beeped, its battery on its last breath. It was now a race as to who would die first, the battery . . . or them.

Levi's gaze met Jane's, and in that single heartbeat something changed for both of them. Acceptance. He reached for her hand as he spoke into the phone. "Forget my job, Mom," he said with surprising gentleness, eyes still locked on Jane's. "I just wanted to tell you that you're right. Jane's my girlfriend."

"Oh! Levi, that's wonderful. Is she sweet?"

"Very," he said.

Jane bit her lower lip and shook her head, needing him to know she was the furthest thing from sweet.

He just held her gaze and kept talking. "She's sweet, she's caring . . . she's everything you've ever wanted for me."

Jane was boggled. Both at the obvious love he had for his mom and also how she should've been embarrassed to be intruding in such a private moment, but instead she only felt . . . fascination.

"I can't wait to meet her," his mom said, sounding so excited that even Jane's cold, dead heart warmed and rolled over in her chest. "Does she live in Sunrise Cove? When can I meet her?"

"We'll do details another time," Levi said. "I've gotta go now, Mom. Kiss Peyton for me. Love you—"

Beep.

Swearing beneath his breath, Levi looked at his cell, expression tight with worry. Jane knew that not one ounce of it was for himself. It was for his family, whom he clearly loved beyond anything.

That selflessness got her. She'd felt it once, with her grandparents. But like most good things in her life, it hadn't lasted.

That's when she realized she was shaking.

Levi sat up with difficulty and leaned against the bench, where he tucked her into his side so that they were sharing body heat, snuggling her in close. "Hug me," he said. "I'm scared."

She looked into his eyes. He wasn't scared—or at least he wasn't letting it show—but she took the out and pretended it was for him anyway, gratefully moving in against his body.

"We're going to be okay," he said softly near her ear.

The guy had an optimistic outlook, like he truly believed someone would come for them. Since she couldn't remember anyone *ever* coming to her rescue, this blind faith was foreign to her.

They were quiet for a moment. Daylight was fading as the snow swirled all around them, blocking out everything else.

"Any regrets?" he asked.

She shrugged. "I hate regrets. I try really hard not to have them."

"Which didn't answer my question," he said.

"Okay, fine, maybe there are a *few* . . ." She drew a deep breath as she thought about her grandpa. "I lost touch with someone important to me," she admitted. "And the more time that goes by, the harder it is to figure out how to find my way back."

Levi gave a barely-there nod of understanding. "I get that. I . . . hurt someone important to me once." His gaze went faraway, like he was lost in the memories. "She wanted more than I was capable of giving her back then."

"And now?" she asked.

"And now it's too late."

She understood all too well. "So we both suck," she said.

He snorted, and they were quiet a moment.

"If you could have one thing," he finally asked quietly, "whatever you want, right now, what would it be?"

That seemed like an unanswerable question. "You should go first on that one."

His eyes were closed, his voice slower than before, worrying her. "I'd want to see my niece, Peyton . . . Her dad just bailed on her and my sister, and she's lost so much. I'd want one more day with her, playing tea party or whatever she wanted to do."

The words warmed her as much as his delicious body heat.

"Now you," he reminded her. "What would it be?"

Maybe to have a family, like he did. Impossible with the life she led. She worked the ski season in Tahoe every year. The rest of the time, she worked for organizations like Doctors Without Borders. Her next contract was in Haiti. The Tahoe gig paid more over these two months than she would earn the rest of the year. Plus, it was easier and had fewer hours, and she loved the snowy terrain.

But none of that was why she really did it. Her reason was her own and deeply personal.

And not something she intended to share. "Well, I was going to say a cookies 'n' cream cupcake from Cake Walk," she quipped, needing to lighten the mood. "But now that just sounds shallow."

Eyes still closed, he smiled. "There's *nothing* shallow about a cookies 'n' cream cupcake from Cake Walk. What else, Jane?"

Maybe it would be to call Charlotte. When Jane was in Tahoe, she stayed in a big old house owned by Dr. Charlotte Dixon. Charlotte was a trauma surgeon who collected people around her like some women collected shoes, and she was the warmest, kindest, most bossy person Jane had ever met. So yeah, Jane supposed if she could do one thing, it'd be to thank Charlotte for collecting her.

"You've got a cat?"

"It's more like an alley cat I feed when he lets me."

"What's his name?"

"Alley Cat."

He gave a small laugh. "Do you let him inside?"

"No, he's an alley cat." Jane knew a home should be warm and cozy and welcoming, with people in it who loved one another. She couldn't offer that to Cat, not when she'd be gone in six weeks.

"Do you let him in at night?" he asked.

"That would just confuse him when I'm gone, and then his alley would seem cold and hard, and that's hardly fair."

He squeezed her gently, his eyes serious now. "See? *Sweet.*"

"If you knew me better, you'd know how funny that is." But her smile faded when she realized he'd tipped his head back against the bench. He was pale, and his mouth was a hard, grim line.

In that very moment, the gondola started moving again.

"Oh my God!" She looked around with shock and relief, having really thought her number might be up. "We're going to make it!"

When Levi didn't answer, she tightened her grip on him. *"Levi."*

But he was out cold.

Chapter 2

FIVE MINUTES AFTER Levi had passed out, their gondola returned to base. They'd immediately been taken to the hospital.

Jane had sat with him in the ER cubicle until his wounds had been cleaned and stitched up and he'd been wheeled off to Imaging. That had been hours ago. She'd since been checked over and at the moment sat in a cubicle on her own, worrying about Levi.

Dr. Mateo Moreno slipped in past the curtain surrounding her cot. He was one of her favorite ER doctors, not just because he treated nurses with respect but also because he lived next door to Charlotte's house where Jane rented a room. He was a friend.

Or at least as much of a friend as Jane allowed herself.

"If you needed a nap after your shift at North Diamond, you could've just said so," he wisecracked as he pulled up a stool. "You okay?"

She snorted in amusement. "Isn't that your job to know?"

His own amusement faded as he met her gaze. "I'm betting your experience was terrifying."

One hundred percent, but it was a personal rule not to do vulnerable. "Nothing I can't handle."

"How did I know you'd say that?" He began to peck on the computer at her bedside. "You call the boss yet?"

This was a joke reference to Dr. Charlotte Dixon, five feet of pure heart encased in hard steel with a Southern accent. "I'm waiting until I'm cleared," Jane said. "Otherwise she'll freak."

He laughed. "She just got off her shift. If you don't leave her a message, you know she'll find out and freak anyway."

"Not if you hurry up and get me out of here. With a little luck, I can go pick up her favorite breakfast and beat her home."

"Just when we all think you don't care at all . . ." he teased.

"How's the guy they brought in with me?" she said with as much nonchalance as she could muster. "Head injury. Is he okay?"

He slid her a look. "Professional interest?"

"Of course," she said.

Mateo shook his head. "You know the drill. If you want info on a patient, see if he'll allow visitors and talk to him yourself."

She sighed. "Or you could just give me a hint."

"I'll say this. You and Levi both got damn lucky."

"You know his name."

"Yeah. I know his name."

"You worked on him in the ER?"

"I did. And also . . . we go way back." And then he went back to typing, shoulders atypically tight.

Seemed everyone had their secrets.

As for her and Levi getting lucky, if Levi hadn't thrown himself across the gondola to protect her, he'd be fine. And she'd be . . . not fine. "I'll take lucky any day of the week," she said quietly.

Mateo's eyes softened. "Same. Your wrist is sprained, and the contusions on your jaw and cheek are nothing to worry about."

"So you're releasing me to go home and take a nap for real."

"Yes. How you going to get there?"

"I don't know yet." The old Subaru she drove, Charlotte's spare car, was still in North Diamond's parking lot. She'd lost her keys at some point between the gondola and the hospital.

"I'll take you home," Mateo said. "I was off thirty minutes ago. I stuck around to spring you free."

She smiled at him. "You're the best, Dr. Hottie Patottie."

He face-palmed. "You promised you'd make all the nurses stop calling me that."

One of the five urgent care clinics she rotated through, Sierra North was attached to the hospital. She knew a lot of the same nurses he did. "Oh, I got them to stop." She hopped off the cot. "That was just for me. I enjoy watching you squirm."

"You're a sick woman."

"Tell me about it. Let's go."

Mateo went to get his stuff, and Jane took a stroll down the ER hallway. She needed to see Levi and know he was okay.

She found him in a patient room, hooked up to an IV, asleep. "Thanks for saving my life," she said softly. "I owe you one."

He didn't give so much as an eye flicker, so she turned to go and . . . bounced off Mateo's chest.

He gave her a look as he shrugged out of his jacket and wrapped it around her shoulders. He didn't say anything, not on the walk out of the hospital and not when they walked across the snowy, slippery parking lot to his car.

He turned on the engine and cranked the heat to high, aiming the vents at her before finally pulling out of the lot.

They stopped at the Cake Walk, Sunrise Cove's local bakery. Jane quickly grabbed Charlotte's favorite muffin and coffee, and then they got on the road again.

As they turned onto their street, Mateo said, "Uh-oh." He pointed to the car in front of them. Charlotte's.

Jane sank down low into her seat. "Just park and get out of the car and leave me in here. I'll sneak out once she's inside."

Mateo made chicken sounds.

"Oh, like you're in the clear. You're still totally in the doghouse with her for clearing our driveway of snow in that last storm."

"Yeah, and maybe you can explain that to me."

Jane laughed at his confused expression. Men were slow sometimes. "She doesn't like to accept help. She's . . . stubborn."

Mateo's and Charlotte's houses shared a driveway that split off at the top. There was enough room for two lanes of cars, but Mateo stopped right next to Charlotte's car.

"Wow," Jane said, still scrunched down low. *"Seriously?"*

"Hey, if I'm going down, I'm taking you with me." He opened his door, got out, and . . . *didn't* shut his door.

Charlotte got out of her car and stood there, hands on hips, in midnight-blue scrubs, her white doctor coat, and a thick pink down jacket. Her blond hair, loose from its usual bun, flew around her face like a halo. She gave Mateo a single nod and said "Doctor" in a tone so chilly Jane almost got frostbite.

"Doctor," Mateo repeated back to her, sounding amused.

Charlotte stared at him. "It's going to snow again later." She said this in that classy Southern drawl of hers. "When it does, don't even think about plowing my driveway."

"Just trying to help," Mateo said lightly.

"Who said I needed help?"

Mateo's lips twitched. Then he slid a knowing look at the strings of twinkling Christmas lights lining Charlotte's house's eaves.

"They're hard to get down," Charlotte said.

"I offered to help you."

"Maybe I just want to be ready for the holidays ahead of time."

"It's only February."

The cold air coming in the open car door was sucking the breath from Jane's lungs. With a sigh, she got out.

Charlotte glanced over and paled.

Jane hoisted the coffee and pastry bag. "Look, breakfast!"

Charlotte drew in a deep breath before sending Mateo a hard look that had something else in it as well, something Jane couldn't place for certain but thought was maybe . . . hurt?

"It's not what you think," Mateo told her calmly.

That was when Jane realized she was wrapped in Mateo's jacket, hood up, arriving home with the guy at just past dawn, like two teenagers trying to sneak back into their house without getting caught. "*Definitely* not what you're thinking," Jane said.

"Thanks," Mateo said dryly, and then turned to Charlotte. "She landed in the ER while you were in surgery."

"*In the ER?*" Charlotte moved toward Jane. "Are you okay?"

With a sigh, Jane let the hood fall back to reveal her small facial injuries and pushed up a sleeve to show the wrist wrap. "It's nothing."

Charlotte aimed a dark look at Mateo.

He put up his hands. "Hey, you should've seen her when she first arrived at the ER. This is her actually cleaned up."

"You should have told me." Charlotte unzipped Jane's jacket to see a set of ER scrubs. She paled. "Where are your clothes?"

They'd been caked with Levi's blood, but that's not what Charlotte was asking. Jane stepped closer, keeping eye contact. "I'm not hurt," she said. "Not in that way." She knew the woman would assume someone had hurt Jane, as Charlotte had once been hurt. "You heard about the gondola that went down last night?"

"Yes," Charlotte said. "No one was on it."

"I was on the gondola just behind the one that went down, with another passenger. We got tossed around some, but I'm fine."

"Why didn't you call me? I was right there at the hospital." She turned on Mateo like this was his doing.

"Yep, and there's my cue to go," he said.

Charlotte's eyes narrowed. "Isn't that just like a man, turning tail and running from a discussion."

Mateo's dark eyes flashed something more than good humor for once. "You're not looking for a discussion, Charlotte. You're looking for a fight. Name the time and place, and I'm there."

The air seemed to crackle.

Jane suddenly straightened and stared at them both because . . . *what*? If she didn't know better, she'd call it sexual tension. Fascinated, she watched as Charlotte seemed to . . . squirm?

Jane eyed Mateo, who looked both amused and annoyed. "Oh my," she said, pointing at them. "You two are doing it?"

Charlotte gasped and put a hand to her chest.

The Southern belle does denial.

Mateo shrugged. "I've asked her out. She's turned me down. Multiple times." He spoke to Jane but never took his eyes off Charlotte. "She knows the ball's in her court."

Charlotte stared at him right back. "I don't play ball."

"Then pick something else. You know where to find me." And with that, he started across the driveway toward his house.

"Hey," Jane called, "you're just going to leave me with her?"

"I've already been yelled at this week. Your turn."

"Excuse me, I don't yell," Charlotte said. "I speak strongly."

"I can't believe I missed all this," Jane muttered. "I thought you two didn't like each other. But it's actually the opposite. You—"

"Finish that sentence and you're doing dishes for the rest of my life." With that, Charlotte strode, nose in the air, toward her house.

"Now who's turning tail?" Mateo asked, almost lazily.

Charlotte, her back to Mateo, froze.

Oh boy, Jane thought. Mateo had no way of knowing that Charlotte had been turning tail when it came to men since her eighteenth birthday, when a string of bad decisions had nearly derailed her entire life.

Jane stood there, caught between two people she cared deeply about, not sure how to help. Thankfully, Mateo's phone went off. He looked at the screen and ran a hand down his face.

"I'm being called back into the hospital," he said.

"No," Charlotte said, bad 'tude replaced with something that looked like worry. "You're too tired. Let them call someone else."

"I'm fine." He gave her an unreadable look, then got back into his car and drove off.

Jane's heart pinched at the look on her friend's face. She knew exactly what to say to the good doctor to redirect her. "Let's go inside. My head and wrist are aching."

Charlotte gasped. "And you let me stand out here dithering on?" She slipped an arm around Jane and drew her inside.

Charlotte had bought the old Victorian to celebrate getting her residency. She typically rented out three of the five bedrooms to hospital staff of the female persuasion, from nurses to cleaning crews. She kept the master for herself and one extra room as a den.

And a bedroom for Jane when she was in town.

For Charlotte, it was a kind of the-family-you-make situation. Her parents lived in Atlanta. And since Charlotte couldn't make herself go back there without experiencing crippling anxiety, she'd created a home and family here in Tahoe as well.

To Jane's eternal gratitude, she was a part of that family.

The house was warm and cozy, right down to the comfy furniture and thriving plants. Just walking inside, Jane could feel her blood pressure lowering. "That was fascinating, you and Mateo."

"Hush." Charlotte took the pastry and coffee. "I'll make breakfast. Then we'll split the pastry and both go get some sleep."

"Sounds perfect. I'll help."

"You mean you'll watch me cook, then do the cleanup."

Jane smiled. "Unless you want my help cooking?"

Charlotte shuddered. "Please, no."

Two women were in the living room on yoga mats, stretching into twisted pretzel poses. Charlotte greeted them warmly and announced she was making breakfast if they were interested.

They were.

Jane waved at them but didn't engage, just followed Charlotte into the kitchen. "What?" she said when Charlotte gave her an amused glance while stripping off her pink down jacket.

"They're our roommates. They've been here two weeks, and you don't know their names." Charlotte cracked some eggs into a bowl, put a pan on the stove, and gave Jane a look.

"Sure I do. Um . . ."

Charlotte snorted. "FYI, it's Zoe and Mariella." She poured the eggs into the hot pan, making them sizzle. "Honey, you're taking lone wolf to a whole new level this time."

"I know. I'm a jerk."

"No. You're an introvert. But even a lone wolf has to come inside and get warm once in a while." She added peppers and onions to the eggs, which made the kitchen smell like heaven. Then she pointed the spatula at Jane. "You're so great with your patients—sweet and personal and caring. But when it comes to making any real connections, you turn all thumbs. Why is that?"

Jane pulled some leftover bacon and chicken from the fridge and crumbled it into a small bowl. "I don't see the point of making connections. Not when I'm going to be gone soon."

"Ah. Right. Your favorite motto."

Jane ignored this and headed to the back door, where she found herself caught in the crosshairs of the biggest cat she'd ever had the pleasure of knowing.

Cat, as she called him, sat on the stoop, a sleek, dark gray predator. He eyed Jane with disfavor for being late with his breakfast.

"Sorry," she said, setting down the bowl. "I nearly almost died, but don't you worry, I've got your food."

"Let him in," Charlotte called out.

"He doesn't want to come in. He likes being free."

She sat on the step with him until he'd finished his food. Then, with a flick of his tail, he was gone.

Other than Charlotte, it was the best relationship she'd ever had.

Back in the kitchen, Charlotte was still working on the food.

"Where's your car, still up at North Diamond?" she asked. "I'll drive you to get it after breakfast."

"Thanks," Jane said gratefully.

Charlotte studied her for a moment. "You want to talk about it?"

"About what?"

"Almost dying."

"I was being dramatic."

"Jane, you're never dramatic. Tell me. I get it, you know."

Jane did know. "I was coming home when the storm hit, it all went bad, and— Oh no." She clutched at her throat where her necklace normally lay. "I lost it," she whispered.

"Your grandma's necklace?"

"Yes." And the only thing Jane had of hers.

Knowing exactly what that necklace meant to her, Charlotte came around the island. "Honey." She slid an arm around her. "Someone will find it and contact the resort."

Jane nodded but knew it would be like trying to find a needle in a haystack.

"How about pancakes with your eggs?"

Jane wasn't the only one who could distract with the best of them. "With chocolate chips?" she asked.

"Is there any other kind?"

THE waves washed over the pebbled sand rhythmically, waking Levi. He took a deep breath. Fresh pine trees and cool, fresh air. Next to him on the beach sat an urn. Amy's ashes.

Lake Tahoe had been her favorite place on Earth. Levi had been her favorite person on Earth. He'd never fully appreciated it.

Guilt washed over him in tune to the water hitting the sand . . .

"Levi? How we doing?"

Something was hammering at the base of his skull. A sledgehammer. He lifted his hands to his head and felt the tug of an IV.

He cracked his eyes open and immediately regretted it because the pain behind his eyeballs exploded. He gasped.

"Take your time. Slow breaths or you'll get sick."

He drew in very slow breaths. The nausea retreated slightly.

He fought his eyes open again. Given the light coming in the window, it was morning. On his right, a nurse checked his vitals.

"I'm fine," he said.

"Of course you are." She smiled at him. "Welcome back."

"Wait." His brain felt scrambled. "Jane. Where's Jane?"

His nurse moved closer. Her name tag said *Daisy*. "I wasn't here when you were brought in. Is she a relative? Your wife?"

He struggled to think. "I just need to know if she's okay."

"All right, hon, I'll ask around. What's her last name?"

He opened his mouth and then had to close it again.

"Hang tight," Daisy said. "I'll get your doctor."

Levi lay back and stared up at the ceiling. The night was a blur, a jumble of snapshots he couldn't seem to put in the right order.

He heard the curtain rings sliding on the metal rod, reminding him of another metal sound. From last night, when the gondola had tipped and the steel rod had slid out of its holder and . . .

Hit him in the head.

Suddenly the images in his head fell into order. Leaving San Francisco for the drive to Lake Tahoe, his childhood home. And then after an hour with his parents, he'd gone to North Diamond, looking forward to the rush he always got from skiing.

Then Jane. Flirting with her while the storm battered the gondola. Then the gondola ahead of them had gone down. They'd both known that at any minute they could fall to their death, and still Jane had remained calm. And damn, that had been attractive.

Lying on the floor of the swaying gondola, Jane sitting with his head in her lap, holding pressure to the cut on his head . . .

He remembered the ambulance ride. Jane at his side, talking in medical jargon to the EMS team. She'd stayed with him in his room until he'd been taken away for X-rays and a scan of his head.

When he'd been brought back, she was gone.

The doctor who appeared from behind the curtain wasn't a stranger. Dr. Mateo Moreno wore scrubs and a face dialed to eight hours past exhaustion. He was Amy's brother and once Levi's best friend. It'd been a few years since they'd seen each other.

Levi's fault.

Mateo's eyes were hooded. "How you feeling?" he asked.

"Good enough to go home."

"Nice try." Mateo paused, then sank into the chair with both weariness and wariness. "About time I run into you, even if it's because you landed in my ER looking like death warmed over."

"That bad, huh?"

Mateo shrugged. "You looked worse when we drove my dad's truck up to the summit and did donuts on the ice and you fell out."

Levi laughed, then groaned at the pain. "We're lucky we survived all the stuff we got into."

"True. And speaking of surviving, you should be good as new in a couple of weeks. Good thing your head's so hard."

Levi snorted, which caused a new stab of pain. "Good thing."

Mateo nodded, eyes serious. "It's been a minute."

"Too many." Levi ached from the loss of one of the best relationships he'd ever had. "I'm sorry."

Ignoring this, Mateo stood and hit some keys on the computer. "I called your mom, told her you were going to be okay. I also told her visiting hours didn't start until nine a.m., so you're welcome and you owe me." And then he started to go.

Levi did owe him. And he'd missed him. "I was a jerk."

Mateo stopped, glanced back. "They say recognizing the problem is half the solution."

"I meant it. I'm sor—"

"You're injured. We're not doing this now."

"I need to," Levi said. "I shouldn't have vanished."

"No, you shouldn't have. It wasn't your fault, what happened to Amy."

"I hurt her."

"Because you didn't let her drag you down the aisle?" Mateo shook his head. "You weren't ready."

"I should've been ready. A wedding was all she ever wanted, and I didn't give it to her before . . . before it was too late."

Mateo sighed and came back to Levi's bedside. "Is that what kept you away? Guilt? You think my family blamed you for not marrying her when she wanted you to? What we blamed you for was leaving and not looking back."

Levi felt his throat tighten. "You deserved better from me."

"Damn straight," Mateo said, voice not as cool as it'd been.

Levi took a deep breath and was grateful he didn't throw up. "I need two more favors," he said quietly. "I want a do-over."

In middle school, when one of them did something stupid, the other could choose to give a do-over. Or not.

But they'd never *not* given each other a second chance.

Mateo took his time answering. "Okay, you get a do-over. I'll take it in the form of pizza and beer when you're cleared to drink."

Levi let out a breath. That was more than he deserved. "Deal."

"And the other favor?"

"I was brought in with a woman named Jane. Is she okay?"

Mateo looked at Levi. "She's in far better shape than you." With that, he walked out, sliding the curtain shut behind him.

Levi opened his palm and looked down at the dainty gold locket in his hands. An old friend on the search-and-rescue had shown up in his ER cubicle after they'd found it on the gondola. Levi had promised to get it back to the owner. He flicked it open now and smiled. The tiny pic on the right was a little girl of around eight with wild dark red curls exploding around her head like a halo. Jane, dressed like a sugar plum fairy. The older woman in the opposite picture could be anyone, but he'd guess a grandmother.

A commotion sounded on the other side of the curtains, and then came a shrill woman's voice. "Where is he? Where's my son?"

"They said the third room on the left, Shirl," a man said.

Levi stared up at the ceiling, not ready for this. But ready or not, his mom, dad, sister, and niece all crowded into his room.

"Honey!" Shirley Cutler cried, rushing to his side. She was dressed up, hair and makeup in place.

Worry lines were etched into her face. "Mom, I'm okay."

She looked him over carefully. Levi always had been the odd man out. His parents ran a sporting goods store, and if there wasn't a ball or a kayak or a tent involved, they weren't interested. Levi loved taking things apart and putting them back together in a better way; gathering data and then creating ways to manage that data.

Bottom line—his brain worked differently from the rest of the Cutlers. They had never really understood him.

And yet here they were, ready to smother him with love in the only way they knew how. "Really, I'm fine."

"Your nurse said you have a concussion," she said. "No one would tell us anything about Jane."

He felt a twitch begin behind his eye. Could one feel a vessel bleed? And if it was bad enough, could he pass out and miss the rest of this visit? "Who's manning the store?" he asked.

"We're opening an hour late," his mom said.

This was a shock. The store his family owned and operated was closed for Easter and Christmas, and nothing else *ever.*

"So," his mom said. "Where's Jane?" She looked around like maybe Levi was hiding her somewhere in the tiny room.

"I'm probably going to be discharged soon," he said. "You guys didn't have to all come check on me."

"We came to meet your girlfriend," his sister, Tess, said.

"Uncle Levi!" Peyton yelled, jumping up and down. "Grandma said you might be getting married soon. Can I be the flower girl?"

Levi looked at his mom, who had the good grace to wince. He shook his head at her, then smiled at Peyton. "Hey, sweetness. There's no wedding on the horizon."

"That's okay!" The six-year-old beamed at him, two front teeth missing. "Hospitals smell bad. Like medicine and burnt toast."

"Peyton," Tess said. "You can't smell all those scents at once."

"Actually, you can," Levi said. "The human nose can distinguish at least a trillion different odors."

His dad tossed up his hands. "He gets his head bashed in but can still cite weird random science facts."

"That's why he beats you at Trivial Pursuit," his mom said. "It's also why he can fix anything and everything. It's how he's wired."

Levi had taken a lot of teasing for being the family fix-it guy, but he hadn't been able to stop Amy from dying or keep his sister from getting dumped by her husband, Cal. And he hadn't been able to fix the emptiness inside that was just a part of him now.

Peyton tried to climb up onto his bed. Levi leaned over and gave her an assist. It hurt his head, but hell, so did life.

"You haz an owie!" she said, pointing at his head.

"It'll heal."

She nodded, then leaned over and said, "I bring you candy from the 'chine. Grandma! We haz to get him some candy!"

"I've got something better." His mom started going through her bag. "Power bars. I made them myself . . . Where did they go . . ."

Tess sighed and shifted closer to Levi. "Thanks for the car ride over here with her, by the way," she whispered.

"Oh, was my near-death experience inconvenient for you?"

His mom raised her head with her ultrasonic maternal ears that could probably also hear his heart rate. "Your *near death?*"

"He's just kidding," Tess said.

"Let's talk about Jane," his mom said. "Where is she?"

"She's been released."

She sat down. "Why isn't she at your bedside? How come you've never mentioned her? What does she do?" Suddenly the hairdo and makeup made sense.

She'd dressed for Jane.

Making up a girlfriend had seemed so logical when he had been staring death in the face, but now . . . "Listen, about—"

His mom put her hand to her mouth. "You were dumped."

"I wasn't dumped. I made her up."

"Are you telling me you'd rather lie to my face about not having a girlfriend just so you don't have to introduce her to me?"

There wasn't enough pain medication for this.

"You having someone in your life was the best news I've had in a long time," his mom said softly, the threat of tears in her voice.

He felt himself cave like a cheap suitcase. "Jane's not been in Sunrise Cove for long. And as for what she does, she's a nurse."

"A nurse," she repeated, sounding impressed. "I'd so love to meet her, and before you say no, I promise to not embarrass you."

"Mom." He reached for her hand. "You don't embarrass me."

"Then you can invite her to our big fortieth anniversary dinner."

Cutler family dinners were a mixture of bickering and disagreeing. His parents' fortieth anniversary dinner, four weeks from now, would be *exponentially* worse. "Mom, that's not necessary."

She sucked in a deep breath, her eyes sparkling with sudden tears. "You think I don't know we could've lost you last night? You've *finally* moved on from Amy's passing and are ready to live your life, and in one fell swoop it could've been over."

There was a single beat of uncomfortable silence.

"You didn't lose me, Mom. I'm right here."

"I know, and I'm grateful. All I'm asking for is a chance to meet the woman who brought your big, beautiful heart back to life."

His so-called big, beautiful heart pinched. Calling home last night had been beyond stupid. But more, it'd been selfish.

"I thought we'd lost you when you left Tahoe," she said quietly. "When you called last night, there was something in your voice. You had love in it. I could tell you were deeply moved. Clearly, Jane did that for you. I want to meet her, Levi. I want to hug her and thank her. And feed her. At my anniversary dinner."

"Mom, that's weeks from now. By then I'll be back in the city."

"Mateo said you'll have to rest for several weeks at least. So see, you *will* be here for the dinner. Tell him, Hank."

Levi's dad turned to him. "You should do what you want, son. You always did."

There was a lot to unpack with that statement, but Levi's head was throbbing and all he wanted was to close his eyes.

"You'll stay," his mom said to him.

Resistance was futile. "For as long as medically advised," he said. "I'll still need to work," he reminded her.

"You're your own CEO. You can work from anywhere."

That might be true, but he needed his own space to function.

And possibly a lobotomy.

Daisy came in, took one look at Levi, and shook her head. "Everyone out," she said. "My patient needs quiet." The room emptied.

Levi nearly asked her to marry him on the spot. "Thank you."

"Don't thank me. They won't go far."

Didn't he know it. He ran his thumb over Jane's locket. She'd want it back, and he'd have to find her. And why that gave him his first real smile of the day, he wasn't sure he wanted to know.

Chapter 3

An incredibly long week of "rest and relaxation" later, Levi finally escaped the family house for a doctor's appointment. After an exam and the removal of his stitches, he walked to where Tess was waiting in the parking lot. He slid into the passenger seat of her car, relieved as hell.

"Well?" she asked. "Is your head still scrambled?"

"Only slightly. The good news is I've been cleared to drive."

"Prepare for the inquisition, then," Tess warned. "Mom's been trying not to hound you about why Jane hasn't checked in on you."

"Maybe we've been texting and calling."

"Maybe." Tess looked out at the parking lot. She asked, "You're going to hightail it out of here now, aren't you."

"Eventually," he said. "But not yet."

She looked over at him, her eyes too shiny. "Really?"

"Yeah, really." He was concerned by her show of emotion. She still hadn't told him what she'd called him up to Tahoe for in the first place. "What's going on, Tess?"

She sighed. "I didn't tell Mom and Dad, but Cal and I didn't have a prenup." She drew a deep breath. "He took all the money out of our accounts before he ran off to Bali with the babysitter."

"What the—" He scrubbed a hand down his face. His anger wasn't going to help her. "What did the police say?"

"Turns out that neither screwing the babysitter nor taking money out of joint accounts is illegal."

Maybe not, but Levi would like a minute alone with Cal to teach him a little respect. That was not the reaction Tess needed, but the money thing, that he could do something about. "I could help—"

"No. I don't want your money. I want my own life back." Angrily she swiped a few tears from her cheeks. Then she gripped the steering wheel tight and took the roundabout on two wheels.

"Maybe I should drive."

"I'm fine!"

"Yeah, I can see that—" He winced as she sped up.

Five minutes later, she pulled into the parking lot of Cutler Sporting Goods. "I've got to get to work," she said. "I'll get a ride home with Mom or Dad. Take my car and go rest."

When Tess got out of the car, Levi moved into the driver's seat. He stopped for a pizza and then at the Cake Walk for a specialty cupcake. He took the pizza to the hospital and asked for Mateo.

His oldest friend appeared at the front desk five minutes later, looking surprised to see Levi. "You okay?"

"Getting there, thanks to you." He pushed the pizza across the greeting desk. "I didn't bring the beer since you're working."

Mateo picked up the box. "I don't need thanks. But I definitely need the pizza." He looked at Levi. "Is this a do-over pizza?"

"Yes. Is it working?"

"Possibly." Mateo started to walk away. "Keep them coming."

Levi left the hospital and drove up to the North Diamond Resort. He parked and stared at the snow-covered mountain.

The sun was out, making the snow sparkle like diamonds—hence the resort's name. At 7,500 feet, the air was crisp but somehow warm, and the sky was sharp blue. He got out and breathed in the harsh, cold air. He didn't mind. Winter invigorated him.

The parking lot was full. Business was booming in spite of what had happened with the gondola a week ago.

The investigation had yielded a decision that it'd all been a freak accident. On the day of the storm, there'd been some construction work done and a piece of debris had been left behind. A small chunk of wood. The vicious wind had knocked it onto the track.

The odds against such a thing were astronomical.

But Levi still didn't get onto the gondola.

Instead, he found a friend who happened to be on ski patrol and hitched a ride on his snowmobile up to the urgent care clinic at mid-mountain. He entered the clinic and asked for Jane.

"She's not scheduled today," the front desk nurse told him.

He drove to High Alpine Resort next. No luck there either.

Two hours later, Levi walked into the last urgent care clinic in the area. This one was in Sunrise Cove, right next to the hospital.

There was Jane, standing in the middle of the room wearing scrubs and a familiar attitude, staring up at the only other person in the room—a huge guy, clearly a fan of daily lifting at the gym.

His entire body was taut with tension. "Hell no," he growled at Jane.

Jane, *maybe* five-four, was clearly not impressed. "We've been through this before, Nick," she said calmly. "You stabbed your thumb on a rusty nail. You need a Tdap shot."

Nick huffed out a huge sigh and shuffled into the lab.

Jane turned to Levi, registering quiet surprise. "Tarzan."

He grimaced. "Tell me you remember my real name."

"Of course I do. I'm not the one with a head injury."

"I'm fine, and you?" He gestured to her wrist.

"I'm good." Her dark green eyes gave nothing away, including how she felt at seeing him again.

"I wanted to thank you for saving my ass."

"You only got hurt because you were trying to protect me."

"I liked the company," he said. While she absorbed that comment, he made another. "You ducked out on me at the hospital."

"Hey, I made sure you were going to live first."

This made him laugh. "Thanks."

"No problem. Are you in need of medical attention?"

"No."

She looked him over anyway. He'd like to think that there was some attraction as well as assessment in her pretty eyes, but she was damn good at holding her own counsel. "Okay, I gotta get back to work," she said. "Make sure the door shuts behind you."

He smiled at being so thoroughly dismissed. "Nice bedside manner. Sexy. Only you're not the boss of me, Jane."

She rolled her eyes. "How did you find me anyway?"

"First, I braved North Diamond's mountain looking for you, only to find out that you weren't scheduled at that urgent care today. Or at Sierra North, Homeward, or Starwood Peak . . ."

That won him a low laugh, but her smile slowly faded. "I'm off rotation at North Diamond for now."

He hated the idea that she was afraid to go back up there, but he certainly understood it. "I nearly had a panic attack at the idea of getting on the gondola," he admitted. "I had to get a buddy from ski patrol to give me a ride on his snowmobile."

She looked at him again, her gaze softer now. "It's not often people try to find me," she said. "Usually it's been the opposite."

That effectively swiped the smile from his face, remembering she'd told him she didn't have family. His family was a huge pain, but he couldn't imagine not having them. "Can we talk?"

Those sharp eyes assessed him, taking in the scar the stitches had left through his eyebrow. "I'm glad you're okay. But I don't know what there is to talk about."

"Maybe I needed to know you're okay too."

"I'm fine."

His gaze settled on the bruise along her jawline. Gently, he ran a finger along it. "I'm sorry about what happened that night, Jane."

She swallowed hard. "None of it was your fault. And I'm sorry, but I've really got to get back to work. So unless you've got another of your fascinating facts for me, I'll see you around—"

"If you burned all the new data from just one day onto DVDs, you could stack them on each other and reach the moon—twice."

She blinked, then looked impressed. "Okay, that's a good one."

"Also, I brought you something." He reached into his pocket.

"At least you didn't ask me to get it out for you this time."

He grinned, and that felt good. He held his hand out to her, palm still closed, and her eyes narrowed. "What is it?"

"Suspicious much?" Reaching for her hand, he dropped her necklace into her palm. "One of the search-and-rescue guys found this that night. I promised to get it back to you."

She stilled and stared down at the necklace, her eyes going shiny before she closed her fingers around the locket and brought it up to her chest. "Thank you," she whispered, voice thick. "You have no idea how much this means to me."

He thought maybe he did. "I'm glad you have it back. Jane . . ."

She lifted her face. "I owe you one."

"Actually, you saving my life trumps me getting the necklace back to you. Can I buy you lunch on your break?"

"Okay. After I finish with my patient, I get a break. Meet me at the hospital cafeteria."

He smiled. "It's a date."

"It's not a date. I don't date."

"Never?" he asked.

"Well, maybe once in a blue moon."

His eyes twinkled with mischief. "Then here's hoping for a blue moon. See you in the cafeteria, Jane."

She nodded, then watched him walk out of the urgent care—which he knew because he looked back and caught her at it.

With another grimace, she vanished into the back, and he smiled all the way to the hospital cafeteria.

Fifteen minutes later, Jane walked into the hospital cafeteria. This was a bad idea. A *really* bad idea, mostly because while she could say she wasn't interested in starting anything with Levi, she seemed to conveniently forget that when looking in his eyes.

Stupid, sexy eyes.

Sandra, a fellow traveling nurse, caught her at the entrance. "Jane! Hi, what's new?"

"Not much," she said neutrally.

"You sure? 'Cause there's a really hot guy waiting for you." Sandra tilted her head in the direction of a table off to the right.

"And?" Jane asked.

"Actually, I was wondering how long you're staying at Charlotte's this year. The hospital offered to extend my contract by another couple of months, but there's no available housing."

Jane had spent part of her life being asked to move along, starting when her grandpa hadn't been able to take care of her on his own. She'd been handed off from one relative to the next.

"Have you spoken to Charlotte?" she asked Sandra.

"Not yet. Thought I'd check in with you first."

The thing was, Jane knew Charlotte would sleep on her own couch to make sure Sandra had a place to stay.

And Charlotte would make more money off Sandra, a lot more, because she never took enough money from Jane to begin with.

But Jane wasn't sure she could handle Charlotte asking. She'd rather leave on her own than face that ever again. "I'm contracted for work until the season is over, but maybe we could work out a shared-room situation. Let's see what Charlotte wants to do."

Sandra squeezed her hand. "Thanks, hon."

When Sandra walked away, Jane drew a deep breath and headed toward Levi's table. He looked up and smiled. "Hey."

"Hey."

He pushed a tray loaded with food to the center of the table. "I know you're short on time, so I got one of everything."

It was ridiculous how much this charmed her, and she laughed as she grabbed a grilled cheese, soup, and French fries.

Looking pleased, Levi took the burger and small salad. "We've got an audience," he said. "Your three o'clock."

She looked and found Sandra, along with other nurses, watching them with avid interest. "Sorry," she said. "They have no idea this is just a lunch between two people who nearly bought the farm together." She laughed.

Levi didn't. "It's whatever we want it to be."

For some reason, this kicked her heart into gear.

He pushed a white box across the table. It had a pretty red bow on it, and she stared at it like it was a coiled snake. "What is it?"

"It's a Thanks-for-Not-Letting-Me-Die present."

"No. I don't do presents."

"Would it change your mind to know it's a cookies 'n' cream cupcake from Cake Walk?"

She gasped. "Don't you tease me."

She practically tore off the bow, making him laugh, but she didn't care. "You actually remembered," she said as she stared at the huge perfect cupcake, lunch forgotten, mouth watering.

"Yeah. You moaned a little when you were talking about it."

Well, that was embarrassing. Uncharacteristically ruffled, she grabbed a knife, cut the cupcake in two, and handed him half.

"You absolutely positive they're even?" he asked.

She eyeballed them again. "You should know, I take these cupcakes very seriously."

"Then I'm *seriously* touched that you'd share." He held up his portion in a cheers. "To not dying."

"To not dying." She took a big bite and moaned. "I can't help it!" she said when he grinned at her.

"Not complaining." He took a bite as well and . . . let out a very male moan himself.

She concentrated on her next bite, not realizing that her free hand had gone to her necklace, back around her neck.

Levi's gaze went there too. "Looks good on you."

Earlier when he'd dropped her grandma's necklace into her palm, she'd had to fight tears. He'd noticed, but he hadn't pushed her to talk. "Thank you again," she said softly.

"The way you touched it when you got on the gondola, I figured it was important to you."

It took her a minute to be able to speak. "Very. It was my grandma's." She opened the locket and looked at the picture of herself, the happiest she'd ever been in her life because they'd just gone to see *The Nutcracker.* "It's the only thing I have of her."

"I'm glad you've got it back." Reaching out, he gently touched the fading bruise on her jaw. "You're really okay?"

"Yes." She looked at the healing cut slicing through his eyebrow. "I should have asked you before how you are feeling."

"Same as you, I imagine."

She drew in a deep breath. She hadn't wanted to discuss with Charlotte what had happened on the gondola, saying she couldn't go there yet. "I'm a master at shoving my hot-mess-ness deep."

A rough laugh rumbled up from Levi's chest. "Same."

Their eyes met and locked. She hadn't been able to talk to anyone else about what happened. But Levi had been right there, so he already knew. She went back to savoring her cupcake. "I'm sort of regretting giving you half," she said around the next mouthful.

He hadn't devoured his. He was taking his time, and casually sucked a dollop of frosting from his thumb.

Jane took her last bite and eyed the baking paper, wondering if she could lick that without embarrassing herself.

"You ever going to tell me why you disappeared on me that night?" Levi asked.

"I took off because I knew you were in good hands and you'd be okay." Plus, the longer she sat at his bedside, the longer she'd wanted to stay. She felt his hand on hers.

"Hey," he said quietly, waiting until she looked at him. "It's normal after a situation like that to bond with the person you survived it with. After you left, I worried about you maybe going through a bad time and not having anyone who'd understand."

She didn't want to be touched, but she was. "I face life-or-death situations all the time for a living. If I formed an attachment to every patient, I wouldn't last long."

He looked at her for a long moment. "What happened up there that night was far more than a patient/practitioner relationship."

She looked into the box, but a second cupcake did not appear.

"You face life-and-death situations every day?" he asked.

He'd caught the one little tidbit she hadn't meant to let loose. "I told you I'm only in Tahoe for the ski season. The rest of the year I'm out working for Doctors Without Borders and other organizations like them." She genuinely loved helping to make people feel safe. But mostly she loved the temporary nature of the contracts she took. No one asked her to leave because she'd become inconvenient.

Levi still had his hand on hers, and he was rubbing his thumb back and forth over her palm. "You keep surprising me, Jane."

"Yeah." She pulled her hand free. "I get that a lot."

"I meant in a good way."

She took in the seriousness behind the playful light in his eyes, behind the several-days-old stubble on his jaw, at his slow smile because she was still just staring at him. "Oh," she said brilliantly.

"Oh," he repeated with a small smile, and slid the rest of his cupcake back toward her. He'd taken only two small bites.

"You're giving it back?"

"I like watching you eat."

"You're a strange guy."

"No doubt," he said agreeably.

She took the half cupcake. Bit. Chewed. Swallowed. And then stilled at the realization. "You want something."

"It's a small thing."

Damn. She knew it. She stopped eating. "What?"

"You disappeared before my parents could meet my . . . *girlfriend*."

Her tummy quivered. "You mean your pretend girlfriend."

"My mom wants to meet the woman willing to put up with me. She wants her to come to their fortieth anniversary dinner."

"Again, not seeing how this is my problem."

"It'd be just one family dinner."

"Oh no," she said, snorting to hide her horror. "No, no, no."

"Okay, great. So you'll think about it."

She had to laugh. "So your Male Selective Hearing is intact."

With a smile, he stood. "Take your time; dinner's not for three weeks." And he walked off. He passed the table of gawking nurses and winked. "She's thinking about it," he said conspiratorially.

The whole table swiveled their heads and stared at Jane.

"No," she said. "I'm not."

The next morning when Jane's alarm went off at four forty-five, she was still doing nothing but thinking about it. She got up, showered, and hit the Stovetop Diner by five.

The early bird always gets the worm, as her grandpa used to say.

Which was why she was really here. Not just the diner, but Lake Tahoe in general.

Last year she'd caught sight of him in this very diner. Too shocked to talk to him, she'd ducked out before he could see her.

This year, she was no closer to talking to him.

But none of that stopped her from wanting a peek at him. So she returned to the diner because her grandpa was a creature of habit.

She eyed the table across the room, where indeed he sat with his cronies telling stories about growing up here in Tahoe.

Jane watched him, heart torn between love and hurt as she sipped her coffee, her ski hat pulled low, coat still on to hide her scrubs. She was in an out-of-the-way booth, not easily seen, sitting with a spare to-go coffee to take to Charlotte at work.

Her grandpa tipped back his head and laughed heartily at something one of the men said, and it both hurt and felt good to hear it. The waves of nostalgia, heartbreak, and guilt hit hard.

When someone unexpectedly sat at her table, Jane nearly jumped right out of her skin.

"Some PI you are," Charlotte said, stealing Jane's coffee. "You didn't even see me coming."

"You need a bell around your neck. And hey, the one in the to-go cup is yours."

Charlotte took both. "I'm stealth, baby. Stealth enough to know that a hot guy brought you a cupcake to work yesterday and that he asked you something and you're thinking about it."

"How in the world . . . ?"

Charlotte grinned. "Heard it from an intern, who heard it from Radiology, who heard it from a nurse at the table with Sandra."

"Wow." Jane shook her head. "And you're missing a whole bunch of details. Your sources are slipping."

Charlotte leaned in, hands on the table. "Let's discuss."

"Sure," Jane said. "We'll discuss as soon as *you* discuss our very handsome next-door neighbor—also your coworker—and why you pretended to not like him when you secretly *do*."

Charlotte choked on her sip of coffee, her heart pounding. She leaned back. "I don't know what you're talking about."

"Then neither do I," Jane said with a smirk. She saw right through Charlotte. They were two peas in a pod, which allowed Charlotte to relax with Jane like she could with no one else.

But right now, with Jane clearly hiding burgeoning feelings for a man, and with Charlotte doing almost the exact same thing . . . Well, it would have been funny if it hadn't been so scary.

They stared at each other. Charlotte broke first. She'd never met a silence she could endure. "I know you sat at Sexy Gondola Guy's hospital bedside for hours before coming home."

Jane went from smirk to . . . unsure? Charlotte's heart kicked. "What does he need from you? Do I have to kick his ass?"

Jane let out a laugh. "Not necessary. Stand down, Dr. Dixon."

"You know I'd do it." She flexed. "I'm tiny but mighty."

This won her another rough laugh. "I never doubt you," Jane said. "But what Levi wants, it's, um . . ." She squirmed.

Jane *never* squirmed. "It's what?" Charlotte pressed.

"When Levi and I were on that gondola and we thought we were going to die, he called his mother to say goodbye."

Charlotte gasped, a hand to her chest. "Oh my," she whispered. She couldn't imagine calling her mom to say goodbye, not without her throat tightening and her eyes burning with unshed emotion.

"Yeah." Jane let out a breath. "The thing was, he couldn't actually do it. He told her he was happy and in a relationship. Now he needs a pretend girlfriend for some big family dinner in three weeks."

Charlotte took this in. Jane was . . . blushing a little. And not making eye contact. Fascinating. "You going to do it?"

"He brought me my locket back."

Charlotte felt a smile crease her face. "You're going to do it."

"I don't know. Wait— How do you know I sat by his bedside?"

"Someone told me."

Jane stared at her. "Now I'm going to have to kill Mateo."

Mateo. The only man who could make Charlotte feel like she didn't know what she was doing. At any given moment of any day, she wasn't sure if she wanted to wrap her fingers around his neck and squeeze or climb him like a tree. Not that she would admit either.

"I knew it!" Jane pointed at her. "You *don't* want him dead."

"Well, I never said I wanted him dead, did I? I said I wanted him to stop flirting with me." A total lie.

"Admit it," Jane said. "You have no idea how to deal with a good man trying to get your attention. I mean, you're not quite as screwed up as I am, but you're close enough."

True. Charlotte had had a good childhood, but she'd also had her share of trauma, which had left her just as awkward and uneasy at romantic entanglements as Jane.

"He wants to go out with you."

Charlotte ignored the butterflies in her belly at that thought and shook her head. "He's a flirt. He flirts with *everyone*."

"Wrong," Jane said. "Mateo's nice to everyone, but there's only one person he flirts with, brings coffee to. And that's— *Ohmigod*."

"What?"

Jane squeaked and ducked low, beneath the table. "I think my grandpa saw me—don't look!"

But Charlotte was already looking, feeling her heart harden. "I want to see the man who deserted you when you were eight."

"He didn't desert me. He wasn't well."

"And you were eight."

"Yeah," Jane muttered. "Hence me being under the table like I'm still eight."

Charlotte stuck her head under the table, softening when she saw Jane's genuine panic. "Honey, what have I always told you?"

"Always make time for lip gloss because we're not animals."

"Aw! You *were* listening." Charlotte felt so proud. "And . . . ?"

"And . . . family is earned not inherited."

Charlotte nodded. "So you have to decide. Are you ready to go there? Open up some old wounds?"

The look on Jane's face said she was undecided.

Charlotte said softly, "And you know that no matter what happens with your grandpa, you're going to be okay because . . . why?"

Jane gave a reluctant smile. "Because I've got you at my back."

"Aw. You've grown up so fast—" Charlotte caught a glimpse

of the tall man in scrubs who strode into the diner. She gave an unladylike squeak and slid out of her chair and under the table too.

"Mateo's here," she hissed.

Jane blinked. "And?"

"And this is not a drill! Congratulations, you've taught me how to be ridiculous. Hope you're proud. Scoot over and make room!"

Jane snorted but scooted just as Mateo spoke from above them. "Morning, ladies. Did you drop something?"

Jane smirked at Charlotte.

"Don't you dare leave—" But she was talking to air because Jane was gone as if she had the hounds of hell on her heels.

Not Charlotte. It wasn't the hounds of hell chasing her. It was her past.

Which felt just as scary.

Chapter 4

Levi woke up to the unmistakable sound of paws scrambling, but he didn't move, hoping he was invisible. Not likely, though, as he was on the pullout couch in the Cutler family den slash office.

A hot, wet tongue licked him from chin to forehead.

"Thanks, Jasper," he murmured.

Apparently encouraged by the greeting, his mom's goldendoodle slash Wookiee leapt on top of him. Levi hugged the silly, lovable dog, not an easy task with Jasper's four massive paws.

He had to laugh. After Tess and Peyton had moved back in for the duration of Tess's ugly divorce, his childhood bedroom had been turned into a proud princess palace. They'd offered to move out for his stay, but he'd refused, saying the couch was fine.

Not that it mattered where he slept in this house, because he'd always felt just a little misplaced in it. He'd been a good skier and probably could've gone somewhere with it, but even though he'd gone to the University of Colorado, where he could have skied competitively, he'd concentrated on getting his data science degree instead. Which of course had baffled his parents. As far as they were concerned, he'd taken his athletic talent and walked.

Looking back, Levi understood their point of view, but he also knew they'd never understood his. He'd worked at the family store growing up, putting in his time, even if he'd always had his nose in a book or been on the computer creating software, then later working in tech to support himself. Now his start-up, Cutler Analytics, was thriving. Yes, he missed the mountain. But he hadn't missed feeling like a square peg in a round hole.

Suddenly his niece Peyton bounced into the room in a tutu and tiara, carrying a bowl of Froot Loops.

Jasper jumped down—finally—and ran to his favorite person.

"Down," the six-year-old commanded.

Jasper lay down like a perfectly behaved dog.

Peyton leaned over Levi. "Uncle Levi! Uncle Levi!"

"Yes, baby."

"Is your girlfriend here?"

He narrowed his eyes. "Did your mom tell you to ask me that?"

"No. Grandma."

Levi sighed. "Can we talk about something else?"

"Okay, let's talk about my tea party. It's soon. You're coming."

He sat up and realized his dad sat only a few feet away, muttering about "crap internet reception" as he pecked on his computer keyboard.

Peyton was jumping up and down, making Levi dizzy as hell.

"Can we have a tea party? Can we? Can we? *Can we?*"

"Peyton!" Tess yelled from somewhere down the hallway. *"Don't wake up Uncle Levi!"*

"He's already awake! Jasper did it!" Peyton carefully picked up her bowl of Froot Loops. "I brought you breakfast," she said.

Levi leaned in to take a Froot Loop, but she held up her wand. "Any color but red," she said. "The red ones are my favorite."

"Thanks." He popped one in his mouth, and she grinned at him, a sweet guileless toothless grin that tugged at his heart.

He started to sit up before remembering he'd stripped down to just boxers last night. "Uh, why don't you get the tea party all set up and I'll come meet you after I shower."

"Yay! DON'T BE LATE!" And she skipped out of the office.

Silence filled the room except for his dad's two pointer fingers continuing to pound away on his keyboard.

Levi stood up and groaned. The bed sucked.

His dad slid him an unimpressed glance. "'Bout time you got up. Here in the mountains, our mornings start before ten."

Levi had always assumed his dad enjoyed pushing his only son's buttons. It hadn't been easy growing up knowing he'd been expected to take over the family business and live happily ever after—without following any of his own hopes and dreams.

Since his stint in the hospital, Levi was starting to realize that maybe the guy was just doing the best he could to get through his own day, and being a cynical ass helped him do that. "What's going on, Dad? What's with all the mumbling?"

"Don't ask when you don't really want to know."

The family store was the only sporting goods store on North Shore, and it did great business. But there wasn't a huge profit margin, and Levi's family had struggled plenty—something he hadn't appreciated growing up because his parents had never let on.

"Dad, just tell me what's going on."

His dad pushed his chair back from the desk, looking disgusted. "The store's books are a mess."

For the past decade, Cal—Tess's soon-to-be-ex—had been doing the accounting for the store. When he took off with the babysitter a month ago, he'd walked away from the job. His dad was now handling the bookkeeping. This wasn't good because he was impatient as hell when it came to the business side of the store.

Levi saw the tight grimness to his mouth. "What's wrong?"

His dad rubbed his eyes. "It's not good."

Levi's heart sank. "I'm going to need you to be clearer. Did Cal mess up the books, or did he help himself to the kitty?"

He looked at Levi. "I'm not sure. But I think the second thing."

"Damn."

"It's just a gut feeling. I haven't been able to find anything."

"The software I sent you last quarter should've alerted you to anything out of the norm going on."

"Yeah, I couldn't make heads or tails out of that program."

"Are you kidding me—" Levi drew a deep breath because, nope, not getting into a fight. "Mom told me it was working out great."

"Because that's what I told her." His dad looked away. "It was complicated, and I never got around to it. Not my smartest move."

A surprising admittance. But the thing was, Levi's program wasn't complicated. No one would have had to do anything but let it run in the background. Levi drew a deep breath. "Dad, why don't you let me take a look and see what I can figure out?"

"What, so you can get it all working, only to go back to the city? I don't want to be left trying to undo something someone did."

"I'm not Cal, Dad. I've never left a mess behind."

His dad sighed. "Sorry. I don't mean to take this out on you. But damn, that jerk left us in a bad place."

"Then why do you always say everything is fine when I call?"

"Your mother didn't want me to bother you. And anyway, you've never wanted the store, so what does it matter to you?"

"Dad, I love it here," he said. And it was true. "I want to help."

"You do?"

"Yes." That he'd not given the store a single thought after Cal had gone had guilt swamping him. "Let me go through the books with a fine-tooth comb and see what I can find."

"I can't ask you to do that."

"You didn't ask. When I'm done, I'll install the software, which will do the job of finding these problems when I'm not around."

His dad put a hand on Levi's shoulder. The Cutler equivalent to a warm, hard hug. "Thanks."

Levi slid him a look. "You must be *extra* desperate."

His dad smiled ruefully. "I was two seconds from chucking the laptop out the window before you woke up."

Jane woke up late. It wasn't often she had a day off.

Lying in bed, contemplating the ceiling, she touched the locket.

There were new memories attached to it now. The way Levi had looked at her when he'd brought it back. She hadn't imagined he could do sweet, and her eyes drifted shut as she smiled—

And then flew open when the bed shifted.

And began to purr.

"What the—" She leapt out of bed, yanked back the covers, and came face-to-face with a pair of gray eyes. Alley Cat.

He stretched, turned in a circle, then lay down, his back to her.

She had to laugh. "You can't be in here." Scooping him up, she strode to the kitchen, unable to resist nuzzling her face against his. If she'd been one to put down roots, she'd keep him in a heartbeat. "Please understand," she whispered against his fur.

Charlotte was at the table, glaring at her laptop. "You'd think that paying bills online would be so much more calming. It's not."

Jane passed by her to the back door and set Cat outside.

She poured a coffee and refilled Charlotte's cup, nudging a chin toward the laptop. "You could double what you're charging people to live here. Then the bills wouldn't be as stressful."

"Not doing that."

Jane tossed up her hands, and Charlotte smiled. "You love me."

Jane rolled her eyes. "I don't love you sneaking the cat into the house and opening the door to the den so he could get on my bed."

"He went looking for you, crying outside your door—which isn't the den; it's your bedroom."

Jane's chest tightened at the thought of Cat crying for her. "You know I'm leaving. It wouldn't be fair to him to live with me for the next month and then be out on the street again." She picked up a piece of paper with a list on it. "What's this?"

Charlotte shrugged. "My family and some others keep asking for my birthday wish list."

Jane looked at her. "Is one of them named Mateo?"

Charlotte pretended not to hear her. "I made the list, but it seems greedy, so I'm not sending it to anyone."

Jane stealthily pulled out her phone and snapped a pic of the list. If Charlotte wouldn't take her money, then she'd give the woman a hell of a birthday gift and make sure others did as well.

Charlotte said, "So, you going to be the hot guy's girlfriend?"

"I knew I was going to be sorry I told you about that. I'm going to shower and then run errands." Jane turned to go.

"Don't forget to buy a bed for Cat to sleep on in your room."

"Sure, soon as you stop taking care of everyone but yourself."

Back in her room after she'd showered and dressed, Jane pulled out her phone and sent the photo of the list to Mateo with a text: *She's made a list. I'm calling dibs on the ski jacket.*

She shoved her phone into her pocket and headed out to Cutler Sporting Goods. Had she picked the jacket to give herself an excuse to go there? Definitely not.

The store was downtown, which consisted of a four-block-long area called the Lake Walk. It was filled with bars, cafés, touristy stores, and galleries. The buildings were mostly from the early 1900s and still held an appealing Old West style. At night, every storefront and tree would be bright with twinkle lights that reflected off the lake and made the place look like a postcard.

Cutler's was done up like an old warehouse with turn-of-the-century skis and sleds decorating the walls. Jane walked in telling herself her mission was to get in, find the jacket, and get out—all without catching a glimpse of Levi. She strode directly toward the ski section, looking straight ahead, stopping at women's jackets.

She found a jacket that matched Charlotte's description and pulled it out. When she saw the price tag, she almost passed out.

Calculating how to cut her food bill down for . . . oh, the next year, she headed to the checkout line. The woman ahead of her was saying, "Don't forget, fifty percent off employee discount."

Employee discount . . . Did pretend girlfriends qualify?

"Good morning," the checkout clerk said when Jane was up. "You find everything you need?"

"Actually, I just realized I need to check on something. Do you know where I can find Levi Cutler?"

The girl pointed up.

Jane looked up. And up. And up . . . The entire back wall was a climber's paradise. The wall was divided into three climbing heights, the tallest being the entire three stories of the building, and there was Levi near the top, and, close as she could tell, the only thing holding him up there was a very thin-looking rope.

The man was clearly insane.

She walked up to the wall and stood next to a tall, lanky guy in cargo shorts and a store employee shirt. His name tag said *Dusty.*

"Can he hear me if I yell up to him?" she asked.

"Dude hears *everything.* We think he might have bat hearing."

"It's true," Levi said, hanging high above them.

"Hey, Tarzan," she called up. "Have you lost your marbles? You've had a concussion. Being a hundred feet up is a bad idea."

"It's thirty feet, and I've been cleared by my doc."

She crossed her arms. "We need to talk," she said.

He grinned down at her. "Sure. Come on up."

"Funny."

He laughed. "Thought you weren't afraid of anything."

Turned out, she was afraid of plenty, including how just looking at him could change the rhythm of her heart.

Kicking off from a rock, Levi suddenly arced into the air, making her gasp. He dropped to the ground, landing lightly on his feet.

Jane went hands on hips. "There's no way you're cleared for rock climbing. Who's your doctor?"

"Mateo Moreno."

She blinked. "Dr. Mateo Moreno?"

"Yep, and he's an old friend. Best friend from middle school. So trust me, he knows me well and realizes climbing in here is tame in comparison to half the stuff the two of us did growing up."

"Huh." How had she not known this?

Levi cocked his head. "You know him?"

"He lives next door to the house I'm staying in. Good guy."

"The best," Levi agreed. "And you're here at the store. Either you missed me or you need something. Or you're here to agree to go to a family dinner as my girlfriend."

"*Fake* girlfriend," she said. "And . . . maybe."

"I like the maybe." He gestured to the wall. "Want to try?"

She opened her mouth to say he was delusional, but he raised a brow, his eyes filled with the unspoken dare. "I'm not trained."

"We've got an expert on staff."

"You?"

He shrugged. "Grew up climbing this wall. And did I mention there are Cake Walk cupcakes for people who climb?" he asked.

She narrowed her eyes. "You're teasing me."

"When I'm teasing you, you'll know it."

She pointed to the shortest of the three walls, the single-story one. "What are my chances of dying on that?"

"On average, there's two point five accidents per ten thousand hours of mountaineering."

"Two point five?" she asked. "It doesn't make sense."

"Neither does the bravest woman I've ever met turning down a simple challenge."

She'd never thought of herself as courageous. In fact, she often felt the opposite. Running scared from connections, ties, roots . . .

Maybe it was time to stop running. "Any tips?"

"Don't look down."

He got her harnessed so quick that she knew he knew she was a flight risk. He said, "I'll be right beside you the whole time. Dusty will be belaying you. I promise you're perfectly safe."

She looked over at Dusty. "Look," she said, "I'm sure you're nice and all, but I'm not big on blind trust. If I fall—"

"You won't," Levi said. "Dusty will be right below you. He's on the local search-and-rescue team and is the best of the best."

Jane stared at Dusty. "I *knew* you looked familiar. You were there that night of the blizzard."

Dusty nodded. "Yeah, and that was the closest you're going to come to dying on my watch. You got your necklace back?"

She pulled it out from beneath her neckline. "Yes. Thank you."

"Don't thank me, thank him," Dusty said, nodding at Levi.

Levi's gaze locked with and held on to hers.

"He said he'd do whatever he had to in order to get it back to you," Dusty said. "You okay with heights?"

Jane jerked her gaze from Levi, a little dizzy with the rapid subject change. "I'm better with heights than enclosed spaces."

Dusty laughed. "Say stop at any time, and we'll get you down."

All righty, then. She began to climb, with Levi right at her side. Whenever she struggled to find the right hand- or foothold, he'd make a suggestion with a quick explanation, and she listened to what he was saying and began to get into the rhythm.

Until she looked down to check her progress. Stupid, stupid move. The ground felt a mile away, and instantly her head spun.

"Jane."

She closed her eyes and gulped in air. "Sorry, can't talk right now, *very* busy having a panic attack."

Levi curled an arm around her. "Breathe," he said softly into her ear. "You can't slip or fall. The rope has you. And I've got you."

And suddenly she was even more scared. Not at the idea of falling. What scared her most was the idea of him having her back.

When was the last time she could say that about a man? She couldn't remember. She took another peek down and let out a wimpy whimper. "It's like the blizzard all over again."

"Except there's no wind, no snow, and we're not dangling seven hundred and fifty feet in the air."

"That night you told me we were at five hundred and fifty!"

"Is there really a difference?"

Good point, but she opened her eyes to glare at him anyway. His gray eyes were a shiny silver. "Unfair," she whispered.

"That I lied?"

"That you have ridiculously long eyelashes."

His lips quirked, and her gaze went rogue, dropping to his mouth, which slowly curved as she watched.

"I'm going to beat you to the top." She had no idea why she said that, but she went back to climbing. It was a huge rush, even when she faltered. And when she scrambled to the top, she found herself smiling from what felt like Mount Everest. "I did it."

Levi grinned at her. "You did."

She nodded and then sat right there at the top because her knees were knocking. He handed her a bottle of water and sat with her. "Turns out, you're a badass in an emergency *and* a badass in a competition." He smiled. "I like it. I like *you,* Jane."

She snorted the water up her nose and then choked.

He rubbed her back until she could breathe. "So you aren't comfortable with compliments. Noted."

Actually, it was the "I like you," which she hadn't expected. "So . . . about that pretend girlfriend thing. I've got stipulations."

"Hit me."

She took a deep breath. "What would this thing entail exactly? I mean, nothing . . . physical, right? Pretend or otherwise?"

When he spoke, his voice was serious. "I wouldn't want *pretend* physical anything from anyone. Especially you, Jane."

She drew a deep breath. Oh boy . . .

"You mentioned stipulations," he said, sounding amused.

She nodded. "You have to promise me that this thing stays pretend no matter what, that you won't fall for me."

He smiled.

She pointed at him. "Hey! It could happen!"

His smile faded. "I have no doubt."

Her heart did a somersault. "Promise me," she whispered.

He was quiet a moment. "I get it," he finally said. "We're both leaving Sunrise Cove soon, and we lead very different lives that would make it nearly impossible to maintain a relationship."

His honesty made her feel a whole lot better about things.

"My turn for a question," he said. "You mentioned not really having a family. What happened to yours?"

She looked away. "I got bounced around a lot as a child between anyone related to me. Kind of soured me on the idea of family." She smiled, though she hated to talk about her childhood.

Levi was looking at her like he felt sorry for her. "My turn," she said. "Do fake girlfriends get the friends and family discount?"

He laughed, breaking the emotional tension, but his eyes remained serious. "Fake girlfriends get whatever they want. Why?"

"I was hoping to buy my roommate the jacket sitting at the checkout counter."

He smiled. "Smart. Funny. Sexy. *And* a shrewd businesswoman. You got it. So . . . we're doing my parents' dinner party?"

"Yes."

He nodded. "We should probably spend a little time getting to know each other before the dinner."

She blinked. "Like a date?"

"Consider it a fact-finding mission on your pretend boyfriend."

At just the thought of what she was agreeing to, she quivered with more nerves than she'd battled while climbing up this wall.

Levi's mouth curved. "You trust me, Jane?"

"No."

"Damn." But he was grinning again, clearly, unabashedly *not* worried. "Then this isn't going to be nearly as much fun."

He stood and took her hand, pulling her to the edge of the wall.

"What are you doing?" she asked.

"My first act as your boyfriend is to get you safely to the ground."

"*Pretend* boyfriend," she corrected, and then screamed all the way down.

Chapter 5

CHARLOTTE MAINLINED A HUGE mug of black coffee as she drove home. She was coming off twenty-four straight hours in the OR.

Car accident victims had arrived on top of car accident victims. Heaven forbid people slow down or take the icy road conditions into account as they leave their cities and hit the mountains.

Parking at the top of her driveway, she glanced over at Mateo's house. No vehicle in the driveway. At the crack of dawn.

Doing her best not to think about whose bed he was in, she let herself inside her house. It was quiet. Empty. Zoe and Mariella were at work. She had no idea where Jane was. There was a stick-it note on the fridge in Jane's scrawl that read *Don't worry.*

In the beginning, Jane hadn't understood that Charlotte actually cared about where she was and if she was okay. Leaving a note now was the equivalent to shouting from the rooftops that Jane considered Charlotte family. Her feral wolf cub was growing up.

After her shower, she pulled on jeans and a sweatshirt and went out into her backyard. Hands on hips, she stared up at the roofline, where her Christmas lights twinkled at her mockingly.

The other day in the staff room, there'd been a pool on who still had their holiday decorations up, and you couldn't bet on yourself.

Mateo had laughingly collected the bounty because he'd been the only one to know that she had hers up.

"They light up my bedroom at night," he told her later when they'd been alone. "Makes me think of you."

What would he say if she told him the truth—that she thought of him too. Way too much. But she hated that she'd lost the bet on a technicality. She pointed up at her lights. "I'm coming for you."

She wondered if Mateo would notice that they were gone.

He'd asked her out multiple times. But she'd declined. Not for a lack of interest. She'd have to be dead and buried to not be attracted to the man whose easygoing mannerisms conflicted with his heart-stopping magic in the ER in the most fascinating of ways.

She dragged her ladder from the garage and wrestled it up against the roof. Not easy on any day, but she still had a foot of snow in her yard, even more up against the house.

She climbed to the top of the ladder and began to lift the string of lights from the hooks in her eaves. Two minutes in, she heard the doorbell ring. Grumbling, she backed down the ladder.

Stalking around the side of the house, she stopped in surprise at seeing Jane standing on the porch, a big bakery bag in one hand. She was in jeans and a thin sweater. No jacket.

Charlotte had met Jane years ago at a medical clinic in Colombia, on a Doctors Without Borders stint.

One night, rebels, guns blazing, had come into the clinic to confiscate all the meds and cash. Charlotte had been by the door, just locking up. The rebel guarding their exit had sidled up to her.

She hadn't understood everything he'd said, but his intent had been clear in the way he looked at her while fingering her hair, bringing a strand of it up to his face to sniff at exaggeratedly.

She'd completely frozen, mentally yanked into an old nightmare of another situation she hadn't been able to control. One of the American nurses shoved her way in front of Charlotte, hands out at her sides to keep Charlotte behind her as she stared up at the rebel. "Take the drugs and money and get the hell out of here."

He'd laughed in her face, but Jane, all five feet four inches of her, hadn't backed down.

And the rebels had finished their looting and gone.

Charlotte had fainted. *Fainted*. Even now, six years later, just thinking about it made her face heat with humiliation.

She'd taken a lot of self-defense classes since then and had also had counseling. She'd like to think if anything happened now, she'd hold her own and be as brave as Jane had been that day.

But she'd not taken on any more of those clinics, instead staying in Tahoe and working at the local hospital. She loved it, loved the people, and yes, okay, it was safe.

But she liked safe. Lived for it.

And the fact that she was living at all was thanks to Jane, and she'd never forget it.

Jane caught sight of Charlotte coming around from the side of the house. "Hey," she called out. "Everything okay?"

"Yes, except for the fact that you're ringing the doorbell. You have a key. You live here, Jane. You pay rent."

Jane thrust out the bakery bag to Charlotte. "Heard about your rough shift. And you don't ever take my money."

Charlotte took the bakery bag because there was stubborn and then there was stupid. And she refused to be stupid. "I could marry you for whatever is in this bag. And I do so take your rent money."

"Charlotte, you haven't accepted my Venmo payment."

Charlotte opened her mouth, but Jane pointed at her. "Did you accept Zoe's and Mariella's?"

Charlotte sighed.

"Thought so." Jane shook her head. "You know I love what you're doing here. Renting to women, making sure they're safe. I know why you do it and want to be a part of it too. I want to help."

"You already have." Charlotte could feel herself getting emotional when she didn't want to. "And what does this have to do with you refusing to let yourself in with your key?"

"Since you won't take my rent, I'm technically a guest. And guests ring the bell." She paused and softened her tone. "It's not my room, Charlotte. It's your den. You could be renting it out and making money. We both know Sandra's looking to stay longer."

Charlotte opened the pastry bag. Her mouth watered at the huge blueberry lemon muffin, her favorite. "Okay, first, thank you for bringing me food. And second, that room is for me to choose what to do with. And I choose to keep it a den slash bedroom. For *you*. You aren't a guest, Jane. You're family."

Charlotte opened the front door and walked inside.

Jane followed her in. "I bring you food because you do so much for me, and I feel like it's the only thing I can do for you in return."

Charlotte turned and put her hands on Jane's shoulders. "Listen to me. You're my dearest friend, you hardly ever try to boss me around, and after long, horrific days in the OR, you make me laugh. So *I'm* the one that gets the most out of this relationship."

Jane blinked. "I . . . didn't know any of that."

"Well, now you do."

Jane took a deep breath and headed through the living room. She opened the sliding glass door, stepped outside, and sat on the stoop. The huge gray cat waiting for her hopped into her lap.

Charlotte stepped outside, too, reaching out to stroke the cat, who allowed it once, then batted Charlotte's hand away.

"I'm sorry," Jane said as the behemoth cat jumped lithely down.

"Why are you sorry if he's not your cat?"

Jane rolled her eyes. "No one owns this cat. Sometimes he chooses to come visit me, that's all."

Charlotte snorted. "Feed your stray, then let me feed mine."

"Are you comparing me to the cat?"

"You have to admit, there are some similarities." Grinning at Jane's grimace, she went into the kitchen. Five minutes later, it was scented with the bacon and eggs she had going.

Jane came into the kitchen, prepared a bowl of food for Cat, and set it down at the back door where he was waiting. She was quiet.

"What is it?" Charlotte asked. "Something's bothering you."

Jane smiled. "Have you met me? Everything bothers me."

"Has something happened?"

Jane hesitated. "I might've done something potentially stupid. I agreed to go out on a date—a *pretend* date—with Levi."

Charlotte gaped. "And the date's pretend . . . why?"

"I told you what he did when we thought we were going to die."

"Yes. He told his mom he had someone in his life so she wouldn't worry. But still not hearing the potentially stupid part."

"Because the *pretend* date is to get good enough at being his *pretend* girlfriend for his parents' fortieth anniversary dinner."

Charlotte stared at her and then laughed.

Jane pointed at her. "Stop that."

Charlotte loaded up two plates and handed Jane one. "I love how you go kicking and screaming into anything good in your life. So if you have to tell yourself this is pretend, I'm all for it."

"It *is* pretend. It's just so that it seems believable and all that."

"Uh-huh."

Jane rolled her eyes as she dug in. "This is delicious. Oh, and I bought your birthday present, so don't go snooping."

Charlotte was turning forty next week and would really rather not. "I told you not to get me anything."

"I didn't listen."

She sighed. "Okay, so let's see this present."

"No way. You don't get it until your birthday next week."

"Spoilsport." Charlotte watched Jane push around the food with her fork. "What else?"

Jane sighed. "I spied on my grandpa's weekly lunch with some of his old work buddies yesterday."

Charlotte studied Jane's face.

Jane sighed. "Yeah, yeah, I'm ridiculous."

"Only if you hide under a table again."

"No, I stayed outside and watched through the window."

Charlotte laughed. "We've made progress."

"We? The only way *we* made progress is if you ran into Mateo today, didn't hide under a table, *and* agreed to go out with him."

Ignoring this, Charlotte went chin up. “How does he look?”

“Sexy as hell, with that leanly muscled runner’s build and—”

“I meant your *grandpa!*” Charlotte said. She didn’t need to know how Mateo looked; he was imprinted on her brain.

Jane thought about it. “He’s a little pale, a little tired. Clearly still recovering from his heart attack. His last EKG showed minor damage, but sufficient blood and oxygen supply to the heart.”

Charlotte’s heart skipped. “Tell me you didn’t put your license in jeopardy to get that information.”

“I didn’t. I eavesdropped on his conversation with one of his friends in the parking lot after his lunch.” She looked at Charlotte. “You’re not going to suggest I go talk to him?”

Hell, no. “I’m still not sure he deserves you.”

Jane gave Charlotte a very rare hug that got her right in the feels. “Better than rent money,” she quipped, making Jane snort.

Jane gathered the dishes. Charlotte got up to help as well, and Jane shook her head. “You cooked. I clean. That’s the rule.”

She made a shooing motion at Charlotte with her hands.

Charlotte laughed and then went outside to finish with the lights. She was back up on the ladder, her headphones on full blast, when someone unexpectedly put a hand on her foot from below. She nearly jerked right out of her skin. Instinctively, she kicked.

And caught Mateo right on the chin.

He staggered back a step. “Nice one, tiger.”

Yanking out an earbud, she stared down at him in horror. “Are you all right?”

“No blood, no foul,” he said. “And a hundred percent my fault.”

Now that she could breathe again, she climbed down. A proper Southern woman looked a person in the eyes while she yelled at him. *“Why in the world did you sneak up on me like that?”*

He shrugged. “When I made myself known the other day at the hospital cafeteria, you ran off. So I figured I’d try a new tactic.”

“You figured wrong.”

He cocked his head, smile fading as he studied her. She knew what he saw. Her eyes were misty; her hands were shaking.

His expression serious now, he said, "I didn't mean to startle you. I won't do it again."

She swallowed hard at the sincerity in his voice and the regret in his eyes. "Thank you." She turned to climb back up the ladder.

"Charlotte."

A sigh escaped her, but she hesitated.

"You're shaking. Give yourself a minute."

"I'm fine."

"I know," he said quietly. "But do it for me."

She hesitated, but eventually nodded because she really was still shaking. Far too revealing, because he slowly drew her in . . . pausing to look into her eyes before he hugged her.

Yeah, she'd *definitely* given herself away, maybe even more than she thought, because they'd never touched before.

And *why?* His arms . . . they were almost as good as his chest, which she had her cheek pressed to.

He drew a deep breath as if he was just as unexpectedly shaken as she by the physical contact, then pressed his face into her hair.

She let herself absorb the feel of a man's arms around her. This man. He was big and warm. And he smelled good. Too good.

Just then, Jane opened the back door. "Hey, Charlotte—" She stopped short at the sight of them hugging. "Ohmigosh, so sorry."

And then she was gone.

Charlotte buried her face in Mateo's neck. She wanted one last big sniff of him before forcing herself to pull back.

He was smiling. "Did you just smell me?"

"I believe it's called breathing."

Onto her, he smirked, but didn't press further. Instead, he looked up at the holiday lights, half still on her eaves, the other half dangling from the roof to the ground. "Need help?"

"No. I—" But he was climbing the ladder. He was wearing work boots, dark jeans, and a black T-shirt with an unbuttoned flannel shirt over it, which flared away from him at the breeze.

Rolling the lights up as he unhooked them, he said, "You could accept help in the spirit it was intended."

Hadn't she just lectured Jane about accepting help? Yes. Yes, she had. So maybe it was time she took some of her own advice. "Fine. But you have to let me do something for you in return."

He glanced down at her, smiling. "You have my full attention."

She rolled her eyes. "I'll feed you after."

He grinned. "Sold."

JANE was on hour sixteen of what should have been a twelve-hour shift. When she finally got a break, she dashed into the cafeteria in the hospital adjacent to Sierra North. She piled up a tray with food and sat with a grateful sigh. She picked up the can of soda she'd grabbed—briefly wishing that it was alcohol—and cracked it open.

It sprayed her in the face. With a gasp, she stilled as it dripped off her nose. "That's what I get for wishing you were alcohol."

"Here." A woman handed her a stack of napkins. "And yeah, a martini would be great about now."

"Thanks." With a wry grimace, Jane began to mop herself up. "And I've actually never had a martini."

"That's a crime against alcohol. Is this seat taken?"

The woman, maybe late thirties, was in yoga gear and had her brown hair up in a ponytail, her gray eyes behind boxy glasses. She wore a welcoming, warm smile that said she liked to talk.

Jane liked to be lonely on her breaks, but she couldn't be rude, so she nodded. Plus, she wasn't going to lie: the woman's tray was filled with desserts. They were probably soul mates.

The woman sat and reached for her own can of soda.

"I'd be care—" Jane started, but that can blew up too.

The woman laughed as Jane got up and brought back more napkins. "Should've seen that coming," she said ruefully.

Jane eyeballed the woman's tray and had a hard time keeping her gaze off the stack of miniature lemon squares.

"Take them," she said. "I've got my eyes on the big brownie."

Jane shook her head. "Oh, I couldn't—"

Her new companion took the plate of mini lemon squares from her tray and set it on Jane's. "For sharing your table."

Jane was not a person who turned down dessert. "Thanks."

"Been a long shift?" the woman asked in sympathy.

"It turned into a double."

"Damn. They always overwork the unsung heroes."

Jane pretended not to hear this. She was always uncomfortable when someone thanked her for her work or referred to the job as being heroic. It was a job, and she loved it, but it was a paycheck.

Her table mate smiled. "My name's Tess. I come here sometimes for lunch before picking up my daughter from the after-school program across the street. How about you?"

"Jane. I'm a nurse at the urgent care clinic next door."

"You must meet a lot of interesting people in your line of work."

Jane thought about how she'd met Levi while hanging seven hundred and fifty feet in the air and had to laugh a little. "Yeah."

Tess smiled. "You look like you've got a good story to tell."

Pleading the Fifth, Jane stuffed in another mini lemon square.

"Sorry." Tess sat back, looking embarrassed. "I ask everyone about their relationships because mine just blew up in my face."

"Oh, I'm so sorry."

"Don't be." Tess shook her head. "I let my soon-to-be ex-husband handle all our financial affairs, which means I don't get to be surprised he ran away with the babysitter and all our money."

"That's awful," Jane said in genuine sympathy. "Men suck." She had a quick flashback to Levi moving to protect her on the gondola. "Well, maybe they don't all suck," she corrected.

Tess lit up with hope. "You have someone special in your life?"

"Um, not exactly. I'm only here for the ski season. After that, I'll be contracted somewhere probably far away from here."

Tess was quiet a moment. Reflective. "That sounds lonely."

"I'm not that great at connections."

Tess nodded. "You've been hurt too."

"Haven't we all?"

Tess laughed a little mirthlessly. "Touché. Tell me you're in a relationship with someone good. Give me some hope."

Jane let out a small laugh. "To be determined, I guess."

Tess knocked her soda can to Jane's. "To the 'to be determined,' then."

Levi couldn't remember the last time he'd felt nerves bubble in his chest, but he felt it now. It was date night—*pretend* date night.

Louie's on the Lake was just as its name proclaimed—right on the water and a popular local dining spot that would be extremely public. He was going to try and remain neutral *and* stay awake. He was exhausted, having spent the past few days doing a deep dive into Cutler Sporting Goods accounting.

The store's situation was bad. He needed to talk to his family but wanted another day to finish going through everything first. His mom and dad were good people, and Cal had clearly taken advantage of them. When Tess found out, it'd kill her.

It was keeping him awake at night.

He could see Jane walking toward him in dark jeans, sexy boots, and a sweater the same green as her eyes. Suddenly he knew staying awake wasn't going to be a problem. Just one look at her and the weight of his stress and exhaustion faded.

Jane sat across from him and, without preamble, pushed her iPad across the table to him. She'd loaded a site called How to Get to Know Someone in 100 Questions. He looked at her. "Seriously?"

"Okay, so we can skip the obvious ones, like how do you react in a life-or-death situation?" She let her finger land on the screen. "Here. Number fifty-two. What's your most unusual talent?"

He smiled. "In or out of the bedroom? Oh, and hi, by the way."

She softened with a laugh. "Hi. Now answer the question. And OUT of the bedroom is all I'm concerned about."

He laughed. "Okay, unusual talent . . . robotic gadgets."

"I said *out* of the bedroom!"

"I was actually being serious. I like to build robotic gadgets."

"Oh." She blushed. "Sorry."

Their waitress turned out to be an old classmate of his. Kendra smiled warmly at him. "Hey, hot stuff," she said. "Heard you made good on that fancy brain of yours. You get paid to tell all those big CEOs in the Bay Area what to do with their data now, right?"

"More like I offer suggestions in a consulting capacity." He gestured to Jane. "Kendra, this is Jane. Jane, Kendra."

"We sweated out AP Chemistry together," Kendra told Jane. "So what can I get you kiddies tonight?"

Levi indicated for Jane to go first.

"I'm trying to decide between the sweet potato fries and the shrimp kebab," she said.

"Take both," Kendra said. "They're amazing. And your main?"

"Oh . . ." Jane paused. "Um, just the apps, thanks."

Levi didn't know if she wasn't that hungry or if she was worried about the prices. "How about one of each of the five appetizers." And then he added a flight of beer, getting Jane to pick the flavors.

"Also, we've got s'mores on the menu," Kendra said. "You take the makings out on the patio to the fire pits and create yourself."

Levi looked at Jane, who had lit up at the word *s'mores.* "I think that's a yes."

Kendra gave him a wink and took off.

"Were you one of the hot guys who had girls throwing themselves at you?" Jane asked.

He laughed. "No. I was the science geek."

"Doesn't seem like it hurt your game any."

"I had *zero* game. Luckily for me, just after I graduated from high school, my best friend told me we were in a relationship."

"Mateo?" she asked in surprise.

"Mateo's sister Amy. They lived on my street growing up, and we were all close. Amy and I got closer that summer after graduation, and she changed colleges to go with me to Colorado."

"How long were you with her?"

"Until the year after college." He really wasn't ready to explain what had happened to Amy because there was no way to do that without taking the mood to a somber place.

Luckily, just then Kendra brought them their food and beer.

Jane picked up a sweet potato fry. "There's no way we can eat all of this. It was sweet of you, but impractical."

That made him laugh. He was the most practical person he knew. "My brain doesn't even know how to compute that," he said. "And you never told me your most unusual talent."

"To piss people off, which is self-explanatory." She picked up a shrimp kebab, dragged it through a mountain of sauce, and pointed it at him. "Stop trying to distract me with all your sexy nerd hotness." She went back to her iPad. "Next question—"

"Oh no." He put a hand over her iPad. "You're not getting away with telling me your talent is pissing people off. Play fair."

"But it's true."

He studied her. "You haven't pissed me off."

"Give me time." She shrugged. "You might disagree with me on stuff. Or not like my opinions, of which I have many."

"There's nothing wrong with disagreeing or having varying opinions. I actually like that."

She looked at him for a long beat. "You're different."

"Now you're getting it."

Jane stared at him, a suddenly wary look on her face.

"Pretend," she said, pointing at him. "This is pretend."

"Are you reminding me or yourself?"

"Both." She shoved his hand off her iPad and read the next question. "Is a hot dog a sandwich—and why."

Their faces were close. Not as close as they'd been the night of the blizzard or when she'd climbed the wall at the store.

"Hello," she said. "Earth to Tarzan."

"You do know that for this to work, we need to know more about each other than how we categorize a hot dog."

"Okay . . ." She studied him thoughtfully. "You're clearly smart and successful. Why do you need a pretend girlfriend?"

He turned to look out the windows. "I spend my whole day at work selling people on the idea that I'm the solution to all their problems. When I get home, I just want to be me. And I guess I haven't met a woman who's okay with me as is."

"I get that," she said, nodding. "And same."

No one had ever understood this about him. He shook his head. "I'm thinking you're one of the most fascinating, amazing women I've ever met. I guess I'm just stunned that you're . . . available."

Her lips quirked. "Are you asking me why I'm single?"

"If you're willing to answer, then yes. Why are you single?"

She lifted a shoulder. "I spend nine months of the year in other parts of the world dealing with real people with real problems. It makes dating seem . . . frivolous, I guess."

This made sense, but it gave him a pang deep in his chest for her. She reached for the iPad, but he gently pushed it away.

She picked up one of the shots of beer, took a sip, put it down.

"You're nervous," he realized. He put his hand over hers. "I was nervous tonight too. Until I saw you."

She gave a small smile. "I wasn't nervous *until* I saw you. Good thing this is only pretend, right?"

"We'll start easy, okay?" he said. "Tell me about your day."

"It was pretty ordinary." She thought about it. "I did meet someone new at lunch. I usually try to eat alone, but today this woman asked if she could sit with me. At first I was irritated."

"Not you . . ."

She snorted. "But she was really nice. She loves martinis, which I've never had, so we're going to go for martinis soon. She's a single mom, getting a divorce, loves skiing . . . Tess something."

Levi froze. *"Tess,"* he repeated, trying to hide his disbelief.

"Yeah. Her daughter's after-school program is across the street from the hospital. She was *very* chatty. Her daughter thinks she's a fairy princess. Oh, and she has a totally annoying brother."

"Really," he said dryly. He really should've seen this coming, but his sister, and undoubtedly his mom as well, had clearly been cyberstalking Jane. He shouldn't be stunned, but he was.

And they wondered why he'd chosen to live in San Francisco.

"Yeah, I guess he's home for a bit," Jane said, "and leaves dirty dishes in the sink. How big is your family again?"

"There's five of us, though sometimes it seems like triple that."

She didn't smile, his first clue something was wrong.

"And they're . . . nice?" she asked.

She was anxious about meeting them. "They're going to be *really* nice to you, and very busy trying to figure out why you're with me."

She gave him a small smile at that, and he paused before bringing up her family again. "You're not close to yours, I take it."

"No. My mom was a teenager when she got pregnant, and my dad didn't stick around. She wasn't ready to take care of a baby.

It was tough for her to keep up with school and have a life, so we bounced around for a while. She burned some bridges."

"And you? What happened to you?"

"When I was two, my mom got an opportunity to go away to college. I was sent to my mom's older sister, Aunt Viv. But she got married and wanted to start a family of her own."

"I can't imagine what that must have been like for you."

"I was fine," she said, as if she didn't want him to feel sorry for her. "Anyway, that's when my grandparents took me in. And that was . . ." She smiled a little. "The best. They lived in Sunrise Cove in a tiny cabin. I loved everything about that time."

"Here?" he asked, surprised. "They're here in Tahoe?"

"Just my grandpa now. My grandma . . ." She paused, her liquid-jade eyes revealing pain. "She died when I was eight."

"Jane, I'm so sorry. Did you get to stay with your grandpa?"

"My grandpa had problems. Grief, and some health issues. My aunt Viv took me back in so I wouldn't put any burden on him."

"Damn. You couldn't catch a break."

"Maybe if I'd been an easier kid—"

"Jane, you were just a kid. Someone should have made you feel wanted. Someone should have *asked* you to stay."

"Real life's not like that. Memories stay. People go."

He put his hand over hers. "What happened next?"

"I bounced around, and emancipated myself at sixteen."

"Do you see your grandpa when you're here?"

"No. Thinking about it, though." She caught the look on his face and shook her head. "It wasn't all bad."

She'd been through hell, and *she* was comforting *him*. His heart tightened at that. "Your family failed you."

"They did the best they could. And I never had to go into the system." She shuddered. "I know people who are still scarred from that."

She was amazing and resilient, and he wanted to hold her. He wanted to make her feel as special as she made him feel.

Kendra came by and gathered up their plates. "Your s'mores platter is ready when you are."

Levi stood and took Jane's hand, pulling her up. "Come on."

There were six fire pits with low benches on a snow-covered patio. They claimed a spot by themselves, and Kendra brought a platter with marshmallows, chocolate bars, and graham crackers.

"I've never done this before," Jane said.

Levi smiled and handed her a spear. "You just load a marshmallow—" He broke off as she loaded not one, not two, but *three* marshmallows on her spear and held it over the fire, looking so excited that he laughed as he loaded his own spear. He held his marshmallow over the fire, too, and gently tapped it to hers.

She looked up at him.

"Thanks for tonight," he said.

"I haven't been out in a long time," she admitted.

She pulled her marshmallows back from the fire and beamed with pride. Perfectly golden. She carefully sandwiched them with chocolate and graham crackers.

She took a big bite, and he became enthralled with the dollop of melted marshmallow at the corner of her mouth.

"What happened between you and Amy?" she asked.

The question surprised him, but he supposed it shouldn't have.

Jane narrowed her eyes. "Did you cheat on her?"

"No. We got engaged." The year after college, they'd played house and they'd been happy. But then she started pressing for that wedding she'd been dreaming of since seventh grade. He made some agreeable noises, but he'd stalled on setting a date.

And then she'd died—without the wedding, which had been all she'd ever wanted. These days he never made promises. Ever.

"Levi?"

There was no getting around this. "She passed away unexpectedly a year after we were engaged," he said. "An aneurysm."

"Oh, I'm so sorry. I shouldn't have pushed—"

"No, it's okay. You learn to live with it. And you move on."

Her eyes were warm. Regretful, but also understanding. She nodded and then went about toasting another perfect marshmallow. Then she created a s'more with it and handed it to him.

That was when he realized that the more he got to know her, the more real he wanted this to be.

"This was a very unusual date," she said, eyes dark by the fire's glow, mouth utterly kissable.

He smiled. "You said *date.*"

"*Pretend* date," she corrected. "You promised me, remember?"

Right. He'd also promised not to fall for her. Guess he did make promises after all. Really bad ones. "I remember."

She nodded. "I'm going to be gone soon. So are you, right?"

"I'm actually thinking of moving back. It caught me off guard, but I've missed connections, and I have a lot of them here."

She looked across the outdoor patio to the lake just beyond, dark and beautiful. "I can see why you'd want to stay here."

"And you?" he asked.

She shook her head. "I'm not really a one-place sort of girl."

Then right now would have to do.

By the time they laughingly gobbled up the last of their s'mores and walked out front, it was snowing.

Jane tipped her face up to the falling flakes. "I never get tired of snow. It's got potential to do damage, and yet it's so beautiful."

He thought that could describe Jane too. "Where's your car?"

"Oh, I walked."

"Let me drive you home," he said, reaching for her hand.

She studied him for a long beat, while he did his damnedest to look like something she couldn't live without. "A ride home would be nice, thank you," she finally said softly.

He followed her directions to an older neighborhood up on the hill. He stopped before two old Victorians that shared a driveway.

"We're on the left," Jane said.

Levi had never been to Mateo's. The front yard was good sized, with two huge pine trees, all of it covered with snow. Levi turned off the engine and started to get out of the car.

Jane looked over at him, startled. "What are you doing?"

"Walking you to your door."

"That's hardly necessary."

He got out of the car anyway and met her at the front of the car.

She was silent on the way to the door, then turned to him on the porch. "You know, pretend first dates don't come with a kiss."

This had him smiling. "But you're thinking about it."

She laughed. "I'm not inviting you in, Levi."

"I know."

"Do you? Because we're pretending for *your* family. The people in my life don't need to know about you."

"Ouch. And I thought you told me you didn't have anyone in your life."

"Fine. I have my landlord and roommate."

The front door swung open. A pretty blonde smiled out at him. "Charlotte," she said. "Landlord and aforementioned friend, though I'll add I'm also her *best* friend. And her family."

Levi recognized the protectiveness and appreciated it. "Nice to meet you." He smiled at Jane. "Seems we have plenty of reasons for a second date." Then he started to walk back to his car.

"Hey," she called.

He turned back to find her standing there on the porch, lit by the glow of a single-bulb light. "What's the first reason?" she asked.

He smiled. "That kiss you want."

And when she didn't deny this, he smiled all the way home.

Chapter 6

It wasn't a real workday until someone yelled at Jane. Today it was a patient named Jason Wells, who'd gone snowboarding off trail—not permitted here at High Alpine—and had hit a tree.

With his face.

She'd been attempting to irrigate the worst of the guy's cuts so he could get stitched up, and all he wanted was his phone. "Phones aren't allowed in the treatment rooms, sir."

"The hell with that." He sat up. "I'm outta here."

His buddy, who'd dragged Jason into the clinic twenty minutes ago, appeared through the privacy curtain. "Dude, calm down; she's just trying to help you."

Never in history has telling someone to calm down worked.

"I don't need medical attention." Jason swung out with his arm, scattering the medical supplies across the room.

Mateo, who had been sent over on loan from the hospital, also appeared in the doorway. "Jane." He gave her a chin nudge indicating he wanted her to move farther back, out of Jason's reach.

Before she could, Jason's friend pushed past her and . . . punched Jason in the face.

Jason fell back, unconscious, and his friend looked at Mateo and Jane. "Sorry, but you should be able to treat him now."

They'd had to call the police, but it turned out that Jason had recently come home from Afghanistan and was suffering from debilitating PTSD. His friend had truly just been trying to help.

She took a late lunch break on the deck of High Alpine's lunch lodge and watched the skiers hurl themselves down the mountain.

Mateo came out and sat next to her, holding a glass container she recognized. "Charlotte made you lunch?"

He grinned. "Jealous?"

He pulled out two forks and handed her one.

"You are a god among men," she said fervently.

"She gave me this lasagna on the demand that I share with you. As she said, you probably packed a protein bar and a soda."

They both looked down at Jane's protein bar and can of soda.

Mateo laughed, and they began eating, racing each other to the middle, because on this job, no break lasted long.

"So what's up with you and Charlotte?" Jane asked.

"Other than that she finally allowed me to help her take down the holiday lights? Nothing."

"She fed you. She only feeds the people she cares about."

Mateo smiled hopefully. "Yeah?"

"Yeah." She jabbed her fork in his direction. "Hurt her and answer to me. She's dead set against opening her heart."

"Why?"

Jane shook her head. "Trust me, she has her reasons."

He looked troubled. "Yeah. I'm getting that loud and clear."

She put her hand over his. "Just don't give up too soon, okay?"

"I won't."

"Good. Oh, and how did I not know *your best friend is Levi?*"

Mateo shrugged. "Until the gondola incident, I hadn't seen him in a few years."

She set her fork down. "I'm sorry about your sister, Mateo."

He sighed. "Me too."

"Why didn't you tell me you knew Levi?"

He looked at her. "Until right this very minute, I didn't realize there was anything to talk about."

Crap. "There isn't."

He laughed. "Uh-huh. You do realize you're about as forthcoming with your emotions as Charlotte, right?"

"Pretty sure I'm worse," she admitted.

He paused. "Levi seem okay?"

She met his eyes and saw genuine concern. "He says his headaches and dizziness are mostly gone."

"I didn't mean that. I mean . . ." He paused. "He cut himself off from friends and family, like maybe he thought he didn't deserve that kind of connection."

"You think he's going to vanish again?"

"Well, not until you go, anyway."

She shook her head. "It's not like that. I'm just pretending to be his girlfriend for some family dinner."

Mateo stared at her. "Oh, man. You're so in over your head."

"Why? Is his family awful?"

"No. They're amazing."

Her phone pinged with a voice mail. It was from the local Humane Society, offering free shots for rescue animals. She looked at Mateo. "Should I get Cat his shots even though he's not mine?"

"Yes, and yes he is."

She hit the number and got an opening for five o'clock.

So that's how Jane found herself after work wrestling Cat into a carrier she found in Charlotte's garage. He went into it willingly but howled his displeasure all the way to the animal shelter.

The woman at the front desk looked up and smiled. "Oh my," she said. "He's got quite a voice."

"Sorry, he does. My name's Jane, and I have an appointment."

The woman's smile widened. "Hello, Jane, lovely to meet you. I'm Shirl. We didn't actually get the name of your lovely cat."

"It's Cat. Short for Alley Cat."

If Shirl thought this was odd, she didn't show it as she had Jane fill out a form and then took her and Cat to a patient room.

Cat stalked out of the crate when Jane opened it, looking royally pissed. "What do we know about this beauty?" Shirl said.

"He lives in the alley behind the house I'm staying in."

Shirl scooped Cat up from the floor and set him on the examination table. "This precious boy needs a real name," she said. "That's the first step in making him yours."

"I'm a nurse. I work twelve-hour shifts. I'd be a terrible cat mom. Plus, I'm here only for ski season; then I'll be gone."

This seemed to startle Shirl. "Where to?"

"I think it's Haiti next."

Shirl paused. "Putting yourself on the front lines to take care of other people. I don't know if there's a more respectable job than that. Your mom must be so proud."

Jane's mom was something all right, but proud probably wasn't it. If she'd had a mom like Shirl, she'd want to live close.

You're living close to your grandpa . . .

At the thought of him, she was hit by the usual colliding mix of emotions. Some she knew—regret, resentment. The other emotions she couldn't name. "I'm not close to my family."

"Oh, I'm so sorry." That didn't stop Shirl from asking another question. "Well, then, certainly the man in your life is proud."

"Um—"

"Oh dear," Shirl said suddenly while still checking out Cat.

Jane's heart leapt into her throat. "What's wrong with him?"

"Well, that's just it. He's not a he; he's a she." Shirl beamed. "She's already had a litter. You might want to get her spayed."

Jane scooped Cat up and hugged her close. "Thank you. Yes, I'll think about getting her spayed as soon as possible."

Shirl smiled. "You're a good person, Jane. If you're worried about her, we've got personalized collars and tags out front. You can put your phone number on the tag. Would you like that?"

A tag that would claim Cat as her own. That seemed a horrible idea and the best idea on the planet. "I'll think about that too."

Levi spent the day in the back office at Cutler Sporting Goods. He purposely waited until everyone was busy to let himself into the stockroom. He wanted to do an inventory check against what was in the system, because as near as Levi could tell, Cal had dipped his fingers into every corner of the family business.

Levi needed to get the authorities involved, but he didn't want to freak out his parents and Tess until he'd finished his audit.

But after last night's date, his mission at the store today was more than just the inventory check. He wanted to ask Tess what the hell she'd been thinking befriending his pretend girlfriend.

But his sister came to him, poking her head into the stockroom. "What are you doing poking around back here?" she asked.

He leaned against a wall of shelving. "Seems to me you're the one poking around in other people's business."

She came into the room. "You've got something to say?"

He just stared at her, knowing the value of silence when it came to gaining any intel from her. She'd fill it, in three, two, one—

"Fine. Clearly Jane told you about our coincidental meetup."

"That was no coincidence."

She shrugged. "One of our customers happens to be an X-ray tech and knows her. It's not my fault you won't tell us anything about your girlfriend. Like the fact that she's *not* your girlfriend."

Never underestimate the depths of deception that an older bossy sister would sink to. "I don't know what you're talking about."

Tess smiled, knowing she had him. "She's clearly single, Levi."

Damn. His sister was better than any lie detector in the land. "Okay," he said. "Let's say I do have a *pretend* girlfriend."

Tess crossed her arms. "Uh-huh . . ."

"What if I wanted to make things real?"

The door opened and nearly hit his sister. Shirl Cutler came in, bouncing with joy. "Guess who I met today during my volunteer shift at the Humane Society!"

Levi turned and thunked his head against the shelving. *"Why?"*

"Don't worry. I didn't tell her who I was."

Mateo came in behind Levi's mom. "What did I miss?"

Levi sighed. "And you're here why?"

"I invited him here," his mom said. "We have leftover food from lunch, and I bet Mateo hasn't eaten a good home-cooked meal in forever. I'm packing him up leftovers."

Mateo was one of the best cooks Levi knew. The guy was actually a huge food snob. There was no way he hadn't eaten.

"Come help me, Tess." And with that, Levi's mom and sister were gone.

Mateo plopped into one of the two chairs in the corner.

"Long few days?" Levi asked.

"You could say that."

Levi dropped into the other chair. "What's going on?"

"What do you know about your pretend girlfriend's friend?"

"How do you know about Jane?"

"I have my ways. Tell me what you know about Charlotte."

Levi shrugged. "I met her last night. She's a doctor at your hospital. Which means you know way more about her than I do."

Mateo leaned forward and put his face into his hands.

When the Morenos had lost Amy, it'd left Mateo an only child solely responsible for his elderly parents. Between that and the demanding job, Mateo had no personal life outside his family. Levi had vanished on him, leaving Mateo without emotional support. He wouldn't make that mistake again. "What's wrong?"

"She's smart as hell, feisty and sassy, and . . . she's the One."

"And this is a problem?"

"She doesn't like me."

"Come on. You've never had to work for a woman in your life."

"Until this one," Mateo said. "When I get home before her, I clear her snow. She yells at me. I leave snacks in her cubby at work. She thinks it's the X-ray tech who always hits on her."

Levi burst out laughing. "Why not just tell her how you feel?"

"Really?" Mateo asked. "Is that what you're doing with Jane?"

"Hey, we both know how *not* an expert I am on this stuff. But what's so wrong with telling Charlotte how you really feel?"

"I'll mess it up."

When it came to getting serious in a relationship, the guy had as little experience as, well, Levi. "You could just take it slow."

Mateo laughed mirthlessly. "Our current pace is a tortoise wading through peanut butter. Any slower, we'll be going backward."

"What's the hurry? Neither of you are going anywhere."

"Tell me you got better advice for me than that."

"Pretend girlfriend, remember?"

Mateo snorted, then shook his head. "We're both dumbasses."

"No doubt."

CHARLOTTE walked out of the hospital at dawn and made her way to her car, a sharp pain of grief stabbing her chest.

A young woman had died on her table last night under her knife.

Cranking on the heater, she turned the vents toward her as she drove home, but all the heat in the world couldn't warm her up.

Talia, a twenty-two-year-old, had been a victim of domestic abuse. Feeling the prickle of tears, Charlotte blinked hard and pulled into her driveway. Which had been cleared.

Mateo, of course.

Drawing a deep breath, she pulled her visor down to look into the mirror, needing to make sure there were no signs of her turmoil. She didn't need a knight in shining armor to save her day.

She would save her own damn day.

She got out of the car, made her way to his door, and knocked.

When the door opened, Mateo stood there wearing red knit boxers. No shirt. Bed head. Eyes heavy lidded. Bare feet.

He blinked blearily. "What's up?"

"Put it back."

"Put what back?"

"The snow," she said. "Put it all back."

He groaned. "I didn't get out of the ER until an hour ago. I've had twelve minutes of sleep in thirty-six hours. Are you crazy?"

"Yes. And you already know that. So you should also know that I'm completely capable of clearing my own snow, even after a terrible, horrible, no good, very bad day at work."

His eyes softened. "I know. I saw her in the ER. I had no choice but to send her to you in OR, but I hated it, because I knew what it would do to you."

To her utter horror, she felt her eyes filling. She turned her back to him, hating that he'd seen her at her worst—vulnerable.

"I'm going to touch you now," he warned in his quiet, calm voice. Then he slowly pulled her back around to face him.

She already knew he was perceptive. It was what made him such a great ER doctor, but it also made him dangerous to her heart, because though she hadn't said a word about her past to anyone except Jane, he'd clearly gotten the gist of it from her own actions.

"Charlotte," he said. "Let me make you something to eat."

She glared at him. "I don't want you to feel sorry for me."

"Good, because I don't." His voice was low. Serious. "You've had a bad night, and let's just say I know what that feels like."

"I'm not fit for company."

"Then we won't talk. We'll just eat. Then sleep." Slowly, he reached for her hand. "But first, I'd like to hug you again. Okay?"

More okay than anything she could think of. Fact was, she hadn't stopped thinking about how safe she'd felt in his arms.

"Yes, please," she whispered, and with a smile he stepped into the freezing cold morning and wrapped his arms around her.

She gasped as her hands came in contact with warm, bare skin. "Oh, you're almost naked!"

"That was a 'you're almost naked' in a good way, right?"

And that was how she found herself laughing and crying at the same time. Going up on tiptoes, she pressed her face into the crook of his neck, slipping her arms around him, holding on for dear life. "You're going to catch frostbite," she whispered against his throat.

He held her close. "Guess you'll just have to keep me warm."

She breathed him in, her anchor in a world gone mad.

He pulled back but held on to her hand. "Come inside, Charlotte. I've got food. I even know how to cook it."

She stared up at him. "Just breakfast, right? Nothing more."

"I'd never ask you for more than you were willing to give."

No one had ever said something so earth-changing to her.

He looked into her eyes. "You in, or is it too much?"

That was when her stomach chose to rumble and grumble like a locomotive engine. Horrified, she pressed her hands to her belly while Mateo laughed and tugged her inside.

She looked around. The big living room had wall-to-wall windows framing the gorgeous mountains. The place was all warm woods and neutral colors and big, sturdy, inviting furniture.

There were noises coming from the kitchen, making her realize she'd stopped in the living room and Mateo hadn't. She followed the sounds and found he'd pulled on sweatpants and a T-shirt. He stood in front of his stove, cracking eggs into a pan. She sat down on a barstool on the other side of his cooking station.

She watched him toss some chopped veggies in with the eggs, then flip the omelet with a flick of his wrist.

Two minutes later, he'd divided the eggs onto two plates, added toast, and served her with easy efficiency.

"You've been doing that a long time," she said.

He shrugged. "My parents worked around the clock. Being the oldest, I was the babysitter. It was cook or go hungry."

She knew he had a big extended family and that he took care of most of them. "Who takes care of you?" she asked.

He sat on the barstool next to her.

"I take care of me. The same way you take care of you. It's who we are; it's what we do."

She nodded. "Does it ever get to you? Always being an island?"

Reaching out, he brushed the tips of his fingers along her jaw. "I guess I don't let myself think about it too much."

"That's usually my tactic too. But sometimes it gets old."

He watched her inhale the food he'd made for her, a small smile curving his mouth. "We could do something about that."

She nearly choked on a bite of toast. "Meaning?"

He just smiled. "You telling me you haven't thought about it?"

She met his gaze. "By *it*, you're suggesting we sleep together?"

"I'm suggesting I'm here to meet any need you have, any time."

If she thought about that for even a second, she was going to crawl into his lap and wrap herself around him. Instead, she stood up and loaded their plates into his dishwasher. When she turned, he was right there, close enough to touch. "That was the only need I'm capable of helping you with at the moment," she said.

"And you?" he asked. "Is there a need I can help *you* with? Want to talk about last night?"

"No." *Definitely not.*

Mateo looked at her for a long beat. "When you're ready, then."

She dried off his countertop. "Thanks for breakfast."

"Anytime." He gently pulled her back around to face him. "But I'm sure we could do much better than breakfast for you."

Her body shifted against his. "I . . . need to work up to that."

With a smile, he cupped her face and brushed a kiss across her forehead. "On your time, Charlotte. Always."

A FEW minutes later, Charlotte walked back to her house, the icy air burning her lungs. But she didn't care. Dr. Charlotte Marie Dixon was leaving a man's house, and she was smiling.

She felt amazing. Absolutely nothing had happened, but it'd been the most intimate she'd been with a man in years.

When she stepped into her kitchen, she found Jane sitting at the table staring at a small, flat box on the coffee table as if it were a coiled rattlesnake. She looked up at Charlotte with obvious relief. "Hey. Where were you? Your car's here, but you vanished."

Charlotte laughed. "Sucks, doesn't it, the not knowing if someone's okay?"

"Wait a minute. Did you just come from Mateo's house?"

"He cleared the snow for us, so I went over there to, um, thank him, and he made me breakfast."

Jane stared at her. "Are you blushing?"

Charlotte clasped her hands to her cheeks. "If I'm blushing, it's because he made me breakfast and didn't expect anything more."

"I like it," Jane said. "I like him for you." She then turned back to the table to stare at the box some more.

"What's that?" Charlotte asked.

"You tell me. You left it for me."

Charlotte gave a slow shake of her head. "Not me. Are you kidding? You break out into hives when I give you a present."

Jane frowned. "You're not playing me?" She opened the box and pulled out a sugar plum fairy ornament, dangling it from her finger. "You're the only one who knows I once dressed up like a sugar plum fairy to go see *The Nutcracker* with my grandma."

"It's beautiful," Charlotte breathed, admiring the dainty glass ornament. "But no. I'm not playing you. Where was it?"

"At my cubby in the Sierra North clinic." She eyed Charlotte suspiciously. "But if it wasn't you, then who the hell left it?"

Charlotte put a hand on her shoulder. "The question is, if it *had* been me who gave it to you, why would it upset you so much?"

Jane sank into a chair. "I don't know. Maybe because it feels like the past colliding with the here and now. The past hurts."

"Is it possible someone from your past left it? Your grandpa?"

"He doesn't know I'm here." Jane turned the pretty ornament in the light. "It's fragile. I'll break it if I take it with me when I go."

"Then leave it here, in your bedroom, for when you come back."

"I don't like taking up your space with my junk. Plus, you never know if you'll need the room for another renter while I'm gone."

Charlotte took in the anxiety on Jane's face and ached for her. "There's always going to be a room for you *and* your stuff, Jane."

"Have you talked to Sandra? She wants to extend her stay."

"Yeah, I'm thinking of buying bunk beds for the downstairs bedroom. Zoe said she wouldn't mind sharing."

"You don't need to spend the money on a new bed," Jane said. "Seriously. The easier solution is for me to head out early."

Spinning on her heels, Charlotte opened her junk drawer and grabbed a Sharpie. Without a word, she headed down the hall.

She smiled grimly when she heard footsteps following after her.

"What are you doing?" Jane asked.

Charlotte uncapped the Sharpie and wrote *JANE* in big letters across her bedroom door. "Does this make it clear?"

Jane looked at her. "You do realize that paint could cover it up."

Charlotte pointed at her with the Sharpie. "Don't ruin this for me. We're having a moment."

"I'm not good at moments."

"No kidding. Now hush, or I'll make you hug me." She snagged an arm around Jane's neck and dragged her in close.

"But what if you need the money?"

Charlotte's throat tightened. "I don't rent out my rooms because I need the money. You know that. I need time with my best friend, the sister of my heart, whenever she can get into town."

Suddenly Jane straightened up. *"Levi."*

Charlotte blinked, confused. "Huh?"

"He's the one who got me back my locket. He knows what a sugar plum fairy would mean to me." She shook her head. "I can't believe I didn't think of it before. *What was he thinking?*"

Charlotte watched Jane pace back and forth. "You're thinking he knows you far better than you're comfortable with."

Jane gave her a *duh* look, and Charlotte felt her mouth curve. "You know you have to thank him, right? In person. It's etiquette."

Jane leaned back and thunked her head against the door.

Charlotte knew better than to laugh, but as it was her greatest wish for Jane to find someone special enough to keep her here in Tahoe, she allowed herself a small smile.

Chapter 7

THE NEXT MORNING, JANE headed to Starwood Peak urgent care.

Starwood was Jane's least favorite of the five, mostly because it tended to draw the hotdoggers. Its high ratio of serious injuries meant calling for the helicopter to get them airlifted to either Reno or Davis, depending on how many minutes they had to save them—a grim reality that *wasn't* in the promo ads for Lake Tahoe.

The clinic was unusually cold today, so she was working in her scrubs with her down vest on top. In the vest pocket sat the sugar plum fairy ornament. Every time the box pressed up against her ribs, a mixed bag of emotions she couldn't name hit her.

On her break, she decided it was time to be a grown-up. So she sneaked into the supply closet—because nothing said grown-up more than that—and pulled out her phone to send a text.

JANE: *Need to talk to you.*
LEVI: *Not that I'm easy, but when and where?*
JANE: *I get off at 6. Leave me a text on where to find you.*

At six fifteen, she headed out to the parking lot and stopped short at the man leaning against her car, boots casually crossed, head down doing something on his phone. He looked up and unerringly landed that see-all gray gaze on her.

She faltered, then lifted her chin and strode directly toward him. *Remember, you're not happy he gave you a present. This is pretend. Presents have no place in a pretend relationship.*

She felt a stirring of frustration with him for standing there looking like the best thing that had ever happened to her.

So she did what she did. She went toe-to-toe with him, pulled the box out of her pocket, and pressed it against his chest. "We agreed this isn't real, so why in the world would you do this?"

He opened the box and looked at the ornament.

She stared into his eyes. Okay, not his eyes. She stared at his mouth. She didn't know why. "Your turn to talk," she said.

"Well, thanks to my niece, I know this is a sugar plum fairy. Although I gotta say, you make a far cuter one."

"Why, Levi?"

"I don't know. Why did you tell me you didn't want to kiss me when all you've done since you got out here was look at my lips?"

Gah! She jerked her gaze off his lips. "I swear, I have no idea."

He set the box with the ornament on the hood. "This is why," he said, and nudged her up against the vehicle. Then he kissed her. Slow. Sweet. Almost as if he was asking a question.

She pulled back and stared at him, her only thought being that this hadn't been nearly enough. Grabbing his jacket, she yanked him back. "This is *just* a kiss," she informed him, her voice soft and breathy.

This had him laughing softly against her as he nibbled her lower lip. Someone gasped. Her. Dammit. She closed a fist in his hair, held on for the best kiss of her life.

Levi was slow to pull back and reveal those sexy eyes.

"Okay." She nodded. "So we got that out of the way."

He looked pointedly at her arms, still wrapped around him.

She yanked her hands from him and turned away while she tried to catch her breath and gather her thoughts. "You make me crazy."

"Ditto." He paused. "And I didn't give you that ornament."

She whirled back and took in the truth in his eyes.

That left only her grandpa. So he knew she was in town.

Guilt flooded her. He was aware of her trips to Tahoe and knew she'd been avoiding him. And then there was the disappointment that he'd chosen to communicate via the gift instead of in person.

"Jane? You okay?"

She dropped her head to his chest. Slowly shook her head.

"What can I do? Name it."

"Feed me."

"Done." He led her to his car and drove them toward town.

In less than five minutes, they were seated inside a pizzeria, near a huge brick fireplace. The heat felt wonderful, the scents teased her cranky belly, and as much as she didn't want to admit it, her dinner companion was a sight for sore eyes.

When they each had a beer in front of them, Levi met her gaze. "I'm guessing you have an idea who the ornament is from."

She gave a stunned nod. "My grandpa. He's the only other person who would know what such a gift would mean to me."

"Can you ask him?"

"I haven't talked to him in twenty years."

Gently, he rubbed the pad of his thumb over the back of her hand. "What do you want to do?"

Maybe it was time to let go of the past and make a present for herself. "I don't know. If I just show up, I might upset him."

Levi continued to hold her hand. "If he's the one who got you the ornament, he already knows you're here," he pointed out. "I'm betting he's expecting you."

She looked into his calm eyes. "But what if he's not? What if he's unhappy to see me. I can't . . . I don't want to be turned away."

Levi gently cupped her face. "Either way, you're in the driver's seat. You can't make a wrong move."

She nodded, empowered by the reminder. "I'm just . . . wary. But I want bygones to be bygones because family matters."

"Family does matter. But it only works if it's a give-and-take."

"He did make the first move," she said. "Sort of."

He nodded, keeping a hold on her hand, gaze solemn.

"When I lived with my grandparents . . . it was the best time of my entire childhood," she admitted.

"There's no harm in reaching out and seeing what's up."

How did he always make everything sound so simple, so right? When she was with him, she felt like she could do anything.

Their pizza came, and she practically fell onto it, inhaling the best-tasting loaded pie she'd ever had.

Levi was working on his own big slice. "Only yesterday, I'd have said heaven on earth."

"What changed since yesterday?"

"I have a new favorite taste," he said.

She blushed. "Are you always such a flirt?"

"No."

"So why me?"

He smiled. "Because when I'm with you, I feel like . . . me."

Everything inside her softened at that. Because the truth was, she felt the exact same way, which meant he was dangerous to her heart and soul. She decided to concentrate on eating.

He told her about his day, how he was balancing his own work with helping out his parents with the store's accounting, making her laugh with the antics of Jasper, the goldendoodle.

She was halfway through the last slice when she caught him smiling at her and realized that his smile was missing its usual wattage. "I'm sorry I accused you of leaving me the ornament," she said on a wince. "Not my finest moment."

"I understand."

She met his gaze. "I feel like something's bothering you."

He blew out a breath. "I came to Tahoe because my mom hinted that she needed my help with something. The store's accountant was my sister's husband. When he left her, he took all their money and vanished. My dad was worried that he'd gotten creative with the store accounting as well."

"Did he?"

He pushed his plate away. "He helped himself to the kitty."

"Oh no." Her heart sank for him. For his family. "Did you get the police involved?"

"Not yet. I'm not quite finished with the internal audit, but it's bad. And my family is going to be shattered when they find out."

"I'm so sorry," she said. "That's a heavy burden to carry alone."

"I don't feel alone at the moment."

It felt as natural as breathing to slide out of her side of the booth and into his to wrap her arms around his strong shoulders and hug him. And when he buried his face in her hair and held on tight, something squeezed deep inside her chest in the very best of ways.

"How do you tell family that *family* screwed you over?"

Jane let out a small mirthless huff of laughter. "I'd say this—just rip off the Band-Aid rather than skate around the truth."

The waitress came by and offered them dessert. They ordered a brownie and ice cream to share.

"You thinking of sticking around Tahoe?" she asked, digging into the brownie, dragging it through the ice cream.

He looked out the window. "I told myself I didn't miss it here. But lately, since I've been home, I feel an ache to be back."

She knew that ache. She just didn't know where her home was.

He took a long pull of his beer. "My mom's been demon-dialing me. They're getting antsy, wanting to know if you're coming to the anniversary dinner."

"Oh." She bit her lip. "I can't think of a good excuse not to."

He laughed.

"It's not funny! But I promised, so yes, I'm coming to dinner. I should bring something. Wine? Dessert?"

"Well, my mom's a great cook, but not a great baker."

"Okay," Jane said, hoping her panic wasn't showing. She was a crap baker. "I'll get a recipe from Charlotte."

"It's only fair that I help," he said on a smile.

"Are you looking for pretend date number three?"

"Yes. Just name the day and time and I'll be there."

She nodded, and he smiled. Then he leaned in and kissed her, his thumb gliding along her jaw. He tasted like hopes and dreams and brownies, and she was breathless when he pulled back.

"Was that pretend too?" he asked, voice low and husky.

She had to clear her throat to talk. "*Extremely* pretend."

His mouth twitched. "Whatever helps you sleep at night."

Charlotte pulled up her driveway at four in the afternoon. It was the first time she'd seen daylight in . . . well, she couldn't remember how long. She got out of her car, noticing that Mateo had at least ten cars in his driveway, with more lining the street.

What was going on?

She followed the sounds of wild laughter around the side of Mateo's house. The snow was deeper here, and her boots made a crunching sound as she moved. Just as she rounded the corner to the back, she realized all noise had stopped. And then . . . whoosh!

A snowball hit her right in the face, breaking apart on impact, its momentum taking her down in the snow.

"Oh my gosh! Did we kill her?"

Charlotte sat up and wiped the quickly melting snow from her eyes and mouth as a tall shadow dropped to its knees at her side.

"Charlotte?"

She didn't answer right away as she was spitting out some snow, so Mateo hauled her upright, and he stared down into her face, his own creased in deep concern. "Charlotte, say something."

She looked past his broad shadow to find a whole bunch of what looked like Morenos of all ages scattered in the yard, clearly in the midst of a killer snowball fight. "Who threw it?"

Every single person pointed to Mateo.

She swiveled her head and looked at him.

He grimaced. "You were tiptoeing in the back way. I thought you were my cousin Rafe. Did I hurt you?"

She bent under the guise of rubbing her ankle. "I think I sprained something. Do you have a first aid kit?"

"Of course." He turned toward the house.

"Mateo?"

He turned back just as she rose, patting the snow she'd just scooped up into a snowball as she did. Which she threw at him.

And nailed him. Also in the face. His family erupted in cheers.

She grinned and took a bow.

Mateo straightened—snow in his hair, dripping off his nose and sticking to the stubble on his jaw—and just looked at her.

"Mateo, can we keep her for our team?" someone called out.

"Charlotte," Mateo said, and swept an arm across his yard, "meet my wild and crazy cousins. Primos, meet Dr. Charlotte Dixon. And she's far too civilized to play with this lot."

"I'm not that civilized. And I want to play against you."

Cheers broke out on one side of the yard.

Mateo's face was lit with humor. "You should know, there's no rules. First one to call 'tío' gets a cease-fire and a loss."

She turned to her team. "Let's do this."

It was mayhem. Snowballs flew so hard and fast that it was a constant, unrelenting battle. Charlotte loved every second.

A snowball took her beanie right off her head. When she looked up, Mateo stood there with a mischievous unrepentant grin.

She threw a snowball and nailed him right between the eyes.

He wavered but didn't go down, so she launched herself at him, and then they were in free fall. Mateo landed flat on his back, cushioning her as she followed him down.

"Say it," she said, laughingly holding him down. "Say it."

His hands went to her hips, his mouth not saying a word.

"Say it, say it, say it," her team of Morenos began to chant.

Charlotte wiggled a bit, getting cold as the snow had slowly seeped into her clothing. Mateo's eyes went from amused to hot.

She stared down at him, time suddenly stopping as she gulped.

"Tío," he said huskily.

She cocked a hand around her ear. "I didn't catch that."

He rolled her to her back and dropped a kiss on her icy nose. "Our next round is a one-on-one," he said for her ears only, and then rose, hauling her to her feet.

After that comment, she felt her knees wobbling, so he held on to her for an extra second. "Yeah?" he asked.

She drew a deep breath. "Yeah."

LEVI was at his dad's desk, putting together a PowerPoint presentation to explain all the shocking accounting discrepancies to his family. He'd come up with a few possible solutions for the store, not to mention a list of the evidence needed to put Cal away.

Cal had gotten his hands on a lot of Cutler money, enough to put them under if the store didn't bring in a lot of money quickly.

And the high-revenue season—the holidays—was behind them. Knowing that, Levi planned to present the info in a way that they could stomach. Or so he hoped.

Making it worse, Cal had gone off the grid. With the right resources, Levi felt confident they'd be able to find him and haul his ass back to Tahoe to face his crimes. But one thing at a time.

The next morning, Levi asked everyone to meet at the kitchen table at eight a.m. sharp.

Levi's mom and dad showed up two minutes past the hour.

Tess came strolling in fifteen minutes later. "Sorry I'm late," she said. "I didn't want to come."

Levi didn't blame her. He didn't want to do this either. "Can everyone see my laptop screen?"

"Why couldn't we have done this in the study?" his dad asked.

"Or in the living room on the comfy couches," his mom said.

"You don't allow liquor on the couches," Levi said, handing out glasses of orange juice. Then he grabbed the vodka from the freezer, pouring a healthy shot into the OJ glasses.

His mom stared at him, looking worried. "It must be bad if my most well-behaved child is drinking so early."

"Excuse me," Tess said. "Most well-behaved child?"

"Focus," Levi said. He handed out folders with the evidence of

Cal's creative accounting, along with Levi's plan on how to steer the damaged ship without going under.

"What is this?" his mom asked, flipping through the pages.

"It's an accounting of where the store stands financially. You're looking at the balance sheets for the different departments."

"Why does it look so much worse than last year?" his dad asked.

"Because it *is* worse than last year," Levi said. "Large orders were placed for store inventory. The money left your account to pay for those orders, but we never received the inventory."

"Well, that doesn't make any sense," Tess said. "Cal was in charge of all of that . . ." She gasped softly. "Oh my God."

His dad ran a hand down his face, then slugged his OJ down.

Tess looked like she wanted to throw up. "Are you telling me that the lying son of a bitch was stealing from Mom and Dad to fund his new life with his girlfriend on some island in Bali?"

He nodded grimly. "It looks like he was creating invoices for fictitious accounts to funnel the money to himself."

"Fictitious accounts?" his mom asked.

"Yeah, there are a bunch. One of them is called Buffy Slater."

His mom drank her glass down.

"What?" his sister shrieked, and leapt to her feet. "Buffy Slater is the babysitter's name! We need to call the police!"

"Yes," Levi said, pouring her another drink.

Peyton stuck her head in the kitchen. She was in Wonder Woman pj's, hair looking like an explosion in a mattress factory. "Hi! I wanna have a drink too!"

His sister drew in a steadying breath. "Not now, baby."

Levi went to the pantry and came out with a box of apple juice.

Peyton beamed her thanks. "Will you come to my tea party?"

He ruffled her hair. "I'll see you in a few minutes," he said.

"Okay, but don't forget to dress up as a girl superhero! Only girl superheroes can come into my room."

He grimaced, but his sister pointed at the screen. "How long?" she whispered. "How long has this been going on?"

Levi really didn't want to tell her. He gave Peyton a kiss on the forehead and gently nudged her out of the kitchen. "Two years."

His mom grabbed the vodka bottle and refilled everyone's glass. Minus the juice.

His dad jabbed a finger at the laptop. "You could've just called me into the office and had a meeting. Man-to-man."

Levi's mom whipped around to stare at him. "Why? So you could hide the fact that our company's going under? And then you'd shoulder all that responsibility and keep it from us?"

"This is all my fault," Tess moaned.

"Nonsense." His dad's fist hit the table. "*I'm* the one who gave that SOB a job. Instead, I should've kicked his ass."

Levi stood up. "Everyone just take a deep breath and look at the PowerPoint," he said calmly. He clicked to the next slide. "Here you'll see I've created a five-step plan to get the store out of debt."

Dad stood up. "No offense, son, but I'm not going to get my store back on its feet by watching a slide show from a tech guy."

"Dad, you *know* he's more than a tech guy," Tess said. "He consults with businesses on how to manage their data, and—"

Their dad shook his head. "This isn't about data either."

"Hank, stop," his mom snapped. "Levi's just trying to help."

"You're right." His dad looked Levi in the eyes with remorse. "We appreciate what you've done. I just need a minute." He took another shot and walked out.

Levi let out a breath. *This isn't about you,* he reminded himself.

His mom patted him on the arm. "He loves you very much. We're grateful for your help, but I better go check on him. When he gets worked up like this, it's bad for his blood pressure."

When they were alone, Levi turned to his sister. "Dad has blood pressure problems?"

"Dad's got a lot of problems." She got up and left, too, and a moment later he heard the shower go on in her bathroom.

Levi looked at his PowerPoint, which for the record still had ten pages left to go on the plan to fix the most immediate problems.

Square peg, round hole.

He eyed the vodka. Tempting. But he had a woman waiting.

Peyton beamed her welcome when he appeared in her doorway, and Levi felt a slight warming in the region of his cold heart. "I don't have a superhero costume. May I still come in?"

"Yes! And here, I'll help you." She pulled off her sash and wrapped it around his head like a bandanna. "Sit!" she commanded.

So he sat at her tiny little table and drank her pretend tea and ate her pretend cookies, and they plotted how Wonder Woman might save the world if she was real.

Chapter 8

JUST AFTER NIGHTFALL, Levi was on a Zoom call with clients when his cell phone buzzed with an incoming text from Jane:

I'm stuck and could use some help.

He immediately got out of his meeting and called her. "Jane."

"Yep."

She sounded not at all like herself. "Where are you?" he asked.

"I'll text you the address."

His gut clenched. "Are you safe?"

But she'd disconnected.

He recognized the street name she'd given him, up the hill just outside of Sunset Cove, so he headed out. A handful of turns and five minutes later, he saw Jane's car. Dark. No lights. He parked behind her and got out, realizing she was sitting behind the wheel. He slid into her front passenger seat. "Why wasn't this locked?"

She let out a mirthless laugh and stared up at the roof of her car. "There's not a lot of people who would ask me that."

"Then I'll make sure to keep asking." He reached out and let his fingertips brush the nape of her neck. "Are you okay?"

Instead of answering, she closed her eyes. "I'm short on brave tonight. You got any to spare?"

"You can have any of me you want. You said you were stuck?"

"I think my battery's dead."

"That's easy enough." He looked around. "Where are we?"

"Up that steep driveway is my grandpa's cabin."

With that, he finally understood. She was going to go talk to her grandpa for the first time in twenty years. "You've got this, Jane."

That got him a ragged but real laugh. "How do you always know the right thing to say?"

Now *he* laughed, thinking of his family and how they might disagree. "I never know the right thing to say."

She turned her head, met his gaze, and gave him a small smile. "You just get lucky?"

Her smile turned his heart upside down. "Once in a blue moon."

JANE drew a deep breath at the way Levi was looking at her. Like she meant something to him. She'd texted him, and he'd shown up, no questions asked. "Thank you," she said softly.

"Happy to help."

She felt some of the tension drain from her. "Thanks for always knowing what to say to brighten my day."

He smiled. "But it's night."

"You know what I mean."

His smile faded. "I do. And you do the same for me." He pulled off his ski cap and unzipped his jacket, even though the interior of her car was cold. She'd turned it off half an hour ago to save gas.

Then he put the ski cap on her head, wrapped her up in his jacket, and zipped it up, letting his fingers brush her jaw. "Better?"

With that single word, she knew somehow it was going to be okay. "Yes. I need to go talk to my grandpa about the ornament."

He nodded, clearly not wanting to influence her on this.

They looked up the driveway to the small old cabin at the top. A light flickered in the kitchen, her favorite kitchen in the whole wide world. The place had always seemed warm, and there'd been copious amounts of hot chocolate made with love. "I've been avoiding this a long time," she murmured.

"I know. Just a reminder, you didn't do anything wrong. No one in their right mind would blame an eight-year-old who was at the mercy of her relatives after her parents walked away from her."

She closed her eyes, then felt Levi's hand slip into hers.

"Come here, Jane."

She leaned in closer, and he hauled her up and over the console.

"What—"

He wrapped his arms around her and cuddled her into him.

She heard herself purr and pressed her face to his throat.

He dipped his head so he could meet her gaze.

"What do you want to do?" he asked.

"I *want* to run away," she admitted. "But I *need* to go talk to him."

"I'll go with you if you want."

The offer surprised and warmed her from tip to toe. "Just knowing you would helps. But I think I've got to do this alone."

"I'll wait. As long as you need."

She let out a breath, not taking that promise lightly. "Thanks," she whispered. She reached for the door handle, then hesitated.

"Quick like a Band-Aid," he said. "You've got this, Jane."

She eyed the little cabin. "You sure?"

"Hey, you survived a near-fatal fall from a gondola. You regularly put yourself in war zones to save people's lives. Trust me, you can handle this. Either way, I'll be waiting right here."

She got out of the car, walked up to the front door, and knocked.

She wasn't sure what she planned to say, and the door opened far too soon, because suddenly her grandpa was standing there. He gasped, put a hand to his chest, and whispered, "Sugar Plum?"

Butterflies took flight in her belly. "Hi, Grandpa."

His smile was trembling, and there was a suspicious shininess to his eyes now as he reached for her hand. "You're actually here."

"Is that okay?"

At her question, a shadow passed over his face. "Yes. More than anything. I'm sorry if you doubted it for even a second."

"There were more than a few seconds," she said, not willing to let herself be moved by his obvious emotions at seeing her.

"I deserve that," he said quietly. "Can . . . can I hug you, Jane?"

The eight-year-old in her spoke before the grown-up in her could, whispering yes.

He pulled her into his arms and pressed his cheek to hers. "Thank you," he said, holding on tight. "You're so much braver than I've ever been."

Leaving that statement alone for now, she pulled back. "Did you get it?" She pulled the ornament from her pocket.

"You carry it with you." He looked unbearably touched by that. "Come in, come in, before you catch your death!"

She followed him past the front room she remembered so vividly. She'd bounced on that very couch, huddled up to the woodstove after playing in the snow. "It's the same," she whispered.

He shrugged. "I like the same." He brought her into the kitchen. "Let me make us something warm to drink. Sit."

She sat at the same scarred wood table where she'd memorized her multiplication tables and learned how to write in cursive.

Her grandpa brought her hot cocoa with marshmallows and whipped cream. "My favorite."

"I know." He hesitated. "I bought it the day I saw you watching me in the coffee shop. I was stunned to see you, and . . ." His eyes went misty. "You were wearing your grandma's necklace." He gave her a smile. "I knew it was you, even after all these years."

"I saw you too."

"I knew after what I'd done that I had to give you the time you deserved to decide if you wanted to see me."

Her throat felt tight. It'd been two years since she'd found him in Sunrise Cove, and she'd hesitated to make contact. But he'd seen her what, a week ago, and hadn't hesitated. "What you did?"

He looked away as if ashamed. "I let you go, Jane." He met her eyes again. "I've never forgiven myself for that. I have a lot to make up for, but I want a second chance with you. I started with the ornament. It was a way to approach you without your feeling forced into something you weren't ready for."

She searched for the right words. "I'm glad you made contact," she said carefully. "I figured that if you'd wanted to see me after all that had happened, you'd get in touch."

"After all that happened?"

"You know, when you and Aunt Viv fought over me and it destroyed your relationship. She told me about it back then, how keeping me would have been too hard on you."

He looked stricken. "She shouldn't have told you that. The truth is, Viv and I *always* fought. That wasn't your fault, Jane."

"It felt like it."

"I'm sorry for that. Please believe me." He drew a shaky breath. "Do you remember what I used to tell you?"

"That Santa Claus was real? Which, by the way . . ."

That got her a small smile. "I meant when I once told you that family is blood. I was wrong. Family, real family, is who you pick. Your aunt Viv and your mom . . . they are who they are. I'm angry that Viv made you feel like you were a burden. But mostly I'm angry with myself that I didn't come to you years ago. You are the family that I'm choosing, Jane. If you'll have me."

Jane lost the battle with her tears, as did her grandpa. They moved toward each other and held on tight for a long moment.

"Are you okay?" he asked quietly. "And the answer doesn't have to be yes."

"That's good, because I'm not sure how I am." She sniffed and gave a slow shake of her head. "I'm sorry."

"Don't be." He looked out the window. "Do you want to talk about that handsome young fellow waiting out in the cold?"

Nope. Definitely not. She shook her head.

"Sugar Plum." He removed his fogged-up glasses to wipe them on his sweater. "It's twenty-two degrees outside."

And she was wearing his jacket and hat . . . "I can't stay."

He nodded. "Maybe next time, then, you'll let him come in."

Was there going to be a next time? "Maybe."

He smiled, still looking emotional. And tired. "When?"

"Maybe we could have dinner one night after work."

"You just tell me when and where, and I'll be there," he said.

She nodded and then put her contact info into his phone, which made him beam so happily it gave her a hard pang. "I'm going to go before *Family Feud* comes on, which you used to always watch after your stretching routine. You still do that, right?"

"Yes. It's a requirement now, ever since . . ." He broke off.

"Since your heart attack?"

Her grandpa winced guiltily. "You know about that?"

"Yes. Your cronies are all on Facebook. They posted pics visiting you in the hospital."

Her grandpa looked pained. "I need to call Facebook and have them delete all the pictures and burn the negatives."

"Yeah, that's not how it actually works—" She wasn't ready to let him off the hook. "I assume you're eating well?"

"I'm fine," he said, waving that off. "It's my damn TV that isn't. My friend Doug's grandson convinced me to upgrade my system. But I can't figure out how to do anything. I'm stuck on some sappy movie channel. I mean, I couldn't get stuck on, say, ESPN?"

Jane walked to the living room and looked his system over. "It's voice activated. We could set it up so you can talk to your remote."

"Talk to my remote?" He shook his head like she'd just said he could visit Mars.

She concentrated on setting up his system and . . . failed. "Okay, I'm going to have to call in tech support," she finally admitted.

"It's a little late . . ."

"Oh, don't you worry, this tech support's open twenty-four seven." She pulled out her phone and called Levi.

He answered with "You okay?"

Her heart swelled against her rib cage. "I am. I'm actually calling for tech support. You available?"

"Always."

She disconnected. "He'll be right here."

The doorbell rang, and her grandpa's brows went up, but he headed to the door. "Are you her fellow?" he asked Levi.

Levi looked past him to Jane, and she felt him taking visual inventory. She knew he could see the trace of tears.

"Right now I'm tech support," he said to her grandpa.

"And later?"

"Whatever she needs me to be."

Jane felt her heart warm for Levi in a whole new way as her grandpa let Levi in.

Levi kept his gaze on Jane, wanting a sign that she was okay. She looked emotional, but more relaxed than she'd been in the car.

"Grandpa," she said, "this is Levi Cutler. Levi, this is my grandpa, Lloyd Parks."

Her grandpa was the same height as Jane, and round and solid as a tree trunk. He had a wild mane of white hair that seemed to defy gravity and a beard that ensured he could pass for Santa. "Nice to meet you, Mr. Parks," he said, and shook the man's hand.

"Call me Lloyd," her grandpa said. "In fact, if you can fix my TV, you can call me whatever you want."

"I'll do my best." Levi put a hand on Jane's shoulder, running it lightly down her arm to squeeze her fingers.

She smiled and squeezed back, then brought him over to the TV and handed him the remote. "Hope this is in your realm of expertise." Then she turned to her grandpa. "Did you have dinner?"

"Yes, and the hot cocoa was excellent."

"Grandpa, when someone has a heart attack, that someone should change his entire way of living, including how he eats."

Her grandpa smiled. "You've got your grandma's bossiness."

She pointed at him. "Don't try to distract me with sentiment. Did you really not eat yet?"

"I had some cookies."

"Grandpa."

"Kuchi zamishi," Levi said.

Lloyd laughed in delight and pointed at him. "Exactly!"

Jane looked at Levi, clearly waiting for the translation.

"*Kuchi zamishi* is a Japanese saying. It's the act of eating because your mouth is lonely," Levi said.

"Hence the cookies," Lloyd explained to Jane.

She narrowed her eyes. "You eat bad because you're lonely?"

"Maybe?"

"You're going to start taking better care of yourself so that when I come back, you can tell me about it."

"I will." He dropped himself into the recliner and looked at Levi with a wry smile. "My sweet, mild-mannered granddaughter."

"She's a lot of things," Levi agreed. He smiled at Jane. "I'm not sure mild-mannered is one of them."

She rolled her eyes.

"I know," Lloyd said proudly. "She's amazing, isn't she?"

Jane went into the kitchen. A moment later they heard her mutter, "Oh my gosh. You're using real butter, cream cheese, and whipped cream? *Seriously?*"

Lloyd cackled, clearly enjoying himself.

As for Levi, he was enjoying watching Jane handle her grandpa. Not giving away her heart, but being far more caring than he'd imagined she'd be. It was clear her grandpa loved it. And her.

He turned back to his task. The TV.

"So . . ." Lloyd said as he worked. "You and Jane seem close."

"Hmm," he said noncommittally. He held out the remote. "Okay, I think we've got it. Let me show you how to use this. I'll also write down the password for you."

"You think I'm old enough to forget things?"

Levi slid him a look. "I don't think age has anything to do with . . . *forgetting* things." Or people . . .

Lloyd held his gaze, then nodded grimly. "Yeah. But I intend to work on that."

"Good."

The old man sighed. "I'm glad you don't want to kick my ass."

"Not my place," Levi said, but didn't offer any empty platitudes about it being okay. Because it wasn't. Not in his book.

Lloyd gave a gruff nod. "Not letting me off the hook. I deserve that. She got passed around more than an offering basket in church. I don't deserve her, but I intend to try and make up for whatever I can for as long as she'll let me."

As frustrating as Levi's own family could be, he knew they'd never treat him like he wasn't welcome. "I hope that's true."

"It is. She deserved more, and I'm hoping it's not too late."

"If you two are finished gossiping, dinner's on the table."

The two turned and found Jane standing there, arms crossed.

Lloyd looked like a kid caught with his hand in the candy jar. "We were just—"

"I know." Jane met his gaze. "I found frozen chicken bowls in your freezer. There's veggies in them, so let's eat."

The old man got a little misty-eyed. "You made dinner."

"Well, 'made' is a bit strong. More like pushed a few buttons. Last one to the table has to clean up."

Her grandpa rushed to follow her into the kitchen. Levi followed more slowly, watching Jane. Something about her was different tonight. She seemed . . . just a little more open.

And right then and there, he vowed to see that look on her face as often as possible. He didn't want to be just another person in a long line of people who'd hurt her, but truth was truth.

She was leaving at the end of the season. And when, not if, he changed his home base back to Tahoe, he knew she wouldn't do the same. She already had a contract for her next job.

They had an expiration date, him and Jane.

And playing pretend wasn't going to change that or keep them from getting hurt. Nothing was. Unless he somehow changed her mind about him being a keeper.

Jane watched Levi out of her peripheral vision as he drove her home. He'd tried giving her battery a jump, but no go.

Tonight had gone better than she could have imagined. She honestly hadn't been sure she could face her grandpa. But then Levi had shown up and soothed a place deep inside her where she kept her vulnerability and fear hidden from the rest of the world.

And she'd faced her past.

"Thanks for tonight," she said quietly.

Without taking his eyes off the road, he reached for her hand, bringing it up to his mouth to brush a kiss to her palm. "After that night on the gondola, I'd probably do anything for you, Jane."

Her heart kicked into gear. She took in his profile by the ambient light of the dashboard. He had a few days' scruff on him that she loved, wavy hair that never quite behaved.

"See something you like?" he teased, and nipped at the palm he still had hold of.

Her insides quivered. "Yes."

"Good, because I can hardly take my eyes off you."

Something deep inside her shifted and clicked into place. Suddenly she felt anchored. "Levi?"

He glanced over at her.

"I'm not ready to go home," she said softly.

"Where should we go?"

We. She closed her eyes a beat. "Anywhere quiet."

He turned on the next road, and suddenly they were going up a hill. And up. Fifteen minutes later, they'd left all signs of Sunrise Cove behind. She could see nothing past the dark outline of trees.

Finally he took a hairpin curve and stopped the truck.

She took in the view and gasped.

A half-moon hung in the sky, streaked with fingerlike clouds surrounded by shimmering stars. Far below lay the dark outline of Lake Tahoe. "It's like we're on top of the world," she whispered.

"We are. We're up on the Tahoe Rim Trail. At ninety-five hundred feet."

She turned to find him watching her. Thoughts hidden. She sensed a careful restraint, a rare hesitation.

She felt neither of those things.

With a nervous laugh, she pulled out her phone. "So . . . I found another questionnaire. It's called Ten Questions to Ask Before Having Sex."

He stared at her for a beat, then let out a smile. "Hit me."

Nodding, suddenly nervous, she looked down at the first question. "Um . . . where's your favorite place to be kissed?"

He pointed to his lips.

Heart pounding, she unbuckled her seat belt, came up on her knees, and leaned over him. She started with a light closed-mouth kiss to one corner of his mouth, her plan to move slowly.

"Jane—"

"Hmm?" She bypassed his mouth for the second kiss because his jaw called to her, and then his sexy throat.

"Jane . . . I didn't bring you up here for this."

"I know, but are you going to turn down your pretend girlfriend?"

His rough laugh made her grin, and then he caught her mouth in a kiss that was soft and sweet.

He hauled her over the console and into his lap. Time passed as he slowly swept his hands up and down her back and into her hair. At one point, he started to say something and then stopped.

"What?" she whispered.

"I actually don't have words."

He wrapped his arms around her, nuzzling at her neck. And with it was the unspoken agreement that this, whatever *this* was, would continue to their mutual pleasure for as long as it worked.

Or for as long as they were both in Tahoe.

Because as she reminded everyone, she was going to be gone soon. There would be no future. She'd made him promise her that. And hell if it wasn't both a huge relief and her greatest regret.

Chapter 9

The next morning, Jane jerked awake at the rude sound of her alarm. She and Levi had stayed up on the Tahoe Rim Trail until two thirty in the morning. Which had been three short hours ago.

She staggered into the shower. Ten minutes later, she was back in her room, hunting for clothes, when Levi called.

"Just wanted to make sure you're okay."

The sound of his low, sleep-roughened voice had her smiling like an idiot. "I think you know that I am."

He gave a soft laugh. Then he asked quietly, "Any regrets?"

"No," she said, and meant it.

"Good. Your car's out front. I charged your battery."

"Wait— You did? But . . . you must have gotten up hours ago."

"Did it after I drove you home. Mateo gave me a ride out there."

That he and Mateo had skipped out on sleep to do such a thing for her boggled her mind. But maybe it shouldn't. "Thank you."

"Anytime. Later, Jane."

"Later," she whispered, wondering why it sounded like a promise. She went down to the kitchen and straight to the coffee maker, staring at it until it produced twelve ounces of blessed caffeine.

As she slurped it as fast as she could, Charlotte stepped into the room. She took one look at Jane and said, "Whoa."

"What?"

"You're wearing a smile. In the a.m. hours. What's that about?"

Jane shrugged, pouring herself a bowl of cereal. When she looked up, Charlotte gave her a brow waggle.

Jane gave her a prim look. "What are you trying to say?"

Charlotte looked into her eyes. "I'm happy for you."

"It was just one night."

"It could turn into more if you let it."

For a single second, she allowed herself the luxury of wanting more. "You know I'm not built that way."

"Jane."

She grabbed her keys and turned back to her landlord, her roommate, and one of her favorite people on the planet. "I'm not."

"People change."

Jane pointed at her. "I will if you will."

"Hey," Charlotte said. Sighed. "And fair."

Jane headed to the door.

"What if being with Levi turned out to be the best thing in your life? You're just going to ignore it?" Charlotte asked.

"Uh-huh. Pot, I'd like you to meet Kettle."

"*I'm* not running," Charlotte said. "*I'm* staying put."

"Physically, sure. But you're holding back with Mateo because you're afraid your past will keep you from leading a full life. That makes you a walking, talking self-fulfilling prophecy."

"So you're saying I'm being a hypocrite."

Jane held up her hand with her first finger and thumb half an inch apart.

Charlotte sat back, looking thoughtful. "Damn. You're right."

Jane laughed. "Duh."

"But we're also both wrong. We're holding back with our hearts on two men who deserve the best of us. But . . ." She bit her lip.

Jane drew a deep breath. "We need to move on from our pasts."

"I will if you will," Charlotte said.

Jane had to admit, it was tempting. On a rough laugh, she left for work. But the smile stuck all day long.

Levi awoke to someone poking his cheek. When he didn't open his eyes right away, little fingers pried one open for him.

Peyton's face was two inches from his, her faithful minion Jasper right behind. "You're awake!" she said. "Tonight's Grandma and Grandpa's anniversary dinner! We finally get to meet Jane!"

"Yes," he said sleepily. He hadn't gotten much sleep the last couple of weeks. The night up on the Tahoe Rim Trail with Jane had started it, but he'd forgo sleep every night just to be with her.

Just last night, he'd met her at her grandpa's house, where they'd made bread with one of Jane's grandma's old recipes.

"Betty's recipe never fails," Lloyd had said proudly as they'd all stuffed themselves with one of the two loaves they'd made.

"Good enough to take to your mom's tomorrow night for their anniversary dinner?" Jane had asked, nerves evident.

"Everyone's going to love it, and you," Levi had promised.

"What's not to love about a big family dinner?" Lloyd said. "I don't remember much, but I know how much I miss those."

Jane had paused. Looked at Levi, who had nodded, then drew a breath. "You can go with me, if you'd like."

Lloyd smiled. "Really?" he'd asked softly, hopefully.

"Really," Jane had whispered back.

Now Levi looked into Peyton's eyes. "I'm going to be an astronaut," she said apropos of nothing. "I'm going to be the first human to land on Jupiter."

"Sounds good," Levi said. "But you can't actually land on Jupiter. It's made of gas and has no solid surface."

She nodded sagely. "Grandma says I'm going to be as smart as you. Which means I'll find a way to land on Jupiter."

"If anyone can do it, you can," he said.

"Peyton!" Tess yelled from down the hallway. "Are you bothering Uncle Levi again?"

"Nope!"

There came a snort from the desk. His dad.

"I really love my community bedroom," Levi said, just as it occurred to him that after tonight's dinner, he was pretty much free to leave. He was healed from his concussion. He'd found the source of the money leak, and they had a lawyer involved now. It was only a matter of time before Cal had to face what he'd done.

But he knew he wasn't going back to San Francisco. At least not permanently. There was land for sale up on the Tahoe Rim Trail.

It was a great investment, but that's not why he wanted it. He wanted to build a house that he could someday raise his kids in.

Not that he was ready to share that yet. Hell, he'd barely come to terms with the idea himself.

"Do you know what your mother is doing?" his dad asked.

"Not my turn to watch her."

"Smart-ass. She's rearranging furniture for tonight's anniversary dinner. She's so excited, and is it because she and I are celebrating the big four-oh? No. It's because we'll finally get to meet Jane."

Levi rose to his feet. "Don't you mean she'll meet her for the *second* time? Yeah," he said at the flicker of guilt behind his dad's eyes. "I know Mom coaxed her into the Humane Society with a fake email."

"Not fake," his mom said, coming into the room. "It was a real email. She got her adorable rescue cat treated at a discount."

Levi shook his head at her. "You met her under false pretenses."

Tess appeared in the doorway, and Levi gave her a hard look as well. "None of you told Jane the truth about who you are. What do you think is going to happen when she shows up later and finds her new friends here? How is she supposed to feel about you guys and the deception you pulled off? Or *me*, for that matter, since I didn't blow the whistle on any of you."

His mom's expression was pure guilt, but she lifted her chin. "Maybe she's going to think you're so well loved that we wanted to make sure she was good enough for you after Amy."

Tess nodded in unison.

Levi shook his head. "I'm going to shower. You might want to work on what to say to her when she arrives. I have my own groveling to do." Because he'd made his own mistakes with Jane, and at some point he was going to pay a high price for those mistakes.

An hour later, he was in the back booth at the Stovetop Diner.

He liked the owner, one of Mateo's cousins. He liked the way everyone left him to his own devices. Mostly, that is. Because just then Mateo slid onto the seat across from him.

At least he was bearing gifts in the way of two plates loaded with bacon, eggs, and pancakes. He slid one to Levi and then waited for him to take his first bite before saying, "Heard you put a bid in for that property up in Hidden Falls."

Levi choked on that bite. "How do you know about the bid I put on those fifteen acres less than an hour ago?"

"Ah, man, you know how it is. It's Sunrise Cove. You can leave your car unlocked, but there's no such thing as privacy."

Levi just looked at him.

"Okay, fine. The real estate agent you're using is my cousin's sister-in-law's mom. And yeah, I know, I've got a lot of cousins."

Jeez. Why did he want to move back here again? *Because even though they drive you crazy, you miss your family.* "Just tell me my mom and dad don't already know."

"They don't know. *Yet.*"

Levi groaned. "If my mom finds out before I tell her, she'll tell everyone I'm going to build a house with a white picket fence and fill it with a wife named Jane and two point five kids."

Mateo laughed. "Come on, no one will believe that."

Right. Because he'd never really made any commitment to anyone. He looked away, out the window. It was snowing again.

"Something's wrong," Mateo said.

"Nothing's wrong."

Mateo shook his head. "Calling bull, man. Is it Jane? She falling for you?"

"You know she's just doing me a favor." Which, for the record, he hated. He never should have started this ridiculous farce.

Mateo studied him for a beat. "It's you. *You're* falling for *her.*"

Levi closed his eyes. "Yeah," he admitted. "I'm screwed."

Mateo shrugged. "You could just tell her."

"She has a contract lined up in Haiti, had it before she even stepped foot into Sunrise Cove. I haven't wanted to scare her off."

Mateo looked at him for a beat. "I think you're complicating this on purpose so it doesn't happen. I think you're scared."

Levi sighed and pushed his plate away.

"You won't hurt her, Levi."

He met Mateo's gaze. "How do you know?"

"When we were kids," Mateo said, "you worked hard at making the people around you happy. Your family. Amy. Often to the sacrifice of your own happiness. But in the years since, you've settled into who you are. You know what you want, what makes you happy. There's nothing wrong with that."

Levi took that in. Realized Mateo was right. He did know what he wanted. "I'm still not convinced it's that easy."

"Why not? All that's left for you to do is to make your move."

"Why don't you follow your own advice with Charlotte?"

"Because I'm like you—I'm in love and terrified to admit it."

LEVI thought about Mateo's parting words for the rest of the day. He worked, then went for a run, showered, and shortly before Jane was due to arrive, headed downstairs, feeling . . . nervous.

Wondering what that was about, he walked into the living room and looked out the picture window. Jane's car wasn't there.

He turned to face the room and found his entire family standing there staring at him.

His mom clasped her hands together. "Levi, I've got everything prepped for dinner and the house cleaned. Does it look okay?"

"The house is always clean, Mom. It looks great. And I thought you were going to order food in so you didn't have to cook."

"I wanted homemade food for Jane. I want her to love us."

"She will, Mom."

The doorbell rang, and everyone jumped. Jasper barked a piercing warning to the entire planet that there was a possible intruder.

Levi got out in front of the whole pack and faced them, hands up. "All of you, try to look normal."

"Honestly, Levi," his mom said, "we know how to behave."

"Do you?"

"It's his *girlfriend,*" Tess said, putting an odd emphasis on the word *girlfriend* that made Levi grimace on the inside. "He's got the right to want everything to go perfectly. Isn't that right, Levi?"

He pointed at her, then the rest of them. "All of you, zip it." He touched his finger to Peyton's nose. "Except you. Never you."

She beamed her toothless grin at him.

To everyone else he said, "Not a single one of you is going to say another word. There's no way I'm letting her walk in here without first telling her about the con you all pulled."

He opened the door to Jane and her grandpa. Jasper squeezed by and immediately put his nose to Lloyd's crotch.

"Whoa," Lloyd said.

"Sorry." Levi pulled the dog away. "Jasper, sit."

Jasper sat, panting happily, smiling from ear to ear.

"Jasper, huh?" Lloyd patted him on the head. "What a big boy you are. Nice name too."

"He also goes by 'don't you dare,' 'no!' and 'stop!'" Levi said. He looked at Jane, trying to figure out how to do this. Like a Band-Aid, Jane would say.

Her smile was a little short of its usual wattage. Levi stepped over the threshold, pulling the door shut behind him. "You okay?"

"Nervous." She sat on the porch step like her legs were wobbly.

"Me too," Lloyd said at a decibel that suggested he might have forgotten to turn on his hearing aids. "But not for the same reason as Jane. I'm nervous because I had bologna and cheese for lunch, and bologna gives me the toots."

"Don't worry, Jasper will have you beat," Levi said, and crouched before Jane. "Don't be nervous. Trust me, they're going to be nicer to you than they are to me."

She studied him a moment. "You seem off too. What is it?"

How did she always know what was going on with him beneath the surface? It made him feel vulnerable like nothing else ever had.

"Tell me quick before I have a heart attack," she said.

Levi really hated that he had to do this. "There're a few things you need to know before we go inside."

"Maybe I should give you two a moment," Lloyd said. He gestured to the front door and then opened it and vanished inside.

"Ohmigosh," Jane said. "Should I go after him?"

"No." If anyone could handle Levi's family for a minute, it was Lloyd. He sat next to Jane, then turned her to face him. Their knees bumped, and he took comfort from the touch. He knew that in a minute she'd be mad at him. "I'm not sure where to start."

"Then I'll start," she said. "You regret asking me to do this. You regret that night at the Tahoe Rim Trail. And every night since."

"No. *No,*" he repeated softly, reaching for her hand. "That night at the Tahoe Rim Trail will go down in history as one of my favorite nights ever."

She drew a deep breath. "Then what is it? I can feel it."

"Remember that night on the gondola?"

"The one I still have nightmares about? No, not at all."

They'd circle back to the nightmares. "When I called my mom and told her I had someone in my life—"

"Because all she'd ever wanted was for you to have love in your life . . . Yeah, I get it, Levi. I've seen the Hallmark movies."

He scrubbed a hand over his face. "They started hounding me about meeting you and got impatient. My mom is Shirley, the nosy woman you met at the Humane Society. My sister is Tess, the nosy woman who forced you to be friends with her."

Jane's mouth fell open, and she just stared at him.

"Jane?" He slid closer, a hand on her leg. "Say something."

She slowly shook her head. "They did all that for me?"

"You mean stalked you? Yes, they did, and I'm sorry."

He had no idea what she would do next, but he was stunned to see her suddenly smile and whisper, "Wow."

"Jane," he said, completely undone. "You should be running for the hills, not looking like you won the lottery. You're not upset?"

"Are you kidding? No one's ever gone through that much trouble to find me before. But your mom and sister did."

He felt like an ass. Here he was, embarrassed by his nosy family, talking to a woman whose own family had tossed her out like yesterday's trash. Wrapping his arms around her, he brushed a kiss to her temple. "Are you really ready for this?"

"Yes. Because who knows what my grandpa is in there telling them." She smiled and squeezed his hand. "Let's do this."

When they walked inside, everyone was lined up looking sheepish, but to Levi's surprise, Jane smiled even bigger and walked right over to his mom, handing over the basket holding the loaf of bread she'd made. "Shirl, it's nice to see you again."

"Oh, honey." His mom yanked Jane in for a hug. "I'm sorry I didn't tell you who I was. I just needed to know that my son had found someone worthy, and then once I started talking to you, I realized that he'd managed to find someone even *better* than I could have ever imagined."

"Thanks for the vote of confidence, Mom," Levi said dryly.

Tess moved toward Jane next. "I'm sorry," she said sincerely. "I should've told you who I was. But you turned out to be so sweet and so funny that I wanted to be your friend for real."

"I get it." She hugged Tess. "Thank you."

His sister pulled back, looking grateful. "For what?"

"For being my first new friend in a long time."

"Hey," Levi said. "Standing right here."

Jane smiled at him, looking beautiful and *happy*.

"Okay, my *second* new friend," she corrected.

Levi smiled and introduced his dad.

"We're just thrilled you're finally here," Levi's dad said. "And that you brought your grandpa."

Lloyd was sitting on a recliner with Peyton. They were reading a book together, heads bent to the pages. He waved at Jane. "No one's ever asked me what my third favorite reptile is before."

"It's the T. rex!" Peyton said joyfully.

Jane moved over there to meet her, and after Levi did the introduction, Peyton immediately pointed at Jane's locket. "Pretty!"

Jane opened it, and from the moment Peyton caught sight of eight-year-old Jane dressed as a fairy princess, their bond was forged in unbreakable ties. Levi's heart warmed.

A timer went off in the kitchen, and his mom clapped. "To the dining room, everyone! Food's ready."

There was the usual mob movement. The Cutlers might be bad at communicating, but breaking bread together was their thing.

Hank started to give an anniversary toast, but Shirl shushed him. "Enough about us, Hank. I want to talk to Jane."

Jane took this all in good humor, even as everyone peppered her with questions. In fact, she gave as good as she got.

Okay, Levi thought, this wasn't so bad. His mom hadn't once asked him when he was going to produce a grandbaby.

"Pass the wine?" his mom asked him, then turned to Jane. "Do you plan to have any kids of your own?"

And there it was. "Mom."

"What, it's just a question," she said innocently.

Jane laughed at whatever look was on his face. Probably horror.

"Why are you laughing?" he asked her. "And seriously, why aren't you running for the hills?"

"Don't pay any attention to him," his mom said. She passed Jane's bread basket around, and just like that it was all gone.

"It's wonderful," his mom said. "It's not easy to bake at altitude." She smiled at Peyton, who was inhaling hers. "And I bet one day, your and Levi's kids will love baking with you."

"Can you die from an eye twitch?" Levi asked the room, pressing a finger to his eye. "You can, right?"

Jane put her hand on his thigh, like she was trying to comfort him, which gave his heart a pinch.

"I do see myself with kids," Jane said. "Someday."

Levi looked over at her in surprise.

She looked just as surprised at herself. "I mean . . . I'm pretty sure. I love other people's kids."

"You'd be an amazing mom," Levi told her quietly. "A kid would be lucky to have you."

She seemed unsure. "I don't have a lot of experience with family. Good experience anyway."

Jane's grandpa looked across the table at her, eyes soft. "Yet you're one of the most warm, caring women I've ever met."

Levi's mom smiled. "Whoever wins you over as the mother of their children should count their blessings." She looked at Levi.

He'd tell her to behave, but she wasn't programmed to behave.

"I'm not sure what kind of a mother I'd be," Jane said. "But I'd love to be a part of a close-knit family like this one. Your son is the best man I've ever known. You all must be so proud of him."

"We are *very* proud," his mom said. "He's so smart. He always knows how to get rid of the gophers in the grass."

He had to laugh. What else could he do?

"I've missed this," Lloyd said. "My wife and I, we had it all, for a long time. I've been blessed, but I miss the family meals."

"How long were you married?" Levi's mom asked.

"Since the ice age." He smiled. "We kept things fresh by writing love notes. My favorite was one she'd left me after a fight. It said: *I considered smothering you with a pillow last night but didn't.*"

Everyone laughed, but no one harder than Levi's dad.

Levi's mom gave him a long, hard look.

He winked at her.

Then she smiled and turned to Jane. "You work so hard. I can't imagine all you go through on a daily basis. I always wanted to be a nurse, but I chickened out. Levi . . ." She looked at him like he was a puzzle she was missing a few pieces of. "I don't think it's healthy to sit at a computer all day."

"I ran five miles this morning."

"I'm just saying."

"You're just saying what?" he asked.

His dad pointed at him with his fork. "Don't sass your mom. She just means you spend a lot of time making big, fancy presentations when you could be doing something else."

"Do you mean the PowerPoint that I created to show you what Cal had done? Because—" He felt Jane's hand on his leg again.

"He was worried about how to tell you all," she said. "I think it's impressive that he was able to lay out the proof in case of prosecution and also to figure out a fix for you."

Everyone looked at Levi as if seeing him for the first time.

"We really are so incredibly happy he brought the woman he loves home to meet us," his mom said.

Levi choked on his last bite of bread and nearly died, but his know-it-all sister pounded him on the back and revived him.

Jane kissed him on the cheek. "Oh, and, Shirl," she said,

"you could totally be a nurse if you wanted. It's never too late."

His mom nudged her husband. "You hear that, Hank? I think I should. I'm going to go back to school to be a nurse!"

Levi's dad was staring at his mom. "If you get to go back to school, then I get to go buy that Camaro I've always wanted."

"Are the car and nursing school free?" Levi asked. "Because as you both now know, you're currently broke."

"But you're fixing it all," his mom said. "See? I read your whole PowerPoint *and* listened in at the meeting with the lawyer."

Levi looked at his steak knife and wondered if he could hit his own carotid artery in one try.

"And anyway," his mom went on, "we're at rock bottom, right? Things can't get worse than this, so why not dream big."

"I'm pregnant," Tess said. "Pass the peas?"

And then she burst into tears.

"Tess?" her mom asked, looking horrified.

"You can stop hounding Levi now," Tess wailed. "I've got your grandbaby number two."

Things deteriorated quickly after that. Levi nearly had to restrain his father from going after Cal to "tear him apart with his bare hands," only to be reminded by his mom that no one knew where Cal was.

His mom was surprisingly serene. Tess's surprise pregnancy gave her two grandbabies right here. Plus, she had Jane on backup.

After dessert, he walked Jane and her grandpa out to her car. Lloyd got in and shut the door, giving Levi and Jane some privacy.

"That was fun," Jane said.

"You have a very odd sense of fun."

Her soft, kissable lips were curved, and she was looking at him as if he were the sun and the moon. Unable to resist, he pulled her into him, cupped her face. "I want to kiss you."

"Please do."

He did, then pulled reluctantly back. "Jane, about tonight."

She smiled. "I think we pulled it off, don't you?"

He froze because that wasn't what he'd wanted to talk about. He wanted to ask if it'd been real for her, but he managed a smile. "Yes," he said, his voice soft. "We definitely pulled it off."

Chapter 10

Charlotte didn't do idle well, one reason she loved being a doctor. Personal time, aka too much thinking time, was rare.

But today she'd actually had the day off and, bored with herself, she'd made a Thanksgiving dinner. In the middle of winter. Sometimes a girl just needed a big, carb-loaded comfort meal.

There was no one home to share it with. Zoe and Mariella were at work. Jane was out, probably somewhere with Levi. There was no one else she'd want to spend time with.

That was a lie. Mateo had called her yesterday. His message had stated he was going to his mom's for dinner, and she was invited.

She was a big chicken.

She looked at the gorgeous meal in front of her, and her phone buzzed. The scheduled OR doc was going home sick, and she was up. With a sigh, she packed up the food and headed to the hospital.

Hours later, she was in a corner of the cafeteria taking a rare break. They'd been beyond busy. Four cars had piled up on roads that had become ice sheets. Two deaths. And then a duo of skiers had hit each other at over twenty miles an hour. Neither had survived.

Sometimes the chaos and trauma she saw hit her harder than others, and tonight was one of those times. Craving the comfort only her mom could supply, she reached for her phone.

"Hey, baby," her mom answered sleepily. "Are you okay?"

Horrified, she looked at the time. It was ten p.m. One a.m. for her parents. "I forgot how late it was for you. Go back to sleep."

"No, I'm so glad it's you." Her mom's voice was more alert now, and there was a soft rustling, as if she was sitting up in bed. "I was hoping to hear from you this week. Is anything wrong?"

"Mom." Charlotte closed her eyes and let her mom's voice

wash over her. "Oh, you know how it goes at work," she managed.

"I do." Her mom had been a nurse, and she'd seen her share of horror. "Remember what I told you to do when it's too much?"

Charlotte found a laugh. "Drink?"

"Find a partner. And jump their bones."

"Mom."

"I don't pretend to understand why you don't want someone in your life. But it's been years and lots of therapists, and—"

"I'm fine, I promise." She rubbed at the tension headache forming between her eyebrows. "Not here."

"Okay, baby. I hear you. How long a break do you have?"

"Maybe twenty minutes."

"You're going to eat, yes? You *need* to eat. Preferably protein."

"I cooked," Charlotte said. "I made turkey and stuffing and brought my leftovers." She opened her glass food container and had to admit, she'd done a damn good job. "I miss you, Mom."

"We miss you too. I wish you'd made it home for the holidays."

"Me too." Charlotte looked out at the sea of exhausted hospital employees around her. "But there are just so many staff members with young kids who wanted to be home with their families."

Charlotte was staring at the floor, trying not to lose it, when two sneakers came into view, topped by long legs covered in green scrubs. She knew those beat-up sneaks. She knew those long legs. "Mom," she said, closing her eyes, "I've gotta go, okay? I love you." She disconnected and pretended she didn't feel the weight of Mateo's gaze as he studied her. She lifted her face to his.

There was no doubt that he took in the ravages the night had brought because his eyes softened. "My mom doesn't understand why I can't always get the holidays off either," he said.

She looked at him for a long beat, quite positive that her reason for not going home was a whole lot different from his.

He looked at her right back. No smile, exhaustion in every line of his body. She knew his night had been as rough as hers. With a sigh, she gestured to the empty chair across the table from her.

He sat, but in the chair right next to her, then eyed her food. "I'll swap you half my dinner for half of yours."

She eyed the huge piece of cherry pie he set in front of him. "That looks more like dessert than dinner."

"It's a dessert sort of night. Straight from my mom's oven. Big family dinner you were invited to, only you didn't call me back."

"I'm sorry."

He chuckled, whether because he didn't believe her or because he appreciated the lie. "It's okay, family can be a lot."

"I need to work up to that."

He nodded. Easy acceptance. That's what she got from him.

He divided the piece of pie and slid the bigger half to her.

Taking the deal, she pushed her food toward him.

With a fork, he scooped up a bite of turkey, dragged it through the dollop of gravy, then scooped some cranberry sauce on top.

She stared at him in horror.

"What?" he asked.

"You mixed everything up!"

"And . . . we don't do that?"

"Absolutely not," she said. "The foods shall never touch."

He ate the bite and closed his eyes in bliss as he chewed. She watched as his entire body relaxed with each passing second.

Opening his eyes, he said, "I'm going to need you to marry me."

She laughed. "You're an idiot."

"Yeah, no doubt. But damn, you're an angel in the kitchen."

She tried and failed to keep the words from warming her from the inside out. "Do you have a lot of family dinners?"

"Yes. I get out of most of them thanks to work, which they pretend to understand. But they don't, not really."

Oh, how she got that, and she relaxed a bit too. Aided by the cherry pie, which really was fantastic.

"So." He fixed himself another bite. "You never go home?"

And . . . so much for relaxing. She shook her head.

"You're not close to your family?"

She took another bite of pie and gave him a vague shrug.

"We're close," she finally admitted, and met his warm, curious eyes. "But it's not that easy to get to Atlanta."

"They don't make planes that fly there several times a day?"

She snorted. "You know what I mean."

He nodded and didn't say anything, and damn if she didn't fill the silence for him like a rookie. "I don't like to go back there."

"Why?" Simple question, no judgment.

"Bad memories. I guess it's hard to remember the good memories over those bad and very loud memories, you know?"

Looking at her with those warm, dark eyes, he gave her a slow nod. He knew. He put his hand over hers.

"You don't have to talk about something you don't want to."

She swallowed hard and nodded.

"But in my experience," he went on quietly, "when the memories get loud, it's because they *need* to be heard."

Her heart skipped a beat. She played with her fork with suddenly clammy palms. Same symptom that assaulted her every time she thought about that night. "Something happened to me. A long time ago. And sometimes I let it affect me now."

"Time's a bitch, isn't it?" He got up, went to the front counter, bought two water bottles, and brought them back, sitting right next to her again. "Sometimes, long-ago memories can feel like just yesterday." He handed her one of the bottles. "Or right now."

She took a long drink. Stalling. But when she made herself look into Mateo's eyes, she saw compassion.

"It's a long, clichéd story about a small-town girl going off to college in the big city. She went out to celebrate her birthday, let herself get taken advantage of." She shook her head. "She was young and naive and stupid. So stupid."

"There's nothing wrong with young and naive, and I have a hard time believing you were ever stupid."

Her laugh held no humor. "He took me dancing. I got drunk."

"Not a crime."

"No, but it made me foolish," she said. "Because instead of calling my parents when I started feeling weird, I stayed."

"Weird?"

She looked away. "Yeah. Not drunk weird. Drugged weird."

"Someone put something in your drink," he said grimly.

"Yes." She knew she needed to say it all out loud and take away its power to hurt her. "I woke up the next morning alone in a strange bed, no clothes, not knowing what had happened."

Mateo sat quietly next to her, calm and steady, but there was a storm in his eyes. "How badly were you hurt?"

She shook her head. "Not badly."

"There are levels of hurt," he said carefully.

As she knew all too well. Charges hadn't been pressed because she'd never been able to ID anyone. "I'm fine. No long-lasting damages." She looked at him again, seeing a carefully banked fury for what she'd gone through. "Well, no lasting physical damages anyway," she admitted with an attempt at a smile.

He'd set his fork down. "And the *not*-physical damages?"

She shrugged. "I've had counseling. I don't hate men. I just . . . I don't like to talk about it, not with anyone."

"Not even Jane?"

"She knows."

"What about in your past relationships?"

She froze for a beat. "I don't do relationships," she finally said.

"Look, there are all kinds of relationships. Like us," he said quietly. "We're neighbors who fight over who plows the snow." He smiled. "It also might be the best relationship I've ever been in."

She was flustered. "But we've never—"

"There are all kinds of relationships," he repeated softly.

He just flashed another small smile and went back to eating.

He'd heard her deepest, darkest secret, and he wasn't scared off.

He was acting completely normal.

"Normal's good, right?" she accidentally said out loud.

He shrugged. "Personally, I think it's overrated." Very briefly, he let his thigh and biceps touch hers. It felt like the very best hug. "Thanks for trusting me," he said very softly.

She turned her head and met his gaze.

He fed her a bite of her own delicious stuffing. "Charlotte?"

"Yeah?"

"What do you need from me right now?"

"Um . . ." She eyed her half of his pie.

"Think bigger," he said.

She looked at his mouth, imagined it on hers, erasing all her nightmares . . . How did you tell the man you'd spent months and months secretly aching for that you wanted to do just as her mom had suggested: jump his bones? "Maybe a hug," she finally said.

He stood, and even though they were in the crowded cafeteria, he pulled her up into his arms. As they closed around her, she sighed out her tension and the memories became muted. For now, at least.

Mateo ducked a little to look into her eyes, a question in his own. *Okay?* he was asking.

"Yes." More than. "I want . . ." She wanted them to be off duty.

"Anything," he said.

She stared at his mouth.

A low groan rumbled up from his chest. "Especially that."

She nodded, then closed her eyes. "I'm sorry, I'm not trying to be a tease here, but . . . I really also like things the way they are."

"Never apologize to me for telling me what you want," he said. "We could tackle what else you might want on your schedule."

Just then they were both texted at the exact same time.

They looked at their phones.

"I have to go," they said in sync, and then laughed a little.

Charlotte gave him a smile and turned to walk off, but he caught her hand, waiting until she looked at him.

"Thanks for the best dinner in recent memory," he said.

"You hardly got to eat."

"It wasn't the food—which was off the charts, by the way." He went back to work. And so did she. But this time, she was smiling.

Two hours later, Charlotte was relieved by another on-call doctor, and she drove home on autopilot. It was just after midnight, and both driveways were cleared. That was no mystery, as Mateo's car was in his driveway.

And in the next moment, she was out of her car and knocking on his door before she could stop herself.

He answered in just sweat bottoms, slung low on his hips. No shirt. Bare feet. Bed-head hair. "You okay?" he asked.

She felt dizzy just looking at him, but she managed a nod.

He shoved his fingers through his hair as if trying to wake himself up. "Let me guess. You've got a problem with the driveway."

She shook her head and found her voice. "Thanks."

He rubbed a hand over his jaw. "Are you . . . hungry?"

"Yes." She took a deep breath. "But not for food."

She stepped across the threshold, kicked his door closed, and pushed him up against it. "Mateo?" she whispered. "You said anything, anytime. Did you mean it?"

"Yes." One of his hands came up to touch her jaw as he lowered his head and brushed a kiss to her temple. "Name it, Charlotte."

"You know what I want," she whispered.

He lifted his head. "Now?" His voice was low, giving her goose bumps over her entire body. The very best kind of goose bumps.

"Now," she said. "I'm sure. I'm surer of this than anything."

JANE pulled up to the cabin and smiled. "That was fun."

Hand on the car door handle, his face lit only by the ambient interior dashboard, her grandpa smiled back.

"Haven't been out past midnight in a long time. Levi's family was nice."

"Very," she agreed, realizing she was still smiling. They were nice. And funny. And irreverent. And . . . pretty great.

"Jane." Her grandpa waited until she looked at him. "You've changed everything for me. I hope you know that."

"What do you mean?"

"I love having you back in my life. I won't be careless with you ever again. I promise. I hope you'll agree to continue to see me."

"I'll be leaving soon, but we can stay in touch."

He gave a sad smile at the reminder she would be gone, and suddenly something seemed off. "Grandpa? You feeling okay?"

"Never better. I promise. Love you. To the moon and back."

Her eyes filled. Her grandma had whispered that to Jane every single night. "To the moon and back," she repeated.

He got out of her car. She watched him walk carefully up to his door, then pulled away and headed back to Charlotte's house.

The house was quiet when she let herself in. Yawning, she tiptoed down the hall and then stopped short in shock.

Charlotte was painting Jane's bedroom door. "Meant to finish this and get in bed before you saw it," she said with a grimace.

Jane shook her head. "It's two in the morning."

"And . . . ?" Charlotte asked.

Jane just looked at the big, curvy letters in blues and greens that spelled out her name. Mountains and trees were also sketched out.

"Paint's more permanent than Sharpie," Charlotte said. "Just to hammer home the point that this room is yours and only yours. And I printed up a billion-year rental agreement for you to sign."

Clearly, Charlotte had lost her noodles. "But—"

"You're not going to freak out, are you?"

"I'm trying," Jane said slowly. "But I think I'm too tired for a freak-out." She grabbed a paintbrush and started filling in a tree.

Charlotte stared at her. "You're *never* too tired to freak out when you think you're putting down roots by accident."

Jane just kept painting, concentrating very hard on the tree.

Charlotte gave a low laugh. "You must really love Levi."

Jane bit her lower lip. "Maybe. But if we talked about it, I'd be putting it out in the universe for karma to mess up somehow."

"Jane." Charlotte got to her feet. "You do realize you deserve to be loved just like any other girl."

Jane hugged Charlotte. "Yeah, and right back at you, babe." She stepped back and took a closer look at Charlotte and laughed. "You want to tell me about the love bite on your throat?"

Charlotte slapped a hand right to the spot. With her free hand, she jabbed her paintbrush in Jane's direction. "You know what? I'm pulling a Jane. We're not talking about it. Because that would be putting it out there into the universe for karma to mess up."

Jane stared at her for a beat. "Fair. Just tell me it was Mateo."

Charlotte grinned dopily. "It was Mateo."

Jane laughed, then stilled at the unmistakable meow right behind her. She turned and found Cat sitting there in the hallway, watching with her sharp gray eyes. "How did you get inside?"

"I've got the basement window cracked open," Charlotte said.

Cat sauntered closer and scratched Jane's door with her paw.

Jane felt the last piece of her heart click into place. "So . . . can we add a pet clause on that billion-year lease?"

A FEW minutes later, Charlotte crawled into bed, satisfied from Jane's reaction to her newly painted bedroom door, but also still smiling about how she'd spent the earlier part of the evening.

In Mateo's bed.

Okay, yes, she'd then sneaked back to her place, but baby steps, right? Besides, he probably hadn't even realized that she'd left. She told herself to go to sleep. She'd just finally drifted off when she was jerked awake by a knock at the front door. *"No,"* she said out loud.

When the knock came again, she blew out a breath and slipped out of bed. She grabbed the fireplace poker on the way to the front door. She looked through the peephole and froze.

Mateo. And he didn't look thrilled.

With a grimace, she opened the door.

"What are you doing here in the middle of the night?" she asked.

"Good question." He stood there in the freezing night wearing nothing but a pair of sweat bottoms, looking rumpled and sexy.

"Normally," he said, "I prefer to share breakfast with the person I just slept with. Instead, you waited for me to fall asleep and then sneaked out. Without so much as a note."

Guilt swamped her, and she sagged, dropping the poker. "I know, it was awful of me, but I didn't know what to do."

Pushing off from the doorjamb, he took a step toward her, still not touching her with anything other than that piercing dark gaze.

Lifting a hand, he traced a finger along her jaw. "Staying the night, that's what girlfriends do."

"I'm not your girlfriend."

"Really?" He shifted in closer now, so that they were sharing air. "Because only a few hours ago it felt a lot like you were."

She reached up and covered his mouth with her hand. "Don't."

Gently, he removed her hand. "Maybe we should talk."

She squirmed. "Talking makes things real. Real things end."

"I'm not going anywhere. Stop running."

"I'm not trying to." She tossed up her hands. "Look, in case you haven't noticed, I'm a handful."

"That's okay, I've got two hands."

She smiled, but her eyes also filled. "I can't sleep in other people's beds. And you know why."

He reached for her, understanding in every line of his body now.

He slipped a hand in hers. "We could always try your bed."

She stared down at their entwined fingers, running her thumb over his palm. "I don't sleep well if someone else is in my bed."

"Then lucky for you I don't mind sleeping on the floor." He reached back out the door and picked up something he'd apparently left on the porch before knocking.

A rolled-up sleeping bag. "This thing has seen a lot," he said. "Your floor will be luxurious accommodations, trust me."

He'd known her problem and had come up with a work-around. As if maybe she truly, honestly did mean something to him.

"My floor is hardwood," she said inanely.

His eyes twinkled. "Doesn't bother me, as long as it doesn't bother you." With his free hand, he tipped her face up to his. "*Does* it bother you, Charlotte? That I want to sleep near you?"

Staring at him for a long beat, she slowly shook her head.

She led him upstairs, heart pounding. Incredibly aware of him at her back, she brought him inside her room.

He shut the door and gestured for her to get in bed. Then he pulled the covers up to her chin and leaned in to kiss her. "'Night."

Then he unrolled his sleeping bag and slid into it. On the floor.

She stared up at the ceiling, waiting for the familiar panic. Or at least unease. Neither came.

She let out a breath and dropped a hand over the side of the bed.

Reaching up, he slipped his into hers. "Sweet dreams."

For a beat, she lay there. If she was going to face her fears, there was no better man to do that with than Mateo. Every time she was in his proximity, she felt a calm wash over her, a sense of anticipation. It was like her body recognized him as a soul mate.

She didn't want to be alone. She didn't want to give one horrific memory the power to steal away the hope of a happy future.

"Mateo?"

"Yeah?"

She slid out of her bed. "Move over?"

He made room for her, and she crawled into his sleeping bag.

Chapter 11

THE NEXT DAY, JANE grabbed her lunch bag from the Homeward resort's staff fridge where she'd stashed it and headed outside. The temp was a brisk thirty-two degrees, but in the sun at high altitude, after five hours in urgent care, it would feel warm and glorious.

She'd grown roots here in Tahoe. Her relationship with Charlotte. Mateo. Cat. Her grandpa . . . And she knew the list wasn't complete without Levi on it, no matter how temporary they were.

Temporary. She'd always considered that word to be a part of her personality. And now that she'd fulfilled her promise to be his pretend girlfriend for his parents' dinner— She froze halfway to a table. *She'd fulfilled her promise to be his pretend girlfriend.*

There was no need for Levi to see her anymore.

The snow crunched beneath her feet as she made her way to a small, empty table. She sat down and closed her eyes.

Was it over? Would she see him again?

And what business did she have wanting to so badly her heart was threatening to pound out of her chest?

When she opened her eyes again, she wasn't alone.

Shirl and Tess were seated opposite her, smiling.

Jane cleared her throat to speak. "What are you doing here?"

"We're not stalking you or anything," Shirl said.

Tess snorted. "We're *totally* stalking you." She looked recovered from her shocking pregnancy reveal last night. Serene and calm. "But . . ." She opened a lunch box. "We come bearing food."

"Thanks, but I brought my own." Jane pulled out a banana, a yogurt, and a package of peanut butter crackers.

Shirl looked over Jane's lunch and shook her head. "That's just sad. How about a meat loaf sandwich?"

"It's her special recipe," Tess said. "It's crackalicious."

Shirl pushed a glass container at Jane.

"How did you know I'd be able to eat with you?"

"Just hoping." Shirl smiled. "I wanted to tell you how good you are for Levi."

Jane's smile faltered as she realized how the deception she and Levi had laid out was going to hurt others. In trying to make his mom happy, they were now about to do the very opposite. "You know I'm leaving soon," she said carefully.

"Yes." Shirl reached for Jane's hand. "You know about Amy?"

Jane nodded.

"He hasn't let another woman in since. That's how we knew before we'd even met you that you had to be special."

"Because I'm Levi's girlfriend," Jane said quietly.

"No, because you're Jane Parks."

Jane froze, feeling that definitive statement clear through her heart. How ironic that all her life she'd shied away from commitments to keep her heart safe, only to fail utterly here. Because what she felt for Levi was shockingly real, and now she was going to hurt his family, who didn't deserve it.

"At least take a bite," Shirl said, nudging the sandwich closer.

Jane took a bite of the sandwich and— "Oh my gosh."

Tess smiled. "Right?"

Jane practically moaned her way through the entire sandwich.

"Here." Levi's mom was going through her phone, tapping away, and then Jane's phone buzzed with a text. "The recipe."

"Are you kidding me?" Tess asked. "I've been asking you for that recipe for years."

Tess laughed, but Jane actually felt her heart tug hard at these two women who'd somehow become a part of her life.

How was she going to let them go? To distract herself, she looked at the recipe. "This might be above my pay grade."

"Levi loves this recipe," Shirl said.

"Mom, women don't have to cook for their men anymore," Tess said. "Love comes from the heart, not the stomach."

"Bull pucky," Shirl said. "Cook the meat loaf, Jane. Trust me on this. I'm still married to the man I married forty years ago."

Jane thought if a man wanted her for her meat loaf, he was going to go through life greatly disappointed. But if said man loved her for her alone . . . and if that man was Levi, she knew she'd do everything she could to make it work. How scary was that?

WHEN Jane got off work, she stopped at the store and bought the ingredients. *Only* because it'd been a most *excellent* meat loaf.

Back home, she entered the kitchen and found Mateo and Charlotte kissing up against the fridge. Charlotte gasped and broke free.

Mateo grinned. "We got hungry."

"Good thing I'm cooking, then."

Charlotte blinked. "Did you say . . . cooking?"

"Ha-ha," Jane said. "Watch and learn."

When she pulled the meat loaf out of the oven an hour later, Zoe and Mariella had joined them, brought in by the scent.

Jane handed out forks, and everyone dug in.

"You've been holding out on me," Charlotte said, mouth full.

"On all of us," Zoe said, shoveling meat loaf into her mouth.

"You know who should have some?" Mateo asked. "Levi."

Just yesterday, Jane would've agreed. But she'd been jerked out of her fantasy bubble after Shirl's and Tess's visit. "I've got someone else in mind for the meat loaf," she said.

Charlotte smiled. "Your grandpa."

Jane touched the tip of her nose and headed out.

When she pulled into her grandpa's driveway, she stared at the truck parked in it. Levi's truck.

Her heart skipped a beat in confusion, but also happiness.

She walked up the driveway and knocked on the front door. When no one answered, she let herself in. "Hello?" she called out, walking through the living room before coming to a stop.

Levi was on a ladder, head into the attic access, so all she could see was a pair of long denim-clad legs. "What are you doing?"

Levi craned his neck to look down at her. "Your grandpa called. He wanted to know who to hire to make this a smart house. I told him I'd do it for him." He climbed down the ladder and kissed her. When he pulled back, he eyed the bag she held with great interest.

"Hungry?"

"Always." He kissed her again.

Grandpa came in the back door wearing a tool belt, and she walked over to him to greet him with a hug.

"Found my hammer," he said with pride, and Jane realized that Levi had clearly included him in the work, which meant that the job was probably taking him three times as long as it should.

Damn. He was truly the best pretend boyfriend she'd ever had.

"Your man's had me working," her grandpa said.

And here was yet another person who was going to be hurt. "Grandpa, you know he's not. That we're . . . not."

Her grandpa glanced over at Levi, who had moved away from them and was cleaning up, then gave Jane a rather impressive eye roll. "Yeah, yeah, I know. It's alllllll pretend."

"I have food," she said inanely.

Levi was back. "What takeout is it?"

"It's not. I actually cooked. It's your mom's meat loaf."

Levi's eyes widened. "She gave you the recipe?"

"She likes me." She took the bag into the kitchen, divided the meat loaf into three portions, and carried them to the living room.

Before Levi, she'd never eaten a family dinner like the one at his house, with fancy china at a decorated table. Here at her grandpa's, they were on the couch, feet up on the coffee table, Grandpa yelling out all the answers to *Jeopardy!*

Even if her life had depended on it, Jane wouldn't have been able to say which dinner had been better. They'd both felt . . . right.

It's still not real . . .

Problem was, it felt more real than anything in her entire life.

After dinner, Levi followed her home. He parked and opened her door before she freed herself of her seat belt.

"This is usually where we argue about me walking you to your door," he said. "But FYI, I'm still going to. I plan on stealing at least one kiss."

"You're going to get more than that." Yes, she was crazy to spend another night with him knowing she could no longer separate her feelings for him from the act of being with him, but she didn't care. She wanted him, even if it was for the last time.

They walked hand in hand to the door. She unlocked it and tugged him into the living room. "Levi, meet Zoe and Mariella."

Zoe and Mariella sat up straight. Mariella pointed at Jane. "Hey, you *do* know our names," she teased.

Jane felt her face heat up and heard Levi's soft laugh, but then there was a loud, demanding meow. The large gray cat unfurled herself from where she'd been lying in front of the woodstove.

Levi crouched down to smile at Cat, who bumped her head against his thigh, demanding to be petted.

Levi obliged, and Jane found herself rubbing her aching chest as she stared down at two of her favorite living creatures. It was an overload of contentment. Which meant she was doomed.

Contentment never lasted.

"Saw your name painted on your door," Zoe said. "Congrats for coming in out of the storm along with Cat."

"Show me your door," Levi said softly in her ear.

She found herself taking his hand and leading him up the stairs.

Levi smiled at the prominently painted *JANE* and the landscape. "Nice. You going to invite me in too? Like you did Cat?"

"It's a little messy."

"I like a little messy," he said, and kissed her softly.

She pushed the door open and walked in. Levi followed, nudged the door closed with his foot, then turned her to face him. "You're an enigma, Jane, and I love that. You have all these secret compartments and hidden locked boxes, and there's no instructions or manual. It's been a thrill of a ride, the not knowing what's around the next corner, but you know what's an even bigger thrill? Being on the inside."

Her breath stuttered in her chest. "You think you're on the inside?" she asked lightly, going for a teasing tone.

"I do." He paused. "I hope."

She dropped her head to his chest to muffle her startled laugh.

"You are in," she said. "But we no longer have to pretend anything so . . ." She shook her head. "What are we really doing here?"

"For me this is real." He brushed his mouth to her temple.

She lifted her head, suddenly having trouble drawing air into her lungs. "How can you be so sure?"

He shrugged. "I've been sure since you stood over me bleeding on the floor of that gondola, stripping out of your clothes."

She choked out a laugh. "I didn't strip out of all my clothes!"

He smiled, but then let it fade. "You're a tough nut to crack, Jane. I've only been able to *hope* that I was slowly worming my way into your heart as well. But now . . ."

"Now what?" she whispered.

"Sometimes I catch you looking at me like I'm a cookies 'n' cream cupcake," he whispered back.

Was he right? No. He was better than a cupcake. "Maybe I'm really just thinking about a cookies 'n' cream cupcake."

He smiled. "You're a cute liar."

"I'll show you cute," she said, needing to change the direction of this conversation.

His eyes said he knew she was holding back, but he didn't call her on it. Instead he smiled and said, "Please do."

THE next morning, Jane jerked awake at her alarm.

A long arm reached over her and hit snooze.

She turned and faced the man in her bed. The man with sexy scruff on his jaw as he pulled her into him and kissed her.

She squirmed a bit, and not just because she didn't know how to do morning-afters. "I'm going to be late."

"I thought your shift didn't start until eight." Levi squinted at the clock. "It's barely past dawn."

She got up and hopped into the clothes he'd got her out of the night before. "I'm meeting my grandpa for breakfast."

He caught her at her bedroom door. Gently he pressed her back against the wood and gave her a drugging kiss so full of longing and desire and affection, she forgot she was in a hurry.

Ten minutes later, she pulled into the Stovetop Diner parking lot.

Her grandpa showed up five minutes later, moving slower than she'd seen so far. She kissed him on his cheek, then watched him slide into the booth as if he hurt everywhere. "What's wrong?"

"I'm old." He flashed a grin.

His mirth didn't go all the way to his eyes. "Grandpa—"

The waitress came by with a smile and a coffeepot.

"Bless you," her grandpa said, and the woman gave him a wink.

"Hey, sexy. Your usual?" she asked.

"Yes, thank you, doll."

"What's your usual?" Jane asked him.

"Two Danish pastries."

"What? No. *Are you kidding me?*"

He waved this off. "I'm like an old phone battery, Sugar Plum. Even when I charge myself overnight for twelve hours, by nine a.m., I'm already drained to forty percent. I need the sugar boost."

Jane turned to the waitress. "Could we get two of your healthy start breakfasts? Hold the pastries?"

Soon as the waitress was gone, Jane turned on her grandpa. "Do you *really* always eat Danishes for breakfast?"

"Unless you're here, yeah."

She sighed. "You can't eat whatever you want anymore."

He reached over and covered her hand in his. "I'm going to bite it and go to the farm someday no matter what I eat."

"Yes, but not any time soon, right?"

He shrugged and dropped the eye contact. "No one knows. That's why it's called life."

She hesitated. "Something's off," she said. "What's wrong?"

"Nothing. I'm fine, relax. And better yet, let me relax, okay? I've lived a long life. I deserve some joy."

She felt certain he was holding something back, but short of pushing him, she didn't know what else to do. "Can you find joy in something other than Danishes?"

At that, he looked into her eyes again. "I can," he said with quiet, warm conviction. "I have."

She felt the threat of tears and gave him a smile. "Love you."

"Love you, too, Sugar Plum. To the moon and back."

An hour later she was at work, running her butt off as usual.

Halfway through her shift, she got a rare lull in patients. She eyed the screen in front of her, where she sat typing her reports. Then she looked around. No one was paying her any attention.

She sucked in a breath and did something she was not allowed to do. She typed in her grandpa's name, accessed his patient records, and began to read.

CHARLOTTE's workday was its usual crazy, so by the time she made it to the break room, she was beyond famished. She crossed the room, heading to the staff fridge before she remembered she hadn't packed herself anything. Damn.

"Whatever is in your bag, it smells amazing when you open the fridge," Sandra said to her.

Charlotte turned in surprise. "What?"

"Your lunch. There's a big brown bag in there with your name on it. Smells like Mexican food, and I'm jealous as hell."

Charlotte opened the fridge and gaped. There was indeed a bag in there with her name on it. "I didn't pack myself anything."

"Then can we pretend it says *Sandra* on it?" the nurse asked.

Hell, no. Because she was pretty sure she recognized that handwriting, and the person who'd written it could cook. So she took the bag out of the fridge and to the counter, and opened it up.

There was a glass container filled with what looked like two enchiladas, a side of tortilla chips, and pico de gallo.

Her mouth watered as she pulled out the folded note.

> Enjoy.
> Love, M

She stood there frozen in placc. *Love, M . . . ?*

Charlotte headed to the ER and pulled Mateo into a corner.

"The note," she said, hearing a touch of hysteria in her voice.

Mateo just looked at her.

"'Love, M'?"

His dark eyes never wavered from hers. "Yes."

"You . . . love me?"

His hands came up to her face. "Yes," he said simply.

She drew in a shuddery breath. "I love you too. But I'm not the girl who dreamed about a wedding and kids." She shook her head.

He smiled into her eyes. "I can do without those things. What I can't do without is you, Charlotte."

Heart. Melted.

He started to kiss her, but someone was calling his name urgently from down the hall, and he straightened. "We're swamped. I gotta go. But I can't until I know we're okay."

She smiled. "We're more than okay."

He smiled back and vanished.

Still smiling, she left the building and walked over to the urgent care next door to share her lunch with Jane.

She found her sitting behind the counter staring off into space, looking pale. And maybe like she'd been crying.

"What is it?" Charlotte asked.

Jane just shook her head.

Charlotte looked around. There was no one waiting to be seen. "Let's take lunch."

They went into the back, heated the container, then sat at the small staff table and shared the food.

"Mateo cooked this?" Jane asked after shoving in a few big bites. "You're going to have to marry him; you do realize that?"

"Yes," Charlotte said, unable to keep the smile off her face.

Jane took in her expression and nodded with satisfaction.

Charlotte set her fork down. "You ready to talk?"

Jane pushed the food back. "My grandpa has cancer."

Charlotte felt the breath stutter in her throat. "Oh, Jane. I'm—"

"—Sorry?" Jane shook her head. "I am too." She stood up and paced the room. "I'm feeling a lot of things."

"You're angry," Charlotte said softly. "It's one of the first emotions to hit with a cancer diagnosis."

"He didn't tell me about it. I had to find out on my own."

Charlotte's first thought was pain and fury for Jane. Her second thought gave her an icy shiver. "Tell me you didn't defy HIPAA."

Jane's face closed off, and Charlotte's heart took another hard kick. "Jane . . ." She broke off when her phone beeped. Work. She was needed in the OR stat.

"Go," Jane said. "I'm fine."

No, she wasn't, but Charlotte had no choice. "I'll call you."

Jane turned away and nodded, and Charlotte had to walk away. One of the hardest things she'd ever done.

Chapter 12

THE SECOND HER SHIFT was over, Jane went straight to her car and started driving. She needed to talk this out with her grandpa. Without jumping to conclusions. It was the logical thing to do.

But she didn't feel logical. Which undoubtedly was the reason that when she parked, she found herself at Levi's house.

Probably because her heart knew what her brain had accepted: that in that moment, she needed Levi. She got out of her car.

Levi opened the door before she got to it, but his smile faded as he came down the steps to meet her. "What's wrong?"

She bit down hard on her lip, but the tears came anyway.

"I got some hard news, but I can't say it yet." Not without completely losing it. "I need a minute."

He gathered her into his arms and held her close. "Whatever it is, Jane, I'm right here. We'll deal with it."

Oh, how she *hated* being vulnerable or seeming weak. But she fisted her hands in his shirt and held on tight.

They stood like that right in the middle of the front yard for a long moment. And then suddenly she felt a gentle patting on her back from hands that weren't Levi's.

And then yet a third person's arms hugged her from behind.

"Jane?" It was Shirl. "Baby, what's the matter?"

"Whatever it is, we got you," Tess said.

"I've got an extra taco. Do you want it?" This was from Peyton.

Jasper was at her side, very gently and stealthily licking the taco shell in her hand. Hank was waiting on the porch.

Jane swiped at her eyes. "I didn't mean to interrupt dinner."

"Honey, don't you give it a second thought," Shirl said. "Come inside, I've got food. And hot tea."

"Yes," Tess said. "And I've got something to lace the tea with."

Levi looked at his mom and sister. There was a silent exchange, and then everyone nodded and went back inside. "We don't have to go," Levi said. "We can go somewhere else, you name it."

She sniffed. "The food smells good."

He smiled. "Here it is, then. Talk, or food first?"

She'd never be able to eat until she got this out. "Talk."

He offered her a hand, and they walked inside. He pulled her through the crowd of his well-meaning family and up the stairs.

Despite Levi's clothes over the couch and Peyton's toys everywhere, the room felt warm and cozy. Levi swiped everything from the couch with a single swoop of a hand. "Have a seat."

When she did, he came up with a box of tissues and sat next to her, pulling her into his side. "Tell me what's going on."

Now she had to say it out loud. "At breakfast this morning, there was something off about my grandpa. He promised me he was fine." She gulped in some air. "But he's not. He's got cancer." Her eyes filled. "I just found him again, and he's going to die."

"Oh, Jane." He hugged her tight, his jaw resting on the top of her head. She sank into him and let his strength seep into her.

"What kind of cancer?" he asked. "So many are curable now."

"Yes, if the patient elects to seek treatment." A little bitter about that, she climbed off his lap and began to pace the room. "It's lung cancer. He was successfully treated two years ago, but it's back and . . ." She swallowed hard. "He is refusing treatment. He's just going to let himself die. How could he promise me everything was okay when he knew it wouldn't ever be okay again?"

Levi rose to his feet and stepped into her path.

She lifted her face to his. *"How?"* she demanded.

He ran his hands up her arms. "You're only just back in his life.

It's possible he hasn't worked up the nerve to tell you yet. Cancer isn't easy to talk about, especially with someone you love."

"No." She twisted away, turned her back on him and his empathy. "It's *exactly* the thing you talk about to someone you love."

"Jane—"

"Stop." Maybe she was still nothing but an inconvenience to her grandpa. He couldn't possibly really love her "to the moon and back" if he'd kept such a huge, unforgivable secret.

"This might have nothing to do with you or your relationship with him," Levi said quietly. "You may have to accept that."

"He still should've told me." She hugged herself, staring out the window. "He knows I'm going to be gone again soon."

"Is it possible that he didn't want to spend the last of his time with you talking about death and being sick? That he just wanted to soak up every moment he could with you before you go?"

She shook her head. "He chose *no* treatment. None. Zero."

"Again, his choice."

Fueled by panic and anxiety and fury, she whirled on him. "Are you actually trying to defend his decision to me? There are treatments available, Levi. There is no defense for what he's doing."

"I assume you've talked to him about this. Calmly. Rationally."

She tossed up her hands. "Of course I haven't. I came straight here." She felt her eyes fill. "I'm just so mad at him."

He nodded. "It's understandable," he said. "But it's possible he made his choice *before* you were back in his life."

His words hit her like a one-two punch to the solar plexus. "So it's my fault for not reaching out to him sooner?"

"No, of course not. But I do think he might've made a different choice now—something you won't know unless you talk to him."

She pressed the heels of her hands to her temples. "You don't get it. Cancer doesn't waste time. There's no fixing this now."

"You don't know that."

"Oh, Mr. Fix-It, but I *do* know it. I accessed his records, Levi. He wouldn't have given them to me."

He was toe-to-toe with her now but not touching her, looking suddenly both incredulous and angry.

"So you, what, accessed them without permission, meaning you risked your entire nursing career, not to mention your license, to avoid a difficult conversation with your grandpa?"

"You're one to talk about avoiding a difficult conversation," she said. "You made up a pretend girlfriend!"

"Guilty. And for the record, I stopped pretending a long time ago. As I told you, this is real for me, Jane. *Very* real."

She sucked in a breath. She was never going to get used to that.

Levi gave her a tight smile. "But clearly you haven't gotten there yet."

"I haven't *let* myself go there," she corrected. Paused. "I do know you're important to me, Levi. Very important."

"As important as your love of going far and wide without any tether longer than the length of your next contract?"

"Work doesn't factor into this."

"The hell it doesn't. Work gives you an excuse to leave."

For a heart-stopping moment, she was eight years old again, too much trouble to keep, to fight for, to want. She'd fixed that, though, by always leaving first. "That's not fair."

"No? You're the one who, in the same sentence about your grandpa's cancer, also talked about leaving Tahoe. Things change, Jane. No one's asking you to leave this time. You could stay here and enjoy the time you have left with your grandpa."

She stared at him, trying to fight rising panic. "I've never lied to you. You've always known I was going to leave."

He looked . . . disappointed. Hurt. "You're running away again, too afraid of getting hurt to even try and build a real relationship."

Is that what she was doing? Finding reasons to take off before she could be asked to leave? She didn't know how to respond.

She was going to lose her grandpa and Levi because of the desperate need to run from anything that made her feel too much.

"Jane, what do you want me to do here?"

"I want you to do whatever you want," she said dully.

He nodded. "All right." He was clearly waiting for her to do something. Walk out, she realized, so she did, without looking back. That was the trick, she reminded herself. Never look back.

But for the first time, she wanted to.

LEVI HEARD THE DOOR SHUT and felt it reverberate in his gut.

He ran his hands through his hair and then asked himself why he wasn't going after the best thing to ever happen to him. To hell with that, and he strode down the stairs and to the front door.

Jane's car was gone.

He turned in a slow circle in the living room, wondering why had he ever made that promise to not fall for her? He stopped when he realized the double doors leading to the kitchen were closed.

They were never closed.

He pushed them open, and his entire family leapt away from the doors, trying to look busy. Only his niece was left standing suspiciously close to the wall next to the kitchen door.

The eavesdropping wall.

"Hi! We were listening to you and Jane upstairs. Grandma was using a glass cuz she said it carries sound better."

Levi cut his eyes to his mom, who had the good grace to grimace. "Kids," she said. "They say the darnedest things."

"Why is Jane mad at you?" Peyton asked him.

Levi crouched before Peyton. "Sometimes adults disagree, and that's okay." He rose to his feet and shook his head at the rest of his family. "You couldn't give me ten minutes of privacy?"

His dad snorted. "You blew that whole thing up in under five."

Tess nodded her agreement. "I don't even think one of your PowerPoints could have saved you."

Levi shook his head and turned to his mom. "And you? The leader of the pack, you don't have a comment for me too?"

"No, because I'm not talking to you," his mom said, nose in the air. "You made up a girlfriend. And then lied to me about it."

Levi walked out of the kitchen, and oh, goody, Mateo was walking in the front door. The guy took one look at Levi, and his smile faded. "What happened?"

"He just destroyed his relationship with Jane," his mom said over Levi's shoulder, having followed him from the kitchen.

Coming in behind his mom, Tess said, "*Jane* dumped *him*."

"Actually, what Jane said was that he could do whatever he wanted," his mom said.

Mateo shook his head. "When a woman says that, you do *not* do whatever you want. You stand still. You don't even breathe."

"Awesome," Levi said. "That was super helpful, thanks."

His mom sighed. "I'm sorry you messed up. Are you okay?"

Levi pressed his hand to his aching heart and shook his head. "I'll let you know if I ever get sensation back in my soul. Not that I *should*—my personal life shouldn't be up for debate."

"Aw, sweetheart." She cupped his face. "Who taught you that your personal life has to be separate from your family?"

"Who do you think?"

Sadness filled her eyes. "I'm sorry," she said softly. "You were just always so private that we tended to do whatever we had to in order to find out what was up with you. I can see now that wasn't always healthy for you. But we just love you so much."

"I love you, too, but you guys couldn't give me two minutes to process what just happened before breathing down my neck?"

She looked stricken. "You're right. We just didn't want you to take so long that you missed out on something that made you so happy." She drew a deep breath. "That night you called me from the gondola. It was to say goodbye, wasn't it?"

The regret was yet another bitter pill.

"But you couldn't do it," she said. "Your last thoughts were to make me happy." She pressed her hand to her chest. "I'm sorry I ever made you feel you had to be something you weren't. I know we overreact, but you uprooted your life and moved away, and we miss you so much." Her eyes filled with tears.

"Mom," he whispered, reaching for her. "Don't cry."

"I can't help it. I want to go after Jane and fix this myself."

"Okay, but you won't, right?"

She both cried and huffed out a laugh against his chest, and he realized that while maybe his family didn't always understand him, he'd never taken the time to understand them either. He never imagined that his moving away would bother them so much. At the time, he'd been desperate, so much so that he'd unintentionally cut the people who loved him right out of his life.

And wasn't that what he just accused Jane of doing?

Why had he pushed a truth she hadn't wanted to hear, inadvertently playing off her worst fear—being walked away from? She'd done the walking, but still. He'd definitely pushed her into it.

He hated that, and at the moment, hated himself too. He needed to prove to her that it was real between them. "I made mistakes."

"Well, who hasn't?" his mom asked. "There are always things in life that can't be undone, no matter how badly you want it. But there are also plenty of things you *can* fix. Like you and Jane."

"How?" he said. "How do I fix this?"

"Whoa." Tess looked amazed. "He's asking for advice. Quick, someone write the date down."

His mom ignored this. "You're going to have to listen to your heart, which already has the answer."

Levi moved to the door. "I've gotta go."

"I suggest groveling," Tess said.

"Ditto," Mateo said.

"Good luck, son," his dad said. "You're going to need it."

Jane pulled off the road for two reasons. One, because her defroster was on the blink. Two, she was crying.

She swiped at her face and eyed her reflection in the rearview mirror. "Since when do you let anyone get close enough to hurt you? Because that's just plain dumb. You know better."

She'd somehow come to believe that she'd been on a new trajectory, where the people she let into her life could be trusted. But the joke was on her. Both the men she loved had just gutted her.

By the time she parked in front of her grandpa's house, the tears were gone. She stormed up the walk and lifted her hand to knock, but the door opened before she could.

Her grandpa took one look at her and sighed. "You always were a nosy little thing."

"How could you not tell me?"

Suddenly looking older than his years, he seemed to cave in on himself. "I knew if I told you, it'd be all you'd want to talk about."

"But—"

"I made my decision about treatment a year ago, far before you came back into my life. Back then, all I could think of was getting to see your grandma again." He looked at her with regret. "I had messed things up with you and couldn't imagine a scenario in which you'd ever want to see me again. I thought I was done here."

She sat down before her knees could give out, right there on the top step of his porch. "I feel like I just found you," she said through a thick throat. "I can't bear the thought of losing you again."

He sat on the step next to her and took her hand. "I'll still be with you. Just like I always have been."

Her eyes filled. "But there are treatments that can make it so you can stay with me longer."

He was already shaking his head. "Jane, I'd rather have three incredible months with you than three painful years." He looked her in the eyes. "Can you try and understand that?"

She had to ask herself . . . if he *hadn't* been her grandpa, if he'd been one of her patients, how would she feel?

If she was being brutally honest, she'd agree with him.

And something else. Levi had said no one was pushing her away this time; she'd done that all on her own. And he was right, painfully so. There would always be another job. There wouldn't be another grandpa, not for her. "I'll be here," she said fiercely, clinging to her grandpa's hand. "I'll be here with you no matter what."

The tension drained from his shoulders, and he kissed her cheek. "Thank you," he said with such meaning, her heart squeezed.

She realized that Levi had simply been attempting to help her understand what her grandpa wanted. He'd put his heart on the line for her, and she'd turned away, doing to him what people had done to her. She'd walked. "I messed up," she murmured.

"Not with me you didn't," her grandpa said genuinely.

She held on to his hand. "Thank you for that. But you're not the only one I hurt today by thinking only of myself."

"Levi?"

"Yes." She swallowed hard. "I walked away," she whispered.

Her grandpa nodded. "After all you've been through, you don't trust love. But people *are* going to love you just for being you." He cupped her face. "It's okay to let them. It's a beautiful thing. You don't have to live in the shadows of your past anymore."

She wanted to stop. She did. But could she? Was it that simple?

"That boy loves you. Go to him like you came to me. He'll listen. Then you'll listen. Just like we did here, you and me."

She covered her face. "I'm not sure he can forgive me."

Her grandpa stood up and offered her a hand, and then a hug that she really needed. "You've got a lot of people here who care about you. This time, *every* time, it's your choice to stay or go."

He pulled back and gave her a *shoo* gesture. "Go."

She turned and started down the path, only to stop short.

Levi's truck was parked at the end of the driveway. She could see his tall silhouette in the fading daylight, waiting for her.

He looked like the rest of her life.

Swiping the tears off her cheeks, she moved closer. "Hi."

"Hi." He looked at her with a self-deprecating smile. "I thought maybe you might need an Uber or tech support."

Though his tone had been light, his eyes were anything but. "Maybe I just need you," she said.

He studied her. "I'd like to think that was true, but you don't often let yourself need anything or anyone."

"I know." She shook her head. "But coming back here this time, bonding with Charlotte, my grandpa. *You* . . ." She held his gaze. "Being alone doesn't hold the same appeal anymore."

"Good," he said. "Because you're not alone. I'm right here."

Her own miracle. "You came for me."

"I'll always come for you. But I lied about the Uber and tech support. I'm here because I forgot to tell you something."

"What?"

He straightened up but still didn't touch her. "I love you, Jane."

She nearly melted into a puddle right there. Stepping into him, she slid her hands around his neck. He hauled her in closer so there was no space between them. Then he kissed her, telling her with his mouth, his touch, that she really was the love of his life.

Just as he was hers. "I left something out too." She drew in a deep breath, because here went everything. "You said it was real for you. I need you to know it's real for me."

His eyes searched hers, dark, serious. Intense. "From when?"

"From the moment you showed up with my grandma's locket. To be honest, I wasn't sure I had it in me to fall in love." She shook her head. "But a part of me knew from that first night on the mountain that you would change everything. I love you too, Levi."

He let out a breath like he'd been holding it for just that. Looking touched, marveled, and relieved, he gave a low laugh.

"You didn't know?" she asked.

"Hoped. Suspected. But no, I wasn't sure."

"I really was going to Haiti," she whispered. "I'm not now."

He rubbed his jaw against hers and nodded. "But even if you had, it wouldn't have changed anything for me."

"Me either. Thank you for loving me, Tarzan."

"You're easy to love." He kissed her again. His lips were cold, and she realized he wasn't wearing a jacket. "You're freezing!"

"Left in a hurry. Jane, there's one more thing."

Her heart stopped at the seriousness in his voice. "Okay . . ."

"I bought a piece of land near the Tahoe Rim Trail. I'm going to build a house. I'd like it to be our house. Our home."

Her heart swelled. "I've never had a house."

"I know."

"A home either," she said. "Though Charlotte's place is close."

He smiled. "So you'll have two now, though I hope you're going to sleep in ours." He tipped her face up to his. "I want you to be mine, Jane. But more than that, I want to be yours. If it means seeing you during ski season when you're here working, or if it means flying to visit you wherever you happen to be, I don't care."

This got her in the feels. "You deserve more than having to follow me around. I think I'd like to transfer from the urgent care clinics to the actual hospital. It's better shifts and more stability."

He was already shaking his head. "Don't do that for me, Jane. I don't want to change anything about you."

"I'm doing it for me, because I need more of us than a visit here and there. You are my person, Levi. And I'm yours. How long can I keep you?"

He cupped her face. "How does forever sound?"

Her heart turned over in her chest. "It's a date."

Epilogue

Five years later

JANE STAGGERED DOWN the stairs, plopped into a dining room chair, and did *gimme* hands toward Levi's coffee mug.

He slid it to her.

She sipped, grateful it was still steaming hot. Smiling, she scooped up Cat, who'd been winding around her ankles.

Levi hooked a foot around the leg of her chair and pulled her closer. Miffed, Cat jumped off, and Levi scooped Jane into his lap, pulling her in for a kiss that had her melting into him.

"*Ew.*"

They broke apart and looked over at Nicole, their four-year-old daughter, who was the image of her daddy. Their daughter was still in pj's, wearing—if Jane wasn't mistaken—syrup. A quick glance around the kitchen told the tale. Waffles had been made.

"Why do you kiss so much?" Nicole wanted to know.

"Because we love each other."

"Is he your boyfriend?"

"Sort of. But we're married, so that also makes him my husband."

"My friend Shelley's mommy thinks my daddy's hot."

Levi choked on the sip of coffee he'd just swallowed.

Jane laughed. "I'd have to agree with her."

Nicole crawled up into Jane's lap, and as she was still sitting in Levi's lap, it was a very tight fit. "Do you have to go to work today, Mommy? Can we go sledding down the hill?"

The house that they'd built had a slope in the backyard—perfect for sledding. Jane kissed the tip of Nicole's cute little nose. "I'm not working today." She was now employed at the Sunrise Cove hospital and loving it. She'd taken the week off because Mateo had finally talked Charlotte into saying "I do," and as her best friend's matron of honor, Jane had a lot to take care of.

But today was all about Nicole. "Sledding sounds perfect. Why don't you go get ready?"

"Yay!" Nicole leapt down and ran to her bedroom. There was the sound of drawers opening and closing as she searched for her sledding gear from Cutler Sporting Goods. Cal had been arrested and had done some time but had never paid back a penny. Still, after floundering for a bit, the store was beginning to thrive again.

Jane leaned back against Levi's chest and sighed as he dragged his mouth down the side of her neck. Then those little feet came running into the kitchen again.

"Daddy! Leave her alone. We're going sledding!"

Levi gently nudged Jane off his lap and stood to face the sweetest little tyrant they'd ever met. "Can I go too?"

Nicole giggled. "Of course, Daddy. Can Peyton come over and sled with us? And Taylor? I promised my cousins."

"*Everyone* can come."

Nicole ran to him. Levi caught her and then snagged Nicole's mommy in close too. "Caught you both."

"Careful," Jane warned. "The syrup's sticky."

"Perfect. Now we can stick together." He pressed his forehead to Jane's. "For always."

Sounded like the perfect plan.

After*Words*

Jill Shalvis is a city girl turned mountain woman. Originally from Los Angeles, she now lives in a small town outside Lake Tahoe, California, in the Sierras. Shalvis loves setting her romances in small towns—both for their charming sense of community and for the plot-handy difficulties of keeping anything secret. *The Family You Make* is the first of her more than fifty women's fiction novels to be set in her current hometown. It's also the flagship story in a new romance series based in the fictional town of Sunrise Cove.

Shalvis has always been a storyteller—as a child, she had an active imagination and loved to embellish the truth. She majored in journalism, but found that sticking to the facts of non-fiction wasn't her calling. After college, she worked in accounting for a while. An avid reader, she took crack at writing fiction after having run out of things to read while pregnant with her first child.

Says Shalvis of her writing habits, "I can't write at a desk. I use a laptop and have to migrate around, from my bed to the couch to the deck to the woods . . . to the kitchen, where I'll stop and eat way too many chips or cookies."

She is a *New York Times* bestselling author, and her novel *The Trouble with Mistletoe* was adapted to film by Passionflix in 2017.

When not writing, she enjoys reading, hiking, paddleboarding, and chasing after her dogs.

FIRST EDITION: Volume 385

Library of Congress Catalog Card Number: 98-640138
ISSN: 1541-0900

Printed in the United States of America

ACKNOWLEDGMENTS

Page 159: David Burnett. Page 289: Courtesy of the author. Page 433: Kate Hannon. Page 575: Susan Zweigle, ZR Studios.com. Jacket and title page image: Westend61/Getty Images.

The original editions of the books in this volume are published and copyrighted as follows:

2 Sisters Detective Agency, published at $31.00 by Grand Central Publishing,
an imprint of Hachette Book Group
© 2021 by James Patterson

The Lost and Found Necklace, published at $16.99 by Sourcebooks Landmark,
an imprint of Sourcebooks
© 2021 by Louisa Leaman

Girl in Ice, published at $27.00 by Scout Press,
an imprint of Simon & Schuster, Inc.
© 2022 by Erica Renée Ferencik

The Family You Make, published at $16.99 by William Morrow,
an imprint of HarperCollins Publishers
© 2022 by Jill Shalvis

The volumes in this series are issued every two months.
Readers may receive this service by contacting us by mail, email, or company website.

In the United States:
Reader's Digest Select Editions
PO Box 50005, Prescott, AZ 86304-5005
bookservices@rd.com
rd.com

In Canada:
Reader's Digest Select Editions
PO Box 970 Stn Main, Markham, ON L3P 0K2
bookservices@rd.com
rd.ca

Some of the titles in this volume are also available in large-print format.
For information about Select Editions Large Type, contact us at
PO Box 37894, Boone, IA 50037-0894 or selt@emailcustomerservice.com.